THE DEAL

A Novel By

G. WILLIAM MARSHALL

BARTHOLOMEW HOUSE LTD.

Publishers

01010913

BARTHOLOMEW HOUSE LTD.
First Printing . . . January 1968

© 1968 by G. William Marshall

Library of Congress Catalog Card Number: 67-30079

DEDICATED

First and foremost: To little Sam—
Merci pour d'être toujours toi

To B.A.C., whose food I ate copiously, whose wine I drank
cheerfully, whose tobacco I stole shamelessly; whose
advice and friendship are invaluable

(Joel 2-25)
The Lord said, "And I will restore to you the
years that the locust hath eaten" . . . and He did.
G.W.M.

The sordid realism of this book may generate a feeling of shock. To this I plead guilty. However, I do not think the book is shocking. I think the people about whom the book is written did some shocking, if not some terrifying, things.

I may be charged with holding out a "lure" to the sensuality of the readers of this book, prostituting my talent (such as it is), presumably with the idea of making money. I have tried to be an acute observer of the corruption that sometimes seems to go along with the making of an independent motion picture in Europe. There is an undercurrent of violence in this story that comes to the surface because it had to.

Everyone, especially women, are always talking about the divinity of sex. Theirs. I don't know about that. I figure you might as well talk about the divinity of digestion or the divinity of changing your pants. Sex is neither more nor less divine than anything else. People feel that the evil and the ugly disappear when exposed. Unfortunately, this is untrue and that is the way that it was with the Deal.

MOVIEOLAS

I should like to explain to you what a Movieola is. It is a machine a little larger than a television set. It is used in the cutting and editing of a motion picture. It permits you to take the new and incomplete film that you have shot and run this film through a viewer—faster or slower, bigger or smaller, backward or forward. This machine is used to cut, to edit, revise, and get into its proper place all of the story points, the scenes and the actors in your motion picture. So in this way I am introducing the characters in this book.

Movieola: *The Baron*

He was the number-one male box-office star in the United States and the world. He had been for the past three years. He was tall, wide-shouldered, small-hipped. He was as lithe as a whip. His profile was as classically beautiful as you could want. He was graceful, like a fast light heavyweight. He walked like a dancer, moving only from the waist up, carrying himself carefully, like an open bottle. He had that wonderful quality of bringing out the worst in everyone. And out of the cat's grace with which he held himself, he could be snarling, spitting, slashing the whole world and the air, then suddenly mewing like a kitten so that the ladies rolled over themselves; purred, cuddled, and warmed him—and before they knew it were "outraged," if they still call it that.

The Baron, however, had a tremendous problem. As he had said himself many times, he was "hung like a stud mouse looking for a lady mouse," so that many of the Baron's widely discussed love affairs and escapades became disasters. Each episode with the sex goddess of the moment became sordid and unsatisfactory for both participants.

Movieola: *The Princess*

She had a figure that would make a bishop kick a hole in a stained glass window. She had a beautiful face. People had been kind to that face. It was lovely and fresh and yet there was a certain wisdom smiling behind her eyes. The face looked as if it had heard all of the answers and had remembered the ones it might be able to use sometime. This looked like it might be one of those times. She smiled. "I have heard of you, Monsieur Jarnigan.

12

THE DEAL

The Baron speaks of you often." Here she crossed her legs. Now I understood a little how she had the Baron locked up and perhaps didn't know what to do with him. It always came to that sooner or later with the Baron. Man, the life, the chances, the girls, and the world he threw away.

As we talked she shifted over onto her other hip and recrossed her legs. The perfume of her drifted over to me from across the desk. Whatever it was, it was the right one. She absolutely radiated sex. She gave me a smile I could feel in my inside pocket. But, regrettably, the Princess never learned to distinguish between moments that are truth and moments that are traitors. So her life was filled with uncertain and sometimes terrifying inconsistencies. She was either very much in love or completely obsessed by revenge upon being thwarted. She used razors in her hating and after the love was dead she wept with remorse, vowed to enter a nunnery—a complete withdrawal from the world. This usually lasted for at least several hours or until she returned to her club, and granting her favors to the next *amant* she was fully aware of their complete unworthiness to be near her.

However, she was very popular with the international set, was sought after from Cannes on the Riviera to the ski slopes in Gstaad, and was one of the rare beautiful girls who are in truth the toast of Paris.

There were many galas and parties given in Paris where the French motion picture industry mingled with the dubious royalty of the City of Light. There the royalty and the French actors and actresses lived gaily, loved promiscuously, drank vastly, sang loudly, swaggered outrageously, lied brazenly, and when caught in the love trap hated dangerously. *"Vive la France et les frites!"* ("Long live France and French fried potatoes!")

At one of these parties I was talking with an Italian countess—a real one, in the studbook and everything. As we watched the Princess dancing by, the Countess said, "The Princess is such a lovely girl. She rides beautifully. You should see her, simply wonderful on a horse."

"How is she in the kip?"

"I beg your pardon?"

"I said, she looks like she's plenty hep. That's American argot for smart, intelligent, grand," I finished.

"Ah, your American argot is so . . . is so . . . *argot, n'est-ce pas?*"

"Absolutely," I said, "absolutely."

Movieola: *Sam Neely*

Now at forty, Sam was still all shoulders and chest. No belly or hips. He walked on the balls of his feet, always moving forward, always physically on balance. For the mental balance and all judgment he relied on me completely, as he had for the past thirty years. He trusted me completely, and you have to be careful with that kind of blind loyalty. It's a responsibility.

Sam Neely, over and above this, was one of the finest men in the world so far as I was concerned. I'd known him since childhood and still couldn't fault him. He sometimes overmatched himself in life. One of the things that he was unfortunately known for was that he was truly, abundantly endowed so far as his masculinity was concerned. Sam was very much like a guy called "Fourteen-inch Freddie" whom everyone in pictures knows. This guy Freddie was a freak who was hired by the various studios and bets were made for and against how grand his proportions really were. Supposedly, he had a dong fourteen inches long. I don't know the other proportions. He worked principally at Jason Wormser's studio and was a pet of some of the more wild and way-out parties and of some of the directors and producers on the lot.

The only rival that Fourteen-inch Freddie had ever had was Sam Neely. Sam, being dignified, would never submit to the vulgar. The bad-taste bets and the phony, freakish camaraderie that from time to time bounced about the studios hit the walls and fell to the ground where they belonged. Sam, as I said, could have given Fourteen-inch Freddie a run for his money, but he never wanted to. Even the suggestion angered him. And Sam in his anger, which was a quiet, smoldering thing, could have been more dangerous than all the elements put together. Certainly at any time he could have ruined the Deal one way or the other.

I trusted Sam and relied on him. I knew that he'd do anything for me. He had about as much use for the people around the studio—the hangers-on, Fourteen-inch Freddie, Saul Baum, and a bunch of the other people who hung around the Baron—as a pig has for a sidesaddle. When he was angry, he had the kind of a face you didn't know if he was holding three aces or a death threat. He read a lot, especially Plato on Socrates. He had a favorite quote, always giving the title and credit to Plato: "To be conquered by self is of all things the most shameful and vile." Now, I went along with that, but from time to time Sam had an annoying habit of using this quote in the wrong places. For example, this is not a maxim to quote to a producer the morning after he has been searching all night for his star and hasn't been able to find him. It's worse than hearing military music for breakfast.

Sam was a guy who had just missed being a world champion. It just seemed that there was no one around because he rang the doorbell of the world from the doorstep and no one answered. The world was empty and cold and the earth had died from a lack of warmth. And Sam was resigned to this as no one I had ever seen. He accepted his lot with dignity. Sam used to say to me in the moments when we were both low and depressed, in the moments when the picture was stalled and there was nothing to do, and I'd be cursing quietly to myself—hating everything, everyone, alone in my anger melting myself down—Sam would say: "Listen, Jarn boy, I'd hate to think that your life will end up in sixty months or seventy months or any months in Malibu or in Jamaica or here in Paris or in any of those houses that you have or houses that you can buy—and to me, boy, it doesn't seem right for me to sit here and *see* you go through all of this—and end up with just some money. What the hell, Jarn, what the hell. What are we going to do?" And I'd look at Sam and would see the affection and the genuine friendship in his eyes, and I'd answer and say, "It's like you say, Sam boy, what the hell, what the hell."

Movieola: *Mlle. Quinze ("15")—the Professional Virgin*

She had a lovely, if oversized, mouth, and when she walked into my office I saw that she was young, much too young. She brushed her hair back from her face with a smooth, preening, birdlike gesture, a thousand years of that graceful movement that no one has to teach them. She had beautiful hair, beautiful manners, her hands were long and slender and she spoke in a slightly husky little-girl voice. She was lean and lovely. She didn't walk, she floated. It was a sensual movement of the hips and legs, pantherish in one so young.

On one occasion, when we had been looking in every likely saloon and watering place for the Baron, I tried again to get some information from "15." I wasn't sure if she'd lied to me on the phone, because she lied just to keep in practice. So I decided to go to her apartment and see for myself if the Baron was there. I knocked on the door. "15" answered. "Is the Baron here?" I asked. "Drunk here, I mean." "15" looked me over, her love-lazy face taking inventory. "I wouldn't be surprised," she purred. "I'm not trying to surprise you, baby, or I'd have worn my leotards. Is he in or out?" She backed up a step, then smiled. "He's in, but not in like . . ." "Don't say it," I said, "don't say it ever again. It's not funny and you're not cute. So pull up your pants and girdle and stay the hell out of the way. This is business." Running her hands down her slender flanks, she said, "But, Jarn, I don't wear a girdle." I looked at her steadily for a moment. "You should wear one—as a muzzle," I said pointedly. She didn't look scared, surprised or nervous at what I had said. She was as calm as an adobe wall

15

in the moonlight. I passed her. As we went into the room she couldn't resist leaning over a bit so one little cute and fifteen-year-old knocker was showing. She gave me an up-from-under look, fluttering her eyes a little. "You're wasting your time, small time," I said. "Make with the feet into the other room, we've got work to do to try to sober him up." She left us to do it. Quietly.

1

I'd been back from France some little time then. I was playing golf at the Lakeview Country Club, not far from Studio City, where a couple of the big studios were. My golfing enemies were, and had been for many years, a long-nosed comedian, who was a grand fellow, who was truly funny, both on and off the screen and on and off television; a doctor whose name was A. Maxwell Dade; and an actor who wore lifts even in his golf shoes, but was nonetheless a fine fellow.

Some years back, when I was still producing films in Hollywood, I had won the Motion Picture Golf Tournament, and I still played a fair but not too steady game. Lately we'd become involved in what we called the "Count Lavoris Open." This consisted of the long-nosed comedian (good friend and fine fellow, who played fair golf) and Max Dade, the doctor. The actor who wore lifts in his golf shoes had been replaced by Count Lavoris. The Count, who was in the studbook and everything, loved to play for high stakes. We'd played many times—it was a beautiful golf game on a beautiful course. The Count was a fellow who liked to gamble even if he had to knock you down with his club to make a bet with you. I had been playing with him a couple of times a week for the past month. Actually, I should have sent a car for him because he was one of those men whose weakness is, he feels he is loved by everyone and that he does everything better, plays every game better, makes love to all the women better, and generally figures that he's really a helluva fellow.

Count Lavoris was a guy who liked to play a fifteen-hundred-dollar Nassau, in which a man could end up losing five, six thousand dollars on a bad day very easily, especially with the side bets. This was a day that I had the Count tapped in for around eleven thousand dollars. We had been betting on everything possible. We'd just arrived at the eighteenth green. On the eighteenth tee I had let him talk me into playing him double or nothing for the eleven *mille*; I had him locked out, so I gave him the bet. By the time we reached the green, we had a little gallery; additionally, all the golf bums came down from the clubhouse, so we were not without an undignified and highly critical audience.

I had to give the Count a stroke on the eighteenth hole, which meant that I had to play this hole extremely well. I figured two ways. If I blew it

17

and the eleven thousand, the publicity would do me good, because I knew the comedian would tell it all over. I also knew that my friend Dr. Max Dade would talk it over with the nice and friendly-wealthy bums at the Club. I knew I'd get more than enough public relations benefit out of my eleven thousand if I blew it, and actually it truly wasn't my eleven, it was the Count's eleven, and if by chance I nailed him, I'd walk away with twenty-two thousand dollars, which wasn't bad for a day's play, and it was always fun, the betting included. That alone would get me the publicity, because I'd given the Count more than a fair bet.

The Count was spraying all around. I was about one hundred fifty yards from the pin. I took out a six iron and stroked the ball. A fortunate shot, it had ended up about fifteen feet from the pin. I was lying three and it was a par five hole. All I had to do was knock that putt in for twenty-two thousand dollars. A goodly crowd, as they say in the movies, was gathered around the green. Among some of the other actors and producers there, all joking good-naturedly and making unnecessarily rude remarks all in good spirits, I was surprised to see the Baron in full makeup. Obviously he'd just come from the studio. He waved grandly, gave me a conspiratorial wink, and said, "Hi, Jarn, how's the boy?" "Fine, Baron, fine," I said, then turned to look over the green.

"Does it bother you to talk? I hear you got twenty-two thou riding on this putt."

"Yes." I smiled. "Yes, I have. Nope, it doesn't bother me." I looked at him.

The Baron had the needle out. "Well, aren't you just a little bit nervous?"

"Yeah, if it makes you feel better, as the fellow says."

I looked over at the Count. The Count was about thirty foot off the green; he grabbed his four iron and stroked at the ball. He skulled it, but the ball went up to about six foot from the pin. It was my turn to shoot. If I'd sink, I'd win. If I missed and he knocked his in, then *he* was going to win. It was an interesting game—an interesting situation.

I knelt down, looking over the putt, which, as I said, was a slightly uphill putt, no breaks, shouldn't be too tough. I could hear the Baron talking loudly in the background. I heard him make a bet against me, taking the long end of a hundred-dollar wager. He'd *pay* to see that I missed. I thought this was funny. Why did he want me to lose? I turned and looked at him, then started to line up my putt. The Baron called out, "Are you nervous *now*, Jarn?" And gave me another wink. I looked at him, returned his wink, went back and lined up the putt.

THE DEAL

I heard a guy say, "Who's the tall guy putting?"

"Name's Jarnigan—Logan Jarnigan. Been working in Europe—just came back."

"Looks like a fighter, don't he? Looks like he's stopped a couple."

"He is, and he has. You better keep your voice down, he's going to putt."

I turned and spotted a producer I knew from Universal. I grinned. "Hi, George. How's it going—and the talk doesn't bother me, I'll either make it or I won't. That's the way she goes."

George smiled. "Keep your head down, Jarn. I'm betting on you to make it."

I stood there a minute. It really wasn't a tough putt. I stroked the ball. It went up the hill. It climbed beautifully, and at the rim of the cup literally rolled over and flung itself into the hole. The crowd broke for the bar.

With the crowd thinned out, there was only my caddy left standing there looking at me, his red-rimmed eyes shining happily at "our win." And he was right. I reached into my pocket, took out two hundred dollars and handed it to him. "Thanks, Irv, you did me a lot of good today, son." "Thank you, Mr. Jarnigan," he said politely, "you sure stroked them today." He took the money, then hefted the golf bag. "I'll clean these myself, Mr. Jarnigan." He would do that and then I knew he'd burn a streak to the nearest bar and have himself a rumba. However, he had packed me plenty of times in a lot of tournaments. Irv was a good caddy and sober as a judge when he was working. I wish there were a lot of other people like that in the picture business—including myself.

After the golf match the Baron came into the bar. We had a drink. We talked awhile. I told him a little about the French motion picture industry. The Baron told me he had heard about my pictures in France and so forth and he'd like to see them. I told him I was running one of them that night in Beverly Hills.

"I'd like to have you see the picture, Baron. It's an interesting one, I think."

He smiled. "It won one of those—prizes in France, didn't it? What *was* the title?" Here he looked heavenward and started thinking of the title. He let me see him thinking. The effect was as phony as a chorus girl's eyelashes.

I let him toy with it awhile, then I said, "Well, the title was *Blackmail*, or, in French, *Chantage*."

He frowned. "I know what it is in French," he said testily.

"Well," I grinned, "I'd like to have you come and see the picture, if you're free."

"I'll make myself free, Jarn boy. I'd like to see what you did."

"All right, Baron. Anyway, you won't be too bored, there are English subtitles on the picture."

"I told you," he said stiffly, "I understand French."

I grinned at him. "Well, don't let that bother you, Baron, because those subtitles are for me. You know, sometimes I lose track of the story. So then I just read one of the titles and then I'm back on the track." I laughed.

He frowned for a minute and then decided it was a joke and laughed also. That was the way we were. And that was the way it was.

2

It was about 7:30 in the evening. I had my chauffeur drive me over to the theater where we were going to run the picture. This was a little studio on Canon Drive. Very swank. Very artsy-craftsy. You know—Claude Venard and Bernard Buffet saving the day in the gallery. Normally, it was a projection room used for art pictures. All of the fine foreign films, French, Italian, were screened there first for the prospective buyers for the art houses. This picture of mine had won the Cannes Award and in Germany the Von Turkheim award. I was proud of it; it showed what you could do without too much money.

I went into the theater. Many of guests would arrive late. But I'd arranged to show a newsreel first. I figured that ought to take care of that. Surprisingly enough, I saw the Baron's mother and father come in and seat themselves down front. I also saw, with no surprise at all, Big Sue, the Baron's mother-in-law, come in and plant herself firmly in a chair just in front of the Baron's, motioning for two girls of dubious breeds that I didn't know, to be seated. The Baron's American attorney wandered in as usual with gaiters, a kind of tuxedo–frontier-pants effect, and loose tie—all smiles, all legal, all bunk.

On the other side of the aisle and down front came Jules Molotov and his wife, followed closely by the Editor, Edwards, and his little fluffy blonde girl friend. They walked in, sat down, arranged themselves, and were waiting for the picture to start. I was not waiting for the picture to start because I knew it wouldn't start until I pressed the button. The Baron, seated on my right, was looking at the people, accepting his due, accepting their admiration—certainly not "fans," but people high up in the motion picture industry. I pushed the button after I'd seen that everyone was in and properly seated, and the picture started.

I must say that, right from the main title with the wonderful music that had been written by René Cloric and from the first thousand feet of film that had been shot by Marc Grignon, a good friend, it was a shoo-in. The picture was really excellent. I say that objectively. It had only cost around three hundred thousand and had already grossed over two and a half million, so it was safe to say that it was a success.

Since it was in the French language, I didn't know how well everyone

21

was getting the picture. I knew the subtitles were excellent. They'd been done in Paris by a woman with a Russian name who had done most of the titling for foreign pictures of Metro, Twentieth, and Paramount. I'd been watching the Baron. I'd been watching the reaction of a couple of distributors and sensing the things you can tell after you have been around a bit. It's a sense. It doesn't take anybody with any extraordinary amount of perception to know that it's a good picture, or it's a bad picture, or a fair picture, or a bomb (a *navet*, as they say in French, which means turnip). Without looking at the screen, hearing the music, I knew every foot of film, I knew every foot of music, and I knew that in about four minutes it would be over. I took a good look at everyone else first, then I glanced over at the Baron. I saw that he was sitting on the edge of his seat, poised almost as if he was ready to jump. I knew that the Baron was "in the box."

The picture finished; fade-out, music came up, and slowly the lights came on. There was applause, I was pleased. And surprised. I hadn't figured that fifty-some people could make that much noise. The Baron, flushed with the success of the film (since he had invited half of the people), stood up, motioned, waved, gestured for silence and said, "I think this picture is —— I think it is ——" here, in a big pantomime of happy speechlessness, he leaned over, put out his hand to shake hands, and then reached over to kiss me on both cheeks, an appropriate Continental expression of admiration. I shook the Baron's hand, turned sideways, the Baron raised both hands—the gesture of the conqueror. It was like winning a prize fight. The applause died down and the people started talking, and the Baron said, "Jarn, I have a little party arranged. I want you to come up; we'll go to my house—you and I have to discuss a picture. Jarn ——" He looked at me, the two yellow coyote's eyes put on a "fix." (I was to know that look, that heavy-menace stare.) "You and I," he continued, "are going to make pictures. We are going to do what should have been done several years ago. I shall immediately have you driven up to my house."

"Well, now listen, Baron, I have a couple of people to see here."

"What!" he exclaimed, rearing back his head. This apparently was a thing that should never be done. If you were summoned to the Baron's house this was an honor, and if he arranged to have you taken there, this was a double honor.

Now in all fairness to the Baron, it must be said that he was the highest priced star in the motion picture business throughout the world. He made approximately a million dollars a year, and through various methods, with the use of many tax experts, legal consultants, counsels, attorneys and business managers, he managed to keep most of the money he made.

THE DEAL

The Baron left after he'd been assured that I would follow within the next half hour or forty-five minutes. I discussed the picture with a couple of the distributors; they wanted to make some sort of a financing deal. I had motioned to Jules Molotov, who came over and stood listening without saying too much. Miriam, his beautiful wife, stood there eyeing me as though this were a different picture than she had seen a couple of weeks ago. But Miriam was fine, Jules Molotov was fine, all the people who had seen the picture were fine. Hell, even the Baron was fine. I was happy, I was "on top."

I knew that if I played it right I could make a deal with the Baron. This, of course, was what I wanted. If I had the Baron under contract and made a picture starring him which would cost me less than a million dollars, knowing that the Baron hadn't made a picture that had grossed less than four to five million, I knew what the break-even point was and I knew I could handle it and more importantly, if I could handle the Baron, we'd both make a lot of money.

I knew I'd give him a fair deal. I just hoped he'd be smart enough to take it. He was . . . and I wasn't. The flaw in the Deal was that I thought I could handle the Baron. I thought that he could be persuaded to do the thing that was correct and right. I knew he loved money. I knew he loved being the big star that he certainly was . . . but I didn't know that the Baron was a rickety-brained, scattered-idea man. He was not up in the clouds, not under the ground. He was a fellow who was not even in limbo. He was a man who was nonexistent within himself. He had the blind vanity that makes men so ready to believe themselves lovable. He thought everyone, everywhere, dreamt, thought, lived, breathed only for the Baron.

Later, I knew that back of that handsome façade, under the glow of charm that he radiated absolutely for a distance of fifty feet, fifty yards, fifty miles, he was not hearing or feeling anything except self-love. Everyone loved the Baron—including himself.

After we had had a few drinks and after we had talked everything over, the Deal was in progress. I thought, let us not pry into this experience of a miracle with whiskey-tangled fingers. Let us leave it to dirtier hands than ours, if such can be found—which I doubt.

23

3

The Baron's house was truly a sultanic affair: swimming pools, naked girls swimming in a dim light, silver-gilded, silver-painted, suffocating. Sometimes going to the bottom like fish, but all very sexy, all very explained, all very arranged.

After a while and a lot of conversation, walking here and there in the party, nodding to this one, listening to a quick and usually lewd story from that one, I moved on to where the Baron was standing next to the mantel in his library—people all around him.

There he was, under a huge picture of Jared Throne—Throne, an actor in the finest Barrymore sense of the word—Louis Jouvet de France, Sir Laurence Olivier of England, the best representative of what every true and real and absolute actor would like to be. The Baron turned, saw me, waved urgently.

I approached, pushing through the crowd, and when I got close to him, he reached out and gave me a bear hug. "Jarn, let me tell you again, it was grand. It was an experience, it was a moment in motion pictures that I shall not forget." Here he struck a pose, then added breathlessly, "No, never." I gave him a quick up-from-under look. I didn't figure the picture was *that* good even though it had made that amount of money. But if he figured it was that good I certainly wasn't going to water him down, so I waited to see what the next move was going to be.

"Now, Jarn," he said—and turning, he called out in a kind of cold voice, "Gentlemen, gentlemen—" Here he was speaking loudly enough to be heard by a group of men who were obviously discussing the Baron's business or the motion picture that they had just seen. "I should like you gentlemen to retire with me to the study. Mr. Jarnigan and I have something to talk over with you."

I watched then to see the Editor, a little fellow with no chin, who was engaged to the fluffy-blonde kitten-type girl, separate himself from the group. Then came the Baron's attorney, then came the Baron's business manager, then came the Baron's French attorney, then came the tax consultant, and before I knew it, there was a group big enough for a football team; with the Baron leading the way we all filed solemnly out of the library and into the Baron's study. There we were all properly seated.

THE DEAL

The Baron walked over to the fireplace, below another portrait of Jared Throne, and said, "Men" (this said in the tone of one of his pirate roles) "men, I want to discuss something with you. I tell you outright and forthright I want to make some pictures with Jarnigan. I want a deal worked out whereby Jarn and I can form a partnership." He turned, shot a glance at me. I was looking at him; I am sure that my face registered the surprise I felt. I hadn't figured that he would cold-deck it that fast. He had declared himself. He wanted to make a picture with me—not one but several. That was fine with me.

I looked around the room, then looked back at the Baron. "That's fine, I had wanted to make a picture with you, but regrettably I know that you are under a firm contract to Jason Wormser and I don't know how we can break it, unless you get your pal Hugh Bloodtest, who's got a lot of power —not only carries a big stick, but can use it—to maybe talk to Jason and get you 'outside picture rights.' "

Here the Baron struck a pose. "I say to you now, Logan Jarnigan," emphasizing my full name, "I say to you now, Jarn, in front of my advisors, my attorneys, and my friends"—in spite of himself he took a little bow—"I want us to be united in friendship and in business. I know that our confederate artistry will consider only the greatest pictures that can be made. We will work together, write together; our pictures will be heralded throughout the motion picture world in every language and in every theater. We will not assign to each his specific labors," he said grandly, "but rather you are my partner, my full partner. I rely on you for the business, and you"—here he took another little bow—"must rely on me for the acting and the artistic achievement we must attain to continue our work together."

After a lot of this kind of talk, the Jamaican maître d'hôtel in full regalia came in and said that the Baron could summon his guests for dinner. We all filed out; this was the first of many dinners I was to enjoy (or deplore) with the Baron. I would have preferred to go on alone, leave this party and have a quiet dinner by myself. I knew now that the Baron was ready to make a deal and I also knew that in the next forty-eight hours, depending upon how the tax consultants worked, I could have the Baron locked up. I thought about leaving, then I thought better of it. Perhaps for the sake of the Deal I should stay.

I remembered in France when I was starting a picture, in the face of many obstacles, and would see the hangers-on and the false friends seat themselves at my table. Even then I did not have the poor man's comfort, because the poor man has many reasons for lack of comfort. I was poor but I was still desiring something. I didn't have the comfort of sitting down to a morsel in peace, at a table uncrowded with flatterers and eaters and devourers. And where I would not be embarrassed with dependents.

I took some comfort, perhaps large comfort, from the fact that along with the dainties of the rich—and in this case that meant making a picture with an unlimited budget—I could escape all the diseases, all of the incompleted completion bonds. The bread or the film that was eaten was sweet or bitter to the taste. The water or the wine that was being drunk was pleasant or unpleasant to the thirst. I wanted but could not limit my desires with humility. I did not want to presume on the riches of the grand producer nor did I want to be as the poor producer and despond over poverty. I needed brains, I needed charm, I needed help, Lord. My cup was running over too fast.

Movieola: *The Baron's Attorney*

After we had had a couple of talks and after the lawyer and I had had a few business meetings and we were "friends," he tried to give me a deal for the Baron. If I let the Baron sign for an outside picture, it would be worth $100,000 to me under the table. I listened and then called the Baron from another room and confronted the attorney in front of the Baron and explained exactly the "sell-out" and the double-cross. The Baron listened to it, thought about it, decided he liked it. "Don't you see what a bastard he is, what a son-of-a-bitch?" he said with pride. "You see, kid, what you don't understand is this—if the barrister here will try to screw me, he's just the man I need, because he will screw all the people I'm doing business with. So even with what he gets from me, I'm ahead."

"You sure are," I said, "a head—and everybody pees on you." I left the room.

The lawyer was Pontius Pilate with a poop, a prayer, and a belch. Wind came out of him from every exit of his overcaloried body. It smelled bad. Even the untruthful words that rolled off his tongue had a purple smell. I didn't like him.

4

Two days later the Baron joined me for lunch at the Club. I tried to show him how to play golf. He lost interest quickly. We went back into the clubhouse—talked of our Deal. We had a drink. Then the Baron had several. Later I suggested we drive home. To my surprise, the Baron agreed. We left.

The Baron and I were riding in the car back from the Club. He was sitting there beside me half drunk, half asleep, half a grin on his face, but wholly full of himself—the star, the idol, riding a broomhandle for the whole world, yet knowing he couldn't do more than stick in a straw. He turned and looked at me, coughed, belched, nothing showy but performed with an easy grace, winked and said, "Let's go get laid. Know anybody?"

"Nope."

"I mean, anybody new?"

"Same nope."

"No new ones?" He frowned. This wasn't good; the star wanted to get laid. He gave me his brooding, heavy-menace look. "You want me to make this Deal or no?"

I thought about it, and him, and everything. "Sure I want to make this Deal—that's what we've been talking about."

He did the belch again, turned and looked out of the car. He was quiet for quite a while. I thought he'd forgotten about it. He hadn't. He turned around, facing me with his back to the door. He fished out a cigarette, put it in his mouth, reached for the lighter in the dashboard. He tried to make contact with the cigarette, missed it by a few inches each time. I reached over to help him, he pushed my hand away, turned and threw both the cigarette and the lighter out the window, turned back and said, "Let's talk about dames."

I looked at him. I wondered how it felt to be a big star, control a big studio by fear, have a beautiful wife, a yacht, a covey of mistresses, starlets, nymphets, and make a million dollars a year. He had all that, but he didn't look as though he were having any fun out of it.

"Okay, let's talk about dames—you start first."

"Ever screw a nigger?"

29

"I might have," I said, "but my luck's okay."

He grinned, "I have—a lot of them, Jamaican girls, the greatest." He thought this over. "How about a chink?"

"Nope, no luck there either, never really had a chance."

This didn't seem to bother him. He continued, "Well, I have, they have a kind of musty smell but they got action, they're the greatest. How about a les—ever boff a lesbo?"

"Nope, there again you have me, never wanted to get around to that."

"Well, listen, kid, how about a virgin? You must have got a virgin."

This talk was getting worse and worse, but I wanted the Deal, so I said, "Well, yeah, I may have, but it never left any marks on me."

He leaned back and closed his eyes. "I have," he said, "screwed virgins, lesbos, everything, they're the greatest." He blinked, his eyes open suddenly. "Ever screw a horse?"

I looked the star over; he didn't like the look. I said, "Not lately, but I know you have and they're the greatest."

He frowned at that, the eyebrows that were full and shapely—the delight of the teenagers—twitched; some were at least an inch long, and when a guy with eyebrows like that frowns he can really do you a frown. "I never said I screwed a horse and I think you owe me an apology. Stop this car." He put his hand on the wheel and jerked it over to the right. I eased the big car over onto the shoulder of the highway and cut the motor.

He opened the door with a violent shove and almost fell getting out. His face under the tan was pale, the end of his nose had a waxy look I didn't like. He was breathing heavily.

"Okay, joy boy," he said, "buzz off, dangle, hit the road."

He slammed the door so hard the big car shook. I just sat there looking at him through the window. He turned away and took two steps, turned back, opened the door and added, "Get lost." He gave me the heavy-menace stare, started to say something, shook his head, slammed the door again and began to walk away.

His steps took him along the edge of the highway. I watched his tall figure striding, erect. Walking away from me was the star, the big picture, the difference between an artsy-craftsy European picture or a big one, and one I wanted to do. I turned the key. Man, I don't know why it was so hard to do. I listened to the motor turning over slowly, took the decision and started slowly down the road after him.

As the car drew alongside of him, I stopped and he stopped. I looked at him. "I'm sorry, Baron, I didn't mean to offend you. I was just ——" He looked at me, leaned down and put his elbows on the window. He smiled at me.

"Scared, huh? It's scared the Deal won't go through now and it's scared." I grinned at him, I made it a big, friendly grin.

His smile changed and he said, "You're a pimp, a prick, and you're not too bright, right?"

I tried to hold the grin in place.

He continued: "A nothing. You make a couple of foreign pictures and you're a genius. Well, you're not. You're a nothing. You know why I'm able to tell you you're nothing? How much money do you have? Enough for the picture or are you promoting it on me?" He nodded his head wisely, spacing his words, with over-enunciation like any drunk who tries to be dignified. "Promoting on me, all you bastards are alike."

My grin had slipped away now. I didn't try to put it back.

He plowed on. "No guts, no brains, no possibilities now, no star to peddle, no Deal, no nothing. You're a nothing." He straightened up. I couldn't see his face now, it was above the top of the car. I opened the door and got out on my side, walked slowly around the car to him. He watched me, the heavy-menace look started to fall off his face, his eyes shifted past me, no cars coming, all quiet. I came close to him but not too close. I turned slightly to my left. I was as tall as he was, in better shape, less belly. A nerve was twanging away in my check like a piano wire. I looked at him.

"What is it, what's the matter with you?" he said.

I didn't answer.

"You look sore." He moved slightly, maybe half a foot back. "Say something."

"Get in the car," I said.

"What?"

"You heard me, Baron—get in the car."

"Now look here, old man, there's . . ."

I moved a little and gently dropped my right shoulder. His eyes flicked here and there over my face, yellow eyes like a coyote's looking at and past me. I said softly, "Baron . . ."

A look of fear blinked out of his eyes for a few seconds. He put his hand on the door handle and half opened the door. He tried to get the menace look but it wouldn't come. He stopped, took out a cigarette, put it in his mouth, took a gold lighter from an inner pocket, lit it and blew smoke carefully past my shoulder, looked down at the cigarette, every movement, every gesture right out of the catalogue, every tired cliché that he'd done a hundred times in his films. He said, "You still sore?" I just stood there waiting. He opened the door completely and got in the car. I walked back around and got in under the wheel.

"Can't you take a ribbing and not get on your damned high horse?" he said. He took a long pull at his cigarette. "You know, Jarn—" this quietly, not looking at me. A long silence. He shifted nervously in his seat. I kept looking at the road. He started to speak a couple of times but gave up finally. It was getting dark, I switched the lights on; the big car glided up between the hills, now in the best residential section. He turned in his seat with his back to the door. He cleared his throat. "Jarn?"

"Yeah."

"I'm sorry I said all that crap. You know me, I ———"

"Yeah, I know."

"Well, what I mean to say is, I really am sorry and I apologize."

"Forget it."

"No, I won't forget it. I hurt your feelings and I don't want to do that." He took in a breath, let it out slowly, "I hurt your feelings and I'm no frigging good."

I looked at him. He was kind of slumped over. I pulled into the driveway that approached his big house. "No feelings, Baron, no feelings at all," I said as I pulled the car to a stop. He started to get out, then leaned back in his seat.

"Jarn," he said, "the real reason I'm sorry is that you're my friend and I'm your friend, we make a great team. You do the business, I rape the women on and off the screen and we make money."

He tried to grin, then he put a serious look on his face. "Will you forget it and shake hands?"

He stuck out his hand. I looked at him. "Monkeys shake hands," I said.

"Jarn, come on, don't stay sore. I mean, shake hands on the Deal—you've sold me. It will be a good picture—after I make some changes, it could be a great picture—so let's shake on our Deal."

Well, there it was—what I wanted.

"We can sign those papers in the morning, the ones you've carried in the brief case so long. We got a Deal, Jarn boy." He gestured with his hands. I put out my hand and we shook hands, but he held on. He had a good grip and he looked me in the eye with a concentrated effort at sincerity. "Jarn, our Deal is made, but I want you to know this handshake is more than that to me, because thinking it over on the ride back, I suddenly found out you're my best friend."

32

THE DEAL

He shook my hand once more, hard, a little sad, but very manly, got out of the car, turned and started up the walk.

He waved once at the top of the steps, the door opened, the sound of voices and laughter came out—another party.

The door closed. I sat quietly in the car for a few minutes, thinking of what he had said. If I was his best friend, God help him. I started the car and drove off down the driveway. The lights of the city were spread out below me. It was beautiful. I looked up; there were stars in the sky who had sense enough to keep their distance from motion pictures. I turned out into the street. A car raced by with three girls in it, laughter spilled out and rustled along behind the car like leaves that follow the wind. I thought I'd go have a drink, maybe two.

"A nothing." I said it out loud. I guessed I'd call a girl. No, maybe drive over and play a game of chess with Doc—no, his wife thought I was a bad influence. I was the snake of reason and that might cause trouble. I drove on, past some restaurants, past the bars and the gin mills, past everything. I pulled in at a gas station, told the kid to fill her up and went into the john.

I came out. What to do? I was lonely, nobody to call, nobody to see, nobody to care if I lived or died or went to Willcox, Arizona. I walked to the pay phone, dropped in the dime, and dialed a number. It rang several times; finally a tight girlish voice answered, "Utter-McKinley Funeral Parlor"—shambles of laughter—then, "Who is it, darling?"

"Is the Baron there?" I asked.

"*Everyone's* here, darling. Who do you want? You sound nice. My name is Joan. Hello . . . hello . . ."

"Forget it," I said and hung up.

I'd almost done it. Almost called to go up to a party I didn't want to go to. One of the Baron's parties, a bash, a swinger, a ball—a nothing. I walked back to the car, paid for the gas and drove out and back along the street toward the restaurants. The hell with it, I'll go home. No one's there now, so go home, boy.

I drove into the driveway of the house I could now afford, opened the door, went in. The phone was ringing, I started to pick it up. Somebody calling. I put my hand out, drew the hand back, looked at it, turned and walked into the library, put on the light, fixed a drink, lit the fire and sat down in front of it.

I took a sip of the drink—it was flat—I stared into the fire. "You're a pimp, a prick, you're not too bright, you're a nothing, you're lonely. But there's something to warm you—you got the Deal."

33

5

Now that I was vaccinated, it became difficult if not impossible, to decline the Baron's parties. Each one took its toll of me. I've often thought what a great movie one of those parties would make. An underground movie—in more senses than one.

Soon after we made the Deal, I was at another of the Baron's parties. After the pot was smoked and boiled, the guests flung themselves with reckless abandon into the soft velvet pit of sexual everything. They sang, chanted and soloed their almed voices toward heaven; they clamored at the jalousied, paneled, ventilated doors of hell. They drank their mead and dipped their wicks in (and to) each other. Deliberately, steadily, continuously.

The Baron had himself and them all fooled with colored baubles. At his tables and in his beds (the standard party wind-up) couples were sprawling, singing, weeping, retching. Those still on their feet danced. Coupling bodies pressed thigh to thigh, belly to belly, tit to chest, in undulant ecstacy. All was a welter of lusts and perspirations. They dinged—they donged. Please ring the rubber bell of hell . . . then enter softly.

And through it all, the Baron moved happily. He boasted of many things. His talk brushed you lightly and well, he said the things all wanted to hear. His evil was well hidden under the charm and polish. He was like an iceberg, only a small part of the evil showed. This had a certain charm. The real evil lurked happily underneath, knowing it was well hidden below the surface.

He floated onward, onward; kissing and touching lightly, a sexual pickpocket feeling his way from group to group, from table to table; a whispered tale in a starlet's ear . . . a scandal pandered to a studio executive. Self-eulogy, self-love in every underplayed phrase. He gathered them in as a thresher the wheat. He pulled down the grapes and was gone to other vines.

His laugh moved on before him, sharp, self-satisfied, smirking, gonging . . . like a leper's bell warning people to get out of his way. He moved on through the crowd, shaking hands, bowing and talking—the bell tolling the way clear before him.

But these winds that inflated his sails carried with them the seeds of his destruction. The windy, breathy voices of the chorus of starlets, laid and unlaid, floated him onward. Later—his voice thickening, the song less clear, becoming muddled, the eyes glazed and reddish, the belly no longer flat—the cry for love became a burden, became a wail, became a long-drawn lonely scream in silence. The over-world is worse than the other. The Baron was unsimply growing older, the emptiness of his brain giving a false and uncertain fullness to his life. A puffy something... to counterbalance the deflated nothing.

His parties always finished up a bent and canted orgy. His guests were all so sex-crazy it had backed up into their heads like a plugged-up sewer line. If you cut open the top of one of their heads like you open a coconut, you could look in and see a dinker chasing a muff around the curved inside of the cranium. Diving, snuffling, snatching. This was life—hot damn!

And the Baron really *was* damned in the final stages of these orgies. I once walked in the famous green door of his corner bedroom, and had a sobering eyeful of the Baron's private hell in that king-sized bed. Hate—self-hate—in the midst of the act of love itself. For during what was passing for the act—bodies interlaced, struggling together—the Baron's face had an almost pained expression.

The mask of true passion or even real sensualism is difficult to hold in place during the act. Thus, as the Baron played out his lonely battles on the breasts, stomach, and between the thighs of willing battle sites, like an evil ghost, the truth slipped out, withered and drew itself painfully from out and between and away from the battlefield—slowly dwindling away into the nothingness it was in the first place. In spite of all his efforts, the Baron was again to be laughed out of the bedroom.

As he withdrew, finally and completely, the lovely-warm and wetly hollow field underneath him demanded fiercely, "What's the matter? You can't stop now. Don't you know that? Don't you know by now how it is with a woman?"

The Baron, now completely withdrawn, his shame wholly insecure, knew and dreaded what was to come, remembering the countless times he had played and replayed this scene. He fell back on the one sure weapon he had, ridicule. "Listen, you mother . . ." he said, "you don't do anything for me. I thought we'd be all right but you're too old for me. You don't excite me. You don't . . ." Suddenly, there in the dark, he felt a blinding slap across his eyes. *Slap* . . . again the woman's arms flashed out; slashing the air like a cat, she mewed and spit at him. His head ached from the blows. Circles of red and green zoomed in and out of focus, his brain reeled and careened wildly out and away, over the dark threshing shape under him, and then careened back giddily. The Baron cursed. He hit her . . . then again. He backed out of her; then up off the bed like a lobster crawfishing back into its hole in the sea. He pulled himself up, wrapped himself in a sheet, turned, and strode into the bathroom. He slammed the door and turned on the light. He stood there looking at himself in the mirror, once again riding a broomhandle for the world and couldn't even stick in a straw. He was shaking, trembling and it wasn't with cold. A solitary tear of sex and sadness trickled slowly down his cheek. Whistling soundlessly under his breath a lonely empty tune, he slowly started to dress.

You can't stop now. I wonder how many times the Baron had to hear that shriveling challenge. He didn't want to stop. He had the drive. He had the balls. But no club. As he said to me during a drunken crying jag, "I've been laughed out of too many bedrooms . . ."

He was lucky if he could smile about it afterwards. As he did in at least one instance, when a famous foreign actress made the corner bedroom scene . . .

As yet she didn't know—didn't know what disappointment was coming her way. She waited in the bathroom with the Baron waiting in the bedroom. She remembered she had left her cologne and perfume in her purse. Not wanting to make a false exit, she took the little can of perfumed bathroom deodorant, shook it and sprayed a little deodorant under each arm, gave a *phsst* between her thighs, and entered the bedroom where waited the Baron. She slid into his arms as he murmured, "Oh, the perfume of you—it's vaguely familiar."

She stirred in his arms.

"No, no," the Baron said. "Don't tell me what it is."

She wasn't about to.

He continued, "It is Rochas or Chanel, right?"

She murmured, "So long as it pleases you."

"It does . . . oh, it does," the Baron answered.

"Then kiss me and let's do the friendliest thing a man and a woman can do," she said in her low, breathless, little-girl voice.

The Baron held her tightly and they lay together—if not well, at least fragrantly.

6

Well, love was love and business, business.

All during these days, the actual contract for the Deal was being drawn up. The Baron's own attorney drafted it, and his own business manager witnessed it.

The Baron was all friendship and optimism when he signed, and when I signed.

Then I was realistic enough to take it to my attorney, Jules Molotov. If I'd had Julie in on the first conference, he would have advised me not to sign, and that was advice I didn't want to hear. Not that it wouldn't have been good advice. The contract called for me to be one hundred percent responsible for the financing. There was no financial obligation on the part of the Baron. Also he had several tax gimmicks, but I knew this could be healed. Jules was a fast man with a contract, probably the best motion picture lawyer in the business.

While Julie was telling me how sorry I'd be, I got into an argument with my star. This was the first of many arguments I was to have with the Baron, at which time he would ask for the advance of a large sum of money not called for or provided for in the contract.

So right here, I told Jules to revise the contract I had just signed with the Baron, and to pack in all his good advice, to make it iron-bound, rock-clad. The Baron would have to "render and complete" his services for Jarnigan Motion Picture Limited Productions, and we were really partners, fifty-fifty.

The Baron would have artistic control; I would make the final business decisions. Of course the Baron was reluctant to sign this revised contract, but he needed two hundred thousand dollars, and he needed it now.

The Baron always needed money. At that point, I hadn't learned what he did with it all. That knowledge came later, and dearer.

Then, we re-signed the contract, and Julie patted himself on the back, just as I had patted myself on the back when I signed the original one.

And the Baron took the two hundred thousand dollars, probably patting himself on the back, too. We shouldn't have taken time out to pat our backs. We had the Deal locked up. The Deal had us locked up. We started the first picture.

7

The motion picture business is something that every man can play but very few men play well. Now actually the right and successful producer is one who has the simple faculty that we call common sense. He must be a strong man who makes sure of his facts, who makes his decisions on what he has seen. The pictures he may or may not have made but he has observed and then he makes his decision on what he has seen. He is thoroughly persuaded of the absolute truth of arithmetic. He knows that there is always a reason, a good reason for a man's having good or bad luck and so making or not making money. Producers talk as if there was some kind of magic about this and in effect believe in this magic, which extends to other parts of their lives as well.

I know that there is only one principle, there is one road, there is one cashier. You pay and you get pound for pound, cent for cent, dollar for dollar, franc for franc and that good luck is just having singleness of purpose, tenacity, holding on, enduring. But it is a lonely life and sometimes you find yourself down on your hands and knees looking in the corners of the world for your soul—like a dropped dime.

The movie we'd begun to shoot was a special case. Basically, we were cutting the French star scenes out of my earlier film, and replacing them with new scenes starring the Baron. Thus, by spending a couple of hundred thousand dollars shooting in Hollywood and Carmel, we would end up with a feature worth two million dollars at least, and in a sense a competitor to the features that the Baron was turning out for Wormser under their multi-picture deal.

It was tricky, since Wormser would surely not stand still for the Baron's moonlighting if he found out about it; but I counted on getting this one in the can fast, and then moving on to Paris for our next film, to be shot completely from scratch of course, which would be the second starring the Baron in his multi-picture contract with *me*. It would be more difficult for Wormser to prevent our foreign operations and, if it came to a court fight, he had more to lose than I would, because the Baron would refuse to work at all.

As for Bloodtest, I figured him to play both sides. He could go on collecting his hundred grand a year off the Baron's contract with Worm-

41

THE DEAL

ser—and he could always justify the Baron's first picture with me by pointing out to Wormser that he had first refusal rights on the distribution of the film. Bloodtest would also get his cut off the Baron's contract with me. The Deal, in other words, might be a problem for Bloodtest and Wormser, but I wasn't too concerned as yet. They both loved the money and their own deal too much to pull their bluff and threat too far. My trick was to keep them on edge, but not mad enough to knock everything off.

So this movie we were shooting had been selected because it was easy to rework, and also because artistically it was right up the Baron's alley, a sort of mixture of Hamlet and of all the Good-night-sweet-prince John Barrymore pictures.

The Baron, who looked very well in tights and who had always longed to play Hamlet, was in his costume strutting around on the stage waiting for the next shot to begin. The reason that he was not in the dressing room was because he was very proud walking around in those tights—the equivalent of leotards. He had been properly padded and his manly effect was artfully exaggerated, so his costume, with the built-in special masculine effect, was something absolutely surprising, and the "ohs" and "ahs" that came from the extras who didn't know of his infirmity brought little squeals of admiration here and there, and of course the Baron, who had already had a couple that morning, was absolutely thrilled until I half knowingly shot him down with, "Baron, you're getting a tan from all those admiring glances. Why don't you go and take it easy in your dressing room?"

His surprised look and up-from-under sheepish grin let me know that he knew what I was talking about. He said, "Yes, let's go in. I did have something I wanted to talk over with you."

We went into his dressing room where the Editor was sitting with Saul Baum, the stunt man. We discussed this and that, all had to do with the shooting the rest of the day. I frankly was very content because the Baron was still sober, the Editor didn't look as though he was going to be whipped today, and Saul Baum was relaxed. I was hopeful that if things continued, we'd get three or four minutes of good stuff on film.

Before long, we were doing the wrap-up of the first picture. We had practically finished all shooting. I had matched up the footage done in Italy and France, so we finished up in Malibu, Carmel, and the Big Sur country. By now I had a tremendous personal cash investment in this picture, with all the new additional footage.

It was then that Hugh Bloodtest gave me the first inkling of trouble. He told me if this picture was released by anyone but Jason Wormser's studio, it would kill the Baron's fourteen-year, fourteen-million-dollar contract. Bloodtest said slyly, "Jarn, I certainly don't want that to happen." This was told to me by that great man just before I was planning to leave for Paris to prepare the second picture. Which reminded me of a thing that happened right after the start of the first picture—a tragic thing that almost stopped the shooting of the picture.

8

The Baron had told his first wife, who was older than the Baron and was a successful early screen star, that he was through with the "extra payoffs." So, from here on in, she was to get her alimony, support for the son, and that was it. The ex-wife, having "discovered" him when she was a big star, felt he should have been more grateful to her for that. And she was still madly in love with the Baron.

However, there was something that he must have been ungrateful to her for, and this for the rest of his life.

She had given Baron his first taste of heroin, or "horse." She had exotically shown him how to smoke opium. She had done this when he was very young and, even then, easily induced to try these sorts of things. But, many years, many films, and many wives and mistresses later, he no longer wanted to keep sending the monthly envelope (that was over and above his regular alimony payments paid by his business office).

While she was out of town at her place in Palm Springs, he carefully and secretly bugged her home; put a tape recorder, carefully concealed, in her bedroom. It was the latest tape recorder. This recording device is almost human. As you start to speak, it turns on, and whenever you stop, it turns off. It has absolute fidelity of tone. It is battery-operated and will record fifty hours of conversation.

Two of the first three sets ever made were given to an RCA director and an Academy Award–winning actor; the third was given to me. The Baron saw me use it shortly afterward to dictate some notes, and of course decided he had to have it. To make a long story short, I gave it to the Baron.

Later, the Baron let me hear what the little machine had recorded. I was horrified. The operation was perfect, and under the circumstances it was like listening to the sound-track of a movie you know so well that you don't have to look at the screen. It will play ineradicably in my memory.

This is how it was inside the Baron's ex-wife's house. This is what she was doing when the tape was rolling—knowing her, knowing her habits well. The tape went like this—you could almost see the movements . . .

"No," said the woman. "don't look at me like that. Tell me, darling"—she held out her hand in what was meant to be a caressing move-

45

ment. He moved his head. He didn't like to be caressed; and anyway it was hot. He wanted to leave this stuffy room that smelled of perfume, powder, and was filled with pictures of actors and actresses. Some of the pictures were yellow and starting to turn up at the edges. All were at least twenty-five years old. She was in most of the pictures in different poses— some smiling, some dignified. She knew everyone else in the pictures by name, and sometimes when she really went on a good one, she'd dig into the old trunk with the false labels, the trunk covered with the faded Spanish shawl that had been given her when she was in Madrid, by a *torero* who was a fairy. He had also given her a couple of cushions, both with paintings of bullfighters on them. One, fringed in leather, showed a lopsided Manolete with a hawk nose and bowlegs, a bull being killed . . . the "moment of truth" on every corner.

He looked at the room. Glory, how he hated it. And the sauna bath, as she liked to call it, this also had an odor that he hated. In the bathroom on a shelf over the mirror that made your face a little swollen on one side even if you were not, and on another little shelf under the mirror which was crowded into one corner, there were jars and tubes and bottles and capsules, boxes and brushes. Some of the jars and tubes were many years old. They were cure-alls for beauty, health, age—they guaranteed to keep you eternally young; also—they smelled.

Sometimes when he'd go into the bathroom, the rubber hose from her douche bag would hit him in the face. This always made him furious. Although she was well kept financially, there were bits and pieces of lingerie hanging on a cord which stretched from the medicine cabinet to the top of the water closet, which didn't help any, either. But he paid no more attention to her than usual as she continued in her voice of distinction which he knew was reserved for the studio, the theater, her latest lover, or if she was getting lousy-drunk.

He was never curious about her lovers, although sometimes he wondered why she still kept him. She had been drinking heavily all day; even from the other room he had heard the clink of the glasses.

The woman said, "Darling, I don't think you're listening to me. I started to say, what shall we do tonight . . . or would you rather we just stayed here and I'll read aloud to you? I know you always like that. I know you know I have always been known for my voice, and even in my latest vehicle, George Gene Weill said, 'The voice of . . .' "

He turned away. It didn't mean anything to him because nothing of hers meant anything to him. He was sorry he was with her, but there it was. He had nothing better for the moment, and although he wished they could go to the country—anywhere to get away from this room and its smells—he felt if he could get out from time to time, it wouldn't be so bad. But he never had a chance. Her latest vehicle, as she put it, had been many years ago and before he knew her, when she was still married to the Baron. He yawned, then walked over to the window.

Two men were going by, following closely on the heels of a girl of about twenty years old. She had a very good figure, and long slender legs, a short skirt. She was leading a dog of a rather dubious breed, but they looked very nice together, and he liked the way the dog followed along two paces behind the sheer-stockinged legs. His eyes followed the girl and the dog until they were out of sight. He never glanced again at the two men and, as usual, he didn't listen any more than he could help to what the woman said. Anyway, it was her tone of voice that gave him his cue. He knew when to act gay and when to play cute and when to be silent, and now was the time to be silent . . .

"You're not listening." She frowned at him. "Sometimes I think you're like all the rest of them. You really don't care for me." Her voice lowered dramatically. "You really don't." She turned and looked at herself in the mirror. She said: "Yes, you're like all the rest. I wonder why I keep you—there's no real love in your heart for me." She turned back to the mirror. She sucked in her cheeks, she arched her eyebrows and then she smiled. Then she frowned. She half closed her eyes and then suddenly opened them. She leaned back, turned her shoulder so that she was half facing the mirror, and with lowered lashes told her reflection in a low, whispering voice: "You're not bad, you know, not half bad. In fact, you're beautiful."

She leaned slowly closer and closer to the mirror, her face almost touching the face in the glass. The woman in the mirror and the face of the woman approaching the mirror had their lips almost touching. Then slowly, the woman kissed the reflection. It was with love. It was a long kiss, full of love and a thing greater than passion—admiration—deep and true and down-in-the-stomach admiration.

The kiss ended. The woman leaned back. "There," she breathed, "that's better!" The imprint of her mouth stayed on the mirror and the moisture started slowly to dissolve. Her fingers automatically opened the drawer and she took out a bottle. It was Queen Anne Scotch. It was also about empty. She poured almost all that was left into a silver goblet that had been given her after it had been stolen from the home of a little parish priest. She drank a little.

Suddenly she stopped. She sat up very straight. She raised the glass in a

47

toast to the reflection in the mirror. She said: "Chin-chin, my lovely, you're not so old. Forty-eight isn't so old. I know women twenty-five who'd give their souls to have a body like yours." She drained the rest of the Scotch, set the goblet down. She knocked a box of powder off the dresser—it spilled in a little pink pile half on the rug and half on the bare floor. The woman never noticed. She looked again at the reflection in the glass. She said: "Why, you look as young and as beautiful as when you played in *The First Lady*. Of course, maybe your breasts aren't quite as firm, but really, you're lovely, still very lovely." The woman got up and went over to the trunk. She swept from it the Sapnish shawl which had come from Madrid, which had been given to her by the fairy bullfighter, and got out a hidden bottle of Queen Anne. This had been "held out" for a special occasion.

He just stood there and watched her and thought to himself, Brother it's really going to be a good one!

She opened the bottle and took a drink from it as she came walking back across the room. The reflection in the mirror approached her and again the two of them sat down. The woman tried to pour the Queen Anne into the goblet, but was carefully pouring about a quarter of the bottle of whiskey on the dressing table. It ran in little rivers and lakes—little snakes of whiskey darted here and there. They hid behind the bottle of perfume, they ran around behind and hid again behind the boxes of powder; finally they met again and, whispering gaily, leaped off the dresser and coiled into the cracks of the floor. With a gulp of breath, the woman changed her aim and soon Queen Anne was in the goblet and the goblet was full and overflowing, and the table was a little lake of whiskey.

The woman leaned over and could see her face staring back at her from the whiskey mirror under her elbows. Little rings of wet formed on her elbows and tried to climb up her arms. As the woman looked up from the whiskey mirror to the good reflection, or the partially good reflection, in the real mirror, she said: "Good little old reflection—darling, you're not so old, you're not old at all—in fact you're young! I don't know anyone as young as you for your age—just a shade over forty—hell, that's not old."

She lowered her eyes and flirted outrageously with the reflection in the mirror. She said softly to the reflection: "I'm going to tell you something maybe you'd suspected . . . but I've never told a living soul." She raised her hand and made a concentrated effort to look solemn.

"I swear to God and Saint Joseph and on my sainted mother that I've never said out loud what I'm going to say to you."

She leaned very close to the reflection and she whispered: "Every time I take two or three little drinkies . . . I get hot pants . . . even for myself.

THE DEAL

There. Now you know it . . . now you know. I told you and you know it and I swear to God and Saint Joseph and my sainted mother that it's true." She raised the goblet and took a long drink—then she banged the goblet down. It hit the dresser with a crash and under the whiskey lake the glass covering the table top cracked. The whiskey, now having several avenues of escape, ran happily in all directions, but mainly followed the cracks in the glass. One little river ran into the woman's lap. She didn't notice it. She was looking into the mirror.

"That milkfaced chippie. Do you think she could have got him if I'd wanted to keep him? He was a nothing—less than nothing. You're damn right she couldn't! She's had so many abortions she can't hold any man. She was as big as the whole world—the whole damn world. But with him it made no difference. He's a diver—a damn diver. I'll tell you something. I'll be honest with you. She was big and she stank." Her face became puzzled. "Or is it *stunk*?"

She continued: "I tried to warn him but he wouldn't listen. Well, would he? He and his damn whore, a white milkfaced whore." The reflection looked back properly sorrowful and listened. The woman hiccuped and said under her breath, so the words came out all at once: "ShewasawhitefacedwhoreandGodknowsshewasandsodoMaryandJosephandsodoI . . . If I'd wanted him, I'd have kept him. I'm still young, I've still got my looks and my figure and they can never take away my voice. George Gene Weill once said to me: 'You know, a voice like yours is a gift to the silver screen and the theater, my dear, you must guard it carefully.' That's exactly what he said to me." She leaned closer to the reflection. "You see, I know he meant it. You probably think he said it to try and get in my pants; but that's not true. You see, he's a fairy. He doesn't like any women."

Here, she changed her expression to pleasure, to admit that she had something out of the ordinary. She corrected herself. "Unless, of course, they have a voice like mine. He said, 'You have a great gift'—and I swear on a stack of Bibles and to God and Saint Joseph if he didn't. May I die this minute, if he didn't say those very words." She leaned back and almost fell off the stool that stood in front of the dresser. Regaining her balance, and leaning very close to the glass so that her breath made little smoky circles when she talked, her eyes now took on a glitter; and, holding the bottle firmly in both hands, she whispered to the mirror: "You think I told you all? You think I told you *why* I let him go? Baron was the prettiest young man I'd ever seen. He was as fresh as a child. Just to look at him could set me off. To kiss him was beyond belief—but then I found he couldn't do the other well—not from lack of trying or wanting—but from lack of the thing a man needs quite a bit of. Oh, don't get me wrong; he had both of *them* and they could have run a stallion—but the rest was a feeble zero. Well, I'll tell you. Damn my soul if I'm not going to tell you the God's truth."

She leaned so close to the mirror that she couldn't see; and then, leaning closer still, she bumped her head. It startled her but finally she pulled herself back into the comfortable society of her reflection; then, after a smile and a wink and a silent kiss to herself in the mirror—the noise of which even made him turn around—she continued: "But who needs him—who needs his big balls and little club? What's all the fuss about—I ask you, what is it? It's something you can do in twenty minutes. When you're young, you can do it standing in a doorway. Kids are made in the back seats of cars, and, after all, what is it? I ask you, what *is* it?"

She turned back to the mirror, her face properly sober. Then she had a thought. The thought impressed the reflection and the reflection smiled back encouragingly. The face became sober again, started to become reverent. She nursed the idea, said softly, "I think I will enter a convent. Yes, I think I will devote myself to religion. I've been good. Think of all the money I've given away!" She looked up from under her lashes into the mirror to see that her reflection was paying attention. She allowed herself a little more liberty. She gave the image a quick look. "Yes, I will take to religion. It's what I should have done all along."

She pictured herself in the white robes of a nun—healing the sick, caring for little orphan children, a sweet suffering smile on her face—helping all. Only for the good. She said, "Yes, that's what I'll do. I'll enter ——" She hiccuped. She turned; she was still playing the nun. She looked back in the mirror. "But it's a lie, like it's always been—a lie!"

She started to cry. The sobbing and the voice and the face in the mirror all went hand in hand. The reflection tried to follow everything that she said. The woman continued. "I'm unclean, that's what I am—unclean." Here she closed her eyes, threw out her arms. Then she opened her eyes, made them very big so that the reflection in the mirror became something horrible.

"I'm unclean . . . I'm a monster! No, I'm abnormal . . . that's what I am, abnormal."

On looking at herself in the mirror, she leaned forward until she was staring directly into her eyes. The reflection stared back and because she was drunk, she felt almost as if the mirror or the reflection was telling her everything she had said. She kept staring at the eyes of the reflection.

Finally, all she could see were the eyes . . . she almost began to be afraid. She turned her eyes away from the mirror and said—and there was something different in the voice that made him listen as she breathed— "Listen, I told you I let him go because he was like he was . . . I let them all go . . . I've kept some, and I've lived with some, and after it's all over . . . Here," she said, and stretched out her hands to him and breathed, "Look at me. Look at me—in my eyes."

She took a false step backward, recovered herself, and dramatically continued: "Here it is—now listen to me; here's my secret . . . it's really terrible, and I've never confessed it to anybody before. I do it with you because we have no secrets and because of the way I feel for you."

She sat down on the little stool. She looked very close and hard at him as she said: "Lately I want no man; no one. I'd rather make love with myself. Yes, sir, that's it! I'd rather do it alone . . . it's kind of . . . well, it's more like . . . I mean, it's more beautiful if you do it alone . . . you know what I mean . . ." She leaned back on the stool and the reflection kept looking at her.

She turned her face back to the mirror without moving her lips. "You're a liar," the reflection said. "You're a dirty liar. You're old and you're ugly, and you're a drunken, dirty liar."

The reflection leaned closer. "I'll tell you something else, you're a les—" The woman picked up the goblet and hit the reflection squarely between the eyes, and it was gone.

The woman turned and stood up. Some of the broken glass and a lot of the whiskey ran off her as she stood up and she said, "Darling, I don't know why I get like that. You won't hate me, will you? You won't lie to me? I swear by Saint Joseph and Saint Mary I'll never lie to you. Darling, come here—please, darling, come here and let me hold you in my arms. You're all I've got, you know, and that's good. Just you and me, and we are alone and we love each other, and we trust each other. Isn't that right?"

She walked toward him with her arms outstretched, her face a mask of tears, of red-rimmed eyes and cracked makeup. Under the eyes were puffs, and each detail showed too many drinks, too many plays, too many beds, and lately, too many invitations to the court of Queen Anne; indeed, the aroma of Queen Anne hung on her heavily.

Her eyes began to fill with tears of self-pity as he avoided her arms. He turned and walked back over to look out the window. He knew without turning around that she had gone back to the bed. He could hear the bed move—headboard hit the wall—and soon he would be expected to join her and comfort her. But the thought of lying next to that body, that fat body, with the heat and the smell!

THE DEAL

He looked back out of the window. It was getting dark. A thin woman and two little girls were coming up the street. A car almost hit them as they crossed the intersection. The driver honked angrily but the thin woman walked on, acting as if she hadn't heard.

He continued standing by the window and she said, "Darling, come and lie close to me. I feel cold and you know how I like to feel you close to me. Please . . . please . . . I'm so alone and you're all I've got and we love each other, and don't lie, and we are true to each other and all those things that people do in love, darling . . . darling . . ." She started to cry.

He had heard it before and it bored him, but this evening had been too much, and besides, her breaking that glass had made him nervous. He didn't want to go to her. All he wanted was to go out and walk, to breathe a little air and to just get the hell out of this place of tears and memories, of whiskey and perfume—the air of powder and peroxide and everything that made up this woman and, most of all, just to be away from her.

It hadn't been so bad when the Baron was around. More luxury, and plenty of action with the Baron. He had liked the Baron. Felt real affection for him. He didn't care what the Baron's problems were, he just liked him, and he knew, and the Baron knew, that he was no fairy. He had no sex axe to grind. He looked back at the woman lying on the bed.

The crying continued and then the woman said quite clearly, "I've said it before, I'll say it again. I've been betrayed, yes, I've been betrayed, and they all have left me . . . and now, even you . . ." She began to sob more loudly. "Darling, don't leave me. Don't be like all the rest. Don't use me and then not love me. Please, please, come to bed . . . Please come here next to me."

Now he knew she really wanted him to come to her; but he knew he just couldn't. He couldn't make himself go to her. It was too bad, but that's the way it was . . .

The woman watched him as he stood there staring out of the window, acting as if he hadn't heard her. She started to call him again, and then suddenly she smiled, started to talk to herself in a high sing-song little voice, like the little girl in the children's plays. "They'll be sorry. Yes, they will. Who will be more sorry than they? I've kept them all, and now they desert me in my hour of need . . . Yes, desert me . . . Well, they will see . . . they will surely see . . . Yes, they will . . . They . . ." The voice broke off because the woman ran out of breath.

She took a deep breath to start again and saw that he was still looking out the window. She slowly got up and went to the little table with no table

52

top, no glass mirror, no friend, no reflection. She opened the drawer and took out a box. She opened the box.

Inside were about twenty-five little red pills with little blue strips of gelatin on them. She poured them all into her hand, then she went into the bathroom and got a glass half full of water and started the long walk back to the bed.

To her it seemed a long way. It was exactly thirty feet.

She sat down on the bed. She turned to him and said, "Of all the ones I've kept since the Baron left . . . the leading man, the other actor, that writer with the lovely chin, and the singer . . . of all of them, you're the only one I never minded paying for . . . Don't you love me? Don't you love me just a little? Please come here and put your head in my lap and let me sing to you or talk to you. Please, darling, for the last time, don't you turn away from me too. You won't do that, will . . ."

The woman stopped. She saw that he wasn't going to move. She lay back on the bed. She turned her head to the wall and said to him softly, "You'll be sorry when it's too late. You'll be sorry. No one will love you as I do, and now no one will keep you as well as I. I wish you had still loved me, I really do. It seems too bad that no one really likes me now . . . I'm still as pretty as I was, really I am . . . I'm not so old. Forty isn't old, and no one has a voice like mine . . ."

She raised herself quickly. She put all of the pills into her mouth with several quick motions, threw back her head and swallowed each time, and she drank all of the water. She lay back down on the bed and she held tightly onto the glass. She waited. She said, "I needed you so much. I needed the Baron too, but he's with Miss Milkface, who doesn't care what he hasn't. I needed everyone tonight, I guess. It's awful to be so lonely . . ."

She began breathing heavily, but he still didn't turn around. Another car passed the window on the way somewhere downtown. Now there was life downtown. Street lights started coming on. A piece of paper was blowing down the street and stopped, wrapped around a lady's foot. She kicked it off and walked on by the window. The minutes went by . . .

The woman turned restlessly and said, "Baron, I don't care if you do think it's wrong, you have no choice, since you won't or can't now. I have to go. Yes, I know I'm making my choice; but that's the way it has to be. You can be a lot . . . and then what if she says I am . . . I don't care because hers is a milk face and . . . of course my figure . . . You don't think I need to wear anything, do you? . . . Everyone knows who I am . . . and they all think I have a beautiful voice . . . It's a gift to the movies from the theater . . . he said so himself . . . He said to me, 'You know, you . . .' And I've . . . and I . . . I swear to Mary . . . and . . . Saint Joseph and my sainted mother it's . . .

He turned away from the window because he heard the glass hit the floor. It rolled away somewhere under the bed. One hand was just touching the floor. She really had lovely hands—they were thin and white and almost transparent. She was quiet . . . no noise . . . only all quiet.

He went closer to her. He could tell now that she wasn't breathing and he knew instinctively that she wasn't asleep. He knew what it was now . . . it was all over. He turned and he walked back to the window. He really didn't care too much. You see, he was a dog . . . and he just stood there and kept looking out the window . . .

He hoped the Baron would come and take him out now, that they could romp together like before. Being cooped up with an old actress is truly a dog's life. He grinned to himself and let out a mournful howl. He thought happily, Now this will bring the Baron . . . OU*ooooooooooo*!

The funeral was over. It had been nicely done. The Utter-McKinley Funeral Home always did it up well. On the Baron's instructions, they hadn't opened the coffin.

The scandal whizzed, rocketed, and hummed around Beverly Hills, Bel-Air, and the entertainment community of Hollywood.

After the funeral, I rode back in the limousine with the Baron, who was properly solemn, properly grieved—properly, but not excessively. He was the perfect superstar in mourning, in proper bereavement at the loss of someone gone before; in this case, the old ex-wife he had heartily hated and whose alimony he could now stop paying.

As the big car threaded its way through the traffic, up Wilshire Boulevard, turning right at Beverly Drive and on up to where Beverly Drive joins Coldwater Canyon and up into the hills, the Baron sat quietly looking out the window, not saying a word.

"You all right, Baron?" I asked.

He just nodded, saying nothing. "Well, it's over now. I think you should stay home and rest the rest of the day. And you needn't come in tomorrow. It's easy to shoot around you for one day."

I looked at him. He nodded again, still saying nothing. And that's how it was, riding back to the Baron's home after the funeral. We'd arrive in about twenty minutes and I was already thinking of getting to the studio and rearranging the schedule next day so that the Baron wouldn't have to work; and while I was thinking this, the Baron's mind was also going, with

THE DEAL

his mind's eye blind so that he was continually tap, tap, tapping through his brain with the white cane, looking, looking, but finding nothing—certainly no comfort—the Baron sat there living over his life with her, remembering the two images of her which he now recalled.

He realized that she was dead. She had ceased to exist and soon would not even be a memory. But right now, because of the tape recorder, he felt ill at ease. It would have been better if he hadn't known how the end was.

He sought to justify his act. What else could he have done? He could not continue this continual deception to himself. This farce that he had gone through, paying out those sums every month, year in and year out. He certainly could not have disposed of her in any way. She had protected herself well in this, leaving letters "confiding in friends," so the Baron would have been the last one to have harmed her. No, what he had done seemed to him to have been the best thing. Was he to blame now that she was finally and completely gone? He began to understand how lonely her life must have been, sitting night after night alone, running old films, rechecking old manuscripts, continually looking over old "stills."

He wondered if his life too would end lonely. He wondered what would happen when he ceased to exist, when he would become a memory. He wondered if anyone would think of him.

The Baron turned away from the window—it was the first movement he had made. The purring engine of the car, the whack whacking of the tires going up the mountain began to cut into his thoughts. He looked as though he'd begun to doubt the reality of what had happened. He looked as though he'd never been to a funeral. No death, no darkness, no pain, no voice could reach him.

I watched him carefully. He worried me. He sat perfectly silent, completely alone. The big car made the broad sweeping turn and went up into the drive. The chauffeur beeped the horn, the door to the Baron's house opened, a small dog came bounding out, overly happy, an actual grin on its face. The car stopped and the chauffeur opened the door. The dog jumped at the Baron. The chauffeur shooed him away, then carefully helped the Baron, unnecessarily solicitous, and we went up the steps and into the house, the dog following at the Baron's heels. So, another problem was disposed of. The Deal would continue.

9

And the Deal did continue . . . with a typical episode.

I sat in the office and waited for the Baron, who was to show at 2:30. It was already 4 p.m. The secretary came in languidly and said, "Mr. Jarnigan, there is a Mr. Tannenbaum to see you."

"Who," I asked, "is Mr. Tannenbaum?"

She put one hand up behind her head to tuck in an imaginary wisp of stray hair. She was another one of the Baron's imports but she was on a knife-blade now. The Baron wasn't getting off with her at all. I knew why. She didn't . . . so she was now hedging her bet and letting me know in a nice, perfumed sort of way that if the Baron didn't . . . I could, or would I? She had a lot of angles to figure but she played them well; she looked them all over . . . she was deciding. Today with her, the fashion show was different.

She was wearing a knit dress that clung to her as if it were wet. It had a sheath effect, a mandarin type, with the slit up the side higher than the censor's office would allow. She wore a simple string of pearls, perfectly matched and the "right" shade. She had little bell earrings, and when she walked, they gonged gently. Her perfume was something. Chanel or Rochas or Givenchy, whatever it was, it was the "right" one. A drop of that behind each ear lobe and the diamonds would fall like summer rain. A large charm bracelet was on her left wrist and a ring on the wrong finger: she couldn't have typed without wrecking the typewriter. Her hands were long and lovely and, I suppose, supple. The nails were pink pearl, the same as the ones around her neck. Through high-heeled golden Italian sandals, her toenails peeked out coyly. They were also the correct pearl-pink. She looked as though it would take a week to get her properly shod and dressed.

Then shyly she looked up and said, "Are you through?"

"I never started," I answered. "You may show Mr. Tannenbaum in, if he's still there."

She gave me a thoughtful look, then turned slowly and walked out of the room like a dancer, moving only from the waist up. She was something.

She came back in a couple of minutes and ushered in Mr. Tannenbaum.

57

THE DEAL

Mr. Tannenbaum looked about fifty. A bad fifty. He sat down in the chair that was oversized as everything in the office was oversized—the desk, the chairs, the windows, the drapes, and the egos. For the Baron, everything was oversized. I knew why. He had talked to me about it but it didn't make me feel any different about him.

Mr. Tannenbaum's feet came just short of hitting the floor. He had small hands, small neat feet. His suit was of excellent material but needed pressing. He had the shape of an egg, and his chin would never hit a wall before he walked into it. He looked like he had walked into a few too.

He sat there quietly looking at me, not fidgeting; his sleeves were too long, but his nails were well cared for. I looked at him politely, waiting.

He looked back at me with sad brown eyes. He said, "Call me Tanny, Mr. Jarnigan, everybody does. I am a Jew, married to a Catholic French girl, and I have had troubles like nobody, but I got my money up . . . like it was agreed upon, and after all this and that, the Baron now tells me that I must go to see you."

"Oh," I said.

He nodded and continued confidingly, "You know, the money is all gone."

"Oh," I said again.

Once more he nodded and sadly continued, "Well, I am here and since the Baron said you handled all the finances I thought that it was time we should discuss the picture."

"Oh," I said for the third time, then added, "What money, Mr. Tannenbaum, and what picture?"

He slumped feebly in the big chair, then very tiredly murmured, "I was sure that was it. When Micheline told me to give him the money to do the picture of the script they had written together . . . I knew . . . I tried to tell . . ."

"Hold it, Mr. Tannenbaum," I said, "now hold it."

He had started to talk faster and faster, like a motor with the governor broken. He spoke in the same unemotional tone, without feeling. He looked up at me.

"You see," he said, in a tired and lonely voice, "It isn't so much the money, it's Micheline—she left with him."

And then Mr. Tannenbaum did a sad and lonely thing. He started to cry . . . not loud, not showy. For him, I was no longer in the room. He kept sobbing deep sobs that came drily out from between his two hands that he had put up to his face.

58

THE DEAL

The little man rocked slowly back and forth in his lonely grief. "It's not the money, it's Micheline . . ."

An old saying came to my mind, "It's not the money, it's the principle." His cry was, "It's not the money, it's my wife." It looked as though the Baron had let me in for another bag of nails.

Well, now, how do I mop this up? I sat and watched the little man for a few minutes. Then I got up from behind the desk and walked carefully over to the wall bar. I picked out a bottle of brandy. I got two glasses and I poured out a stiff jolt into each of them. Then I walked back over to the quietly crying man. "Here, Mr. Tannenbaum," I said, handing him a glass.

He didn't look up; he took the glass without saying anything, but he didn't touch the brandy. I knew there was no "quick-cure," no "get-well pill" for a cracked heart.

After a few minutes he leaned back in the chair; he was taking it better now. He carefully leaned over and set the still untouched glass of brandy on my desk. He turned his round little fat face and looked at me piteously. He said, quietly, as if it were important, "I don't drink, Mr. Jarnigan." The armed soul dwelling in a feeble body.

The meeting, the social graces, the prelims, the talks, the con, the dinners, the drinks, the arranged boffs . . . the pseudo tax discussions, the giving of gifts; at last the party, and the public relations man for the Baron announces the partnership between me and the Baron.

"O.K., keed . . . O.K., Jarn." He breathes happily in my face. His breath is bad . . . it would be . . . so was the Deal.

10

Movieola: *Hugh Bloodtest*

He was like an Arab, velvet fat covering his body, eyes that flashed; he considered himself a "great layer of women." Many times I had heard him tell of his "named conquests." I had always told him and his brothers that he was no "layer of women" but was rather a "screwer of horses," and was loved by the brothers accordingly. And in the agent I had, in truth, no friend.

The agent was always talking about giving his stars and clients "service" or having them "serviced." When I was young I grew up on a ranch and my father or my uncle was always talking about getting the stallion and having this or that mare "serviced." Sometimes they'd have Tom Condell's Hereford bull come over to service some of the cows. So from youth onward any time I hear an agent or lawyer talk about "servicing" their clients, I know they, the clients, are in for a "paid screwing."

You know how it is early in the morning in southern California. A summer fog is still low and will never force its way up through the smog to disappear. The grand houses along Crescent Drive in Beverly Hills peer elegantly at each other, the drive takes an elegant lazy curve, and then you come to the really big estates. Most of them have high walls around them. From behind the drive, long rows of eucalyptus trees give off a tomcat smell and, once in a while, you can smell the ocean in the air.

Beverly Hills is not that far from the sea, but inside the walled manor houses the sun becomes filtered and gentle, daring to brush only lightly against the skins of the sheltered dwellers within. A special brand of atmosphere, perfumed, untainted—if you could bottle it in soundproof, anti-everything bottles, even Dr. Brinkley could sell it.

So the pure and the impure sleep the sleep of the innocent, the guilty and the doped, and I shouldn't forget to mention the two-million-dollar drugstore, where the pharmacist gets tennis elbow from pouring out sleeping pills to give his Beverly Hills clients.

Sleeping pills, the great pacifier, the great help over the rough bumps—

61

THE DEAL

Little grains of quiet,
Used with trembling hands.
Can make the world look lovely,
As you leave for promised lands.

—and after that verse, these pills, if properly taken, can gently and absolutely remove you from the Hollywood dream, when it has become a nightmare. I'm allergic to pills or I might have taken the trip myself, just for the ride.

I had walked out of my house, the lovely French Provincial one of fourteen rooms, two pools—one very small, I'd had it put in for my son—with hot and cold water. Luxury was in that house. A countess had done the interior decorating—this made it perfect, of course. I looked up and down the drive. Yeah, Beverly Hills. I wanted to be a part of it, but not as a foreign-type producer, a maker of artsy-craftsy European films. I walked down to the garage to get the car—a Cadillac, special body, black, long, low; it looked as if it had cost more than the house.

I passed between two hydrangea bushes just as a yellow butterfly with brown spots on his wings took off lazily, full of perfume and flowers—full of himself. He flew heavily, but with dignity, off to some butterfly appointment. They have them too.

I got in the car, started the lovely, heavy-throated motor, let it idle for a minute, then drove up the driveway, turned into the street. The Adohr milkman was just pulling up in front of my neighbor's home. My neighbor was a motion picture producer. Mr. Adohr's man got out of the milk truck in a uniform so white it made me feel cleaner just looking at him. He knew me; he waved casually. I waved back. I was a solid citizen, democratic too. The Adohr man carried the milk tenderly, like a baby. He put it down on the big side porch in the shade and walked back to the truck. I hoped he'd get paid. The last picture the producer made was so bad, if it had been human they would have buried it. He'd gone broke so many times it didn't hurt any more. But he lived the same all the time. I guess it was because he was, after all, a gentleman, and people let gentle people get away with almost anything if they wish, and they usually do.

I drove off down the street. The big car guided itself but I held the wheel just to be friendly. I was on my way to see Hugh Bloodtest, the president of the biggest talent agency in the world.

He had been a shoe clerk as a boy (was conscious now of all shoes, and his own feet) but by dint of hard work—that is, by lying, cheerfully cutting all his friends' throats (soon running out of friends but running in the money)—he had obtained a seat of infinite power. His marriage to the

THE DEAL

daughter of the head of a major studio hadn't hurt. At first he was nice to her, but then as the children and the money came, he tolerated her because by now he no longer needed her money, nor for that matter his father-in-law, the studio head. Where before he had been the soul of respect and solicitude toward his father-in-law, even to chanting Sir this and Sir that, now as time went on, taking a little bite further, a step longer, the Yes a second sooner changed to Yeah. Yes, he had made it big.

As I tooled the big car into the parking lot of the templelike building, I thought I should be polite, firm, dignified. Things were a little different now. I got out of the car and approached the building. I walked up the steps between a lot of Spanish grill and ironwork, painted white. I looked back toward the parking lot; there were two Rolls, a Bentley, a lowly Jaguar, and a Negro dusting them off now, a flick here and there. He almost sneered at my Cadillac—it was a domestic car—flick, flick.

I looked at my shoes, shined, but not too much. Good. He would notice it—they were not newly shined for him. I would be showing my independence. Ha!

I reached for the handle of the door, a huge brass ring coming out of a lion's mouth, and pulled. A bell chimed with proper solemnity. I was calling on fifty million dollars. But I was making my own . . . now. Bloodtest had asked *me* to come by. This was like being summoned by the Pope. I answered the call. Here I was. I went in, proceeded through a foyer.

The elevator soundlessly brought me to the tenth floor. Inside, as my eyes grew accustomed to the reception room's dim elegance, I could see several people waiting, three women and two men. The girls looked gay, sexy, charming, and properly dramatic. Whatever the occasion might call for, they had it. A brilliant-looking man, Noel Coward with a Vandyke, posed dignified and a little angry. He looked me up and down, decided I wasn't worth the effort and turned languidly away, as bored as a French aristocrat who has married money. The next number was a slim dark man; he had mean little eyes and a long foxy nose; he sniffed as if he were constantly smelling something he didn't like—and with a nose like that he could certainly smell plenty.

I finished the looking-over and approached a desk that was so dainty a puff of air would have blown it over. It would have taken much more to blow over the cool-looking girl who looked distantly at and past me. She said, "Yes?"

"I haven't asked you yet," I answered.

She parried it easily, "Whom do you wish to see?"

"Mr. Bloodtest," I said. "By appointment."

"And who . . ."

I cut her off politely, "Tell him Mr. Jarnigan."

"Does he know you, Mr. Jarnigan? Have you been here before?"

"Yes, but you had better check that."

"I will," she purred. "Please sit down."

I stood still while she looked me over. She had warmed up a little, but she was still no heat wave. She picked up the phone, one of the four on the desk. "Mrs. Menifie?" Sound bubbled softly out of the phone. "Yes, I understand, Mrs. Menifie. There's a Mr. Jarnigan here to see Mr. Blood-test"—she paused—"by appointment." The phone bubbled pleasantly again; she hung up. "Someone will come to take you to Mr. Bloodtest."

I said, "That would be nice."

"You can't do it," he began loudly through his false teeth, or as loud as he could without losing them.

Hugh Bloodtest said this as he slowly turned a deep shade of purple. The color rose from his shirt collar up to his ears and then around and the color chart of his kisser gave me the go-ahead. "Do what?" I asked quietly, and then, "Hugh man, you take it easy."

He lisped, "I'm easy, I'm easy."

"And you're a nice fellow, too," I said. "Now let's start this meeting off right. First, Hugh, I'm damn glad to see you." And I was. I was because this was the start of it and with him giving me the purplefaced light, I knew I was in. I knew I had the Deal. What was more important, Hugh Bloodtest, the Baron's agent and mentor, also knew I had the Deal.

He walked back past and around about eighteen hundred dollars worth of big black teakwood desk. He aimed his bottom at the black leather chair and sat down heavily. He gasped, "I'm getting too old for this. Anyway, Jarn boy . . ." Here he brightened up a little. Mr. Big. Mr. Big, taking care of everything. "I'm glad to see you too, Jarn boy, you've made a lot of progress and I've seen two of the pictures you've made. Very good. In fact, one was excellent." Here he permitted himself a little smile. "Now, Jarn . . ." As he said Jarn, he put his hands up in a gesture of mock sur-render. He then leaned forward and planted his elbows on the desk, looked at me in a friendly way and said, "Now, let's talk."

Well, here it was. Hugh Bloodtest, with fifty million dollars behind him, fifty million dollars that could be used for this and that. He had control of a good part of it and could certainly do everything that he said he'd do.

As he leaned forward and said, with a calmness I didn't like, "I got your letter, Jarn. How can I help you and the Baron?" I smiled at him affectionately. And I watched him reach into a humidor and take out one of those coffinlike cigars, taking one for me also and sliding it over to my side of the desk. He made a big business of opening the little coffinlike case; he glanced at me carefully for a minute, and I started to open mine with equal caution. This cigar was a nice cigar, Bloodtest was a nice fellow, I was a nice fellow. Hell, we were all nice fellows. But now I had a firm multiple-picture deal with the Baron. This made a big difference.

I thought back on a time, not too long ago, when I'd wanted to talk to Hugh Bloodtest just before I had signed the Deal. It went something like this: I had written, phoned, and practically begged for an appointment with respect to the last picture I had made, which happily had turned out a success. It was only then that I got a letter from Hugh Bloodtest on the gilded and muchly encrested stationery. There were *écussons* all over it. It looked like it would take a week to read only the crests. The letter was full of glowing terms and little friendly anecdotes and finished that I should come and see Hugh Bloodtest. Well—hm—here I was, but not in exactly the way he had expected to see me. I had answered the letter; it went something like this:

"I was pleased and flattered to receive a letter from so distinguished a person as yourself, being very unaccustomed to favors or letters from the great. I'm not exactly sure how to receive them or in what terms to acknowledge them. Once, some time ago, overly encouraged, overly enthusiastic, I first visited you and was overpowered, like many others, by the enchanting way you addressed me. You made me feel important, and as a young producer from France who had just won the Cannes Film Festival Award, I was certain that I could be *le vainqueur du vainqueur de la terre* (translation: the conqueror of the conqueror of the world). I remember you calling in the rest of the men; these were the high-collar white-collar boys, not just the white-collar boys. But once I had said my piece and had addressed them and yourself, I had exhausted the art of pleasing or being charming and I tried to retire, knowing that I had absolutely not sold with my soft sell the proposition of your agency being behind me. I had done all that I could and no man is very well pleased to have his 'all' neglected, be it ever so humble, or so little.

"A few appointments, some time, and many feet of film have passed since I waited with anxiety in your outer office, or since I was gently, but with a social grace, dismissed from your door. During that time, I pushed on with my work, as difficult as it may have been, and it's useless to complain although I didn't receive from you, or anyone, one act of assistance, one word of encouragement—the smile I never expected. But the treatment I did not expect was what I received. Any appeals for help, which I desired and solicited and literally sucked and begged for, fell on deaf ears. I was looked on with unconcern. It was like watching a man struggling for his life in deep water and once he has reached the shore, overburdening and encumbering him with help, with too much help.

"After my two awards from the Cannes Film Festival—which is admittedly a lopsided success because I too concur with the thought that unless you are a success in Hollywood, you are not truly a world-wide success with respect to the picture business—I was grateful that you noticed my efforts and were very kind. Nevertheless, this notice which you have finally given me, if it had been a little sooner, if it had been a little kinder—as the fellow says, 'one second sooner, or one inch farther'—but this was not the case.

"This, whatever it is you're offering me now, has been delayed to the point that I am happily, completely, indifferent to it, and I can't enjoy it.

"Still, being only a lopsided and partially successful producer of foreign films, I must say here, with a little cynicism, I must not confess to an obligation or a debt to you where no benefit or help has been received. What little efforts and what little success have been received by me have only been D.L., or perhaps you would understand the word *providence*. 'Providence' has enabled me to do this for myself.

"Having carried on my work so far with very little obligation to anyone, certainly to any favored one of learning or any high-placed agency, I think I will try to content myself with merely struggling onward and trying to get by on a million or so a year. But at least I won't wait in anyone's outer office . . ."

This went through my mind while I sat there watching Hugh Bloodtest unwrap his coffinlike cigar. I said, "Now let's talk about my deal with your star client, the Baron."

He looked at me with hatred. I grinned at him.

Then, with an effort like lifting the Empire State Building, he carefully, brick by brick, built a smile on his face. "All right, Jarn," he said with calculated deadly politeness, "let's talk. What do you want?"

"Well, Hugh, since you put it like that, I'm grateful for your help." He watched me as motionless as a basking snake. I continued, "What I want is . . ." And we both knew he'd try and give it to me . . . both ways.

"Naturally, what I want," I said, "is going to interfere with the Baron's exclusive contract with Jason Wormser's studio—a fourteen-year deal at a million dollars a year."

THE DEAL

"This could break his contract," said Hugh, frowning at me.

"Hugh, I know that, but the Baron wants to break his contract and screw Jason Wormser."

But it would also screw Hugh . . . out of his tremendous agency commission, and his complete control over the Baron, which enabled him to barter the Baron's services for other stars—"trading," as they choose to call it politely. This would considerably cut down the Bloodtest activities, since the Baron was the number-one box-office star of the world.

(Number one or not, I might point out that in many of the Baron's business discussions with me, in some cases when he'd get angry, it was like dealing with a child. When he didn't have his lawyer and business manager and/or moral support from both of them, he truly was not normal. His thoughts were not rational. He'd become angry and confused.

I'd explain the situation as I saw it, the various things that should be done, the differences with respect to certain tax shelters that we could take advantage of by working outside of the continental United States, by using a corporation—all legal, but a little complicated. When I'd ask the Baron if he understood these, he'd say of course he did, but was angry because he had not thought these things out in the clear precise fashion of normalcy. He still thought, even at his age, child fashion, all instinct and intuition, but that didn't make him feel any less unhappy. In fact, it was the contrary. The sweets of life were bitter to his taste. They were unhappily poisoned by the constant knowledge that he was as he was. His complexed shame was ever with him, ever increasing. This was why, after I knew the problem and many times tried to cheer him up—although usually this fell on a deaf ear—I finally told him that the world doesn't hang by a dong and certainly not his. I said, "The world doesn't hang by a dong nor your dong in particular."

Dongs and lawyers. The combination had occurred to me before. The actor-star producer always carries a lawyer with him everywhere; to business conferences of a certainty, but also to every luncheon, dinner, cocktail party. They call them several times a day. I am sure that even from the bathroom, they call their attorneys to check and see if they'll clear their right to make the normal move that they'd like to make there.)

Meanwhile, Hugh Bloodtest wouldn't approve the Deal. "Jarn," he cut back into my thoughts, "you may be as sharp as plate glass, but I can still have a hole put in you." He laughed, then leaned back in his chair, all fifty million dollars of him. There he sat, the Big Man. "The reason I sent for

67

you is, you could be getting into a little trouble." He smiled. "And Jarn, it was nice of you to come."

I grinned back at him. "Well, Hugh, it's a pretty big deal for me."

He smiled again; that was two in one minute, more than I thought he'd use in one day. The smile broadened a little. "Unless you use one of our other stars, I won't let the Baron make the deal."

"That's where you're wrong, Hugh. The deal is already made."

Now, a deal with Hugh Bloodtest fell something short of a guarantee from Lloyds of London, and I got to thinking about the claptrap cunning of a movie agent's heart. Then I got to thinking somewhat about my own heart. And finally I got to thinking about my Uncle Newt's old and foxy heart, all scheming Arizona-Kansas-clever.

One time Uncle Newt and I had made a funny little deal. We shook hands on the "solemn word of a Jarnigan." Although my part of the deal had to do with a girl, Uncle Newt's part had to do with money. But what it really had to do with, I recalled vividly, was a Mexican saddle.

My Uncle Newt had asked me to meet him at the local drugstore. We were sitting in one of the little booths which were just an extension of the soda-fountain counter when my Uncle Newt started to unfold his deal.

"Listen, Uncle Newt, I don't know about this—that last 'permanent' part you mentioned and all. I'm seventeen now and I'd like to figure out part of this for myself. You know that last . . . that marrying part and all."

"Boy . . . you hear me. You want to help your daddy, don't you? Why he even gave up his diamond ring this morning." This said while squeezing a cherry Coke, which he did by simply reaching backward where our booth joined the soda fountain. This was done with considerable dexterity on my uncle's part, and had to be done swiftly since he must complete this maneuver before Virgil the soda jerk came back from behind the prescription counter. My uncle served himself "ammonia Cokes" on the house which the house knew nothing about. Virgil was always suspicious, but then Virgil had a suspicious nature. Uncle Newt carefully squirted the soda, then added ammonia in the glass. Of course, again Virgil didn't see him do it. He didn't approve of my uncle in any way.

My uncle continued sliding down into the booth with one smooth continuous motion, took a sip from his ammonia Coke, and said in a conspirator's voice, "Listen, kid, you've got a rep around town as a dong kid. You're around screwing all these little girls . . ." (and their mothers, I thought proudly, but wisely said nothing, waiting for the deal I knew was coming) "Well, nephew," my uncle's whisper continued, "here is what you can do to help your dad out of a fix." He didn't add that if Dad was really in trouble, Uncle Newt was dead, because everything he had, he got from Dad. "You know how your dad is, with his religion and all." The voice dropped another notch lower, to the businessman's level: "You see, Jarn boy, this would have to be between us. Your dad would never stick for it."

"Well, what is it, Uncle Newt?"

He set his glass down in front of him, took his glasses off, polished them thoughtfully, put them back on and leaned closer, practically whispering: "Well, I know, or I hear, you been around with the Herford girl."

"Uh-huh."

"Well, here's what I was pondering over," he said, giving me the beady stare, his eyes weirdly magnified by the glasses. "If you was really to be serious about Della Herford, and marry her or something like that . . . well . . . old man Herford would be better and kindlier disposed toward us—I mean, your dad."

"Judas . . . Uncle Newt, I sure don't like that Della like that."

He leaned closer toward me. "You took her over the jumps, your cousin told me," Uncle Newt put in conversationally.

"Yeah, but it was . . . I mean that was for a bet and anyway I just don't like . . ."

"You love your dad, don't you, boy?" This said fiercely.

"Sure, but I . . ."

"But nothing. Here you got a chance to help out your family and you try to wiggle out of it."

"I'm not wiggling out. I just don't like . . ."

"You're wiggling." This said sternly. "You're letting your dad, your mother and brother down, way down . . ." Continuing sadly, "That's a pretty mean boy that would do a thing like that to his own close-blood kin." Then, with dignified self-pity, "I'm not asking for me." He paused. "Jarn, I can see you're upset; your Uncle Newt don't want to rush you into anything you really don't want to do . . ."

"Well, I really *don't* want . . ."

"Don't interrupt, Jarn. It's bad enough that you are ungrateful without on top of it being rude to your uncle and not hearing him out when he's only thinking for the family . . . and for all our goods . . . I mean," he said quickly, "for all our good," completing the phrase incorrectly. I started to interrupt him. He said, quickly and quietly after glancing over his shoulder, looking around to see that no one else was in the drugstore, that we were alone so that he could tell me what obviously was on his mind, "You see, Jarn boy—" he said confidentially, hitching himself over a little closer to me.

THE DEAL

He arranged himself carefully and crossed his legs. I noticed that one of his shoes had a hole in the bottom. He saw me looking at it and, still non-chalantly, crossed his legs the other way.

"You see, Jarn, I've been giving this a lot of thought and I think I've got her figured out."

I acted like I was looking out the window of the drugstore but I glanced at him sideways. My Uncle Newt, the big operator. If he had planned it out, it was sure to go wrong. Uncle Newt was a born loser; he never gave up trying, he never had any truly good deals. He was my father's older brother and had, by dint of keeping close to my father, made certain money, had always done fairly well and, although some of the deals that my father made when I was very young were good for us, he had always split fifty-fifty with my uncle. My uncle's contribution was always very nebulous, consisting mostly of meeting men and finally bringing my father in to discuss the deal. Things hadn't gone too well for the past few years because my father had certainly taken his religion seriously and now neglected business to the point where there wasn't any. When the deals and the money stopped coming in, my Uncle Newt was forced to fall back on his own resources, which unfortunately, were very meager.

While I was thinking this over and looking at Uncle Newt out of the corner of my eye, the door to the drugstore opened and in came two of the kids that I went to school with.

"Hi, Jarn."

"Hi, Susan," I replied to a tall, lean beautiful girl with long brown hair. She was the daughter of one of the men who had struck it rich. He had a lot of oil production, had been a rancher prior to that but now he rested comfortably on his oil, on all of the money he'd made; no longer a rancher wearing the clothes, the boots and the big hat that most of them affected. He now was addicted to, as he called them, "Hick Freeman" suits. He was still trying to be one of the boys although he was proud he had Hickey-Freeman suits and Florsheim shoes and went to Chicago, had even been to Europe.

Susan Howe was sixteen years old. She was the cheerleader in the high school and on cold days when leading our class of students through the various yells, wore her dress what I considered attractively short, and in jumping displayed an abundance of slender leg which I, along with the rest of the fellows, appreciated greatly. But old Foreman Howe—"the Fore-man," as they called him—was plenty strict with her, never let her out of his sight. I had tried to date her on a couple of occasions, had taken her to

70

the movies, but it hadn't worked out too well, the old boy always being on the lookout...

"... the way I have it figured out," Uncle Newt said.

I could tell from the disgusted look on his face he'd been talking to me while I'd been thinking about Susan Howe. Apparently I hadn't reacted properly to his big idea, which I still didn't know too much about except he wanted me to get locked up with Della Herford. "So you see, Jarn," Uncle Newt continued, "if you was to just get friendly—you know, a little more friendly than you have been—this would put your dad and me in a position to go in there and talk to the bank. Why, hell, in just a short time we'd be right back on top and your dad could go ahead with this preaching idea that he's got—which I'm certainly in accord with," he added judiciously. "Now, here's what I think you should do, Jarn. You see, I've done a lot of checking and, believe me, old Mr. Herford really checks out; he's in great shape in the money department, with his bank and all—and that's where you and I want to come in strong, right, boy?" Here he reached over and poked me not too gently in the ribs.

"Well, I like the money part and all, and I sure want to help Dad and my family, as you put it, but how about you getting friendly with Mr. Howe and lemme do this plan with Susan? Now, I'd like that," I put in eagerly.

"Now, you can just forget about Susan Howe and you stick to what I'm telling you. Susan don't check out at all. Old Foreman is a tough old son-of-a-bitch, he don't check out at all."

"Yeah, I know, Uncle Newt, but I like Susan pretty good and I can probably do the same thing there, I think, but ..."

"Now you just listen to me," Uncle Newt said harshly under his breath. "You listen to me, boy, because I tell you I have this thing figured out. It's not for pleasure we're doing this, it's for the family, remember?"

I didn't quite get the term "we're doing this," because the way I had it figured out, Uncle Newt had me locked in the barn and wanted to turn Della Herford in with me.

We must have sat there talking for quite a while. I know it was quite a while because my Uncle Newt had time to go up to the soda fountain when Virgil had gone back in the back to fill a prescription, which gave my uncle time to steal another one of his ammonia Cokes. He again shot a dash of cherry by standing on tiptoe, and reaching clear over the fountain, he could get a pretty good squirt of Coke. And then when Virgil would come out he would say, "Virge, would you add a little soda to this, you know I like soda, it's good for my stomach." Virge always looked suspiciously at the

71

glass, which was full of the concentrated Coke syrup, but he never said anything because my uncle was kind of a noisy fellow and wasn't ashamed to start a commotion anywhere, so Virgil figured that a couple of fingers of Coca-Cola syrup and a squirt of ammonia wasn't worth the commotion in the drugstore, which was the focal point of the local society, especially on a bad day like it was today. And in more ways than one it was becoming a bad day for me.

"So you see, Jarn," Uncle Newt said persuasively, "I got it all fixed for you, all you got to do is sweet-talk this Della a little. Hell, from what I hear I don't have to tell you what to say and all this and that about things like that, because hell, from what my boy tells me, you're a regular stud. He says you prong 'em all—how about that, boy?" he asked, leaning down and looking in my face.

The bald eyes, magnified now, had a glint in them I didn't like. Uncle Newt licked his lips and I turned away. He clapped me on the shoulder, friendly, uncle to nephew. "You know, Jarn boy, you're a lucky kid. I'll tell you what else your old Uncle Newt is going to do for you. You know my car?"

I knew the car, I did indeed. It was an old Pierce-Arrow, a convertible touring car. It was long, looked like a hearse, and was very high. It was a familiar landmark in the county.

"You see, Jarn," Uncle Newt continued, "I'm going to loan you my car. She's full of gas. And I've got ten dollars for you. Now I want you to sweet-talk Della into driving down to Nogales with you. Then you take her over the border and you know there's a lot of those cocktail places and so forth, and you kids'll have a good time." Here he poked me again in the ribs. "You know what I mean."

"Yeah, I know, Uncle Newt."

"Well, here's the idea, kid," he said eagerly, warming to the subject. "You take Della over and you keep her over there all night. Then the next day, you call me and tell me you're worried and all this and that and you're afraid to come back. Then I'll tell you to come on back and I'll go with you to see Mr. Herford and we'll just face him together and make a clean breast of it."

"Make a clean breast of what?"

"Well, Christ, son, what do you think I've been talking ... I mean, shucks, son" (this in deference to my father) "what do you think I've been talking about? You take Della over there and you two kids, you know you like each other—you've been to that poontang place before with her—so stay over there together all night, in the same room, register and

72

everything. Then, when you get back, old Herford will listen to reason. I mean," he put in quickly, "old Mr. Herford will help us work out the problem."

"Listen, Uncle Newt," I said. "What if I knock her up?"

Here Uncle Newt took a deep breath. He looked all around the drugstore; there was no one close by. He leaned over and whispered in my ear, which was unnecessary because no could have heard us, "What did you say, son?"

"I said," I repeated, "what happens if I knock her up?"

He slapped the table with his fist. He smiled and whispered fiercely: "That's it, boy, that's the ticket, Jarn boy, you've hit it. You've hit the nail on the head, right on the money button. You see, then you'll probably have to ask Della to marry you, the old man will have to agree—and your daddy-in-law is the richest man in town—and, what the hell, she's a nice girl, a little wide in the beam for my taste, but then a fellow can't have everything he wants in this life, and like I said before . . ."—here his voice dropped two notches lower and he was down onto the organlike and solemn family level—"sometimes a feller has to make these little sacrifices for his family. I know"—he shook his head sadly—"I've made mine."

"Well, Uncle Newt, if you'd like to take Della over, I'm all for it. I'll try and help you explain it to Aunt Esther and . . ."

"You trying to be funny, boy? You mocking your uncle? You making fun of me?" This fiercely—his eyes had an evil glint I didn't like. But then I never liked Uncle Newt very well anyway. I drew back from him and he saw that maybe he'd gone a little too far. He didn't want to do this since he was already in so deep he couldn't retract the proposal that he'd already made. He tried another approach, "Now, Jarn, let's don't you and your old Uncle Newt lose our heads and go off the sidetrack. We're just kind of excited about this . . ."

"I'm not excited, Uncle Newt. I just don't like the idea very much at all."

Uncle Newt looked at me thoughtfully for a minute, and then a grin spread over his face. His voice changed musically; here he was the good old Uncle Newt. "Jarn, boy, I'm going to do something I was waiting for your birthday to do. Do you know that saddle I got down in Sonora, Mexico—the one with all the silver on it?"

"You mean the Noponee saddle?" I asked, a little surprised.

"The Noponee saddle," he said with dignity.

Well, I sure knew the Noponee saddle. I guess it must have cost an awful lot of money. It was the thing my uncle owned of which he was the most proud, although he never rode any more. Once in a while in a parade, but that was all. It was heavy black and hand-carved leather; the silver work and engraving on it were done with loving care. Since I was a little boy, the height of my dreams was to own a saddle like the Noponee.

I never knew how my uncle had gotten hold of this saddle, but he loved it. I heard he came by it in various ways. I'd heard the story how he'd won it in a poker game; I'd heard the story how he'd traded his two quarter horses for it; but I'd also heard the story how he'd just picked it up and got it back across the border. This was the story we never talked about because everyone in our family was very correct and certainly honest, while Uncle Newt did a lot of things like changing the numbers in oil leases and taking commissions on both sides of a cattle deal and little things like this and that. I'd put two and two together and figured the third story might be correct. He had maybe "borrowed" that saddle from some rich Mexican a long time ago, got it across the border—and the Mexican couldn't get across to claim it. Anyway, that was years ago, and so far as I was concerned was beside the point. It was just the most beautiful saddle I'd ever seen.

Uncle Newt never knew what a great card he'd played when he told me he'd give me that saddle. I didn't trust him too much and I wanted to make sure of what he'd said. I wanted to make sure he'd give me that saddle if I did what he wanted me to.

While I'd been thinking about this, Uncle Newt's face had taken on a somber expression, his eyes fixed on me. He sat there in the drugstore booth, a rumpled and dusty old hawk looking at a young rooster. I turned and looked him straight in the eye. "Uncle Newt," I said, "you mean you'll give me that saddle with no strings attached if I do what you want with Della Herford?"

He returned my look, swallowed and made a sincere effort to look me directly in the eye. "That's what I mean, Jarn boy. You have my word on it."

This, of course, didn't reassure me too much because I'd had Uncle Newt's word on a lot of things; so had my father, and it hadn't worked out too well. "When could I get the saddle?"

"When you get back from Nogales," my uncle said grimly. "When you come back from your trip, boy, bringing Della with you."

The minutes went by. "Well?" my uncle said, "what do you say, boy? I ain't going to keep this offer open forever."

I looked around the drugstore. Susan Howe was just leaving. She waved goodbye. I waved back, thinking I'd sure like to take Susan with her slen-

THE DEAL

der legs to Nogales even if I didn't get the Noponee saddle. I turned back and said to Uncle Newt, "Uncle Newt, if you're telling me the truth, I'll do it."

"The *truth*, boy!" He reared back, looked down at me with as much dignity as he could muster. "I give you my solemn word. *The word of a Jarnigan*. You've got that saddle when you get back from Nogales with Della Herford and here's my hand on it."

With that he stuck out his paw, I put my hand in his, and we shook on it. The drive to Nogales in the Pierce-Arrow I'd like. The staying all night in Nogales and maybe going to one of those clubs, I'd like. The thought about Della Herford I wasn't too keen about, but I thought I'd enjoy the trip back in the Pierce-Arrow and when I got back home—then I'd have the Noponee saddle.

I shook hands again with Uncle Newt and I closed the "deal."

11

Movieola: *Jason Wormser, Studio President*   •

He wore his hair brushed forward in a kind of upsweep, a vain attempt to cover his bald spot. The hair, defying gravity, clung precariously to his skull as a cluster of flowers with no roots cling to a cliffside. He pushed his scanty black hair over the vacant spot on his head—his fleshy red nose a large button in the eggshaped surging jowls of his face. He was a big man. He had a small high voice. Little eyes, too close together, stared out coldly over the nose. He had tight thin lips and spoke in a high fluted voice, incongruous for such a big man. He had beautiful white teeth, but they hadn't grown in his mouth.

And it came to pass in the City of Hollywood in the days of Darryl the King, a wise man came from the East, a "maven" from New York. The name, Jason Wormser. He was a phony up to his eyebrows and his biggest trouble was that he wanted to be loved. His joy was hearing a good joke or story and he would invariably try to top it. Unfortunately, he had a twelfth-century mind for most everything; even his jokes should have been told with "thees" and "thous."

I remember when Jason Wormser had to get rid of his nephew, so he exiled him to the wilderness of television. Never had a general with such absolute fearlessness sent a human pig through a mine field of kinnybombs. Certainly that pig would be blown to smithereens.

> The General was content
> but the pig survived,
> is still alive,
> and the films came fumbling after.

He was a Lazarus who laughed and returned, knowing it was for more than three days.

A man without credentials? Send him through the mine fields. A pig runs and has two chances more to step on the fuse—so run, man—run, pig—run, pig—man. *Bam!*

Having gone a few rounds with Hugh Bloodtest, I was ready for the main event with Jason Wormser.

THE DEAL

And Jason was not long in summoning me. Actually, I could have summoned *him,* but Jason was still playing the game like he held the winning cards. So I played along and went to his office.

He ordered me up to his desk with two spastic jerks of his head. Another jerk, and he sent away the secretary who had brought me in. I was hardly seated when he informed me that the politics in our country were lousy, that the weather was reported rainy and that that was right because his left knee hurt.

After I had explained the first part of the Deal, the easy part, that still didn't please him. He started shouting and saying a lot of things. When he ran out of phrases and cuss words of a sort, he still had some wind left. So, he used it on me, shouting, "Don't you know any better than to talk to me like that?" From then on, it got worse. I didn't say anything. "Well?" he concluded in a whining tone.

"Listen," I said, as though talking to a crazy child, "if you don't yell and holler I can hear you. My deafness is a lot better since I've been drinking milk." I put my hand out and touched the trophy on his desk—a tennis trophy. "Mean anything?" I said, "or just for show?"

"Hell," he roared again, "I'm . . ."

"The hell you are," I said. "I'm damned glad to meet you." I stuck out my hand.

He grinned and gave me his beefy paw. We shook hands and he walked back around the desk, aimed his bottom squarely at the executive chair, sat down and waved the other paw. Then he coughed. It sounded like calling up a dog. *Heyumph.* But I knew he meant for me to sit down. I did. We grinned at each other, and there we were, as friendly as puppies again. It would probably last all of two minutes.

"Now," he said, "let's get to work."

Even though I figured I had been as busy as a Japanese juggler, I agreed, and we started to work on the Deal. He pushed some buttons and the production people came in smartly, almost saluted, and sat down. He looked at them. He sat back and talked elegantly from the high celestial plane of his $800,000-per-year income. His voice carefully brushed and combed for his listeners, each one receiving lovingly his well-modulated tonal ablutions. His advice was well meant—if ignored, brought certain disaster. All listened carefully; all ignored it.

"Listen, Jason," I said. "Pride ruined Judea, it conquered Rome, it pooped off Greece; Hollywood isn't even a mouse-fart compared to those cities."

"Balls," he sneered. "Hollywood is the greatest city on earth and I am

78

the greatest man in Hollywood. You don't do what I want in this deal and you are dead—worse than dead, finished, through, *kaput.*" When he said *kaput* the false teeth started to go. He clapped his hand to his mouth and covered it beautifully with his handkerchief. "You think you've got that deal with the Baron," he said through the loosely separated teeth, "Oh, you . . . you . . . I could spit . . ."

"Don't spit, Jason," I said, "don't blow the Deal." I grinned at him. I had him cold and he knew it. "Now, let's start over," I said. "You asked me here to get things straight. Well, in my book they *are* straight."

His eyes glared at me. "I'll have you knocked off," he hissed. "I'll have you beaten up, I'll have them cut the balls off you," he yelled. That did it. He was worse than Bloodtest.

"You can skip the mushy talk, Jason. Don't overmouth it. You may have to eat it, and crap don't taste good. I know—I've eaten enough, keeping the lid on this pot. And I've got the contract."

That shook him. For the first time he started to calm down. The dirty talk impressed him. "You going to bull it through?" he asked.

"Yeah," I said. "Better get on the winning team." I looked at him coldly. The winning team is me."

"Well, kid," he breathed, "you know me . . . I could be with you all the way . . . *if,*" he finished slyly, "you're a winner. Sometimes I blow off, but you know I'd be with you. Remember the time . . ."

I patted him on the shoulder and said gently, "I remember, Jason. I remember. As long as we understand each other."

"Oh, we do . . . we do . . ." he hummed.

He turned away from me, strangely older, and sat back in his chair. He pushed a button, and an office waiter wearing white gloves came in. Wormser ordered drinks. When the waiter returned, I relieved him of them, walked over to Jason and said, "Have a drink." I looked around casually. "Nice office, nice service."

He sat there staring at me, not saying a word, not touching his drink. He breathed, "I'm too old for these arguments." Then more calmly, "Do you really have a signed contract with the Baron, son? Not just a talk-deal—an oral contract."

I grinned at him affectionately. I reached my hand slowly up to my inside pocket. I took out a signed copy of my deal with the Baron and threw it on the table in front of him. He didn't touch it, that paper that he had screamed, ranted, and raved about, that contract that could change his studio's plans, and that was now there for him to read. He looked at me for at least three minutes, thinking, wondering, scheming. Finally . . . nothing ever moved more slowly than his old hand going out to pick up the contract. He whispered softly to himself, "Well, let's see what we've got here." He began to read. He read it with no pleasure. Then he looked at the back cover, which was blank, and "read" it just as carefully. What he had read was very clear: a short, well-drawn contract that said exactly what it said. No other interpretation could be arrived at reading that document. I had a firm five-year multiple–motion picture contract with the Baron. Jules Molotov, the finest motion picture lawyer in the world, had drawn that agreement. He was paid one of the highest fees an attorney could ask, plus a small percentage of the budget of each picture, and after the break-even point of each picture he'd get a piece of the producer's share. For that, he was retained by me for the duration of the contract to act as my personal attorney.

Later, much later, to help him get more money (because Jules Molotov's young, pretty, and sexy wife was going to divorce him), I agreed to let him represent the company—the partnership of the Baron and me. That gave him bigger fees and a bigger percentage (and gave him his wife back, for a time). But it proved to be my second biggest mistake, because when the dike broke, he couldn't represent me *against* the Baron, so I had practically disarmed myself. My first and biggest mistake was in making the Deal at all.

Jason Wormser said, "Can I have a copy of this agreement?"

I looked at him for a moment. "So far as I'm concerned, you may. I'll ask Molotov to give you one."

He nodded, still looking at me as though he wasn't too sure about me or about what he had just read. It wasn't so much that he was surprised, and he certainly wasn't afraid. It was just moving a little too fast for him. So he'd try to slow it down.

He gave me the fatherly Jason Wormser smile and confidential tone, "You know, Jarnigan, I've been meaning to talk to you for a long time, especially since your last couple of French films. Hell, son . . ."—here the fatherly warmth and charm—"you belong back in the family, here at the studio. You were here once," he nodded nostalgically, "right?"

"Yeah, but you didn't know it. However, I'm glad you've looked it up."

A couple of layers of the fatherly charm peeled off, since he saw I wasn't buying it, but plowed on: "Jarn, why don't you come to the house for dinner tomorrow night?"

I looked at him and smiled. "That would be nice, Jason. I think I can make it."

But I'd check with the Baron first.

12

The Baron had been bothering me a little lately. He was irritable and snarled at everyone. He was still very friendly with me and talked a lot about many things. But he'd begun to question me about our picture and about our Deal, about what he felt, about what he wanted, about what he thought. He wanted to change the script. And I was the one guy who didn't "yes" him. I think that was the first reason he really started to depend on me.

"Jarn," he said, after a long and boring session, "I want to talk to you about a new part Jason Wormser has boxed up for me. I want . . ."

Now, maybe it was because all of this "moonlight" night-shooting had made me tired, or perhaps I was overly worried about my meeting with Wormser, but I said coldly and firmly, getting up from my chair, "Baron, you talk too damn much. And it's too damn much about you." I turned away from him and started for the door.

"Jarn," he called after me. "Jarn . . ."

I kept going, but called back, "I'll see you at the studio tomorrow."

"O.K., boy . . . Get some sleep. Sorry I sounded off so much about me. See you tomorrow," he called.

I just threw up my hand in a wave, without turning around, and left.

The basic and prime flaw in the Baron's personal makeup was that he believed, in spite of his own self-knowledge, that he was as formidable, as virile, and as potent as the studio publicists had made him.

The next day, when we were sitting in the Blue Room at the studio— where only the stars and major executives were allowed to water, feed, and muddle their brains at lunch—the Baron looked over at me with a confused and painful expression, so I knew he was thinking about himself and was worried.

"Kid," he said quietly, "Jarn, like I told you, Leo Walsh wants me to do his next picture, but I don't know . . ."

"Don't know what?"

"Well," he continued. "I don't know if I should do it, because in the story I play a man who's . . . who's impotent."

I looked at him. He was being honest. One of the rare times when he was trying to decide something correctly, that is, correctly for himself. I

THE DEAL

wondered, if the Baron were given a private screening of himself—if I'd taken some footage of his private hell in the green bedroom the night he gave me that party to celebrate the beginning of our Deal—would he still be asking me, could he *play* a man who's impotent?

"Aside from the impotent part of the character, how's the role?" I asked, looking around the room and nodding to Jason Wormser, who nodded back, his great fleshy face florid from his "tea"—a potent vodka martini served to him from a blue teapot in a large blue cup. His mouth formed the words across the room: "See me in my office after lunch." I nodded a Yes. To continue the pantomime, he gave me a wink and the thumbs-up, A-OK signal of agreement, and went back to his tea, his round red button of a nose a cherry, shining and hanging on for dear life over the teacup.

". . . so what I'd like is your opinion." The Baron had continued talking. I realized that I hadn't been listening to him, but he didn't notice, being so full of the problem at hand.

"Well," I welled, "I'll read the script, but I remember a saying—if a guy doesn't have too many nuts in his basket, he shouldn't walk through the same woods again. This saying may or may not fit." I looked at him thoughtfully. "I think it does."

I went back to my looking around the dining room. I knew it would never stop there. The Baron had the germ of an idea and was carrying it carefully in his head the way you hold a sick baby. So, knowing we would continue this conversation after lunch, I said, "Baron, I should see Blood-test; he's in the corner, so I'll see you back on the stage. O.K.?"

"Sure, kid," he said, hardly looking at me, "I think I'll go and have a cup of tea with the Pres."

I looked steadily at him for a moment. "Yeah, do that. But be nice and be careful, you know . . ."

"Sure, kid," he assured me again.

I got up and walked among the tables, saying Hello here and there. I wasn't worried about the Baron getting drunk. I knew the president would only give him one cup of "tea." I continued to cross the dining room; the faces read like a movie star tourist's map. I gave a nod here, a kiss there. So, nodding and kissing my way, I was making progress across the room to where sat Hugh Bloodtest at the head of the ten-million-dollar agents' executive dining table. I finished my walk hearing him say, "Atttention, men, the boy genius, the foreign-type producer, is in our midst." Bloodtest

82

had a stupid, infantile smile on his face, a fixed grin of polite idiocy. The smile of a baby that hadn't been born.

It must be remembered that the Baron had admitted he was hung like a stud mouse. In truth, I think this was really the greatest cause of many flaws in the Baron's character. I know me. I have pooned a few of them . . . but would never have done . . . never have started . . . the "run down the slanted stairs of love." You pooned them because you loved it, because next to the first and greatest thing you wanted in the world was just that, and maybe the poon was the best. Remember how it was, in or out of school? But at that age, remember, the teachers pooned and the choir leaders, and the girl in church who played the organ. (Now, this is symbolic in many ways, but it seems to me there was a definite hazard in being a church or choir organist. They were always getting seduced, raped, or murdered in the choir loft. I am sure that the insurance risk of being a choir accompanist is bad, and the premium high.) You pooned them and you loved it and were proud of your dong and your wiggle, and your worldly knowledge. You were a teen-age man and you had proof, if needed, and it was needed; and you were damned happy to gratify and crawl over, climb up or down, sneak through or warm up to any cause, any need, for one more of them. Especially if she was beautiful and was young and the skin went together with a lot of rules that you put up.

But with the Baron, it was different. He was like a great brain with no outlet, a great orator and no tongue to speak. He had the drive, the desire, the allness that drove him on to conquer any girl or any woman in the world he saw and desired. But when he got there, the cupboard wasn't bare—but the key just wouldn't fit the lock. He had a needle, and what was required was a spike. The drive in, like the drive home, would never be accomplished by a ghost.

One night at the studio when we were shooting late, we were talking about the problem, and I said, "Baron, I am sure glad everything's going well and want to thank you for the last few days. Man, the rushes look great, and your scenes in the fight and on the docks are just sensational. I know I've hollered at you and bitched about the delays and all this and that, but boy, you're just great in there the last few days and I'm sure for you."

And I meant it. He'd been working the last few days like it was his first picture, nobody could have been better. He made some suggestions during an action scene that were splendid, and even the cameraman said, "Jarn, no matter what he does wrong, how can you help but like the son-of-a-bitch when he's like he's been for the last few days?"

"He's fine. He's great," I agreed. "Listen, Marc, brag on him a little. Tell him you appreciate the good work he's done and his suggestions. Tell him that and encourage him."

"Hey, Jarn boy," he grinned, "what's the matter with you? You're the nervous one."

"Ha, ha," I laughed with him in the corny way. "Hell, Marc, you know me, I'm the 'Iceman,' the same old s.o.b. whether the work goes good or bad."

"I know . . . I know," he answered with that half-smile, "I know, Jarn." And he gave me a look of steady friendship and affection that had endured nine years and thirteen motion pictures. He knew me . . . and I knew him, and we were genuine friends who respected each other by knowledge; but, more important, by work under fire . . . and again fire.

As the picture progressed, going better every day, the rushes were so good that even I started to dare hope we'd grabbed onto a "big one" and then, not prearranged . . . not destiny . . . nothing spectacular . . . *it* happened. It was as simple as though you had just put a dynamite cap in a cap pistol. Everything went up. It had to . . .

Possibly the only person in the world who cared more about the Baron's dinker than he did was the reigning sex goddess of the industry, an Academy Award winner and number-one box-office draw.

Needless to say, she had never seen it—either the real one, which would have calmed her down, or the Frankenstein one, which would have frightened even her—but the idea had already become an obsession with her. When she'd look at the Baron, it was like a setter pup watching a bug: she really put a fix on him.

Here was a woman who could have had any man in the world (and indeed, she was known to have denied herself many presentable candidates who came along); and yet she had this particular thing for the Baron. After a while, you could see it eating her up.

I had seen men who had it bad, who absolutely had to have this or that woman. I have seen old guys sick with a letch for a young girl. These were all-enveloping passions that completely obliterated everything else. But her passion had an abnormal tone. She was really hooked.

I was uncomfortably in the middle of this campaign because I had negotiated with her almost to the point of signing a firm three-picture deal. But she had given me an absolute condition that the first picture would have to

THE DEAL

co-star the Baron. She had made it quite clear that I would have to "arrange things" so that she could "get to know him better," even before the shooting.

Obviously, if I could lock up these two number-one stars in one film, it would be an international blockbuster, so I had become her not-too-unwilling general in the campaign to get the Baron—also her courier, runner, aide-de-corps, fellow conspirator, *maquereau*—not to put too fine an edge on it, I felt like a pimp in a Mexican whorehouse, except I was pimping for the world's number-one sex goddess. Which didn't make it any nicer, only more air-conditioned. I was busier than a hustler working two bunks.

At this time, the sister of a studio head gave a tremendous cocktail party on the estate next to mine in Beverly Hills. Since the Baron and I were partners, we were invited together, and as we set out I thought I ought to warn the Baron that this was just another move in the sex goddess's chess game . . . and that she was trying for a checkmate.

As the Baron and I crossed the huge lawn, there was much babble, drinking, dancing, twisting and all of those new African-type Negro dances. As we came to the door, the sex goddess, who had been on her way to the powder room, stopped dead in her tracks, as if someone had pulled a trigger in her. She gave a look to the Baron that nailed him in place, waving and shouting Hello to me over the heads of the crowd.

Torn between the necessity and immediacy of the powder room and her letch for the Baron; drunk enough to be twitching and waggling her cute *derrière* in time with the music, and with a sweet and simple girlish smile on her face, her legs spread, rhythm in every part of her—she started peeing daintily, but with serene dignity, her body moving in time to the twist.

As the golden stream darted and ran happily through the flowered impressions of the new white rug, the studio head's sister gave a scream of rage and pain; but the sex goddess, her feet of clay now very damp, very soggy, floated happily, oblivious of everything and everyone but the Baron. Now, the Baron and I were quite close to her at this point of the peeing. She was still dancing and, as the Baron looked down, he saw the streams coming toward him, jumped agilely aside, and was immediately grabbed by a young girl to dance. So away they twisted, farther and farther from the by now very damp and somewhat dispirited sex goddess. She was hurriedly, if not affectionately, rushed away by three protectors to the safety of the Taj Mahal–like powder room. But it had the startling effect of a disaster so far as the sex goddess–Baron picture was concerned.

The Baron had been frightened of the sex goddess anyway. Her reputation alone would have been enough to shrink him into humiliation (and

85

then he would have been nonexistent). But the effect of this golden-stream episode was all that was needed to frighten him right out of any bedroom, the house, and my super-Deal, for sure.

In all my years in Hollywood and Paris, I never had been so near and yet so far. Neither had she. In the end we were all like empty paper bags, blathering at nothing.

I hoped we could now get on with the shooting of our first movie, as I was already blocking out the second in my mind and eager to move our operation to Paris. At the same time, I was beginning to suspect that there were going to be many more nightmarish episodes in my life, now that the Baron was a part of it.

13

What had started as a quick off-the-top-of-the-head idea became an absolute mad-scientist-and-the-monster fabrication. When, as the producer of the picture, I had received an interoffice memo to come to the makeup lab, I couldn't guess the reason. I knew that there had been a conference between the Baron and the head of the makeup department, and I couldn't understand why I was to be consulted, since so far as I was concerned all the makeup problems on the picture had been solved in advance.

I had seen the Baron talking with the head of makeup off and on for the past three or four days. Then one day I saw the Baron take him to lunch. Although Frank Eastman was a very nice fellow and had been the head of makeup at the studio for years, I had never known the Baron to be particularly friendly toward him. He was just a nice normal fellow so far as I knew. Actually, I might not have remembered him so well except that I knew he was responsible for the fabrication of an interesting brace of gifts from Jason Wormser to Hugh Bloodtest and to the president of another major studio. I had first seen these objects on the desk of Jason Wormser and later seen them in the office of the president of the other major studio and, of course, had seen this "masterpiece" many times in Hugh Bloodtest's sanctum sanctorum.

The object was a gold-plated Oscar-type award. It was a huge oversized hand, cast in bronze. The fingers were closed into a fist, with the middle finger pointing straight up. This was set in a heavy black marble base. The golden fist was there in all its splendor, giving the golden finger to the world. It was engraved in the truest tradition of disrespect from Jason to Hugh Bloodtest, and from Jason to the president of the rival major studio.

When I first realized to what lengths the fabrication of this other situation might amount to, it was truly another education I received. I thought I could no longer be surprised by anything in Hollywood. I walked into the laboratory, all white and disinfected and in the truest sense simulating an operating room in a fine hospital—all fluorescent lights and the proper laboratory smell. One door in the research lab was marked Private and guarded by a studio cop. You'd have thought they were constructing a secret weapon. As it turned out, they were.

THE DEAL

As I walked into the room, my first impulse was to give a whoop of laughter, but there was a calm and strained serious atmosphere. Eastman and the two lab men, all in white smocks, were discussing with deadly seriousness the thickness, the length, the rigidity, the movable parts . . . In brief, what was lying there in the spotlight, was a rubberized plastic false dong about thirteen inches long and of unbelievable proportion . . . . Then Frank Eastman looked up at me with his sharp little eyes, smiled nervously as though he had just delivered a baby, and said, "What do you think?" The two lab men were leaning over the table under the lights, looking at me tensely, as though what I might have to say would have an effect on the future of the race.

I couldn't stand it. I howled with laughter. Frank Eastman leaned back and for a moment looked resentful, and then grudgingly started to grin. Being a knowledgeable man, though full of self-importance, he was waiting for my reply.

I looked down at the thing and back at him and said, "I think it looks like what it is."

"Yes, I know," Frank said, "but don't you think it's a great job?"

"I suppose so, but the only one of those I'm interested in is mine. It may sound selfish, but that's the way it is. If this is what I think it's for, I think you should have padded his tights with a banana."

Frank looked at the two lab technicians; they returned the look. He said, "Why don't you fellows go to lunch. I want to talk to Mr. Jarnigan." They walked out without a word. After the door had closed, Frank said to me, "I guess you think this thing has gotten a little out of hand."

"Yeah . . . I do. I know there was a lot of trouble on the set the other day because the padding in the Baron's tights slipped during the fight scene and his dong was on his knee. I know you two guys have been talking the last couple of days, but I never knew you were coming up with anything this realistic."

"Listen, Jarn," he said. "This is serious."

I would have laughed again, but the look on his face made me realize that I had to find out what the hell was going on.

"Jarn, the Baron's been down here the last two nights. I think he's slipped a cog but I can't tell him that."

"You can't tell him what?" I asked. "And turn that light out and cover that thing up. It looks like somebody's just been dissected." I started to laugh again, a little sourly.

"Don't laugh, Jarn," he said gravely. "This could develop into a serious problem."

THE DEAL

"Well, what the hell is so serious and hush-hush about padding the Baron's tights?"

"Well," Frank said, still much too serious for my liking, "after the Baron and I started talking about this and how he could wear it and prevent a recurrence of the thing slipping off, he got an idea which I didn't like but you know the Baron when he's a little high. He stuck to his point and he paid me enough money on his own to work this thing out for him, and paid the lab technicians enough so that the three of us are keeping quiet. That's when this thing began to worry me and that's why I asked you to come down here."

"Well, what the hell is this? I don't know anything about it. I was sorry he was embarrassed on the set because of that difficulty with the tights, but I never thought it had affected him that much."

"That's what I say." Frank turned away, and walked back to the small desk in the corner of the room, began to take off the white smock, then sat down.

"Listen, Frank, this is ridiculous. Get rid of your smock—you're beginning to look like Madame Curie after a bad night. Let's go over to the Club and have a drink. Then you can tell me everything the Baron said. You're so bloody serious that you worry me. This is one time the Baron hasn't said anything to me about what's going on. When I first saw that thing, I thought this was another gag that Jason had figured out, like that golden finger you made for him last year."

Frank got up and walked over to a door, got rid of the smock, then took his coat out of a closet, put it on and said, "Jarn, I'll take you up on that drink, we can talk better outside. Just a minute." He walked over to the table and carefully picked up the huge false dong like he was handling a sick baby. He wrapped it in white gauze, towels, and padding, and put it in a large box. He then went over to a big safelike contraption which he opened up, carefully put the coffinlike box inside, closed the door, locked it carefully and then, shaking his head, said, "Let's go and get that drink."

I shot a quick look at him and he was strangely pale.

"Jarn," he said, "I've got a hunch about all this, and it isn't good. And after some things the Baron said . . ." His voice trailed off.

"What things?" I asked quickly.

"Just things. Now, will you for Christ's sake buy me that drink?"

"Sure, Frank . . . sure I will, boy. Just take it easy."

But *I* wasn't taking it easy. Frank had me worried. Well, hell, I'd be able to handle it. I didn't doubt that for a minute. After Frank had a couple I'd get the truth out of him.

THE DEAL

Well, Frank didn't have two drinks, he had five. He didn't like them. And I didn't like what he finally told me.

In the end, it was the false dong that threatened to ruin us and truly kill the Deal.

The mechanics of the Baron's false dinker was a distasteful and yet an astonishing thing to see. It looked as though it were a combination garter belt and jockstrap. I began to worry about this when I discovered by accident that the Baron didn't confine the wearing of this object to his movie-making. He was wearing it, properly "battened down," in private life. One night the Baron explained to me the whole, unhealthy, unsavory situation and idea. He said, "Jarn, I'm through being laughed out of bedrooms. This is the foolproof way."

He continued savagely: "Jarn, in the night when I get them going I can touch them with a baseball bat or a pickle and they will still go off. I just say to them I have a complex and don't want to be touched, on my dong, anyway." I thought, He don't like to be touched, a feces complex. He can't afford the complex, but he's the feces part, all right. I looked at him in amazement.

While I was studying him, he went on, as if he were alone. He told me of the night with the sex goddess star. They were boffing hard . . . then, a disaster . . . the false dong broke. "Christ," Baron said to himself, "It's still in her, what can I do?" The Baron had jumped up and away from the girl, away from the bed; he ran into the bathroom, locked the door, and stood there in abject terror. He stared down at himself, at his straps, his empty harness—it looked as though a small midget had slipped out of a parachute. He couldn't go back to face her—What to do? He told me he'd never been so terrified in his life. I believed him. Good Christ, what a nightmare. (I withdraw that, Blessed Christ. I've got no right to even think of You or call your name . . . in this dirty business, I'm even afraid to pray . . .)

Afterward, I understood the Baron's ridiculous, yet horrible plan. He told me how he was going to practice and everything. It was then I knew how far the Baron was off balance with respect to his infirmity. His obsession had carried him out, and out further. He was beyond sanity.

I remember a friend of mine taking me to a Paris precinct station and into their "collector's room" concerning sex criminals, deviates, and perverts. Here was a collection of the most far-out and sadistic sex instruments I had ever heard of—devices no one but a madman or woman could think up.

90

THE DEAL

There was a bicycle with a false dinker where you sat, pedaled, and got yanced. There was a false wall, full of protuberances and holes, forward . . . or backward . . . pleasures modern and ancient joys, joys modern and ancient pleasures. All of this filth and horror was brought to mind when I first saw the Baron's plan proceeding.

He began proving himself with his false and yet *fidèle* friend. Then while making violent love—bogus love, hocus-pocus love—the Baron lived for these scenes and the pleasure he got looking down at the girls' reactions. These beautiful girls! He "came" because they gave such shocked, painful, sexually jarred, uncertain moans of ecstasy; knowing the Baron was kissing them, knowing the Baron was riding them, and that they'd never felt such size, such pain, such hurting passion. Wasn't he the biggest star of all! He "came" when they "went off." He dewdropped pitifully, feebly, within his plastic dinker walls. His six-year-old-sized self slobbered a nothing inside the mastodon *bête* he'd made for himself. The false yet reigning dinker had truly felt as much as the Baron . . . only it didn't get excited and cry afterward.

> Small is the dinker hanging from me,
> Never been shown in a whorehouse.
> I thank no father, mother dear
> That I am hung like a stud mouse.

The Baron had practiced much and well, like a man who has received a new artificial limb. First he walked about in the privacy of his own room. Later, becoming more bold, he walked through the house, stomping from the bedroom through the corridor into the great hall, into the living room and back and forth. Stomp, stomp, stomp. Practice, practice. Soon he might be able to try it outdoors with any degree of privacy.

This was a technique you had to pay to learn. The Baron had taken frequent trips down to Mexico and there, with the young ones to practice on, he was diligent and apparently successful. Finally, the big night in Hollywood—he had taken a new, young, and voluptuous starlet to a première. Later, in his home high up in the hills, after the usual champagne, soft music, and the lights lowered routine, after the dialogue that both played very well—she surprisingly enough knew all the words, words he didn't think she should know—came the gentle undressing and the lights turned completely out, with the Baron saying he truly couldn't be touched.

By this time, after many kisses, the girl was completely submissive and at the Baron's mercy and, as he boasted, he could have touched her with a

91

baseball bat or a dill pickle and she'd have gone off like a rocket. With this false sword that he now fenced with so beautifully, now was the time.

He went in softly, slowly at first, then drove mightily all the way home. Her eyes widened with disbelief and pained shock—she fainted. Then pulling out and removing himself to the bathroom, he saw that everything was well in place; apparently his many hours of practice had paid off. Later, the Baron couldn't help feeling highly elated; he bathed in the absolute shock and amazement of this young girl. She looked at him with astonishment and awe. She had never felt anything like this, quite obviously; and didn't quite know now how to accept the Baron. When the Baron was smiling down at the girl she finally got up enough courage to breathe, "Baron, you're a . . . there is nobody like you. Nothing like you. You're a king." And she was right. The Baron was certainly unique—not eunuch anymore.

I wonder what she would have thought if she could have seen his face in the dark as he opened the bathroom door and came into the bedroom—the culture of two thousand years ground down into dust and smothered beneath this false animalism of the Baron, this overly large and disproportionate thing that was now as much a part of the Baron as his own arms and legs.

He would approach ready to be cruel, exact, precise, absolute—and fully aware of taking his rights. He had practiced enough, and if the girl could have seen this, she might have been revolted, but perhaps she would have been more surprised, waiting, maybe even with anticipation, for what was to come. Whatever the unknown was, whatever his demands would be, they would be met and satisfied; because she had her own little row to hoe, she had her own little things to overcome. With her, "business was business." She was glad, gratified, and thrilled to be in bed with the Baron, because this would justify everything. There was no question it would have its profits, its fringe benefits, its definite result for her. And it kept the Baron happy.

> Baron laid a little girl,
> He laid her on the shelf.
> But he had nothing to dip in.
> She only screwed herself.

The Baron's confessions as to his sexual disasters seemed candid enough when he recited them to me. He laid them about. He spread them like a steel-wool blanket on a cold and rusty bed. The real interest, I thought, would be to hear the other-side-of-the-bed's story. The willing yet-empty-wombed tale.

14

The next problem on the agenda was also out of the ordinary film makers' realm—but this too I was able to use to keep shooting the films. I guess I would have used anything.

The Baron had found some old aluminum-type records of his father talking. His father had been a windy but nice old guy. After he died, whenever the Baron was lonely, disturbed, or just drunk, he listened to these records each day. The sessions had gone on for quite a while. The Baron listened to these records and searched out each phrase for advice. It was interesting but at the same time pitiful. He'd insist that I go with him and listen, so we'd enter the million-dollar den with the paintings and all the over-elaborate furniture and hear again and again these recordings, the Baron making every effort to get more out of it than was possible, busy at the tremendous recording and hi-fi machine, adjusting knobs, reading dials, as busy as a sparrow. He would listen for a while, then look up at me and say, "Kid, do you hear *that*? That's what Dad is saying to me."

"Yeah," I agreed the first few times, and listened. To me it was all babble.

After several repetitions of this scene over a period of some weeks, and the closer we got to the end of the picture, the more disturbed the Baron became. He kept trying to get something extra from those recordings. I got to know each inflection of the old man's voice, and suddenly I knew a way to play it with the Baron, depending on how drunk he was or how "horsed" he was before I could put the plan into action.

Since the Baron seemed to be trying to get messages from his father, I knew for sure that, properly used, I had found a way to keep the Baron in line. The following day I had the secretary call all the character actors we had on the books. I interviewed them privately, heard their voices, and finally selected Vinton Hayworth. He was excellent. With some rehearsing, a lot of work, and some judicious editing, this guy could duplicate exactly and imitate to perfection the voice of the Baron's father.

From then on, the actor, who was a nice guy, rehearsed and rehearsed, read scenes over and over again, with me furnishing him the dialogue. He was thinking all the time that he was reading for test scenes and various parts in the forthcoming pictures. I had conned him with the idea that it was a father speaking to and giving advice to his son. He agreed to do his

93

readings in that way, since he wanted the part. He finally said, "I think I've got it exactly now," after he'd heard one of the actual records of Baron's father. "I think I can do the part."

"Yeah, I know. I'm sure you can. But let's keep on doing the test scenes and from here on in you're on salary." I told him to keep this in confidence, as it was to be a surprise picture.

Finally, by use of those records, I was able to get the Baron to do almost anything according to the advice of the "voice from beyond." Since we were getting into the last days of the picture, I had carefully seen that many records were "discovered" by the Baron. I used old letters, old stamps and an old gun case. The markings on the leather case indicated the records came from Paris and from Jamaica.

This phase of control of the Baron worked successfully for several weeks. His father's voice tolled, "Son, integrity, dignity. Help your fellow man." The long-dead voice, perfectly imitated, droned on: "Baron, my son, be true to yourself, be true to your work. Honor must be served at all times. Beware of false friends. Remember, if a man has one true friend in a lifetime, he is fortunate." It was sugary. It was sickening. It kept my film going. I was content. I was a producer. I was the Baron's true friend. I was a bastard.

That was another aspect of the Baron's character, his susceptibility to supernatural incidents. The case of the Vinton Hayworth records, I used *for* him, or at least for the Deal. (Why lie?—I used it for my own selfish interest.)

But there was one time when I wasn't even a part of it, when a group of the Baron's friends played on the supernatural for a practical joke, and almost scared him to death. Which would have made it truly a doubly deadly joke.

It was after ten in the morning, and I was in the library of the Baron's home. I had been called there by the Baron's lawyer for the signing of the new agreement of my partnership with the Baron, but the big star was still asleep. I was sitting in the big leather chair in front of the fireplace over which hung the Van Gogh. Facing directly opposite the Van Gogh was an oil painting of Jared Throne by John Fitzdocker. Jared looked loaded and had a nice four-highball glow on his face. His gaze was properly severe and tightly dignified. His eyes looked accusingly at me sitting in his chair with the name plaque. It had some bizarre memories for me.

After Jared Throne's death, a few of the Baron's friends had stolen the body from the morgue—his soul having no further need of it—and had carted it up the hill at night and placed it neatly, if somewhat stiffly, in a sitting position in that personal chair. This was the day before the funeral . . .

After placing a drink at Jared Throne's side, Saul Baum, the stunt man from the studio, lit a cigar and placed it carefully between the dead man's fingers. Then all the friends stepped back, admiring their handiwork. They carefully, happily, adjusted the lights, then one of the lighthearted and lit-up friends of the Baron called out to him in a loud voice: "Baron, come forth."

Now the Baron had been asleep and was intertwined with a girl or something. Upon hearing this stentorian, theatrical voice calling, "Baron, come forth," he untwined himself and staggered to the door. He opened it and peeked out fearfully. And rightly so! There sat Jared in front of the fireplace, a drink by his side, a cigar burning in his hand!

The Baron screamed shrilly and promptly fainted dead away. Jared Throne, who was beginning to limber up from the heat, leaned over slowly, staring incuriously into the fire, looking deader and deader. After all, he had been cold for three days.

With a delicate sense of neatness, Saul Baum propped Jared back up, arranged his borrowed hat, took the now-dead cigar from the dead fingers, relit it, blew out the smoke and said, to no one in particular, "Let's get the big star back to bed." By that time I had recovered enough to get them all the hell out, taking Jared with them. I knew when the Baron came out of it, I'd have a nut on my hands for a week, persuading him it wasn't true. Man, what a Deal—the charm was unraveling fast.

The director of the funeral home was always puzzled as to how the corpse of the famous actor had suddenly limbered up and taken a walk during the night—had put on oversized shoes. And the shoes had mud on them. "How passing strange."

But it wasn't "passing strange." The insane things were becoming "passing familiar," "passing impressive." The lie of this Deal with the Baron was a terrifying thing. It was like a blow; the pain came slowly, then with a jolt. It ekes off, tries to separate itself, pulls out from and up through the back hairs of your neck; it pulls out through your collar up beyond, and beyond your brain like a bicycle chain clanking and screeching down the white-tiled corridor of your mind. Somebody was going to pull that chain . . . somebody did. It turned out to be the Editor.

15

Movieola: *The Editor*

A film editor is a man who works closely with the director of a motion picture. He is an important man on the sound stage because he is the one who cuts the picture and has some considerable influence with some directors as to how scenes are to be completed. It is the custom that a major motion picture star can ask for the same editor on each picture. The film editor gets to know what angles he is best photographed from, which is his "good" profile, and thus it was that the Editor had worked closely with the Baron for fourteen years on every picture that the Baron made.

He was a mousy man with no morals, ethics, or chin. He was a cringer in spite of his profession, born to be the Baron's victim. He held a stop watch next to the camera and at the end of each close-up scene, regardless of the quality, he would look at the Baron, flash the O.K. sign by putting up his hand and making a circle with the thumb and middle finger, pursing his lips and saying, "Sensash ... sensash ... wonderful, baby ... you have a choker for forty-two seconds." (Meaning that the Baron's handsome and classical profile was alone that long on the screen, many times larger than king-size.)

Movieola: *Sam Baum, the Stunt Man*

He was well-muscled, wide in the shoulder, narrow in the hip. He was well-tailored but ran to a very pressed-in-the-pants look, very shiny in the shoes. He had a long lean hawk face and a nose that went with it. His eyes were close together, with bushy black brows. He always looked fierce, as though he were just ready to enter into battle and to do it well. His face, while it wouldn't scare children, bore witness to the fact, however, that it had not been overly exposed to gentility, kindness, and a well-bred upbringing. He wore his hair very long and never used his head for any little thing like thinking, but rather as a thing to carry that hair and to hold up in front of the women who usually hung around the Baron for their admiring glances. He walked around under his brain and under his hair, not hearing anything except the clankings of the workings within. They clanked because there wasn't much in there. It was an unfilled space. Only acknowledging that it must do the Baron's bidding.

Saul Baum, the stunt man. This guy had all the charm and appeal of a hit-and-run driver, but he worked for the Baron, that was sole reason to be— the sole *raison d'être* for Saul Baum.

I can never forget the time that the Editor got married. The Baron, in one of his generous and expansive moods, to celebrate the conclusion of shooting of the first picture under the Deal, had decided to give the wedding for his friend. There would be a fair-sized reception at the Baron's home overlooking the Beverly Hills canyon. There would be the false friends, the Baron's crew and the usual hangers-on, the pickers-up of the crumbs that fell regularly from the Baron's table.

As I drove through the huge iron gates and up the long curving driveway, a lad in a burgundy-colored coat came to take the car. I walked up the steps and was greeted at the door by the maid and by Sue. She greeted me warmly, gave me an overly affectionate kiss, said how glad she was to see me. I mumbled something or other. I was always surprised to see Susan still in the Baron's home. This had become too Noel Cowardish for me. You see, Susan Hamilton III was the former mother-in-law of the Baron.

She was in her middle forties, but well-preserved, and was immensely wealthy. She had an ample bosom and ran to low-necked dresses and push-up brassières, which sometimes gave her a pouter-pigeon effect. She had lovely skin, wide-set eyes, a sensuous mouth. She had a smile. I couldn't help but remember another wedding in this same house where Susan Hamilton III was the weeping mother, but properly, holding fast to her undeniable good breeding.

Susan Hamilton III's husband, Roderick Hamilton III, gave his daughter, "Little Sue," away at the wedding. (I think it was the only thing he ever gave away cheerfully.) He didn't like the wife and was truly surprised he had ever had a daughter. But he appeared at the wedding to give her away for the sake of appearances, and at the same time to pick up his quarterly separate-maintenance check from Susan Hamilton III.

"Big Sue," as she was familiarly called by her close and intimate friends numbering hundreds—me being one of the lucky ones—had grabbed hold of Roderick when it looked as though he might really turn into something. His father, Roderick Hamilton II, had a seat on the New York Stock Exchange and had at one time left Roderick III a tremendous amount of money and a junior partnership in the brokerage firm of Mervin, Lewis,

THE DEAL

Fenster, Hamster & Clunk—the name they said sounded like a trunk falling downstairs.

But it was Roderick III who fell downstairs too many times, after which Roderick III was politely but firmly told three things: First, he was no longer associated with the firm; second, his investments, which had in truth been handled by a senior partner of the firm, were now of small consequence by reason of Roderick's bad judgment—or so said the senior partner from his lofty position; third, Roderick no longer qualified for the social role that his name implied. Thus, little by little, he was relegated to a separate maintenance from Susan Hamilton III; and, on the condition that he remained quietly and discreetly out of the way and only showed up at check-receiving time, the money would continue to come to him quarterly. Actually, this hadn't bothered Roderick Hamilton III too much. He was always too deeply involved in his own peculiar pleasures.

So in the social whirl of Beverly Hills, Palm Springs, Sun Valley and then over to Paris, Biarritz, and the Riviera, the two Susan Hamiltons, III and IV, were well, if not affectionately, known as Big Sue and Little Sue. Nothing more corny than that except butterfly kisses, which they used on the various escorts with whom they covered the *boîtes* and the proper sunning, skiing, and gambling places.

Little Sue Hamilton was introduced to the Baron by Big Sue, much to Big Sue's regret, because the Baron, with his fetish for small young girls, never looked back once he saw Little Sue. So eventually they were married, with Big Sue, of course, giving the grandest and most elaborate wedding reception possible and vicariously going through the wedding and the honeymoon. After a short while, as always, the Baron's relationship—and in this case, the marriage—petered out (in the strictest sense of the word) and Little Sue picked and chose, fairly discriminately for her, the young French, Italian, or Middle European studs that thundered her way; the Baron usually ending up in the casino at Cannes or at Monte Carlo, gambling with Big Sue.

So the mother-in-law and the bridegroom spent more time together than the bride and the bridegroom, and eventually Big Sue moved into the Baron's villa with the newlyweds, and from then on was a permanent member of the household.

I viewed with interest and a touch of amusement, the three of them together. A common joke around Paris when they would arrive together in all their elegance—the Baron, Little Sue the wife, and Big Sue the mother—was the real and ersatz French royalty welcome for them (under their breath): "Here come *tiercé, belote et rebelote.*"

". . . so I'm very glad you came. The wedding wouldn't be complete if you weren't here. Weddings always make me cry. Don't they make you . . . Ha, ha, ha," she laughed, "of course not."

I realized that Big Sue had been talking all the time, that I hadn't been listening—a bad habit I had gotten into lately, because of the Deal and all—and even as I had replayed the scene in my mind of the *tiercé, belote et rebelote* wedding, Big Sue was to be congratulated because she had fortitude and staying power. You couldn't take that away from her, or her hold on the Baron. In some ways she had become as nearly indispensable as anyone could get in the Baron's inner circle. He used her harshly, cruelly—from time to time bombarding her with charm. So she stayed and was probably the most beautifully gowned, best-dressed housekeeper and overseer in Beverly Hills, Paris, or Biarritz. She was always there with a quiet word, a cool hand on his brow, and was grateful for any small and tender mercies he, from time to time, elegantly bestowed upon her—making sure that she realized at all times, even in the kip, that she was completely unworthy to be this close to the Baron.

More people were coming in. I said Hello here and there. I was escorted firmly by Big Sue down the hallway, down the three steps into the sunken living room. There was a further spattering of Hellos. Beautiful girls with scarlet mouths and scarlet fingernails waved and gestured and put more energy into saying Hello and holding up their bosoms than you would expect from paid mannequins—which some of them were. The perfume, the cigarette smoke, the smell of Scotch, champagne, the inevitable hors d'oeuvres, seemed to press in on me more than usual, but I plowed on across the room and congratulated the Editor, who stood there in a weak-chinned, glassy-eyed, loose-mouth sort of way. A sloppy smiler, he should have kept a sterner look on his face, but this was impossible for him to do. He walked three steps toward me, grasped my hand in both his damp little paws and said, "It's great, simply great, that you came. Like the Baron says, you're the old Iceman! I was afraid you wouldn't show."

I grinned down at him. "No, this is an important day for you, and I figured I'd better put in an appearance. I want to wish you a lot of luck"—not adding that he'd need luck, among various and sundry other things.

He gushed, "Jarn, you have to meet my fiancée. She's wonderful! She's . . ." He never got any further because, walking across the room escorted by Big Sue, came the Editor's fiancée. It was amazing. I could have picked her out in a crowded room. I saw her, with the sinking feeling you

100

THE DEAL

get when the elevator starts down too fast, leading the Baron safely through the crowd; him trailing happily along in her wake, a five-highball grin on his face.

When they got close to us, he bowed from the waist and said solemnly, "The Iceman cometh. I didn't think you'd be here." The Editor interrupted: "Jarn, I want you to . . ." The Baron turned, a look of pathetic regard on his face. "Allow *me*, dear boy, allow me to present Jarn to this lovely girl." He backed up half a step, gave a slight courtly bow and said, "Joanie, may I present my partner, my mentor, my best friend—Mr. Jarnigan—Joanie Brooks."

I looked from the Editor to the Baron and turned to acknowledge the introduction to the girl. I can never forget the look on the Editor's face; like he had been allowed to see something beautiful; following each word with silent lip movements as though he were dubbing a picture. The little blonde, fluffy and cute, hardly bigger than a child. She had skin like a pearl, shining and yet transparent; a lovely little body with everything in its proper place. A perfect child-woman. It was so obvious what was going to happen with this threesome that it clanked, boiled, and bubbled during the introduction.

By this time the minister from the Beverly Hills Episcopal Church came forward. He was exuding kindness, benevolence; and had obviously been showing his tolerance, since he had a two-highball glow on. Mouthing little niceties, paying due attention to the social graces, the minister nodded and bowed and waltzed his way across to where we were standing.

After paying his respects to the Baron, he was introduced to the Editor and his fluffy little fiancée. He talked nicely; he had a beautiful voice and was fully aware of it. Questions were asked and answered and it was obvious the wedding was now to begin. Solemnly, the Baron took the arm of little Joanie, the bride-to-be. Saul Baum, the ever-present stand-in for the Baron, escorted the Editor toward the far end of the room where the ceremony would take place.

The minister made me a little bow and I made a little bow back. It seemed to call for that sort of thing. He walked in the direction of the prospective bride and groom, fully conscious of his importance. I trailed behind and, as he paused before performing the ceremony, he said to me, "I want to congratulate you, Mr. Jarnigan, I have heard about the contract between you and the Baron. May I say that I am gratified; may I say that I am very pleased for both of you? May I . . ."

"Thank you very much," I put in pointedly.

"It is to be hoped," he continued as though I hadn't interrupted, "that the Lord's blessing will be on your contract, on the marriage of these two young people, and on everyone at this gathering."

"I'll say Amen to that," I managed. He smiled at me benevolently. He gave me a celestial pat on the head, a sort of religious rubdown for being gracious and obviously in accord with his thoughts. He turned and walked over to stand in front of the Editor and the girl. When we were all properly nailed in place, everyone sorted into wavy little rows under the oversolicitous direction of Big Sue, the wedding ceremony commenced, and the Editor and little Joanie Brooks were married.

"I pronounce you man and wife" was hardly spoken when the Baron took a half-step forward to dominate the scene as usual: "I claim the privilege of kissing the bride." He did so, overlong, overzealous, and over the tentative but quickly restrained objection of the Editor. The Baron stepped back and with a little gesture said, "My boy," and the Editor finally grasped at his prize, missed kissing her the first time, finally accomplished it in an unconvincing way. Everyone laughed, applauded. I was looking at the Baron and he turned and caught my eye. He shrugged as if to say, "Well, what can you do?" I knew what *he* could do, and I knew what the bastard *would* do. I looked back at the minister, who was intoning some sort of benediction and he finished what in my view was an overly long prayer—especially over this crowd, nothing would help—with the wind-up, "So blessed be this house and blessed be this couple."

The wedding march started and I added softly, "Unblessed are the poon-tangers, for theirs is the hymn of the rumpled bed." Aloud, I said congratulations and best wishes to both, shook hands all around, and started for the bar. I had pointed my tongue on the soft anvil of hypocrisy. I knew bloody well that if the Editor ended up in bed with his new wife that night, it would be by accident. The Baron already had it reserved. And with the strains of "Here Comes the Bride" in my ears I felt sad for the Editor because "Here Comes the Bride" would be as close as he came to any coupling or connection that night. . . .

I crossed the huge living room, then I took the two steps down into the sunken level bar. I went in, looked around. There were the usual amount of people there, saying the usual things. Everybody a little glassy-eyed. Everybody with a fixed grin of polite idiocy on his face.

I glanced over in a corner where there was a low leather-covered bar. A girl was sitting there. She was lovely. She leaned on her elbow and looked up at me thoughtfully, with no particular expression. Reserved maybe . . . Yes, I guess that's what it was. But she was certainly grand to look at. And she knew it—and that made her prettier. She bridled pleasantly and said, "You're taller than I am, standing there. Can you reach me a drink?"

I took a glass of something from a waiter's tray as he passed by, stoop-shouldered from carrying drinks. I handed it to her. She inhaled half of it and murmured, "You're cute."

"Well, fine now," I said. "And . . ."

"And what?" a voice like a foghorn said in my ear. "What's your problem, Jack?"

I turned around and took a look at him. He was a tall, thick bird with a mashed nose and little foxy eyes. He was one of the ugliest men I'd ever seen. He had a face like a ruptured kidney.

"Oh," I said, "your girl asked me for a drink. And now I see why she needs it. If you will excuse me?"

"Huh?" he said, looking puzzled.

I walked away before the dime dropped.

A group of three slender long-legged virgins walked by; their ages added together would hit about forty. So would their chest measurements. They walked past, chirping and purring; all needing, wanting, desiring a real—or visual—rubdown. The Baron chirped once, purred twice, and let himself down into their midst. Their feathers and furs—*plumes et fourrures*—enveloped him, softly, warmly, and expectantly. *Quelle déception.*

I went into the other room. And there the noise was about three drinks higher. Everyone talking in three- to four-highball voices. Everybody babbling . . . not watching his partner. But all had a stranglehold on a cup of the flit and were relaxed only because they knew there was more to come. The stomach relaxing, the smile easier, eyes flashing; the cheeks above the neck and below the navel sweating. A gauge—how much had gone down and how much needed to go out? The alky or the pee, I mean. Somebody put on a Sinatra record. Great . . . just great. The party was great. The drinkers were great. And Sinatra singing . . . great! A wonderful party. Hot damn!

The Baron's parties had a sameness as though they'd all been planned at the same time—they always finished with the usual group of very young, very slender and tiny girls. All were grist that came to his feeble and puny mill.

I was glad I was leaving for New York to set up the financing deal. Anything would be a welcome change after this.

16

After I had arrived in New York and after the first of three meetings with the French banker and the Suisse Syndicate man, I asked Jules Molotov, my attorney, to fly in. Then, after three days of meetings the Deal looked pretty well set. The Baron was in Hollywood, making another one of those sword-and-dagger, crossbow-and-lance pictures, where the men are all seven feet tall and the women have callouses on their *derrières* from working on the love-bench overtime. Although I had the right to, I didn't want to sign the final agreement until I was certain that the Baron completely understood and was in agreement with the contracts.

Up to now, even though it had been a difficult, a delicate, hazardous and certainly an uneasy time, I didn't want us to start off on this financing contract with any problems from the Baron. I had been over to "21" for lunch with Alfred Rice, Ernest Hemingway's young and extremely clever attorney, trying to conclude buying the rights for a story which would be ideal for the Baron. I gave Rice a certified check for fifty thousand dollars to option it. He had agreed to hold this money until I was certain to clear the Baron from his present studio commitment and to make certain that the studio would not pre-empt the Baron's services. This would allow me sufficient time to complete the shooting in Paris, with the exteriors in Italy.

It was a good lunch, made better by the company. Al gave me a humidor of Uppman panatellas that Ernie had sent up from his place in Cuba. I opened the present, gave Al one, and we sat there smoking over brandy and coffee. Al looked thoughtful for a minute, carefully regarding his cigar, then said, "Jarn, you've got a lot of money riding on this film. I don't want to step out of line, but I'd like to give you a little free legal counsel."

"Fine," I grinned. "I know that legal counsel is the most expensive in the world, so any time I can get some free, especially from a guy like you, I'll take it. Incidentally, I'm picking up the tab for the lunch, so make this advice worth while."

I laughed. He gave a very brief smile. I could see that something was disturbing him. "Remember when we were in France last year?" he asked

"Uh-huh."

"Remember when you were telling me that you were flying back to Hollywood to try and lock up this deal?"

"Yes."

THE DEAL

"I asked you then, even though the Baron is the hottest male star in pictures, is it worth the candle?" He reached over and gently knocked the ashes off the end of his cigar and continued. "I met the Baron twice, once here in New York and once down at Ernie's place in Cuba. I saw them fish together, talk together, booze together. I told you he seemed like a great guy to do those three things with, but in my opinion left a little to be desired as a business associate."

"I remember, Al. I remember you told me that. I also remember I told you that I was tired of just making French pictures; that the artsy-craftsy movie was fine, but I didn't want to be a lopsided success; and unless you make it big in Hollywood or with Hollywood stars, you are an art-circuit foreign film producer." I leaned back in the chair and asked the waiter for some hot coffee. He came over and served it with many little flourishing movements.

Al continued: "You know we get along fine and I know you have some small regard for me. Your deal's signed, so that's that and you are going to have to play it out the way it started. But I think you'd better use wisdom and keep a tight rein on everything. If a fifty-million-dollar major studio can't control this guy, you are going to have to be pretty alert—I use that term nicely—to keep everything under control—and *everything* in this case seems to be the Baron."

"Well, he's not that bad," I protested. "Al, this guy is all right. Sure, he's temperamental, and sure, he's hard to handle sometimes—but hell, that's one of the reasons he's the biggest box office star in the world today. He's news, and happily when he was in France two years ago, he saw a picture I did in Cannes and liked it and talked about making a deal then. Then last year, when I was making the picture in Madrid with the bullfighters and that star he liked, he hung around for two or three weeks and we got pretty friendly. You know the routine. We were wearing *espadrilles*, eating *paella*, taking in all the bullfights. He was a real *aficionado*. There was nothing phony about that. I know he got a lot of that from Ernie but he sure as hell knew what it was all about."

Al said quietly, "Yeah, Jarn, but that isn't making motion pictures and he wasn't your partner then."

"Listen, he came to see the rushes every day while we were shooting in Madrid. He came down to Barcelona where we did the wrap-up of the picture. He was interested in the budgets; he asked all the right questions. He seemed amazed and pleased that we were turning out this kind of film for that kind of money. Why, hell, the last three pictures I made in Europe

106

never cost as much as that last costume epic he made in Hollywood."

Al said, "Sure," with a little wry grin on his face. From time to time he gave me the "Christmas tiger," nodding his head as though he were agreeing with me but had many reservations. It cost nothing to grin or to have the other, either.

"You know, Al, I've got a pretty good contract with the Baron. You should know. You've seen it. You wanted to see it before we made the deal for Ernie's story. What's wrong with it?"

"Well, nothing's wrong with it, except it's like all contracts. The human element gets in there and when I see the financial responsibility you've taken on, with every safeguard against financial loss for the Baron and none for you, it seems to me that you wanted the deal more than the Baron did."

"Well, maybe I did. Maybe I did, but that doesn't prove it's a bad contract."

"Whoa . . . whoa . . . Jarn boy. I didn't say it was a bad contract. I'm only pointing out in a friendly way that there are certain precautionary measures that in my view you should take. I know on the Baron's side he's got that studio behind him who'd love to cut your nuts off since they've found that you have the Baron tied up on this multiple-picture deal. I know the Baron's got nine lawyers who are pretty clever. They won't make too much from your deal, but they'll make plenty from the Baron on his studio deal. I know that Hugh Bloodtest doesn't like your deal with the Baron, because he told me so. So it just seemed to me that you were giving away a little too much weight.

"Also, Jarn boy," Al continued, "You better not let him get into another morals rap. That rape stuff will blow your deal right out of the water." He grinned at me to try and soften the blow.

He had a lot more behind his vest than his shirt and I liked him; and even though he was making me very uneasy, some of the points he made were well taken—maybe all of the points he made—and I began to wonder if Jules Molotov had miscalculated or had I, perhaps, oversold Jules . . .

"But I don't want to worry you, telling you this," Al was continuing. I grinned back at him. For a long time now they had called me the "Iceman" in business. I must say I didn't feel like any Iceman right at the moment. I think Al regretted having opened the conversation, but I knew that he had an earnest and sincere desire to help me. I knew that from the way that he had said what he said; that he was only trying in a friendly way to caution me with respect to my long-range association with the Baron.

THE DEAL

"When are you coming out to the house for dinner?" Al went on. "My son is quite a young man by now. I know you liked him and he'd sure get a thrill out of seeing you again."

"Al, I'll try and make it on my first trip back from Paris, but I'm going to call the Baron in Hollywood today. I'm having him fly in before I wind up a couple of things so that I can go on to Paris and start the pre-production on this second picture of our deal. Then he can return to Hollywood and finish the one he's doing now. But let me keep a raincheck," I added, "and say hello from me to the family."

I got the waiter and got the check signed, and together we left "21." We walked up to Fifth Avenue. We shook hands and Al turned to the right to walk back to his office down Fifth Avenue. I turned to the left and started walking back up to the Hampshire House.

I walked slowly along Fifth Avenue even though the air was chilly. It was a dry cold—the wind was sharp against my face. The snap in the air was like the brisk crackle you get on the Spanish plains before you reach Burgos. Talking to Al about Spain brought back some memories of that— some pleasant, some not so pleasant, but all interesting. I couldn't be this wrong about the Baron or the Deal. Yet the shooting in Spain without the worry of a superstar had been grand. I remembered . . .

I'd come up to Burgos from Madrid alone because I wanted to visit its famous cathedral. I parked the car and walked down the narrow cobble-stone, overhung street. The stones gave off a tomcat smell in the hot sun. The plumbing in Burgos left a lot to be desired, but the town had everything so far as I was concerned.

I walked into the Gothic cavern of the quiet cathedral, one of the most beautiful in the world. An old priest was at one of the altars at the back of the dimly lit church. I walked toward him. He turned and very politely bowed. *"Señor,"* he said. I explained to him that I could only understand a little Spanish. "Father, do you speak French?"

His face lit up. "But, of course. I was one of the fortunate who spent some time in a parish outside of Paris. I should be gratefully pleased to speak French." So, with the language barrier comfortably overcome and the priest being glad to converse—with boyish glee in one so old—he insisted on showing me all the treasures of the cathedral. After the tour, he motioned me to follow him.

Then, with the joy of a conspirator, he led me down a flight of darkened stairs and into a cavern which was closed off by a heavily barred iron gate.

THE DEAL

Reaching into the folds of his cassock, he took out about twelve pounds of keys, selected one, and with a flourish and much creaking of hinges, swung back the heavy iron bars. Then, in the very dim light, he led me down more stairs and into a room about thirty feet square.

Here he showed me a marble coffin, the last resting place of Queen Isabella, and a smaller carved-marble sarcophagus with the figures of children resting stiffly yet comfortably on it. In the far-off corner, where no light touched it, was a pitifully small, carved, white marble sarcophagus. Since it was so very far away from the others, I asked the priest to explain.

"You see," he answered politely and with dignity, "one was never sure of the parentage of this child of God. Decorum *exige*—demands," he corrected himself—"that the distance separate the last resting places." He gave a little bow. I had heard a bell ring in the upper part of the church. "If you will excuse me, I permit myself to leave you for a brief moment. I will return almost immediately." He left quietly. I couldn't figure how "decorum" was helped by burying the body of a little kid twenty feet away from its mother. Two people lay together and there's a child—it's not theirs anyway, but God's. And God truly doesn't mind the parentage, or where the small lump of clay lies buried. How unimportant we all are.

But there was also in the little town of Burgos happiness, and sometimes there were dances. At those dances everyone was kind of polite at first. You know, not really dancing with the one they wanted to. Later . . . some of the wild ones—the *toreros* who never made it in the ring but tried to make it every other way—at intermission would furtively drop pepper and Spanish fly on the floor. It looked like rosin.

At first, I never saw too much difference in the women. Most of the ones that were there had been "laid" in advance anyhow, but some of the rest of the young *señoritas* got pretty hot and fancy as the flamenco continued, with the heels drumming on the floor, raising a lot of dust and Spanish fly. For an observer, it got to be a pretty amusing situation. Every once in a while you'd see a couple head for one of the exits. They'd be back again in about twenty minutes for more heel tapping.

I was wondering about this and remembering what I'd heard a *señorita* say: "It's a mortal sin, but so agreeable . . ." I wondered truly how much of a sin it was. It seemed hard to reconcile the fact that Christ would squash out these young coupling people, so close, so screwing together . . . It must have the same importance as when you go out a screen door on a hot day and see two flies locked together on the screen. You watch them for a moment and let them live. Or when you from your observer position watch the dancers on the floor, seeing the lovers go in and out and not hiding it too

109

well; beautiful flies screwing on a screen. It would be unkind to let any door slam on them . . .

"Boy, you're thinking again tonight," *Someone* said.

"Yeah," I answered.

"Well, just don't get profound."

"O.K., O.K., no profundities. I think I'll wander back to the hotel."

Someone agreed. "It's safer there . . ."

So I walked on up the Fifth Avenue street of "Burgos," turned left onto Central Park South and continued to the Hampshire House. The doorman said, *"Bonjour, Monsieur Jarnigan."*

"Buenas dias," I answered. And left Spain to go upstairs and put in a call to the Baron.

17

I had called the Baron in Hollywood, but was unable to reach him at the studio. Later, I got him at home on the private number that rang only in his library and bedroom. When he answered, I knew that he had been drinking, but not badly. "How are you, Baron?" I said, taking the temperature, wanting to find out for sure that he was in a position to talk business.

"Great, Jarn, just great. How's the boy?" he said, in a happy three-highball voice.

"Fine, Baron, everything goes fine. I'm going to have to take a decision within the next forty-eight hours and I thought it was worth while to call you to see how the picture was going and how tight your schedule is there."

"Well, you know Jason," he said, pronouncing the name as though he hated to. "It's pretty tight. However, I could make it as loose as a goose—loose as a goose—get it?"

"Yeah," I said, "but let's don't kick up any dust if we don't have to."

"What's on your mind, Jarn boy? You didn't call to ask about Jason's picture."

"Nope. I called because I'm ready to lock up this Deal and I am of the opinion that perhaps you should get on a plane and fly into New York, and we can lock it up together."

He laughed. "Jason would scream like a ruptured duck. He'd never permit it. He'd forbid me to go . . . I'll be there."

"Well," I answered thoughtfully, "you don't want to get in a position where he could sue you or exert some pressure."

"Screw him." The Baron's voice cracked over the wire.

"No, seriously, Baron, we don't want, at this point of the game, to get anybody's back hair ruffled. This thing will work out. I just thought you might like to be here. I know I'd like to have you here," I added, to assure him that I wanted him to know and understand every phase of the financial business that went on. I continued with, "If Jason gets up on his hind legs, he may cause a little trouble."

"Frig him," the Baron said.

I said quietly over the phone, "Baron, you must not continually say 'screw him' and 'frig him.' Be polite and speak nicely."

"Of Jason?" the Baron asked in shocked and justified surprise, "Jarn, that's a crock of the well-known article. You know that."

"Well, anyway," I laughed, "talk to him; see if they could reasonably shoot around you for the next two or three days."

"When would you want me there, Jarn?" he countered.

"Well, I'd like to have you here in time for the meeting tomorrow night."

The Baron laughed. "If I asked Jason, if only to annoy me he'd say 'No, absolutely no,' and he would finally conclude with 'I forbid it! I forbid it!' " The Baron laughed again. "I shall leave promptly on the first plane out in the morning."

"Well, now wait a minute, Baron, don't you think—"

"Jarn boy, the Baron has spoken. You want me there. I'll be there. How are all the broads in New York?"

"I don't know, Baron, I haven't had time to do any looking around. I've been working pretty—"

"Remember my theme, Jarn—Always time for the poon."

"Yeah, I know," I laughed. "Well, I'll wait for you. Have the secretary give me a call what flight you are on and I'll meet you at the plane."

"Done, my boy, done and done again," he said happily.

I knew he was glad to come but I knew he was more happy trying to slip it to Jason every time he got the chance. We said a few meaningless phrases and after a minute, hung up.

I sat there for a while looking at the telephone, wondering if I should call Paris; but then I decided I'd wait for another forty-eight hours. Better to be absolutely sure. I called Jules Molotov at the Plaza. When I rang they put me through, "Yes, Jarn, what's the problem?"

"Does it always have to be a problem?"

"Well, I didn't expect your call."

"What's *your* problem, Julie? You sound a little upset."

"No, no. My wife came in a couple of days early and we've been having a little . . ."

"Yeah, I know. Well, what I had to say is not important. I thought if you were alone, I'd take you up to a little French restaurant I know and we could have dinner."

He sounded relieved. I didn't know if I was helping him to get off some hook, but it always seemed to me that every time Miriam was around, especially when we had business to discuss, Jules wasn't as clear and precise as he normally was. I never knew whether it was trying to impress his wife, or because he instinctively reverted to the big legal counsel, the high-priced

112

THE DEAL

lawyer routine, which either kept her at a distance or kept her close to him. I hadn't been able to figure it out.

Jules only stood about five feet four. He had a giant soft egg of a belly, was completely bald; affected heavy, horn-rimmed glasses. He had a beautiful low voice, an overly large nose, and at many times looked like a heavyset, intelligent Jimmy Durante. Miriam, on the other hand, was one of the most beautiful Jewish girls I'd ever seen. The right schools, the right education, the right charm, the right everything. Whatever was needed in that department, she had it. And she had Jules so madly in love with her it was about the only chink in his armor of intelligence, craftiness, and all-around good judgment. When I mentioned the French restaurant, he grabbed on to it as though I had invited him on a cruise to the Mediterranean. He said, "Great, Jarn boy, we'll go."

"Wait a minute," I said. "Why don't you and Miriam go somewhere? I'll have dinner here in the apartment."

"No, no," he said, too hastily. "Let's all go, the three of us. We'll pick you up in twenty minutes."

"Take it easy, Julie. Can anybody hear me talking?"

He answered softly, "No, everything's fine."

"Well, then, just answer this with a yes or no. Can I help you if I take you and Miriam to dinner, or wouldn't you prefer to be alone?" I asked hopefully.

He replied, "I think any help I can get in connection with this contract would be useful, and any cooperation that can come from your side will make the deal go easier."

"Fine . . . Julie . . . fine," I said tiredly. "I'll come by and pick you up in an hour."

"Great, Jarn boy, great. We'll be ready."

We hung up. I thought wearily, Man, I hate to go through another one of those dinners with Jules and Miriam. I knew he would talk and try to be charming and it always somehow missed with his wife. I knew she would flirt and try to play "kneesies" under the table, and between listening to Jules talk with the misplaced charm and ducking the not-too-subtle overtures of Miriam, I knew it was going to be a hell of a dinner. I turned back to the telephone and almost called back to say I had received an overseas call and couldn't make it. Then I remembered that I needed Jules in the Deal, and anyway I know how it is when you have wife trouble. Any agreeable help you can give or get during one of these times is more than welcome. Nodding my head soberly, I walked into the bedroom to change clothes and shower, and I remembered the old phrase, "A nod is the same as a wink to a blind horse." In connection with Miriam, Jules was a blind little fat pony.

    This is what was happening in their suite when I hung up after talking to Jules. Jules stood there, looking at the telephone. Miriam came in. She was wearing only a half-slip and garter belt, her long and slender legs gleaming beautifully in the soft light of their living room. She was completely naked from the waist up. Jules felt a thickening in his throat, his mouth suddenly dry. He tried to swallow, couldn't. He ran his tongue over his lips.

    Miriam stood there looking at him, conscious of the effect she always had on him—it still surprised her even though she knew he was unworthy of her. "Who was that, dear?" she asked quietly, standing closer to him now. Jules opened his mouth, no sound came. She saw his look and quickly tried to avert what was coming. "Business again—no one exciting ever calls us unless it's business." She pouted and turned away.

    He came up behind her, started to slip his arms under her arms to clasp her breasts, his hands already curved into the clasp of ownership. He made cups of his hands. She sensed the move and turned to face him. "Well, who was it?"

    Jules said hoarsely, "It was Jarnigan. He wants us to go to dinner."

    Her face lit up. "Oh, that's nice, that's good; it will be fun." Jules didn't answer, he was staring at her breasts, which were just at his mouth level—he with no shoes, Miriam in stiletto heels—which usually annoyed him because it made him seem shorter, but he wasn't annoyed now.

    He said, "Jarn's got a great deal and I locked it up for him—that's why I asked you to come to New York—and that's why you get the Rolls . . ."

    In spite of herself, Miriam took a step closer to him impulsively. Her gesture was not lost on Jules, who continued, "I've decided to quit the firm, give up the partnership. I want to do only picture work from now on—no trials, no studio deals. Just set up these foreign deals, like I did for Jarnigan."

    Miriam's voice took on the little-girl tone that Julie liked. But for Miriam, this was her "business voice"—it got her what she wanted from Julie. "But, daddy," she breathed, "is it wise to give up your practice? I mean, the security, the sure money, and all?"

    Jules looked at her closely. "Yes. I think I'm going to branch out. I think I'll go it alone. What do I need Lou Geisler for?"

    She watched him. "For keeping us in the big money, daddy, the real big money," she said, shooting him down, but not too seriously.

    "What's the matter? Is it you don't have faith in me . . . I mean me alone?" Jules said, painfully, his pride hurt.

THE DEAL

"Nu," Miriam said smoothly, "I got the faith in you. I just wanted to see you stay on top—stay big."

Julie grinned now, reassured. "The only thing I want to stay on top of is you. And I *am* big. Let's get to bed." He said this stiffly—or as stiffly as a fat man can say anything. Miriam looked thoughtfully at him, shrugged—gave a sharp look of annoyance, which he couldn't see—and went to the marriage bed. She hoped he wouldn't take too long.

While this was happening, I was thinking of Jules and of Miriam, and of the few minutes of Julie's not too muted pleasure. Miriam would endure it, would support his weight and would echo his bleats of love; with Jules on top, wallowing and dipping his wick in his own (he thought) private and velvety-moist jewel box. It was costing him enough for his pleasures. Pleasures that truly only youth—or what is left of youth—can know. Now, thinking of them, it left a faintly unpleasant scent in the nose, like something not exactly clean—like something that you smell from across a river, not too clean, from far off. And Jules' earth would die one day of cold . . . (a lack of warmth).

18

I received a call from the Baron's secretary in Hollywood telling me what flight he was taking and when he would arrive in New York and although I had a Cadillac and chauffeur, I now hired a Rolls-Royce because I knew that little things like that pleased the Baron. He liked everything to be overluxurious and with the kind of money we made we could afford it. So now I leaned back against the seat cushions in this luxurious car and on the drive to the International Airport, I closed my eyes and went over everything that I could think of in connection with the Deal that might be a problem: the contracts and the contacts, the distribution setup, the financing setup, the money exchanges from soft to hard currency, the Swiss bank accounts, the French lawyers, the Suisse Syndicate man—the whole setup. What it finally came down to was my personal relationship with the Baron. *Could* I control him? Would he do what he had agreed to do? Would he "render and complete his services as a star" in these pictures we were starting out on?

Up to now he had made some little demands with respect to some money he wasn't entitled to but they were small enough amounts and they didn't matter too much. Now he wanted to surprise the Princess, who was the current fiancée, with a chinchilla coat when he greeted her in Paris. The first real argument we had was because he wanted the expense to be put on the wardrobe budget of the picture. I disagreed, and for the first time the Baron employed those phrases that I was to hear for so many years and that are written in bronze inside my head:

"Listen, Jarn boy. Aren't I a partner? Don't I have as much to say about this Deal as you do? I am the star—I have the artistic control, you take care of the business, and we produce the pictures together as partners. We share everything."

"Yeah, but that don't mean we have to share paying for a twenty-five-thousand-dollar chinchilla coat for your girl."

"Jarn boy," he grinned, and the grin wasn't particularly friendly, "these are the little things in life that as an American producer you must learn to adjust to now. When we signed our Deal, did I ask you for fifty thousand

117

dollars under the table? No. Did I ask you to buy me a sports car as a present and an inducement to sign the contract? No." He nodded, obviously pleased that he hadn't made these demands.

"Did I, for example, as I did with my friend Jason Wormser, ask you to visit an art gallery with me and finally let you persuade me to accept a Van Gogh painting as an inducement to sign the contract?" Again, and practically talking a bow, he answered the question himself, "No. Well then, for a guy who's stepped out from producing artistic pictures, some of which were good, but some were crap, to step into producing pictures with *me*, with being able to make a two-million-dollar picture instead of making a half-million-dollar picture, it would seem to me, Jarn boy, that somewhere in that extra million and a half that you have to play with, that *we* could afford to take on the price of a lousy fur coat." Of course he carefully avoided saying the "lousy fur coat" was chinchilla and cost twenty-five grand.

Well, there it was. I gave in because actually some of the things he said were true, and then again, I have to admit that I wanted this Deal more than anything. I could see prestige, I could see making good pictures, I could see a lot of money, and losing myself in those thoughts the dangers and the importance of this test of wills escaped me. I had made my first big mistake.

I said, "Baron, some of the things you have said are true, but nonetheless I think you should know exactly how I feel about that."

He looked at me. "Did you say 'nonetheless'? "

"Yeah, but don't let that bother you. There is such a word."

"I know there is, dear boy, but I didn't know that you knew it."

"I know it."

He gave me now the old friendly charm and lovable grin, the real Baron trademark. He clapped me on the back, put his arm around my shoulder and said, "Partner, we'll get along. Remember what I said: You do the business, we produce the pictures, I rape the women, on and off the screen, and we make money all over the world. Partners . . . we split everything fifty-fifty. We share everything . . . Don't forget that."

I didn't say anything, but I grinned back at him. I knew he had "slipped into the easy lie, he made his bread and butter by." This was a line I'd used in several pictures. It seemed to fit in this bit of dialogue with the Baron and it was a phrase that was to be used over the years in my experience with the Baron. However, I didn't know it then.

I was roused from my reverie and none-too-pleasant reflections by the chauffeur. "Mr. Jarnigan, which airline?" I said, "I think it's American. You have the note." He fumbled around on the seat beside him. "You're right, Mr. Jarnigan." He tooled the big car into the airport and pulled up to a reserved parking space. We were early. I wasn't going to go out to meet the Baron until just before the plane arrived. "Will you go in and check to see if the plane is on time. Also, send the public relations representative out to the car. Tell him Mr. Jarnigan wants to check with him about the arrival of the Baron from Hollywood."

About twenty minutes later I got out of the car and went in through the terminal, and with the PR man leading the way we went out on the Tarmac as the big jet taxied up toward American. As it stopped, they pushed the stairwell against the fuselage. The front-section door opened, two or three people got out, and then here came the Baron. He stood there and surveyed the airport and New York, and he owned it all.

I have to admit I was glad to see him. He came down the steps with that particular agility and grace that he had in person when he knew he was on display, and on the screen. As he started along the red rug from the jet to the building, I walked toward him. He waved and hollered: "Jarn boy! How's the kid?"

"Hi, Baron, I see you made it." I was glad to see that he only had on a mild happy glow.

But before he said anything further he grabbed my arm and said, "Kid, that hostess is the greatest. Now, I promised her dinner and a screen test. Can we do it?"

"Well," I laughed, "I don't know about the screen test. The dinner—of course we can do that." I grinned and said, "Let's not worry about that right now."

The Baron looked back and said, "Hold on, Jarn, I *want* to worry about that right now."

I gave him a sharp look. "Now take it easy, Baron. I'll have the public relations representative get her name and we'll get the necessary information and she can call you or you can call her."

"Oh, I already have that information," he grinned back, cutting me off. People were going by us now, eager to get into the terminal and get their bags and go on running. The trip had finished. As they passed us, I could see them casting curious, and sometimes envious, glances at the Baron.

"There he is, Sadie," I heard a little man say. "I told you he was on the plane."

"Looks like a fag, don't he?" said a guy with a thirty-dollar Legion convention smile to his pal.

119

THE DEAL

"Naw, he don't look like a fag . . . but they ain't his shoulders."
"Sure," said the pal, "hell . . . anyone can pad out a suit:"

A little girl came rushing right by me and up to the Baron. "Oh . . . oh Baron . . . is it really you . . . can I . . . may I touch you? I mean you being here and all and right before my very eyes . . ." and she ran out of breath; it had been a long sentence.

The Baron looked at her and smiled. He bridled pleasantly, "Madame, I don't think we've met." Now, I knew he'd never have done that "Madame" bit unless he was hooked. She was young and she was little and his coyote's eyes and the handsome foxy nose crinkled at the same time. One good thing I have to say about the Baron, he was genuinely unmoved by fans or the adulation he received. He wasn't concerned with the gushy type of woman or man (and there were plenty) or really ever got a kick out of the worship he received (and he had plenty of that too). What he really used the fame for was . . . just what had happened and was happening with this little girl. She had thrown herself at the Baron . . . she hadn't had to . . . he was there before, long before, trying to get off with "that" before this little gushing girl in front of him had been born.

"Listen, Baron," I said, "the chauffeur will get the bags, let's go on out to the car."

"What?" he said vaguely. "Oh, sure . . ." Then looking back down at the little girl, "What's your name, dear? You can ride in with us."

The little girl looked around. She wasn't afraid—they never are—but it was moving a little too quick for her. Things were happening a little too fast. "Well . . . I . . ." She hesitated and look down at her hands.

The Baron, smiling, reached down and lifted one of them. He moved back a step and moved the little girl's glove down from her wrist, leaving about an inch of space between the glove and the suit sleeve. He said in a voice to charm the dead, "I truly hope you'll drive in with us," and with that he bent over and kissed the little girl's wrist on the inside.

She acted like someone had pulled a trigger in her. She swayed . . . it had shaken her. I hoped she wouldn't do anything silly.

The Baron smiled with complete self-satisfaction in what for him had been an easy and complete success, then with a slight bow he stepped back. "Well, if you are not going with us, call me. I am at the Hampshire House. By the way . . . what name?"

The girl wailed softly, "It's Virginia and I'll call . . . I'll call . . ."—this trailing after us as we were walking out toward the car. The driver had taken the baggage checks and was now installing the Baron's grips in the back of the Rolls. We shook hands with the public relations executive and started the ride back to New York.

Once inside the car the Baron leaned back in the seat, leaned his head against the cushion and closed his eyes. Now that I could see him closely I thought he looked a little pale. "What I want—" I started to say, but he stopped me with an airy wave of the hand.

"It's what *I* want, Jarn boy. What I want . . . I came here because you asked me and it had better be all right."

I looked at him. Well, it was all right. I knew it was all right, so I sat back and relaxed. I didn't say anything. He opened his eyes and looked at me. He looked surprised that I hadn't said anything. I grinned at him and in a few minutes, nodding his head, he closed his eyes and seemed to go to sleep. The Rolls purred on toward the city. I knew he was tired . . . I was glad he was here . . . now it's really started, I thought . . .

19

When the Baron and I arrived at the Hampshire House, the Rolls pulled up to the entrance on Central Park South and the doorman immediately announced to the assistant manager, who immediately informed the general manager, that we had arrived and the Baron was on the way in.

There was the usual hubbub in the lobby. Most of the residents of Hampshire House were sophisticated, but the Baron still drew a number of pleasant Hellos—most of the people were trying to act as though they were unimpressed yet pleased to see him. The general manager gave the assistant manager orders as though royalty had arrived—which indeed was the case—and with many instructions and much pomp and circumstance we were ushered to the private elevator and shot up to the penthouse suites. The manager showed us in with many little bows and many little courtesy speeches of welcome, pointing out this and that, the Baron taking it all in, feeling it was his due.

The manager left, the assistant manager left. Then with astonishing rapidity the room began to fill up with bottles of Scotch, bottles of champagne, and a tremendous floral display. The maître d'hôtel came up from the restaurant, saying that hors d'oeuvres were on the way. Forty-five minutes after we arrived at the hotel you would have thought we'd been there for several days. The Baron was carefully installed in one of the huge armchairs in front of the fireplace, a Scotch in his hand. He had eaten copiously of the hors d'oeuvres, saying he had not felt like eating on the plane. He was in an expansive mood and wanted to talk.

I said, "Baron, how long can you safely stay in New York without causing an absolute blowup at the studio in Hollywood?"

He dismissed the question with an airy wave of his hand. "No particular time, Jarn boy. How long will you need me?"

"Well, it would be fine if you could stay two or three days. However, I realize that is asking a lot."

"A mere bagatelle, my boy. I shall inform the studio that I will return at the end of three days. When I left I told the director, who is a pal"—(he said this sarcastically)—"I told him to prepare to shoot around me, that I had urgent business, and since I have a couple of downs on him anyway— plus the knowledge that he wants to direct my new picture there—I feel we will have no difficulty."

THE DEAL

"Well, that's fine," I said. "That certainly is fine." And I meant it. "Then Jason Wormser knows you're here in New York?"

The Baron glanced at me with a little frown of annoyance. "I didn't say that. I said I didn't think we'd have any difficulty and that's what I meant. I don't inform that son-of-a-bitch about what I do."

I watched him for a minute. "Well, Baron. Why don't you rest and freshen up? I'm going to the office suite. I have an appointment with the Suisse Syndicate attorney. He's got the money."

The Baron grinned broadly. "Jarn, my younger brother," the Baron intoned, in the finest Jared Throne actor's voice, "remember my theme, Always time for the poon. However," he added judiciously, "we must give the dollars, the francs, the pounds their proper place. So for this I amend my theme." He grinned boyishly, but not a very young boy. "Always time for the poon—always time for the pound. Get it?" He continued to grin.

"I get it."

And I did get it. I also wanted to leave him in that good mood.

I left for my own suite. I knew the Syndicate man would be on time. This was business; I knew exactly how to handle it. I could close this deal.

The secretary showed him into the library. He gave the characteristic little bow which they all have. *"Enchanté, Monsieur Jarnigan."*

I said, *"Je suis content, Monsieur Roulot."* He looked a little like Neville Chamberlain; he even had an umbrella. He ran to a derby hat, a silk raincoat. He carefully removed some rubbers from his feet. I made a motion to show him where he could hang his things.

He said, *"Ca ne fait rien. Ca ne fait rien. Ici ça va."* He put his things carefully on the small settee, walked over and took a chair in front of the desk. I sat down as he fastidiously wiped his hand on a beautiful linen handkerchief, looked it over carefully, frowned as if he was displeased to see dirt, put it in his pocket, looked up at me, gave me a smile that never reached his eyes. "It is a pleasure to greet you in person," he said, speaking French. "One is sometimes surprised at meeting one with whom he has corresponded by letter for so long a time. You are a younger man than I had thought—*c'est mon plaisir."*

"I am equally pleased," I said, "and am grateful that we are finally able to meet face to face. I see that you have brought your brief case and would be grateful if we could immediately start conducting our business since our *avocat* must return to California late tonight."

124

THE DEAL

"I should be ravished, Monsieur Jarnigan. Practically all has been done by letter, as you know. It is simply that we should confirm our agreement. I would be desolate if anything at this late date should mar our tremendous and grand business friendship."

"I am in complete accord with you, dear friend, and I equally should be desolated if anything should interfere with our affairs. I am sure they will not falter. However, in spite of this, one must not lose the North, for, unhappily, in the heat of winding up these affairs one is prone to forget where one's best interests lie."

He said quickly, "I am in accord. I am in accord. I think it is only for you to sign on behalf of your Société and for me to sign on behalf of our Syndicate. The initial check is prepared and we can conclude in the briefest time possible. However"—he hummed on, looking shyly around the room, although there was nothing shy in his manner—"there is one slight change." Here he paused, then continued, looking past my right ear.

"I permit myself only to mention it by reason of its unimportance. But with respect to the second payment I feel, that is to say," he corrected quickly, "our Syndicate feels that the second payment should not become due until the first day of the actual photography of the film." His gaze wandered back to me and he looked at me carefully. I didn't say anything. My not saying anything seemed to surprise him. He coughed; he changed position in the chair.

I reached over on the desk, took a cigar out of the humidor, offered one—he declined politely—I trimmed the end off the panatella carefully. I lit it carefully. When the cigar was burning to my satisfaction, I looked up at him quietly, still not saying anything, waiting for him to continue. He said, "There are many deals made where the second payment after the initial payment upon our signatures on the original contract is not made until the first day of . . ." Here he paused, thinking seriously—he looked up to see that I was noticing that he was thinking seriously, and he continued, ". . . I think you call it 'principal photography.' " I nodded, still not saying anything. We sat there looking at each other. I continued smoking and he started to fidget. The moments drifted by and he smiled at me solemnly and said, "May I have your reaction to this, Monsieur Jarnigan?"

"You may," I said. "It's quite simple, Monsieur Roulot. This was not our deal. We were to receive three initial payments: the first on the signature of the contract; the second on the start of the preproduction, which was to be no later than forty-five days after the signature of the contract; and the third payment on the first day of principal photography, which was to be no later than ninety days from the start of preproduction," I finished, looking at him.

He shifted uncomfortably in his chair before speaking. "I realize that there had been some discussions in that regard. However, my confreres and I have agreed that in our best judgment the payments should be the initial payment now and the other payments lumped together in one sum and given on the first day of photography."

I smiled at him, "Well, that may be what you and your confreres have agreed. However, that is not what you and I have agreed and in this case, as we say, 'I must keep all my reserve.' "

He looked at me sincerely and coldly, and said, "Monsieur Jarnigan, you must allow me to say, you must permit me to demonstrate, that sometimes *les affaires* have a tendency to be 'slightly' changed and we should feel more comfortable in our association if we could disburse the money to you in the fashion I have just outlined. Since the sum involved for our Syndicate is of an immense and astronomical figure, we feel that we should in all friendship impose this unimportant condition." He leaned back in the chair, looking me over carefully, and waited.

I looked my cigar over for any flaw, any birthmark. I thought over briefly what he'd said. I looked up at him and replied, "In all friendship, monsieur, unless my Société and the conditions we have agreed upon are met to the letter specifically, and since we are allowing your Syndicate to be financially interested in a picture starring the Baron where the financial success is a certainty, I regrettably permit myself to inform you that we are not in accord with respect to your suggestion; and I must further advise you that as desolate as I should be if this 'condition' were to be a condition, it would bore me to open negotiations and start discussions in another direction and another channel."

He looked at me, deadly hate now coming from his eyes. "Monsieur Jarnigan . . . Monsieur Jarnigan . . . we are men of affairs, we can discuss, no?"

I didn't say anything.

He continued, "I say to you in all honesty and in all simplicity, remembering our long correspondence, but especially from our brief personal acquaintance, I permit myself to say I have a profound sympathy toward you."

I nodded my head, agreeing with him. "I equally have a sympathy toward you and your confreres."

He continued, "My suggestion was one that I had been advised to give you by our *avocat* but since I can see that his advice is not the route we should follow, may I, on behalf of myself and of my confreres, assure you that there is no need for you to divert yourself in other directions or other channels. I further assure you that I, Roulot, and our Syndicate will honor all of the conditions that are on paper by our letters and are contentedly correct. I am disregarding the suggestion of our *avocat*. So may I assure you there is no disinclination from my side—our side—to not go ahead with *l'Affaire*."

He was warming a little to his subject now; continuing with, "So elbow to elbow we can vanquish our competitors, our possible detractors, and conclude our Deal with happiness and with all our salutations very distinguished toward you, your star, and your constituents. I hope I have made myself clear?"

He was a little red-faced and out of breath when he had said all of this. He took a deep breath, leaned forward, looking directly and dishonestly into my face. I returned the look. My hands weren't too clean in this Deal anyway but in spite of both of us, the French side of the Deal was made. He opened his brief case and took out the papers. I took my set of papers out of the drawer in the desk and looked over both sets of papers, comparing them very carefully and after looking them over, feeling they were correct, they were the papers I had sent to him, the little JM on the bottom of each page, I knew these were the original Jules Molotov contracts. I got up, walked around to his side of the desk; I pulled out an extension shelf, placed both sets of papers before him, reached over and took up a pen and gave it to him. He took it delicately in his hand and then did a strange thing. He carefully pushed his chair back from the desk; standing up, he took a monocle out of his pocket and then lowering himself to one knee so that his face was not more than two inches off the desk, he read carefully every word of the contracts as though he had never seen them before. I walked across the room, turned and looked back. There he was in the kneeling position, his lips moving as he was diligently dissecting each word of the contract which he had had, and his attorneys and his Syndicate confreres had had, for two months. Looking him over carefully, I noticed for the first time he had on an absolute celluloid collar, the gray morning pants had a blue-bottle-fly green cast to them. I could see the sole of his left shoe as he was forced to hold his foot in his kneeling position. I had never seen feet so big on so small a man. I had time to finish my cigar. Then very carefully he signed the papers with the pen I had given him. He could have signed them with his nose, it was that close to the paper. After he had finished signing all six copies, he awkwardly straightened up, turned to me with a little bow and said, handing me the pen, "Monsieur Jarnigan, all is in order."

I walked over and signed three copies. I turned. He put out his hand to

THE DEAL

take them. I said gently, "Monsieur Roulot, as always we must conduct our affairs as men of affairs. There is the matter of the cashier's check."

He looked at me sadly for a moment, "But, of course, certainly." He reached down into his brief case and took out a heavy manila envelope. He handed it to me. I opened it and there it was . . . one half a million dollars, a certified check drawn on the Chase Bank. I looked at the signatures; everything seemed in order. I had known the check was issued, since I had called my friend Theodore Williamson, who was a vice president of the bank, and he had confirmed that the check had been certified. I handed M. Roulot his three signed contracts. As he put them in his brief case he looked with something more than sadness in his eyes as he saw the check disappear into my wallet and into my inside pocket. He swallowed, and smiled gamely. I put my three signed copies back in the drawer of the desk, locked the drawer, looked at him. He stuck out his hand. We shook hands solemnly, and I said, "Would you care for a brandy or a drink to acknowledge the signing of our agreement?"

He looked around uncomfortably, "Do you have a Perrier?"

I said, "I'm afraid not."

"Evian?" he suggested.

I shook my head.

"Well, in that case, Monsieur Jarnigan, I permit myself to refuse. I never touch spirits. A little wine with water during the repast, but the alcohol you Americans have is too brisk and too strong and is not good for my digestion. But I pray you to continue and have a drink; you celebrate for both of us."

I smiled at him. "I must decline, Monsieur Roulot, since I have much work to do and in any event I am looking forward with anticipation and pleasure to the company of you and your confreres for dinner this evening."

"I equally am looking forward," he answered. He put his copies of the contracts in his brief case, walked over to the settee and carefully put on his rubbers.

I walked over, picked up his raincoat and said, "If you will permit me."

"That is very amiable of you," he murmured. I helped him into his raincoat, walked him to the door. We again shook hands ceremoniously and with a little bow he backed out of the door, saying, "Until tonight."

I said, "Until tonight, Monsieur Roulot. My secretary will inform you at the hotel at what time our driver will come to search for you at your hotel."

He bowed again, and murmured, *"A ce soir."*

I said *adieu* and gently closed the door.

128

20

The Deal has been signed; now it's all in order, I thought. I had called my attorney, Jules Molotov, to wrap up the details; then went back to the other suite. I wanted to shower and change my clothes. When I came back I walked in and took the private elevator to the 33rd floor. There were only two penthouse suites on this top floor. Lounge rooms beautifully furnished, paneled libraries, real fireplaces. They looked like what they were, suites for royalty or for millionaires. When I walked in that door with the gold key they give you for the Tower Suites, I felt like both royalty and a millionaire. I was already bowing with dignity to the crowds who wanted to be near, to touch and maybe try to spend some of the millions I was counting. As I strolled into the huge living room I was preparing a speech of acceptance for these beautiful bounties that were now mine. I was brought back to reality by the voice of the Baron saying, "Jarnigan, you look happy. It's done then, I presume."

"Right, Baron," I said, "done and done again, and all for us, partner."

"Did you get all the points I wanted—artistic control, choice of director, leading lady, etcetera, etcetera?"

"Baron, it's like you wanted, only better. The money and the percentage are better, and *we* have the control."

"*Who*," he asked coolly, "has the control?"

"Why, we do," I answered.

"*Who*?" he asked again, giving me a look which meant he thought I wasn't too bright. "Don't you get what I mean, Jarn?"

"No," I lied, getting perfectly well what he meant.

A look of grave concern came over his face. The star was now going to shine, was going to brighten up my evening, was going to tell me the facts of life. "I," he stated—taking advantage of the setting: the fire in the fireplace, the high-beamed ceiling, the soft sound of the hi-fi playing, the unmistakable feel of richness and solid security—and the Baron was playing a scene. The ruler absolute, laying down the law, dispensing orders and favors. The giver of gifts, the withholder of the world's pleasures—to be donated or denied. Life to be given or taken away by installment. "*I*," he repeated, "have the control. I have the final say on everything."

"Baron," I said, "you have all *artistic* control. But I have control of the *business*. Remember how the contract reads?"

"Yes, Jarn boy, I remember very well," he said, letting me see him remembering. He frowned in concentration, remembering, thinking. Even from our first meeting years ago and especially after our first business talks I knew that thinking was always going to be a problem for him. A gray and foggy experience, like when he was truly angry. His brain flared and smoked inside his head, like a fire in a changing wind. He wandered alone through the smoke of his thoughts, never truly understanding anything. Finally not even remembering why he was angry. Then, frightened at his own anger and confused doubts, trying to retire his argument with dignity—at times he had that, and I didn't want to take it from him; not yet, anyway. Because after this full day I was suddenly tired. Suddenly I didn't feel as elated as when I had entered the suite, savoring the elegance, taking the bows, preparing the speeches, counting the money. The main title in color, "Produced by *Jarnigan*," not only didn't shine on the screen, it also went out of focus. Again—suddenly I became the Average Man.

Actually, none of us is an Average Man—we are all special. Because the average man is a tired and scared man, and a scared and tired man makes bad decisions, he can't afford the largesse of ideals. His morals—what he has left of them—decline because they, like many things of value, are prone to slip away, through the fingers or out of the mind. You no longer—being a scared, tired, and average man—can expect, nor do you expect, quality in your ideas, ideals, or *yourself*. You substitute a phrase, neatly turned, for want of an idea—a good one. For running scared, the ideals are slipping by —posts along a highway seen from a fast car. But I didn't want to get on that merry-go-round. I'd been on it before, and it was too fast a ride, too much mileage—cost too much—so I put that smile on my face. I worked hard at it. (You simply raise your face, tighten the muscles in your jawbone, let your mouth widen, and your lips, slightly open, relaxed, come back slightly over the teeth so they are exposed in friendliness.) The smile, if that's what it was, wouldn't stay on, it was as empty as a new-dug grave. It peeled off, never reaching my eyes. I strained and tried again.

"Listen, Baron." This said in a firm tone, trying to get what had started to be a good Deal going again. "We've much to be grateful for. We have over four million in the revolving fund, yours and my salaries are now in numbered Swiss bank accounts."

I reached in my pocket and gave him a wallet I had picked up at Dunhill's. Beautiful leather with his initials on it. But more important, a deposit slip in his own numbered account for two hundred fifty thousand dollars. He stretched out his hand, took the wallet, looked at it, liked it, thought about it. But when he read the deposit slip and saw the amount, the first real smile I'd ever seen him have spread over his face, a smile that went clear up to his eyes. It was a nice smile. I smiled back. I could tell from the feel of my face that I was grinning. Damn, I thought, my mouth smiles. It has been saying things. Little purring nice things to try to keep the lid on this Deal. My mouth will say anything. Christ, I thought, now hold it, hold it, Jarnigan, stop getting mad. This isn't what you came here for. So I dealt out the rest of the replies to his questions like cards—expertly, efficiently—and the minutes pattered by on dainty little feet.

I listened to more of the Baron's conversation. About this time, the telephone rang. I went over, picked it up. The operator burbled, "Mr. Jarnigan, there's a Mr. Jason Wormser on the phone."

"Oh," I ohed, "just hold the line please. Don't say I'm in or out."

I went over to the Baron. "Well, you know who's on the telephone."

The Baron reared back. "You mean that son-of-a-bitch is calling already?"

"That's what I mean, Baron. He's on the phone. What shall I say?"

The Baron, all dignity intact, said, "It's not for you to say, Jarn my boy. It's for *me* to say. I shall take the call." And with that he strolled determinedly over to the phone, said to the operator. "This is the Baron speaking. Put Jason Wormser on."

After a little while there were a couple of murmurs from the Baron and finally the Baron said, "Hello, Jason. Yes . . . Yes." The Baron continued saying Yes very politely. Finally he shouted, "Are you telling me to come back . . . Don't you curse at me, Jason. I won't put up with it . . . You dare to give *me* an ultimatum?" The Baron said this loudly. Then, much to my surprise, he was calm for a while. The conversation continued, with the Baron usually saying No and sometimes only just shaking his head and listening. Suddenly the Baron completely lost his head and started shouting insults at Jason Wormser. He held the phone away from his ear, and I walked over closer to the Baron. I could hear Jason screaming. I heard him yell, "I'll sue!" From the conversation between the two, and what I could pick up on the phone, Jason was going to sue the Baron for millions of dollars as a result of stopping the picture. He was threatening the Baron with his contract. The Baron shook the phone as he would a dumbbell, hoisting it back and forth, strolling back and forth, kicking at the long cord tangling around his feet.

The Baron said, "That picture isn't stopped, the director told me he's able to shoot around me for four or five days. Don't scream at me." Finally the Baron said, "You Jew . . . you pharisee . . . you've sucked my blood . . . you've drained me dry for fourteen years." The Baron continued ranting and raving, shouting a verbal barrage at Jason Wormser.

Suddenly the Baron swerved around. He looked at me. There was a puzzled, pained look on his face. Without a word he fell straight over backward, the phone clattering to the floor. I rushed over, grabbed a pillow off one of the chairs and put it under the Baron's head. I picked up the phone, said "We'll call you back," and hung up. I immediately flashed the operator. I told her, "Listen, get Dr. Kurt Lindbaum. The number is Circle 7-7000. Yes. Tell him it's an emergency. It's for Logan Jarnigan. That he must come immediately to the Hampshire House. Yes. Give him all the information. Now connect me with the manager."

In a few moments the manager's voice came over: "Yes, Mr. Jarnigan, what is it?" He sounded concerned.

"We've had a little problem up here and I'm waiting for Dr. Kurt Lindbaum. Will you see that he's brought up immediately when he arrives."

An hour later: Dr. Kurt Lindbaum had been in the room and finished his examination of the Baron. The Baron had suffered a coronary. Nothing too serious, but just the same it was a warning. The Baron was conscious. He looked at me and said, grinning weakly, "Jarn boy. Did I tell that son-of-a-bitch off or no?"

I looked back at him. I tried to muster up a grin . . . couldn't. "You told him, Baron. You sure did. But forget that and just take it easy."

."This is a damned silly-ass thing to do," the Baron continued, almost talking to himself, tiredly.

Kurt looked at him and said, "Baron, you must lie quiet for a while and then we're going to get you to bed."

The Baron wasn't in any condition to argue. He lay there quietly. Kurt motioned to me and I walked over to the other side of the room. "Listen, Jarn, this is serious. He's had a bad attack. I've got to get him to a hospital."

The Baron overheard that. "No, no hospitals. That's all that pharisee Wormser would want. He'd like to think that he'd put me in the hospital." His voice rose two notches: "If I were dying I wouldn't go to the hospital."

I turned and walked over to the Baron. I said, "Don't worry. Don't worry, Baron, you're not going to the hospital." That seemed to quiet him for a moment. I turned back to Kurt and said quietly, "Listen, Kurt, this is important. Forgetting about any expense, you bring any equipment that you need here to this apartment. This has to be kept absolutely quiet."

Kurt owed me some favors and I knew in any event he'd help me. He walked over to the desk. Picked up the phone. Called the hospital. I heard him giving some instructions.

Another hour went by and one of the bedrooms in the suite started to look like a hospital room. There was an oxygen tent, oxygen tanks in the corner—and a nurse all very white and proper and absolutely thrilled to death at being able to minister to the Baron.

As soon as the Baron was safely installed in bed—holding tightly onto the nurse's hand in what, in my view, was an unnecessarily close relationship for a fellow who'd just had a heart attack—I walked into the library talking to Kurt.

Kurt said: "Now listen, Jarn, I still say that he should be in a hospital. He's got to have the nurse for the next three or four days, plus absolute quiet. No booze. No broads. No excitement. No anything... get it?" Kurt was frowning, looking me dead in the eye. "No *anything*. You've got to keep this guy quieted down or he's liable to step off."

"Kurt, we'll do it just like that."

I had called Jules Molotov, told him the dinner was off. I also called the Suisse Syndicate man, their French attorney, their American attorney, and told them the dinner was off but that I would see them the following evening. I decided to stay in with the Baron and see that he was all right, although the nurse looked to me as though she was taking very good care of him.

After the Baron heard Kurt talking to me, after he had questioned Kurt strongly with respect to his condition, after he'd questioned the nurse—it looked as though he was going to be able to get everything out of the nurse, in every sense of the word—the Baron now wanted to talk. He had been scared. After some discussion with him I realized that he had gotten very thoughtful. It looked as though he might want to go through a brief religious repentance, judging by the kind of questions he was asking me.

"Jarn," the Baron said quietly, "tell me about... some of those things that you were telling me, about your father being a preacher and all ..."

"Well, Baron, there's not much to tell. I have, or used to have, certain religious convictions but I don't know that I know too much about religion. Why?" I had thought this was a little out of place, since I didn't figure that I was going to be able to help him too much. But I wanted to talk to him. I wanted to help him, and I wanted to see if I could tell what was troubling him. I sure didn't want him to be worried to death, and if this religious talk was going to help him—well, then, we'd have a religious talk. Nor had I abandoned my beliefs. Because I figured that the funeral of God is always a premature burial.

THE DEAL

The false and "artistic" producer, the new-money-heavy producer, is not really a deep thinker because he will not consent to be more than superficial. He is bewitched by his own artsy-craftiness . . . stares at it, but cannot see through it, only around it. He cannot believe that true art is a slight, light thing; a feather that should not be clutched at with heavy-handed, money-lending fingers that try to claw and grasp their way to something they are unable to really touch or understand . . . ever.

The Baron said, "Jarn"—and here he got a serious look on his face. His voice was quiet, he looked at me directly, and for once seemed to have a truly sincere expression in his eyes. "Jarn, I'd like to talk to you about something serious, about something that—well, I wouldn't talk to anybody about it except you. You know what I said—you're my best friend."

I didn't say anything. I just nodded. "All right, Baron," I said, "shoot. What is it?"

The Baron started to tell me.

I figured the Baron had been engaged in half-truths all his life. He charmed truth, he waltzed truth, and then tried to seduce her. He bent her over backward on the bed, and couldn't . . . truthfully couldn't . . . do anything. *Quelle tristesse, Quelle Sagan.* So it went. They had only a nodding acquaintance—a limp lob, a limper truth. So, as the Baron smoked and fumed his way down to hell, I wondered if even *Someone* wanted to help him.

On that day and on the day following the Baron talked about religion, about wanting to change. He told me of the many times he'd tried to pray but couldn't. He had never done it. He didn't know how. But now he truthfully wanted to try to pray. What the hell, I'd try to help him take a cut at it, it sure wouldn't hurt him any.

21

I have never understood, nor could ever quite believe, how the Baron finally convinced me that he wanted to change. His plea for help at the time couldn't have sounded more honest, beseeching—a deep crying-out from the heart. In retrospect, I can't convince myself he fooled me, because before we prayed, in the far-off, far-back corridor of my mind a little bell rang—I think tolled would be a better word—and I believed him. What the hell, I'd pray with him. What the Baron didn't know was, I needed it worse than he did.

So, as we knelt to pray, me half believing him, I looked closely and absently at the design, subdued and discreet, bravely dissecting the dark green rug beneath me. My knees completed the pattern and formed a triangle. I was waiting for him to start . . . I was quiet. He said softly, "Kid, can't you start us off?"

I said to myself, Lord, help me do this right, help me. It may save the Deal and even, who knows, save this son-of-a-bitch. I withdraw that, I thought, and repeated out loud, "I withdraw that."

"What, kid . . . did you start? Have you started praying?"

"Listen, Baron," I said, "let's just be quiet for a minute."

"Oh, sure . . . quiet . . . huh . . . right . . . quiet . . ."

I took a peek at him from under my hands. He was pale and wan-looking, but strangely he looked better than he had ever looked in his life. He was kind of gazing up and maybe waiting for something. He looked half scared but happy. Like he was waiting to be tapped on the shoulder or hit, but wouldn't mind because he deserved it—it would be part of his purification. We kept kneeling. My stomach rumbled.

Christ, dear blessed Christ, I thought, after I'd peeked at the Baron again. He had his eyes kind of closed. Listen, Lord, I don't know if this crap is right. I don't know, I thought, if this son of a bitch is sincere, but he's half sold me . . . maybe whole sold me . . . so I'd say—Lord, help this guy. I can then get through this picture and this Deal one way or the other. I have slid down so low and so bad that I don't know if I can get through to You, but since this is a selfless prayer, Lord, just help this man—Christ knows he needs it—and help me to pray to convince him and . . .

"Kid, do you mean all that?"

135

THE DEAL

"What's that?" I said. I opened my eyes, I was looking at the Baron. I had been talking out loud. I got up and walked over to the fireplace. Slowly the Baron followed me. We stood there a minute. Then he stuck out his hand.

"I've never really prayed before," he said. I looked at him carefully. I was convinced in spite of myself that the Baron might be sincere. But again, far off in the back corridor of my mind I kept thinking, he may be only playing a scene. I could hear him say to the Pope, "I have changed. I want to turn." "Yes, my son," the Pope intones. I can see the Baron now, playing a scene like Spencer Tracy in a monastery, white-robed, sincere, low-voiced: "I am sure I can find myself in His service." "Yes, my son, yes," the Pope dreams on.

The Baron walked back over and half knelt by his chair.

And then I was back inside my head and I stopped. What the hell's wrong with me? Maybe the Baron *has* changed. It's happened before. Not to the Marquis de Sade, not to Jack the Ripper, but maybe it could happen to the Baron. I looked at him. His face had the surface numbness of a man who is in a fight, yet with him, no hurt, no striking back.

Yes . . . as I watched him I could see him flexing the muscles of his soul, like an oyster, feeling the lemon juice squeezed from above, the all-powerful hands doling out the acid—waiting to be eaten, to be swallowed. How can you digest the soul, how do you get through . . . how . . . God doesn't need another oyster, He doesn't even like them. And anyway, there is no "R" in the month of Soul.

I don't know how long we stayed there. It was some little while. Then I heard the muted bell of the telephone ring. I looked over at the Baron. He was still half kneeling, his head on his hands. He hadn't moved or changed position. I thought he might really be doing a little soul-searching. When you almost step off after a heart attack you reevaluate things. If he got down to it, it might really shake him up. One thing sure, all it could do would be to help him or let him break even. I turned and went out of the room, carefully and quietly. I walked over to the desk and picked up the phone. "Yes," I said.

"I haven't asked you yet," the girl's voice said over the wire. She continued, "Who is this, darling?"

"Who were you calling?" I asked. "Normally, calls are announced and since you weren't, well . . . " I let my voice trail off.

"I'm a guest in the hotel, sweetie. I told them I'm an old friend of the Baron; they know me, so they rang through."

THE DEAL

"Well, that's just fine, so if you'll tell *me* then we'll all know who you are," I said, still speaking quietly.

"Darling, you're as fussy as a dance director. I'm Joyce." She gurgled.

"Joyce who?" I asked again.

"Hell, I'm Joyce Dahl, everybody knows me."

By now I knew she was a little tanked so I let her down easy with, "Miss Dahl, I'll call you back, or the secretary will. We're in a meeting here and . . ."

She cut in on me. "I've been to some of the Baron's meetings. Can I come up?"

"Not now, Miss Dahl."

"Call me Joyce."

"Not now, Joyce," I said firmly.

"Yeah, I know those meetings take a lot out of you. If I don't hear in an hour I'm coming up, okay?"

"Not okay. I'll call you . . ."

"Who are you, darling, if one may ask?"

"Just a friend, just a tired friend."

"Oh," she ohed. "So you're in the meeting too," she said happily. "Well, don't break the chain, go on back." I started to hang up. "Hey," she yelled, "you'll call me?"

"You will be called, Miss Dahl. Goodbye."

I hung up and went back into the library. The Baron was still down on his knees. He didn't look comfortable enough to have fallen asleep. His body was half tense, almost in the crouched position of a runner about to start a sprint race. Every once in a while I could hear what seemed to be a whispered word, but I couldn't be sure. I went over and sat down in one of the deep chairs that were carefully arranged in front of the fireplace. Three logs were burning pleasantly, it was a nice fire. The room was nice. The cold gray day that was outside the window was nice, the Baron was a nice fellow, I was a nice fellow. His idea of wanting me to pray with him was— well, I'd like to say "nice" to keep the phrase going, but it wasn't nice. It bothered me. I don't know why it should have to such an extent, but it did.

A couple of hundred years ago my father had been a minister. So I had been dunked in it, baptized in it, and heard it for the first years of my life. Every day, every hour on the hour. It was Communion every day. Every meal we ever ate became so holy from being prayed over and blessed and thanked for that all the taste went out of it. My brother and I were half scared to eat it, since it seemed that Jesus or one of the Disciples had just delivered it to the front door. When you're eight or nine years old, it's hard to reconstruct Christ's body out of a hamburger. Now, if you're hungry you'll try and forget that you're eating holy food. With fish or turnips I remember I didn't have too much trouble. But to try and reconcile Christ's thigh being ground up, put on a bun, and served with an onion was a pretty tough thing to swallow. My father said the blessing long enough for everything to get nice and cold. My mother added what her Father in Heaven would like and what wouldn't be vetoed or criticized by our father at the table—"a prayer on a knife-blade." My brother had his turn; he had fifteen words to say and he said them faster or slower as the case seemed to call for. When my turn came, since I was the youngest all I had to say was, "In Jesus' name, amen." I always got through mine fast. What I'm trying to say is, I came from a fairly religious family.

I don't want to give the wrong impression about my father. He was the kindest, gentlest man I ever knew, and if he didn't understand things too well as they were, I never blamed him, because he always blamed himself too much. He was just never quite with us. He had been a good business-man. But now he was a saint, a Protestant saint, a part-time minister. The only trouble was, he never could get the people to agree with him. But my father could cure a cold or stomach-ache, he could fix anything, he could talk to birds, and every dog that ever saw him laughed and grinned affectionately at him, even from across the street.

He didn't preach well. It took him too long to get his idea across. His prayers were too involved and kind of trailed off, lost in the absolute sincerity of his idea. He knew it would be good for them to understand but he tried to put over too much in one gulp. When he preached (without pay) the good people in the church knew what he was trying to say, and they slept peacefully and lovingly during service. The evildoers, for that's what he called them, listened vaguely for a while, soon lost track in the maze of goodness that flowed around them, and finished up figuring my father was a religious dope, if he hadn't been an unpaid preacher (or perhaps because of that), a nut.

Over the years, however, a lot my father told me sunk in, had a certain practical value. Sometimes his prayers were answered. Material stuff never arrived, but the health came through fine. We grew up fine, my mother is fine. (My brother, a question mark.) But one day my father got a fine cancer. Had a prayerfully fine death. Out of his multitude of friends, five came to the burial. It was a fine funeral.

I guess I had dozed off in front of the fire. Thinking nice nice things. I

THE DEAL

had a fine fine dream. That certainly is fine. I looked up. The Baron was sitting opposite me, staring into the fire.

"How're you feeling, Baron?"

He didn't answer for a while. He turned and looked at me, his face very serious, not silly serious as usual, but thoughtful serious. "Kid," he said, "I'm going to try that faith and belief and prayer idea. Do you realize we've lived over half our lives, that in less than the time we've already lived, we'll be dead?" He paused for a moment. "Can you realize that?"

I could see something was bothering him. He had hold of something he'd never really touched before. It was completely unfamiliar to him. But he didn't want to drop any of it. I had known him so long and so well it was hard to listen and figure this new facet. Which might last . . . here I gave up. He said solemnly, "Yes, kid, in less time than we've lived up to now we'll be dead."

"Well, what the hell, Baron," I answered, "what the hell."

He looked stern. "You don't think I'm serious, do you?" he said, looking away and then turning back toward the fireplace.

"Well," I said, "I . . ."

He stopped me. "I am, kid. I am and I want you to help me. Really help me." His voice rose. He got up swiftly from the chair and started walking back and forth in front of the fireplace. He talked on. "I'd like to start again. I'd like to change. I'd like . . ." Here he ran out of breath, but I saw that for once he retained what he was thinking about. The familiar gestures, the handsome profile, were submerged in this new idea. He turned and walked over to the mantel, leaned back—forgot to strike a pose, take an attitude. His voice came out naked: "I want you to help me; you're my best friend, please help me."

For the first time I saw a real tear slide furtively out of the Baron's eye and move stealthily down past his nose. He never noticed it. He never saw the effect his apparent sincerity was having on me. He didn't brush the tears away—a gesture he wouldn't have missed, would have made the most of and had the whole theater reaching for their towels. He stood there dead-sober, unashamedly crying. Stretching out his soul for help. Man, he convinced me. "I'll pray with you now, Baron," I said softly.

Without a word he turned and dropped to his knees, his head on the chair. I didn't kneel. I stood there and looked down at him, kneeling on the other side of the fireplace. I listened, and heard the Baron whisper . . . "God, I never prayed before and that's the truth. What I want is . . ." Here he choked, but swallowed and went on, "What I want is to try and . . . just . . . well . . . try to be . . . to have you know that . . . *Christ!*

139

this is hard." He stopped, raised his head, turned to look at me. I looked down at him. I could only nod. It didn't seem like much help; he just shook his head and gritted his teeth; he put his head back down on his hands, then moved one hand up and tore his tie and collar open—a button fell off unnoticed and half buried itself in the soft rug. He wasn't saying anything now. He was quietly crying. I sat back down in the opposite chair. I was quiet. But by damn I was moved. It's something to see a man truly come of age when he's forty-two.

I looked into the fire. The logs were mistily blurred. The Baron's quiet whispering started again. I heard: "So if you'd do that, I could try it because I never asked that. I don't understand and I'm afraid . . . I'm afraid . . . I don't want to know some things. I want to be better. I want . . . and then if I do that, maybe you'll help, see . . ." By now he was shaking with sobs. Dry heaving sobs. "It's that I can't and you know I can't. God knows I can't, and I don't even want to and I try but it's just . . ." He cried aloud, "By Christ, this is tough. I can't let them know, the bastards, they'll kill me, they'll tell . . . you've *got* to help."

Suddenly he stopped; he raised his head and looked directly at me. I've never seen a face like that in my life. Whatever it was, it had him completely. He was inspired and torn apart by something. I'd known him for years and never once saw even a faint glimpse of this intense self-hating, this wanting, this exposed fear. He looked insane. I tried to calm him, to soothe him. I said quietly, "Go ahead, Baron, go ahead, boy. Nobody will ever know, get it off your mind. Pray it out now. There's nobody here but you and me."

He looked at me in open pain. "*God's* here," he corrected me firmly and quietly. "And I'm going to tell Him."

He dropped his head and stayed there—quiet. From time to time a whispered word came out. Once I heard, ". . . and help my son, too . . . help . . . need . . . please, Christ . . . regret . . . pay back . . . help . . . please help . . ." Then—quiet.

I sat there and watched him for a minute. Then I quietly got up and walked softly across the room. At the door I turned around. The Baron hadn't moved. I hoped God would help him. I left.

The following day, I was in the Baron's suite when the telephone rang. It was Jules Molotov. I told Jules I'd be over to his hotel later, to sit tight. I could see that the Baron was going to stay in the apartment. If he felt that way I sure as hell wasn't going to insist that he come along. I knew he was in a funny mood, and I didn't want him to crack out at the dinner with the Suisse Syndicate *directeur*.

"You go ahead, kid," he said, "I'll have dinner sent in if I feel like anything, but I think I'll just stay in and hit the kip early. I've got a lot to think about."

I turned and started out the door. He looked better now, but was still talking quiet and subdued. When I got to the front door he called out to me. "Wait a minute, I have to tell you something." I stopped putting on my coat, turned back around and leaned against the front door. He came walking out from the library, down the hall and over to me. His face had a little more color now, he looked calm, calmer than I'd ever remembered seeing him.

He walked right up to me, looked me straight in the eyes and said, "Jarn, I want to thank you for that in there. I mean, truly thank you. I told you before you are the best friend I have. I trust you, I believe you and I don't believe any son-of-a-bitch in the world (I've got to cut out that swearing). You know—you saw what happened to me in there. I'd never let anyone but you have that 'down' on me. I'd have you chopped if I thought you'd ever breathe a word about it. I know you won't so we won't talk about it. But, kid," he continued, "I'm going to change—not *going to* —I *have* changed. You saw it . . . didn't you see it?"

I shook my head. "You sold me. I think it was . . ." I never got to finish what I thought. He was too full of it. Whatever he had, he certainly wasn't going to let it go. He went on with, "Yes, I've changed—I won't go back. You saw, and by damn you stood by me and helped me through the most tremendous, the most . . ." he faltered, trying to fish up another word. He grappled with himself, and it, and continued, ". . . terrifying, wonderful experience of my life. I feel pure. I feel different. I feel maybe I have a chance. Don't you think so?"

"Nobody," I answered, "can take it from you; but this one you have to play alone."

"Yes, I'm sure of that. I'm sure and I'm ready to play this out alone." Here he raised his face as though he were heading into a strong wind; his chin thrust forward, his face stern, already solidly in control, his destiny no longer hanging in the balance. It would have been ridiculous if he hadn't been so deadly serious. The Baron Saul "on the road to Damascus" was experiencing a change. It was quick, but then maybe it was true; what the hell, anything was better than having him kicking up dust all the time. His was worse than fall-out. All the dust from his anger, his tantrums, his irrational behavior, contaminated everything around him. The periods of "niceness," doing things like making pictures, reading scripts, acting like the star that he was, the top of his profession—all this, and all the money he made for himself and for our company, didn't dilute, didn't water down enough the times when he was on his down-swing period. Then he poisoned us all with his own special brand of radiation.

He said quietly, "Do you have to go just now, or can we talk a minute more?"

He started slowly back toward the library. I followed, saying, "Well, I should get on down to this meeting since it's ready to be signed—the distribution contract, I mean. The money deal is already locked up." I could see he wasn't listening.

He said, "You know, kid, I want this feeling to last. I feel great. I feel different. Nothing bad, the old fear, nothing, can get to me right at this minute . . . that's why I've got to hold on to it, don't you see?"

"Yeah, but I just wonder if you . . ."

The Baron looked around like he'd misplaced something, not worried, just looking as if he were trying to orient himself with his surroundings.

"Listen," he said, "listen, let's talk this over . . . I'd like to . . . just be sure . . ." He turned around and stared at the fireplace for a brief moment, then turned to look at me. I don't know if he thought I'd say anything or not; however, my not saying anything didn't seem to matter either. He started to light a cigarette, held the cigarette thoughtfully for a moment, then tossed it into the fireplace. He went over to a chair and sat down, leaned back and stared thoughtfully into the fire with half-closed eyes.

I walked over to the window and looked out over Central Park. Here and there lights were going on, through the mist you could see the headlights of the automobiles moving through the park and on toward Fifth and Park Avenues. It had been a strange afternoon. Looking back at the last couple of days, the last couple of hours, it was difficult to believe that it really had happened, as I knew it had happened.

The telephone rang and I went out to answer it. The operator said Mr. Molotov was calling again. I said to put him on.

"How's the boy?" he asked.

"Fine, Jules, fine." I said, looking back into the library and seeing that the Baron hadn't moved from his staring into the fire position.

"How's the Baron? Sleeping, drunk, or poontanging?" You see, he knew the Baron well.

"Jules," I said quietly, "where are you?"

THE DEAL

"I'm still at the Plaza. We are waiting for you, but we can come right over to perk you up."

"Nix," I said, still quiet. "Nix, Jules, we've had a little problem over here. I'll meet you at the Oak Room for a drink and you bring me up to date on what happened this afternoon on the Deal, and we'll meet Venard and the Suisse banker fellow . . . uh . . . Monsieur . . ." I'd forgotten his name.

"Roulot," Jules supplied. "Say, boy, what's wrong? Why the hell are you talking so low? And it's not like you to forget the banker's name. Hell, any guy who's giving you two million cash you have to be polite and remember his name and little things like that," he added sarcastically. "Well, where do we meet you?" he finished.

"Like I said, we've had a little problem here," I repeated patiently. "I'll be over in a while. I've got to wait and see how the Baron feels; he has . . ."

He cut in on me, his voice now as low and quiet as mine. "Is he blipped? Is he "horsing" it?"

"No, nothing like that."

"Well, what the hell is it then? Listen, boy . . . I'm coming over. You sound like you need me; you know, old Uncle Jules . . . tell old Uncle Jules every—"

I said, quietly but firmly, "Don't come over, Julie. Now, for Christ's sake let's do something right for a change. Stay there or take Miriam on to dinner. I'll change and go directly to the dinner. I'll call you if there are any changes." I hung up before he could say anything. I put the phone down. My hand was cramped; I'd been squeezing it tight enough to crack it. I hadn't noticed it until then. I called the operator and told her not to put any more calls through from in or out of the hotel until I told her different, and to give the word to the other girls at the board.

I went back into the library. He hadn't moved. "Baron." No response. No sign that he had even heard me. "Baron, I have to go over and meet the men from France and the Suisse man." He nodded. "Then we're supposed to go on to dinner. How do you feel?" He glanced at me for a brief moment then.

"I'm not going anywhere. I'm staying here." The way he said it, I knew he meant it.

"Well, I'm going in my room and change, I'll see you in a few minutes." I started out of the room. "Just take it easy, Baron, don't worry, everything's all right."

143

THE DEAL

"Sure, kid, sure everything's all right," he said in a voice I didn't like. "You go ahead, I'm staying here." As I left the room, he called after me, "Don't you worry either, boy."

I went across the study and down to my bedroom, one of four in the suite. I closed my door, sat down on a chair and started to take off my shoes.

That religious thing had really hit the Baron hard. Since it was the first time this had happened, I had no way of knowing how long it would last. A picture, a love affair, another rape charge—I'd been vaccinated with them all and knew the amount of time each sickness lasted . . . all ways. However, this thing had jarred him worse than anything I'd ever seen hit. Well, it was something to think about. Could the Baron really change? A change is something that can happen fast or slow. It was a son-of-a-gun to try and judge, especially with the Baron.

I believe time and truth never change. It doesn't matter that men try to evade and discredit that irrefutable evidence. Plainly, the minute hasn't changed, the second hand proceeds at the same pace it always has. Would the Baron really accept or respect this change if it came to him? It should here be remembered: "No one is entitled to respect, if he doesn't have any for himself." And that was the bitch-dog in the Baron's manger.

22

I showered and dressed. I went out into the main hall to the closet. I got my topcoat, a muffler, my hat, not making a noise, but still not trying to be quiet, trying to get back into a sense of normalcy. I put my head in the library and said to the Baron, who was just sitting there quietly in front of the fire, "I'm going now. Still feeling okay?" He nodded. "Sure you don't want to meet us over at the restaurant?" He shook his head. I told him I'd see him later. I left.

It had been decided that we'd all have dinner at El Morocco. It was one of the Baron's favorite watering places and had been chosen for that reason. That, and to celebrate the closing of one of the finest independent financial deals in the history of motion pictures.

We now had practically an unlimited revolving fund in dollars or Swiss francs; full artistic control; and absolute control of the money as long as we stayed within the limits of our budgets, which had been properly made up and gone into to be certain to allow for some delays. I had to take into account the Baron's peculiarities. Within certain limits I had explained them away in part to the Suisse Syndicate *directeur* who had carte blanche to make the deal, and since he was getting his off the top, he wasn't too hard to convince. The Baron was the biggest male star of the past few years, and when I finished with these money men his escapades came off no worse than a spirited boy's pranks. The rape and morals charge was glossed over as *chantage* (blackmail). The holding up production was never because the Baron was loaded or "horsed" to the eyebrows—it was "temperament."

You know there is no such thing as collective honesty. A group of men, or a board of directors, will cheerfully ruin a man, create a run on the market, have a guy Sent Over, all under the mantle of (cough, ahem, arhurrmph) . . . "big business." And we are all a hell of a bunch of fellows—men of the world, with the collective dishonest urge, the desire to stick your dinker a mile deep in the womb of the business and break it off. So each group has the paternally satisfied feeling that they have properly seduced the other side ("screwed them" is the term). Then, properly

145

frigged, you lead each other off to a business dinner. The Picture Business Beatitude: If I'm going to be fucked, I want to be kissed too.

Well, here we were, sitting in El Morocco. I wanted it to be a good celebration. I looked around the room. There hadn't been a strange face in there for a long time. At the dinner were the Syndicate man M. Roulot, Jules Molotov, and his wife Miriam. Two starlets were also very much present. One was from Columbia, one was from Fox. They wore the usual "pained and hungry" expression. Arched eyebrows, pushed-up bosoms—and all their brains in their faces. There was an Arab-sheik-type lawyer, whose name I never did catch, who did some money-changing in hard and soft currency for the Syndicate man. He'd latched on to one of the starlets. So the dinner had progressed.

The battle was continuing. All were screwed in advance. I leaned back in my chair far enough away from Miriam so she couldn't get a hammerlock on me, and started thinking. Living in Europe, but especially in France, an American has a tendency to become maybe more of a Continental man, because it seems if you live in one place a long time, you've deposited something of yourself there. You've left, or you would leave if you left, a lot of yourself. So to a sensitive man—and we are all sensitive men—the French thing gets into your being; it is not as though it were a new, unwalked-on and unspoiled land—the sun has shone, the wind has blown, and the rain has fallen. There are a million corpses in the sea and death rotting underfoot at every hand. And here sat old Jarnigan at El Morocco.

I wondered what I was doing here and what could happen next. My superstar was on a religious kick and half nuts back in his apartment. My attorney and his sexy wife were getting blipped in a studious and judicious manner. And here sat old Jarnigan.

I excused myself and got up from the table. The Arab was gnawing on the starlet's shoulder. I walked into the small alcove and used the telephone. I called the Hampshire House. I rang the Baron's room. There was no answer for a long time. Finally he answered the phone, very quiet, very subdued.

"How are you doing, Baron? How do you feel?"

"I'm all right, Jarn," he said with dignity, "I'm fine."

"Where's the nurse, Baron?"

"She's resting. I told her to. I'm all right."

"Well, now listen, Baron, why don't you get some sleep? I'm going to finish this dinner and send these people off."

THE DEAL

He interrupted, saying, "Well, don't hurry, Jarn, on my account. I like being alone. Anyway, I'll call the nurse if I need her."

"That's all right, Baron," I said. "I'll get through with these people; then I have to get Jules Molotov to the plane, but I should be back to the apartment by around two o'clock. Now get some sleep, will you? Remember what Kurt said."

"What?" he asked.

I repeated slowly. "You know the doctor said you should sleep a lot. Now, I'll wake you in the morning and the doctor will be by to see you around ten o'clock. Okay?"

He murmured something. Said, "Fine, good night." And we hung up. I was terribly sleepy. I wondered where I could buy twenty-four hours of sleep. But I went back to the table. The dinner was finished. I signed the check.

We all walked out into the street. Jules Molotov and Miriam were to be dropped off at the Plaza and then I was to wait for Jules. During that time the starlets would be dropped off one by one. The banker and the Suisse Syndicate man could go with them or not as they chose. (I later learned that the Suisse Syndicate man was a fagola, who apparently was going to make it with the lawyer.) There were a lot of false and empty farewells. Pledges of happy and lasting futures. Monies and pleasures to be taken easily and lightly. *Quelle farce, quelle comédie.*

I sat in the lobby waiting while Jules went back up to his suite with Miriam. I hoped he wouldn't take too long. I dozed there in a big leather chair. Boy, would I like to go to sleep. Then I started to think sleepily.

Listen, I said to myself, if you keep this "dealing" up you're going to end up a dirty old man. You'll live in a stinking house on a dirty street. You'll wear false teeth, they'll become loose and they'll click in your mouth when you try to eat, if you can find something to eat. You won't be able to get yourself a woman because nobody will have you, so you'll end up to jerk off. You will filch half-finished drinks off any bar or club they'll let you into, and then you'll end up in the gutter. Worse—under the gutter, I thought, half asleep. I didn't know why I was browbeating myself like this, but I was.

"Man, you sure give yourself a pep talk. That's some sales pitch," *Someone* said.

"Well, hell, I'm just tired of it . . ." I answered.

"Tired, son? Why, you haven't even started. Doing unclean work and evil things are finally the hardest work of all, and the result, as you say, Jarn . . . no payoff."

THE DEAL

"Listen, will you just knock it off. Just for Christ's sake leave me alone?"

Someone answered quietly, "It's precisely for His sake that I am *not* letting you alone. I'll be around, Jarn. You'll need me one day."

"Yeah, well don't call me, I'll call . . ."

"I know the phrase, Jarn, and I'll call you."

I must have slept. "Mr. Jarnigan," the chauffeur said, "Mr. Jarnigan?" Respectfully tapping my shoulder.

"Oh, yeah, I must have dozed off." I looked up at him and asked, "Listen, where is the car?"

"It's right in front on the Fifth Avenue side, sir."

"Well, I'm going out. You call Mr. Molotov's suite. Tell him I said we must leave for the airport at once."

"Yes, sir, Mr. Jarnigan."

He went over to the desk while I went out to the car. I got in and sat down; then I almost corked off again. A few minutes later, Jules joined me in the car. The chauffeur put his bags and brief case in the trunk, and we started out to the airport.

I almost dozed again riding back from the airport. Jules Molotov had to be back in Hollywood the next morning. Miriam had stayed in New York to do some "shopping" and then would follow him to California, and by damn the surprises never stopped. Just before he boarded the plane, Jules said seriously, looking up at me with his fat round face, his jowls glistening, "Listen, Jarn, look after Miriam. You know she's just a kid . . . headstrong and all, but she's just wonderful. Huh, Jarn?"

"She's grand," I said.

"Well," he continued, "I told her to call you if she needs anything. You know I'd do the same for you if you were still married."

I looked down at him quietly. "Sure, I know you would, Julie." I thought, Judas, how could a guy be so smart one way, and be so incredibly lopsided the other? It was hard to believe that he couldn't see Miriam . . . really see her. He had told her, "Call Jarn if you need anything." He didn't know that she had been calling me since the night of the celebration party when we signed the Deal with the Baron long ago. And this "headstrong kid," as he put it, wanted to get involved in things regardless of the outcome. I am sure not a monk, but Mrs. Jarnigan didn't raise any boy sappy enough to lay the wife of his lawyer—especially a smart one

148

whom I needed like I needed Jules. That was one *boute de miel* that I wouldn't touch.

"Mr. Jarnigan . . . sir . . . Mr. Jarnigan."

"What . . . oh yeah . . . thanks."

The driver had awakened me as we arrived back at the Hampshire House. "Pick me up at nine a.m." I said. "Don't bother to open the door. You go on and get some sleep." I got out of the car, took two steps and turned back. "Oh, here . . ." I handed him a ten . . . "Get a beer and relax." He grinned at me, gave a casual salute with his hand, and said, "Thanks, Mr. Jarnigan. I hope you sleep well too. Sure thank you, sir." I walked away, waved good night, and went into the lobby. I started directly over to the elevator.

"Mr. Jarnigan," the clerk at the desk said, "there's a call for you."

"Oh." I walked over to him and took the slip of paper he handed me. It read, "Mr. Jarnigan. Please call Mrs. Molotov. Urgent." I looked at the clerk. He was a thin, pale man with a thin blond mustache that didn't show too well—he had touched it up a bit with a too-red pencil, but it didn't go with the rest of him.

"Will you be good enough to tell the operator I'm out and no calls until tomorrow morning."

"Yes, sir, Mr Jarnigan Oh, Mr. Jarnigan, could I speak to you before you go up? You see . . ."

"Not tonight," I answered. I walked over to the elevator, got in, pushed the button for the penthouse floor and read the note again on the way up. "Urgent." Hell, I thought, Jules is hardly off the ground. The plane's hardly in the air and here we go. Christ . . . women! They are wonderful, they are divine, you can't do without them, and yet they are the only true and absolutely complete sons-of-bitches on earth. I grinned . . . "Urgent."

Sleeping with her wasn't urgent, it could be done any time. There was no question that she'd be great, but not great enough. Nobody would be great enough. My Deal was the really great thing . . . the Deal was the thing that was . . . urgent. The elevator stopped at the penthouse floor. I got out and threw the "urgent" message in a blue vase big enough to cage a tiger. I walked down the hall to the door of the suite. And that's when the blast of noise hit me.

I opened the door. I didn't know what I expected . . . no . . . that's a lie . . . I knew what to expect and I was afraid of it. However, I didn't think it would be as bad as it was. The door swung open and that's the way the people were inside . . . everything swinging, everything open. There were about six couples in the living room, some dancing, drinking; two of the couples were laid out on the two davenports, in the strictest sense of the word. The big stereo in the corner was going full blast. I looked the room over quietly. There was no one there that I knew. I walked over to the corner of the living room and pulled the cord out.

The quiet that came after the loud music seemed to make more noise than when everything had been going full volume. The dancing couples turned in different degrees of rapidity toward the stereo, and of course saw me. Slowly it began to dawn on them that it was no accident, that I had turned the music off deliberately. Some of the people walked over and sat in some of the chairs. A beautiful girl of about eighteen who was almost in a dress of chartreuse or one of those colors that you can see through, came over toward me. When she was about six feet from me, she stumbled and came the rest of the way in a canted angle and fell against my chest. She looked up, breathing my Scotch in my face. "You're cute," she murmured. "Been here long?" I put my hands on her shoulders, straightened her up and turned her around. About that time a long narrow bird with a thin angular face marched up and said, "Get your own girl, Jack. This one's mine." I looked at him thoughtfully. He was tall and slender and dolled up in what the well-dressed "girl-man" should wear. Sharp-eyed, sharp-faced, with one of those mustaches that get caught under your fingernail.

By now one of the men who had been in the laid-out position on the couch untangled and arranged himself, then walked over drunkenly toward me. When he got close enough he halted, peered at me sullenly, looked at the tall bird, then back at me. Then, in the New York tough-guy act, he said out of the corner of his mouth, "Who is this clown, Shep?"

Shep, who was evidently the tall, thin bird, answered in a nervous falsetto, "I don't know, Monk, but he's trying to flirt with Dixie. He's trying to take Dixie from me." He finished with a bleat.

The guy called Monk had on a violet-colored tux; he was a square-built man with a strong neck, the eyes too close together, a drunken smile, and all his brains in his dark and ugly face. He stepped over in front of the tall thin number, turned back to look at me, dropped his shoulder and threw a right at me that would have taken at least two minutes to get anywhere. "I'll handle this, Shep," he yelled, completing the swing. I leaned back and let it go by. He turned with the force of the swing. I grabbed him by the neck and the seat of his pants, then started him fast for the door, which was still open. I was cold-angry . . . this was a disaster.

I didn't know what all this would do to the Baron and my Deal. I thought this as I gathered momentum. I threw this guy out into the hall so hard that when his head and shoulder hit the wall on the other side, the building rattled. He moaned once, then slid down the wall onto the floor and never moved again.

"Let's see you handle that," I snarled and turned back into the room. By now, the rest of the people were getting to their feet and coming to the center of the living room. Dixie, the little blonde girl, came over to me and said, "Wha . . . wha . . ." I pushed her aside and went over to the tall bird.

"Listen, Sonny," I said, "you and your friends get the hell out of here—and I mean right now, or do you want me to help you out?"

"Christ, mister, what the hell did you do to Monk? We was invited here!"

"If Monk's the guy I pushed out in the hall, unless you want to join him, take off and take your friends with you." I added, softly, "Don't make me tell you again."

Then I walked over to the couch where one of the girls who had been laid out was still taking everything in from a horizontal position. I yanked her to her feet, picked up a coat—I didn't know if it was hers—grabbed another coat, threw it at the other girl and said, "Out. I'm going to turn around twice, then I don't want to see anybody in this room."

The guys, if that's what they were (they had the long hair and the high-heeled boots and the look of disappointed girls), were trying to make up their minds what they should do. Maybe if they all got together they could cause a little trouble. I didn't give them time to think anything over. I walked over to the fireplace and picked up the poker. "For the last time, out." They broke for the door. A couple of coats and a couple of purses were left on the floor. I walked over and picked them up, went to the door, and threw them out in the hall. I could see by now they had rung for the elevator. They were babbling among themselves, the girls scared, the guys confused. Monk was still out on the floor.

I slammed the door and as I turned around and went back into the living room, the door to the library which led into the master bedroom opened and out walked one of the most beautiful Oriental girls I'd ever seen. She was small and delicate and par for the course. It didn't take any genius to figure out what was going on. She walked toward me quietly, delicately, like a little cat, softly. I noticed she had her shoes in her left hand. She moved daintily closer, walking like a small yellow cat on a wet floor, picking up her tiny feet and placing them carefully on the thick and heavy rug. When she was about five feet from me she stopped and leaned over and said quietly, "Where are the rest? Are you of the party . . . yes?"

I didn't say anything. She took three more small delicate steps. Now she was standing very close to me looking up. She was still very tiny, still very beautiful. She asked questioningly, "You with the party, no? All others gone . . . ?"

When I still didn't say anything, she glanced carefully around the room, then back around the other side, and then looked up into my face again with her little slanted opaque eyes. "I am Yoko . . . who you?" She looked down for a moment and then looked back up at me shyly and tilted her head in a little birdlike movement. She fluttered her eyes. When I still didn't say anything, she cooed, "You want to take Yoko other room?"

"Listen, Madame Butterfly, take off. Get on your shoes and get your things and leave."

"Whassa matter . . . whassa matter?"

I pointed to the door and said quietly, "That's the way out, now take it. I won't tell you again."

Without a word she stepped back a half-step, bowed her head a little, then minced softly to the far side of the room, picked up a little coat, hastily put on one shoe and then the other, walked to the door, opened it, turned and looked back at me thoughtfully for a moment, then quietly backed out of the room. She closed the door without a sound.

Remembering the talk I'd had with the Baron before I left earlier that evening, remembering the prayers and the tears and the con that I'd really taken in, I walked deliberately over to the library door, pulled it open and walked in. I took a look at the three people in the room. They were something to see. They all looked up in various stages of surprise. It was as though you had put a stop-frame on the picture.

There was a beautiful Jamaican-type girl on her knees in front of the Baron. There was a Swedish-type girl with long blonde hair that hung clear down to the middle of her back, on her knees at one side of the Baron, and in the large chair, properly enthroned, sat the Baron. He had a silly, sappy, stunned look on his face. His eyes were glassy, no pupils. He never moved. It was as if they were cast in bronze.

I stood there looking at the three of them, but mostly at the Baron. I noticed, as though I were looking at them from outside myself, that the knees of the Jamaican girl and the knees of the Swedish girl were practically in the exact spot where the Baron had knelt to pray . . . had asked God to help . . . had said, "Christ, this is hard . . . by Christ, this is tough . . . I'd like to change . . ." And he had. He had changed from worse to worst . . . The brief repentance hadn't lasted long enough to even get the prayer properly through.

THE DEAL

I walked over toward him and for the first time the two girls moved. The Jamaican girl fell over on her side and on her hands and knees went backwards away from me. The blonde girl with the long hair down her back made some futile gestures, trying with a scarf to cover up the Baron, who was overly exposed. There wasn't much to cover but she· did it anyway. What the two of them had found to work on was difficult to find. If you did find it, it was certainly not enough for one, let alone two.

I stood there for what seemed like an hour but couldn't have been more than a minute. By now the girls had crawfished back as far as they could go. The Baron still sat there looking at me, his mouth open. He looked like a blowfish trying to get his breath. One of his shoes was off, and he never moved, with the exception of blinking his eyes very slowly from time to time as though trying to see through a mist. I said quietly to the girls, "Do I have to tell you what I want you to do now?"

When they didn't move I made one step toward the Jamaican girl, who slithered like a fish into the corner, braced herself up and shot for the door like she'd been fired out of a gun. The blonde girl ran to the other door thinking it was an exit. I followed the blonde girl into the room. She kept backing up, little whinnying noises of fear burbling out of her mouth. I must have looked like a crazy man to her. I reached over slowly, took her by the arm. She flinched away from me and I said softly, "Now you get out . . . get out now." She stumbled. I reached to help her in the direction of the door, she shrank away from me, then finally ran through the door.

I never heard the door to the living room close but I was sure they were gone. I walked back in and stood in front of the Baron. By now he was shaking his head and looking up at me. He croaked, "Is that you, Jarn boy? That you, Jarn?" I looked down at this man. I thought of the things that we had said a few hours ago, that I had had a true desire to try to help him if I could. It wasn't that that bothered me. It was that he had really gotten through to me. I really had prayed for him and for myself. But, seeing him the way he was now took away something important from me. Because I realized that not only had it not done him any good, but I hadn't got through either. I was no better than he was, and that's what shook me.

"Jarn." I looked back at the Baron. "Jarn, I'm sorry. It didn't last long, did it?" He tried to sit up a little straighter in his chair. I still hadn't said a word. For the first time he noticed the condition that he was in. He threw off the scarf that was still in his lap, tried to stand up, couldn't; arranged the zipper on his pants, then reached down with the over-slow, over-careful movement of the drunk; put on his shoe, leaned back and rested his head for a moment on the back of the chair. He closed his eyes. When he opened them they were a little clearer. Whatever he had taken was starting to slack off.

"Jarn, listen to me," he said. "Listen, I . . . I got lonesome and I slipped, I sent the nurse away. And, well, that's it, Jarn boy . . . I slipped. I got lonesome and I called my friends." He looked at me seriously, or as seriously as he could look in the condition he was in. "Jarn, I—"

"Baron, don't stand up or I'll cool you," I snarled, looking down at him. "You're filth . . . you're lousy filth. Why you had to include me in that religious shit earlier this evening, make me start to think maybe I could change . . . Not *you*, you lousy bastard . . . *me*! But when I see you now, you remind me of every rotten thing I've ever done . . . of every nasty, mean, disgusting part I played to get to this Deal. You're worse than my conscience. You're a living chancre, man. You sit there and show me first hand what I am and what I have been. For a few hours tonight I thought maybe I could lift out of it. I ricocheted off that lousy prayer you made—I tried to claw up with it. Christ, forgive me." I looked at him with a dead stare. "But now it's straight—you're filth and I'm filth. I'm worse than you for even trying to pray my way out of it."

I leaned down and looked him directly in the face, "But there is one thing, baby, we are going to do. We're going to finish this Deal. We're going to finish these pictures and we're both going to go to hell—but we're not going together. You'll take your poison—I've already got mine, because I have to work with you."

What I had said got to him in spite of the condition he was in. A semblance of the old frown came back, a vague glimmer of the old big-star sneer started to come. "Now look here, old boy," he wheezed, "I think you're a little harsh. I think you've no right to talk—"

I snarled, "Baron, if I didn't need your face in front of the camera you wouldn't have a face. This proves I'm worse than you. I want the Deal and the money worse than anything. But you cleared it up for me. You've made me see how rotten I am. That's what I love about this Deal, a little old truth-maker. That's what I despise about what you've done, what you did earlier, man. When I think about those prayers and those tears, I could puke. Good Christ, what happened to me? Me . . . me, taking on a sinning son-of-a-bitch like you when I can't even pray my own way out of a wicker basket. Well, pin-prick, well, sonny boy, you roll your hoop . . . and I'll roll mine from now on, except we got the Deal and I got you and that's the way it will be until it's finished. But, man, I hate you for showing me to myself—this plain. No excuse now."

I was out of breath after I said all this. I turned and started for the door, then I walked back over to the Baron, leaned down and stared him in the eye and snarled, "But don't you forget it . . . don't you push me too hard after this and don't you ever mention anything to me about religion—" I choked—"ever again."

• • •

I turned abruptly and walked out of the library. I slammed the door. I walked into the living room, went over to the bar next to the fireplace, poured myself a large brandy and walked back to drop down into one of the big leather chairs. I sat looking into the fire. I took a big drink of the brandy. I looked at my hands. They were trembling. "That's anger," I thought, "that's anger, and fear of what has happened . . . another form of drunkenness."

I knew my next thoughts would be toward self-justification but since I was only talking to me inside my head, I knew that this was one I wouldn't be able to rationalize. Any guy that needed to grab a hold of that cock-eyed, rickety, slanted, irrational prayer that the Baron made, and then to blow up like I did, needed a keeper. Well, I figured, I can always blame it on God. That's the ticket . . .What kind of a Creator created such a mixed-up, complicated, evil, and lousy world when, being the only Cause and Creator, He could have made such a nice easy one. And after death . . . Paradise . . . we all go home—horse shit. Some escapees like me don't want to go home, because we've had our hell there. So to die and go home to hell after trying to live a good and pure life would be an unjust reward; an unwelcome punishment.

You can't think that God is just a nice old man with a long white beard who examines your soul for marks and bruised scuffings as you hockey your way through life. You can't think your soul resembles a scruffy white volleyball with your sins plainly in evidence on its surface. A white volleyball if you were a big man. If you were a different man, a Baron man . . . the tennis-ball size will do. But then the different Baron-man had played too many sets with his "tennis-ball" soul. It wasn't so bouncy now . . . If you've got a volleyball soul or a tennis-ball soul, precisely and judiciously black-marked, you go directly to hell.

Now, it would be unfair to see a baby that hadn't been baptized, or a jungle native who'd never even heard of, or had a chance to see the light, go to hell. But you, yourself—you've fornicated, lied, drunk, and "dealed" your way through life. So you'll pay, and you'll enter accordingly. But would the baby and the native just end up there? You can't blame God.

You shouldn't take Him in a literal sense, saying, "God can't be omnipresent, omniscient and omnipotent . . . He can't be troubled beyond creating the world." Is this incorrect? Nope . . . I don't want to figure that God has long days, bad days, or good days, like a bad golfer.

I took a drink. I looked into the fire. I saw things I didn't care to see. I took another drink. I felt pretty low and pretty filthy, but it was the first time that I couldn't wash myself off within myself; sucker myself with what little feeble thoughts I had way off in the back corridor of my mind, saying to myself, Some day you'll change back, some day you'll be like you started out.

I took another drink—I could feel my face getting numb, my cheeks cold, like in frostbite. "Jarnigan," I addressed myself sternly, "you must now cleanse yourself. Keep yourself pure. Learn to wash and soap your soul in alcohol. Be brilliant. Be as bright as a struck match. A Lucifer ablaze with unkindness. You'll get there, boy . . . you'll get there . . . Hell . . . it's your Deal."

23

The Deal was now ready to go European.

I was headed for Paris, to arrange for the start of the second picture. The Baron was headed back to Hollywood, to work on Jason Wormser's picture, and this year's million dollars.

In my last talks with the Baron before I left for Paris, I saw to it that the conversations were on a strictly business basis. I told the Baron how the Deal would work. Needless to say, we did not discuss religion. As I've said before, the old clichés are true. You can't break the rules; you can't ignore the world.

When I arrived in Paris, I phoned the French co-producer. The Baron would have been proud of his class. His first instinct was to give a party for the press, to celebrate the signing of a multimillion-dollar "Baron film"— to be made entirely in France.

I spoke to the Baron in Hollywood from Paris a couple of times during the next few days. We only discussed briefly the preproduction work as it went along. The Baron was sober, tactful, and speaking correctly. It was then that the French co-producer gave a party for the press.

The party was in his large apartment on the Quai d'Orsay. Prior to that we had a meeting. He was talking quietly to us. The "us" was the French producer, the French lawyer, and a guy from the Centre du Cinéma. The guy looked and talked like a cadaver. His eyes looked like two burnt holes in a blanket. The "state secrets" he pandered from the Centre were supposed to burn holes in the brains of his listeners. He was a tortured, noisy, windy man; he ran to dysentery of the mouth and peritonitis of the soul. I listened only because he had to sign the license to permit us to shoot the picture we were already shooting. A waiter passed by—he clawed a glass off the tray. His fourth since we'd been talking. I hoped he'd either finish talking or pass out. Yet I couldn't be rude, since earlier we'd had an argument, and I didn't want it to flare up again. It's always best to let the enemy clear away the dead after a battle—not too much dust kicked up then, like the fellow says.

After what I considered was a polite period, I excused myself, accepting a date for lunch with this "great man" the following day. I started back for the main room, looking for a good writer, a friend of mine—the Tolstoi of Brooklyn and The Cloisters.

After the serious discussion with that Centre du Cinéma *con*, even this party would be a relief. Walking back into the main room, where the cocktail party for the press was in full progress, for the first time in several weeks I started to relax, knowing that for the moment the Deal was all right.

I looked around the room and saw this girl. Like the fellow said, everyone has loved her somewhere, the trick is to find her. I could feel my throat thicken. I was surprised at the effect she had on me. She must have felt me staring at her, for she looked directly into my eyes; then nodded her head in acknowledgment of the look, neither smiling nor giving anything away. She turned back to listen to what her companion was saying. I thought, I should be ashamed of myself. A reader of Mencken, an admirer of Voltaire, an advocate of moral rearmament, to stand here and lust after this little-titted, flat-bellied, soft, warm-looking frou-frou skirt.

While I had been looking at this girl, a writer from Hollywood who was still surprised to find himself in Paris was earnestly telling me the story idea for his latest screenplay. I was half listening, trying to be polite. Why not? I felt good. I kept looking around the room, I saw Darryl Zanuck in the corner talking with Irwin Shaw. John Huston came in and said Hello; he introduced me to a jockey who would go about four feet tall; he was riding John's horse in the Derby. Tola Litvak came in with Sophie, looking lovely as usual. It was always grand to see them. I turned back and gave half an ear to the apparent windup of the story: The writer had a self-satisfied, sappy grin on his face as though he had just finished *The Greatest Story Ever Told*.

I am still always amazed at writers, even very good writers, who will sometimes during the "hour of the amber" get the cocktail braggies and insist on telling you their story. Any great writer when talking about his childhood stops; then childishly submits, "I wanted to be a brave writer" or "Some day I thought I should write this." At that point, hang on, reader, you're going to get three paragraphs of sobs, tears, and flapdoodle. If you're really looking for an idea, sometimes you can pick something up, but in most cases it's just a question of babble.

He wound up the story, which I truly hadn't heard or understood. He asked seriously: "Well, that's it, Jarn, what do you think . . . do you think it's too deep for them?"

I mumbled some meaningless phrases; then I said to him, "Don't worry, boy, it isn't too deep for anybody . . . Tolstoi is resting easy. He's still way out front."

THE DEAL

He looked at me and he said, "Well, Jarn, I have to live too."
"Why?" I asked.
"Well, I work for my pay. I have to eat, you know."
"In your case, the laborer is worthy of his mire, because that's what you write."
He continued as though I hadn't said anything, "Well, I just do, that's all, and anyway what business is it of yours?"
"None," I answered, "none at all. I just think you take up too much room in the world. You're too big . . ."
"Hell, I'm not as big as you . . ."
"I know," I said, "but you . . . you are a lousy writer. You use every little emotion you feel in those lousy scripts, then your full but empty self just clutters around."
"You're crazy, Jarn."
"Uh-huh," I agreed.
"Completely crazy," he muttered, gave me an insincere grin and walked off to join the rest of the party.
I excused myself to myself and walked away.
I went over to talk with Jean Dupont Durand, the Baron's French *avocat*. He was talking to a couple of men, one of whom was the character actor we had hired for a three-week role. He was okay for it if we could stand him for the three weeks. We had taken this dubious risk; had added the dubious talent of Shamus Girkin to our picture. He was a narrow ugly man, with long arms and a large misshapen nose. George Arliss in a bikini, with a bikini brain to match. He was given to waving his arms in large gestures when he spoke. He ran to a conformist type of politics. He was a fool. I greeted him falsely—warmly. He spoke with an "actor-lawyer's" smooth voice: reasonable, logical, and lugubrious. He was not a Hamlet I had known and loved.

For the first time in several days I began to relax. Then all of us started to discuss politics in the usual expert manner of the inexpert. The discussion started to warm up into an argument, but nothing loud, nothing showy. Then, right on cue, in stepped the French co-producer and the former head of the Centre du Cinéma, looking more cadaverish than ever. He'd heard the last of our discussion. He was full of gas and ready to go. He was not loath to inform us, he disliked all Americans with an intensity. But his dislike and his opinions were like himself, unstable, and were based on emotionalism, exaggeration and insecurely based facts. He also was a fool. He spoke De Gaulle's name as though it were going to explode in his mouth. He then cursed all Americans. I almost popped him. But I caught myself in time.

159

THE DEAL

I was mad, but I tried to smile my way out of it and the very thinnest edge of skin on the front of my face moved. It must have been a smile, they were all half-smiling back at me now. Whew . . . it had been close, all on the edge of the blade. I felt my stomach muscles start to relax. A nerve was twanging in my cheeks like a piano wire. No one noticed it. The French producer led the ex-government official away. "Let's get on with our friendly argument," my writer friend said.

I grinned. "Well, just not let him get superior and ex-governmental."

"The hell with him," my friend said.

"He spends a lot of time there and I'd like him to stay there for good."

The writer grinned, "All in good time, my boy. All in good time."

My friend the writer, who was a self-exiled American, was a good writer, but not a great writer; but he was kind, enjoyed life, and was able to sit back and take a good close objective look at his co-workers. That was all right because he took the close hard look at himself too. This should have made him a great writer but it only made him a good writer.

After a few goodbyes, I went to my host, apologized for the little "discussion," was given a verbal rubdown that all was sweetness and light. I left. But the evening ended up in a fight anyway. As it turned out, it was my one fight in Paris that was good for me.

24

I went to the Halles to have a drink alone and maybe some onion soup. I ran into my ex-wife and an AC-DC actor who escorted her from time to time. She called me over to her table, I was reintroduced to the guy for the umpteenth time. *Enchanté* and *au plaisir* were bouncing off the walls— it always seemed to call for that sort of thing. I was invited to sit down. I sat down. I had that "adrenaline feeling" you get when you've just missed a fight. I expansively ordered champagne . . . It was a Baron-like gesture and I almost canceled it to order brandy. But my ex-wife got sentimental, the way they do, because I had ordered the mark and year of Dom Perignon that I always used to order for her.

I ordered it from long habit, but if she wanted to think I remembered and ordered it because of her it was jake with me. AC-DC made an unnecessarily rude remark in French argot he didn't think I understood. I did . . . My ex-wife knew I did, but I acted as if I hadn't heard. He shot me a quick look, saw nothing wrong, and relaxed back into the bitchy mood they get sometimes. Maybe it was his "period"—I didn't know or care—but he was walking on a cobweb and didn't know it. He affected a loose white shirt, lace-cuffed apparel. He was tall and wiry, an over-long nose, muddy eyes and wore a gold earring in his right ear. The bottle of champagne was gone, so from long habit of doing the wrong thing I ordered a magnum . . . I was benevolent . . . trying to make up for my outburst at the party, which was in no way connected with this bag of nails.

AC-DC babbled on, almost as if he didn't know what he was saying. With each little liberty he took—and got away with—he became more brave. Pretty well lit up by now, eyes flashing, he was getting his revenge "on the way he was," and on the American producer, the ex-husband of the French star seated next to him whom he couldn't make . . . because *en toute simplicité* he just couldn't . . . but now he had started to become a bore.

My ex said to him a couple of times, *"Fais attention . . . fais attention; il comprend tout."* AC-DC didn't believe I understood everything so he chirped right on. Finally his jibes got a little too ripe. I had been sitting there quietly talking English to my ex once in a while . . . this was what had spurred the fagola on. I leaned over and said to him, none too gently, in French, "Listen, *con*, you've been babbling on and I haven't flushed you down yet . . . Dont 'Oh' and 'Ah' and say 'How interest-

161

ing' for any half-thought-out piece of Freud or Plato you have misunderstood in some book you've read. You're trying to bring out the *man* in you, yet those pieces have only muddled you up more, if that's possible, which I doubt. Now maybe the world is full of discarded husbands, wives, and lovers, but they are all not interchangeable, as your cross-circuited mentality seems to indicate."

He bleated . . . "Oh, you . . . oh . . . you . . ." He hissed, he half stood up, reached over and slapped me, looking and spitting at me just like an angry woman . . .

I stood up slowly. My ex-wife said, "No, Jarn . . . no." I reached out and caught the actor by his lacey shirt, "You filth," I snarled. "I put up with your perfumed crap all evening . . . but you didn't know when to quit . . ." I shot a look at the terrified girl at the table. "Even she tried to stop you . . ." I shook him a little. He was pale, but had a nasty look in his eyes. He watched me, not fearful . . . but with girlish insolence . . . I reached up my hand, pulled hard, and jerked the gold earring out through his ear . . . the pierced lobe split like a grape, dripped blood. He turned green. He looked like he was going to faint. He bleated. I shook him roughly out from behind the table; I slapped the bloody earring in his hand and snarled, "This will look better in your nose. Now get out of here and check your eye shadow." I shoved him toward the door.

Spittle ran down his chin. He ran out through the tables, which were happily almost empty now. My ex-wife was looking at me with her mouth open . . . "Close your mouth, angel," I said quietly, "someone might think you are about to scream . . . but we know you're not." With that I reached out my hand and gently put it under her lovely chin. Her mouth went shut. She closed her lips . . . she looked at me strangely. I sat down, saying, "Not too thinly disguised within you, *madame*, is all that wonderful sex they talk about. I'm sorry I hurt your friend . . . I'll have to apologize sometime. But I was speaking of sex, and ours was the greatest. However, both the sex and I are ashamed and can try to withdraw . . . I can . . . sex can't. That's why it's all so sad or happy or *triste* leaving "a head" when there is truly nothing left at all. Like the fable that a snake with its head cut off dies at sunset . . . untrue . . . all untrue." I shook my head, sadly.

She sat there watching me; quietly. She looked lovely. She said, "You're drunk, Jarn." "Yes, dear . . . how about a date tomorrow night?" I asked.

She preened herself. "Can we talk about my part in the Baron's picture if I go out with you?" she asked coyly.

I looked at her with mock tenderness . . . "You mean you don't love me for myself?"

162

THE DEAL

She looked at me as though she were going to say, "I love you." She said, "You stink. You only think of your lousy picture and your damn Deal."

"The picture can't be lousy," I said. "It hasn't been finished yet."

"Your *deal* has been made, though, hasn't it, Mr. Big-Shot Producer?" she spumed.

"Not completed yet but it looks promising," I answered. I frowned at her right knee. It was a nice knee—it was nice to look at.

She stopped me with, "So listen, Mr. Big-Shot Producer, I'm not one to suggest that your good looks and Continental charm won't make someone turn themselves inside out for you, but don't take those men for granted. I know more than you think I know. And even though I hate you, I don't want you to get killed. They *are* tough, like other people *think* they are tough."

I smiled at her. "You mustn't be scared of the Syndicate men, angel. You mustn't let them sandy you. I know that all the "snow" doesn't go up the Baron's sneezer. I know he's been talking to you, but don't go for the gold ring, darling. It just isn't there. They're doing their job, I'm doing mine. We will be all right."

"You be careful, Jarn," she breathed. "You think you're so damn smart and clever; I'm afraid one day you'll go too far."

I grinned at her. "One day maybe, but not tonight. Now do I get that date? I'd like that."

She looked at me with those beautiful eyes. She gathered her things and started for the door. She turned back. "Yes. Shall I dress, or what?"

I smiled at her and said, "Just be ready at eight, darling. Dressed or undressed, you would still be the most beautiful. Now run along, I've got a guy to see." She opened her mouth to say something else. I said, nicely but firmly, "Run along, darling." She left.

Life with her, and love with her, had been like a runaway train roaring down strange tracks. You wondered how fast . . . how long . . . before love jumped it. And it did. It left so quickly, you only missed it after it was gone.

I left the restaurant after paying for all the champagne. I couldn't pay for the other, I'd pay for that later . . . and I did.

* * *

I walked down the dark streets toward my parked car. There was still a light on in a little bar so, again with my good judgment, I went in. The bar was filled with a lot of butchers with bloody aprons . . . all full of suet—I

163

mean the butchers, not the aprons. I motioned to the barman, who acknowledged my order. He was a beauty; he had a pocked-marked face and wore a cap with a sweatband—which had not been misnamed in this case. He had on what at one time must have been a white shirt. He drank a lot of red wine. If you couldn't tell by his nose, you could tell by the huge purple patches of sweat underneath his arms . . . I figured it was that or he wore a burgundy undershirt. I quaffed freely of the bad brandy he served me. After I had given him more francs than were good for him . . . he became my *serviteur* friend . . .

As the brandy went down in my own personal bottle, everyone was becoming more friendly. A guy with a cast in one eye wanted to get me his girl friend . . . first it was for two hundred francs, then, later, because I was his friend, it was for free. The bottle was finished. I ordered another. My bar-owner friend said this bottle was on him . . . He said this with a tear in the eye. I didn't know if it was from the brandy, or the happiness of the occasion. My cast-eyed friend said he would consider it an insult if I didn't accept the favors of his girl friend . . . and what was more, offered to drive me there. I declined. Then cast-eye offered to bring her to the bar. Again I declined. Now cast-eye was angry. I had insulted not only his girl friend, but, cast-eye said, I had insulted him. He sadly threw a punch at me. Only to make him feel better, because I truly did not wish to hurt him, I let the punch drift by, and sank my fist gently but with a certain firmness about ten inches into his belly. Cast-eye looked at me in pained surprise and vomited a brandy-and-onion soup mist which happily I was able to avoid.

The joyousness that had reigned supreme became a *bagarre*. It was sad, because I was just starting to like it there. By a lucky stroke of fortune I chose the right exit. I found myself in an alley almost dark; smelling like anything but Helene Rochas. I had only taken about three steps when I saw a figure move in from behind a barrel. I figured it was the ped, back with a bandaged ear, another earring, and reenforcements. I was trying to make up my mind, and another few feet up the alley, when a shadow in a doorway interrupted my brain work. The shadow moved and a voice went "Psssssst." I didn't jump more than ten feet. I heard a voice from far away mumble, "Jarnigan."

I swung at the shadow. I swung at the voice. I was not being overly cautious, I figured it would take more than the lightfoots to get me. I wished my brother were here. I wished I hadn't drunk so much. I wished I was in the land of cotton. Then I wished I hadn't connected with the blow as well as I did. My fist felt as if it had hit an adobe wall. I heard a grunt; I heard the start of my name "Jar—." I went to work . . . and, man, it was cut out for me. The guy I was fighting was like a dancer, only he hit like Joe Louis . . . he kept yelling my name. I figured he was calling for the rest of the ped's gang, so I bored on in. I didn't like the work. The pay was too low, and this bastard was all over me. With luck, and that's what it was, I caught this guy with a right that I can still feel whenever I clench my fist. He sailed out into the light. Blessed Christ . . . it was *Sam Neely*!

I rushed over to him. "You big bastard, what the hell were you doing?"

"Judas priest, Jarn, what the hell is wrong with you? Man, I called your name . . .

"Hell, Sam, I thought it was some other guy calling for the dogs. Are you okay?" He stepped out farther into the light. I said, "Sam, you son-of-a-gun, it's great to see you, but what the hell are you doing, trying to cold-cock a guy in the alley?"

"Judas, Jarn," Sam said, breathing heavily. "I heard you was in that restaurant with the ex-wife. I figured I'd wait and see you when you came out. Then just after she left, I heard two guys talking about how they was going to nail you when you came out. They drifted down to this little alley. I drifted right along behind them, but not too close, and we were all being so careful of you, we plumb missed you until you came out into the alley, which, in my view, was too frigging quiet."

By now we had walked into the street and I got a good look at Sam. "Christ, it's good to see you," I said, and I meant it. This guy was like my brother, only he had drifted some . . . and he never would let me help him. "Sam," I continued eagerly, "let's go back to my place and talk. I want to know where you been, why I haven't heard from you. Hell, boy . . . I want to know everything."

He grinned at me, the old Sam-grin, the old brother-grin, full of affection. He looked at my clothes; I was pretty mussed up and bloody, clothes and shirt torn. His grin widened. "Jarn," he said quietly in that soft voice he had, "you wouldn't be a bad kid if you dressed a little neater." We both laughed. I had never been in such a fight.

"C'est mon ami parce que je l'aime: et je l'aime parce que c'est mon ami."

25

We were sitting in my apartment after the fight. I had just said, "Sam, you're still the best fighter."

"Don't kid me."

"No, I'm not. I think you fight very well, like always."

"Listen, don't kid me, you were lucky."

"Right," I said grinning, "I was lucky. Anyway, I'm hog-fat and out of shape. Sam, you stepped into one, that's all."

"Really?" he said, wanting to believe me, wanting to reestablish his absolute confidence in himself that for just a moment was slipping badly.

"Of course," I reassured him. "Any other time you'd have killed me."

"Well," he said, looking away, "I did kind of take it easy on you at first, but . . ."

"That's it, that's exactly it. I thought it was funny, me nailing you and all. Now I know why—you were taking it easy."

A smile came from between his split and broken lips, the one good eye staring bravely at me with a twinkle—the half-closed one bravely glimmering, but watering too much to be effective. "Hell," he said, "if I'd work with you a little, nobody could ever lay a paw on you."

"Great, just great. Sam, could you work with me on that from time to time? You could get me in shape. I know we could work out a deal that would be good for both of us. We always used to."

A look of quiet disbelief came over his face. "You mean," he said quietly, "you want me to go back to work for you—like a trainer maybe?" His gaze fastened itself on my face as if I were deciding the fate of the world; and I was—*his* world.

"Well," I said, "I don't want you to come to work for me." The face fell—the eyes dimmed out, an old man peeped out shyly from behind the good eye. "What I meant was," I continued, "that you'd come to work *with* me, not *for* me. Because the way I figure it you're going to be doing more good for me than I can do for you. So will you do it? Will you start to work with me?"

"When?" the question shot out. He looked past my right shoulder. "I mean—well, I'll have to think it over and besides . . ." He was talking fast to keep from breaking.

I turned away and picked up my case. I took out a cigar, a panatella, bit the end off and lit up. I handed him one, still not looking directly at him. I could see him giving me little up-from-under looks from the good eye, his head turned so he could see past the swollen one. He took the cigar and gingerly put it in his mouth. I flicked my lighter at him and we made a big thing out of lighting his cigar. Making more out of it than it was. I could see he was getting himself back under control. "Listen," I said. "I sent out the word for you before I left the States. Man, I tried everywhere and I'd sure appreciate it if you could start right away. You see, I've got this tough picture going on, and—say," I said quickly, "you could even work out with the Baron."

His face fell again. Really clouded up. "Jarn, that's no good," he said, "I'll go to work with you or for you or any damn thing you want because you're the only one that's been square with me all my life. But since I got stuck here in France trying to start that chauffeured limousine rental business . . ." his voice trailed off . . . "I've always been a little short." I thought he was stating that mildly, but I said nothing. He took confidence from my not saying anything. Continued with: "Like I said, I'll do anything for you but I don't want to train or to box with the Baron." He looked away and then back to me, his eyes looking about two inches over my head.

"Why not, Sam? Why won't you work out with the Baron?"

He shifted his gaze down the two inches, looked me square in the eyes and said softly, "Because I'd kill the dirty son-of-a-bitch, that's why."

Well, that's the way it was the night before the first big blowup came, and that's how Sam Neeley came back to work *with*—not *for* me—and he still does. It was always my brother, Sam Neeley, and me.

So again Sam was safe and "at home." He knew I'd always look out for him, as I'd done most of his life. He always thought I could do anything. He trusted me implicitly. By nature he was a joyous man. He was a guy who would go festive with one drink, then dance happily to his own singing. He was my friend. It was grand that we could work together again.

26

I don't talk about Sam Neely much, because Sam Neely was a part of my growing up, a part of my childhood and a part of everything I knew since I grew up. Sam Neely's dad had been a boxer and we were all very proud of him. We were proud because he represented us. He was our champion. A Dempsey or a Carpentier or a Louis or a Sugar Ray, for us, could never have laid a glove on him. I mention these fellows because they're all fine men, all fine gentlemen. I like every one of them and I'm proud to be a friend of theirs.

Sam Neely's daddy had married a Jamaican girl—and she was lovely. At least she was lovely from the way I looked at her when I was a boy. I was alone that summer, when I was nine. The first of several big hurts came and Jessie Neely was the one I ran to; I hugged her and I buried my face in those ponderous breasts. She hugged me and said, "Little Jarnie, little Jarnie, nothing is this bad, boy, nothing is this bad. You just be quiet. Don't let Sam see you like this. And y'know what, Jarn?" I looked up at her, furtively wiping away a tear. She acted as though she never saw it.

Then she said, "Listen," her voice conspiratorial. We were together . . . two thieves away from childhood. "Let's don't let Sam see you like this. Sam looks up to you, Jarn, so you have to be right—even if you're littler than he is and younger. Because my Sam always says to me, 'If Jarn says it, that's the way I'm going to do it, Mom.' And I just smile to him because Jarnie, you're a good boy and I love you like I love Sam. So, there are lots of things you have to be careful about. You can't bruise them and you can't tangle them up. They are very important things. So now will you listen to your Aunt Jessie?"

"Yes, ma'am," I said, "I sure will."

"Well, now, isn't that nice," she said. "You know, Jarnie, you're a polite little boy and you're a pretty little boy. Now you remember what your Aunt Jessie tells you. You be polite and you stay pretty and there's no place that you can't go. No, sir, no place."

"Could I go with you and Uncle Brian to the Carnival?" I said, craftily, in my nine-year-old wisdom.

"Bless you, sure you can," Aunt Jessie said.

"Listen, Aunt Jessie," I said, "when people die and you cover 'em up, does that cut 'em off from everything? Does that mean that they gotta dig themselves out to get up?"

Aunt Jessie just looked at me with the prettiest face that you could see and said, "But, Jarnie boy, it's not that you have to dig up and up, because you're already up. You're already there. And do you know what I think, Jarnie?"

"What?"

Here she leaned that beautiful face over and said, "Can you keep a secret? If I told you something, could you keep the secret and not tell anyone?"

"Oh," I said, and shivered in excitement, "No, ma'am. I wouldn't tell anybody, if you told me not to tell anybody."

"Well, then, Jarnie, you listen." Here she looked out and away from where we were. She adjusted me carefully on her lap by moving her two tremendous thighs. And there I was, in the lap of love. I knew instinctively, with my nine years of living, that this kind, this wonderful lady was going to tell me a good thing.

"Jarnie," she said. Her voice was low, soft, and lovely. "You have to listen, boy. You have to listen for truth because truth is beautiful and you'll hear it. And you know what you must listen for, son?"

"What? What?" I said.

"I listen for a someone who talks to me," she said. "I listen to a someone who tells me things." Here her eyes looked out and I knew whatever it was she was seeing, it was the truth. She said, "Jarnie, I listen to this someone, and this someone says to me, 'Jessie, now here's what you have to do with your husband. You tell him this, and this is the way to go, Jessie. No, Jessie, don't do this'—and, Jarnie, do you know what I call this voice?"

"No . . . no. What?" I whispered, shivering. I was excited.

She leaned down and she said, "I just call him—*Someone*, because every time he speaks and every time I listen, the truth is there—and you know what, Jarnie?"

"What?" I asked, shivering again.

"The truth happens, boy—that's what happens—the *truth*. So every time I hear *Someone* say something, way off in the back corridor of my mind, I listen. Now, I'll give you this present. I *will* this to you. Here." At this point she raised up her arm and took my hand in hers and we had a pact. Gripping my hand slowly, she said, "Jarnie, would you listen to *Someone* if—*if* I told you the secret?"

"Oh, yes, yes, I would. I would," I said. "I swear, Aunt Jessie, I would."

THE DEAL

"Well, you just listen and if *Someone* says something to you, you *do* it. And if *Someone's* arguing with you, you know you've gotta do it because of *Someone*, and that *Someone* is the important one—you understand?" Here she nodded her head.

I nodded mine too, because I was trying to understand.

"Jarnie, Jarnie boy, little pretty boy that I love," she crooned. And she hugged and kissed me. "Would you promise something to your Aunt Jessie?"

"Yes, ma'am. Yes, ma'am, and I'd like to hear a little more about this *Someone* fellow."

"Well, you do me the one thing. Will you do it now, boy?"

"Yes, ma'am. I'll do it," I said quickly.

"Well, in your life—and you've the furthest way to go from all of us, you've a long ways to go, Jarnie—when *Someone* talks to you, and when *Someone* says something to you, will you *listen*? And will you listen good, and will you not do anything against what *Someone* says?"

"Well," I said practically, being practical at nine years old. "What if he tells me to do something I shouldn't do, Aunt Jessie?"

"He won't, honey. He won't. You just promise me, since I told you the secret—will you do what he asks?"

"Yes, ma'am."

"All right, I'll tell you, when *Someone* talks to you and when *Someone* says something for you to do, you can argue with him; you can say to him, 'Listen, why do I have to do this?' Or, 'I don't want to do that.' And *Someone* will say to you, 'Listen here, you do this, boy,' or, 'You do that, boy.' And you know something? Every time he says that to you, he's right. And I *know* he's right, and you know your Aunt Jessie wouldn't tell you anything to do that wasn't right. Is that right?"

"Yes, ma'am. I know that. Well, now, Aunt Jessie, when am I going to talk to this Mr. Someone?"

"Well, honey, he's not a mister, he's just a kind of a mind-voice that you hear in your head." Here she looked out and away; it wasn't a frown, but it was a faraway-inside look. "Listen, honey, you just figure it's Aunt Jessie talking to you with love, or you figure it's your Uncle Brian talking to you with love. You just figure the love-and-the-Aunt-Jessie, and the love-and-the-Uncle-Brian, and the love-and-that-*Someone*—all lumped together in a big dumpling—are saying to you, 'Jarn boy, *this* is what you have to do.' Now, will you promise?"

By this time I was so carried away and I loved her so much . . . "I promise, Aunt Jessie, I promise. I'll sure listen to this *Someone* fellow."

171

Then she hugged me, and I guess that's about as close to Heaven as a nine-year-old wanted to get.

• • •

Everyone had arrived in Paris that I truly needed to be able to start the picture. I was grateful to have arranged for all of the suites, the elegant offices in the studio. I had arranged to have the Baron's name inscribed in bronze, and this plaque was fastened to the office door next to mine.

Sam Neely had notified me that the Baron was on the way to the studio. I hadn't expected that he would arrive this early. I knew that I had arranged everything for his comfort and convenience on the estate I had rented for his use during the production of the picture, a lovely estate in Saint-Cloud, only fifteen minutes from the studio.

I had been doing some work and wasn't sure when the Baron would arrive. I had been sitting in the office waiting for the final work schedule and budget breakdown on the film—not a "top sheet," but the complete budget. It was a beautiful day outside. Everyone believes that Paris is so lovely in the spring—and it is, but to me it's more beautiful in the autumn.

I was in the process of discussing a tax problem with Jules Molotov when in walked the Baron. He was something to see. He had on a tweed suit, suede walking boots, and a huge brown suede overcoat thrown over his shoulders; the hat was pushed back on his head in the best John Barrymore tradition. He looked handsome, charming; he was enthusiastic, he was full of beans. He made his entrance smiling—all charm, all confidence—he must have slept well. He said to everyone and no one in particular, "Well, to business. Let's get down to business; or better, let's talk about poontang." He turned and looked at me, "Now don't frown, Jarn. It's too early in the day to frown." He took off the hat, sailed it in the general direction of a chair in the corner, threw off the coat, walked over in front of the big fireplace, turned around, faced the room, struck a pose and said, "As I said, men, let's talk about poontang."

This was opening up the act. "Not now . . . now is not the time," I said.

"Always time for the poon, Jarn. Always time for the poon." He grinned at me. "You know, I can be looking at a beautiful painting, I can be drinking a lovely wine, I can even be hungry and, blooey . . . it hits me—the poon." He hummed a moment and started to sing:

172

THE DEAL

Poon, poon, beautiful poon.
Poon, poon, glorious poon.
Poon's all I live for,
It's captured my soul,
I love poon . . . poon . . . poon.

(This sung to the melody of that wonderful old hymn "Peace, Peace, Glorious Peace.") The last two lines of this poontanged hymn were sung in barber-shop harmony. The Baron was lustily joined by the Editor, Saul Baum, and Jules Molotov, and they all finished, singing much too loudly, "We love poon . . . poon . . . poon." I had to laugh. Old Baron was really grand when he was right. I knew we'd get a good day's work. So I grinned at him. He winked at me. "How's the boy?"

"Fine, Baron, just fine."

"Great, kid," then continued his theme song . . . "Poon, poon, beautiful poon" . . . and the day's work started.

27

After a good day's shooting, and the milk of human kindness flowing, not curdling, the Baron asked me to his place for dinner. He said only the Princess, he, and I would be there. The Princess tipped the scale; I said I'd be pleased to come, and I was. So, that night in the Baron's apartment we'd had a late dinner and had discussed the week's work. I had explained to the Baron about the trip to the south of France that should be made prior to the whole company's leaving Paris and going down to Nice. It had been a nice dinner, very relaxed. The Baron wasn't drinking too much and the Princess was looking lovely, even more desirable than usual.

I looked at them both talking quietly over coffee. It was a relaxed mood. As I sat there seeing those two beautiful people, knowing both of them well, I was surprised to realize how quiet the whole evening had been. It was such a change from the hundreds of other evenings that had been noisy, useless, colored baubles. The Baron was talking earnestly to the Princess, who was listening with a little half-smile on her face. It was an amused smile, an indifferent smile, but tolerant, as though she were listening to an eager small boy. I had to admit Baron was certainly charming that night. He was grinning boyishly at her. He had pulled out all the stops. It had been a good party.

I think this was the first time in the many years I had known the Baron that I envied him anything. In the long time that we had been together, knowing his faults, knowing him as a man as well as I knew myself, I could truthfully say I had never envied him his fame, his wealth, certainly not his "affairs," not the adulation he received, and not the life that he had led, that he was living now; but I envied him this girl. I coveted her. I was concerned about this. I couldn't let anything interfere with the Deal.

In the many years that the Baron and I had been in Hollywood and Europe making pictures there had been girls, many girls, lovely girls, exciting girls, certainly too many girls—no comfort, no warmth there—but I had noticed to my surprise little danger signals here and there about this girl during the past few months.

I would catch myself watching her when we were on the yacht together at one of the Baron's parties. I would notice the way she water-skied and watch her dance and move like no one I had ever seen, her lovely lithe body flat-bellied, high-breasted. She moved with sinuous flowing movements; never out of time. She did everything gracefully. I remember when she'd leave my office after coming up on some business or other, inquiring about something for the Baron; after she'd left, I would, for no reason, walk over to the window and watch her walk away toward the Rue Pierre Charron. It was grand to watch her move. The sun shone on the dark auburn-colored hair with little glints of chestnut and gold. Then I'd look away and walk back over to my desk, knowing I was getting too much out of just seeing a beautiful young girl walk down the street. I can truthfully say the "Princess" part never got to me. I remember an actor friend of mine, a big star, had once slept with one of the ugliest women I'd ever seen because she was a countess, and I said to him, "Man . . . how could you do it? She should sing the song 'I'd rather be dead than naked.' " She was such an ugly woman, it seemed indecent that she had breasts. Worse, she wore a kind of uplift brassière to accentuate her mammaries; like calling attention to two boils on an ugly face, two carbuncles on a cold-ridden and muchly blown nose.

"Hell, Jarn," he answered seriously, "I've boffed 'em all but I never laid a countess before. Me and a countess, get it . . .?"

I got it.

But I was remembering when we were in Deauville. The Baron and I had entered the live pigeon shooting meet. It was for the championship of France. I've loved to hunt and loved to shoot all my life. The Baron was an excellent shot but better with a rifle than with a shotgun. I could scarcely conceal my pleasure when on the seventeenth bird, the Baron missed and was eliminated. On the twenty-first the two Italians and one Spanish shooter went out, leaving only the Comte de Lion and me. The Count had won the National Pigeon Shoot in France, in Spain, and in Italy. He toured the circuit like a golf pro, was immensely wealthy and really a fine fellow. When it came to the twenty-sixth bird he shot and missed. By now everyone at the Sporting Club had gathered on the terrace to watch the finals. My name was called and all of the people gathered around the clubhouse walked toward the shoot, as close as they were allowed. I could see the Baron and the Princess standing close by, the Baron smiling good-naturedly with a thumbs-up gesture, the Princess giving me a steady thoughtful look. I walked up to the mark which was the handicap. I said, *"Prêt?"*

"Tire!"

THE DEAL

The trap on the right opened and the Spanish pigeon—*zurita*—shot out of the box quail-high.

You have one-sixteenth of a second to make your kill or else the bird is beyond the barrier. It was one of those days when everything went right. I snapped a shot at him, saw the feathers fly, and hit him with the other barrel before he touched the ground—and I had won the National.

It was a big deal. The American flag was raised over the Sporting Club. The corny cocktail band played "The Star-Spangled Banner." I was being congratulated on all sides, the Baron taking it very big—he was as proud of me as if he'd won it. I have to say for all that kind of thing there was never a better sportsman than the Baron. I didn't know until then that the Princess had been designated to present the cup. While I was being congratulated by the other shooters and the various and sundry celebrities who were down, not so much for the pigeon shoot as for the gambling and the regular Deauville season, I shook hands with the *président* of the Tir aux Pigeons de France. He gave me a certificate, a plaque and a check for eight hundred thousand francs (at that time about twenty-five hundred dollars).

As I was led into the clubhouse for the presentation a little later, there stood the Baron and the other celebrities. Pictures were taken and the Princess came up. A steward handed her a large—in my view, overly large —trophy; a cup with a guy standing at the ready, with a shotgun in such an awkward position he couldn't have hit a bull in the behind with buckshot. But it was properly engraved—from the time of the finish of the contest until now they had had my name engraved in the proper place.

I stood there watching the Princess as she walked toward me carrying the trophy. She said in her lovely low voice, quietly, "Jarn, I'm so glad. I was praying for you to win." Then she turned and said aloud, "On behalf of the *président* of the Tir aux Pigeons de France I present you with this trophy for the *Championnat de France.*" Here she handed me the trophy and very tenderly reached up and kissed me on both cheeks. I could smell the perfume of her, and then there was that feeling. It was as if no one else was there. It was almost all that I could do to keep myself from grabbing her. I looked at her. She got the look and, while she didn't return it, she seemed to be puzzled by it. All of that was shut off when the crowd started calling, "Speech, speech."

I said: "*Monsieur le président, mesdames et messieurs,* I am most grateful and very moved to have won this trophy. I was fortunate today, since I know at least six of the shooters present shoot better than I—but it is a grand sport. I guess today was just my day. We all can get even at the shoot in Barcelona next month."

177

THE DEAL

"Hear . . . hear . . . bravo . . . bravissimo . . ." were the mixed shouts of camaraderie, all by now a little drunk. I turned back to look at the Princess but she had stepped away and was talking to the Baron. I handed the trophy and my gun to Sam Neely. He whispered, "Great, just great. Man, did you ever slaughter them!"

I laughed at Sam. "Don't worry about the trophy, but watch the gun."

"I know, boy, I know." He laughed again and went off through the crowd, happier than if he'd won that himself. A slap on the back that rattled my teeth turned me around. There was the Baron, full of brotherly love, full of good cheer, and plenty of whatever he had been drinking.

"Jarn, dear boy, you did it! You did it! You shooting son-of-a-bitch, you did it! I knew when de Lion went out you'd nail it." He was talking too loud.

I said quietly, "Thanks, Baron. Thank you."

"Let's have a drink, Jarn boy."

"Hey, hold it, we've got a whole evening to celebrate."

"Hell, we're celebrating now. My partner is the champion pigeon shooter of France." He looked at me, deadly serious. "By the way, partner, half of that twenty-five hundred dollars is mine, right?" It was so much the Baron: In spite of the booze, the championship, the camaraderie, the whole ambiance of this sporting event, the Baron came through . . . he wanted his fifty percent of the money. I laughed loudly, partly from the exhilaration of winning, partly because I saw the Princess standing there and smiling, mostly because the Deal had been going beautifully lately, and I said, "Baron, you're dead right. Fifty-fifty. We split *everything*, partner."

"Partner," he roared at the top of his voice, "we share everything." He stuck out his hand, grabbed mine and I thought he'd break it off. I looked at the Princess, who was looking at me with a thoughtful gaze. This time *I* got a message—and there was no puzzlement in *my* eyes. I returned that look, and for the first time in I don't know how long, it seemed there was something almost as important as the Deal. I had forgotten about it for a few seconds.

I was aroused from these thoughts to hear "Jarn . . . Jarn . . . are you asleep?" She had leaned over and was gently pulling on my arm. I realized I had been absolutely in a reverie. I turned and looked at the Baron. He was absorbed in smoking his cigar, finishing his brandy.

I said, "Excuse me, I must have dozed off."

"Do you always doze with your eyes open?"

I smiled. "Sometimes, sometimes."

THE DEAL

The Baron stood up. He walked over, looked out the window. Far below you could see the Seine. The *bateau mouche* was making probably its last tour for the night. It was now after one o'clock. No work tomorrow, being Sunday. The Baron said to no one, "Well, it's been a nice night, nice dinner; let's go to bed."

I stood up, walked over to the fire, threw my cigar in the ashes, and said, "I'd better be leaving."

"Have one for the road, Jarn," the Baron said.

I laughed. "The road is only a hundred meters down the street and I'm going to walk. I can make it on what I've already had."

The Baron smiled. "Well, good night then, kid. I'm going to bed. I'm pooped." With that he gave me a wave of his hand, walked over and kissed the Princess on the cheek, and said, "You're coming, darling?"

"In a minute. I'd like to finish my brandy," she said quietly.

"Anything you say," he said, walking away. "Night, Jarn." And he went out of the living room down the hall in the direction of his bedroom.

There was a large couch in front of the fireplace. The Princess got up and walked over to the couch carrying her brandy with her. She sat down with that graceful movement, leaned back and stretched out those long and beautifully slender legs toward the fire. She had on one of those short cocktail dresses that she looked so well in—and she knew it. She crossed her legs—a little casually, I thought—and the dress came up a little higher than usual. She didn't seem to notice it. I noticed. I stood there in front of the fire looking down at her. She was gazing steadily into the fire. She said quietly, "Join me in a nightcap, Jarn. I'm not sleepy." I looked at her steadily for a moment. Her gaze shifted upward. She looked me in the eyes and said, "Get your drink and come sit beside me."

"All right," I said, more calmly than I felt. I walked back over to the table, poured myself a small brandy and came back and stood in front of the fireplace. She merely looked at me quietly for a moment, then looked back into the fire, put her hand upon the couch and carefully arranged her dress close to that beautiful thigh. She patted the couch.

I walked over to her and sat down, but not too close. We sat there quietly for a while, just looking into the fire. The music from the stereo was coming in softly. It was a dangerous time. Slowly, she changed her brandy glass to her other hand and put her hand on mine, still looking into the fire. I glanced sideways at her and held my breath.

"Do you like watching the fire?" she breathed.

"Uh-huh."

"I do." She continued softly, "I love watching the fire and I love watch-

179

ing the sea. Those are my two favorite things since I was a little girl." She shifted her position and gently leaned back lower on the couch. She gave a little contented sigh. "This is nice."

"Uh-huh."

"What do you do when you get talkative, Jarn? Wiggle your ears? Haven't you ever sat in front of a fire with a girl before?"

"Yeah, but—I've never sat in front of a fire with you before."

I could feel that she turned her head and was looking at me. I kept staring straight into the fire. "You know, Jarn," she continued, as if I hadn't spoken, "we ve never gotten to know each other very well. We've never truly become friends and I want to be friends."

"Fine," I said.

Then after a moment she continued, "Don't you want to be friends?"

"Sure. Fine," I said again.

"You don't sound like it's fine."

"Well . . ."

"Is it that you don't like me?" I didn't answer. "Is it that you've got a mistress hidden?" she said gaily. She laughed a gay little laugh. "I can be very jealous, you know."

"Listen, Nicole . . ."

She turned abruptly and said quietly, "Jarn, it's the first time you've ever called me by my name. It was always 'hi' or 'hello' or 'your highness' when you were sarcastic and mean, like you are most of the time," she continued, as though she'd won a point. "I know the Baron calls you the Iceman. *Are* you an ice man, Jarn?"

I looked at her, took a big drink of my brandy and said, "Well, I don't feel like an ice man right now." I laughed, wanting to brush it off.

She whispered, "Jarn, you . . ."

"Yeah, the Iceman. I'm the fixer, the trouble-shooter, I'm the business-man, I'm the perfect partner—loyal, trustworthy, courteous and kind, and there is some other part to that speech but I forget it." I turned my head and looked down at her. Her eyes had a violet look, her lips were slightly parted. I could see the long line of her throat that went on down and down, and suddenly, as though she had nothing on, I could see that body. As though she could read my mind, she changed her position and stretched. I turned back to the fire and said carefully, "I'm going to have another drink—want one?"

She didn't answer. I got up, walked back over to the table, poured myself a stiff one, drank half of it there, and walked back and stood in front of the fireplace and looked down at this girl whom I wanted more than

180

anything. I think for the first time since I was a boy, all thought of business and money, of making it big, had completely gone out of my head. I knew that it was corny and nobody knew better than I how dangerous it was. I was beginning to feel the effects of the brandy.

She said quietly, "Sit down beside me, Jarn."

"Now, Nic, you listen," I said harshly, "Listen," I repeated. Her eyes widened; that mouth, the lower lip that would be warm velvet, that I could describe anywhere, any time, was there. I could feel her as though I were touching every part of her, and yet we were several feet apart. I was warmed by her. The fire was nothing beside that warmth. She looked at me. She knew it . . . and I knew it.

She half straightened up and leaned forward.

She whispered softly, "Would you kiss me, Jarn?" I rubbed my hand over my face and squeezed it so hard my hand felt numb. I took my hand away from my face and looked down at it. The fingers were trembling. She hadn't moved. I took the three steps toward her slowly and leaned down; her face, that face, came up toward me. I could hear her breathing—her breath was as fresh as the wings of a wish—she half closed her eyes, her mouth opened gently. I leaned closer . . . she closed her eyes and her breathing came faster . . .

"Hey, honey, are you coming to bed?" The Baron had called loudly from the other room. Neither one of us moved; it was a stop-frame. Then, slowly, I straightened up and took two steps backward toward the fireplace. She still hadn't moved but her eyes opened slightly. The Baron said, "Hey . . . out there, aren't you coming in?"

She sat up a little straighter and leaned back in a sitting position on the couch. She called back in a voice that to me was surprisingly calm yet firm—I don't think I would have been able to say a word—"Not now, Baron, I'm not sleepy. I'll be along in a while." All this said looking me directly in the eyes. I looked down toward her. Everything was quiet.

"Well, that's it . . . that's it," I said, hoarsely. "Listen, Nic, you must forgive me. I . . . it was the . . ."

"Don't say it was the brandy, Jarn," she said quietly. "Don't say it."

"Listen," I said. "Things are like they are and you better go on in."

"Not just yet," she whispered.

"Look, Nic," I said, more calmly than I felt, but more in control. "I have to leave and you'd better go on in." Then I turned around, suddenly angry, angry at myself, angry at her. I could have cheerfully killed the Baron. Frig it all, I thought, frig all this lousy Deal, this life, this confusion, this . . . Aloud I said, "No, the brandy *did* get to me."

"Jarn," she whispered.

"Listen," I said, "now let's get things back in focus. He's calling you and you'd better go in. You better go in and thread the needle," I added cruelly.

She said, "Jarn, please."

I growled, "Go on in, Nic, there's nothing out here but trouble for both of us."

She stood up slowly, walked the three steps over to me at the fireplace, turned, and looked directly up into my face. She said quietly, "You feel like I feel. I know you do." And there went that feeling again.

I said, "Listen, that won't get it. I don't know how you feel. I don't know if you know how you feel. No, 'like' won't get it; sure I like you; but maybe there are things that . . . that I . . . that I like better . . ."

"What things?" she whispered.

"Well—things," I said, "just things . . . the Deal and . . ." I was trembling. I looked down into that beautiful face, then I pulled back and said, "Will you for Chrissake just *go in*." I took a step away from her.

She gazed at me thoughtfully for a minute, then the little half-smile that I loved came on those lips that I had almost kissed. "I love you too, Jarn," she said. She turned and left quietly.

I watched her as she walked away—down to the bedroom of the Baron. I whispered—to her and to myself, Every guy that's ever seen you before loves you. The trick is to find you. She disappeared down the hall. I turned back to the fire, thought about getting another drink, then thought I'd already had too much and set the brandy glass on a side table, put both hands on the mantelpiece and leaned down, looking into the now half-dead embers of the fire. Myself said to myself, I've made a lot of pictures; I've read a lot of books, too many books; I've seen on film about every love scene there is; I have read scripts where the love scenes would make you cry, erotic, or just nervous; and now I am nervous. I didn't know if I loved the Princess, but whatever it was it sure had hold of me.

I went home. I went to bed. I did not sleep.

28

Yes, there are various kinds of love. Like gold, it is extremely rare in its pure state. It is often mixed with the baser elements, like lust or greed; again, it can have a more sophisticated alloy.

For example, you might have lust and gratitude mixed. I've heard it said, a stiff dong has no conscience. Maybe that's true, but sometimes the man leaves conscience to the woman; and so, who can judge? Plenty can . . .

Anyway, I remember an aging star who was grateful to me for a few minutes of that kind of situation . . . My difficulty was those few minutes. It was the casting couch in reverse . . . but we needed her in the picture.

Starting an affair with this woman, this overly ripe sex symbol, was sort of like cross-collateralizing between virtue and vice; as if a woman is allowed to be vicious provided she not be a pain in the ass. It's at this point that gallantry ends, and infamy begins; and one way or another, you're lost. You've done what, in your view, had to be done at the time.

So this was needful to be done, to further the Deal. The shame of it is more or less hard to overcome. But if the sex part is in your favor, it gives you, afterward, not too much trouble. You've only got yourself to deal with . . .

You can live your whole life waiting for a disaster, but when it comes be so unprepared that it stares at you openly, like a newly dug grave that is waiting but not yet open for you.

The thighs that you don't know yet, the unexplored and untamed, inviting ones, may not be the exact ones. All swell, huh? All fun—so fool the world and yourself with colored baubles! Sort out the beads, and string them. You are a charmer—you know all the words. Yet—ha! ha!—you have nothing to say.

> Meander, meander . . .
> Where shall I pander?
> Up the hill
> Or down in hell . . .
> Or in some baby's chamber?

The Baron had insisted that this lady play his young aunt in the picture. She was truly a fine actress, as well as a former sex symbol. She did not go for the Baron-type picture. She would need persuasion. I was the persuader. She had invited me to dinner in her lovely home.

Driving through Bel Air, the car went soundlessly up and down gently curving lanes. High walls covered with ivy hid the mansions that grew luxuriously everywhere. The carriage lamps before many of the estate entrances glowed softly and pallidly through the mist; even they looked expensive.

When I arrived in front of this mansion, I looked over the floodlit grounds. It was a big colonial house with more tall white columns than Mount Vernon. A long flowing lawn ran around everywhere. Magnolias and hydrangeas were arranged to make it what it was—lovely. The Chinese houseboy opened the door, bowed, and took my hat in one smooth motion, and was through for the night. Without a word we started off down a corridor that was over-long and over-high. We reached another door with a knob as big as a cannonball, which opened and I was bowed in.

It was a large oval-shaped room with a large oval-shaped rug on the floor. The furniture was in dark yellow leather, the walls a lighter yellow. There were four highbacked wing chairs around a large teakwood table. A fire was burning in a fireplace big enough to park a car in.

There she was, seated in all her glory and deserved splendor. She looked every inch the superstar. She was sitting in a lovely diffused pink light. She had a long nose and her eyebrows grew in a straight line across her forehead. She blew her nose from the inside—a crying, sobbing sound. She made up her narrow mouth over-large and very red. She had a smile. She had beautiful hair, beautiful manners; her clothes were something; her hands were long, slender, and properly jeweled and she had a slightly husky, childish voice; but it had been a long time since she was a little girl. Although drinks were set out on a large low coffee table, she sipped delicately from a pink-gold and silver flask. It was either vodka or distilled tiger's breath. Whatever it was, she was getting on beautifully with it.

We played the game we both knew well. We had a drink. We went from dignified theater talk to Hollywood politics.

We had a drink. We spoke of music and art . . . and of the latest scandals.

We had a drink. We had the inevitable grand dinner properly served, with the proper wines. We retired to the living room again. She invited me to sit next to her for coffee. I did.

We had a drink. She asked me to kiss her. I did.

With her leading me, we drifted languidly down a huge corridor; then into a bedroom a little smaller than the Colosseum. White rugs, white drapes, white silk sheets on a bed big enough to play tennis on. She did not have tennis on her mind. Nor did I. The preliminaries over, we settled down to the last act. We both knew our lines. We both played the love game well.

"Listen . . ." she said. "Oh, Jarn, this is wonderful! I'm very grateful to you for this."

"Don't talk," I whispered—the "this" being, I was on top of her, pounding down, and in; trying not to be out of breath when I talked, knowing how she was . . . and it was. Trying to remember her as she had been. I tried to close my eyes and think of that, but she kept talking . . . murmuring. Not to me, not to anyone but herself. I didn't flatter myself that I was that good, but I lay on top of her and thought of many things . . . in a sweaty sort of way . . . and she lay under me breathing out little moans of mock passion, a "nothing make love." The new and the old, the *faux jeton* and the "then make love." "Now . . . make love," she said.

"It's . . . well it's . . ."

"Oh, just wait a minute," she moaned.

Why . . .? I thought. "Why . . .?" I said. "Why . . .?" I came. We needed her in the picture. It was as simple as that.

She talked as though she had truly made love. The voice dry with the after-love hoarseness, the juices gone. The break in the voice was pure artistry. The love was . . . well . . . the love. Yes, the love; that was another thing. The wild music of the humping time broke and washed over us. We were as naked as a pier at low tide. We are naked now—and lonely now, and do you know, we never once discussed the Baron's picture. It was all prearranged. *Quelle comédie.*

I looked at this women who gestured, who did everything so gracefully, whose hands were so delicate that they should be struck in bronze—in more than bronze—in gold slightly impure, pyrite, fool's good. But seeing them I was filled with regret and remorse that those hands, in the soft, fluffy, quiet dark, had held the Baron's false dong. Had fluted lovingly up and down that plastic bat and was carried away with herself holding all in firm yet delicate hands, had taken the trip alone on a rubber-plastic-unvisaed passport. "Oh, you . . . you . . . you," she gasped, which came out in French, *"Oh, toi . . . toi . . . toi."* A lonely trip, and later on the bidet nothing to be washed down except herself alone; alone, vinegared alone; she had firmly clamped him between her thighs with her eyes. He didn't know it, but he had been enfolded in a warm, moist envelope of calculated passion—if they still call it that.

•   •   •

185

THE DEAL

I first began to know *Someone* was around when I was pretty young, after Aunt Jessie told me about it. I'd been to church and all that stuff but he—*Someone*—had never really bothered me except for little-kid stuff.

S. Well, why did you have to shoot that bird?

J. You crazy . . .? I got this BB gun from the hardware store. I sold those magaznes, sold those milk bottles I hooked from Powell's Dairy, I got this gun and what the hell else for but to shoot birds?

S. I've tried to talk to you about that, but you're pretty headstrong. However, we'll get to know each other better now that we've established contact.

(Then, a couple of years later)

S. Do you really want to do this? Is this really what you want to do?

J. Judas! Knock it off, and yeah, I'm going to screw her, I've worked hard enough for it, haven't I?

S. You have, but not with my agreement.

J. Well, screw you and screw your agreement and lay off now, just leave me the hell alone.

S. I can't do that, Jarn.

J. Well, if you think you're going to louse *this* up . . . you can drop dead.

S. No, Jarny, I can't . . . but you can.

J. That's it, go ahead . . . that's it, try to make me scared, try to ruin it for me like you do everything else. Boy, I wish I could shut you out.

S. Not really, Jarny. You may think you can shut me "off" very temporarily . . . but you can never shut me "out."

J. Well, I'm a son-of-a-bitch, keep it up . . . just keep it up; you think this girl's going to lay here like this all night, you think she's stuffed? Now lay off.

S. My fear, Jarn, is that she *will* lie there all night. You see, actually, Jarn, you are a good boy. I know it and she knows it. Listen; I've talked with her Soul and, "boy," as you say, has he got his work cut out for him.

J. What the hell are you talking about? (Fourteen-year-old scared.)

S. Jarny, you know I can't really stay around talking with you if you use language like that.

J. You can't?

S. No, I don't think it's proper.

J. Well then, hell, hell, screw, hell and take off.

186

THE DEAL

S.   I guess I'll tune out for a while. I won't "take off," I'll be right here. I can see you're not really listening.

J.   Man, you finally got it. Take off, I'm not listening now, next week, next year, or ever.

S.   We'll see, Jarn. We'll see. If you want me or would like to talk it over, I'll be . . .

J.   Listen, you said you were going . . . well, *go* then, go to hell.

S.   No, I won't go there, Jarn, and I'm trying my best to see that *you* don't, either.

J.   Listen, don't try that scaring crap again. You can't scare me with that bunk.

S.   Maybe I'll let you take a *closer look at it* one day, Jarn, but you're not that far gone yet. However . . . there are no lengths that I will not go to keep us together, to keep you safe.

J.   Oh, man, what a son-of-a-bitch; will you just clear the hell out? I got to concentrate.

I looked down at the girl. "Now listen, baby." The girl stirred herself, stretched, and looked up. Her love-lazy face all there, all mine, all inviting . . . just waiting.

"Jarn," she said, "You were gone away from me for a minute."

"Not me, honey, not me, kid," I said. "Nothing could take me away from you." I looked around furtively, then satisfied that no one was there, leaned down to kiss the girl. "That son-of-a-bitch," I said to myself.

"What, Jarny?" said the little girl.

"Nothing—I just said, you sweet little son-of-a-bitch."

One day the Baron had been lounging around Sam Neely's office; probably to offer him some inducement to keep his eyes open for promising little *poules* he might see while driving around the studio, or something like that.

Sam hadn't come in, so when the phone rang, the Baron answered it.

It was Jean-Claude, the studio production manager, speaking with great urgency, and in his haste thinking he was addressing Sam.

It seems my brother and Jean-Claude had been looking for location sites to set up and shoot some "bar" footage on the Boulevard St. Germain. Knowing my brother, he had undoubtedly been testing, and tasting, as they joyously carried on their work. There had been a jam-up at the Deux Magots in St. Germain, and my brother had now been jumped by a gang of *les*

187

durs. The Baron curtly told Jean-Claude that he'd be right there . . . and he was better than his word.

He dashed right out of Sam's office into the street, commandeered a passing auto (it must have been a grand scene, with the Baron playing it to the hilt), drove first to the studio, where he "volunteered" a couple of stunt men who were every bit as tough as Saul Baum—and then they hit St. Germain. All hell broke loose!

French toughs flew through the air like a prearranged *apache* nightclub act. By the time I got there my brother was all dusted off and having a little victory drink, while the Baron, victoriously sipping brandy, was colorfully acting out and retelling the whole episode for the benefit of some attractive little girls who just happened to be at the bar. Joy reigned, tightly and supreme.

A little gruff, because I didn't want to sound corny, I said to the Baron, "Of all the people in the world, you're the last guy in the world I'd have figured to save my brother in a street brawl."

The Baron grinned (with his "good" profile to the little girls). "I don't know why you say that, Jarn. Aren't you my partner? Don't we share everything? Aren't you my best friend, besides?" The little girls loved it all.

Well, whatever the Baron was up to before and after that little fracas in St. Germain, he definitely saved my brother and me from getting worked over that time.

But the Baron couldn't stand the straight and narrow for long. I guess to him it seemed too uncomplicated. So he ran me through the wringer this way. The Deal should have been a musical.

The Baron played too many instruments in the jazz band of his life. It wasn't always the jazzy flute of sex. He also played the *piqure* piccolo of "horse." They definitely did not make beautiful music together. When the Baron played his "jazz" and rode his "horse," I'd check his eyes for the mud look, and the waxy end of his nose for a barometer reading. Then I'd end up calling my friend the Doctor.

This time the Baron had found his "horse," which I had hidden, . . . and had used most all of it in the bathroom. I'd never have known if I hadn't walked in on him as he was finishing with the needle. His face was white and sweaty. "Kid," he said, "don't ever try this . . . don't ever try it . . . me, I . . ."

The Baron never got to finish. He reached up quickly for the shower curtain, a swift movement; with his left arm flashing out and up, like he was hanging a cat, and didn't want to be scratched. He fell into the shower, accidentally turning on the water. I got wet hauling him out . . . I pulled him over to the bed. I stretched him out on it and covered him up with towels and some blankets . . . He lay there as if he were dead.

I called the Doctor. He came shortly afterward. He looked at me. Then stood looking quietly down at the Baron.

"Well, what the hell do you think I wanted you to see him for—so you could meet a star?"

The Doctor looked at me and smiled; he was big, like a bear; he would go about five-eleven and would weigh in like a hammered-down heavyweight. He had a long dish-face and a lot of black hair. He wore thick glasses that neither helped nor hurt his appearance. He listened while I ranted a little more, then he frowned. The frown helped; but it made him look as harmless as a big woodchuck, only a lot more friendly. I liked him . . . I liked everything about him; and I should have. He had once saved my life.

"He looks," Doc said, "as though he is in a state of alcoholic shock."

I looked at him. "Yeah, he's in shock; but I don't know if it's alcohol or the Black Mallack."

"The what?"

"Black Mallack. And I don't know what the hell that is either. But listen, he's the big one in my picture and I need expert help and no noise. I figured I could get them both from you," I finished, and stood watching him.

"How long has he been this way?" he asked, picking up the Baron's wrist and doing a lot of heavy thinking. I'm sure that's what it was because, you see, I knew him very well. I told him what had happened.

He went to work on the Baron. He even got a few answers from him. He gave him a shot of something to let him climb down off the roof easier; he told me to call him later. He left. After about an hour the Baron started to babble softly, then stirred a little. I waited.

The Baron started to move; then he started to sit up. He looked around bleary-eyed. "Kid," he said, "is that you?"

"Yeah, I'm here . . ." I answered.

"I'd like a drink," he said. "I don't feel so good."

I figured this was an understatement. "Take it easy, Baron . . . and I'll tell you what the Doc said." I looked at him. He grinned.

"What doc, Jarn boy? What doc?"

"Don't remember, huh?" I said, looking at him closely. He grinned again. It was a sappy grin.

"You're trying to frighten me, Jarn boy, and it won't work . . ."

189

"Maybe, but let's wait for the Doc's report. He's going to phone me and tell me who we should see if he can't make it." I looked at him calmly. "I've got to keep you in good shape, you know.

Then there was the time that the sixteen-year-old virgin (they were all virgins) came to see the Baron. This time he truly didn't do it; this time he had passed out; but to secure her position—to gird up his loins, such as they were—the girl got back in bed with him. Morning came and she dramatically threatened to expose the Baron for rape. She declared she was going to call the police to demand an examination by a doctor. Well, there it was; the Baron was hooked. He came to see me, frantic—explained he had to have help—I helped him. He paid by promising to work continuously.

I knew he'd be convicted of rape *if* the girl had been laid—I knew the police were really after him. Baron swore he never touched her. He got down on his knees and swore. I told him I believed him, acting all the time like I didn't. He didn't lay her, he repeated over and over, I couldn't let him take the fall. I needed him. I couldn't just say the hell with him; he had been guilty plenty of times, but after the last "near-miss" he would be finished. I knew it. And it was still fresh enough in his mind so *he* knew it.

He kept repeating in his three-highball voice, with the fear only half out of it: "I don't remember. I don't remember."

I looked at him coldly. "Forget it," I said. "I'll take care of her, and it. Don't I always?"

He gave me what started to be his drunken leer. "You do that, Jarn boy. Take care of it, kid."

I looked at him with my leaden stare. "It's not fixed yet. I don't know, maybe you . . ."

He got three shades whiter. "Don't kid about this, Jarn. I can't handle another one. Don't forget, it will ruin your picture too."

I grinned at him, I had him now. "I'm beginning to feel sorry for you again," I said, "half smart—half hung and half smart. Maybe the thing for me to do is let you take it."

He gave me one of those smiles you see in the operating room. "Nah, you won't . . . you won't do that; you want the money too bad." Part of a sneer hung weakly on his face. He was right; I did. But I didn't want him to be too brave.

"Take it easy," I said quietly, "we've got a lot of hard work to do, with everybody working hard, and everyone on time and all. Right?"

"Right," he echoed quickly. "Right, Jarn," he said again.

THE DEAL

I gave him a thoughtful look. "Well, Baron, it will be handled like always." I started for the door, but not too fast. He let me get to it before he stopped me.

"You're not sore, are you, kid? I didn't mean that crack about the money. Can't you take a rib from your partner?"

I said, "You rib too deep sometimes; don't bear down on it too hard, Baron, or I might forget to handle it. We'll see."

I opened the door and walked out. As I looked back, he was taking a big one. But pouring it into it . . . all that fear. The Baron wouldn't get drunk too fast tonight . . . not tonight.

I think it was that night that I got the idea how I could really control the Baron. I'd have to set it up right. But I could do that. The Baron would be an all-too-easy victim; a willing lender of himself, ready to do anything to try and get close enough to one more of those little girls who (maybe) might set him off, let him truly and absolutely take the trip for once. I'd keep an eye open for the right one. I'd be able to handle it . . . *(Yes I would).*

Ever since the Baron had arrived in Paris, it had been one thing after another. The women, the "horse," the money. And if it wasn't the Baron, it might be Bloodtest, or Goldin, or Edwards. Especially; it might be all three of them together. By the time we were shooting down at the studio in Nice. these "emergency conferences" were coming up with some regularity. I'd get the call around eleven, and the three of them would be waiting. Then the Baron would come in . . .

The room suddenly seemed empty except for the Baron and me. "Hi, boy," he said in a husky five-highball voice. "Sit down, sit down." He had overlooked the fact that I was already seated and was waiting for God knows what. He went over to the bar. I knew it was too late to make any sense of anything. Bloodtest would listen, Mitty would suck, the Editor and I would watch the ball for a while, and then, depending on what the problem really was—if there was a problem—try the hell to sort it out. The Editor was too scared and owed too much to let go. I was too young and wanted too much to even think about letting go. I could always get off when I wanted; *yes I could.*

Once I said to the Baron, "Don't you get 'em mixed up sometimes? I mean, screwing the mothers and the daughters and things like this and that?" He grinned at me, all under control, all full of himself, whatever that means. I continued, "No kidding, Baron, you and your personality. You

191

mow 'em down like nine-pins. Man, the variety. Because, when you look at it, with these little girls, it's just like masturbating in one way or another; except the couple of times when you've outfoxed yourself."

He winked, "Jarn boy, fill 'em full of gysum, then they won't complain. Fill 'em full of gysum." I didn't want to mention the couple or four young ones he had or had not "filled full of gysum" and the trouble it caused. He was winging now, no trouble now, so why shoot him down? We still had the picture to do, there was still a lot more crap to eat.

Like once when the Baron caught the measles from "15" . . . a childish disease . . .

The Doctor came out of the Baron's bedroom looking properly serious. Bloodtest stayed in with the Baron . . . worrying.

I asked, "What is the matter with him, doctor?"

"Well," he said. He cleared his throat. "I don't like to make this diagnosis until I have made a few tests."

I grinned at him. "He's kind of swollen up, isn't he?" I said, knowing that he had started to look like a balloon.

"Well," the Doctor said, "I think I know what it is but . . ."

He never got to finish what it was—out walked Bloodtest. "What do you mean, he has measles?" Bloodtest snorted. "Hell, I figured he could have syphilis, but measles . . . he ain't clean enough to catch the measles."

I looked at Bloodtest, and from habit wanted him to worry. I gave him a look of grave concern. I said, "Hugh, maybe you're right; maybe it is syphilis and not the measles. However—"15" is in bed with the measles. It's probably the most harmless thing she's been in bed with for some time."

He looked at me, a long look. "Hell," he said. "You're kidding—oh no, the measles." He looked again at me. It was kind of a sincere, yet sad look. "You don't like the Baron anymore, do you, kid?" There was nothing in that for me so I let it drift with the rest of the smoke that was slowly blowing into the air conditioner from Bloodtest's cigar. He shook his head sadly. "I can see that you don't really feel sorry for him."

"Balls," I said, *en toute simplicité*. "At least, Hugh, we'll know damn well where he is the next few days."

Hugh was looking at his cigar—I was looking at everything, at nothing. Well, I thought, I'll go try to shoot around him for a few days. Hell, I've shot around him so much up to now the film will have to be shown in a "round" theater. I grinned, and thought—At least I can get some good work out of script number 1.

THE DEAL

"Take your licking, Jarn, and get to work," *Someone* said.
"O.K.," I said, "I'll do just that." I left for the studio.

While I was driving along, I remembered certain things that the late Jared Throne had said, which the Baron repeated as though inscribed in bronze.

Over and above the fact that Jared Throne was probably the finest actor of his time, he'd made many brilliant statements. He was a sad and humorous man when discharged, which he frequently was by his studio, on morals charges. Many serious comments were made that had been proved false and, as he said, "perilous." Also, many private and frivolous comments which were valuable and ought to be immortal. When he spoke, striking a pose looking stage right, stage left, then piercing his audience of four thousand, or one, he struck dead the stiff and false psychology of the unprepared actor. And with that it suggested that in the number of theaters and the number of public houses where he had appeared before drunks, he was always completely, thoroughly in charge. Jared Throne was a master. He said that in the many bedrooms of his life, none had made him sleepy. This in itself was a sort of tribute to the character he played. On his deathbed, when the nurse had come in, he threw back the sheet, looked at her and said, "If you're the best I can do, get in." An empty, terrible, lonely death, yet not without a flair. On his death, fate for once seemed to pick out his particular situation in plain black and white, not in color. It was an allegory. The words said over the coffin filled with "a nothing," with an emptiness not even "an act." They were spoken over his box, a tragedy of appalling platitudes. The heroes were the heroes, the villains were the villains; the common tangle of life, in which good men do evil by mistake and bad men do good by accident, seemed suspended and we knew or were advised that the Almighty would take it under advisement: the judgment of Jared Throne . . . the judgment of the Baron.

I remembered, as we left the funeral sadly and with dignity, we thought our thoughts. We had had to do things in the picture business to make deals that not only were vile but they felt vile in the making. We had had to destroy men who not only were noble but who looked noble, such as Jared Throne. For he had been killed surely and definitely, and yet with a lack of dignity. Because in the last years he had only been offered roles which were parodies of himself. But Jared Throne on his deathbed had made an epitaph by the refusal of an epitaph . . . with a gesture, he flung out his arms hoping to enfold any tune that he might carry to heaven with him.

193

THE DEAL

Like his agent in many respects, on his deathbed he, and in his lifetime his agent, mixed their metaphors, saddled with two separate careers, one boxing on one side, one in-fighting on the other—the *plunk, plunk* of the well-padded gloves bouncing off the calloused foreskin of their souls.

I knew that the Baron had modeled most of his life after Jared Throne. He regarded Throne as the atheist innovator in an atheist age. The great new precedent of his acting was just a fraud and would have been broken had not Jared Throne himself been a great man and a great actor. But the Baron, within the bubbled limits, was completely immersed in his plastic dong, which never reached out with clawing sperming hands for the reality that he always tried to attain. This was the first act of the tragedy; yet unhappily the Baron wanted to continue in that vein, wanted to follow with the second act. It would have been fine if we could have left Jared Throne there, but we were not done with this fellow, because of his splendid work. For the Baron ran and reran his old films. Had clothes and costumes made exactly patterned after Jared Throne's. He spoke in a satanic manner whenever he assumed the "Baron Throne" pose. He used many terms of abuse. He was a tempter. He dragged the other actors to "partake of the body of Jared Throne." He wanted them to learn the meaning of any acting mass that Jared Throne had left as his legacy. The trumpet of resurrection had blown, yet only a few arose. There, standing quietly in his lonely loneliness, was the Baron . . . his limp and unfurled flag tattered at every corner . . . being fastened to a mast which wasn't too rigid in the first place.

The second act of the drama came when the Baron decided, in all good grace and in all good spirits, to become my partner and, with all benevolence intact, bestowed upon me certain death—as though he had shot me between the eyes, or stabbed me in the heart. What was worse, I didn't know that the Novocain of the money anesthetized thought; the Metrecal of the fatted calf had thinned my thinking, warped my wisdom, clouded my cleverness and jammed up my judgment. So, all in all, the Deal that I had made was a treachery unto myself. I was a man who unknowingly was swimming the ocean, and my destiny was to drown in three foot of water off the Santa Monica pier.

When the Baron and I were discussing business, even though common sense tried to make itself felt, I listened intently to his ideas . . . this was before we had made the first picture. His ideas, I thought, were mad, were completely unbalanced. But they held a certain exhilaration; by their loose license, they fell into place with my thinking. I was willing to polish the bar, to shine the glasses for his thoughts. His drinking at that time didn't annoy me. I had only thought with canny incorrectness that I could use his drinking to my own advantage. I was a poor bourgeoisified innocent. I was a thief who was after filmed property, not lives. I drove to the studio. I walked onto the set. I went back to work.

Things were going from worse to worse. Late that afternoon, I walked from the studio to the Aviation Club, on the Champs Elysées. I was tired, I was disappointed by what I knew had been a bad day's work for everyone. I had not used my head well, I had not reasoned things out correctly.

In the Club bar, unfortunately, I was unable to avoid a casual acquaintance, a well-known crippled producer. His high wheel chair was so angled at the bar that he looked like a heavyweight fighter ready to take on the first comer for the first round. He said Hello to me and, from my habit of doing the wrong thing, I answered.

We got into a stupid discussion that turned into an argument, which I shouldn't have let happen. But finally I was sick of it, and of him. In one way, he reminded me of the Baron. He said, "If I weren't a cripple, I'd . . . I'd . . ."

"If you weren't a cripple," I snarled, "you wouldn't be talking that way—you'd already have been flushed down the toilet. Now, that's the same in English and in French. You're a turd . . . I'm no sport, Hector . . . to me you're just another bent prick. You open your mouth again to me and I'll shove that cane of yours so far up you, that it will splinter and you can pick all your false teeth with one move."

His face paled; he shut up and recoiled back against the bar like a struck snake. He made a furtive half-wave motion with his hand and was wheeled away by his male nurse, who, turning his head around, thanked me gratefully with his eyes, and as he started slowly away, said, "Monsieur Jarnigan."

This crippled European producer—very broad in the shoulders, huge muscular arms; but from the waist down, an unfortunate situation—overcame any pity or sympathy you might have had for him by his arrogance and his reliance on the fact that he was a cripple. This guy was one of the worst sons-of-bitches I ever knew. Without his infirmity, he would have sunk beneath the slime of his own being. With his crippledom, he was like a wounded turd; crippled and filled with enough gaseous air to keep afloat. Although he was suffering from the smell of his own inadequte, useless, "above the surface" life, he filled the air with a lame-walked conversation; jerking himself off every time he used his cane; caressing himself with each painful step. He pussed and yellowed his way through the studio, the theater, and life, hated by all—the thoughts of others were medical. When could the core of this chancre be squeezed out from between our even lightly touched selves, by his crippled presence, his life?

But I had other things to worry me. I had called a meeting for 5 o'clock in my office with the French co-producer and the Suisse Syndicate banker representative. They were late with the money; and, by Christ, if they didn't come up with it by tonight, after my warning of yesterday, I'd flush *them* down the drain. I walked over to my office, went in and sat down. And in about five minutes, in they came. But I didn't see any brief cases; that meant no cash. And I was through taking their checks . . .

I motioned them to their chairs. Nailed them in place with a cold and calculated look, and started to speak quietly:

"Alors, mes amis (this conversation was carried on in the French language)—my friends, let us speak seriously, for it would be easy to fence with you for an eternity—to parry every point you attempt to make, every thrust. I refuse to continue along the course that you have indicated up to now. There is, to say the least, a great deal that is wrong with the Deal—with *l'Affaire* that you have proposed. It should not be forgotten, even in the full blaze of your marvelous mistakes and your disaster-prone contracts, that our current business relationship—between you and myself—has not been—again, to say the least—completely satisfactory. The collapse of your finances and the deflation of all your promises leave a yawning gap. Your ineptitude places me in a perilous situation. Your mistakes are matters of absolute fact, and to enumerate them does not exhaust the truth, nor does it leave me speechless."

Here, both the French attorney and the Suisse Syndicate man glanced at each other; started to say something. I said, "I pray you, let me continue because otherwise I must take my leave. I have heard your tales, your lies, until exhausted; so I propose that you listen to me, and then—deliberate. Take the time necessary to give me a firm reply. Verbal assurances and verbal money will be insufficient. I will only accept hard cash, hard francs . . . or soft, as they may be.

"I will outline the various ways in which you have defaulted on our agreement. I have selected them on a principle, a principle which in my view cannot fail to interest you—although undoubtedly it will not please you. On the many occasions that we have had dealings, you have been very wrong indeed and I have been wrong in accepting your assurances. However, in my earnest and sincere desire to continue with the Deal, I accepted these things; going along, hoping that you might eventually come up with your part of our definite and concrete agreement. I am now returning to the studio. No . . . you needn't get up; there's nothing to say for the moment, since I see you have not brought the cash. I shall expect word before the close of the day today. I will be in the Studio Boulogne until eight o'clock. If I have not had concrete examples of cash in my office by that hour, then, as you say in French, *je garde toutes mes reserves*—I keep all my reserve."

(The following was said in English)—"And I'll keep everything else; you babies are going to have troubles that you've never dreamed of."

"Is that a threat, Monsieur Jarnigan?"

"Listen, sweetheart, you take it any way you want. Now, I've gone along on the stilted French . . ."

"Pardon," the little attorney said, "I don't quite . . . would you speak slower . . ."

"Look, if I spoke more slowly, it wouldn't help, so I say to you in English—have the money there before eight o'clock tonight or that's it! And if you don't have it there, be missing. Get out of the world!"

At 7:30 p.m. I was in my office at the studio. I truly hadn't been waiting . . . they still had another half-hour. There was a discreet knock on my door, the friendly rap of the old-time bootlegger, with the beer-froth smile and the friendly, deep pocket. The secretary had left earlier; I was alone.

"Come in," I called. The door opened quietly and in slipped the French producer; he came through the door quietly, another wise cat; he came swiftly, silently toward me, put a brief case on my desk and sat down all in one smooth motion.

"You're early," I said, opening up the act.

He looked sad. "Monsieur Jarnigan . . . Monsieur Jarnigan, you know that you may always rely on me; I had indicated the course my confreres were to follow. They chose to ignore my advice, and you acted in the manner in which I told them you would react. You were splendid—yes, splendid . . ." he hummed on, "you carried it off with flying colors."

"Carried what off?"

"Tut . . . tut, Monsieur Jarnigan," he tut-tutted, "you were bluffing and we both know it." Here he winked. I didn't say anything. He nodded . . . for him I was becoming more wise each minute. He gave me his undertaker's smile. "Are you a closed-mouth man? Can you keep your own counsel?"

I shook my head. "No, I like to talk."

"C'est formidable, vraiment formidable." He grinned at me. "You know," he said, "you and I are really going to get along."

THE DEAL

I returned his grin. You dirty bastard, I thought.

He smiled. "I'd like to make you a proposal, Monsieur Jarnigan, since we are men of the world." He kept the smile squarely on his face.

"Does it have to do with this money you are paying me?"

He nodded.

"Well, then," I said, "I'd better have you talk to Maître Gautrat; he's about as worldly as I get." I stood up. "By the way, I suppose the money is all here," I said, picking up the brief case.

He smiled at me coldly. "The money is there, Monsieur Jarnigan."

"But you didn't say positively."

"Positively."

"Grand. So I'll bid you good night," I said quietly, "and thanks for being early."

He looked daggers at me. "I see you are in no mood to discuss a proposal that could be beneficial to you."

"See Gautrat," I said. "My conversations with your group without my lawyer holding my hand have been, to say the least, difficult. Again I bid you good night."

He stood up. He looked at me quietly. "We shall see . . . we shall see."

"Yeah, let's do that. *Bonsoir, cher ami.*"

He left, again quietly, a cat picking his way through cactus.

And so we were ready to continue the shooting in the south of France.

It was after the next day's shooting, and we were ready to see the rushes. We were all there. We had finished the shooting about 7 p.m.—the Baron, the Princess, the actors and a worried producer.

How are you, darlings! were splattered all around as we were waiting for the projection room to show the first filmed sequences with the rest of the cast.

Just as we started to go into the projection room, the door flew open and a lot of French actors and actresses came out, having just seen the rushes of the French-language picture they were making at the studio. There were actors and boors, French producers and whores. The "new wave" was just trying to get started up the beach, so they waved out of the projection room.

I was looking at them as they went by. The star was a displaced American actor who had a badly acned face, a worse toupee, and the flustered look of a "flop-swat" actor. He was very full of himself.

They talked in high voices . . . talked not to each other but to themselves, in the worst sort of dream. It would fog off later, but after the heat and

198

glow of the projection room . . . hell, this was life. This is what they had been born for. Pitiful . . . pitiful.

I was looking them over, and I glanced up and saw the Baron looking at me. He was standing on a step, so he was a little above the rest of the people. He had on a yachting jacket and a blue scarf. I couldn't see what else because the Princess came up on one side and his new "find" came up on the other. I glanced back at the Baron. He was the perfect superstar. He was smiling at the French actors and actresses; nodding Hellos here and there—very dignified and completely aware of the obvious adulation, which he accepted as his due. His hair was in careful, but not unstudied waves. He was giving each one a smile so brief it was no smile at all. Just then, up came the French co-producer, who insisted on shaking hands right away. And we all went into the projection room.

It is true Gilot hadn't liked his previous meeting with the Baron in Paris on account of the condition the Baron was in when I introduced them. The projection room darkened as I was thinking of the Paris meeting. The Baron had been surrounded by five adoring fagots. All were seated in the bar of the George V. This, of course, wasn't my fault, but the producer seemed to think it was a bad and "Hollywood-type" atmosphere. The French producer, who spoke very little English but understood practically everything, had been further annoyed by the Baron's introduction of his "friends." The Baron had looked around his circle of fagolas and said, "Sows . . . I want you to meet our co-producer, Monsieur Gilot."

This first fag stood up—a blond-type fellow, big-hipped, cow-eyed. He shook hands with M. Gilot and lisped, *"Enchanté,"* and then I realized what we were in for. Since the first fag had gotten up, showing off its manners, I knew that the other four would stand up and insist on shaking hands too. They are like that. After many handshakings, many coy laughs and flashing eyes, also some unnecessarily rude under-the-breath remarks, the Baron sat down, and the French producer and I excused ourselves and walked out of the bar.

The French producer said, *"Les salauds."*

"No," I said, *"salopes."* Walking on out of the lobby of the George V, we said goodbye, solemnly shaking hands again, ready to meet first thing in the morning. I said, speaking French, "You know, Monsieur Gilot, I regret that you had to meet the Baron under these conditions. I am sure you are aware, being a producer of many films, having dealt with stars of every category, that the Baron is under quite a strain. He has only just arrived from Hollywood; you didn't see him at his best."

THE DEAL

That was the understatement of the week, but I stood there and the French producer nodded with dignity and said quietly, "I understand, Monsieur Jarnigan. I have heard of some of the problems which you have had, and have dealt with admirably. But in all sincerity, I must confess I had not fully appreciated their complexities until now. It is to be hoped that we will not have a typical Baron-type *carnaval en dehors du film.*" He finished with a throb in his moist voice.

I answered, "I am in complete accord with you, *cher ami,* and am certain that this will not occur." We again shook hands solemnly. And the little producer turned and walked away, a little sad, but with dignity.

My partner, the Baron, hadn't made too good an impression at that meeting. He hadn't looked good at all, not at all. This and many other thoughts were going through my mind as the projection started. But I was already in my "furrow," which would have to be plowed whether we made the picture in Hollywood, in Rome, Madrid, or here in the City of Light. Everything was fraught with hidden rocks. Old Jarn, the plowman.

The film was "screening" now and happily looked all right. As I watched it I couldn't help thinking the Baron had been spending too much time with the fagolas lately. There was this pederast who'd got his hooks and things into the Baron. The ped had a flair, was colorful, and an excellent designer, and one of the greatest con artists I'd ever seen. The Baron finally latched on to the ped like a drowning man clutching a straw. Before, where he'd treated them with a touch of amusement and indifference, now it was with true interest. I don't know what went on, but for the Baron from that time on, whatever was needed, the ped—"Milord the fairy"—had it. Everything went well. I didn't care what they did. "It was their mouth; they could carry coal in it" . . . but when the ped started interfering with the Deal . . . goodbye, old ped.

When drunk and on the flit, this fag was an old swish who wanted to play "up the dirt road" with any teen-age boy he could find, liberally dropping phony checks along the way like used "pansy-type flowers." Of course, they were made good later—the checks, I mean—and with luck and the studio's help he had just never ended up in the"blimp." Sober, he was just a nice old fagola, shooting around a lot of superficial charm, hitting nobody. When they passed the law in England that pederasty was legal between consenting adults, he had wanted to marry an English knight who had special tendencies. They were seeking marriage in England, or perhaps "adoption," and when they came to join us on the picture in France I thought it was funny . . . I could just see myself introducing them as Sir Hector Pomfret-Jones and Lady Marcel LaRoche. Marcel and Hector were a couple of lulus.

THE DEAL

When this Marcel was in bloom and was really aflame he caused a lot of trouble on the picture. When he was the temptee, not the tempter, he was too much. Then he'd say to the Devil, "Get thee behind me, Satan." It was that, hopefully, Satan would yance him. *And he did.* Goodbye, old ped, you're leaving Cheyenne . . .

Well, it may be all right, I thought. I knew the next day my brother was supposed to fly in from New York, bringing the rest of the cast.

The boat has sailed, Jarn boy; so suck in your belly, tighten the reins, and ride the bitch out. You can do it . . . *Yes you can.*

29

Movieola: *The Brother*

Mo was a handsome man, a little too heavy but at a glance you could see he had great power. He had worked with me for many years from Hollywood through Europe. He was the eternal big brother—over-protective, yet he needed to be told what to do. He had been an All-American football player, an amateur heavyweight boxer, had been very proud of his physique and was formerly a health addict. This in the past few years had faded considerably.

The Baron regarded him as only my older brother, and with the usual indulgent Hollywood-star contempt for a relative working for a relative. The Baron, who at times thought himself quite a boxer, had boxed a few times with my brother but later had wisely and rightly declined, saying my brother was too rough and too heavy. What it really was, my brother didn't make the Baron look too good, as most of the Baron's "clown fighters" tried to do. My brother didn't make the Baron look too good because I had purposely refrained from telling my brother to go out of his way to *make* the Baron look good. I didn't want my brother to be the Baron's "other stunt man." But he would drink with the Baron and try to keep him out of trouble and in that he was invaluable to me, because although the Baron was truly afraid of my brother, he also liked him.

How many nights I had seen my brother put the Baron to bed, with Saul Baum helping—the Baron completely out. Then my brother coming over to me and saying contentedly, "Well, kid; got him home all right." I would look at his poor whiskey-bruised face and feel sad. Continuing, he would grin and say, "This keeping your star in shape takes a lot out of a man." Then he'd turn, look around the room, and say brightly, "Well, I think I'll have one for the road and then I'll be off."

I'd say, "I don't think you need one for the road."

He'd put me in my place with a drunken accusing stare, saying, "You know, little brother, I'm doing this for you."

Not wanting another argument, not wanting any more trouble, I'd dismiss it and say quietly, "Sure, kid, sure. Let's go get some coffee and go on home. I have to be at the studio early."

"I do too. I do too," my brother would say unhappily. We'd leave.

The sad, the unfortunate thing was, that this drunkenness finally betrayed Mo. He became an angry man but kept it carefully hidden—that was the flaw in his character, which I didn't see in time, and was too selfish and unwise to remedy. It was not that he didn't have ability, but the false dignity he carried when he was drunk stole away completely the charm and common sense he had when he was sober. There were times when I'd regret having had him come to Europe, but he was my older brother and I loved him.

My brother—another tragedy of the Deal.

It was after the next day's shooting, and again we went to the projection room to see the rushes. Now my brother, whom I was waiting for, had met the Baron many times in Hollywood—he'd seen me try to teach the Baron golf at Lakeview Country Club, watched his feeble attempts to play the game. He came to know, as I knew, all of the Baron's coordination was in his stunt man . . . the jumps, the swinging from the top of a mast, the fencing, the firing of a cannon, and—best of all—the fight scenes. The Baron just wasn't . . . that's the way to say it . . . he just wasn't. He was always "missing" . . .

We had finished shooting about 6:30 p.m. It was now almost seven. My brother had just arrived—he had flown in from New York. He had brought with him a fag actor who played himself very well. He had also brought along the actress who was a little past her prime . . . but was still sexy in a musty-fusty sort of way. She still had "the name" and was always a lady, which was the hardest and most difficult role she'd ever played.

I hadn't met them at the plane . . . but now, here was my brother, a little too happy and "fine" from the martinis during the flight. All of them knew Paris was gayer because "they" had arrived. How do you tell your brother that you don't need him that way? That you don't need another drinker, or another problem on the picture? You don't. He was so happy he'd brought them, you'd have thought he piloted the plane, and carefully nursed them here to help me.

He said, "Boy, it's good to see you . . ."

"Yeah," I said. I looked at him quietly. "Your eyes are glassy, son." Like said our father. Not God, just our father . . . who was a good man . . . who always wanted to give his sons the best . . . except there was a little problem that got in the way.

The door to the projection room was open now. We went in. No point in getting mad. I couldn't pray my way out of this, so I went over and sat by my brother . . .

"Now why don't you just be quiet and watch your picture? It's costing you enough, in more ways than money," *Someone* said.

THE DEAL

"Oh, man, are you here again? Can't you, for Christ's sake, take a night off?"

"Jarn, when will you learn that for His sake I can't take the night off. We have a much stronger, a more "devoted" union than you producers do. In my view, we are also more closely aligned with Good," *Someone* finished primly.

"Listen, knock it off you . . . you . . ."

"Jarn, I shall knock it off, and leave you alone to watch your film. May I add before leaving, I don't care much for your script? It's too violent, and certainly suggestive; a little too involved, perhaps. Of course," *Someone* added, "that is an unprofessional opinion."

"Well, for Christ's sake," I said, "are you a critic too?"

"For His sake I am everything and anything that will help you," *Someone* answered.

"Listen, I've got to watch this film, so fly off," I growled.

"What did you say, Jarn?" my brother whispered.

"Oh," I whispered back, "I just said I'm sorry I cracked about the glassy-eyed part. I'm just tired but I'm sure damned glad to see you, big brother."

He put his arm around the back of my chair and patted me gently on the shoulder. It felt "home"—it felt good. He didn't say any more. I glanced at him out of the corner of my eye. I whispered, "You all right, kid?" He turned his head around and looked at me. In the dark projection room his eyes gleamed brightly. He smiled.

"When we're all right, I'm all right." His smile changed to his warm big-brother grin. "Now, watch your picture, little brother—it's costing you enough, in more ways than money." He patted my shoulder again. I watched my picture, the picture that cost me . . . everything.

This picture we were shooting in France was the second step forward for the Deal. But now something happened which was a step backward—indeed, the start of a fatal reverse action that was never to stop . . .

Jason Wormser discovered that the Baron and I had completed that first picture right under his nose. He now sent an emissary from Hollywood to Paris to talk with the Baron—to inform him that any work in my picture, and any future work the Baron would do for me, violated the contract Wormser held with the Baron. Wormser threatened to sue the Baron for fourteen million dollars to enforce that contract—let the chips (such as the Deal and me) fall where they might.

THE DEAL

This represented a severe conflict of interest for the Baron's unskilled and infrequently used business brain; but he was experienced enough to see one thing: The negative of that first picture was a danger to him personally as well as a tremendous source of money. He wasn't going to let Wormser ruin it. He just figured he'd steal the complete picture, negatives and all . . . and wait for the moment when it would be best for him to decide, for his own interests, what to do. The hell with everyone else! He'd hide this first negative . . . and hold it, blocking any move that Wormser—or old Jarnigan, his partner and "best friend"—could make.

The Baron figured he could pour oil on the troubled waters of the fourteen-million-dollar contract, and also go on making pictures with me, *if* he stayed away from Hollywood once the first negative was no longer an exposed pawn. The Baron didn't have to move up his knight to protect it—the Editor had already done that.

I was soon to discover what followed, through a report from my own man, who locked the barn door after the horse had been stolen. The Baron had sent Edwards, the Editor, not to Wormser, but to the laboratory where the negative was held.

He had the Baron's strict instructions, he had the use of the Baron's name—and he had a roll of cash as well, to convince anyone who might be reluctant to take the word of the Baron's well-known alter ego. Heaven help anyone who refused the persuasion and the cash; Edwards was known to be a crony of the Baron's "enforcer," Saul Baum. He was the Baronpope's emissary.

So, the Editor went to the laboratory where the negative was, and accomplished his mission of theft. He took that negative and sealed it in a vault in one of the many properties the Baron maintained throughout the world.

When I found out most of this, I realized there was nothing I could do right away, since we were in the middle of a multimillion-dollar motion picture. I would be ruined if the picture stopped for any reason—the more so without the security of distribution money from that first negative.

I felt—mistakenly, as it turned out—that I could remedy the situation after we completed the picture. On the surface, therefore, I was as friendly with the Baron as I had ever been, but a current of calculated hatred now began to flow not too far under the surface. And the Editor was in way over his depth now. It was as though he were at the bottom of the sea . . .

We had been shooting in the studio of Boulogne and the picture hadn't been going too badly. Then, right on cue—as it always happened—I got

206

the call from the production manager and the first assistant director to say the Baron was wanted on the set at seven o'clock that evening. I had told them to keep me personally informed when the Baron was needed. Then, I'd reel him in from wherever he was. I knew we had some night shooting to do, but it didn't seem to be anything too difficult. It was only four o'clock in the afternoon. I'd been doing the wrap-up on some film that we'd received from the second unit, shooting backgrounds for us in the south of France.

As usual, the cry for help started the same way. I got the call from Sam Neely, who said, "Jarn, you'd better come up here."

"Better come up where?"

"Well, you know. I've been keeping an eye on the Baron like you said. But it's not a question of keeping an eye on him now. You oughta be up here to see what's going on. And the way things are, I doubt if you'll have him around tonight. You told me to have him there for sure at six o'clock. Right?" he asked.

"That's right, I did. What's the problem, Sam?"

"Well, that American lawyer, the friend of the Baron and the Editor and two or three of the other crew—you know, Saul and some of the other fellows—have got a thing going on here that I don't think is very good. I can't handle it without causing a ruckus here in this hotel."

"Well, Sam, can't you tell me what it is, because I'd have to drive clear back in from Neuilly."

"Jarn, this is something only you can handle. Besides, I can't explain it to you on the phone. It's just that you . . . Well, I think you should come on in right away," he finished urgently.

"All right, Sam." I knew the way he said it something serious was up. "He's not . . . Is he blipped?" I asked.

"No, Jarn. He isn't. I'd have told you that. This is an entirely new kind of a situation and I just don't know how to handle it. There's so many people here and all . . ."

"Well, Sam, for Chri—stop being so mysterious and tell me—at least try to tell me what it is."

"Jarn, listen. Please come over. Please come up to the hotel."

"All right, Sam. It must be something or you wouldn't be acting like this. I'm leaving now." I hung up.

Not knowing what was going on, I told the secretary I'd be back in an hour. I went out of the studio office building, talked to the guard for a few minutes, made arrangements for setting up the shooting for the night. Told him to be sure and check with the production manager that everything was in order for the lynching scene, got in the car and started back to Paris.

It was beautiful driving through the Bois and I wondered what new son-of-a-gun of a thing could happen.

I drove up and parked the car in front of the George V. I went in, said hello to a couple of people I knew, got in the elevator, went up to the fifth floor. I knew where the Baron's suite was; but if I hadn't known, I would've been guided there by the noise. As I walked out of the large grilled elevator and turned left and started up the hall, walking on the heavy plush carpet leading to the master suites, several French people, couples, were grouped in the hall—laughing, giggling—it seemed to be a very gay affair. They were all speaking French, of course, and this is the way some of the conversation went:

"What a magnificence! Have you ever seen anything like it? Who would have believed . . . who would have believed . . ." a little girl with big eyes kept bleating.

Another Frenchman, who also had a chin that would never hit a wall before he walked into it, was saying, "I still think it's a very crude American joke. *Ils ne sont pas cultivés.* They have . . . they're not cultured at all, the Americans . . . *les sauvages* . . . *Ils sont tous des sauvages* . . ."

"You may think that is *sauvage*," said the little fluffy blonde, "I thought it was . . . I thought it was magnificent!"

Getting past this little group and their dippy conversation then, I saw a lot of other people—there must have been twenty in the other hall by now—laughing and talking. I saw that the end group, trailing like a bunch of ants, was banking to the right, into the living room of the Baron's suite.

At this moment, out pushed Saul Baum from the Baron's living room. "Hi, Jarn," he yelled drunkenly, "we've got something you'll be very pleased about."

At this, he was pushed aside, and the American attorney came out. Loaded. Full of himself. Full of over-slippery words. Another one of the guys who have the blind vanity that makes men so ready to believe themselves lovable, and capable, and full of the well-known article. He kept walking on, bumping the wall when he didn't bump into people, and said, "Jarn, my boy . . ." And as he said this, he was taking on some of the Baron's act of Jared Throne. "Jarn, we have come across a way to raise a considerable amount of money. You're a man who likes money, and who says, 'Now we have to sell this territory for this much' or 'We have to sell this country for this much.' We have come across a foolproof scheme of making money!" He leered at me drunkenly. \

By this time, I'd pushed past him and was in the living room. There they

THE DEAL

all were. I saw first of all my brother, looking around glassy-eyed, sitting there and smiling as if he'd just made a touchdown against Michigan State. He hardly noticed his girl, seated next to him, who was out, in every sense of the word, although she was sitting there.

It was then I saw that she was steadily and firmly holding onto my brief case, with all the bank notes and the distribution contracts in it. Her dress was up—but then, it always had been up. But my brother trusted her; that made it perfect.

The legal-eagle came over from across the room. He hiccuped. "Jarn boy," he said, "you can stop worrying. Old Iceman, I inform you that we have arrived at a foolproof way of making back the money that has been unfortunately misspent—shall we say—by the Baron's sometimes indisposition."

I gave him a look that should have killed him. I said coldly, "Well, what's going on? And why the hell couldn't you bring the Baron out?"

"Ahh," he said, taking half a step back and giving me a courtly little bow.

I had noticed that everyone took on the Baron's little picture-mannerisms when they got tanked. It seemed contagious.

"Out is exactly what the Baron is. But even in a prone and out position, he is making you money."

I pushed past him and went farther on into the suite. I could see everyone drunk—all of the people trying to be at ease, all very motion-picture and Paris royalty–wise. They were eating at the trough, daintily dropping hors d'ouvres on all the rugs—and all of this, of course, on the budget of my picture. There was a guy sitting on the floor in the corner, talking loudly into the telephone. He kept saying, "Operator, operator . . . *non, non, anglais* . . . I want the overseas operator . . . I just been cut off from California. I've just been cut off. Now, I want . . . I said I want . . . Now listen, sister, do you know who . . ."

I walked over behind the davenport and pulled out the jack to disconnect the phone. This guy never noticed. He kept right on talking and said continuously, "Listen, sister . . . am I connected? Now, speak louder . . . I heard you laugh . . . speak louder. Get hot . . . snap it up."

I pushed through the rest of the people, walked down the corridor of the suite and went into the little library. Happily, no one was there except a very pretty girl who was out, completely, and lying on the floor in what I thought was a very casual position, her dress up to her hips. The noise and the babble that was going on in the room and in the far room had pumped up drunken laughter. Good Christ, I thought, I can't blow it now. I just can't blow it now. I've got to keep the lid on this thing. The wrap-up on this picture's almost complete. But, good blessed Christ, I'm tired. I'm tired of it all. I'm tired like a criminal trying to write a letter begging for his life. An important letter—but the pages are damp, and the writing's blurred. The film's out of focus. I'm blurred. The whole lousy world is blurred.

At this point, the babble became so loud at one end of the room I took a last look at the girl, who hadn't moved, then walked out of the library and down the hall to the Baron's bedroom. This obviously was the main attraction. "Well, it can't be any worse than some of the other times." I prayed my lopsided prayer. I took a deep breath, walked into the bedroom and there they were. They were something to see.

Pushing my way past about fifteen people in the room, I saw the Baron's king-size bed, and on it—in a state of complete drunkenness or horsedness; or any one of the things that got him blipped—the Baron was out, and lying so flat on the bed he looked like he'd been pressed. A few drunks were there, a few very distinguished-looking people; then, looking around again, I was surprised to see standing in the corner the Editor, and somehow or other, Saul Baum had come in the other way. And here again was the Baron's American attorney. All in high spirits. All completely loaded.

It was a gala atmosphere—that is to say, for all except me. Now I understood why, in meeting, the French couple down the hall had laughed and why the two or three other couples had been giggling and laughing uproariously. Because only now did I notice that the Editor, Saul Baum, and the American attorney each had a fistful of French francs. The bills were intertwined in their fingers as though they had been in a crap game. Then I got the whole picture as I saw Saul Baum delicately remove a hundred-franc note from a man, and another hundred-franc note from a woman—and he grandly gestured them past the foot of the Baron's bed as though they were walking past a coffin to pay their respects to a corpse—a loved departed one.

I went a couple of steps closer, and saw that the Baron was carefully dressed in his dark blue silk pajamas—and there, disguised, was the plastic bat, the false dong, peeking coyly out from his pajamas. And, about four inches down, tied around the middle, there was a blue ribbon, properly bowed—all arranged with the Baron's bathrobe. It was the most fantastic, nightmarish sight you could see.

This obviously had been a work of art. I could see from the gibberish and the gibbering that was going on among Saul, the Editor, and the attorney that this had been their idea. They were all in high spirits, happily

THE DEAL

continuing to take in the hundred-franc notes. They had been selling tickets to anyone in the hotel; and had told them to pass the word. Anyone on the Champs Elysées or in the George V who would like to see the Baron quiet; and would like to see the dong of the Baron, the celebrated movie star— one hundred francs, and you can take your look. Bring your girl! Bring your friends! What an afternoon! What a chancred hell!

It seemed that the tour started in the living room, through the corridor into the Baron's bedroom; then back through the Baron's bathroom and into the hallway that led through the living room and outside the door—it was a sort of full circle. Saul Baum had by now taken in quite a bit of money; he'd been the business manager.

I couldn't believe it.

It was at this time that a young woman who'd paid her hundred francs walked past the Baron, leading her boyfriend. She leaned down closer. Her lover jerked her back. "What a *splendide . . . quel monstre!*" Her eyes glistened. The guy jerked her around and led her forcibly out of the room.

I turned around, slammed one of the doors and said loudly, "All right. Out! Everybody. *Sortez!*"

There was a confused yet shrill babble starting. *"Mais; mon argent. J'ai payé . . ."*

Everyone laughing (a hell-scene by Brueghel). But then they saw the look on my face. They became vaguely uneasy and not a little disappointed. Slowly, they began backing up and wandering down the hall. I slammed the other door. There was no one left except Saul Baum, the Editor, the attorney, and myself. The babbling continued—about how many fans would be disappointed. French and American clientele would be so pleased to see something they could truly boast about and remember. The attorney told me that the agent had now said this was a foolproof way to raise money at any time, if we wanted to make more pictures.

I stood there, numb. This was more of a nightmare than I could believe. I turned to the attorney and said, "Listen, come over here. I want to talk to you. . . . Saul, you know you'd better get the Baron straightened out."

Just then there was a rapping on the door and, forcibly entering, there appeared the French attorney of the Baron, Jean Dupont Durand. He had now become a bosom buddy of the Baron's American attorney. So they were both there, looking at me, seeing my anger.

They watched me carefully. I went over and grabbed a blanket, threw it over the Baron, and said to Saul, "You'd better start to sober him up. Now I'm not going to tell you again. And get that thing away and clean him up."

There was another loud banging on the door and in walked Hugh Blood-

211

test's brother (actually, he said he was his nephew; but he looked like his father). As an actor he had failed. As an agent he had made it. But his success was qualified by his big weakness. He had a crude, undisciplined, yet crafty mind. He was vain, too self-assertive and a liar. Yet he was gangster-style smooth. A slick and pretty licker lad, a braggart who was at the mercy of his own egotism. *De la merde dans un bas de soie.*

He pushed his way in and said, "What's this? What's this? I heard about this. It's all over Paris. What a disgrace. Jarnigan, do you know that this could break your contract with the Baron? The morals clause, you know."

"Listen, just either get out or sit down. Because I've got a couple of things to say to this baby here"—indicating the American attorney.

At this time, Jean Dupont Durand said, speaking French, "It would seem to me, Monsieur Jarnigan, that we all must, at this point, keep our heads. If I may, I should like to point out the certain difficulties that have arisen in the past between the Baron and yourself . . ."

"*Merde,*" I said. "I don't want, and I do not permit conversation now. Too much has to be done."

Hugh Bloodtest's nephew-brother said, "I insist that . . ." He lost his head for a minute. We started to have an argument; and the argument became a little louder and a little more bitter.

Then young Bloodtest, who was the Baron's guardian on behalf of the big agency in the United States, started to say things. Things and words came out of his mouth; he was surprised how brave he was. He finished this vocal tirade with, "And listen, Jarnigan, you may be the hot boy-genius producer here, but to carry on this way and think you'll continue to shoot the picture, I say No, and No again. I won't stand for it!"

I took a look at this fellow and looked at the rest of them in the room. I walked toward him three steps—he backed up two, and couldn't go any farther because he had hit the wall.

"Listen, sweetheart," I said quietly. "You'll stand, sing, jump for Jesus, or ride a bicycle if I want you to. Have you got that straight? Now, I don't want any more crap!"

At this, the tough guy Saul, whose bread and butter was with the studio and with the agency, who made his living from the big operations he thought he was helping the Baron out on, stood up quickly. He wasn't sure he was going to do anything, but being a big man, he felt better on his feet. He growled, "Somebody is going to get somebody's face pushed into the floor. Did you say crap?"

I spun around and looked at him. I must have been more mad than I thought, because Saul took a half a step back. I snarled at him, "Crap, and more crap! Crap's what I said, and crap's what I meant; you save your tough-guy dialogue for the stunt men in the back room. And keep the rest of the mushy stuff to yourself."

He said uncertainly, "Jarn, did you ever get knocked on your ass?"

I looked at him for a minute—something had to break. I grinned, coldly, "Not by anybody your weight, baby."

Here the agent half turned. Then Saul Baum turned away and said, "Oh, you're always kidding. You know, Jarn, sometimes you get a guy so upset."

"Well, now, you just take it easy, Saul. Take your boyfriend and get out of here, after you've sobered up the Baron. You'll be around a long time, Saul boy. You know where it's buried. You've got your wick dipped in here. So, take it easy . . . yeah, take it easy."

By this time my cup was really running over because, right on cue, in walked the French associate producer. So this made our group, after the departure of Saul and young Bloodtest: the French banker, the French attorney, and the French producer.

I stood there and looked at the producer; then I started to hear the static. He was annoyed and said, "Monsieur Jarnigan, you are violating my rights with this—display."

"Display, hell," I said. "What did I display? I came up here to try and break up something."

"I must insist again on my rights. This is not the way to conduct a motion picture of this magnitude. If one more thing happens, or if the repercussions of this are too devastating, I will be forced to withdraw."

I walked over to the other side of the room, looked around for a cigar, couldn't find one, took a deep breath, and came back; said, "Now I want to tell you babies something, and I'm speaking to you, Monsieur Dupont Durand, and your French producer-friend here, who hasn't produced anything except children the last five years that I've known him. This is the first time he's had a chance to really be associated with a real film, and up to now he's had a cakewalk."

The French producer drew himself up to his full height of five feet four and said, "This is not the manner in which you should address me and my *avocat*."

I looked down at him coldly. "Well, now, I'll tell you something—it's like this with me. I'm a *gangster américain* producer and nobody likes me. And if I don't have enough problems with this picture, I've got to have you cutting up on me. Now it's not bad enough that I have to deal with gangsters, syndicate men from the Swiss group, fags, pimps, former government officials from the Centre du Cinéma; I have to deal with stars, actresses, whores, phony nurses, lawyers of every breed, and distributors of every ilk. I spend my life here in Paris going over dirty deals, under-the-table pay-offs, bribes; listening to purple lies, smelling lousy breaths. If I finally get the picture through, it's the star, it's the Baron, or it's the director, or it's the French producer who made the picture good. But if it's bad, it's *my* picture—the script was no good, so I'm in error, it's the American pro-ducer's fault. Then, some shyster lawyer—and we're standing awfully close to one—finds ten ways to get out from under the distribution contract, and then sues me. But that's not enough. With all of this, I've got to have you giving me the double cross. *Quels cons!"*

I walked out and down the hall, leaving them standing there. I looked in the library. The pretty girl had apparently pulled down her dress and had gone. There was only Saul Baum. He walked out and I saw young Blood-test. He'd changed from the arrogance he'd had when he made the entrance in the Baron's bedroom. He didn't quite know what was going to happen. I looked at him thoughtfully for a minute; I didn't say anything. I saw the sweat start to break out underneath the hair that he had painted on over his head.

"Jarn," he said. "I'm sorry I blew up in there. I got excited. But you know, the Baron being our big client and all—you know how Hugh is . . ."

"Yeah, yeah, Nathan, I know how he is."

"You're not gonna tell him everything I said, are you?" Nathan said ner-vously.

"I don't know. I don't know."

"How can I square this, Jarn? How can I make this up to you? You know I don't want any more trouble."

I looked at him thoughtfully. "Well, maybe there is a way you can dig yourself out of this," I told him.

"How, Jarn . . . how?" he said, too quickly. "I want to watch my step."

"It's not your step you should watch; it's the back of your lap."

He looked fearfully at me. "You know," I told him almost affectionately, "this independent picture racket is not for stupes. You've got to have both money and brains and the ability to handle people. One doesn't work with-out the other. But you know, blowing up at a producer—especially in front of some people who are halfway important—and probably being in on this deal with the selling of the tickets for the Baron's dong-showing, little things like this and that . . . it don't make for a friendship and understand-ing and compassion between us."

THE DEAL

He looked at me nervously. "I understand, I understand." He trembled. "What can I do, Jarn?"

"Well, for openers, you can reach down in that brief case of yours and give me the amendments to the Baron's contract. I know you've got them. You've been carrying them around for the last three days." He looked at me with frightened eyes. "Okay, Nate, if that's the way you want to play it. I guess I'm gonna call Hugh and blow the whistle."

He grabbed the case. He rooted around in it for a while. Snorted around some more. He raised his little pig head, looked out of his little pig eyes and oinked, "I don't seem to find it, It doesn't seem to be here."

He was a short half-square-shaped fellow, getting shorter and squarer by the minute. His face was now gray-green. He looked like a small bazooka, and to complete the illusion, he leaned backward when he spoke. He aimed carefully, blooping his words at me. The words whizzed and whooshed and shot forward from the pig snout of a mouth; he would have liked to spit— cannoned me to death with his agent's talk—but he knew I had him. And this time his face really paled.

"I don't have it, Jarn. I don't have it." He looked at me.

I just stood there staring at him. I turned my head to one side and said, "I heard an ambulance siren."

"Hell," he said, "there aren't any sirens around here. This is France. They have that *wha-wha*—What are you talking about, Jarn? Anyway, I don't hear a thing. Ha, ha . . ." He laughed weakly.

"Well, that figures," I said, looking at him sadly. He got the look. "You'd be the one guy in the world that wouldn't hear it."

He became more pale. "You're making that up. You don't hear any ambulance. You don't hear anything."

I gave him a steady, thoughtful grin and walked out. He was worried. And so was I.

When I got back into the living room, my brother got up, came over toward me. He handed me my brief case and said, "There, everything's there. I've been sitting here waiting for you."

"Fine, boy, fine," I said. My poor brother . . . he hadn't even seen me come in.

Sam Neeley came through the living room door. "Jarn . . ."

I said, "Everything's all right, Sam. Help me get these people out of here. The Baron's in there. Saul Baum says he'll get him sobered up. Will you see that they get to the studio? I'll have something else lined up, ready to shoot. But get him there by eight o'clock. Ready for work. Can I rely on you, Sam? Or a call from you by seven?"

"You know me, Jarn," Sam said, looking at me less worried now. "He'll be there. He'll be there or I'll call. You look worried."

"Ha. Not me, not me. I'm going on back now. Have him there, huh?"

"He'll be there, Jarn, I promise."

My brother looked at me again. "What can I do, kid? What can I do?"

"Well, why don't you stick around and help Sam, and I'll see you back at the studio, okay?"

"Okay, boy. I'm glad that everything's under control."

"Sure, everything's fine. Everything's just fine."

I walked out the door. Rode the elevator down. Walked through the lobby. Same faces. Same babble. The only strange face that was in that hotel lobby was the occasional dog that got in by accident.

I was out on the street. Got in my car. Drove up the Avenue Georges Cinq. Took a left. Went up the Champs Elysées. Around the Arc and the Etoile and down the Avenue de Neuilly on the way back to the studio. I was grateful to be alone. But, as always, I had to start thinking. An artsy-craftsy producer. What was I in now? Praise the soulless producer. Damn the soulful writer. If you try both, you're lost.

> Mingle, mangle, mingle . . .
> How my chances tingle.
> Down with gold and up with Hell.
> My thoughts ding—dangle—dingle.

Well, old Jarn praises God for "perhaps" some dingled-talent to now go to work on script number three for the Baron, and sort the leprosy out. I know the Baron won't be in any shape for the good script tonight, but I thank God, and feel to kiss that gentle hand that has led me into this written world, even though it's empty and lonely. I don't want to come and go only once through this world, to trifle and piddle away dignity, love, everything, for the sake of fifty thousand feet of film. It's a thing to weep over. I wonder how I do it. I sit back. I watch me eat, drink, dress, love, hate. I watch me act. I hear my voice, well controlled . . .

"Actors," I hum beautifully, "how simple and unaware you are of your good fortune to be in the same world as I. Actors, here is some free advice: When dealing with deadly producers, avoid flatterers, con-men, and the quick and ready lovers. They are thieves in disguise. Their flattery is expensive. They lie to flatter. They flatter to cheat. They flatter to lie. And what is worse—you believe them."

216

THE DEAL

Here I was jarred out of any more thinking, because I had almost hit a truck. No loss there. "So, actors, don't let your opportunity go wandering on the wind, because then you are loose and unguarded. You do wrong to others and to yourself." I thought of the Baron.

I knew if he was sober I would tell him tonight, before we started shooting . . . *if* he was sober . . .

"Baron, some of you is still a man. However, most of you is not a man, but rather a shapeless pigmy who walks asleep in a fog, searching for his own alarm clock fixed to a bomb. And you, Baron, somehow manage to find it, then set it off, always. You are like an old serpent that can't shed its skin; so you call all others naked and orgylike and try to emulate them. You call them shameless while you, in your own lonely and uncertain security, stand in the sunlight with your back to the sun, and see only your own shadow and are guided by it. Break up the chill that encloses your understanding of others, because your pain, your hell, is self-chosen. It's selected with love, but your kind of pick-nose love. Baron, let's finish this picture, then you go your way, and I'll go mine. Roll your own hoop, and I'll roll mine . . ."

O wind from the south,
Blow mud in the mouth
Of the Baron, the Baron, the Baron.

I've found all the old clichés are true . . . You can't break the rules. You can't ignore the world.

The Baron was the guy for whom they coined the phrase "as ignorant as an actor." How much more could I take? How much more could I support? I had so much wanted this picture to be good, to be worth while. A man has to, at some time in his life, fix all his brain, all his strength, all his soul, all his being, on one thing. A deal, a woman, or a thing that must absorb him completely. It wasn't a woman or a thing in my case—it was only the Deal . . . this mother-of-a-Deal.

● ● ●

We had finished shooting the interiors of the picture in Paris and were returning to the south of France to take the exteriors—all on a boat. The Baron had made arrangements to have his yacht moored in the yacht basin at Monaco.

Just at this time of strain and resentment at the Baron's behavior, I had

217

a fluke accident, and it was the Baron who showed some right and decent manners in the emergency.

I was riding in the camera truck. We were photographing the Baron in some scenes on street location sites, when we were sideswiped by a little red sports car.

It was a terrific-looking wreck. Members of the crew were stretched out in the street like stranded starfish. Most just had the wind knocked out of them; but you would have taken them for victims of an Afrika Corps tank battle.

Both my legs were banged up pretty severely, but by the time the story hit the French newspapers and international wires, a notorious American producer was dying in Nice.

The Baron was on the transatlantic telephone instantly, calling my mother in Beverly Hills; while I was still in a rage about how much money this delay would cost us.

"Dear Lady Jarnigan"—I was able to reconstruct his call without too much difficulty, as the Baron could draw an audience even in a telephone booth—"it's the Baron. I want you to know that the news of Jarn's unfortunate accident is greatly exaggerated. He's bruised a little; but no worse than after a football game. In a couple of days, we'll call you again, together. Meanwhile, you needn't worry, I'm staying right with him. After all, he is my best friend as well as my partner.

"But, if you feel any anxiety at all, do not hesitate to call me at my private number, which is Balzac 45-46. I am leaving word that whenever you may call, they are to locate me at once, so that I may be at your complete disposal. I do this because I have respect and feeling for you; in fact, a feeling as if Jarn were my own brother. Good night, Lady Jarnigan . . . or, as we say in French, *bonsoir*."

By the time I was back on the set, the Baron somewhat undid the splendid impression he made on me at that time by going AWOL; and I had to send out Sam Neely to drag every bar in town. But I couldn't deny that he had really done the decent thing in fine style when that red sports car hit the camera truck.

He was a hard guy to hate. Just as you had him labeled a hundred percent son-of-a-bitch, he'd come on with some performance like calling my mother so she wouldn't worry. It sure kept you up on your acrobacy.

About this time, a sex goddess from Italy had caught up with him, and being fairly smashed at the end of one of these parties, he had been unable to make his getaway and leave her peeing on the rug as he had with the Hollywood sex goddess.

And, unlike my own ripe-superstar episode, when I'd wanted an actress's talents rather than her body, the poor Baron wanted any female body small enough to complement him.

Yet he had been absolutely trapped by this Italian overblown, over-eager beauty. I almost felt sorry for him. She made her mouth and her eyes up with broad, overgenerous strokes. I had been told she had a big overgenerous everything. Her sex, like her mouth, was overworked. She had a smile.

Later, upstairs in the big house where the party was going on she finally, literally, trapped the Baron in the bedroom. This is what was happening then . . .

They were both pretty tight and she was trying to get him to do what he would never be able to do—and, if by some horrible accident they did—"nothing."

After "nothing" happened, she left. When she didn't come back right away, the Baron stumbled up and out, went to look for her. He came back . . . he'd never be satisfied. He knew she was gone forever, even if she came back. But back she came, and now the payoff. She lisped, played cute, said, "Baby's got to widdle." This pearl was tossed over to the Baron, who was by now back on the bed. He watched her leave for the bathroom. She went out with almost everything sagging.

He got up off the bed and lurched over to the large mirror in the *placard*. He looked at himself, and he turned away, his chin, his belly and his morals slipping lower with each breath. He looked back in the mirror at his bloated face and he knew that he'd be too tired to accept what would certainly be offered him.

Later . . . together . . . he, trying to do what he couldn't do; and between them, all the love that could be generated by hot sweat, hot breath, hot love, and a lot of blemishes disclosed—they swung along in a tight-assed, girdle-packed, gut-shot stupid way . . . not even worthy of dying.

The Baron turned over on his back. His eyes were out of focus, but he forced the look to come; as he hadn't been able to force the other to do. But he was still the big star, was still ready for the big deal, and he'd just got laid. Not lovingly, not nicely, not even very successfully; but he had halfway taken the trip, and that was great for him. This was the life . . . hot damn!

● ● ●

THE DEAL

I was still looking for the Baron. Sam was trying a couple of other spots. I had been waiting hopefully a long time for Sam to return from his search. We had looked everywhere for the Baron. Finally, I gave up but Sam Neely wanted to try one last place. This was the Mars Club—an American club on the Rue Marbeuf. Now, the only reason Sam wanted to look in there was the piano player, a grand fellow named Art Simmons, a friend of ours who played songs from time to time from some of the Baron's first pictures. And at a certain level of drunkenness, the Baron went nostalgic, thought of his younger days and would sit there in maudlin silence nodding his head with the rhythm.

I had had my secretary call the Mars Club earlier and check. No Baron. I knew the owner well and knew that they would say the truth if he was there and lie with a clear and innocent face if the Baron said "Don't you tell Monsieur Jarnigan." But old Sam wouldn't give up. He knew how important it was for me to have the Baron at the studio the next day. Now if I had wanted the Baron hunted down and beaten up, it would have been the same thing so far as Sam was concerned.

The waiting continued. The rain started. It beat down heavily on the top of the Rolls. It was a heavy constant muted hum. It started to mist up the windshield. I switched on the ignition and started the air blower so I could see out. The patch of glass cleared so that I could see framed perfectly a large photograph of General Charles de Gaulle in a stern yet arrogant pose; this was in a window across the street from where the Rolls was parked. Looking more closely you could see his dislike of the Americans and everything that wasn't French. This *constipe* expression was in every wrinkle of the sneer. De Gaulle for France. France for De Gaulle. He would sneer tall and heavy-footed, trying with an arrogance to stamp his rubber-heeled marks on the pages of French history. He needn't worry. He'd be in all the books . . . one way or another.

The time kept going by. The rain kept coming down and I was getting cold. I didn't want to turn on the heater. I remembered I had a flask of brandy in the glove compartment for emergencies. I declared a state of that, opened the glove compartment, reached in and lifted out the heavy silver-and-leather flask, a gift from an admirer who happened to have the same name as myself. Myself gave myself a drink. It warmed me and I looked out at De Gaulle. The rain was still coming down heavily and De Gaulle looked wet and disgusted, but he still had the sneer. "Sorry, Charles," I said, "I can't offer you one." I treated myself to another libation and that took part of the sneer out of Charlie's face.

The minutes pattered by and the rain pattered down. I sat there quietly.

THE DEAL

As the brandy went down in the flask, warmth and high good humor arose. I waited and drank, and drank and waited. De Gaulle's sneer changed to a look of benevolence, of kindness. If he'd been real I'd have gone over and offered him a drink and now I was certain that he would have accepted it with good grace—grand old Charlie De. So would a lot of Frenchmen offer him a drink with good grace—if he were real.

I heard the sound of footsteps. The door swung open. Sam had come back at last—"empty-Baron-ed." I poured him a drink, then I made my proposal with respect to Grand Old Charlie De. I wanted to make him a present of my flask. One head of state to another. Now Sam didn't agree with me that we should leave the flash for Charlie De. I made another suggestion which Sam vetoed. I succumbed to Sam's wishes and good judgment. He had pointed out, with remarkable restraint, "You know, Jarn, the *gendarmerie* might take a dim view of pouring brandy under De Gaulle's picture and lighting it as an honorary flame. I don't like your suggestion, Mr. Jarnigan, sir, no matter how festive we both might feel and no matter how festive you think the occasion is. And besides," Sam added with his usual clear-headedness, "with all this rain it wouldn't light."

I nodded my head in agreement and saw wisdom in Sam's point of view. Whereupon I promptly appointed Sam an associate producer on the picture for his grand ideas, his ingenuity and calmness in time of stress. Sam took the honor with dignity and calm, properly aware of the solemnity of the occasion. You see, Sam had been promoted and demoted so many times, the escalator moving him up or down, that his titles as producer or associate producer or his position left him strangely unmoved. Sam realized with his cold and absolute wisdom, his superb confidence in himself, and his thorough knowledge of me, that he was a sought-after motion picture executive. He also knew that at any time if he or if I, Jarnigan, wished, he could knock anyone on their ass. So with this self-assurance and our eternal friendship securely locked and bolted, Sam was probably the most well-balanced person on the Deal. Certainly the nicest.

Old Sam didn't need to knock anyone on his ass on this occasion. Later we were called to pick up the Baron, who was now at the Mars Club as Sam had figured, only a little behind schedule. He was gloriously drunk in a back room, with Art Simmons playing that great piano. We got the Baron back into the picture; and the Deal went on to our second movie—our next location right in Paris.

• • •

THE DEAL

It was a lovely morning. There is a smell, or rather a scent, about Paris that in spite of all the words written can never truly be described. I walked down the Rue Pierre Charron. I turned right at the Rue François Premier. Just across the street a man was taking out a huge piece of ice from the back of a wagon. The horse stamped his feet casually at the early morning flies, his hooves, rubber-shod, making very little sound. The man crossed the street, careful to avoid the calling cards left by the dogs who for some reason chose this spot to relieve themselves. They were being walked by the *jeune assistant* to the hotel concierge, the porter from the George V Hotel. I guess it was a kind of "dog sporting club." The iceman tenderly placed the block of ice beside the five other blocks and went inside the *crémerie*.

A few moments later he came outside with a sturdy girl in a white smock, black heavy wool stockings, and wooden sabots on her feet. She checked the ice. The man nodded, then touched his cap in a salute, leaned over and whispered something to the girl. She laughed and gave him a playful shove. This social exchange completed, he turned around, took one step, then stepped back and smacked her familiarly on the *derrière,* then started back to his wagon, laughing. She turned to look at him, a look of false indignation on her face, her arms akimbo. He saluted again and clucked to the big horse, who started off down the street with slow dignity. The girl watched them a moment, then she turned and went back into the *crémerie.*

Down the street and across from the *crémerie* there was a *boulangerie.* Out of its door came a fat girl in a blue work dress. She was loaded with bread. She had two loaves high up under each arm. These were the long thin loaves commonly called *baguettes.* As she walked she continually kept hitching them up higher under her armpits. A sack which probably held *croissants* was daintily carried in her hand and as she passed me, I looked again to make sure—yes, I could see after a little more walking with the bread in the position it was, it should be well buttered with Mum or Arrid or some other deodorant—if she used any.

As she walked across the street directly in front of the *crémerie,* she carefully walked around the puddle of water from the melting ice. The large puddle of water on the sidewalk was augmented by a small dog, not of the George V variety, not a walked-by-the-hotel-porter type, but a real French mongrel. He looked around carefully, walked by the ice, looked it over for birthmarks, and then, stepping nearer, raised his leg and peed daintily over two of the blocks of ice. The girl with the bread, now a little soggy under her arms, chided him gently, absently, but the *crémerie* girl came charging out of the store and chided him with a kick in the butt, losing a sabot in the process. The dog left hurriedly with no dignity whatsoever, the *crémerie* girl limped over to get her shoe, then coming back she took a broom from inside the door and "dusted off" the two blocks of peed-on ice. The spray, faintly yellow, wafted away pleasantly in the new gentle warm air of the lovely Paris morning.

Taking all this in I walked past the *crémerie* and down to the corner of Rue François Premier and the Rue Pierre Charron to the Frontenac bar and the outside café where the waiters were just starting to put out the chairs. I walked over and sat down. I was tired. We had worked on the picture all night. I knew that I would be unable to sleep after all the excitement that had taken place during the past twenty-four hours.

A waiter came over, looking sleepy. He said, *"Monsieur?"*

I said, *"Je voudrais café."*

"Okay," he said, showing me he knew that I was an American. He knew that the Paris American Legion was only four doors away. See, the French are linguists too.

He came back in a moment with the coffee and I said, "Would you bring me a large brandy."

"Okay," he said again and turned back to get it. In a moment he returned with a large cognac, a siphon of soda, and a little bucket of ice.

I took a sip of the strong black coffee, looked up at him casually and said, *"Pas de glace . . .* no ice."

"Oh," he looked at me. *"Monsieur est anglais?"*

"No," I replied in French, "it's just that I am an admirer of dogs and have profound respect for those noble beasts." His eyes watched me warily. He looked me over carefully.

"Comment?" he said.

"No ice," I continued, *"pas de glace.* It's bad for the digestion, especially this morning."

"Okay," he said again. He walked away from me and back into the restaurant. I watched him through the window and could see he was explaining this to the other waiter. With the window open, I could hear them talking; then the other waiter took two steps toward the window so he could see me better. He turned back, saying to the first waiter, *"Alors, qu'est-ce que tu veux? Il est un Americain."* I laced my coffee with some of the brandy and took a sip. I was thinking of the party on the set last night, or rather early this morning, when we finished the shooting in Paris and were getting ready for the whole company to go down to Cannes and Nice to do the exteriors of the film. The party was to have been co-hosted by the French co-producer and the Baron and myself. I stood there shaking hands, smiling, talking, I was a thousand miles away. I could tell from having seen the first hour and forty minutes of the picture that there was much to be done. The film was almost over and unless other tragedies struck it was certain to be a commercial success, my friends and my critics would like it, especially if it made money, and I would make myself a lot of money—but as I looked sadly into the glass of brandy I knew within myself: the story stank, the stars stank, the Deal smelled. It was all turning into something kind of piddling, a nothing. But we have to say it like it is, there will always be someone to tell you better. So in this early Paris morning and along the quiet street, not a creature was stirring . . . as the fellow said. I sat there and got quiet, like the street.

I was trying to get a great writer to write me out of the corner I had gotten myself into. For enough dough, he might do it—and he was vain and arrogant enough for it to be a challenge. As I put in the overseas call to him at his ranch, I remembered a story about him . . .

Ernie Bush had walked Walter Winkler to death.

· Bush knew that Walt had a dangerous heart condition. But Walt had made a picture from one of this great writer's short stories. It was a success. Walt was married to one of the most beautiful singers in the world. Bush had always liked her, was jealous in a bearlike way; always saying to Mrs. Walt, "Daughter, if I could only rid myself, and you, of this husband! How, then that you were free, would I spirit you off to my cave in the mountains!" Then he'd grin and hit Walt too hard on the back. Walt would accept it all with pained good grace. Mrs. Walt would look sweet and sad, and you didn't know what she thought. She would sit there and look from one man to the other . . . weighing, judging, deciding. She had one . . . she could have the other . . .

They had finished talking and turned to her. She gave them the nice, yet inviting smile—the secret looks, one for each—and agreed they should all go on to dinner. But, that was then, this was now . . .

And Bush was up at his ranch in Arizona in the Cochise mountains. Snow, skiing, fires, brandy, every agreeable thing that Bush loved—and that Walt loved, too; but it would kill him, and he knew it. Still, he would risk it because he had to have Bush's other stories. Bush was going to give him the stories . . . for a price. He knew it would probably kill Walt. But, hell . . . weren't his stories, Bush's stories, worth dying for? By Christ, he had almost died writing them! No help or friendly-lighted friendship then. Bush laughed, Walt laughed—Bush set out to kill him.

He started systematically to do this after he got the call. Susan, Walt's

THE DEAL

wife, called and told Bush that Walt's doctor had said: "No booze, no excitement, no exercise—or he'll step off. He'll take the big one." Bush laughed and said he understood. He hung up. He grinned.

He went back into the living room, got out a bottle of brandy, said, "Walt, let's have a charge . . . what say, boy?"

"Can't," grinned Walt, in that sick grin he had now—not the brash, cocky smile he wore when on the *New York Banner* and was younger, dumber. "The doc says no booze, broads, excitement or exercise." He glanced at Bush, then continued, "Yeah, he gave me my four 'don'ts'. No B. B., no E. E."

"Sounds like a shit," Bush said dryly, "a real dry-assed doc. Hell," he boomed, "my doc says brandy is great for a heart condition, and he's the best." Here Bush looked coldly at Walt, then said conversationally, "I hate soft people." He added quietly, "I don't like to drink alone, either."

"Hell," Walt said quickly, a flush rising to his pale face. "I'll take a little charge with you, Ernie. The damm sawbones only says No to everything and sends a bill; sometimes I think he'd give me an aspirin for a brain tumor, ha, ha." He brayed weakly, then got a look of the concentrated tough-guy-producer manner: "Hell, I'll take a couple with you. A drinker I am, soft I ain't." He glanced quickly at the great writer to see how he was taking it.

Bush just stood there, a little dry amused grin on his face; and poured them each a big one. "After a couple more—"Walt, there's a slope I want you to see. Did you ever ski at night?" Ernie asked.

"Oh, no, Ernie," Walt said quickly. "I don't ski well, or at all, anymore. You know . . ." he finished weakly.

"Well, hell, Walt, let's don't ski then. If you're weak and can't ski, hell, I'm not going to force you—but, you can *walk*, can't you?" he asked sullenly, his deep voice filled with disgust.

Walt looked furtively around the room, then up at Ernie's glowering face. There was no escape. He gulped down his brandy, then stood up. "Hell, yes, I can walk," he said, more loudly now, his face dangerously flushed from the brandy. He took three steps across to where Ernie was standing and thrust out his glass. He leered. "Let's have another charge of that brandy, Ern, and then show me your damned ski slope."

Ernie poured Walt the brandy, then filled his own glass. From then on, they had drink for drink. Later, bundled up against the snow, with heavy shoes on, Ernie said to Walt, "You're my kind of man, partner." He slapped Walt heavily on the back. Walt felt a little twinge in his chest.

"Let's go, pard," Ernie roared and started out the door, into the cold and the snow and the beautiful night. "It's only about a mile, Walt boy. Let's hit it!"

Walt looked around the shelter of the huge living room, with the warmth of the fire quiet and inviting. All calm.

"You coming, partner?" Ernie called back loudly.

"I'm with you, Ernie," Walt called back, more quietly . . . and walked out the door to his death.

"Come Dancer, come Prancer, come Donner and Blitzen . . . On Comet, on Cupid—hold it! On second thought, we won't need the reindeer," Ernie said, to no one. "Just take Old Dobbin and the sleigh . . . the producer-man isn't going anywhere. Tom!" he roared to his handyman, "Go down and pick the body of the producer up—the son-of-a-bitch dropped dead on me! You don't need to hurry—he won't get any colder—put him in the saddle room on a trestle. I'll take care of the rest tomorrow." The "rest" being the producer's body.

You see, the producer had left everything and everyone down there on the snow-covered ski slope. He was no longer here, so what was done with the rest—faster or slower, sooner or later—was exquisitely unimportant to the writer, to anyone.

Ernie stood in front of the fire, thoughtfully drinking his brandy. He said aloud, "I guess I'd better go call Susan Winkler. She'll need someone to console her now that Walt is gone. Poor Walt. Terrible. Terrible." He went over and picked up the phone. He smiled, and gave the number.

• • •

Now, I must admit we were making pretty fair progress on the second movie. The trouble was the Baron was also making progress in the wrong direction with these little European girls. He was not overly discreet. In fact, he was over-donging it from Paris to Monaco—as always, more and more interested in his off-stage life.

It didn't take a genius like me—ha! ha!—to know that his luck was running out, and that one of these little bastards might blow our Deal right out of the water. The Baron was horny and stupid—I was arrogant and stupid—and the great axe fell. The mini-cooze and the frigging booze were running us out of time . . . out of the world, on the Baron's "horse."

The latest was in the little French coastal town of Villefranche. A thing happened which is unbelievable but none the less true. Far off in Paris, over twelve hundred kilometers from the scene of the "rape," I was

226

trying to finish up some work on the distribution contracts for the film and making arrangements where to place the money. I was sitting in my beautiful private office with the paneled walls and antique furniture and the fireplace burning the wooden blocks that the French had taken up after the war and stored in various fuel yards. (The wooden blocks had been on the boulevards completing the Etoile and had for years been soaked with gasoline, oil, etc., and burned beautifully.) It was a cold day, not quite making up its mind whether it would snow or not. Old Felix the concierge came in, arranged the fire quietly and went out, and as the dictation progressed the French-Italian secretary from the outer office came in and said, *"Monsieur Jarnigan, je m'excuse* . . . excuse me . . . There is an *avocat* with a *gendarme.* They say they await to see you on a matter of great urgency."

I looked up from my desk, wondering what the hell could this be about, and as the secretary continued telling me this, the door to my private office was suddenly pushed open and in walked a lawyer about the size of Toulouse-Lautrec. He wouldn't go more than four feet tall. He had a beard, a watch chain, and three steps behind him was a *flic,* a real Paris policeman in the thick heavy corded-wool blue uniform with the thick heavy-duty shoes commonly called *écrase-merde.*

"Toulouse," the *avocat,* stepped forward, made a little bow, and said, "Monsieur Jarnigan, I am René Lenet, *avocat à la cour,* I present you with this *papier bleu* which I think in your country is what you call a bench warrant, *n'est-ce pas?"*

At first, looking at this team, they looked like a hammered-down road company of Laurel and Hardy. Had I been in a better frame of mind I would have been certain that they were a couple of actors who had been hired as a joke—that this was to be the great gag of the week. Seeing that I apparently didn't regard him with the esteem he felt was due him, he took the necessary steps, approached my desk and dropped the paper on my hands. I had been holding a contract of distribution. The blue summons from the Tribunal of the Seine stared up at me and I knew it was no joke.

"Et voila, Monsieur Jarnigan." He turned to the cop. *"Vous êtes témoin,* a witness, that this paper has been duly and correctly served according to the laws of France. Do your duty."

The *flic* took two steps toward me and I stood up: *"Attendez un peu*—now hold on; since this isn't a joke, suppose you explain what this summons means. I don't need to read it," I said.

Toulouse answered in a superior and judicial manner, "You must go with the gendarme. Your summons is for statutory rape of Mademoiselle Dubois and I, René Lenet, am the *avocat* of the family Dubois."

I could see this little bastard was serious. I decided to go the other route. "Please to be seated," I said, speaking French politely and smiling.

"*Non, merci.* We will stand," he said severely.

"Well, as a matter of courtesy you should give me a little more information, and since this seems to be a matter of importance . . ."

He cut me off with "*C'est très grave,* very serious, very serious."

"In that case, I had better call my *avocat* Maître Gautrat."

"Oh," he hummed, "the *maître* is your *avocat.*"

I could see he was impressed. I tried again to ask him to be seated, received the same stiff "*Non, merci,*" and called Gautrat. After a few minutes my secretary was able to get the great man on the phone. "Maître," I said, "I'm in trouble."

"Surely, *cher ami,* you didn't call me to inform me of this. Call me to give me news when you are not in trouble." Here he permitted himself a little laugh. It was his joke for the day.

"Quit the clowning," I answered. "There is an *avocat* who looks like a painter, a short one. He's making sounds as though I am under arrest. He also has a solid and burly policeman with him. They have served me a *papier bleu* and I am on the way to the Bastille apparently. What's the word, maître?" I finished.

"What's the charge?" he countered.

"Rape."

"What?" he almost shouted, astonished.

"Rape, *en toute simplicité.*" He began to sputter. Gurgling came over the phone. "*Mon cher* Jarnigan . . . do you . . . you couldn't have . . . I mean . . ."

"Listen, maître, using the words of the great man Gautrat, nothing can be gained by continuing this conversation, so get the hell over here and see what these crazy bastards want."

I knew this rumpled his dignity a little but I had a lot of work to do that day and I didn't want to be bothered with what I didn't understand. Gautrat was a great fixer. I knew I hadn't raped anybody, but I knew the French legal situation pretty well, having been baptised under fire by reason of my dippy and lawless partner, the Baron.

"Lautrec," being properly impressed because of the importance of my attorney, Maître Gautrat, agreed to wait the half-hour and would restrain the officer of the law from taking me down to the clink immediately. I bowed and thanked him properly. I gave the officer of the law a cigar, a Havana, which impressed him more than the importance of my *avocat.* I escorted him and Lautrec out of my private office into the reception room and through the alcove, where I kept for the staff and the Baron's and my special friends a well-stocked bar and some hot coffee. Five minutes later, after overcoming the weak protestations against having a drink, or a "glass," as they call it, I got to them with "Well, this is the hour of the aperitif; allow me." I took down a bottle of Napoleon brandy and their eyes followed it as though I had shown them a masterpiece. I poured out a good charge for the cop. Lautrec, seeing the pinch-bottle of Haig & Haig, asked if he might have a Scotch. I complied with his request. So, upon getting them comfortably seated, a drink and a cigar in hand, with two or three bons mots I walked out of the bar-waiting room toward my private office, helped along by cheery laughter and their camaraderie. I was a hell of a fellow . . . I could have run for president . . . I was a rapist . . .

After what seemed like two hours, but was more like twenty minutes, in came Gautrat, puffing and blowing. Without a word of greeting he marched over to my desk and picked up the *papier bleu*. I still hadn't read it, knowing I was innocent. I was only vaguely interested in who raped whom. Gautrat quietly looked up at me and said, "*C'est tres grave*. Did you do this?"

"For Chrissake, don't give me the lugubrious language—what the hell does it mean?"

"*Ecoutez*, my dear young and very valued friend. This document states clearly and firmly that you have raped one Mademoiselle Dubois on the night of the twenty-second in the city of Villefranche, département de Nice, France. You raped her not once, but twice, and you are going to jail."

I stepped back and sat down quickly. This was a new one. I remembered quickly that I hadn't been in Villefranche for over three weeks. This had happened five days ago. I didn't know Mademoiselle Dubois. I knew that somehow this was a mistake. I looked up at Gautrat, who was commencing to nod his head.

"Oh," he ohed, "I begin to see *la lumière*. The light is appearing."

"Well, hell, let's don't all be in the dark. Enlighten me. I'm just Jarn the raper sitting here."

He nodded solemnly. "It seems that while you are named as the rapist and the complaint is correctly filed by the parents of the victim, also named in the complaint is the partnership of yourself and the Baron's film company, naming the Baron individually and you individually."

"Well, Christ, Gautrat, my company never raped this girl . . ." We looked at each other eye to eye, then both started nodding our heads, he with a properly severe and judicial look in his eye, me with a Christ-what-else-can-happen look in mine. We both nodded and said at the same time, in chorus, "*Le Baron.*"

"Well, what do we do?" I asked, opening up the act.

"What do we do," he intoned. "What do we do," he echo'ed himself. "We comply with the law. We must immediately go to the tribunal where this writ was issued. Happily, I know the president of this court, this tribunal, but we must go immediately. If you will permit me a telephone call."

"I'll permit you," I said. He walked over and picked up one of the phones on the desk and started, his organlike voice demanding this or that from whoever was answering on the other end. After being switched here and there, he finally made contact with someone and I heard him make arrangements that he would present himself, bringing along the Hollywood rapist, Jarnigan, at two o'clock in the Palais de Justice and for the period of eleven o'clock in the morning, which it was now, until two in the afternoon he would personally hold himself responsible and accountable for the conduct of the criminal. This was getting worse and worse.

I walked over to the large windows and looked out over the Champs Elysées. It was a cold morning and yet people were walking up and down the street. Paris was the same. Beautiful girls properly bundled up were going off to meet their lovers for lunch. I looked directly below my office and saw my brother laughing and talking with Sam Neely. I wondered if they had heard about this. All thought of working on the script and continuing with the contracts was out the window. I had told my secretary to cancel any appointments for me until the end of the afternoon. So there I stood, old Jarn the raper, staring out the window wondering how this was going to work out.

After my attorney finished with his telephone calls, he suggested that we call in "Toulouse-Lautrec," the victim's lawyer, and my arresting officer. I sent the secretary for them. They came along in about five minutes and introductions were made. I could see they were about two drinks more relaxed than when they had first made their entrance into the office. Lenet was fawning and servile with *le maître,* who sternly nodded to the gendarme and said briskly, "Wait outside, *s'il vous plaît.*" The cop, with an unhappy look on his face, made a thoughtful and sad exit to the door, bowed carefully, and walked out to take up his post in my bar so that I couldn't escape if I left by that way.

After the gendarme had left, Gautrat, with charm oozing from every pore, said, "I'm pleased and gratified that you are handling this unfortunate and unjust affair of our young friend here. I have heard of you, René

Lebet." He nodded contentedly to himself. "Yes, I've heard of you, Maître Lebet."

"Lautrec" smiled uncomfortably, flattered and appreciative of the title *maître*, but gently in an undertone corrected Gautrat: "Lenet, L*enet*—not L*ebet*."

"To be sure, to be sure," hummed Gautrat, airily dismissing the inaccuracy. "Yes, I've heard of you, Maître Lenet," as though he hadn't been interrupted. "It was on the case of . . . of . . ." He raised his face heavenward as if searching for the case number of the Dreyfus trial.

Lautrec gave him the cue. "You mean," he slobbered, "the case of Dutru *et* Dubec?"

"Exactly," intoned Gautrat. "That is exactly the case I mean. You were superb."

"I didn't actually handle that. My partner did the most." Lautrec said primly.

"You are too modest, my friend. It never pays to be too modest. A man should receive the just consideration and appreciation that is his due." Gautrat said that and a lot of other things like that, until I was ready to kick him right in the ass. I didn't see what all this was leading up to. I didn't see why we just didn't go the hell down to court and prove that I hadn't done anything and let me get back to work.

While Lautrec was admiring some of my paintings (he especially liked a Van Gogh I had) I whispered to Gautrat, "What the hell are you doing? Is this necessary? Can't we just tell this little bastard we didn't do anything?"

"Your use of the word 'we' is ill-timed," quoth Gautrat, giving me an evil smile.

"Listen," I whispered, "this isn't funny. I never raped anybody."

"Well, *I* certainly didn't," Gautrat said.

"I didn't mean that," I almost shouted. "I know you didn't. But *I* didn't either."

"I'm sure you didn't, my boy, but this must be handled with dignity and finesse. If I may use your American *argot*, you don't want to spend the night in the clinker, do you?"

"Not clinker—clink," I said.

"Clinker, clink, you'd still be in jail. Now just let me handle it, will you, *cher ami*?" asked Gautrat, still much too calm for my taste.

"All right. But does he have to stay here? Can't we just meet him at the jail until they drop the axe on me?"

"Patience, my boy, patience. It would be more *politique* to ask him to accompany us to lunch; then in all *amitié* and friendship walk into the president of the tribunal together, showing there is no animosity, certain that this grave injustice can be remedied."

"All right," I said. "Do you invite him or do I invite him? Which is more *politique*?" I added sarcastically.

"I think that since we are adversaries and at the same time confreres, I should invite him."

"By all means invite him." I gave up. I went back over to my desk, sat down, took a cigar from the humidor, lit up and thought how happy I was to be in the picture business, to be in Paris, to be a very-loved partner of the Baron, and to be a rapist at eleven o'clock on a Tuesday morning in the City of Light. We left for lunch. And another day was wasted.

In order to show completely the chaotic state that the picture was in and in order to show the ultimate in confusion that was taking place when the French attorney and the French policeman came to my office to arrest me for statutory rape—at that time I had an overseas call going to Hollywood, and I had an overseas call to Majorca, trying to locate the Baron, who had disappeared with the yacht. While talking simultaneously on both overseas calls, finally realizing the gravity of the situation so far as the French attorney and the French policeman on the rape charge were concerned, I had my secretary call the studio to cancel my day's appointments there. The frantic goings-on in the office are easily understandable, since there were two overseas phone calls, my French attorney arguing with the other attorney regarding the rape, with the French policeman standing by; and then who should come in but the French co-producer, demanding to be seen and heard because the French Government Motion Picture Division was going to withdraw our license to shoot the picture because they had heard the picture was stopped by reason of the Baron's absence.

In order to obtain the license to shoot my picture in the English language only, I had made a deal with the French government motion picture agency, the Centre du Cinéma, that if I were allowed to shoot my picture in English only, I would upon completion of my picture start a French-language motion picture within ninety days, which would cost in money the equivalent amount spent on the American picture. So the license which was granted me to shoot my picture in English only was a temporary license or, as they say in France, a *license provisoire*. If there were any default on my part or on the part of my French co-producer with respect to the American picture or the French picture to be made following the American picture, I would be held liable, as would my French co-producer. And monies which we had coming from the Aide de Cinéma would be confiscated, since this money, amounting to several million francs, had been offered as a sort of security bond to guarantee completion of the pictures. It is clear that when the Baron left the picture, forcing me to try to continue with the use of a double, it had a disastrous effect on the picture and my agreement with the Centre du Cinéma. If I failed to complete these pictures I, of course, would be unable ever to make pictures again in France.

It was at this point that Hugh Bloodtest prepared to fly to France with an offer from Jason Wormser that he would take over the picture, buy up my multiple-picture contract with the Baron, and settle up what had been spent on the picture to date. When I got into the discussions, since I had already made a previous distribution arrangement with another major studio, I asked what would happen with respect to that contract. Bloodtest said that Wormser or his agency would advance me the money to buy back the distribution contract. All this was worth listening to, until we got to the point of completing the picture in France and my obligation to start within ninety days the French-language picture. The Hollywood studio, of course, wanted no part of that, so I was on the horns of a dilemma. If I sold my contract with the Baron, accepted the money and allowed them to complete the picture, they would immediately complete the picture in Hollywood. So not only would I ruin myself in France but would also ruin the French co-producer with me.

All these things were going on in the office, with decisions to be made whose consequences could be disastrous, and it was at this exact moment that I was to be dragged off to the Bastille for rape committed by the Baron, but because of my being the Baron's partner and financially responsible I was considered, as I'd begun to call myself, "old Jarn the rapist."

We got the rape charge "killed" by settling with the "Lautrec" lawyer. But it was the first time, I'm sure, that a producer was arrested for rape without have been within a country's length of the "rapee." I left the court and went home. Tomorrow was coming. *Yes it was.*

30

"He was neither imp nor angel, cur nor king; part hero—part ham." He was a good fellow. A fine theater actor, who knew all the words. He was an actor who starred principally in costume dramas. He ran to very Shakespearean dialogue, wore long flowing robes and spoke in long flowing sentences. He was continually sniffing the air as if testing the wind for the scent of something or other. Being in Hollywood he would have to have been pretty discriminating to distinguish the various things that came his way. But, when he sniffed with his nose, which was overly long and slightly bent—the bending having been done when the nose was into something which it shouldn't have been—he had what the movie fans call a sexy look. The feminine movie columnists in Hollywood and the feminine movie columnists outside Hollywood felt that this actor was the perfect Renaissance sex symbol.

However, time went on, and the costume movie with flowing robes and the flowing phrases started to be passé, and the long-nosed actor found it more and more difficult to obtain roles which measured up to his rigid requirements. Thus one day his agent, during a moment of heated discussion about the "at liberty" periods of the actor, threw caution to the winds and said to his client, whose name was Basil Vincent, "Listen, Bas baby, the parts don't come, the parts are tough to get because unless you are walking around under one of those powdered wigs and fooling with a sword, the nose just don't look believable, baby."

Basil cut in with, "Dear old chap, in the heated discussions where money must be brought into the conversation, I think we would both be well advised to remember where our best interests lie. Yours, clearly, quite definitely and positively, is to obtain for me the starring roles that have been my lot for the past decade. Since nothing has been forthcoming for a long period now, I feel, in spite of my warm affection for you, that I must regrettably change impresarios." He used the term "impresario" as though he were speaking of a symphony conductor.

The agent, in spite of himself, was a little overcome by this language, but the fact that he might possibly lose Basil as his client did not seem to disturb him too much, shockingly enough for Basil. "Look, Bas baby, I'm talking to you like a brother, better than a brother even, I can't get you

235

romantic leads in these new pictures because of the big beak. It's too long. It makes the kids laugh and no casting director or director even considers you unless it's one of the cloak-and-dagger or Louis, King of Italy pictures."

Basil sniffed haughtily and looked down that nose at the agent, "It would be Louis, King of *France*," he corrected.

"Yeah, I know, sweetheart, but what we want to do is get you back in pictures, right?"

"You are absolutely correct," Basil smiled haughtily.

"Well, I have the solution."

Basil beamed, "Really, dear boy, well why didn't you say so? What is it—a Broadway play, a television special? Details, I want details." He gave the agent the look of a man who is waiting and definitely interested in details, to whom details mean something.

The agent frowned, turned around and walked away from Basil, back to his desk and sat down. He picked up a pipe, lit it, smoked hurriedly for a moment and said, "Bas baby, we've got to take a decision."

Basil took two graceful steps toward the chair in front of the desk and sat down on about three inches of it, his back erect, as straight as a rapier. "Well," Basil said, looking hard at the agent who was sitting there puffing at his pipe, "what would you recomend?"

"That's just it, Bas—it isn't a play, a picture, or television. I think you've got to have the beak bobbed."

Basil shot out of the chair as though he had been stabbed in the rear by the rapier. "What?" he said breathlessly, thunderstruck by what he had heard. "What?" he said again, incredulously. "Do you mean that . . .?"

"Right, Basil," the agent said, for the first time calling him by his full name and not adding "baby." Then, a little more softly, with even a hint of friendship in his voice, he continued, "I have talked to all the producers. I've taken every studio casting executive to lunch. I am convinced that there is only one thing to do. You've got to have a nose job."

Basil sat back down in the chair and almost wailed, "What do you mean? What are you saying? Me, Basil Vincent, after twenty-six years in the theater and films? Everyone knows me, my profile—you should hear what has been said of my work."

The agent cut in quietly and said softly, "Basil, I know all that. Remember me, I'm the one who's been your agent for the past fifteen years. I've sold you, although honestly in many cases you've sold yourself. You're a fine actor, Basil," he said placatingly, "but we've got to change the image, and in this case the image is the beak."

THE DEAL

"Never," Basil said, back on his feet again, walking gracefully back and forth across the room, "never. I'd sooner give up films."

The agent, at this point truly feeling sorry for Basil, felt it was unnecessary to remind him that pictures had already given up Basil—which was the whole point of their conversation. Basil walked over to the big couch by the window and for once slumped down miserably, dejectedly and looked out over Sunset Boulevard. "Listen," said the agent, "I have a great gimmick. I have an idea which will put you back in the headlines and when you come out of it, there is a new you, a new Basil Vincent." Basil never moved. The agent continued, warming slightly to his subject, "Think of it, Bas, headlines, follow-up stories and you getting all the publicity that you need, especially at the time."

Basil raised his head and looked up rather slyly at the agent, "What's the gimmick? What idea do you have?"

"Listen, Bas baby," said the agent, now hot on his subject and full of the idea, being completely carried away. He pushed back his chair, walked quickly around the desk and said, "Are you ready?" Basil half sat up and looked at him. He was ready.

The agent ducked his head in a sly movement—the cunning dog who has successfully deceived the master (here a large wink). He grinned dishonestly, and said, "This is it. You are driving your car up from Malibu toward Carmel. You take your Jaguar, that's fast, then we fake an accident, see? Headline: Basil Vincent in horrible car accident. Second headline: Basil badly injured—Basil's face disfigured. Third item: Doctors say Basil's face will be as new, even more handsome. Fourth headline: the unveiling, and *tra la!* . . . a new Basil Vincent!" Here the agent half fell on his knee with his arms outflung in a typical Jolson finishing gesture. It was quite a performance. The agent got awkwardly back to a standing position and looked at Basil as though he were waiting for applause.

Basil looked at him coldly for a moment and said, "You stink. The idea stinks; and from here on in consider yourself no longer employed by me." He walked over and picked up his homburg, picked up the cane which he always affected, and started to stride elegantly from the room in what would be another of his famous exits.

The agent gave him a steady thoughtful look and walked deliberately back to his desk and sat down, noticing that Basil was not going through the door. He was hurt and spoke a little heavily, "Well, Bas, I may stink but you don't work. You don't work, you can't pay me. You can't pay me, our friendship hangs by a hair." He continued, "Here I rack my brains thinking of ways to get you back in the business; because you are out of

237

the business, Bas baby, whether you admit it or not. Sure I can get you a few personal appearances with some pictures you've made—sure I can get you on a rocky television show. You can play them crazy kid guessing games on TV till you're ninety, but not the way *you* like to live, Bas baby, not with your little peculiarities. You're a guy that likes to swing. You're a guy that likes to live high. Don't let me recite to you what can happen. Don't let me toll the bell." The agent went on reciting and tolling just the same: "First the house in Beverly Hills goes—this is after the money's gone. Then you give up that collection of phony antique cars. Then when you are really scrambling, they'll cut any guest-appearance price I can get for you. I don't have to tell you how this town is. There's no mercy, baby, no mercy at all. Next step you'll play summer stock in a parody of every lousy costume picture you've made."

Basil, standing by the door, his exit completely ruined by now, looked back at the agent terrified. The agent continued, "Should I go on? Bas, I don't want to go on, I shouldn't have said what I did, but when you told me I stink you got to me, sweetheart. So now, since I'm fired as your agent, I don't have to give you this advice but I'm going to anyway. Whether I service you or some other agent services you, you'd better get the beak bobbed. This is my considered and professional and friendly advice, and you don't owe me a quarter," he finished grandly.

Basil walked slowly back toward the couch by the window, stood there for a moment watching the cars whizzing by on the Boulevard. He turned back and looked at the agent. He said dejectedly, "Is there no other way?"

The agent looked at him, then looked up, as though appealing for aid, awaiting advice, then said halfheartedly, "Well, maybe we can frame it that maybe you got in a fight with a pro." He started to warm to this, then said, "Nah, that wouldn't get the coverage."

Basil wailed in the proper tone, "I don't know, I don't know." He shook his head despondently, then threw his hat and cane down on the couch. He sat down awkwardly. Then for the first time the agent saw how dispirited and humiliated the actor was. Basil looked up and asked quietly, "You honestly and sincerely advise me to do this?"

The agent said again, "Bas baby, it's for your own good. Forget what it would do to me."

Basil looked at him thoughtfully for a moment. They sat looking at each other for a few moments. After what seemed a long time, Basil got slowly to his feet, walked over to the mirror, set his hat at a rakish angle, picked up his cane, tapped it lightly against his leg for a minute, looking down at the rug, then with a quick glance at the agent he said, "I'm leaving, dear boy. I'll think about it." His face was pale and the agent felt bad for him, but not too bad. Basil's exit, if slightly delayed, was carried out this time. He walked out of the office, through the anteroom, past the girl at the switchboard. She said, "Goodbye, Mr. Vincent." Basil's usual charm and debonair smile were missing. He half-nodded soberly to her and without a word walked out the door. The girl at the switchboard thought he looked like a man in shock from an automobile accident. Basil Vincent walked down the steps of the building out to his car and knew that he was going to have the prearranged, publicity-covered, part-getting promotional automobile wreck. He also knew he'd have the nose job.

The agent threw himself into the conspiracy with a real promotional flair. He spent more time in Basil's home planning it than he'd ever done for any one of his client's Shakespearean productions.

The staging was excellent.

Then, as agreed, prearranged in the misty dawn, Basil's beautiful sports car (without Basil in it, of course) roared and zoomed off the cliff highway down into the surf. A terrible wreck. Amazingly, with perfect timing, an ambulance materialized. Stretcher-bearers "pulled" Basil Vincent out of the "wreck," they carried him delicately up the cliff, and sped him off to a private clinic.

Meanwhile, the agent dashed up to a beach house and gave his carefully rehearsed, terribly affecting story—how he had been following the great actor along the highway to Carmel—watched with horror as the sports car went out of control. The natives, who had of course heard of Basil Vincent, were thrilled to be in on the drama. They telephoned their neighbors and the nearest ambulance—this done in all innocence. They also called the police. They even forced a few quick brandies down the throat of the agent, who, nothing loath, played the scene so well even Basil would have been proud of him.

When the police arrived they found Basil's effects strewn around the wreckage in the surf. The second ambulance arrived; its driver heard the agent's story about the lucky coincidence concerning the first ambulance, which the agent had not mentioned to his benefactors.

And since this was early morning, the afternoon papers would have sufficient time to do really-banner headlines and many follow-up stories —especially since the agent had taken the precaution of being ready to give all the press and wire services the best background on Basil that a grief-stricken friend can be expected to create on the spur of the moment. The following day and the days afterward, stories leaked out that Basil

239

THE DEAL

Vincent's face had been mutilated but that the plastic surgeons had every hope of saving his classic profile and good looks.

Months later, in France, Basil Vincent came to see me, to request a part in the Baron's picture. Since the "accident," Basil had been unable to secure any parts for a truly tragic reason. The doctor who had performed the plastic surgery on Basil's nose had used either insufficient skill or bad judgment. He had snipped off much too much of Basil's aquiline profile. Where before Basil had looked like a handsomely evil Roman senator, he now had a little pug nose that gave him a continually surprised look. One of his sexy attributes on the screen had been that during the love scenes with the leading lady or sometimes love scenes that he played alone (he played those best—it took no acting), the critics would say, and especially the lady columnists would say, "Basil's nostrils flared with passion." Now, Basil could really do you a flare. His nostrils, which had not been small to begin with, now looked like two mouseholes. When he opened his mouth, which was disproportionately small, giving him this surprised look, it looked like he had three mouths—all open.

Receiving no parts in the United States, he had finally taken one or two "character" roles in some foreign costume pictures. As he was telling me this tragic and unfortunate tale, as he was moaning his fate, he said, "Jarn, you've always been my friend. What shall I do? What shall I do?"

I don't know why I was always singled out. It seemed to me I was a sort of six-foot-two-inch wailing wall. In making pictures with the Baron I'd had troubles I hadn't even heard of yet; but I was continually beset and besieged by American actors who for various reasons were not making it too well in Hollywood and would land on me as a displaced American producer doing films in France or Italy. It was as though these particular actors and actresses thought that Paris was in the middle of the Sahara Desert, with no communication. That the producers, directors, and distributors in Europe were completely unfamiliar with the decline and lack of box-office appeal of these stars.

It is true that Europe and especially France is very *fidèle* and loyal to their stars as well as American stars, and it is true that the Europeans are not so afflicted with the "eternal youth" problem of the American film makers. If a star is good at thirty in France, a star is equally good and perhaps more loved at fifty. However, if an actor is a hambone and second-rate in Hollywood, he is unfortunately a hambone and second-rate actor in Europe too—with rare exceptions. And while Basil was certainly not second-rate and was truly in every respect a complete actor, his unfortunate problem was well known to the producers; had caused no little comment in the motion picture community throughout the world. As he continued talking to me, I tuned in again on "Jarn, you have to help me. I know there's a part in the Baron's picture I can do. Hell, I'll wear a false nose in this costume drama," he said.

I looked at him closely. For the first time I realized that he was a little drunk. Up to the present time I had only thought him to be terribly upset and a trifle windy, which wasn't unusual for most actors; but I had known him in Hollywood when I was younger. He had always been pleasantly polite and friendly; I did want to help him. I knew that there was nothing in our picture for him but I let him down easy with, "Listen, Basil, I'm damn sorry about this new film with the Baron. The part that you could play must be by a very young, athletic and frankly unromantic character."

He looked at me thoughtfully for a moment and said, "Jarn, that's crap. I've read the script. I got it from Jack Clement."

I knew Jack Clement was the second assistant director on our picture, and remembered also that Jack was a second unit director who had done many pictures in Hollywood and had worked on several of Basil Vincent's pictures when he was a big star. I said, "Well, Basil, I unfortunately must disagree. I don't think you're right for it." I said this knowing how the Baron felt about Basil. That the first thing the Baron would say to him was, "Don't put your nose—what's left of it—in my picture." The Baron had a down on Basil ever since he had played a minor role in one of Basil's pictures when the Baron first came to Hollywood. There was no point in having Basil completely destroyed; I was afraid this would happen if he caught the Baron in one of his "off moods," which were becoming more and more frequent.

We had been sitting in the bar at the studio and I asked Basil to take a walk with me to the office. Once we were inside he asked for a brandy, which I gave him. I asked if he wanted a cigar. He declined.

"I never liked them," he said, "a nasty habit, I always thought." He finished the brandy and without my asking him poured himself another. Walking over toward a painting I had in the office and pretending to study it closely, he tossed off the second brandy, turned, and said, "Jarn, you are my last hope. I am unable to work in Hollywood. I have made no headway at all in getting any type of role here in Europe." He went over to a large leather chair, fell into it, saying, "What's to become of me—what's to become of me?" He put his head in his hands.

I walked over to my desk, took out a cigar, lit it, knew I shouldn't be wasting any time in the office, but you just can't turn your back on a man when he's that down. You can't grind it into him when he has already done that to himself. He looked up and said, "Jarn, if I don't get a picture I'm going to take the big one. I'll step off a bridge or in front of a car, or maybe off the Eiffel Tower—more headlines, you know." He said that with a gay sardonic touch. I didn't know how much was acting and how much was real. But one thing I did know. He might talk himself into it—he was that much of an actor.

He got up from the leather chair, went over and poured himself another drink. He walked over to the window, looked out, raised the glass to the outside world and in the best typical-Hollywood gesture, said, "To *la belle France*, to motion pictures, to my friends. To hell with all of you." He flipped the drink down, walked over toward the fireplace and made a gesture as if to throw the glass and break it—every gesture right out of any of the pictures he had made.

I caught his arm. I took the glass from him. "Basil, sit down. I want to give you a little heart-to-heart." I figured maybe a little tough talk would snap him out of it. The half-drunken and badly played hysterics were not going to help him. He might throw himself into the part, really throw himself off the Eiffel Tower. I pushed him, not too gently, into the big leather chair and continued, "Basil, maybe in the next picture there's something. It starts in four months. How much dough you got?"

"Well . . ." he colored slightly, "well . . . I'm not too well fixed, any way . . ."

I stopped him with, "Listen, this is Paris. You don't have to live at the George V or the Plaza Athenée. You don't have to keep your Rolls to go around in."

"The Rolls has gone," he said quietly.

"Great," I said, "nobody here likes a pretentious American actor. There are plenty of good places you can live, and not expensive. Try to learn French, forget trying to make the kind of pictures you were used to. You won't be able to, so forget it. You've got to start a whole new deal."

He looked at me searchingly. He said softly with a break in his voice, "You will help me, Jarn . . .?"

"Listen, Basil, you got to stop feeling sorry for yourself. You've told me the story. You tried something. It didn't work but it's not the end of your life. Your life wasn't your nose, or was it?" I probed, trying to get him angry, get him out of the dangerous self-pitying mood he was in. I could see he was thinking over what I was saying but the over-large eyes now filled with tears. It seemed I was doomed to get the crying ones. He sobbed, "But nobody likes me, nobody will use me. Even my fiancée has left me."

THE DEAL

I thought wryly that I truly wouldn't know of his "fiancée." I never really knew whether Basil was AC or DC. I had heard both. It didn't matter to me one way or the other, but he said fiancée, so I said, "Hell, if she's any kind of a woman she'll like you better if you show a little backbone and don't let this nose thing completely throw you."

"But she . . . but she . . ."

"Listen," I snarled, purposely over-tough since it seemed to be working, "what kind of a dame is she?"

He cut me off completely with a pitiful gesture, raising his hands in supplication, "But we're not making out any more. She won't let me touch her."

"Well then, frig her," I said. "If all you were to her was a nose, blow her off. Be tough; make her come after you. Cut off her dough. If I know you, you were keeping her too good."

"Well, I have been spending a little too much on her . . ."

"I don't want to hear about that. You've got to stop feeling sorry for yourself. Get a haircut. There's enough hair on the back of your head for a snood. Cut it off; it'll make your nose look bigger. As for your girl, your fiancée, tell her your dong's growed since you had your nose nobbed. You may start a fad."

He stood up, "Jarn, if you . . ."

"Listen, Basil, it's this simple. You know the picture business, you've been in it thirty years. I'm going to help you if you do three things. Stop feeling sorry for yourself . . . forget you're a matinee idol, stop trying for the juvenile long-nosed leads that you will never get . . . stop living like a movie star and start acting a man. Get yourself a normal apartment and the normal girls will come. Do you speak French?"

"Yes, I do" . . . he faltered, "yes."

"All right," I said. And to myself quietly: Man, what are you letting yourself in for? You're not the brother of the world. *Stop acting so frigging pure!* You're helping this poor bastard because it could have been you or your brother—and if this picture keeps going like the last two it *could* be you very quickly. It's your insurance, Jarn boy, spiritual payments on your escrowed property in heaven, I said to myself. I swung around, looked Basil Vincent straight in the eye.

"You want a job, you got a job. You won't wear a muffler or spats. You won't be worrying about your profile. I'm offering you a job as technical advisor on the picture. You've made enough of these costume epics, you can certainly help the director . . . when you are asked," I added sternly. "You can break into this end of the business and still have one hell of a

243

life, believe me. There are problems on both sides of the camera but on my side at least you don't have to be in makeup."

The look of gratitude on his face, whether it was real or only for the moment, was worth it. He started to say something, couldn't, and turned back to the window; he said, more to himself than to me, "I've always wanted to be in the production end of the business. I've always wanted to be on the other side of the camera." He was giving himself the hard sell. He swung back around, "Jarn, I know I can be of help to you. I'll work hard . . . I'll work the way you've never seen anyone work . . . Why, the pictures I've made, I can help you . . . Do you remember when I did *Captain from Castile* . . . do you remember *The Sea Hawk*—do you remember . . ." he was talking pretty loud.

I didn't want to shoot him down but I said quietly, "Basil, I remember, I remember; and get this: I'm not doing you any favor. I think you will be a help to me and a help to the director. You'll earn your dough, it's hard work. Now, I expect you to be at the studio in this office next Monday morning at ten o'clock for a production meeting. Incidentally, we're not dressing—no spats, no cane, no homburg—any old tweed suit will do."

A grin came over his face that even the badly operated nose couldn't detract from. "I'll be there, Jarn, I'll be there, dear boy," he said with part of the old flair. Then softly, "Thank you." He turned and started out the door; he paused, "Jarn . . . could I . . . I . . ."

Thinking this might be a touch, I was prepared to help him, to a certain extent, so I said quietly, "What is it, Basil?" I was prepared to go a grand; he was certainly worth that. He took a hesitant step back toward me and said, "Jarn," then looking down almost shyly and then glancing back up to my face, "Would there be any . . . I mean, do you think I could have . . . I was just wondering . . . if a technical advisor gets screen credit?"

I don't know if I grinned in relief at not having to pop for the grand, or in relief at this modest request. I couldn't help but wonder after this whole conversation—his destiny back and forth like a ping pong ball, off a bridge, in the river, or off the Eiffel Tower, and now, it was technical advisor, screen credit. I walked over to him, stuck out my hand, grinned, and said, "Basil, the screen credit will read, Technical Advisor and Action Sequence Supervised by Basil Vincent."

We shook hands. He smiled at me, reverently took two steps backward, made the little bow I'd seen him do a hundred times on the screen, turned, walked to the door, opened it, then came back; quickly took the steps toward me, grasped my hand again. He started to say something and

THE DEAL

couldn't. I turned away. I didn't want him to see that I saw him as exposed and disarmed as he was. I gave him a slap on the shoulder, walked over to the window, and said more harshly than I should have, "Okay, Basil, ten o'clock Monday morning, right?"

He said quietly, "Thank you, Jarnigan," and walked out, closing the door softly.

Ten o'clock Monday morning was a catastrophe for Basil Vincent.

We were shooting a dueling scene. Basil forgot himself, being so caught up in his memories, and emerged from his advisor's niche to make a comment or two about the Baron's foil technique.

The Baron, who hated the old-timer anyway, launched right into a tirade, ending with, "Who gave you fencing lessons? The clown who sliced off your beak?" It was terrible.

The Baron then challenged Basil to a real duel, with the buttons off the points, and before anyone could intervene, the Baron was advancing across the stage, slashing away, and actually cutting Basil every few strokes.

"I could kill you," Basil sobbed, any "new chance" in motion pictures pathetically beyond him now. "Try it, try it," shouted the Baron, pressing and slashing wildly at his opponent, who did not dare counterattack.

Poor Basil gave ground all the way back to the edge of the stage, and finally fell backward right off the scaffolding, the Baron standing over him and shouting down that he was fired. By the time I calmed the Baron a little, Basil had disappeared.

What followed was worse. Basil got back to his little apartment literally humiliated into shock. It seems that he took out his most precious possession—the costume he had worn in *The Sea Hawk* and had carried with him afterward from place to place. He put the costume on. Then he arranged himself in a big leather armchair, pulled up close enough to the gas fireplace so that he could arrange what had to be arranged. He put a rubber hose in his mouth, and a blanket over his head, to make sure; he did it carefully and well. His last act was a complete success. He may have heard just the first few rings of the telephone . . .

I was at the other end of the line, ready to hand the phone to the Baron, who by now, after our private talk, had had a change of heart. But the apology and reinstatement in the picture were not destined to be heard by Basil in this world. Basil had taken the big one. He had stepped off; and out.

On getting the terrible news shortly after, the Baron and I rushed to

THE DEAL

Basil's apartment. The Baron's expression when he pulled the blanket off Basil's head and looked into those dead eyes was not pretty. Neither was Basil. The Baron was stunned.

He vowed on the spot to give Basil a fine funeral, and make him look as he had in earlier days. He figured he would have liked that. I thought it was silly, but the Baron wouldn't rest until he got the makeup man to guarantee a perfect reproduction of the classic Basil Vincent nose.

"I'm going to send him on his way happy," swore the Baron—Jared Throne-like—after a few drinks to calm himself. The Baron—the swordsman with whom Basil Vincent fought his last duel—was now dueling with himself. A lonely unpaid occupation. However, he did take over all funeral arrangements. The sad thing was, the Baron really did feel grief for what he had done. It was one time I think he was truly sorry for an outburst. He did want to show publicly he regretted his actions. It was a grand, if a somehow slightly warped, gesture that the Baron was determined to make. But as always, the Baron's mighty effort turned into a piddling nothing. The funeral ended in a second, posthumous catastrophe for poor Basil Vincent.

It seemed we were in over our heads with disasters these last days, no shortages in that department.

The big funeral was followed by a wake. Then, after the eulogies were read, and as most things with the Baron, it turned into a dirge-type cocktail party, with the coffin resting on two large planks covered with flowers so that anyone present, if he wanted to, could pass completely around the coffin and get a last look at Basil.

But it was a transformed Basil they were looking at. The Baron had had a wax nose made from stills of Basil and there he lay with his former classic profile intact. It had been as good a job as you could want and with the wax nose Basil Vincent had his old aquiline, evil-Roman-senator look. A few of the American actors who hadn't seen Basil in his bobbed-nose state, said, "Why, my goodness, he looks exactly as he always looked . . . he looks very well indeed . . . let's have another drink."

Later on, again, which was par for the course, the Baron and his friends got into a fight. Then a horrible thing happened: The fighters knocked over the casket, the casket tumbled off the trestle, and Basil slid gracefully out onto the floor. Unfortunately, lit on his face; and as they turned him over, the nose came off. Everyone was horrified. Then the Baron, who was completely drunk, dropped to his knees beside Basil and kept trying with whiskey-tangled fingers to replace and restick the wax nose on the dead face. The Baron, by now out of his mind with drink or "horse" or shock, kept saying, looking up at me pitifully, "If the son-of-a-bitch don't like the way he's being buried here, let him go somewhere else. I'm picking up the nut for this funeral." He continued his work—still trying to mash the nose in place. "Shouldn't he be grateful, Jarn?"

I couldn't take it anymore. He was crying now, terrified. The nose looked like a potato now on the poor dead face. Basil didn't mind—but I did! I walked out of that madhouse into the street, left my car where it was and kept walking, Dear God, I'd had enough of it—I was sick to death of it.

As I walked along, ignoring the cold and the fact it was starting to rain (I had no coat or hat), taking any empty street that caught me—happily the streets were deserted—I thought I couldn't take this constant hell any longer. Even if I knew how many men have been through this "every-day, every-night hell," this "death by installment," it wouldn't cheer me any. Because it is me these things are happening to, it is me passing through these times, these days and these hours. I am not impressed with what has happened to other men in similar circumstances because I would have bet my life there were no similar circumstances; the things that had happened and were continuing to happen were unbelievable, and unbelievable in the most terrifying sense of the word. Had I known that it was possible to get worse, had I known what was to come, I would have kept walking until I reached the sea; then kept right on walking.

31

About this time, the trail of nymphets the Baron was dropping from Paris to Monaco to Villefranche struck a dead end. Or, at least, he pushed the odds too far after the "Lautrec"-Gautrat affair by trying his luck with the one little girl who had no trouble written on her at all. It just seemed to work out that way . . .

It started soon after we got back to Paris. It was almost a miracle the way these things happened. No one could have planned it, either way—for or against. But the happenings were guaranteed to rip the keenest mind asunder. Especially the deal with Mme. Dumont (Danielle's mother) and Mme. Dumont's lawyer. The act opened up like this . . .

Mme. Dumont had actually, with her *avocat*, caught the Baron with Mme. Dumont's beautiful and fifteen-year-old daughter, Danielle, in a very practical and absolute *flagrante delicto*.

• • •

Mme. Dumont had been married to Rossi Dumont, a fine production manager, who had worked for me for many years in Paris. Unfortunately, he became ill and passed on. Fortunately, during his long illness, I was in full production, so I managed to keep him on the payroll without much difficulty, even though he had kept to his bed for almost two years.

The fifteen-year-old Danielle Dumont was an absolutely ravishing young girl. About five years earlier, she used to come to the studio to meet her father and walk the short distance home with him, and even then, as a child, you could see that she would be a beautiful girl.

When we had started this picture with the Baron, and were shooting at Billancourt Studios, one day Danielle came with her mother to pay me a social visit and to thank me for the kindnesses with respect to her dear departed father. She very sweetly told me that I was always in her prayers, and had been since she was a little girl. The Baron was watching this from the other side of the sound stage. His antenna picked up this child-woman as surely and as deftly as radar. I think he would have known she was there if there had been a ten-foot-thick wall between them.

249

Mme. Dumont had been an actress. She was part Canadian. She was a fluttering, buxom woman, given to much makeup, her cheeks heavily rouged, her eyelashes like small iron railings. She perspired a good deal and reeked of cologne, but was, nonetheless, a nice woman and I'd found no fault with her until this difficulty with the Baron.

I remembered that day at the studio when the Baron had come bounding lithely across the stage, ducked in front of the camera, walked directly up to me and said, in a charming voice, "Jarn, I'd like to talk to you about this next scene." He smiled boyishly.

"Fine, Baron, fine," I said. "Incidentally, I'd like to have you meet Madame Rossi Dumont and her young daughter, Danielle. They are very old and close friends of mine. Monsieur Dumont was a great friend of mine."

The Baron swung around half surprised—acting as though he hadn't noticed the little girl; still carefully avoiding looking at her directly, he went into the act. "Dear Madame Dumont," he purred, bowing over her hand, "it is a pleasure . . ."

"*Enchanté,*" Mme. Dumont beamed, responding to the act; and managing to blush in spite of the heavy coating of rouge. "*Et ma petite fille, Danielle.*" She turned, to include this beautiful child in the introduction.

The Baron now turned and allowed his gaze to fall directly onto the face of the girl. "*Mademoiselle,*" he purred, his voice getting lower and more mellow each time, "*vous êtes une petite fille ravissante.*" He took her hand.

Danielle made a curtsey, which she was still child enough to do, with dignity, although I thought it was too deep a curtsey; then, bowing her head, she said, "*Monsieur, je suis enchanté.*"

The Baron, still holding onto her hand, helped her up from the deep curtsey, and we all stood looking at one another. I could hear the clanking and the smoking going on in the Baron's head and under his hair. To break the silence and to tear the Baron's gaze away from the little girl—for by this time he had put a "fix" on her (I was sure she would have been unable to move or say a word)—I spoke her name. But simultaneously the Baron said: "*Mademoiselle,* you would permit me to show you the rest of our set? The action in this scene is really quite exciting . . . I should be pleased to show this to you."

Danielle first looked into her mother's face. The mother gave a permissive nod. Danielle then switched those beautiful, guileless eyes at me and I said, "If you'd like to, Danielle."

She smiled. "Oh, I would. I would, Monsieur Jarnigan."

"Well, you go ahead. By the way, Baron, what did you want to talk

250

about for the next scene?" I said, deliberately wanting to let him know I knew what he was planning.

He looked back over his shoulder as they were walking away. "Later, Jarn boy, later," he said airily. "We can discuss it later. I must show your little friend about the studio."

With that, they walked off. I must say, it was quite a sight. He was handsome, tall and lean and with makeup looked twenty years younger than he was. She was lovely and slender; not yet in full bloom, but a delight to look upon and, although fifteen, looked older . . . she looked at least seventeen. They continued walking away and I was jarred out of some thoughts that I would prefer not to have had, by Mme. Dumont.

"Monsieur Jarnigan," she burbled, "Again, you must permit me to thank you for your extreme generosity, your extreme thoughtfulness, your extreme gentleness, in continuing the payments to my poor Rossi, my poor . . ." Here she broke down; her plump hands reached into the front of her dress between her two ponderous breasts, where she sought a handkerchief—she flagged it out, waved it in the air a couple of times and made little delicate dabbing gestures at her eyes. The wave of cologne that came from the handkerchief almost made my eyes water, but she was being kind and grateful. She knew one thing with a certainty—that I had really been a friend of her husband's, who had been a good man. I was thinking this and she was still murmuring, "My poor Rossi, *pauvre, pauvre garçon.* You must forgive me, *monsieur,*" she finished, with another wave of the cologne-handkerchief—with the raise of her hand, it disappeared again somewhere below the neck of her dress. "Is there some way I could repay you . . . because the family Dumont is eternally in your debt." You see, she was half Canadian and was fully aware of the social graces.

I turned to one of the production assistants going by and said, "Bring us two chairs, please." Two director's chairs appeared suddenly and I asked Mme. Dumont to be seated and said that I would sit with her for a few minutes, but then must continue with the work. "*Mais certainement,* Monsieur Jarnigan. We only came to pay you our respects."

"Conditions now go well with you?" I asked.

"It goes, it goes. One must keep trying," she intoned. I could tell from the way she replied that this was a sound-track she used often. We were interrupted then.

The assistant director, Jack Clement, came over. "Jarn, we're ready to do the fight scene. You said you wanted to watch it. We have the doubles ready. We've already run through it a couple of times. Would you like to see it before we shoot the first one?"

"Be right with you." I got up from my chair. "Madame Dumont, if you will permit me. I must now attend to my work. I hope to have the pleasure of seeing you again. If there is anything . . ."

"*Mais non, mais non.* You have done enough; but if there is anything we can do . . . we are at your disposition . . ."

I bowed, excused myself, and started away. She called after me, "Monsieur Jarnigan, you'll send Danielle to me?"

"I'll not fail to do that at once, madame."

"Well, until soon then, until soon . . ." she called after me.

I walked over across the sound stage to where we had constructed the big set that was to be where the fight scene between the Baron and the "villain" would take place. As I got near the camera, I saw that Marc, our cameraman, was checking angles and the setup. He saw me come up, and only grinned, the same old dry grin. I said, "How's it go, Marc?"

"Average, Jarn, just average."

"You're set?" I asked.

"You know me. If we're not, I'll holler."

"Fine, Marc, fine," I answered and walked over and took one of the director's chairs, sat down, ready to watch the action. It was at this moment I saw Danielle, standing delicately poised on a parallel, with the Baron holding her—in my view, unnecessarily close. She truly was not paying too much attention but had been interested in the stunt men who were rehearsing the fight.

I watched the last two minutes of the fight and I had to admit it was really tremendous. The action was violent and exciting. It could be a good scene. Saul Baum, as the Baron's stunt man, went through the paces several times at various speeds, with the Baron watching carefully. I had to admit they worked well together, and this was as it should have been—they had been doing pictures together, with Saul taking all the lumps, for the past fourteen years. Lately, here in France, he had started to go Continental and was taking a little more on himself than he should have. I knew that when necessary, I could snap him back pretty fast, but I didn't want to have him say anything that might upset the Baron. The picture had been going fairly well for the last two weeks. I was keeping everything crossed, praying that this good period of filming would continue.

The rehearsal of the fight scene concluded. Saul Baum, with a tremendous heave, had thrown the villain through a false window. This, of course, had only been done with paper for the rehearsals, but would now be done

252

with false glass. At the end of the fight, the Baron was to heave the villain completely through a plate-glass window.

From across the set, the Baron saw me. His grip on the little girl became less tenacious and he carefully and tenderly helped her down from the parallel. They both walked across the set, carefully avoiding the big cables, and came over to where I was now seated, directly below the camera. When they were still several feet from me, little Danielle, who was in an absolute champagne of excitement, said, "Oh, Monsieur Jarnigan . . . can I . . . may I . . . could I . . ."

The Baron, following two steps behind, nodded his head, looking me directly in the eye. I grinned up at the little girl. "May you, can you— what? We are trying to work. You have to go back to your mother."

Her face had a look of childish distress for a moment. "Oh, no, Monsieur Baron said I might stay. Mother will wait. I want to see Monsieur Baron do this fight!"

Well . . . there it was. The fifteen minutes I had spent with the mother had handed the Baron the equivalent of fifteen weeks with this child and he had things locked up in the box. I could tell from the way he looked, and from the absolutely guileless and unspoiled happiness on this little girl's face. She would have done anything the Baron said. If the Baron had said to her, "Jump off the top of the studio," she would only have asked, "When?" Well, to hell with it. I'm not the girl's keeper. Am I my brother's keeper? Am I this son-of-a-bitch's keeper? All this went through my mind and I said, "All right, Danielle, you stay here with me. Baron, you'd better go ahead now. Marc wants to line up once more on you. We'll walk through it and then try one."

He gave me a mock salute. There was also a mocking glint in his eye, but he gave me the boyish grin, saying, "Anything you say, Jarn boy. Anything you say."

He walked away. I saw him go over and say a few words to Saul Baum, who again showed him briefly the intricacies and the "dance steps" of the fight. I told one of the assistant directors to go get Mme. Dumont and to get her a chair to sit where she could see the action, but well out of range of the crew so she wouldn't disturb anyone.

By this time, the little girl had walked over and was standing close by my side. I remembered when she was about ten years old, she used to do that—stand very close to me . . . sometimes put her little hand in mind, and sometimes I'd let her ride on the camera boom. At that time we'd had that sort of friendship . . .

THE DEAL

The assistant director was putting the actors in position; setting them with their light cues. Saul Baum was explaining to the rest of the stunt men what they were to do. I could see him making the broad gestures he used in explaining anything. The finale of every one of his talks was, "The Baron's in here. My boy's in here, so take it easy. Take it easy or you'll have me to contend with. Do it like we danced it before . . ." He always said, "Easy's how it goes. Get the picture, men, easy." I watched him finish his hymn—he sang it lovingly and well—before the Baron went into any fight scene. He knew if anyone really roughed the Baron up, his job would hang by an eyelash in spite of his fourteen years with the Baron.

The assistant director called, "Start your action in the background!" and then, almost in slow motion, the two "villains"—stunt men—waltzed carefully and delicately toward the Baron. I knew they wouldn't hit him hard enough to crack an egg, but they had to make it look good. This first run-through was only for position.

Something went wrong in the background. The Baron stopped. His double came over; and the Editor came rushing out to say, in a very ineffectual way, "I think you would look better doing *this*, Baron."

Baron gave him a sarcastic nod and shot a look over to where I was standing with Danielle. When he saw her look was absolutely riveted on him, he sucked in his belly, which was already flat, put a little more spring in his step—and was certainly going to prove in the next scene that he was really what he was . . . a Something that made the women holler, and made the little girls faint with delight.

The extras, the stunt men, the actors, and the Baron were all in position. This time they hit all of the lights; the big sound stage was lit up. Action started and—if you looked at it without knowing what was happening—it looked like the damnedest fight in creation. The Baron was throwing the stunt men around as if they were flies. When it came to the part of the fight scene where the Baron was to knock one of the villains out and past the camera (which would then pan up to get a close-up of the Baron) the Baron, overenthusiastic, careless, and free with his swings, knowing he could hurt, but would certainly not be hurt, glanced quickly at the girl, flexed his muscles, and threw a right at one of the stunt men. He got him on the side of the head with a sound like a grocer's sack exploding. The big guy went over backward, fell underneath the camera and, if it hadn't been for one of the crew, could have seriously injured himself. As it was, he landed like a sun-stroked bull.

Everybody was yelling "Cut! . . . cut!" and the Baron rushed over with a little, evil, sarcastic grin on his face which quickly changed to mock sympathy and camaraderie as with a voice full of affection he said, "Clyde, Clyde, are you all right?"

The big, sandy bruiser raised up; two of the crew helped him into a sitting position and he sat there shaking his head. One side of his face was already beginning to swell. His eyes didn't focus any too well for a second. He shook his head again, and when his head became still, he ended up looking me right in the eyes. "Oh," he said, in a gravely voice, "hi, Mr. Jarnigan. I guess I stopped one, huh? Clumsy me." Then his gaze shifted and he saw the Baron looking at him with a friendly smile on his face. This warmed the cockles of old Clyde's heart. Poor old punchy stunt man Clyde—a good-natured man, a kindly man, for all his looks. He was a wind-blown thistle of about two hundred fifty pounds. He had a cough of a voice, a shock of red hair, and a lot of spots on his face. When he opened his mouth to smile, which he did often, even his teeth were freckled. He shook his head again and raised his left hand and roughly massaged his face. The Baron reached down, all friendliness, all concern, for his friend Clyde, the stunt man. He stuck out his hand from a standing position and said, "Come on, boy, lemme help you up."

Clyde grinned as though the Baron had given him a present instead of just clobbering him in the head. He grinned that freckled grin again and stretched up his beefy paw and the Baron helped pull him to his feet, all concern, the soul of thoughtfulness, the big star looking out for "his men," "his crew," "his friends."

By now the hubbub had died down. I stepped back, bumping into Danielle, who was looking up at me with a pale little face. "Is he all right, Monsieur Jarnigan? Is he all right? Oh, the Baron hits so hard! He is so terrifying. Is that big man all right?"

"He's all right," I said. "Now you sit over here out of the way and you can watch for a few minutes and then you must go with your mother. I have much work to do."

"But Monsieur Baron said I could . . ."

I cut her off with, "Danielle, watch this shot and then you must go home with your mother."

"All right," she said quietly, completely subdued, looking more like five than fifteen at that point. She sat down on about three inches of one of the director's chairs. I sat next to her. The lights were hit again—the extras, actors, stunt men, and the Baron all in place—and now the actual scene started.

"On action." The whole turmoil started again. The false plate-glass

255

window had been installed and the Baron was thrillingly and magnificently knocking everyone about and generally making his way, with the help of the stunt men, toward the window. I must say he looked pretty good—those stunt men could make anybody look good. The fight was progressing tremendously at one point, where the Baron knocked one of the stunt men over two false tables that collapsed with a roar.

Little Danielle shot to her feet as if she had been pricked. There was so much noise she was almost ready to join in the screaming. She quickly glanced at me to see how I was taking it. I knew everything was going well and it only remained now for the Baron to knock Saul Baum through the glass. This was a cakewalk for both of them and should look great.

As the fighters, with the Baron, of course, winning—but winning dangerously—progressed down the stairway prior to the big crash, the little girl was watching the Baron as though he were something not of this earth. He was feinting and boxing; he was strutting around; he was throwing punches; he was flexing everything that would flex. "Ooh," said the beautiful little girl, taking everything in, "he's so wild . . . so fierce . . . isn't he splendid, Monsieur Jarnigan? . . . But he's so big . . . isn't he terribly dangerous in a fight?"

"Only if he falls on you," I answered politely and truthfully. For all of the Baron's coordination was displaced; and if the stunt men hadn't been helping him, he would have fought like his joints were put on backward.

The roar from the extras became louder; one stunt man went flying, landing on the balance of the tables, and here Saul Baum, the "villain," stood trembling, awaiting his doom in front of the Baron. The Baron delivered him a mighty blow on the side of the head. Saul did the prettiest back swan dive I've ever seen and exploded directly into the middle of the huge plate-glass window. You could have heard the crash of that glass breaking clear across Paris. In a tremendous roar of "paid" approval from the extras, the Baron looked down through the hole where the villain had gone. The proper intelligent sneer was on his face. He looked camera-right, he looked camera-left—giving us the benefit of his falconlike profile, admired the world over—did the standard Baron "lurch," and dove at the rest of the extras, who broke for the opposite side of the stage like a wave of frightened sheep, the Baron in hot pursuit, running beautifully, delicately—a false cat on a cold iron roof.

I looked up at the camera and saw Marc giving me the traditional thumbs-up gesture. You couldn't hear with all the noise; nor could you see very well with the smoke from the smoke-bombs that had been released in

256

the last minute of the fight. I knew we'd staged that fight with five cameras, so if Marc said O.K. I knew we had gotten plenty of footage.

Marc's cousin crawled out from under the rubble of the fight with an Aeroflex, grinning from ear to ear. I knew he'd gotten some good film. I caught Jack Clement as he went by and said, "Jack, will you take Mademoiselle Dumont back to her mother and see that a car drives them home?"

Danielle turned to me as though I had betrayed her. "But, Monsieur Jarnigan, but . . . I'm not going to see the Baron . . . no?"

I looked down at the beautiful little face. "You are not going to see the Baron, no," I said. "We have work to do and we've had a nice visit. I hope to see you again soon. Now you run along with Mr. Clement."

The look of disappointment slowly changed. "I thank you, Monsieur Jarnigan, you are always so *gentil.* I will go. Say *au revoir* to *Monsieur le Baron* for me?"

"I'll do that little thing."

With a dance in her body, she took the four steps over to me, kissed me quickly and lightly on both cheeks, then went off across the stage followed by Jack Clement. She turned and waved. I waved back and two grips who were moving a wild-wall hid her from view. I turned back to the business at hand.

"Jarn boy!" I heard the Baron bellow over the excitement and noise and through the smoke, and suddenly he appeared from behind a group of extras. "Went well, my boy, it went well, *n'est-ce pas?*—as we say in French. Where's the little mademoiselle?"

I gave him a look of surprise and after a second could see that he wasn't buying it. "She left. She had to leave with her mother."

"She's nice, Jarn boy. She's nice," he purred. "What was her name?"

I tried to kid him out of it. "Listen, Baron, she's just a baby and her father was a good friend of mine. Her mother is, too."

He gave me a slight frown. "You don't get the picture, Jarn boy. I like her."

"I get the picture, Baron," I said quietly. "But this one you shouldn't fool with. This one's not the type."

He kept his grin in place, but a veiled look came into his eyes and anger peeped out. "They are all the type, Jarn boy, and especially this one. You know me, Jarn. That's my type, that's my type."

"All right, Baron. But let's talk about it later. By the way, that was a damn good scene. Really great. You looked fine in there today."

He said coldly, "Jarn, this is the Baron talking. Remember me? Don't

257

try to change the subject. I liked that girl. She likes me. What's the matter, something wrong with me?"

I could see nothing in that for me so I let it drift with the rest of the smoke that the blowers were by now trying to fan out of the studio. I knew there was only one way to stop it. But I wouldn't do that. I wouldn't stop the Deal.

• • •

I should never have let the Baron out of the studio, knowing perfectly well what he had in mind for Danielle. And I knew that Mme. Dumont knew what the Baron had in mind for Danielle. And that Mme. Dumont's *lawyer* knew what the Baron had in mind for Danielle. News of the Baron's *fétiche* was all over Paris.

The two of them knew so well, in fact, that they had simply staked out the Baron's apartment, and at the right moment made their entrance.

The Baron had enough sense to call me at that point; and I kicked myself over there, cursing every step of the way my stupidity in falling into this particular trap.

Mme. Dumont's lawyer-friend had induced Mme. Dumont to follow his advice and counsel. He had assured her that this was a way to receive a tremendous amount of money. And didn't they want to marry? *D'accord.* Didn't they need the money to buy the little shop in Cannes? *D'accord. Alors! c'est très simple,* said the lawyer-lover-dumbbell. But Mme. Dumont bought it, and him—and the start of a disaster for me.

The lawyer and Madame found the Baron and little Danielle half nude. It was clear what had happened.

Now, how could this be settled? With money, of course—now hell, I'd have *never* thought of that. . . .

I saw Mme. Dumont downstairs. Her leave-taking was a properly grateful, yet touching thing. She had simpered, *"Vraiment, Monsieur Jarnigan,* it has been a difficult evening. A very trying period. I am so deranged and disturbed."

"And rightly so, Madame Dumont," I said with the proper sympathetic tone, "it is a terrible ordeal that you have gone through, but happily having confidence in me, which you say you have . . ."

She cooed on, *"Ah, oui, Monsieur Jarnigan, beaucoup de confiance*; you are my protector."

"You honor me, madame," I said, thinking that it was not she, Mme.

Dumont, who had truly gone through the "ordeal," if that's what it had been. It was Danielle. And she hadn't seemed to be too much the worse for wear. She had been seated demurely in a large armchair in the far corner of the room as though she was completely unaware of any disturbance or discussion with her mother or her mother's "on-the-spot *avocat*." The *avocat* had already been disposed of with me duly explaining to him that there was a "possibility" that he could do some motion picture contracts for my company, that in this way his judicial efforts on behalf of Mme. Dumont and her daughter would be salved in a material way. He had confidence in me. He had departed, with Mme. Dumont's instruction that all arrangements were to be left to my discretion alone. She had *grande confiance* in Monsieur Jarnigan.

With my hand on Mme. Dumont's ample arm, I was slowly and sympathetically ushering her toward the door. I said gently and warmly, "You will feel better, dear friend, when you've had a good dinner and a little of the glass that cheers—in fact more than a little glass."

She turned her face up to me. She beamed. "Oh, you . . . you can do as you want with me, I am in your hands." I thought to myself, this would be truly a handful, but in her own way she was being friendly about this and in truth she trusted me. She told me she would never do anything to hurt me. But she did love her lawyer, and the Baron had so much money, and I would help her, wouldn't I?

I would. It was perfect. In front of the door I said, *"Chère Madame Dumont,* allow me to order a dinner for you and something grand in a good Burgundy which I hope will please you and rest you quietly over your dinner. As soon as I have straightened things out correctly here, I shall be down to join you," I finished.

"And Danielle—*et ma petite fille?*" she asked piteously—but I could see that the thought of the good dinner and the bottles of wine that were forthcoming were uppermost in her mind.

I smiled, "Confidence in me, madame."

"In everything, in everything," she intoned.

"Well, then, shall I escort you downstairs to the restaurant or do you . . ."

"Oh, I know the way, I know the way. You see . . ." here she leaned her head toward me and spoke in a conspiratorial voice, *"Mon avocat* and I watched diligently from in front of the restaurant waiting for Danielle and *Monsieur le Baron* to arrive. In fact, I ventured in alone to use the . . . telephone." Here she blushed delicately. "It is a restaurant of exquisite beauty."

"Then you have never eaten there?"

259

THE DEAL

"No, but I . . ."

I said firmly, "Then this must be remedied immediately, madame." I made a little bow, opened the door; she walked into the hallway toward the *ascenseur*. I waited until the elevator came; I bowed her in, and said, "Take your time over dinner. These arrangements might consume a certain period."

"Oh, *je comprends*. I understand. Well, I will await you below in the restaurant, do not fear. I understand."

I pressed the button for her, closed the grille, and the old elevator on the water-hydraulic lift oozed slowly toward the ground floor. As I watched her slowly descend, as though she were sinking into a swamp, her happy tear-stained face was below me and she looked up as the elevator descended. I leaned over slightly, she took the ever-present cologned handkerchief, dabbed gently at her eyes and said in an open-mouthed, tremulous way, *"Monsieur Jarnigan, j'ai confiance, j'ai confiance,"* and with me nodding to let her know I understood, smiling, sadly, she sank from view.

I turned around and went back into the apartment, closed and locked the door. I slipped the chain so that we were secure and no disturbance could take place. I walked quickly back down the corridor into the bedroom and there was the Baron. The excitement, the alcohol, or the mainline had tapped him none too gently on the brow. He was sleeping the undisturbed sleep of an unsuccessful "raper."

I went out of the room, closed the door, walked back down the corridor and into the living room where sat the "rapee." Danielle was not only not nervous but was calmly sitting there sipping her drink. She had removed her shoes and her tiny head rested delicately on the back of the huge armchair. This scene I had deliberately set about to accomplish was a calculated plan to make the Baron do as I wanted; namely, just to finish the picture and the Deal. But what a thing it was. Although the Baron had wanted Danielle to do everything, many things she possibly would have refused to let him do, she didn't get the chance to refuse . . . each time he got down to it, he couldn't. Not for a lack of trying, not for a lack of wanting to get next to this one more—he had kept at it until he was absolutely weeping from exhaustion.

He had her half naked . . . he had her submissive, and the battle flag of his passion . . . or lust . . . or anything you want to call it . . . unfurled only slightly, then opened further to reveal the tattered, limp, and completely useless flagstaff. A warrior without a weapon. The new battle site, if not ready, was unresistant and so could be fought over, and upon. But, the straw was never in the wind. There was nothing to blow. The sperms that

260

must have surely been there were turning, or already turned, to vinegar. There was a place for them to go, unaware that it was waiting. But there was no way out for them, no firm passioned bridge, no rigid canal to pass through with a lurch, then to fling themselves through, and in and up . . . and up farther. Climbing then of their own volition, spurring and clawing sweetly to the natural warm and moist and welcoming place that was certainly where their destiny was. But it was not to be with the Baron.

I stood looking down at this beautiful child. My mouth was dry. I licked my lips. She must have felt me looking at her. She gave me a shy yet inviting up-from-under look. She had definitely grown up. She sat there watching me—her lips slightly parted.

I went over and stood in front of the fireplace and finally walked over and sat on the large divan opposite Danielle. "Would you like another drink?"

"If you want . . . if you are having one."

I got up, went over to the bar, mixed myself a drink, mixed her another light one and walked back. I handed it to her, she took it and set it down on the little table beside her chair. I walked back over to the divan and sat down, inhaled part of my drink and said, "Now, Danielle, tell me what happened, and I want the truth."

"Well, Monsieur Jarnigan," she said primly, "The Baron brought me back here after we had had dinner at the Elysée Club. It was very nice. He introduced me to people of great reputation. I was so happy to see all of the *vedettes* in person. I started to ask for a signature but the Baron refused to allow me."

"Listen, Danielle," I said, a little more roughly than I meant to, "I'm not interested in what stars you saw or whose autograph you got. I want to know what happened here that got your mother, who apparently was all primed, to crash in with this little lawyer—by the way, who is he?"

"Oh," she said, "he's a close friend of *ma mère*. She rarely performs any act without him."

I'll bet, I thought to myself. Aloud I said, "Danielle, will you tell me what happened?"

"Well, when we got here, first the Baron asked me to have a drink and then asked me to take a pill, but since I had no headache, I told him this was *inutile* because," she continued in this reasonable voice, "I had no headache. I felt fine. I think he was annoyed with me, because he left me for a while and when he came back he seemed terribly gay and happy."

"Did he talk a lot when he came back?"

"To my mind, his speech was rather excessive, and he said me some stories which were not in the best of taste." Here she paused, took a sip, and sat looking at me quietly.

"Well," I nodded, *"alors, et après . . ."*

"Well, we went over on the divan where you are seated and the Baron was kissing me."

"Did you resist this?" I asked.

"Oh no," she said, childishly and honestly, "He was nice, even if a little rough, and he had let me see him at the studio, you remember?"

I was afraid she would stop again. I said, "I remember, I remember, please continue."

She glanced toward the fireplace, "Oh . . . he just roughly kissed me again and again and then wanted to do other things. He tried to pull my blouse off. It's a very nice blouse and must not be treated roughly."

"Danielle, will you tell me what really happened?" I said, trying not to yell at her.

"When I resisted the taking off of the blouse, he jumped up rather quickly and made me another drink, which seemed very strong. He insisted that I drink this and I did. He resumed his place beside me on the divan and again commenced the removal of the blouse. The room became very hot *et j'avais une chaleur épouvantable*, so it was agreeable to me to remove the blouse. You understand?"

"I understand," I nodded encouragingly.

"We sat there for a while and then the Baron became very rough and angry. I didn't understand why; I knew that he was very agitated."

"So?" I said, wanting her to continue.

"Well," she welled, "I kissed him soundly and at his insistence—completely."

"You what?"

"I kissed him completely," solemnly she gave me a little wink as though we were fellow conspirators. "You know," she said in her breathy little-girl's voice.

"Yeah, I know," I said, "well now, what about the rape?"

"Le quoi? . . . What?"

"When the Baron violated you."

"Well," she started again, "you see . . . well, I finally let him try to love me but we were unsuccessful."

"Listen, Danielle, can't you hurry this on a little? I'm trying to find out what happened."

THE DEAL

"*Rien*," she said, childishly, "nothing. He couldn't. He even wanted me to *faire l'amour* in a perverse way, from behind"—here she took a quick glance at me to see how I was taking this. She added quietly, "It's truly not a sin, you know, just making love in the back isn't a sin; they said this was so."

"Who said?" I asked grimly.

"Well, *ma mère et ma tante*, they said I was to protect my virginity at all costs, because of our religion, you know," she finished, primly looking down, then looking back at me shyly. "The Baron said my mother and my aunt were correct, that I should just relax and all. The Baron then just roughly went ahead and tried to do things with me and you know what?" Here she laughed nicely and quietly behind her hand.

"No, what?" I snarled.

"Well, Monsieur Jarnigan, you don't have to be mean with me and angry."

"I'm not angry, I just thought I was going to throw up."

She turned away and said in a little tight girlish voice, "Very well, since you are not nice, I won't tell you any more."

"I am nice, I'm the nicest fellow you know."

"I know," she said demurely, looking intently at my face, "and I like you very much, and profoundly have a sympathy for you."

"Listen, Danielle," I sweated, "please finish telling me."

"I will if you are nice . . ."

"I am nice."

"And sweet," she continued.

"And I am sweet," I said.

"And would be a little more gentle toward me."

"Danielle, I'll be so gentle toward you that you can't stand it, but please finish about the Baron."

She glanced at me and then glanced away. "Oh—to hell with him."

"He spends a lot of time there," I said under my breath.

"*Quoi* . . .what?"

"Danielle," I said, "Little daughter of my heart, finish about the Baron."

She got up from her chair, she walked over and sat down very close beside me. She looked up into my face, "Then you will be *gentil?*"

"Yes, then I'll be . . ."

"*Très bien*. Very well then," she cut in. "*Alors*, the Baron tried to do me many things, every way, but he accomplished nothing, all his efforts and agitation defeated him. He seemed very disturbed."

I'll bet, I thought.

She continued, "But finally all we did was kiss and I did kiss him completely but . . ."

Here she stopped, "May I speak in confidence to you?"

"You may," I said quietly.

"I don't understand. He's so tiny. *Vraiment . . . un garçon . . .* just a little boy . . . he couldn't hurt anybody . . . or do anything." I leaned back against the couch. "So you see, Monsieur Jarnigan, that's all, that's all that happened. *C'est tout,*" she finished, and took a sip of her drink. For her the episode had ended long before. It might as well never have happened. She leaned over toward me and was now resting her head on my shoulder. "*Je suis fatiguée,* I'm tired now from all the talking. I'd like another glass."

"Another drink?" I said.

"*Oui,* another."

"If you will excuse me," I said getting up.

"I'll excuse you," she said with a little smile, very gay but very tired.

I walked over and fixed the drinks. I went back and handed her her drink. She had now stretched out on the couch and was half reclining, looking at me and from time to time looking into the fire. She thanked me nicely for the drink, she made a little movement as though I were to join her, she smiled at me. It was a lovely inviting smile. I smiled back with whatever kind of smile I was wearing at the moment. Then I walked away from her and the couch over to the fireplace and stood there looking into the fire.

Well, there it was. It does no good just to say you are a son-of-a-bitch; just admitting it doesn't change anything. I had some unclear, unclean second thoughts about this girl. The unclear part, I could sort out the beads and string them, the unclean part was another hole in the dike. No finger would help this because I was giving it (the finger) to what little decency I had left. Gone now . . . all gone. No dong with a hopeful bell to ring . . . I was interrupted by the little voice saying, "Jarn." I half turned around and glanced at her over my shoulder.

"Excuse me to call you by this familiar name, but I heard the Baron who is your friend call you in that way." I turned back, listening to what she said. Danielle said many things. She went on to tell me in her little breathy voice how many times she had thought of me after her father had died. Her father had loved me as a son, he had told me many times.

"Jarn"—and when I didn't move I heard a rustling from the couch and pretty soon I felt her standing beside me. I turned and looked down at this beautiful child. "Jarn, do you think I am *soule?* Do you think I am 'tight,' as you say?" When I didn't say anything, she continued, "I could only tell you this since I perhaps am *soule*. My father," she confided, "who is in heaven, has spoken to me many times. I know he would be happy if I would be with you."

I turned to look at her. The plan was too easy. It was going as I wanted it to go. The act, that had to be done to accomplish what I wanted, this move in my lopsided chess game with the Baron could make a clean sweep of the board, I thought. And yet, I was disturbed that this girl was as she was. Honest, direct, no sham, no pretense, she was offering herself because of her father's *amitié* and affection for me; she had heard of me and seen me since a child and this was her payment. She put her hands on my shoulder and standing on tiptoe in her little stockinged feet she kissed me gently on the cheek and said, "It's all right, Jarn, I invite you. It's right, Jarn . . . I want . . . *j'ai envie.*"

When I still didn't move, she set her glass on the mantelpiece and leaning down came under my arm that I had been resting against the fireplace, then taking two or three dainty steps, she pressed her small body against mine. She stood there welded against me, looking up into my face. *"Embrasse moi . . . embrasse moi . . ."* she whispered. Her little arms came up and around my neck and she pulled herself up toward me. I think it was probably the most wonderful kiss I'd ever had in my life. It was tender, yet passionate; softly warm, yet demanding. Her little mouth was open and she was searching, pressing hungrily . . . continuing the kiss, no words were possible, no words were necessary. I leaned down, she kept her lips firmly pressed against mine and tightened her arms around my neck. I picked her up, she had no weight at all. I walked, carrying her lightly, across the room. I knelt down and laid her on the divan. The kiss continued without interruption. I started once to move my head back, a sound came out of her throat and through half-open lips, *"Non . . . non."*

I thought of old Rossi for one brief second, the celestial *pouvoir* . . . of his heavenly go-ahead to let the bars of virginity down. My friendship and my French francs cast upon the waters of a poor old man that I had liked, were now bearing virginal fruit, in th. strictest sense of the word. I pulled my head away from her, looked down at the little face, and said gently, "Danielle . . ."

She breathed, *"Ne dis rien . . ."* Then fiercely, *"Embrasse moi encore et encore . . ."*

Then there was the agreed-upon rape . . . the deflowering of this child . . . I covered her. She split and cracked gently like a new peach. Moaning and sliding warmly under me. I could feel her breath against the back of my throat. It was as fresh as a delicate perfume, as she moved her head and whispered in my ear quietly demanding, "Is it done . . . Is it done? Am I . . . did you . . . are we finally, did we finally do it . . . completely, I mean . . . completely?"

"*Oui*," I said quietly, "absolutely . . ." I breathed again. "Yes, Danielle. *Oui, ma petite*." And we continued together.

Then . . . we lay there. Her arms around me, and I around and in her. After a while—"Jarn?"

"Yes, little one."

"Am I doing right . . . is it pleasurable to you?"

"Uh-huh . . ."

"You are so *gentil* and it doesn't hurt now and I want to be good at this with you." Then quietly, after a few moments she kissed me gently and whispered, "Can you suggest anything that I can do to make the movement better? You could give me a suggestion to aid the movement?"

"*Oui, mon ange, sois tranquille* . . . be quiet."

"*Fais moi tous ce que tu veux*," she moaned again, threshing slightly under me. "*Oh, toi, . . . oh, toi . . . tu es à moi. J'avais envie de toi depuis si longtemps, si longtemps*."

"And I you," I whispered . . . "and I you."

She moved her head back and took my face in both her tiny hands "*Vraiment, vraiment?*" she questioned.

"Really," I said, "truly and absolutely." And we continued together.

Later . . . much later. She lay there in my arms, her small body nestled tightly and comfortably against me. I could feel her tiny breasts that never would need a *soutien-gorge* . . . she was all lovely, all desirable, all there, if you wanted it again . . . you wanted it. For right now, she was my eternal one hundred pounds of flesh, which I hoped would not be taken away or extracted too soon. The biblical pound of flesh . . . given one hundred times. How fortunate I was, I thought, to have a hold on this perfect, tiny hundred pounds.

You see, I knew this hundred pounds was going to recover for me one million pounds . . . not flesh, but sterling.

This little girl who lay there gently, lovingly, in my arms . . . this girl that I had wronged because she trusted me and was trying only to pay back my kindness to her family. She had done it with childish dignity . . . and done it well.

She moaned sleepily and snuggled her little head closer on my shoulder.

266

THE DEAL

"Jarn," she whispered. "Could we . . . I mean . . . would you . . . oh, please, let us try again . . ." I kissed her, and hungrily as if for the first time we were together—lightly, sleepily, lovingly. Later we slept.

●　●　●

Afterward we were both velvety-exhausted. I say *we* because little Danielle was the best . . . the most . . . well, better than you could dream of. Now thoroughly tired, she was sleeping pressed tightly against me. I lay there quietly thinking . . . I thought about sin . . . about rape . . . about a thoughtful kind of "pay back and getting paid back" blackmail.

Danielle stirred. I looked down at her. Her child's face was beautiful as she lay there sleeping quietly. Gently resting her head on my shoulder, a warm, lightly loving, lightly breathing thing. Too young yet to softly know that this truly was the most important . . . the gentleness, the love, the real warmth. But I wasn't warm; I was cold, numb-cold, drunk-cold.

I thought of the sins done, justified each one, argued each one through: What does it profit a man—? I'll tell you what it's done, what it's profited me; it's saved my life. How? . . . Well, now, I'll finish this last picture, finish the contract with the Baron, and then I am through. No more pictures, no more worries, no more Deals. I will also see to it that this child lying here in my arms is always all right.

I was consoling myself with my own "goodness," a pitiful source of ugly comfort; as I said, it does no good to say to yourself you are a son-of-a-bitch—just admitting it doesn't change anything. I had some "unclear," not "unclean," other thoughts about this little girl. She slept beautifully, the lovely quiet sleep of the young. I slept fitfully with whatever kind of sleep I could get out of this. We slept.

I awoke. I wondered how long I had slept. Where I had been, time didn't have much meaning and yet now that I was awake, I knew that I would have to put the rest of my idea to work. I moved my left arm very slowly so that I was able to turn my wrist, glance at my watch, and see what time it was. It was almost five o'clock in the morning. I had made arrangements with George, the maître d'hôtel in the restaurant downstairs, to see Mme. Dumont safely home. I'd had Sam Neeley, my best friend and driver, standing by in the car in front of the restaurant, ready to take Mme. Dumont as soon as she had finished her dinner. I had also instructed Sam to tell her I was sending Danielle home later, after I had had the doctor "reassure us," if necessary, that little Danielle was all right.

THE DEAL

Very quietly, without disturbing the tiny figure, I disengaged myself and very slowly got up. Danielle never moved; only one slim arm now extended out from the couch, the little hand gracefully open, the tiny fingers relaxed as though they had just given a gift. I looked down at this sleeping child. She was truly exquisite, the long lashes like a fawn's made her face more lovely, if possible, in sleep. I quietly tiptoed over to a closet where I had a large velour car robe. I came back and very gently covered her up with the robe. I tucked it in around her tiny shoulders and as I stood there looking at her she snuggled down luxuriously into the robe and then slept quietly. I walked back softly across the room and down the hall and very quietly opened the door to the bedroom where I knew the Baron was asleep. I walked in. As I approached the bed I realized that I could have entered with a brass band. You could have stampeded a herd of buffalo across the room and he'd have never turned a hair.

He was lying there fully dressed, his mouth open, his face sweaty; he had a pale green color, the nose again having that waxy look I didn't like. That nose was my barometer, my true guide to tell me that the "horse" was slowly galloping into the sunset. I knew I couldn't pry him out of bed with a pipe wrench, and that was perfect for what I had in mind.

I walked out of the room, closed the door, went into the bathroom, took my shirt off, turned on the faucet. I leaned down, ran cold water over my head, wet a large towel and wiped my chest briskly. It woke me up completely and was the best I could do until I got home, because now I had more important things to do. I walked through the bathroom into the Baron's dressing room, where I took one of his shirts, grabbed a tie from one of the many hanging on the rack and in fifteen minutes I looked fairly presentable.

It was now almost six o'clock in the morning. I walked back down the hall, peeked in; my little ex-virgin was sleeping peacefully. I closed the door softly and went into the kitchen, made myself some coffee. I was very careful about this because while I was making the coffee I was thinking over exactly what I was going to say to my friend the doctor. I boiled some water and carefully measured the good French coffee into the *filtre*, poured the boiling water over it, and waited for the coffee to drip through.

I poured myself a cup, got some cream from the icebox, and walked back into the library. I walked over to the mantel and got myself a panatella, went back into the kitchen—the coffee was ready—so carrying the coffee on a tray I went back into the library and set it on the coffee table in front of the fire. I threw three or four logs into the fireplace, it was already

268

set up, touched a match to it and stood there quietly smoking, sipping coffee, feeling the warmth from the fire, and after a few minutes was ready to put the rest of my "security bond" plan into action.

I looked in my little telephone book and got out the private number, the home number, of Dr. Levine. This doctor, with the improbable first name of Goya (his mother had loved a Spanish painter, hence the name), was one of the nicest fellows I'd ever met. We had been friends since right after the war, when he'd been assigned to the American Hospital in Paris. He liked to do the two sports that I liked most, which were live pigeon shooting and golf. We were pigeon-shooting friends first and then golf-playing friends. Later, I realized he had a lot more behind the stethoscope he wore on his chest than his shirt.

He was a dark intense fellow. He had dark crisp hair he wore in a brush cut. He was stocky, yet well built. He wore rimless glasses and always looked calmly at the world, his French wife, and his friends. He looked at you as if he'd slept well and didn't owe too much money.

I had, without thought of recompense, helped him out with the adoption of a child. His wife had been ill; for a brief time she had been confined in an institution after the death of her own child. They had applied and reapplied at many places to adopt a child but unfortunately the history of Mme. Levine was the deterrent to their adoption plans. A friend of mine, a lovely woman who shall be nameless, had had several adopted children of all nationalities and all ages. She ran a sort of school and home for war orphans in an old chateau about fifty kilometers from Paris. She had been an entertainer, a grand one, and I knew her to be one of the kindest ladies I was privileged to know. I had driven out and spoken with her on several occasions in connection with Goya and his wife adopting a child. In short, through the good offices of this woman, and her love of children, I was able after several interviews among all of us to help the Levines adopt a small boy.

This morning, while not wanting to extract or demand payment for any kindness I may have done Goya, I knew that he would refuse me nothing. I dialed his number. Ruth Levine answered the phone sleepily. "*Oui . . .?*"

"Ruth," I said quietly, "it is unpardonable for me to derange you at this early hour. I only permit myself to do so because of the urgency of the matter."

Her voice came back quickly, "Jarn? . . . *C'est toi?* . . . Is it you, Jarn?"

"Yes," I said.

She gasped over the phone, "You are hurt, Jarn, something is wrong?"

"Ruth," I said quietly, "I am all right, but the matter demands the attention of Goya; please put him on the phone."

"But immediately, Jarn, but immediately. Tell me you are in *sécurité*."

"I'm fine, only I pray you, put Goya on the phone."

After a few moments, the voice of Dr. Goya Levine said, "Hello, Jarn." His voice was sleepy but all business, no nonsense. "Jarn . . . Jarn boy, have you had an accident? What's the trouble?"

"Goya, I'm fine. It is not me personally that is in trouble, but I must ask your help immediately."

"Where are you, Jarn?"

"I'm at the Baron's."

"Is it the Baron?"

"Goya, I can't explain over the phone"—this very quietly—"but bring your tools and your discretion and get the hell over here right away. You know the address, don't you?"

"Yes, I know . . . 7th floor, right?"

"No, 8th floor, the top floor. Goya—"

"Yes, Jarn?"

"Don't be too formal about this. It's urgent, you don't have to dress too well, just get on over here now."

"You can't tell me a little—?"

"No, Goya," I said firmly. "Will you please come *now*."

"Jarn, that's me you hear at the door." There was a click and I knew Goya was on his way.

For caution's sake, feeling like a warden, I walked out of the library and back down the hall and took another peek at the Baron. He hadn't moved. I closed the door and went back down to the living room, and there I opened the door softly. I figured it would take Goya about half an hour to get there, making it about 6:30 a.m. Now as I walked into the living room I faced the one part of the problem that was unpleasant to me. I sat down softly on the huge couch where little Danielle was still fast asleep. I kissed her on the cheek and then on the lips. Her beautiful eyes opened slowly; without a word she smiled a lazy, sleepy smile and returned the kiss warmly, lovingly. The little arms came round my neck. Her breath was as fresh and pure as a child's. "Danielle," I whispered softly, "little one. You must awaken. I have something I must talk with you about."

She moved her head back so she could see me better, her eyes becoming more alert, more awake. "*Bonjour, Monsieur Jarn. Bonjour, toi*. I am awake. What may I do for you?"

THE DEAL

I looked down at her. "Danielle, this is serious, I must talk to you very honestly."

A slight look of concern clouded her little face. "You are not . . . you are not . . . unhappy with me, Jarn?"

I couldn't help but grin. "No, *mon petite ange*, of course not. But do you trust me, really?"

She gave me a pained little smile. "How can you ask? How can you even ask to me this?"

I said, "Even if I ask you something which is not of the usual . . ."

She looked frightened. "Jarn, what is it? Of course you may ask me anything." Here she sat up. She was without any blouse, without anything on, and so little, so lovely. She was completely unconcerned that she had no clothes on, until she saw me looking at her, then she smiled happily, "Am I shameless? . . . Do I shock you?"

In spite of the circumstances I grinned. "No, you don't shock me."

She slid over quickly into my arms and kissed me firmly on the mouth. "There," she said, "I'm approaching you now . . . now do I shock you?"

I gently took her tiny arms from around my neck. I looked down. I looked down at the perfect, tiny breasts—the dainty nipples as hard and bright as coral.

"You see . . ." she said, "I *do* shock you with my forwardness."

"No," I smiled, "but if I wanted to be shocked I'd know right where to come. Now listen, child, seriously listen to me. You must get dressed now . . .*immédiatement*. I will escort you to the bath, you must take your clothes and you must return immediately. No makeup, no hair comb, just wash your face, put your clothes on and come back immediately. *Tu comprends?*"

"I am at your orders, sir," she said mockingly. She stood up, clutched the car robe around her; she gathered up her tiny things, she started to pick up her shoes.

"Leave them."

She looked at me. *"Oui, mon général."*

"Danielle," I said, more severely, "this is not a *comédie*, it is important, little one. Please go wash and come back to me immediately." As she started out the door, I said, quickly "Wait! you stay here, I'll go to the bath for you and bring you a damp cloth and a towel. You dress." She looked at me questioningly. She started to say something. I said, "Sssh. You dress. I'll be right back."

When I saw that she was starting to adjust her skirt and put on her little blouse (she wore no brassière), I went out of the living room, down to the bath. I ran some warm water, put a little soap on the washcloth, grabbed a towel and came back. When I got back into the living room she had her skirt and blouse on; her shoes were still on the floor where she'd left them. She was now seated on the couch looking in a small mirror from her handbag. I gently took the mirror away from her, placed it in her bag and put the bag on a chair beside the couch. I sat down beside her, took her little face in my hands and said, "Now you must wipe off your face and when you are fully awake I must explain something to you." She did this and when she had finished drying her face with the towel I took them from her, threw them over by the chair.

"Danielle, you must be quiet and listen. I ask you solemnly, Will you do as I ask you, even if it seems to be strange and even if you don't truly understand the reasons?"

"Yes, Jarn," she said simply. "I told you last night, I tell you in the brightness of this beautiful morning—because this morning is more beautiful than any I have ever known—I'll do anything for you. You have only to ask . . ." Then looking down shyly, "But you know that . . . I would do exactly everything the way you want." She looked back up at me, waiting expectantly.

I looked away. Christ, what kind of a son-of-a—I swallowed, turned back to her and took the plunge. "Danielle, I have a doctor coming here."

Immediately she looked alarmed. "Jarn, you are ill . . ."

"No, *ma petite*—please, please let me explain."

Danielle said, "Just tell me one thing. You are not *malade*?"

I answered, "I am not . . . I must explain this to you but with a rapidity. There is a doctor friend of mine coming. There is an important reason for this. You see, the Baron . . ." Here she looked almost alarmed again. I said soothingly, "Now, Danielle, just listen. Don't be afraid . . ."

"Oh, I'm not afraid, Jarn, as long as you are here, as long as you are with me."

I said, "The Baron has me in an affair of business which could lead to complete disaster for me, cause me great trouble. I could lose everything, and I need your help."

She looked at me quietly for a moment, then said, "I don't understand . . . but I'll do anything for you, or anything you tell me to do for you."

Then I said quietly, "Danielle, I am going to have this doctor—who," I added quickly, "is a true and trusted friend of mine—examine you. He will, of course, know that . . ." Here I stopped. "I don't embarrass you?"

She looked at me steadily, "No, Jarn, are you afraid for last night . . .?"

272

"No, child, just listen."

"Yes, Jarn."

"It's important to me that for a brief time this doctor will think that the Baron made love to you. That he violated you, that he took you by force."

"You mean I should tell the doctor what he tried to do last night?"

"No, *mon ange*, you should tell the doctor that he *did* do what he tried to do to you last night. You must tell the doctor that the Baron made love to you by *force*."

"But, Jarn, I don't understand."

I got up, I walked across the room, turned and walked back. "Danielle, you said you trusted me. You said you wished to help me. I ask you to do this—to do what I say. Once again, will you do exactly as I say?"

She looked at me steadily for a few moments and then with dignity said, "Jarn, even though I do not understand, I shall do as you say. I shall do what you ask even though the thought is unpleasurable to me . . . I mean about the Baron."

"Well . . ." I said, going back toward her and sitting next to her on the couch, "you must do it exactly in the manner that I indicate. It is very simple and I will help you. I'll be right here while the doctor is here."

She looked relieved. "That was the next request I was going to make of you, Jarn . . . that you wouldn't leave me with this man."

"This is not just a man. This man is a doctor . . . and, more important, he is my friend, *mon ami fidèle* (I wondered if *fidèle* sounded a little stilted, a little too dramatic); however, I promise I will not leave you. Now do you understand?"

She nodded slowly. "I am to say," she repeated quietly, "that the Baron made love to me against my desire, that he forced me to submit to do what he wanted to do. Is this as you wish me to say it?"

I nodded seriously and firmly, "That is exactly the way I wish you to say it, Danielle."

"Then that is the way I shall do," she said quietly.

I whispered "*Bon*, it is very good."

"Jarn," she said ". . . I know . . . I am sure you have a valid and good reason to ask this, but . . . it won't get you in trouble?"

I smiled down at her. "My little Danielle, no, *mon petite ange,* not only will it not get me in trouble; it will disperse and get me out of my troubles. I am grateful to you for helping me."

At this moment there was a brisk three knocks on the door. Danielle looked up, frightened. I stood up. She quickly started to her feet. I walked

273

over toward the door. I had taken two steps, and she was beside me. "Jarn," she whispered, "kiss me once, please, before this doctor, this friend, comes in."

I looked down at her. "I kiss you, little one, not because you are afraid. I kiss you because *j'ai envie* . . . because I want to." I kissed her strongly. She walked back to the couch, sat down, curled her feet under her. I threw the robe around her and went to the door. I opened it and in walked Dr. Goya Levine.

Goya looked at me questioningly and said in his quiet voice, "Okay, Jarn, lay it on me. What's the trouble?"

I looked over at Danielle, then turned back to the doctor. "Goya, let's go down to the library, I want to give this to you quick." I said to Danielle, "We'll be back in one minute." Then, starting to walk out the door, I turned back to look at her. "Are you all right?" She looked at me, then nodded her head slowly.

Goya and I went into the library. I said, "Listen, we have to do this, and we have to do it fast."

"We have to do what fast?"

"You know about the troubles I have been having with the Baron on this picture?"

"Hell . . ." he said, "who doesn't know about those. You damned sure didn't wake me up and make me race over here like a fool to tell me that you are having trouble with the Baron. What else is new?"

"Listen, Goya," I said, "this is serious. You know the Baron has been up twice now on the morals charge."

"Yeah, I know," he said, leaning back against the desk.

"Well, the Baron had had a final warning from the prefect, one more morals charge and he not only would be *persona non grata* in Paris, but will take the fall. They'll put him in the clink and he's terrified of that."

"Well . . . so what's your problem?"

I walked over and sat down in one of the chairs. "Sit down, Goya, and let me give you the whole picture. But it has to be done fast."

He pushed some of the things back on the desk, half sat down, and looked at me quietly. "Go ahead, I'm fine. Shoot."

I shot. "The Baron has raped the little girl that's in the living room." I looked at Goya, waiting for his reaction. He made what for him was an abrupt gesture of surprise. Where anyone else would have jumped up or climbed the wall, Goya simply unfolded and then refolded his arms the other way. This for him expressed shocked surprise.

THE DEAL

"Well," he said calmly, "as I said before, what's the problem? You didn't call me over here just to tell me this. What's the punch line?"

"No, I didn't, but you know some of my troubles. All of the money I've got in the world is in these pictures—if this baby folds on me I've lost everything and am in hock for one million, two hundred thousand dollars. In short, I am finished. I've got to keep control of the Baron. I need you to help me out of this fix."

"Christ, Jarn," he said, "I haven't got any money. I don't know any rich friends. Roll it out in front of me—let's hear the story."

I plowed on: "I want you to examine this little girl. I want you to verify that this child has been raped. I want you to examine her thoroughly, take specimens, and then give me the certificate and a doctor's report. Then I want . . ." I looked at him steadily, and took a deep breath. "I want you to keep quiet about it. It can go no further than you and me."

He looked at me thoughtfully for a minute—a little coolly, I thought. "What about the girl?" he asked conversationally. "Is *she* going to keep quiet?"

I got up, walked over and got a cigar, lit it, turned back to him, and said, "Goya, leave that to me. I've got the lid on that one." I turned away from him and continued, "You can really save me on this, boy if you'll do it. If you can't, or if there's something about that oath, that 'hypocritic' oath . . ."

"That's *Hippocratic*," he corrected.

"I know it's Hippocratic in every other case. In this case, it's 'hypocritic.' " I turned back and said roughly, "Listen, Goya, I'm giving it to you straight. I am asking you to give me a chance to save myself on this Deal. If I've got this certificate I can make the Baron finish the picture fast. I can see to it that if the Baron doesn't work, doesn't do exactly what I want and complete the picture so I can get out from under, then I can use your report; give the paper to the prefect of police and help them slam the gate on him."

He looked at me quietly for a minute. "What about the date? How long do you need this 'hold' over the Baron?"

"I will be through the picture in three weeks. Can't you leave it undated? I promise you I can take care of the girl. It's all arranged."

"What do you mean, it's all arranged?" he said; his voice now was definitely cold.

"I mean," I said roughly, "I have already made a deal with her. I didn't figure I'd have to make a deal with you," I added, returning the cold look. "I know this is a little out of your line."

275

THE DEAL

"A little," he said thinly.

"I know it's a rough one. I only asked you because were the situations reversed, I know I'd do it for you." Then quietly, "However, Goy boy, you are off the hook if you want to be. Just walk on out the door and forget I talked to you about it. I can handle it some other way."

His face got pale. "That's a lousy thing to say to me, Jarn."

"Well—"

"Well, nothing," he cut in. "You sprung this on me kind of quick, you know. I never said I wouldn't do it. I only wanted you to be sure that you know what the hell you are doing."

I looked at him. It was a tense moment. "Goya, I know what I am doing and I am asking you straight out, Will you do it? Give me a Yes or a No and then we are going to forget about it, either way you answer. That's the only kind of a deal I want to make with you."

He stood up, walked over toward me, looked me straight in the eye. "You want a straight answer, you got a straight answer. I'll do it, Jarn; then I'll try to forget about it—both ways. Let's go in and talk to the girl." We stood there looking at each other coldly. Without a word I turned around and walked out the door. He followed me, carrying his little black bag.

We walked into the living room. Danielle was still seated on the couch, the car robe still around her. She looked pale and frightened . . . just the way I wanted her to look. "Danielle, you needn't be frightened, *mon enfant*. This is Dr. Levine, a very good friend of mine. There is no cause to alarm yourself, but you must allow Dr. Levine to examine you and you must answer his questions." Goya nodded.

Danielle looked at me, then returning Goya's nod, said, "*Docteur . . .*"

Goya leaned down toward her, speaking French quietly: "Mademoiselle, I am desolate that you have had this unfortunate experience but you must not be frightened. Monsieur Jarnigan has explained to me this *chose mauvaise*. He has told me everything. Would you please stretch out on the couch so that I may conclude certain perfunctory examinations in order to see if you need *majeure*—medical help." Without a word she turned, leaned back and stretched out on the couch. Goya said to me, "Where may I wash my hands? And do you have a sheet?" Danielle lay there looking at me. I led Goya from the room, took him into the bathroom, where he started washing his hands. I grabbed a sheet from the linen closet, went back into the living room. I went over to the couch. Danielle stood up and said, "Jarn, is everything . . ."

276

THE DEAL

"Little one, everything is all right. This will be over in a few minutes. You mustn't be afraid."

"I am only a little frightened. What will he do to me?"

"Nothing, child. He will just examine you. Please don't be afraid."

She looked at me quietly. "If you are here . . ."

"I am here," I said gently.

Goya came back into the room, looking very professional. By this time I had spread the sheet over the couch. Goya said to her, "Mademoiselle, you must disrobe." She did this quickly. She was now lying on the sheet with the other half of the sheet over her. Goya had opened his medical kit and was busy taking out slides and little wooden swabs, laying them out very orderly on a white towel from his bag. He said, "Jarn, if you'll excuse us now." I backed up two or three steps.

"No," Danielle said, "no. I want Monsieur Jarnigan to stay." She looked at me desperately. Goya looked at the little girl, then turned and looked up at me questioningly. "Well," I said. Goya continued looking at me steadily for a moment, shook his head and then turned back to the girl. "All right, mademoiselle, Monsieur Jarnigan can stay. Now, will you please relax."

For the next ten minutes Goya was doing many things with swabs and cotton; from time to time he used other napkins and glass slides. I was standing in the far corner of the room, looking out the window and from time to time glancing back to see what was going on; they were talking quietly. After what seemed to me to be an hour, but wasn't more than ten minutes, Goya stood up and said quietly, "You may dress, mademoiselle. Then you should go in the bath and follow my instructions with the medicine. Then I must ask you a few more questions."

He walked over to where I was standing by the window. We both had our backs to Danielle but I glanced quickly over at her. I saw that she was dressing. Then she walked to the door looking very tiny and forlorn. Goya stood looking out the window, saying nothing.

"Well?" I said.

"Well what?" he frowned.

"Well, what's the report?"

"It's what you said it was," he said quietly.

"Well, what does your report show?"

"Clinically or ——?"

"Clinically, like it's going to show on that medical certificate." I whispered.

He answered like a professor. "Well, her hymen is broken. There is semen present, a lot of semen. She has definitely been involved with rough

277

intercourse. There is minor bleeding present. That's the clinical report, the rest depends on what she says." He turned and looked at me coolly. "What *is* she going to say, Jarn?"

I returned the look. "Ask her," I said quietly.

He gave me another thoughtful glance, then turned abruptly. Danielle had returned to the room. Goya walked back over to the girl. "Now, Mademoiselle Dumont, I must ask you to tell me what happened."

Little Danielle did as I had asked. She stuck pretty close to the truth, but hearing it from this child's lips made it sound even worse than it was. She said the Baron had brought her home, and made her drink something, had given her a pill for a headache that she didn't have, and that he had made love to her against her wishes repeatedly and when she awakened she was alone and . . . Her voice started to falter. I walked over and cut in, "Yeah, we had an early call at the studio. I stopped by to make certain that the Baron would be up and able to work this morning, since I knew he had been out on the town last night. I let myself in and found Mademoiselle Dumont half conscious."

Goya looked up at me, completely ignoring the girl, "And you could tell exactly what had happened?"

I looked down at him coldly. "Yeah . . . that's right, doctor . . . I knew exactly what had happened . . ."

He glanced at the girl and then back at me. "I think it's pretty clear, Jarn. All right, young lady, that's all." He got up, made some notes in a little book, went over, put the things in his bag, and said, handing her a slip of paper—"You must get this at a pharmacy. The directions will be on the bottle. And now, mademoiselle, you must excuse me." He said to me, "Jarn, may I speak with you a moment?"

We excused ourselves. Danielle took a comb from her handbag, and began to fix her hair as Goya and I returned to the library. This time he went around and sat behind the desk. He took out a book, opened the pages, took out his pen. I had gone back over to the mantel, got another cigar, stood there in front of the fireplace smoking and looking at him. He sat there quietly for a couple of moments, then he turned and said, "Jarn, you sure you want me to do this?"

I looked at him. "Uh-huh."

"You don't have anything else to tell me, anything else to add to that in there?"

"No."

"You want me to write it down like she told it to me?"

278

THE DEAL

"I want you to write down what you heard," I said coldly. He looked at me for a minute and then looked down to the page and began writing. I walked over and stood behind him. The blank that he was writing on looked like a large prescription blank or stock certificate. It had file numbers, it had a space for remarks, diagnosis. It looked very clinical. He made the report and I read over his shoulder as his comments were written. He wrote exactly what I wanted: Mademoiselle Dumont had been examined by Dr. Goya Levine at 6:57 of "blank" date. He had found that she was female, Caucasian, age approximately fifteen. She had had violent sexual intercourse, hymen broken, semen present. Being questioned, patient reported she had been assaulted, violated. She named the Baron, of Hollywood, California, U.S.A., as the felon. I read this over his shoulder.

He had stopped writing, he read it through carefully, signed it, then pulled it out of the book. He got up, walked around the desk, waving it in the air as though it were a large check. He walked across the room, turned back, then walked up to me and handed me the paper. "Jarn, here you are." He looked at me steadily for a moment. "I figure you and I are square. All paid off . . ." I took the paper, I took out my wallet, put the paper inside and put the wallet back in my pocket. Without a word, he picked up his bag, his coat and hat, and started for the door. I followed him. He would have gone out of the door.

"Goya . . ."

He turned without saying anything.

"I am grateful to you."

He didn't nod, he didn't acknowledge what I had said. He said in a dull voice, "I'm grateful I didn't have to examine *you* this morning. Remember Jarn, from now on we don't owe each other anything." And without another word he walked out of the room, down the hall, and I heard the front door slam.

I stood there looking into the fireplace, wondering what else I could have said to him. I knew he had hated to do what he did. I knew that I had done a shabby thing in forcing him to repay a moral debt. After he had done it, what could I possibly have said? . . . How feeble words seemed in this case. I sat down in the big chair in front of the fire and was just sitting there when I heard a rustle at my side. I started and turned around. Danielle slid softly and quietly into my lap, put her arms around me and whispered, "Did I do all right, Jarn? Did I say the things to the doctor that pleased you? Does it make you happy—will all be well for you now?" Then turning around so she could look directly into my face, she said,

"Did I do all right?" She smiled . . . a weak, yet beautiful little-girl smile. "You did fine, honey . . . you did just fine."

She put her little head on my shoulder. *"Je suis si contente."*

"I am equally content," I murmured thoughtfully, and we sat there looking into the fire, with me waiting for the Baron to awaken. Now *I* had artistic control. This is a raper's right. Now I could finish the Deal.

32

During these money troubles, when it seemed that our *licence provisoire* was in danger, and that our Aide du Cinéma funds might actually be confiscated, I wanted to line up an extra seven million francs for the next week's shooting.

I was apprehensive about the bank, which had absorbed about all it wished to of the niceties and charm that I could trade for cash, because the current Parisian studio gossip about my troubles with the Baron left little to the imagination.

Worry had got the better of me to such an extent that I left a note on the subject for the Baron, explaining everything and expecting nothing. To my amazement, however, the Baron was in my office an hour later. He was in formal attire . . . having been on his way to a private party which he was quite vague about.

My note had hinted that he would be doing me a big favor by making a personal appearance at the bank; to try to give our activities a solid image. And that is exactly what the Baron did.

In a monster French touring car—which the Baron had probably selected for its romantically spacious back seat—we drove to the bank, where the Baron summoned the president to a conference in a truly lordly yet delicately diplomatic way. We were accordingly ushered into a room that would have made Louis XIV happy. The president and his directors could not have doubted that the Baron's formal dress was a gesture of respect for the bank.

Well, by the time the Baron finished charming those august gentlemen, the Baron could have carried our seven million francs out through the portals in gold bars. I knew he was improvising—because the Baron had never in his life delivered a speech that long without an "idiot card"—but it was really a beauty.

The French have always been susceptible to men of action who are also orators. And the Baron's action was, in fact, mostly oratory. Maybe he could have ended up a member of the Académie . . . if he had just stayed around long enough.

However, frightened about the consequences of the "rape" of Danielle, he

281

took off on his yacht for the balance of the shooting for the next week—and ultimately, for the balance of the entire picture!

The Baron felt, and perhaps rightly so, that I had not been properly grateful for his help. The Baron was a one-at-a-time-shot do-gooder—then he always had to take time out to pat himself on the back and acknowledge his applause. None forthcoming, the Baron's anger was always unjust; it marched swiftly, but without transportation. It was never within—the quality of mercy.

I knew that much of the evil in the world consisted of the disagreement between the object and the appetite. In the Baron's case, it was always the appetite for which he had no knife or fork of sufficient size. With shame, he ate from that table with fingers and mouth. What a man has, he doesn't desire; what he doesn't have he desires.

After the Baron took off from the picture, echoes of old phrases filled my mind: "I am fallen into the hands of publicans and sequesterers, pharisees and farts! They have taken all from me. What now? Let me look about me—what friend have I? They have left me the sun, the moon, fire and water, an ex-wife and friends to pity me." I could still sleep and digest, eat and drink, read and meditate; but if I did all these on script number three—the "leper" script—I'd really be in bad shape. Old Jarn the Iceman would have to do one of two things—warm up a little or freeze to death in his own loneliness and anger. The run-out like the sell-out taught me to be cool and crappy, industrious and evil. I took care to spread the manured malice around, and after all this, found it was no good in itself. The treasure had already been snatched—like the negative of my picture.

I wondered—how few producers in the world are prosperous? How many are slaves and beggars, persecuted and oppressed? We fill the corners of the earth—Hollywood, Paris, Rome; we groan to high heaven; we weep prayers; we have sad reminiscenses—and we all need just that extra completion bond—we need the inch farther, the second sooner—we need help.

At least, brother, *I* need help. I weep with want, I am sick with oppression, I am desperate by a too-quick sense of constant infelicity. I am in the studio. I am on my own sound stage. I see the empty sets. I am in a place of sorrow and tears, of great evil and constant calamity. I should like to remove myself. The pills—or the great pacifier, the .45 that I keep in my room—cure all nightmares, quench all dreams.

There's a lot of noise. I doubt if you care. I doubt if you hear it. The wound doesn't really hurt until you twist the knife and let the air in. Then, brother, you've got it—no film, no problems, no Deal! You have successfully delayed things. For what? I could deal my way out of this; I had the know-how; I had the faith in myself. *Yes I had.*

Again faith seemed to pick out a situation in plain black and white, like an allegory—a tragedy of appalling platitudes.

For the Baron could not "ring fancy's knell." His knells held no gayety, no substance.

The advice of Hamlet about "holding the mirror up to Nature" is always quoted by earnest critics, as meaning that art is nothing, if not realistic. But it really means that art is nothing if not artificial. Realists believe the mirror—and therefore break the mirror.

Now, although the Baron loved to play Hamlet, he had a particular abnormality (over and above the personal one which plagued him through his life) which nowhere is mentioned in the play *Hamlet*. The Baron as a player was bewitched because he was thinking of Hamlet as a real man—with the background behind him three dimensions deep—which does not exist in a looking glass.

The Baron, when he wasn't playing Jared Throne or when he wasn't trying to play Hamlet—when he was trying to be a man—many times did succeed. But, unhappily, his flaws—already described—trapped him. He was known as a man who wanted to be a producer-star, not a star-producer; and at times he wanted to be a gentleman. But trying to be a producer-star-gentleman produces a very grave weakness in such characters.

So, for me it had become, like running down the slanted stairs—worse, riding a horse down the slanted stairs, a horse that ran away with me, that rushed on down, down through wilder and to wilder places until finally I knew that what I was riding was my own Deal, my own nightmare. I was trying continually to outfigure and outguess my superstar, the Baron.

This star asserts that all other creatures on the earth are morally bound to sacrifice their interests to his, on the specific ground that he possesses all noble and necessary qualities, and is an end unto himself.

But the star, when climbing a tree, is less graceful than the cat. Nor do true lovers or poets urge the star to sing all night, like the nightingale. The star also, when submerged a long time underwater (scuba diving, which the Baron was prone to do), was somewhat less happy than the haddock. And, should the star be cut open, pearls would less often be found in him than in an oyster—which has been previously (soulfully) described.

The star is not content to answer criticisms or even tolerate them. Being a muddleheaded star, he does not have the correct answer. He feels that since he is as he is, he is more than a giver of pearls, an underwater creature, or a nightingale bursting into song. His actual self is more valuable. He reflects on the cat.

He at last discovers in the cat one characteristic of the star; a quality of the caudality of the tail. In this, cats are stars, and wave on every treetop the tail—the star's banner.

The Baron's puny and feeble banner had difficulty in unfurling. There was no rod to support it. So why should that singing star, commonly called the songbird of the night, or that climbing star, hitherto known as the cat, fall down and worship other banners? Because they have starmanship, they have the ability to relax in front of the camera—this puts them above everything.

Trying to reason with my star, my Baron, was impossible—unless I caught him on the upswing. My star flings up his heels and kicks the cat. He crushes the oyster; he eats the haddock; he pursues the nightingale. And this is how the war started, Hector—specifically, between "Jarnigan the Raper" (or "Old Jarn the raper") and the Baron.

•　•　•

My story of the Deal with the Baron is not the heart-rending tale of a mouse before a cat, but rather, as it finished, mine was the ripping-asunder, heart-rending tale explaining the luck of a rat; who had a cat with no dong. I had an incomplete man—as we are all incomplete men. And I also have now an incomplete picture. And it isn't "passing strange"—I know what caused it.

33

Well, there was nothing to do but go back to my office, take my lumps, and wonder which way the cat would jump this time . . .

Having tried every way to locate the Baron, I was glad to get any sort of news, even bad. I wasn't disappointed.

Mme. Henriette buzzed me in my private office (my thinking parlor) to inform me that the well-known French attorney, Jean Dupont Durand, was on the phone with private information of a personal nature to impart to me. I said to put him through.

A voice came over the wire, oratorical, musical; a voice pleased with itself, being guided by a brain that told it, it was good. "Monsieur Jarnigan."

"Yes."

"This is Jean Dupont Durand speaking." The sentence rolled off his tongue with him tasting it sweetly at every word. He hated to let them go, but continued. "I permit myself to inform you that it would be most advantageous to appear at my *bureau* . . . office," he corrected quickly.

"In what form would this advantage to myself take shape?" I questioned, putting the ball back on his side of the court.

"My address is 181, Rue St. Honoré. Again, allow me to inform you of the advantages—"

I cut in on him with, "I should be gratified for just a suspicion of what the matter concerns itself with."

"You yourself, monsieur. It's an affair not easily discussed on the telephone. *Malgré cela*—in spite of this—I permit myself to advise—"

I stopped him again. "I'll present myself in your *bureau*, office, at five o'clock."

"It will *certainement* be to your advantage," he concluded solemnly.

I hung up. I knew him to be the finest and best-known motion picture lawyer and *avocat* in Paris. I knew he had represented the Baron on another rape charge, and had gotten him out of a couple of peculiar scrapes that could have made the Baron *persona non grata* in Paris and its environs. I knew he had called about the Baron. I felt, with enough money involved, he would be on my side. If I had a side . . .

I tackled some business about the distribution contracts. God knows it

285

was going to be a cliff-hanger. I was selling off distribution rights for cash in huge sums—for a picture that was only one third through, the star having disappeared, and the finish of the picture still an uncertain quantity. But I kept on selling—the Baron was the hottest thing in pictures. The money was rolling in—with me rolling it into the bank like golden hoops. Some rolled as far as Switzerland and came to rest in numbered accounts for the Baron and me.

• • •

At 5 p.m. precisely, a secretary showed me into M. Jean Dupont Durand's library. This was to make me fully aware of M. Durand's affluence. I looked over his art collection.

Studying the walls in this luxurious office, I realized this man had spent a fortune on paintings. He had some rare and grand ones. A Velázquez, a Brueghel, a sad and despondent Goya. On one wall was a brash and colorful Van Gogh; on the opposite wall over the fireplace two Buffets, in that artist's gray, dead-rabbit period. And in the far corner, beautifully lighted, there was a Claude Venard.

I turned and started out the door into the main conference room, and was caught by the fragile beauty of a small and exquisite moonlight scene by McMath.

Then a gray mouse of a man appeared. He grayly showed me into the sanctum sanctorum.

I looked Jean Dupont Durand over carefully. He was a little man of about sixty, looked fifty, and was probably seventy. He had slightly cocked eyes, light slate in color. He had a lean and probing nose that would be into things; a thick-lipped fleshy mouth that moved continuously, like he was tasting something hot. He wore a Vandyke beard, waxed to a point. The hair that grew out of his ears was long enough to catch a fly. He was wearing a morning coat and gray trousers and gaiter boots. He looked intelligent, and as neat and as nasty as any situation called for.

After the gray man had backed reverently across the inner sanctum, then had gone out, closing the door, Jean Dupont Durand settled himself more comfortably in a straight-backed chair that was high enough so that he could stare down at me. His gaze put the lock on me for a minute; then, nodding his head as if pleased with what he saw, he intoned, *"Monsieur, cher monsieur,* I am ravished to make your acquaintance, and am humbly gratified that you have had the intelligence to come to me for the benefit of my advice and counsel."

THE DEAL

He was more melodious and organlike than in the morning's conversation on the phone. I listened politely, not saying a word. He paused a moment, then smiled wisely, contented that I showed the good sense not to interrupt him. "Permit me to say in all honesty to myself and to yourself that, as we grow more acquainted with one another, you will note the enormous benefits of following my judgment to the letter. I permit myself the following immodest observation, continuously dwelling within the bounds of humility—possessing a true and absolute sense of *fidelité*. And, monsieur, should I lower myself to conceal the idea that one may never find a truer friend, both with respect to the law, yet bending only where I may justly temper friendship, and my duty as a *Bâtonnier des Avocats à la cour;* a known champion of my friends, my clients and—yes, even of my confreres."

The organ kept playing and he kept humming these phrases. He had plenty of them and he gave of them freely. "I have a position of prominence in Paris—may I go so far as to say, Europe?" I didn't contradict him. He nodded again at my wisdom, singing on with, "I shall not reproach myself too severely for discussing freely a problem which, if solved, can only be of benefit to us both. I am putting aside with dignity and disdain, the trivia of accepted precedent. I know you to be a man of the world, a businessman of repute, a man of delicate judgment. So, as candidly as though you were my son, I advise you to retain my services as your *avocat*—your friend and *avocat*."

I opened my mouth for the first time since I'd entered his office. "Retain you for what matter and at what price?"

He leaned back in his high chair as though I had uttered a dirty word in church. A shocked look, a grieved tone, accompanied this reply: "Money— *l'argent*—has no importance. While we must give it its rightful place, it must be secondary if our new-found friendship is to flourish. However," he hurried on, as though he might have gone too far, "it must not, dear friend, be neglected."

I said, "I have not the idea to neglect that or you, but, *maître* (that's "master" in English) . . ." He looked at me lovingly; pleased that I knew the niceties, that I bowed to the social graces and was aware of the lofty position that he held. He brushed and combed me with his eyes. I grinned at him affectionately. "We are"—I made it a big, friendly grin—"talking about the Baron, of course."

He looked as though he had swallowed a fly. "Levity has no place in our conversation, *cher ami*. The Baron is my client; I could never discuss, nor permit myself the laxity to allow you to obtain from me, any privileged information that *Monsieur le Baron* has entrusted to my care."

I rose from my chair. "I regret the trouble I have caused you, *cher maître*. I permit myself to be excused and will retire from your *chambre*." I started for the door, but not very fast.

For a guy of his age, he moved like a ballet dancer. Suddenly, he was in front of the door, effectively preventing my leaving.

He threw his hands out as though to block my way, then dropped them to his sides. "Monsieur, do you not see that our interests are coincidental—that our paths must coincide?"

I allowed him to escort me back to my chair. He made little clucking tsk-tsking sounds and, when he saw I was safely in the chair, he reascended his throne. "It is entirely possible that you do not comprehend the difficulty that faces you." He said this, nailing me firmly in place in my chair. "I," he intoned, "Dupont Durand, *avocat à la cour*—I alone have the answer to your dilemma. Can you doubt the veracity, the absolute *vérité*, of my statement?"

"Who would dare?" I answered in cadence. It seemed to call for this sort of thing.

"I," he sang again, "I, Dupont Durand, will present you with the answer to our problem tomorrow morning. Yes, don't stop me—I will have the solution tomorrow morning."

I hadn't moved. I wasn't going to stop him. The foxy old French son-of-a-bitch knew where the Baron was. So, I'd play his game and he damn well knew it.

He said, "*Cher ami*, shall we say eleven in the morning?"

"Couldn't we say eight a.m.—or even tonight?"

He looked at me and sighed, "Ah, the impetuousness of youth. Ah, the—"

I stopped him with, "It isn't the youth, *maître*; it's the money—*l'argent*."

"That again," he sighed like an aging prima donna on a farewell tour. "We shall discuss that in the morning at eleven. You will find I'm very reasonable, *très raisonnable*—and I know you will be properly grateful. There are many ways friends can help one another. *Par exemple*, I'd like to know more about your *deal;* I also wish to visit your studio when the dance girl sequences are being *tournées*—filmed," he corrected himself. "I, too, have the remnants of youth." Here, he almost winked at me. He ushered me out of his office with a dismissing nod. "*Bonsoir, jeune homme. Demain, à onze heures*—eleven o'clock."

I looked back as I went through the door. He had returned to his throne. He sat, smiling happily. His small hands made a steeple and, nodding to himself, he dwelt on his own pleasures. I left.

THE DEAL

But upon leaving his office, I thought he was full of "hiccius-doccius." Hiccius-doccius is a canted phrase for a wordy-windy, a "hickey-dockey" fellow. One who plays fast and loose with the truth. *(Example:* He was a hickey-dockey talker and the truth was not in him. *Example:* He was a species of "hiccius-doccius.")* A rare piglike bird. He didn't chirp or peep his lies. He grunted and oinked them. Nonetheless, they rang as false as he did. "Peep-chirp-oink-oink." I don't believe you, Jean Dupont Durand.

I knew I had an appointment back in my office with the French co-producer. He was so far behind in his payments and money for the film, he was out of sight.

I got back to my office about twenty minutes ahead of him. The secretary opened the door for him and said quietly, "Monsieur Gilot."

He came into the room slowly, almost daintily. His eyes were puffed out of his head. He looked like a dyke. He was about at that level. But in talking to this guy, I had to play it carefully because he had, with his devious ways, managed to hook onto some of the money that had been destined for my picture.

"Now listen," I said, "I'm going to say this to you in English—and if you don't understand, you'll tell me. We have to come to a decision. We have to decide to decide."

"What is it, Monsieur Jarnigan? What is troubling you?"

I looked at him quietly. "Now, we can dispense with all of that. I want to give you a couple of hints of what's going on. First, you lied to me—with ease and with nothing to follow—in connection with the signing of our contracts. Second, you gave me a check that bounced higher than the Eiffel Tower, then made it good in slow sections—much too slow. Third, you sold off distribution rights "by the territory" to my picture, and you kept the money. Fourth, you reapplied for the Aide du Cinéma subsidy here in France in your name alone, and not in the name of my company as agreed. Fifth, at this moment—as of ten o'clock this morning—you have tried to borrow money on my picture, which isn't even finished yet."

He interrupted, much too calmly for my taste. "That's very precise, Monsieur Jarnigan."

"Yeah . . . and I'm not through being precise. Sixth, there is again that question of your lack of delicacy in trying to retain these new funds—earmarked for my Deal."

He interrupted me again, this time starting to sweat. "Monsieur Jarnigan, I assure you . . ."

"Your verbal assurances fail to reach me, monsieur. And now—

conducting business as business and not French diplomacy—I'd better have that money by bank time tomorrow morning or I'm pulling the chain on you and down you'll go. Flushed of face, but flushed, baby. *En toute simplicité, vous pigez?* Down you'll go—to Merdesville! The Swiss group has come up with theirs, now I want yours. I want it by tomorrow morning," I continued conversationally. "I won't ask you again."

During this time, I had sent detectives and the production managers by plane to every port I could think of, trying to locate the Baron. It now was becoming more difficult to shoot around him. I had another call from Jean Dupont Durand. No news.

I had sent my brother and Kaminka, the production assistant, by car all around the seaport towns, to locate the yacht. The Baron knew all the bars and bistros from Cannes to San Remo; from Biarritz to Beaulieau. My brother knew them, too. And my brother knew the Baron (So, send a thief to catch a thief, I thought.) . . .

Actually, my brother was a wonderful fellow. He had just remained a football hero, an All-American with all the rah-rah still in him, a composite of college boy and forty-year-old man—one vying with the other, but the college boy winning out in every respect, including lack of restraint and good judgment. To completely obviate this, my brother gave love. He loved everyone. He treated *les mendiants avec un verre dans le nez*—like the American ambassador and the embassy staff.

As it turned out, the search was needless anyway. The Baron turned up right in the middle of the search, all on his own—not at all embarrassed that I'd actually had to shoot the final sequences of our second movie without him.

Perhaps now we could re-shoot it with him in the close-ups. The son-of-a-bitch just gave me his boyish grin. "Glad to be back, Jarn boy," he declared magnanimously. "And you're the guest of honor at a party I'm throwing to celebrate the start of our third picture, old partner," he finished grandly. "How's it been going, Jarn boy?"

I could have cheerfully killed him—but that was the Baron, three parts charm and one part pure gall. Anyway, I was glad to see the bastard. Now maybe I could do the wrap-up of the picture as it should have been done. Then, I had to get things straight . . .

It was all I could do, when the Baron pulled a stunt like that, to keep from taking a punch at him. But I'd hold it in, I'd even smile. I'd give the Baron another chance . . . and I'd worry.

THE DEAL

I went home to shower and dress for the Baron's party.

●　●　●

You're troubled, so you go into the bathroom, lock the door; and while sitting on the throne, decide to give God a little of your time. "God," you begin the afterthought prayer—like throwing your last chip on the wheel when all your real money is gone—"here's the problem. You see, I need this and that . . . I want this. I must have that." Well, don't strain yourself, especially where you're sitting. God don't care for a corny prayer, like the fellow says. He doesn't care for a last-chance, badly scented one, either.

I knew that the Lord couldn't possibly be on our side—the Deal had certainly not been made in heaven—but I still hoped that *Someone* might pull off something . . .

34

The party was like most of the others, only more so. A Scotch mist of cologne, sweat, too much babble—and no brains. Those unlaid in advance were searching out new couplers. Someone, or two, to get locked and bolted with. Some new position to explore, some new nothing to check out. Sex—a muchly read, a muchly worked-over story that wasn't too good in the first place.

I watched the fat man from the Syndicate eating. He literally threw the food into his mouth with grand high glee. He talked well but windily, his mouth opening like a fire-bucket, for conversation or food. It slapped, and then closed contentedly on its own wind. What you needed as a respite from him was a long and deadly Victorian peace.

Earlier, just before the party, we had talked in the private conference room of the hotel. It was concerning the final payment of the money, now that the Baron was back.

The French co-producer, the Suisse Syndicate man, and a new guy, or "something," who had waddled into the room, following breathily on the heels of the Suisse Syndicate man, had all taken their seats around my chair. They had closed the door.

When this fat guy sat down on the big heavy davenport, he'd wheezed out, and the leather moaned pitifully. I had heard of this guy, I knew why they were bringing him in. He was the one who really held the hard *gelt,* could give it fast; and take it back, faster. He was worth a look.

As he sat there looking up at me quietly, in a sweaty sort of way, the pale smell (not scent) of overly used cologne came floating over my way in ungentle waves. He blinked behind thick lenses. His suit fitted him like a tent; you could have covered a garage with the coat. He ran to a manicure and a dye job. He wore a hairpiece. It was like fitting a toupee on a hog, and just as attractive. He smiled, giving me the benefit of a freckled-tooth, sloppy grin.

"Monsieur Jarnigan, I have some money for you," he'd said—and he gave me a brief case.

I had counted the money carefully. It was all there. I arranged to put it carefully away . . .

Then, I saw a French actor, a lopsided European star, standing there in all his glory. He looked at each girl who came in. "Oh, the wonder of it all!"

293

was in his eyes. He had his little peculiarities and, I'd heard, a lack—almost like the Baron's. But this French star had a long and golden pompadour that he groomed with love.

He'd combed his hair so much, his follicles were down where his testicles should have been. The follicles he had—the others were missing. He made futile movements when with women. In truth, he could have combed his *cojones*—everything—very thin; including his talent.

The next *numero* that caught my eye was a threesome who were truly only a "onesome" together. I looked away.

The next act was a French newspaperwoman, supposedly clever, but surely *con*. She danced up to me; she gushed . . . flowing over onto everything around her. She turned her spout on me and trickled, "Your new deal with the Baron, the publicity and all, the supposed fights between you two . . . isn't it just too exciting for words?"

"It isn't too exciting for some words I know. But," I continued, less savagely, "some of the words I know are too harsh for a beautiful and gentle lady like you." She smiled, spouted a small personal gush just for me. I excused myself.

I wondered how much more of this I could take, now that I had the money secure and locked in a safety deposit box in the hotel—in my name alone and with me having the only key—I was ready to call it a night. I was happy to see the party starting to dissolve, the French people leaving, like tired lovers after the first juice is gone.

The Baron's other guests were leaving, too. People were starting for the door, good-byes were bouncing around the walls. The Baron stood there nodding; seeing them out politely with his eyes. "So long," he called to a girl, "keep your legs crossed." I walked over to the Baron. He asked, "Kid, how did you like your party?"

"Oh, it was about average, about par for the course," I answered, wondering what was troubling him.

Most of the guests had disappeared. Up to now it hadn't gone too badly. He walked over and sat down in one of the huge armchairs and said quietly, "Kid, what do you think those people think of me?"

"Oh," I answered, "you rate like everybody else—some people like you and some people don't, and some people don't have any feeling about it one way or the other."

"You mean they don't all love me?" he said sarcastically. "The men jealous, and the women think I chase everything that is hot and hollow, the lousy bastards."

"Sure they are," I said.

THE DEAL

He turned his head and looked at me. "Don't *agree* with me," he yelped. "No, they aren't," I said solemnly. The Baron burbled on, "You think I'm stoned. Well, I'm not." (Here, the dignified, half-drunken stare.) "I'm sober, cold sober. I just think they're . . . I think they're . . . bastards."

"You're O.K.," I grinned.

"You're not making fun of me?" the Baron asked seriously.

"No. But I ought to be," I continued, keeping the grin in place.

He watched me carefully for a moment, then dropped it. "Jarn, I'm taking my French attorney and some of the others with me to the Club Salome—want to come?"

"No. I don't go so much for the fag joints." I added, "You shouldn't either."

He grinned at me. "You worried about my image? Well, don't worry, Jarn, I watch my step."

"It ain't your step you should watch, it's the back of your lap."

He laughed. "I've heard you use that phrase before."

"It still applies, Baron, it still applies."

"Well," he said brightly, having gotten his second wind and getting up from his chair, "I'm off to Salome's. Sure you won't change your mind?"

"I'm sure."

"Well," he said again, "I'm off."

And he was, to go up there. But I knew it would only cause trouble if I tried to stop him. "Baron, you've got to work at two o'clock tomorrow, so take it easy, huh?"

He gave me a look of pained surprise. "Jarn boy, Jarn—my partner, have I ever let you down?" He gave me a wink, and his Baron-charming grin. Then, using his "voice to charm the dead," he walked past me, giving me a good hard jolt on the shoulder. "Sleep easy tonight, Jarn. I'll try to make it . . . I'll try . . ."

He grinned at me drunkenly, then went out chanting, "I want a glass of milk. I want a tit. I want milk from the source." Here he hummed and made a little tune:

> I want to drink the milk
> That came from the tit
> That shows in the picture
> *That Jarn makes.*

He laughed uproariously. His voice trailed off, and he trailed out. I stood in the big empty room alone. The party was over.

295

THE DEAL

The "guest of honor" left. Quietly.

I walked toward the entrance. Now, escorting the Baron were his agent, the French co-producer, and the Syndicate people. The cars were being driven to the Club Salome by Saul Baum and Dupont Durand.

I was happy to beat a retreat to the door myself. But just as I hit the entrance to the hotel opening on Avenue Hoche, I was hailed loudly, pleadingly.

Up the stairs came "15." She was beautifully gowned, and beautifully loaded. She simpered, "Jarn, you have to take me home. The Baron left me. He went off with those men." In a little-girl, purring kind of voice: "What's going to happen to *me?* You'll take me home, Jarn?"

I had been having enough serious trouble with the Baron, and I truly didn't need any more. I was really running out of gas so far as the Deal was concerned. I had had enough, and enough again, for the rest of my life. I had had enough of the picture business and particularly this picture— enough of the Baron and his peculiar pleasures—of the Baron and his unpredictable, irrational behavior. I was weary to death of the many problems which needlessly arose. I was just fed up. I looked at "15" thoughtfully. I walked down the steps, went around to my side of the car, opened the door, and got in behind the wheel.

"15" rushed to the other side and stuck her beautiful tawny blonde head in the window. "Jarn, you're not leaving me! You're not leaving me. You must take me home. The Baron would want you to." Then she said, childishly threatening, "I'll tell the Baron if you don't take me home!"

And that did it. "Get in, *Quinze*. Get in, little "15," I purred gently; trying not to yell. "I'll take you home."

I leaned over and pushed open the door. She got in, carefully snuggled down in the seat, exposing a needless amount of leg—but they were nice legs. I pulled her mink coat around her, braced her in the corner, and hoped that she would promptly go to sleep. I started the car and drove up Avenue Hoche, past the Arc, round the Etoile; and started out the Avenue de Neuilly.

We had rented a lovely estate not far from the racetrack and golf course of Saint-Cloud. It was closer to the studio for the Baron, and I had hoped it would, in the long run, pose fewer problems during the picture, since once he got home from the studio, he could have dinner at home with his friends, drink at home and not be exposed to the temptations of Paris, which, in my view, were always too close to the Baron.

"15" stirred, reached down and turned on the radio. She fumbled

296

around, and fumbled around, and finally got some music. "It's nice. Could I have a cigarette, Jarn?"

I looked at her. "I don't have any," I lied—not wanting to have her smoke and fall asleep and burn something.

"You're right, Jarn. I shouldn't smoke. I think I'm a little drunky." She laughed softly to herself, as though this were something exciting and new. As though she were giving me this startling bit of information for the first time. "Yes, I think I'm a little drunky." She moved over and leaned her head on my shoulder. "This is comfortable . . . this is so nice. Jarn . . ."

"Uh-huh."

"What do you think of me?"

"You're a nice child," I said. With my shoulder I moved her over, not too gently, into the corner, pulled her coat around her again and said; "I'll wake you when we get to the Baron's."

She pouted. "But it's cold over here."

"Well, I'll turn the heater on."

"I don't want the heater, I want where it's comfortable."

With that, she fell back across my shoulder and gave the impression that she was half passed-out. I tried pushing her with my shoulder once more, but she pushed back, snuggled contentedly and gave every semblance of being asleep.

It was late, there were no other cars going through the Bois; the head-lights caught the lovely trees, a mist was gently rising off the ground. It was quiet, the car making scarcely any noise. I reached over and turned off the radio, and with that movement "15's" head slipped off my shoulder. She snuggled down; and there she was, with her head in my lap, with me driving along. She sighed contentedly, snuggled deeper into her coat and looked set for the night. I looked down at the young face touched by the light from the dash. She was lovely, all right. But she had sure the hell caused us a lot of trouble—the Baron had rutted after her like a stallion, virtually forgetting the Princess.

Now, driving along, glancing down at her from time to time, I thought, "this wild-looking, hot-looking, beautiful 15-year-old piece of trouble is only going to give us more and more trouble." I wished I could put her in a letter and mail her somewhere far away. She was almost small enough for me to do it . . . the Baron liked that.

Thinking of the Baron got me thinking of other things, and I could feel the old anger swelling up inside me. Suddenly, from out of the night, the headlights picked up a bicycle with no reflector—I had to swerve the big convertible out and around—I narrowly missed knocking a Frenchman off his bicycle and was loved by him accordingly. He cursed after me with precision.

"15" stirred gently, moaned; opened her eyes for a moment and looked up. I looked down.

"Jarn, are we there?" she murmured.

"No, kid, in a little bit," I said.

"That's nice," she breathed. "I'm so comfy." She squirmed again inside the mink coat to prove how comfy she was. She moved her head back and forth a few times, to get more comfy. She said again, "This is nice" and promptly went to sleep. I drove on.

The mist had turned into a rain; it became a little heavier now, pounding on the soft top of the convertible. Another French cyclist with no lights was either getting home awfully late from work, or going to work plenty early. He rode his bicycle from side to side, carefully avoiding the puddles. He paid no attention to my blinking the lights, so I gave him a blast on the horn.

This scared "15," who raised her head up abruptly from my lap and bumped her head underneath the steering wheel.

"Oh," she said, "that hurt."

"Look, kid, why don't you get over in the corner and you won't bump your head."

"But it's comfy here. It didn't hurt, really it didn't," she said in her little-girl voice. "But, you know, Jarn . . ." She moved, at the same time saying this; then, reaching up with one delicate little hand, "if you want to blow the horn any more, I can do it for you. See? . . ." And, suiting the words to the gesture, she pulled the rim of the horn two or three times. The echoes of the klaxon shattered the night.

"Knock it off," I growled at her.

"Well," she pouted, "I'm only trying to help you and I don't want to be frightened anymore." So far as she was concerned, this concluded her side of the argument. She continued, "If you want to blow the horn, you nudge me, and I'll pull. That way the horn will blow, I won't be frightened, and everybody will be happy, see?" She giggled gleefully.

"Listen, kid, for somebody who is supposed to be sleepy, you're pretty talkative."

"Oh, no, Jarn," she said hastily. "I am sleepy—honest I am—except I was frightened." I looked down at the little face. She looked back at me with what was, I guess, a cute-and-frightened look. I returned the look with whatever kind of face I was wearing at the time. Other thoughts were going through my mind, delicate little cloying thoughts that normally I wouldn't have had.

"Are you mad at me, Jarn? I don't want you to be cross with me . . ." she finished, childishly.

"Just be quiet," I growled. "Just be quiet . . ."

"I'll be quiet, Jarn." And she snuggled her head back into my lap, and we drove on.

We crossed over the Pont St.-Cloud. Then, leaving the bridge, I turned the big car up the hill that leads through the Parc de St.-Cloud. No lights were showing anywhere now, and the car continued to wind farther up. As we reached the top of the incline, there was a sharp hairpin turn to the right, going away from the river.

"15" still had her hand on the horn rim and, as I turned the car brusquely, she swayed and the horn blasted again. She said sleepily, "I know you didn't nudge me, Jarn. It was an accident."

Thinking of all the trouble she caused, I wouldn't have minded nudging her with a right cross. When I straightened the car up from the turn, her hand slipped off the wheel, and she was fumbling around, half asleep—but not all that asleep. I leaned over, because the big car swayed, straightening up from the turn, and it helped. It was automatic, it was necessary, it was beautiful.

Hate comes out one way or another, and maybe this had been necessary. We were ready. There was no traffic. "15" nuzzled around like a pup looking for something and finally found it. All of the anger and everything was going out of me now, so I took the last turn that led to the estate, the long way. I parked. I gripped the wheel tightly. She was still acting half-asleep, half-drunk; but was being pacified. So was I. I remembered what she said. I'd nudge her and she was ready to blow the horn. There was no trouble.

I didn't have to nudge her, yet she blew and blew. She tooted and tooted. The music was relaxing. No loud-sounding klaxon here. I wondered about "15." I knew now she played bass beautifully well; I wondered how she did with the piccolo. It must have been sweet-tweet—because she had obviously played music for the Baron. It must have been a song called "Music from a Faroff and Tiny Flute."

Afterward, completely relaxed, I started the motor and drove on. I turned the car into the big driveway that led up to the house. I pulled her head up from under the wheel and off my lap. Then, I moved her over into the corner, tried to tidy her up a little. Her lipstick was all smeared. I gave her my handkerchief.

299

THE DEAL

By the time we got to the door and stopped the car, we both looked a little neater. I wrapped myself further into my coat, shot a look at her. "Are you all right, kid?" She nodded.

The door to the big house swung open and here came, right on cue, the Old Guard—that is to say, Big Sue. I got out of the car, walked around to the other side, pulled the door open. Big Sue came down the steps.

"What's the matter, Jarn?"

"Nothing. The Baron left "15" at the party. She was flying the mail. She was loaded. So, I brought her home." Then I added, "At her insistence."

By this time I had opened the door and pulled little "15" out and to her feet. She leaned against me, weakly. Big Sue looked at me and back to "15"—then back to me again. I looked at her steadily. She gave me back the look.

I said quietly, "Well?"

She sighed, "Well, I guess I'd better get her upstairs."

"You do that," I said. Then, holding "15" by one arm, and Big Sue by the other, I helped them up the first couple of steps and to the big front door.

"15" said, in the little-girl breathy voice, "Thank you, Jarn, for bringing me home." Then, more sleepily, "Thank you for everything."

I didn't say anything. "Are you all right, Jarn?" Big Sue called after me as I was walking back to the car.

"I'm fine," I growled, "old Jarn's always fine."

"You worry me sometimes," she called, a little louder.

"Yeah—well, get "15" upstairs and undressed—then put her to bed."

"Jarn," she called, still not wanting to let the thing go, "the Baron will be grateful to you for looking after her and bringing her home and all."

"Yeah. Sue, you give him all the news. Tell him I said she's pretty young to leave out alone at night." Then, as I got into the car, I said, "Sue?"

She turned back, looking at me thoughtfully. "Yes, Jarn?"

"Tell him he ought to wean her."

Big Sue just stood there, staring at me. I started the car and drove out of the grounds and back onto the road of the estate which would lead me back to the City of Light and my own apartment on the Ile St.-Louis. "I love Paris . . . ," I thought, the music of that song going through my mind. "I love Paris every moment . . ." Especially when it's raining. I drove on.

"You lousy bastard," *Someone* said.

"Yeah, I know," I answered.

"Well, you ought to be real proud of yourself," *Someone* continued.

THE DEAL

"Yeah, I know. I know. Knock it off for tonight, take a night off, huh?"

As I was crossing the Pont St.-Cloud, going back through Neuilly, I remembered what "15" had said when she was trying to blow the horn. Then I remembered another children's song—because, "15" had said, in a voice like "Little Chicken Little"—"You see, Jarn, I can blow it . . ." And she did.

Then, I thought of "15"—of her lovely, lazy face that wouldn't change for quite a while. The body would change, the love-laziness never, and that's the way it was. I was ashamed after I had let her do it—an empty feeling, not at all happy. I thought of the Deal—it sure didn't make me happy, it didn't make me feel any better—but part of the empty feeling had gone away.

Today is only one day in all the days that will ever be. But what will happen in the other days could depend on what you decide today, so think it over, Jarnigan, decide right for once, I told myself.

And *Someone* answered, "Have you ever decided right?"

"Sure," I answered. "Will you knock it off about the 'have I ever?' Sure, I have, and did, and will decide this one right!"

I drove on home. The streets were quiet and lonely. I didn't feel quiet. But I felt the other.

35

Days went by, slowly. And then, another blow fell. My brother had had a severe heart attack and was rushed to the American Hospital in Neuilly. I got to Goya Levine, who told me, brusquely, clinically, "Jarn, your brother has had a massive coronary. He must stay here for several days, maybe weeks, Jarn, that's all I can tell you, now." He finished coldly and walked away.

My friends and members of the cast who had rushed to the American Hospital with me could see that I was at a loss because of the suddenness of my brother's attack. I was not surprised at Dr. Goya Levine's coolness. I didn't like it, but it couldn't be reworked now. My friends tried their best to change my mood and suggested a way.

In the same hospital was Jay, the American star who had been stricken with cancer while on a vacation and would never get out of bed again. He wouldn't need to, in the other world. They talked me into paying Jay a visit, and I hoped it would do him some good. We went into his private suite. All started to babble. "Are you O.K., Jay? Are you O.K.? . . . Everything all right with you, Jay?"

I watched them as they all hovered around the cancer-stricken actor—not too close, and yet close enough to hear everything. They mouthed little sugary niceties, pushing their words along like pieces of cake from a heavenly overhanging table. Pearls of condolence, clichés of sympathy, fell like crumbs off the table. If you were the sick one, it got you or it didn't. In this case, I'm sure it didn't.

The poor sick fellow knew that he was now the sought-after and the observed; not knowing he was looked upon in a horror-smelly way. The onlookers leaned down, mouthing their personal little crumbs of solemn farewell too early. The grave had not yet opened for him. It would, of course, in a short time. For some of the people hovering, maybe shorter, maybe longer . . . old Jay was a dinker's length from home. It was sad; all were enjoying their goodness—their aliveness. They were swell.

At the premature wake, the food and drinks were served at the heavenly table, feeding all, keeping up the escrowed payments, each one fearing to lose his mortgaged property in heaven. The heavenly crumbs continued to

THE DEAL

fall—and they, and we, and all, gobbled them up, making excuses for the good and the bad all together—a nothing. Thinking these thoughts and others—of Death and Dongs—your mind is tossed, and careens wildly; then, veering giddily around, tries to get back inside your head. We left the hospital.

Well, we had passed a milestone . . . but it was beginning to look more like a millstone . . . to hell instead of to the promised land—the promised anything.

We had cut up my French film and re-shot the Baron into sequences for the Deal's first production. And we had now wrapped up our second film.

Maybe the third film would bring something more than money in a numbered account. Maybe it would let me out of this unbarred, velvet insane asylum . . . if I could just finish this film, the Deal—and escape.

I returned to my apartment. I thought of my brother, who was too ill to be seen. I thought of everything that had happened to bring me to this point in my life. I was even ready to talk to *Someone* . . .

- I was alone and naked in the bleak winds of eternity—the child's choice making the man's necessities.

It is aloofness and detachment that life demands of us. The demand becomes most insistent when love cracks and runs down the slanted stairs; then our puny thoughts, our inner resources, are at their lowest ebb, are the least adequate.

On what a frail structure; on what a feeble horse sits our love, rides our hope. So, becoming Continental, speaking French and all, we try to discriminate between the people and things—the loves and vices—to which people attach themselves.

I believe the Baron finally felt the fascination of evil to the full. I believe the funning, charming, happy evil he sought after, found him. He finally had chased around the track so fast that he lapped evil, and caught it. When he finally caught it, and held it close, the shadows of this lovely thing closed protectively around him, shutting out all else. The rhythm of evil-making; like the rhythm of lovemaking—the rapture of the love-evil rest; the saint-sinner star . . . loving togetherness. The Baron prayed his "priest with a switchblade prayer," so menacing, that any good cowered fearfully inside him. When cornered, his was the nature that flees. And when he did flee, with frantic eyes and clanking brain, looking over the shoulder at his enemy in mock or non-pursuit, you felt to say to the Baron—Throw off the evening burden of your past and walk softly into the glad morning of tomorrow.

THE DEAL

It didn't work . . . It didn't work for me, either.

The Baron's women had always been bad medicine for me—the old ones he didn't like any more, like the wife whose suicide had been caught on the tape—the young ones, like the Princess and little "15," with whom I had certainly been indiscreet, to say the least, that night I drove her home after the party celebrating the first shooting of our third picture—and, now especially, the very young ones, who began showing up in my office with their pathetic "contracts." This was a nasty game of the Baron's. It usually went something like this . . . I would be sitting in my private office; it would be about eleven o'clock in the morning.

My private wire buzzed; it was Mme. Henriette, my secretary. "Monsieur Jarnigan," she said, "there is a person here who presents herself with a contract that has obviously been given her by Monsieur le Baron. I think it may be another of the contracts with which you are familiar."

I thought this one over. Mme. Henriette had a delicate way of alluding to "another one of the Baron's contracts." I was familiar with them, all right.

The Baron had a habit, when dining out or attending a party late at night, in the rosy five- or six-highball glow that he would usually get, of opening a case of the evening "braggies" far beyond the hour of the amber mood that he was often in. When he'd seen a beautiful girl—usually very tiny—he would, after a conversation and agreed-upon "trial," give the girl a contract with our company, Baron & Jarnigan Productions Ltd., Paris. He would fill in an amount, depending on how extravagant a mood he was in; normally, it went for around three or four hundred dollars a week.

But it was an interesting contract. It enabled the Baron to do what he wanted with the young lady in question, and it left his partner, old Jarnigan, with the problem of getting rid of each four-hundred-dollar-a-week "actress."

I thought of all of this, but I said to Mme. Henriette, "Well, tell her to come in. What time's my next appointment?"

"About twelve o'clock."

"All right, shoo her in, then in about ten minutes buzz me on the phone so that I can gently get her out of the office."

"*D'accord, Monsieur Jarnigan.*"

So, in a couple of minutes—much to my surprise—in walked one of the tallest, thinnest girls I had ever seen. She approached the desk in mincing, prancing little steps. She was something to see. Not only was she tall and

305

thin—she almost wasn't here. Her feet were so thin, they looked like coat hangers. She said, "Monsieur Jarnigan?" in a closed-mouth, tight-lipped sort of way.

I said, "Yes, what may I do for you?"

"Oh, I have come with respect to my motion picture contract which was granted me by Monsieur le Baron yesterday. He told me I was to come to the office, where I should receive the money and would be assigned a role in the cinema."

"May I have your name, mademoiselle?"

"Oh, yes. My name is . . ."

She said Yvette while I was thinking Yvette. I knew it would run to Paulette, Poupée, Poupette or Francine. "I am enchanted to meet you, mademoiselle. Would you be seated."

She would. She very carefully and somewhat stiffly, in my view, sat down in the large chair in front of my desk. She crossed a pair of the longest legs I have ever seen—she would have made a great basketball player.

Yvette looked at me, gave me another tight-lipped smile. "Are you Monsieur Jarnigan, yourself?"

"Yes," I said, "I am Monsieur Jarnigan, myself, why?"

"Well, from the way Monsieur le Baron spoke of you, I had thought you would be a much older man, a much more . . ." Here, she paused for lack of description.

"Well, I can imagine what Monsieur le Baron told you of me, and I imagine that now you wish to discuss your contract." She nodded, looking at me carefully. "Well, you see, Yvette, the Baron does not have the entire right to sign a contract with respect to our motion picture company. That is in my department."

She looked at me fiercely. "You mean, I have to do it with you, too?"

I stopped her. "Mademoiselle, you don't have to *anything* with me. I'm only trying to make clear the situation."

She flared. "The Baron told me you were a mean and nasty man, that even if you made uncomplimentary remarks toward me I should disregard them and insist on *mes droits*."

"It is not my intention, mademoiselle, to deprive you of *vos droits*, but it is certainly, equally, not my intention that you should be in any production of mine. Now, I must inform you before I speak further." Here, I stopped, reached over into the right-hand drawer of the desk, opened it up; and pulled out several forms which I had. I pulled the light over, so the light was shining on the papers, and I said, "Mademoiselle, you see these contracts—which are like yours?"

She leaned over closely, very carefully not touching the papers, as though they were unclean. She saw immediately they were indeed contracts like hers. "Well," I plowed on, "Yvette, these are contracts which Monsieur le Baron, in moments of reckless abandon, when he feels generosity, when he feels he must express himself, he gives to girls who are attractive."

"Oh." She gave me the benefit of the closed-mouth smile again. "Monsieur Jarnigan thinks I am attractive?"

"Indeed, mademoiselle . . . indeed. However, may we resume our business discussion?"

"Oh, yes, Monsieur Jarnigan. I am at your entire disposal."

Here, in a sudden burst of girlish charm, of overenthusiastic enthusiasm, she smiled. Now it was clear to me why she had previously smiled in a closed-mouth sort of way. She, in displaying the smile, had the worst set of teeth I had ever seen in my life. They were dark. They were freckled—and very unattractive. She showed a great deal of wisdom in keeping her smile a closed-mouth smile. However, turning on an excessive burst of charm, she now simpered, "Monsieur Jarnigan, is it that my contract has no value?"

"On the contrary, mademoiselle, it has a certain value. Now these other papers that I have shown you are, as you can see, for Paulette, another Yvette, Francine, Poupette, and many others. These are young ladies who have been equally led astray and *deçues* by Monsieur le Baron. However, to arrange things on an amicable basis, and let our relationship remain full of *amitié*, I propose to you the same arrangement I have had to make with the other "actresses" who have been signed to a contract by Monsieur le Baron. So, if you will take this slip to Madame Henriette outside, she will give you the money . . . the normal amount."

Here, Yvette jumped to her feet, her hat falling askew on her head. *"Baron m'a dit que vous êtes un monstre . . .* that you are a monster."

"Now, be careful, Yvette, don't lose your girlish charm," I said.

This time Yvette gave me the open-mouthed smile, with the menace of the freckled teeth. Even as it was, I did feel sorry for her. But then she began to say things that brought her down to the level that she must have been on before she came in the door. Things that shouldn't be said, certainly things that I wouldn't accept. This was my office. I had to spend the biggest part of my life in this room since my Deal with the Baron. And all of a sudden, I was sick of the whole thing. I wanted her out. "Listen, sister," I said, *"écoutez, ma fille, je dois dire que vous êtes une putain. Je voudrais que vous partiez immédiatement."* Briefly—I told her to get out.

Again that smile, and she added another dirty word. I said, "Listen sister, you got laid, that's all. You're getting some francs, that's all. If you don't want the francs and don't sign the paper, you don't get anything. All you did was lay a star—so get on out and dream about it."

"*Mais* . . . Monsieur Jarnigan . . . He hurt me. *Mais* . . . *mais* . . ."

I snarled at her. "*Mais* . . . *rien* . . . nothing . . . *Fichez moi la paix. Sortez immédiatement* . . . I won't tell you again!"

She left—not quietly. I was sorry for her. But not that sorry.

So that was the kind of side deal the Baron was always lining up with girls as we got into our third picture together. After paying off a steady stream of them, I got to feel a little like a pimp bookkeeper.

One day, a girl came into my office who gave me a special pang, because she happened to remind me of a girl I'd known when I was twelve. Not just "a girl" either, but really, my first sex experience.

She had wanted to be an actress, just like these Yvettes, Paulettes and Poupées, and I had played along with that game, too, just as the Baron did. Only in the case of Florence, she was way ahead of me, and in fact, gave *me* a few little bits of advice—absolutely sound—along with her physical favors, about the making of deals. I was sure I was in love with her. I knew she was, without any doubt, a "woman of the world," one to be reckoned with, a giver of advice that, if not heeded, could lead to disaster. Also, she taught me—for the first time—how to make love, a thing that was wonderful to know, wonderful to feel—and was also very useful.

• • •

Florence and I had been out riding the horses. We raced over by the auction pens, then started for the Hall-Mar ranch. It was a lovely old place, full of trees and—private. It was good and private.

"Listen, Jarn, how long can we stay out?"

"I don't know—long as we want. I figured we were going to talk about that kind of stuff you been telling me about. Well, we're here and I let you ride the Queen horse—you're not changing, are you? Don't make me wish I'd let Susan Howe come on this ride."

"No, Jarn, I didn't mean that."

"Well, then, dammit," I yelled, "let's go! Clamp your legs and let's make that fence! *Hah*—"

"All right, Jarn," she screamed—wild as a young Apache. Our horses hurtled on down the hill, hit the level, and then gathered speed in a flat-out run. When they reached the high, white-rail fence surrounding the

THE DEAL

Hall-Mar stables, the lean horses, with only our light weight on them, soared over the high rail easily.

Safely over—I was glad. For a minute, I thought I'd pushed the horses too fast on the flat-out, that they'd never make the height. For one sickening instant, I felt the muscles tense in the back and shoulders of Satan, my father's stallion. I leaned down, past the giant shoulder, smelled the good familiar mixture of horse sweat and wet saddle leather and, as I lifted for Satan to clear, saw the ground go away very far. I knew we'd make it.

We rode over into the shadows of the huge trees that lined the Hall-Mar property and got off. I loosened the saddle girths, and let the horses drink from the huge tank that was now full from the spring rains. Florence casually took off her plaid shirt (with nothing underneath)—slowly started to bathe the upper part of her body in the cool water. Still more casually, she said, "Why don't we take a swim . . . raw?"

I looked around. "Where's your brother? You said he'd be here to watch the horses and see that nobody comes . . ."

"Jarn, I told you. Hugh don't like you anymore, on account of Susan Howe. He thinks you're not being fair with me. And Hugh can get awfully mean," she added ominously.

"I can take him, if that's what he's coming out here for."

"That's just it, Jarn. Hugh isn't coming."

I looked at her, not saying anything. She had been quietly taking off the rest of her clothes—laying them on a little bush. I kept watching her. I was getting nervous, and kind of itchy.

"Listen, Jarn," Florence said. "I told you how Hugh is."

"Yeah, I know you told me, and I'm trying not to let that worry me too much. Listen, Florence, we ain't engaged. We ain't anything—so?"

"Where are my pants?" she asked.

"God Almighty, I don't know. Now listen here, Florence, do we hide the horses?"

"Get undressed," she said.

"Judas priest!"

"*Jarn,* how come you said 'Judas priest'?" Now completely naked she looked at me questioningly. I'd never seen the girls in Hollywood, except in pictures, and I don't know how they were then. I only tell you that Florence was not only the most beautiful girl that I'd ever seen—it was beyond that. She was a flat-bellied, not-so-big-titted . . . real *un*-Coca Cola poster type girl.

"Are we going to?" she asked quietly. "You remember, Jarn, you promised," she said, watching me and whisking her little butt around.

309

THE DEAL

"Hell, I don't know—when do you have to be home?"

"Why?" she asked, "who comes home?"

Her eyes were funny-looking. She didn't even know what I was saying. I took a good look at her. She started ripping at my clothes—she tore my shirt, helped me pull off my pants—and then pulled me down and guided me straight into her . . .

Later . . .

"Here're your pants, Florence. How can you get your ass into a little dinky bit of silk like that? What's it for? Sure as hell can't keep you warm . . . Florence, you have to meet Mr. Morehouse."

"Who's he?" asked Florence, eyeing me and at the same time trying to put her pants on. She got one leg in the pants—the other came down around her ankle—she got mad; waggled her toes as though they might have been her fingers.

"Listen, Florence, if you don't screw it up, I'll introduce you to Mr. Morehouse. Mr. Morehouse is a very important man down here, from Tucson. You always holler around here that you want The Theater—you told me what you told me—and I wouldn't never be anyone who held anyone back from the theater or the films, although I think the last is harder to make."

Florence said, excited now, "Jarn, *would* you talk to Mr. Morehouse for me?"

"Yeah . . ." I answered.

"Do you want to do it again, Jarn?" she breathed.

I looked at the flat belly and the little knockers. I tried to swallow, but it didn't work too good—the swallower, I mean—the dinker worked great, or was trying to. I leaned over and she grabbed me. I grabbed easy. I let her pull me down and guide me into her, like we'd done before. This was the second time in my life that I was being a man, so I wanted to do it well. I was trying to be suave and calm—and many things—but I just couldn't think or concentrate too well. I was going away—warmly—floating around under the trees . . .

While I was warmly, lovingly—and thrill-scared, surprised at this wondrous thing—I went away again, floated too high, bumped my head on a branch, was trying to make up a loving phrase for Florence, my beauty, my flat-bellied, little-titted first boff. I had a wet-phrased dream of a thing; and I had to say Now, and Now again, but I couldn't get my mouth to work. The hot-and-ropey, wild-and-smooth thing under me was bucking me off and drawing me in; all legs, all suction, all warmth, all and all, and really all again! I heard a moan—felt a flutter of the little flat-belly—the moan turned to a cry; and I drifted in the tide of it . . . back and forth, high tide, low tide—the world changed places with itself, and a voice said, "Christ, Jarn, that's good!"

"Don't say 'Christ'—it's a mortal sin," I said, "say 'Judas priest.'"

"Judas priest, Christ—that's good!" Florence said again, taking care of the mortal sin and the other one, too.

This was great. I wanted to practice some more. I tried a couple of phrases, very sophisticated, on Florence. "Listen, Jarn," said Florence in her thirteen-year-old wisdom, "use the gooey talk before—now, you can skip the mushy stuff."

"Why, Florence?" I asked. "I *mean* it."

"Sure you mean it, but save it. It don't cut any ice after the dinker-business is over. You see, Jarn," she continued, "gooey-talk first, sweet-talk and rub 'em wet second, and then the dinker business. Drive it in, keep it up as long as you can, then pull out, dry off, and shut up."

I pulled out. I was hurt. I furtively looked for my handkerchief, and Florence threw me her pants to use. She started to sing under her breath, "Yessir, that's my baby . . ." etc. I finished the drying, gave her back her pants; she took them without a word and put them in her sack. She half stood up now, under the low trees. I stood half up and carefully looked out, seeing if all was clear.

We finished dressing. I motioned to Florence all was O.K., and we both stepped out into the open to walk the few yards to the horses. She turned on me sharply.

"Let me look at you, Jarn. Fly buttoned—yes. And brush that dirt off the knees of your pants." I meekly did as she asked. She turned around. "Brush off my shirt in back," she commanded, clearly in control. I brushed her back off, feeling the little butt, free of any pants, under the dress.

My throat thickened and I said, a little hoarsely, "Florence, do you think . . . do you want to try ——"

"Can't," she cut me off. "Can't. Have to be home now."

"O.K.," I said quietly, "if you don't want . . ."

"Listen, kid, I do," she said, "but we can't now. It's too late. Maybe tomorrow night. If you remember what I said."

"Yeah." Then, remembering, "Oh, about the no gooey-talk, and a long time, and——"

"Dry up," she said, "and don't always say 'yeah.' Now, about Mr. More-house, you won't forget you're going to——"

"Listen, you asked me to help you, right? Well, then, don't ask me how

THE DEAL

I'm going to help you. I don't know, exactly, but I got a pretty good idea how it's going to go," I said.

You see, I didn't know right off. I was connected with the theater myself—I was an usher. I never knew Mr. Morehouse that well . . . maybe nobody knew Mr. Morehouse that well.

One night he walked into the Eris Theater . . . I figured it was him. Also the cashier, Miss White, who always had a runny nose, looked at me through the glass of the ticket booth, and signaled that this was the new manager. Mr. Leek, the assistant manager, looked over like he had just been given the band mastership in Forest Park. Mr. Morehouse was looking around the lobby . . .

I rushed up to get his coat. This was not an usher's job, but I wanted to get ahead . . . I was very polite. I lifted off the heavy coat. Lifted is the word—he was about five foot high. In taking off the coat, I had lifted him off his heels. He broke wind, said "Excuse me." He wanted to see the inside of the theater, so I took him down the aisle and put him in a good seat. When he sat down, he broke wind again. I said, "The picture's like that."

He said harshly, "What's that? What's your name?"

"Jarnigan," I said. "I'm an usher here, and this picture isn't worth a mouse-fart—let alone a theater manager's."

Mr. Morehouse kind of rose up in his seat (I hoped it wasn't anything serious). "Boy," he said, as he started to settle down, "I'll be leaving soon. Have a taxi waiting."

I whispered, "All right, Mr. Morehouse, I'll call it right now; but don't be disturbed because you . . . uh . . . you know . . . during this film. We had a lot of complaints . . . a lot of them."

"What do you mean, a lot of complaints?"

"Well, it just seems that everyone says the theater smells bad . . . or they leave . . . like the picture wasn't good. I haven't been able to figure out exactly the average . . . but I sure have been trying to keep tabs on all of this." I continued whispering. "By the way, Mr. Morehouse, I only been working here a little while . . . I wonder if I could see you tomorrow—you know, before the amateur show starts."

Mr. Morehouse raised his tired eyes—and a more tired spirit. "Why?"

"Well, there is this friend of mine who wants to meet you . . . name is Florence . . . knows all about the theater . . . wants to be an actress. She will do anything. She's young and sure pretty; but she can look old-as-hell when she wants, maybe even eighteen."

312

THE DEAL

Mr. Morehouse looked at everything and nothing. "How old are you?" he asked quietly, looking about two inches over my head.

"Fifteen," I lied, "but it doesn't show—I can look sixteen easy, and she's about fifteen sure."

He grunted. I waited. I knew I had him now. "We'll see," he said. Then, leaning back, "How is two p.m. at my hotel?"

"We'll be there," I said.

"Service and showmanship."

I grinned.

"That's the ticket," he breathed. "Fifteen, you said?"

"Yes, fifteen," I answered.

"Service is what I'm after," he leered.

"What I'm here for, Mr. Morehouse."

He walked out. He didn't wait for the picture or the taxi. I walked back up the aisle. This was going to be my first "deal."

I thought about all this, and later said to Florence, "You may have to be pretty friendly with him."

"How friendly?"

"Hell, I don't know. You know the theater—you said. You read enough of them magazines. Be theater-friendly. You always see about those actors and producers and stars kissing each other and all. Hell, I'll bet you any woman star would sure be grateful to kiss Mr. Morehouse. Why, dammit, do you know he manages two theaters here, two in Benson, and he even has one in Phoenix," I said grandly, saving the best for last. Florence was bowled over by this magnificence, this overwhelming theater background. Mr. Morehouse took on the aura of a Goldwyn or a Ziegfeld.

She was standing there in the fading light, thinking, figuring. I got the horses and we rode back to town, talking quietly.

"Will you let him, Florence?"

"Huh?"

"Will you do it with him? I think he kind of wants . . . I mean, the conversation might get around in that general direction."

"Oh, shut up. Just you dry up."

"I remember—dry up afterward."

"Naw, I mean dry up now. I don't want to talk about that." She looked worried.

At the edge of town, Florence dismounted, and I kept the horses standing. "I'm going," she said quickly.

"All right, Florence."

"Listen, kid," she said firmly, back in control, "Don't forget what I told you, and I'll see you here tomorrow night after choir practice, understand?"

"Fine," I breathed. "I understand."

She walked away. I watched her until she passed under the far street light. "I'll see you, Florence," I yelled.

She threw up her hand in a gesture of dismissal, but didn't look around. She disappeared from under the light and was gone. I would have felt hollow and empty, but I was too happy exploring my new-found "treasure." But that still didn't quite let me get over the deception and disappointment of how easily she'd regained her control over me.

But then I was glad. I'd found a face-saving happiness. After all, she was an experienced woman. She had lived, and knew all about those things. I had a mistress. I was a businessman. I was full of beans. I was twelve.

I got on Satan and, leading Queen, I rode back to my folks' place. By now it was dark. I unsaddled the horses and went inside. My mother said, "It's late, Jarn. Where have you been?"

"Yes, ma'am . . ."

She watched me. "A Mr. Morehouse called here for you; said he is from the theater. You're not in any trouble, are you, Jarn?"

"No, m'am."

"Well, what's he want with you?"

"Nothing, Ma. Him and me has got a "deal," that's all," I finished, proudly and mysteriously. "But don't tell Dad."

"Why not?"

"Well . . ." I began, wondering what would stop her, then hitting on the perfect answer, "it's a surprise."

My mother loved surprises and I knew she'd not say a word. "That's nice, son."

"Yes, ma'am."

"Want some dinner?"

"Yes, ma'am. I'm sure hungry, hungrier than usual."

We smiled. Gee, life sure was big and wonderful! I ate supper.

36

Now that the Baron was getting some good footage into the can, we were all in pretty fair spirits. Even the French co-producer began to warm up to the Deal, and the Syndicate men were starting to count their pharisees' wages. What doth it profit a man? Well, if we got through this film it would profit them plenty. We had all lost our souls along the way and not gained the world; only, perhaps, another film of the Baron's. A high price for guitar picks.

We had finished shooting early one afternoon, since our plan was to start at 8 o'clock next morning for some exterior shots on the outskirts of Paris. Normally the shooting in Paris started at noon and finished around 7 p.m., but the next day being a "location day" we were going to shoot from 8 a.m. until 6 p.m. That evening, since one of the actors was returning to the United States, he invited the cast and crew to an on-the-set cocktail party after the shooting. This is the custom in France. It was a very agreeable party and after about an hour I cornered the Baron and told him I was going home since I had some work to do on the script, and he said, "Jarn boy, it's early." Then, in an expansive and affectionate gesture, he flung his arm around my shoulders, "Let's you and I have dinner together. Let's go out on the town, let's be a couple of tourists."

I leaned back and took a good look at the Baron and to my surprise, he wasn't loaded. "O.K., Baron. Let's have an early dinner and then you hit the kip early, I can do a little work, and we'll both be on the set first thing in the morning."

"Done and done again," the Baron laughed. "Old Jarn the Iceman. Never enthused about anything."

I grinned at him. "Where will we meet?" I asked him.

"I'll send the driver for you at 8 o'clock. I want to stop by and see the Princess for a moment, but no women tonight, huh? Just you and me and . . ." It was at this time he saw Jules Molotov just coming out of the executive offices with the French co-producer. "Hey, Jarn," the Baron said in a burst of boyish enthusiasm, "Let's show old Julie the sights. He's the squarest motion picture lawyer I've ever seen. Let's give him a 'French vaccination.' Let's show him the naughty side of Paris." Laughingly he called loudly to Jules, the little attorney, who came walking over sedately.

315

"Yes, Baron," he said in his best legal voice, prepared for any eventuality.

"Julie," the Baron laughed, "old Jarn and I are taking you out on the town, a real Paris nightclub tour. What do you say?"

Julie shot me a quick glance, I nodded; he turned and with dignity said, "I accept, Baron, I am most grateful for your invitation. It pleases me that you include me in your group."

"Christ," the Baron whooped, "he even makes a legal speech when you ask him out to dinner." But he threw his other arm around little Jules and we planned the evening. The car would pick up Jules at his hotel, pick me up at my apartment, then get the Baron. He would stop by and leave a present for the Princess and then we would go on our "tour de Paree."

After a good dinner at the Elysée Club, where we talked to many of the French motion picture people who congregated there nightly, we ended up around midnight in Montmartre. There was a new club called Le Dinerzade. Its entertainment was widely known around Paris and it had lately brought in burlesque strippers from every part of the world. There were dark girls from Africa, beautiful Oriental girls from everywhere, French girls from everywhere; but the high point and the headliner of the show was a "Lilliputian," a female midget supposedly so perfectly formed that she was a tiny woman, slightly over three feet tall.

So there we were, firmly entrenched at a ringside table, the Baron, Jules, and me. The headwaiters hovered around making a big fuss. Champagne was ordered, the Baron was drinking copiously. There were a lot of naked girls running here and there, but what was holding the Baron's attention was the fact that he was finally going to see the tiny woman he had been told about—La Môme Michele. After a suitable time and after many girls had come out and done a dance, then they ran back and changed the costume they almost had on and they did the dance again; then they came back and did the dance a third time with nothing on, there was a fair amount of applause—but apparently everyone was waiting to see the tiny featured performer.

After the master of ceremonies had given the introduction in French and in English, the lights went out, a spotlight hit on the far side of the raised stage, the music of the orchestra swelled to a crescendo and out walked two huge Nubian slaves in costume. Their oiled black bodies shone like ebony in the glare of the spotlight. Their arms extended straight up over their heads. And there, on an ornamental silver tray, was the most beautiful little

THE DEAL

female of indeterminate age that I had ever seen in my life. In contrast to the tall blacks, she seemed smaller than a doll. The group circled around the stage, which was extended into the middle of the audience, and paraded so that everyone could see this perfect little jewel of a girl.

Then delicately—it was obvious she was as light as a leaf—they lowered the silver tray from its great height down on the center of the stage. La Môme Michele finally stood up on the tray and looked up at the two black giants standing on either side of her. The effect was tremendous, and the roar of applause and the shouts of "bravo" which greeted her echoed through the nightclub. I glanced over at the Baron to see how he was taking this and I could see that he was intrigued. He was hit hard.

The music from the orchestra started up and the little figure began to dance looking like something on top of a music box. She had beautiful rhythm, beautiful coordination. She danced as lightly as a feather and weighed about the same. Her little white thighs glistening in the spotlight, moving back and forth out of the light as she performed an exotic and strangely erotic dance.

After what seemed a very short time in my view, she started to do a perfect impersonation of a stripper, taking off the filmy silk things, throwing them here and there on the stage, until she was down to a bikini and a brassière smaller than the tiniest cocktail napkin you could imagine. Finally, after more dancing, she removed these daintily, prettily, and there she stood . . . as naked as September Morn and a lot less coy. She raised her arms over her head, absolutely proud of herself and of her figure. She was a miniature woman, absolutely perfect. Her figure could give you a small lustful wish . . . or a big lustful wish, depending on who you were. The Baron sat there with a glassy-eyed look on his face. He followed her tiny body through every movement. He licked his lips, he could have swallowed her easily in one gulp.

The little figure in the spotlight kept making sensuous little movements, the music became softer and softer; the Baron turned to the maître d'hôtel who was standing just next to our table. He motioned him over, whispered in his ear and gave him several bills. I knew what was happening and hoped this wouldn't get out of line. The orchestra was becoming louder, the dancing becoming more frantic, and with a tremendous crescendo from the orchestra the little figure, spinning like a top, completely nude in the center of the floor, suddenly threw up her hands and fell gracefully, as if unconscious.

The lights hit the two Nubian slaves, who came forward with the silver tray. They lifted her easily, each one picking up one foot and one hand,

317

and like a delicate and lovely bird they laid her quietly and easily on the large silver tray. They extended the tray at arms' length over their heads, the lights went out, the spotlight stayed on the two black bodies and, holding La Môme Michele aloft, they exited from the stage. The lights went out, the house lights came up, and all hell broke loose with applause. The Baron almost upset the table jumping to his feet, shouting, "Encore, encore, bravo, bravo, encore, encore." I didn't get up nor did Jules Molotov. I gave the Baron an uneasy glance but he was too full of the act to notice it. He leaned down, breathed champagne in my face and said, "Wasn't she great, isn't she divine? I've never seen anything so lovely—never!"

"Yeah," I answered, "I'll bet the Princess would get a kick out of this act too . . ."

He shot me a look of dislike, dropped back down to his seat, and started to pour himself some more champagne. The waiter took the bottle from his hand and filled his glass. "Yes, more champagne, *garçon*," the Baron said, and looked at me threateningly. This was another version of the heavy-menace stare, the threatening look to put me in my place and show me that my partner shared everything fifty-fifty.

He drank the champagne off at a gulp, and gave me another sullen look. I said tiredly, "Don't frighten me tonight, Baron, I'm only an innocent boy. If you want to get drunk and be so plastered you can't work tomorrow, that's not, as you might think, your business; it's *our* business because if you don't work, the picture doesn't go ahead and it costs *us* money . . . partner," I added grimly.

It was just at this moment that the headwaiter rustled up and whispered in the Baron's ear. The Baron shook his head. "Tell me in English." The headwaiter told him he had gone to see La Môme Michele and she would be delighted to join the Baron's party. The Baron said, "Can you arrange for her to come out right away, before the second show?" The headwaiter said he could. And she did.

In a few moments I felt rather than saw someone standing beside my chair. I turned around and still had to look down at this beautiful little woman. I stood up, and the Baron jumped to his feet, knocking over his champagne glass. Jules Molotov got slowly to his feet, steadily but politely staring at La Môme Michele.

She extended her little hand up to me. *"Je suis La Môme Michele, monsieur."*

I took the hand, which was not as large as a child's, but rather the hand of a porcelain doll. I bowed over it. *"Je suis enchanté, mademoiselle. Je pense que vous êtes formidable*, really wonderful. Permit me to present to

THE DEAL

you *Monsieur le Baron et notre avocat, Monsieur Jules Molotov."* Jules made a little dumpy bow.

The Baron pushed back his chair and smiling down at her walked completely around me and came up next to her side. "Mademoiselle," he breathed. "It's so gracious of you to join us."

"Un plaisir, monsieur, un plaisir."

Taking her by the hand, leaning down to enable him to do this, he escorted her around behind me over toward his chair, where immediately a higher chair was brought by the headwaiter. It looked like a velvet-covered high chair. La Môme Michele started to climb into the chair and the Baron, with a smile of satisfaction, unable to resist getting his hands on her immediately, reached down, saying, "Permit me, mademoiselle." Then he picked her up like a doll and placed her gently in her chair. She was now practically on eye level with the both of us.

I looked around at the other tables, some of the people watching us, others completely unconcerned. I thought to myself, We are really a team *quelle brochette,* because I was looking at the Baron smiling down happily at La Môme Michele and then glancing up to look at me. I felt like a perfect fool with the two of us sitting there with this miniature but ravishing doll on a high chair between us.

The Baron was all studied, casual charm. "Mademoiselle," he breathed again, "champagne . . .?"

"Oui, monsieur."

He poured her a glass. She took it in her little hand and it looked like a *flacon* that held a quart. She sipped at it daintily, now holding the glass with both hands, and started to place the glass back on the table, but the Baron took the glass from her and did that. And there we sat, looking at one another and down at La Môme.

I took a quick look at Jules Molotov, who was sitting there absolutely hypnotized. I guess we were something to see, all right. While the Baron was trying to converse with her in his bad French, making all the mistakes, yet oozing with boyish charm, I had a chance to study her at close range. From twenty feet away she had been beautiful; up close she was breathtaking.

She was dressed demurely in a high-necked evening gown that would have fitted a doll. It came clear up to her tiny throat and was fastened with a delicate pearl clasp. The dress fully covered her two tiny breasts, no larger than small plums. There was no back to the dress. The clasp had a collar effect. She was bare from the nape of her lovely little neck clear down to the small of her back. Her waist could not have been more than eight

319

inches around. The dress had a sheath skirt and as she crossed her little legs very casually on her high chair, the sheath opened and you could see she was perfectly formed. Her little legs were long and slender, with the most beautiful thighs I'd ever seen. She was something . . .

She was all attention toward the Baron, nodding, smiling, from time to time uttering phrases of two or three words. The Baron plowed on, mixing French and English, not understanding everything he said himself. I noticed that from time to time La Môme Michele would turn and give me a quizzical little up-from-under look. It was a pretty movement, tiny and delicate, like herself. When the Baron paused for breath, she leaned over gently toward me and said in French, "I know very much about Monsieur le Baron, but who are you? What do you do?"

"Well, for the moment I am sitting here admiring you."

"It is a lovely phrase," she said, still speaking in French, "but other than looking at me, what do you do?"

"I produce the Baron's pictures."

She looked at me quietly, "Is that all?"

I laughed, "Well, at the moment it seems to be quite enough."

She joined in the laughter, a little bell-toned laugh. We talked jokingly for a few minutes. The Baron said, "Mademoiselle Michele," and when she didn't turn around he very gently removed the champagne glass from her hand, set it on the table and without a word picked La Môme Michele up and set her on his knee exactly as you would an infant child. I thought this might embarrass her. She was absolutely calm, she watched him thoughtfully. She sat there on his knee, coolly looking up at him, and said, *"Mon champagne."* The Baron hastily adjusted her on his knee, reached over with his left hand, his right arm being around her, and handed her the glass. She took a sip and looked coolly up at me and said, *"Et alors . . ."* The Baron looked down at her, a fixed grin of polite idiocy on his face. He truly didn't know what to do.

The Baron could have worn her on his watch chain. But I knew after a few minutes talk with her that she was also intelligent and dignified. Of course she knew who the Baron was, and moments later as though a signal had been given, the table was surrounded by three or four photographers and pictures were taken of the Baron with La Môme Michele sitting on his knee—a sternly handsome ventriloquist with the beautiful creature—elfinlike, but no dummy at all. During the taking of the pictures, from time to time she'd look at me and smile a little understanding smile as if she were outside and above all this. The photographers went away, she shifted herself over to her other tiny hip.

THE DEAL

The Baron said quickly, "Are you comfortable?"

"Oui, monsieur, très confortable," and sat there looking around the room.

I leaned over and picked up my glass and in doing so was very close to her and from here she was even prettier than I had believed. As I moved my head back, very quickly she said in my ear, *"Parlez-vous Allemand?* . . . Do you speak German?" I shook my head no. *"Moi . . ."* she whispered, "I only speak French and German."

About this time, Jules Molotov said, "Baron, it's getting late and if you will excuse me, I'll go back to my hotel."

The Baron glanced at him quickly for a moment and dismissed him with "Fine, Jules, fine."

Jules knew he was dismissed and looked over to me, "Jarn, are you coming with me or do you want to stay?"

I looked at Jules steadily for a moment, "You go ahead, Julie. I'll come a little later with the Baron."

He bowed, said *"Enchanté"* with a terrible American accent but it charmed La Môme Michele. She thanked him prettily and he gave another little bow, turned and walked off through the tables in the direction of the exit. So there we were, me sitting at the table next to the high chair, and the Baron seated with La Môme Michele on his knee, and gayety was all around us.

A little later, La Môme Michele turned to the Baron and asked, "May I resume my chair, please?" The Baron, who at this time had to go to the men's room, placed her gently in her chair, said *"Pardonnez moi"* and added to me, "Remember, Jarn boy, she's mine." He leered down at the little dancer, turned and walked over toward the waiter.

When he was out of earshot, La Môme Michele asked, speaking French, "Is he always like this?"

"Always like what?" I answered.

"It does not have importance," she threw away.

"Well," I welled. "Tell me about you."

"Oh, don't play the tourist—tell me about you."

"Then I *would* be playing the tourist," I said. "Are you French or German? You speak French beautifully."

"I should," she smiled, "I was born in Alsace-Lorraine. It's lovely there."

I smiled. "I am in accord with you, mademoiselle. Does your family reside there?"

"Yes, my father is in the affairs of wine in Alsace."

"That's interesting. I may have been through his vineyard."

"I doubt that, monsieur, it is a very small vineyard."

I didn't say what I knew she expected me to say—"small like you."

She continued without my having said anything. "I have two married sisters who are normal, with lovely families"—and then proudly—"I have a brother who is a great champion bicycle rider. He finished fifth in the big six-day race of bicycles at the Palais des Sports last year." She talked on and was very amusing. She told me little things about her family like an ordinary French girl; she was very proud of them.

While all of this was being told me in her agreeably low voice, unlike the tinny voice of the normal Lilliputian, we were interrupted by the Baron returning to the table. He slid into his chair. I could see from his face that he had had a couple of quick ones at the bar while he was away. Without a word he gently but firmly picked up La Môme Michele from her chair and again placed her on his knee, holding her very close, looking down at her fascinated. The Baron scarcely breathed or moved as he watched her.

La Môme sitting demurely on his knee had reached over with both her tiny hands and was daintily sipping from her champagne glass, from time to time looking up in the Baron's face with a friendly, appraising look. She looked like a beautiful, tiny bird perched on the Baron's knee. She glanced carelessly around the room, nodding now and then to friends or clients; she was as at home where she was . . . as if she were at home. I could hear the smoothly sliding thoughts, the silken entrancing ideas, unclothing themselves in the Baron's mind. He leaned over and whispered something in La Môme Michele's ear. She leaned back, gave the Baron a cool yet thoughtful look, then turning to me said casually in French, "Your friend is a rare one and strange, *n'est-ce pas?*" I smiled down at her. She returned the smile warmly, "*Mais toi* . . . you are a *gentil* one and you haven't answered my question."

"Thank you . . . no, I haven't."

"*Alors,*" she purred, leaning over toward me, "*Dis-moi.*"

"*Je ne dis rien,*" I smiled. "I'll tell you nothing on that question. I have no opinion." I smiled down at her, "*Quel âge as tu?*"

She leaned back, smiled like any woman and said, "You must never ask a woman her age, even a little one like me"; then she continued, "They would only tell you *un petit mensonge* . . . the smaller the woman . . . the smaller the lie. *J'ai vingt-cinq ans,*" she continued. "*Et toi? Quel âge as tu?*"

"I am thirty-five," I answered. "But you never arrived to be this beautiful in twenty-five years."

"*Quel compliment.*" She preened like a tiny cat.

During this exchange the Baron kept glancing at us . . . darting looks from one of us to the other like a dog driving two sheep down a narrow lane. He said, "Jarn, what's the score?"

"I don't know, Baron. I don't know what you are playing."

"Listen, kid," he whispered, "will she go?"

"Go where?"

"Well, Christ . . . what have you two been talking about?"

I looked down at La Môme, she was watching us but didn't seem too concerned. I looked back to the Baron. "We've been talking about her family, who are wine makers. She has two sisters who have children and are happily married and . . ."

"Frig all that . . . did you tell her I want her to go with me?"

"She has a brother who finished fifth in the six-day bicycle race."

"Are you making fun of me?" he snarled, getting red in the face and almost knocking La Môme off her perch. She fluttered her arms and lit back safely on the Baron's knee.

"No," I answered, "but I ought to be. Christ, Baron . . . you can't walk out of here with a female midget. Or any midget. Before morning you'd be the laughing stock of Paris. And anyway we've got our own midget. We've got Julie Molotov to walk out with . . . nope," I corrected, "Julie's left and we should have gone too. We should have left with the lawyer"—trying to joke him out of it.

But the Baron wouldn't play. "Listen, Jarn, I'm serious. Now you ask her about later."

"Ask her yourself . . . she's on your knee. She's close enough."

"I did, but she didn't answer."

"Well," I said, "that's your answer. Maybe she doesn't dig you, Baron, and anyway it's late and we have to start shooting early in the morning."

"Who's we?" he snarled.

Well, here we were again. I was going to hear the "partner" song again, again the "fifty-fifty" song, where the Baron had artistic control.

During this exchange the beautiful tiny woman La Môme watched both of us, glancing back and forth at each face, following the conversation. She looked up at the Baron, then smiled at me and in French said, "Tell your friend I won't go with him but I will go with you . . . if you want." She added casually, "I understand a *little* English." Well, there it was. I didn't know how much French the Baron understood but I did know here was more trouble and I sat there looking at the Baron with La Môme Michele on his knee. The three of us casting glances. All trying to avoid breaking anything.

THE DEAL

The Baron and I left the nightclub. We had said good night to La Môme Michele, and Sam Neely was there, ready to drive us back home. I said, "Well, come on, Baron, we've had a nice evening. Sam and I will drop you off . . ." Then I saw he was looking out the window of the car, not listening to anything I said. "*Baron*. We'll drop you off, and then we'll go on home."

He turned and looked at me coldly. "Jarn, I don't feel like going home now. Why don't you let Sam drop you off and then he can run me out to the Halles and I'll have something to eat; then I'll go home. I'm fine, I'm fine." He said this and turned and looked back out the window to see the few people who were walking down the streets close to the Rue de l'Etoile.

"All right, Baron, if that's the way you want it, fine. Sam," I said, "you drive me home."

"Yessir, Jarn," and Sam tooled the big car down toward the Seine. across the Pont Neuf, and took a left down toward the Ile de la Cité.

The Baron still wasn't saying anything. I didn't see any reason to keep trying to pry him out of his moment of silence, but I knew he had something on his mind. At least he wasn't drunk, so maybe with luck I'd get a chance to shoot in script one or two and please, good Christ, not number three.

By that time the car had pulled up in front of my apartment. I got out and grinned at the Baron. "Fine, boy. I'll see you in the morning, right?"

"Right, Jarn," the Baron said, looking past my right ear.

"You okay, Baron?" I asked.

"Fine, fine," he said looking the other way. "Let's go. Sam," he said quickly.

"Good night, Jarn," Sam said, looking at me, shaking his head sadly.

"All right, Sam, pick me up at seven-thirty in the morning, right?"

"Right, Jarn."

And the car drove off. I went inside, went up to my apartment, stirred up the fire, lit a cigar, sat down in a chair, and tried to sort some of this out.

It was only the following morning that Sam Neely told me what happened, and for once I truly felt sorry for the Baron . . . genuinely sorry. You see the Baron had made Sam drive him back to the nightclub where La Môme Michele was appearing. He told Sam to wait and he went in. Now Sam couldn't know what happened inside but from the way the Baron came out he knew he had talked to La Môme Michele and she'd refused to have a late supper with him.

324

THE DEAL

Sam sat in the car outside watching the people leave the club. By now it was very late. He saw La Môme Michele come out with one of the tall Negroes. He walked off, she stood there under the lights for a moment and in a few minutes a car came around with the Negro driving. He jumped out and helped the little lady into the back of the car, the way you place a jewel in a jewel box, closed the door respectfully, and drove off.

The Baron came silently out of the club, walked swiftly to the car, said, "Sam, follow that car that just pulled away with La Môme in it."

"Who do you mean, Baron?" Sam said.

"Listen, Neely, don't play cute with me. I said follow that car and you know who I mean," the Baron snarled, his forehead pale.

"All right, Baron. Yessir."

"That's better," the Baron said, back to par. At least he knew he could lay it on to Sam.

The car was easy to follow. It was a long Mercedes phaeton, and it hadn't gone too far before it turned into a small street which was a cul-de-sac. So the Baron knew that at last he'd find out where La Môme Michele lived.

He saw a light go on, a door opened, and La Môme walked into an apartment. The light went out, the Baron sat in the car watching. Pretty soon the Mercedes made the turn, the giant Negro driving past without glancing at the Baron or Sam sitting in the car. They watched the car go out of sight.

The Baron got out. "Sam, turn the car around, then wait here for me, I don't know how long I'll be."

"Well," Sam said, "you know Jarn had thought—"

"Now listen, Sam, I'm not asking you what to do, I'm telling you what to do. Turn the car around and wait for me. You understand?"

"Yessir, Mr. Baron, I understand," Sam said grimly.

The Baron stalked off quickly. Pretty soon Sam saw the light go on. The door opened and closed. From here on it's not too difficult to surmise what happened . . . and this is what they were talking about in the apartment of La Môme . . .

You see, the Baron had bribed the concierge to tell him which floor La Môme lived on. It was the second floor. He went up and knocked on the door. Surprisingly enough, La Môme herself opened the door.

"Monsieur," she said, *"Monsieur le Baron!"*

The Baron just looked at her for a moment, then without a word pushed the door back firmly and walked in . . . he closed the door. La Môme stood with her back to the door and watched him. He walked over toward the fireplace, then abruptly took off his overcoat, threw it on a chair, and sat down.

La Môme watched him, quietly leaning against the door not saying a word. Finally the Baron looked at her, smiled—with an effort put the charming grin on his face—and said in a "voice to charm the dead," "Mademoiselle, please come and sit by me, I wish to speak with you."

La Môme, still not saying a word, walked quietly toward the Baron and seated herself in a chair on the opposite side of the fireplace, folded her little hands, crossed her feet at the ankles, and sat there looking up at him quietly. She nodded and smiled, *"Monsieur le Baron . . ."*

The Baron sat there looking down at La Môme. The room was dimly lit. The fire cast flickers on the large shadow of the Baron, and the slight, slender and definitely lovely shadow of La Môme Michele. It was like seeing an oversized figure and an undersized doll. The shadows leaned forward as though they were listening to what this conversation would be about. And they were . . .

"What did Jarnigan say to you about me?"

"Quoi?" La Môme said, "what? I do not understand, Monsieur Baron, since your French is not the best, and my English is a disaster. But I'll try, if you speak slowly."

The Baron looked at her for a minute, sighed deeply, slumped down further in his chair and looked into the fire. "I mean," he said, "what did Jarnigan tell you of me?"

"He said nothing that was not complimentary and fine. He . . . he seemed very nice, as you're very nice. I think you're both very interesting . . . very . . . very *sympathiques.* You . . . I . . . I feel you have *sympathie."* (Sympathy in French means niceness and friendship, not pity.) This was of course the wrong thing to have said to the Baron. Sympathy was not what he was there for.

What he *was* there for moved in his mind's eye, that was usually blind, the same shadow with the white cane went tap . . . tap . . . tapping down the corridor of his mind . . . again he blinked his yellow coyote's eyes. He shut her out completely, thinking. (If I could just do it once, right . . . if I could really feel, once, how it is . . . now this one has to be right. She *has* to be.)

He shot a look at La Môme Michele, who was gazing into the fire. The brisk movement of his head caught her eye and she turned to look at him.

"What were you saying, Monsieur le Baron?"

"I wasn't saying anything . . . I think . . . Look, how much money do you make at your club?"

THE DEAL

"Oh, that is an indiscreet question, but I do very well thank you. I have a sufficiency."

"That's not what I mean. I'd like to . . . I'd like to . . ."

"Monsieur le Baron, may I make it easier for you?"

The Baron almost snarled at her. He leaned forward in his chair, "I don't want you to make it easier for me, I want to talk to you. I want to make a business arrangement with you." Here he swallowed, looked back into the fire, and said, "Might I have a drink?"

She looked at the Baron for a moment, got up carefully from the little chair, walked over to a sideboard, to a bottle and poured a large glass of brandy, took a smaller one herself, walked back, set it carefully on the little table next to the Baron's chair, then turned gracefully, walked back and sat down without saying a word. She watched him thoughtfully.

The Baron picked up his glass and emptied it in two huge gulps. He swallowed several times, cleared his throat and said, "I want to make this arrangement. I want to sleep with you. I'll pay one thousand dollars, but you must really be with me."

"But, Monsieur," the tiny girl said, seeing the fixed stare in the Baron's eyes, "don't you know that this is impossible . . . this is impossible. There's . . . there's . . . something strange about you. I think it would be wisdom if we finished our drink, finished our talk, and I'll look forward to seeing you again one night at the club, *avec plaisir.*"

La Môme didn't know exactly what was bothering the Baron, but what made her uneasy was he had offered her too much money. This was the Baron's *faiblesse.* His continued overplaying was not a delusion of grandeur, because he actually lived on that grand plane; to him everything was oversized, everything except himself, and his problem. And this of course was the bastard road he had to finish. The hand that was dealt him was unplayable. But, he fought against it in every way that he could, ultimately choosing the wrong way each time.

The Baron leaned toward La Môme. "Listen, we have to do that . . . I have to do that."

La Môme nicely and with dignity said, "Listen, monsieur, I do not feel this with you. I am not in a position where I must be forced to feel this with you. And again, let's remain *amis*—friends. I will tell you good night." This said as she stood up quietly.

The Baron looked at her for a moment, but the damage was done. The Baron was furious. He stood up. He was loud and vulgar. He was determined. He looked down at the little figure. "You know, don't you, that I could take you by force."

THE DEAL

She looked at him coolly. A little up-from-under look, completely composed. "Yes, perhaps you could; surely you could, but I have the impression I know what the problem is, and in this case this would not help you at all."

I would have understood then, and I understand now. The Baron wanted to try to make love with this little body, without even thinking of using the false dong. He was certain La Môme was the ideal one to try with. He was certain he could satisfy this tiny woman, but more important, he was certain that she could, in every sense of the word, realistically, warmly, but most important, tightly, satisfy him. An act which had never normally been done.

The Baron looked as though he might become violent. La Môme very carefully walked toward the door, still with a kind smile on her face.

"Monsieur, it's true you could possibly force me, but as I said, this would have not the same effect. I am sure—and I have heard little murmurings regarding you—I am sure that I know what you need. I know your feeling and I am in sympathy with your . . . with your problem . . . with you. But here, *mon cher ami . . .*"

At this moment the Baron studied her closely. She was speaking in English very slowly, sometimes with errors, but he understood everything.

"You see . . ." La Môme began, standing close to a chair, looking tinier than before. Then she paused, as the Baron walked over to the chair and sat down. Even sitting there he was looking down at La Môme. He stretched out his hand and impulsively she took two little steps forward and took his large hand in her two tiny ones. I think this was the first time the Baron really saw her as a person, as another human being.

"Mon cher ami, Monsieur le Baron," the tiny woman said, "we are at an impasse because, you see"—here she continued kindly—"you like, and you need little women. I . . . I understand. But in my case, *pour moi-même*, I like —I need—only big men. Normal big men." She turned her face away from him and said sadly, "You see, we are opposite. No, my poor friend, you are not for me, *Monsieur le Baron*, nor I for you."

This was said in such a friendly way, a nice way, that the Baron sat back in the chair. La Môme turned and walked daintily over to the sideboard, picked up another glass, poured brandy into it, walked back, and carefully handed him the glass. Standing up she was still not as tall as the Baron seated in the chair. And she continued gently, "You see I have a problem too. Few men want to make love to a tiny . . . I guess you'd call me an unnatural woman." This said sadly, with resignation but with a sort of dignity. "I realize that I would not appeal to normal men; so you and your

328

problem and me and mine—*nous sommes les perdus.*" She walked over and standing very near patted him gently on the cheek. She had to stretch up her little arm to do it and her hand against the Baron's face, soft and gentle, was like the hand of a child. It was truly a loving gesture.

The Baron sat there looking down at her, hypnotized.

"No," she continued sadly, "you are not for me, Monsieur le Baron, nor I for you. But you must not take it as though I feel unkindly toward you. It is just that we are an impossible situation, *vous et moi,* and this could only lead to more hurt for you and possibly new hurt for me." By now the Baron was completely devastated. He finished his drink quickly. This was the fourth large brandy he'd had since he'd been with La Môme. He was now almost completely drunk. Tears formed in the corners of his eyes. Words that wanted to be said were shining in the tears, pulled at the corners of his mouth, tugged again at the eyes. But no sound came. He was near the crying stage now . . . now he *was* sorry for himself. It was true, and it was sad.

He finally stood up and stretched out his hand. He took La Môme's tiny one in his. He looked down at her and said, "*Je regrette, mademoiselle. Je regrette de tout mon cœur.* And now I shall go." This said with a strange dignity. With that he straightened up, walked over, lifted up his coat off the chair and without a backward glance walked over to the door, opened it and walked out into the street. And for him, the street was dark with something more than night.

When the door closed, La Môme stood there looking at it for a long minute, then slowly turned and walked back over in front of the fireplace, sat down in a tiny chair. She had a brandy in her two small hands. She took a dainty sip and was sitting there looking into the fire; slowly, this lovely little figure started to shake her head from side to side, saying quietly, "*Le pauvre garçon . . . le pauvre, pauvre garçon.*" But the damage had been done.

Sam Neely saw the Baron come out the door. He got out of the car, opened the back door and stood there. The Baron got in the car, sat down without a word. Sam closed the door, walked around, got in, started the engine, then drove slowly.

"Well, sir, shall we take you home?"

The Baron said, "Drive me to the studio."

"Yessir."

Sam watched him in the mirror and saw that he was sitting there absolutely dazed, but the funny part was, he didn't look drunk. Sam, of course, didn't know exactly what had happened in there. I only found out later. Bits and pieces that the Baron disclosed when he was either blipped to the eyebrows or when he was, as usual, on the flit.

The rejection and the refusal of La Môme Michele to have anything to do with the Baron was the last straw. When he knew that this was an impossibility, that even with a small woman he'd never truly be able to make love, it was more than a humiliation. He did not want to accept that fact, as the pauper accepts the condition of being perpetually moved on. Unhappily, the Baron was being "moved on" from another possibility of perhaps feeling normal. This thing with La Môme had really jarred him. And in spite of all that he'd drunk, he was sober, cold sober. He began to play back in his mind the conversation with La Môme. It was terrible . . . it was sad. He was more than sad.

The car moved slowly through the streets of Paris, following the route next to the Seine, in the direction of Neuilly. Sam from time to time looked at the Baron in the mirror, saying nothing. The Baron sat quietly and pulled his sorrow, his frightened feeling, his hurt, farther out into the light of his mind so he could examine it better. He didn't like it. It wasn't what he wanted to see.

"Sam," he said, "pull over at the next *bistro*. I need a drink."

Sam looked at him for a moment and said, "Yes, Baron. We'll do that. There's a place I know just before the Pont Saint-Cloud.

The Baron said nothing. He sat quietly, thinking, grieving, completely wrapped within himself.

Later, after Sam had driven the Baron to the studio and saw that he was getting ready to sleep in his dressing room till time for shooting the next day, Sam pulled out quickly and got me on the phone.

It was then four o'clock in the morning. I answered, half asleep.

"Listen, Jarn," Sam reported, "I'm sorry as hell to wake you, but I figured you oughta know what had happened." And he explained to me on the phone as much as he knew about the Baron's visit to La Môme Michele's from what ramblings he had gleaned from him on the drive from the *bistro* to the studio.

So there it was—and there we were. I thought for a minute. Said: "Sam hold the line for a minute, will you please?" I got out of bed, went into the bathroom, sloshed some cold water onto my face, dried briskly with a towel, came back, picked up the telephone. "Well, Sam, listen, why don't you stay there, somewhere—you can sleep in my office. I'll drive the other car to the studio, don't worry. Just stick around and make sure that the guard at the gate tells you if the Baron tries to leave. I'll be there in a couple of hours anyway."

"Right, Jarn. Just as you say, Jarn."

Sam hung up. I knew I could get him in the office, and I knew he would do exactly what I said.

I put the phone down and walked back into the library and stood there. It was cold out and certainly cold and damp in the apartment, but it's always like that when you're close to the Seine at this time of the year. Four, five o'clock in the morning, the mist hangs over the river and it's beautiful, if you have the chance and the time to look out and see it. I'd been blind to most of these things ever since this particular Deal had been going on.

It was almost four-thirty now and I figured I couldn't go back to sleep, so I walked into the kitchen, started to make myself some coffee. When I saw that the coffee would be ready in a few minutes, I went back into the bathroom, took a quick shower, dressed, put on a pair of slacks and an old sweater, walked back into the living room, got a cigar off the mantel, lit up, and paced back and forth, thinking.

Then I went back into the kitchen, poured myself a big cup of coffee, returned to the library and sat down.

I felt sorry for the Baron. Maybe not as sorry as he'd like to have me feel for him, but sorry. It was a hell of a situation to be that way. I sat there drinking coffee, smoking quietly, waiting for it to get completely light. Five o'clock now. I'd be leaving for the studio pretty soon. I leaned my head back against the big leather cushion in the chair and thought . . . well, we are hung as we are hung. Should make no apologies or excuses either way. I can't help nor regret it that I'm hung like a stud, like the Baron can't help it—although he regrets it, with good reason—that he's hung like a stud mouse, as he so gracefully puts it.

I say it's only important if you give it importance. It's like I told him once, "Baron, the world don't hang by a dong, and your dong in particular. So take it easy." But, in all honesty, I'd rather be the stud than the mouse, but I figure it's as hard to find a good lady mare as it is to find a good lady mouse.

I must have dozed off at last because when I looked at my watch it was almost six-thirty. It's hell to go to sleep thinking lousy, evil thoughts like that.

37

I was in my car driving to the studio, taking the road through the Bois. I knew I'd be there in fifteen or twenty minutes. I was trying to get what brains I had left in some semblance of order. At the studio gates, the guard said, "*Bonjour.*" I waved at him, parked, got out and walked over to my office, knowing that there would probably be a difficult day ahead. I walked into the outer office, finding Mme. Henriette already there—my steady, loyal secretary.

"*Bonjour, Monsieur Jarnigan.* They're all in there."

"Who's all in where?" I said.

"Everyone, they're in your office. It seems to be some sort of a meeting. I asked if you were to be present or if you knew about it, and they told me I should call you. I tried, but your line didn't answer."

"Well, it has no importance now. Thank you—*merci.*" With that I headed for my office.

We had been having trouble for two weeks. More trouble than usual. The picture was of course behind schedule. One of the actors had quit because of the Baron's harsh treatment of him. He was legally within his rights and had to be replaced. But now two days' work had to be re-shot.

I opened the private side door to my office and walked in. There they were. There was the crew, the wrecking, parasiting mother-of-a-crew. This time they consisted of the two stunt men who thought they were stuntier and tougher than they were, the French lawyer, the Editor. And there was the Baron, looking better than I figured he would look. The arrogant sneer was back on his face and he was sitting in my chair, behind my desk, dead sober. Ready for business and full of gas.

"You're late, Jarn," he smiled benignly, ready to forgive.

"Balls," I said, "*en toute simplicité.* And I know, I know, I owe you an apology."

The Baron leaned back in my chair, threw his head back and sniffed as though I'd hung a week-old mackerel under his nose.

"My," he sneered, "my, we're in a mood, aren't we?" This said like Jared Throne in a bad play.

I looked at him for a moment, then I remembered there existed no cure, no get-well pill for being the way he was. No sense to grind it in. No sense to look for trouble with a lighted match.

Then suddenly I remembered. I was the Iceman and the reason for this

333

session this morning was to discuss the best way to finish the picture, to try and make up the time that had been lost. That was why I was so surprised to see the Baron and everyone there. There was a writer whom we'd hired from Hollywood to try to do some editing for us on the script—that is to say, on the good script; I never let anyone see script two or three. We were to discuss seriously how, and what, would be the best way to finish the picture.

This writer made a few suggestions, the assistant director made a couple of suggestions, the French lawyer sat and watched. Surprisingly enough, the Baron put in a couple of ideas, very logical, well thought-out, very good. He hadn't been in the picture business twenty years not to have picked up something. He made some very astute remarks. Then something that the writer said struck him wrong. He looked at him for a minute and he said, "I disagree with you. What do you think, Jarn?"

I said, "Go ahead, Baron, you've got the floor."

That, for no reason at all, seemed to be a go-ahead to the Baron, for he started to harangue and beat down this writer—I guess, because for once I hadn't said the Baron was wrong. So, being armed with the right of righteousness, he tore into the writer. During part of this business conference, he had not said too much, which was a rare thing. And his not being drunk was rarer still. And he was sure of his facts, which was still more rare. So I listened to the conversation and the rebuttal, with the poor assistant director and writer thinking and then talking wistfully about how the screenplay should be wound up and the picture should end.

The Baron listened quietly for a minute, put a sneer on his face and tore off the wings of the idea like a fly, and watched it spin one-winged in a circle around the table of conversation. The Baron wanted no nonsense. He was going. He was winging. I didn't want to shoot him down, number one. And number two, he had been right for once. I thought, Boy, if having a session with La Môme Michele, successful or unsuccessful, inspired him like this, I'll go and have a talk with her myself.

The meeting was breaking up. Everyone looked sad but manly, and filed out the door. The Baron got up, waved good-bye airily and walked out. I walked over and sat down in my own chair and said, "Hello, office. Hello, files. Hello, books."

I was glad to be alone. I began to see that we finally might be able to get through this picture and I could quit without having to deal the rest of my life away.

The poor and inadequate producer is dishonest without knowing it. The fairly successful producer is dishonest because he's not exactly sure what to

THE DEAL

be honest about. In producing, honesty is an art. And if you are let alone and can practice it you may come off with a good picture. But, if you are put upon by

> Syndy men, prick men, money men, harems,
> Lawyers, actors, starlets, and Barons . . .

you'll never be a man, my son.

You'll just be a son-of-a-bitch who is running down the slanted stairs to your own private hell, dragging your films behind you.

It was at this point that I heard someone open the door and walk in. I looked up and there was my ex-wife standing there in all her glory.

She said, "Jarn, I heard words, interesting words. I was intrigued."

"Well, go some place else and be intrigued. I'm busy," I said.

"My, we are in a temper this morning, aren't we?"

"You must have been talking to the Baron. That's the same dialogue he used."

"Well," she said, with her lovely accent, her beautiful figure, and her eyes that everyone talks about, "I did happen to meet him coming in."

"I'll bet," I said. "How long did you wait for him? Well, since you're here, sit down and let's see what it is."

"What it is, is very simple, Jarn. I'm supposed to have that part in the picture. We discussed it. You told me I would."

"Listen, you don't need to be in my picture. I don't know why you insist. You're not right for the part. You're a wonderful actress. You're a beautiful woman. You're the sexiest thing I've ever seen. But you're not right for the part. You're a big star, you don't need it. Now, you have certain claims on me for reasons that we're both aware of. The biggest claim that you had is gone and you know why. But the most important claim that you've got is our son—that's the claim, and that's the reason I'm ready to make this deal with you. Now, are you sure there's nothing else I can do for you except have you play this part in the picture? Isn't there anything I can do?"

"Jarn, I have already told my friends that I was going to be in the Baron's picture. I told them it would be splendid working with you again."

"Yeah, just grand. Simply grand."

"Well, you do intend to let me have the part, don't you?"

"I don't know," I said truthfully.

We had been talking for quite a while now. We had talked over the picture. We had talked over the possibilities. We'd talked over "her role." I was sorry I had started it. Actually, it was my fault, because I did start it. It

THE DEAL

was another one of those deals that you make with yourself. I wanted to see my son and there were certain reasons that I was unable to. It's a thing you couldn't explain. Hopefully, I would have liked to have had her cooperation. So, that was how I got into this bag of nails. . . .

We'd been sitting there talking, as I say, for over an hour, seeing what arrangements could be made. Truthfully, I was still undecided whether to give her the part in the picture or not. I knew I'd have to go over on the sound stage pretty soon. I stood up (nicely, I hoped) to indicate that I really did have to go to work. I smiled at her and said, "Look, angel, I have to get over on the set, but I'll certainly give you a call later today." With that kind of talk dying out, I just stood there waiting for a good chance to leave.

After a long silence she looked up at me. She was beautiful, she was lovely, she had the most beautiful eyes in the world. *Et alors*, I thought. We'd had some beautiful times. Beautiful moments are hard to come by because most everything fades quickly away. Anyone can show you that life is rotten, how silly love is, but you hate to have the one you're lying next to show you. It's too bad that after marriage, words become tender, slippery things, leading to poetry, love and lies. I was thinking this looking down at her and said to myself, "Listen, don't let your mind go wool-gathering from the past and present. Just stick around, Jarnigan. Stick around, be with us for awhile."

"Jarn, Jarn."

I realized she was talking to me. She said, "Excuse me. You had such a strange look on your face. What were you thinking?"

"Just the work, just what has to be done."

"Jarn," she continued softly, "sit down. Sit down here on the couch beside me and let's talk. Truly and nicely together. We did once."

I walked around and sat down on the big leather couch. So there I was.

"Jarn."

"Yeah."

"You still say 'yeah.' Can't you say anything to me besides 'yeah'?"

I looked at her and then I looked back over toward my desk. As I sat down on this couch, it sagged. Love or something like that had broken its back, was breaking the back of this conversation.

She turned sideways on the couch so she faced me. She leaned closer. The perfume of her that I remembered drifted faintly over toward me. She gently raised her hand and touched my cheek, and rubbed back and forth, saying, "Jarn, you need a shave."

"Uh-huh."

THE DEAL

She looked at me quietly for a moment, then said, "Do you love me, Jarn?"

"Sure."

"No, you don't. You hate me," she said passionately.

"Sure."

She looked at me imploringly, the false overemotional teary look shining in her eyes. "Doesn't our seven years mean anything? Doesn't it stand for something?"

"Yeah, six years and fifty-one weeks of hell. The first week was jazzy, but the rest was shit."

"Don't say that, *cheri*. You know some of it was good."

"You're not listening," I said. "It was *merde*. You understand what that means. You speak French. You know all the words."

"Oh, you bastard . . . you lousy bastard," she breathed, less quiet now.

"Now don't lose your girlish charm. Listen, angel," I said to her, glad it was done, glad it was over . . . the little whatever was going there for a minute completely stopped, but not wanting to hurt her beyond herself . . . You see, I still cared for her in a way; she had killed the other but I cared for her. "Why the hell can't you take it easy?"

"Take it easy," she said, "take it easy! Mr. Big Shot—Mr. Young Genius Producer says, take it easy."

"Yeah, take it—" I never got to finish.

She stood up, reached over to the desk. There was a small box of papers there. She threw them at me.

I liked that better. That was getting her back to par. I tsk-tsked, and went over to her.

"Now, don't overdo it, or I won't be back and I won't be talking to you, and there won't be anything." And that stopped her. It wasn't what you think. It wasn't "cat-man" talk. It wasn't a "big-donged daddy." It was me, leaving and walking out; she knew that I truly cared for her in my way and you don't find much of that in our circles. Dongs and cats that ding each other, but no real love . . . no real caring . . . ding . . . dong . . . dang it.

•　•　•

She looked at me for a moment. Her eyes were moist with unshed tears. She looked truly sad and more lovely than ever. "I'm sorry, Jarn," she said quietly. She turned and started for the door. And without looking back said, "Call me if you want to." And walked on out the door.

I wanted to—and I would call her.

337

THE DEAL

So now I walked on over to the sound stage where we had reconstructed all of the sets from the outdoors; the wild-walls were in and it looked like a country estate. Earth had been brought in, it was cluttered all around the buildings. And this was where the Baron would make his big entrance, walking over the earth into the big estate, king of all he surveyed, and I thought: a man walks the earth cloaked in his own fears and is more dangerous than all the elements put together. Especially a man like the Baron.

When I got over on the set, the Baron happily was ready, madeup. He waved, gave a thumbs-up gesture. Man, it looked like we might get some footage today. Here came the nice ripe actress, overly madeup. Eyelashes long enough for an owl to roost on. They looked like little iron railings, a little iron picket fence. She came over, gushing musically.

"Jarn, Jarn, oh, what a lovely set. Isn't this wonderful!"

"Grand," I said, "And you look lovely. I like the costume. I think your makeup could be a touch lighter because, with your complexion and all, you truly don't need that much."

"Oh, Jarn," she lisped, "you mean I could just be natural? More the real me?"

"Well," I said, not wanting to swing the pendulum too far the other way, "I think you could have a little less eye makeup. Your eyes are lovely, and you truly don't need it that heavy. I remember pictures where you wore no makeup and you were breath-taking."

Under the praise and compliments she spread like a lap catching all the flowers. She gushed, "Jarn, since I'm leaving tomorrow I'm giving a little party tonight. The Baron's coming. He really is."

That's grand, I thought; if he really is, that will be the first time in a long time. Aloud I said, "That's fine and it's very kind of you to include me. Now if you'll excuse me."

"Oh, Jarn, I will, I will. But with regret." She trilled off into a peal of girlish laughter—but not a very young girl.

I went over and talked to Marc, the cameraman. The scene was rehearsed and rehearsed. And for the rest of the day everyone, including the Baron, worked well and happily together . . . which is the only way to get a fine picture. How I regretted the days and weeks that seemed so terrible. And yet even one good day cleared the air a lot. I was almost happy.

Later, walking back to my office from the sound stage, I caught myself whistling. "Jarn boy," I said to myself, you're cracking up. I grinned at my own joke. The real grin felt funny. I hadn't used it lately. I went in and worked on the script.

38

It was late one night after some of this good shooting. Sam Neely had just brought me back from the studio. We were sitting in the apartment having some coffee. I was tired—ready to go to bed. Sam was just leaving when the telephone rang . . .

It was from a fagola joint up in Montmartre. The headwaiter knew me because he had worked as a "swish headwaiter" on a picture I had made in Paris the year before.

"Monsieur Jarnigan, a *situation très grave* . . . very serious, has arisen here. I think it is urgent that you present yourself here," he said in halting English—then asked, "Might one speak in French?"

"One might," I answered. *"Parlez, d'accord."* From the excitable way in which he talked, I knew something was wrong, radically wrong. "I'm waiting," I said, continuing in French. "What is the problem? What seems to be the grave thing that presents itself?"

"Monsieur Jarnigan," he wailed. "I should not have called you, nor presumed to arouse you at this late hour, to *dérange* you at a time like this, unless it was a matter of the utmost urgency." He was talking very fast. He continued, *"Monsieur le Baron* is here." Then, more quietly, "He's causing quite a disturbance. You know that star, *la vedette* from Hollywood, Rip Cooper, the tall American—*très suave et très beau—alors*, they're having an argument about who's dancing with which boy. They're arguing— should they dance with the two-thousand-franc boy or the three-thousand-franc boy! Now, me," he continued conversationally, "I never have this difficulty, since I have not the francs to dance with these boys. However ——"

"Ecoutez—listen, my friend," I said firmly. "I am appreciative of your call but get to the point." I said this with an urgency, because in the background I could hear loud talking, and once in a while a glass breaking.

The headwaiter went on, a little hurt. He camped some; then said girlishly, "I only desire to render you a service, Monsieur Jarnigan. May I continue?"

"I pray that you do."

The headwaiter, all dignity intact, now went on as calmly as if he were standing there discussing the weather. *"Alors,* it seems that one of the two-

339

thousand-franc boys became angry and actually struck—I mean, *il a frappé un grand coup, contre la vedette Américain*. Then, *Monsieur le Baron* struck the two-thousand-franc boy with a rapidity that was beautiful to behold . . . *Et alors*, there is this fight which looks as though . . . this ferocious *bagarre* may continue . . . I permit myself to request you to come at once, if you permit me."

"I permit you." I hollered. "What is the exact address?"

He answered primly, "It is twenty-five, Rue du Cherche Midi, à Montmartre."

"I'm on my way."

I hung up the phone. Sam looked at me, knowing something was wrong. We hit for the door together.

Sam started the car and we were driving up toward Montmartre—he had heard that much. I filled him in on the way. "Now, listen, Sam, I don't know what the problem is; but we can't afford to let the Baron get in any difficulty. You know that Rip Cooper—that 'Mary.' Well, this he-man from Hollywood doesn't care what he does, although he should, being as big a star as he is." We missed a truck by inches. I went on, "Man, oh man. Well, it's his mouth. He can carry coal in it if he wants to; but I don't want him cutting up over here and getting the Baron in trouble."

I looked over at Sam, who was listening but still paying attention to his driving. He shot me a quick look and said, "How strong do we go?"

I watched him miss another truck by an inch. "Watch your driving."

"Yeah, Jarn."

"Well, Sam, we go as strong as we have to go," I said, pulling my feet out of the floorboards. "We've got to get the Baron out of there. You know these fags . . . it isn't like they're all powder puffs. I've seen some of them that could throw a guy over a building. So, let's first use this diplomatic approach and then we'll do the necessary, okay?"

"Anything you say, Mr. Jarnigan, sir," Sam said—not sarcastically, just the way he talked when he was worried or when we were in front of other people and he wanted to be very respectful. We shot up the hill, winding through little narrow streets. Sam drove extremely well but I was pleased to see us pull up in front of the Place du Montmartre in one piece.

We got out of the car. We didn't need to ask which was the place because you could hear it from half a block away. I ran for the door with Sam. It was with wisdom that I paused diplomatically—just at the time I would have stepped in, three glasses and a chair came flying out. We waited, then I crouched down and peeked in carefully. In the far corner of the room on the dance floor, was the Baron, half under a table. On the

THE DEAL

other side of the room I could see two fags keeping a hold on Rip Cooper, the "feminine-type" he-man Hollywood star. The fight was really progressing. It was a beauty . . .

There was a lot of scratching and spitting and kicking. It was like looking in on a very unclean, furry, masculine-woman's fight. Anger and high falsetto voices bounced around the room like pink smoke—the ugly perfumed kind you get when you have to make the female star look sexy taking a pink bubblebath on the sound stage. By now, one of the fags had snatched up some sort of a bottle, and was swinging it fiercely at Cooper; from time to time, he would lean down and take a cut at the Baron, who, in my judgment, used wisdom in drawing his head back in under the table— like a turtle pulling his head back into the shell. The fag kept screaming, his voice kind of tripping over itself, becoming more and more girlish.

By this time Sam and I were inside the club. I could see that the fight had centered into this one area, with two "girl-boy" dancers against Rip, and Baron in his foxhole under the table. Now the Baron, surprisingly enough, used excellent judgment, because it was at this time he stood up, throwing over the table with a tremendous roar, looking magnificent—the way he does in the fight scenes in his movies. His violent movement scared the hell out of the two fags, which was probably the best offense he could have made. While the two dance-fags were still in shock, the rough Hollywood-type star—who had these certain peculiarities—used what was probably the best move he'd made all night. He very quickly, and with admirable precision, hit one fag deftly on the side of the neck with a huge tray. He was a big fag, but he fell as though he'd been hit with an axe.

I yelled, "Let's go, Baron—this way!"

The Baron shot me a look, laughed loudly, turned to Rip and said, "Let's go, girl, let's go!"

All four of us hit for the door, Sam Neely running blocking tackle and mowing down a couple of the fagolas. By now, all the starch had gone out of them. I don't care how tough they are—no pansy has too much iron in his bones—or anywhere else.

We shot out the door. A few glasses and some bottles came floating after us—a lot of screams and a lot of very rude and insulting things wafted out on the night air. By this time, Sam was in the car, had the motor started. I pushed the Baron and Rip Cooper into the back seat, jumped in the front, and the car shot off with a roar.

I turned around and looked at the Baron, who looked at me half grinning and half sheepish. I must say that it had been a funny sight. I was glad we got out of it this easy, without any scandal. The Baron looked at me. "Jarn boy, as always, was I glad to see you!" He reached over and clapped old Sam on the shoulder. "Boy—the three of us—we can do anything."

He was still excited. He turned and looked at the other star sitting in the back seat, who was very carefully and daintily nursing a cut lip. He had some sort of a handkerchief out now, and, as he dabbed at his lip and wiped off the inside of his wrists, a perfume came out that wouldn't just stop a horse; it would stop a runaway truck. As we started back down the hill I said quietly, "Listen, Sam, we just got out of one problem—let's not have another one with the car. Would you just drive a little slower?" I leaned back in the seat, waiting for my pulse to get back down in the low hundreds.

The Baron, leaning forward, took a grip on my shoulder. "Jarn boy," he said, "my partner—you really pulled me out of one." Then, "But y'know, for once—I'm innocent."

I twisted my head to look at him. He managed with his grin to look painfully innocent. I have to say I was glad that he was sober, and when the final story came out, it was true: he really had tried to help this other star—this fag, who had called him saying he was in trouble. Apparently the trouble was, the Hollywood feminine-type star had refused to pay one of the two-thousand-franc boys more than a thousand francs. Then, when he wouldn't make with the dough, the two-thousand-franc boy refused to let him dance with a thousand-franc boy, saying that he was a cheap pederast. Then they asked him to leave. This was more than "Rippette" could bear, so he started to take it out on them physically, which was a mistake—but then this wasn't the first one he had made. Anyway, the Baron was out of it.

I asked, where could we drop off the fagola (only I didn't call him that). With thanks, we dropped him off at the Plaza Athenée. As he got out of the car, he said, "Mr. Jarnigan, I'm very grateful for your help." His voice had lowered about four notches, and he was being very masculine. He invited us up for a drink. "Really," he said nicely, some of the charm starting to come back in his voice, "wouldn't you come up for a nightcap?"

"No, thanks." I said.

The Baron started to say something. I said, "The Baron won't come up either. We have a lot of work to do. An early call, you know."

"Right-o . . . rightie-o," he chirped cheerfully, now completely back to normal. "Well, thanks again, chaps," and turned away and walked briskly into the hotel.

The Baron looked after him and said, as we drove away . . . "Man, Jarn old Jarn, my savior . . . I am truthfully glad I'm not like that guy. I am as I am, and I'm hung as I'm hung, but by Christ, I'm not a fairy." At this he laughed uproariously, and I must say, Sam joined in wholeheartedly and so did I.

I said, "Listen, let's go down to the Halles and have some onion soup and then everybody go to the studio and get a couple of hours sleep before we have to work. Whad'ya say?"

"Done, Jarn boy, and done again. And thank you again for tonight."

"Listen, Baron, tonight was a swell bag of nails. Let's not get into one like that anymore, huh?"

"Anything you say, Jarn boy. Anything you say. Sam," the Baron said regally, in his best John Barrymore voice, "Sam, my lackey—to the Halles. The onion soup awaits." Then he laughed uproariously, and we all joined in.

Sam tooled the big car down the Avenue Montaigne. We turned right at the Rond-Point and drove toward the Place de la Concorde on the way to the Halles. It hadn't worked out too badly, I thought. With the Baron in this rare mood, if only I could keep him from drinking any more that night, we had a fair chance tomorrow to maybe shoot on script number one. I said a prayer.

Somebody said: "Don't overdo the grateful part. You slid through easy this time."

"All right. You don't mind me being grateful, do you?"

"I don't mind," *Someone* said. "Only you should show it at the proper time."

"I'm showing it. I'm showing it."

"It's a start," *Someone* conceded. "It's a start."

I grinned to myself as we drove along toward the Halles.

●　●　●

Sometimes on weekends, or between pictures when I couldn't get away or get out of going along without absolutely ruining the Deal, the Baron would insist that I go out with him and his friends on the yacht. The "friends" included actresses from the French film industry and the Italian film industry, and various starlets of unnamable breeds. Then there were the "crews." The first crew was the Baron's attorney, stunt man Saul Baum, the Editor, and the latter's fluffy blonde little wife.

The Baron's French attorney had obtained, and was taking along with him on this *voyage,* an absolutely astonishing Chinese girl. He never let her get more than a foot away from him. I had my ex-wife along so we'd have two anchors on the boat. There was also a painter from Villefranche and a fagola the Baron had picked up, or vice versa—the "vice" part stands. He was a tall thin bird with a nervous way of walking, as though he continually expected a kick, or something from behind. He had wispy blond hair, a long, foxy nose, no lips or chin. He looked like a disappointed girl with a beard.

I had a suite at the La Réserve. When in the south of France, I always lived there. The Baron had a suite at the Sporting Club of Monaco, but preferred to stay on his yacht in the harbor of Monaco. I must admit he lived in splendor. It was one of the most beautiful yachts in the world—one hundred forty feet long—three master staterooms with full baths and bidets. In the Baron's master suite, which was done in mahogany and teakwood with dark blue velvet drapes, there was a bed you could have played polo on, and a ceiling entirely in mirrors; a black-tiled bathroom with gold fittings; a steam room and a massage table.

From the first two pictures we had made, we had either hired or sometimes leased antique ship's furniture worth tremendous sums of money. The Baron, with his casual approach, his total disregard of property (other people's), had systematically stolen, picked over, and confiscated any good and valuable piece that struck his fancy. Of course, I had to pay for it . . .

The Baron would report it stolen from the set and then promptly steal it. After the first couple of times, the insurance adjuster came to see me and demanded return of the furniture—or else the police. The Baron raised hell . . . "Listen, kid, this is your baby. Tell them it's destroyed; tell them it fell overboard. You're the business manipulator—*do* it."

"Well, Baron, I don't think that—"

"The hell with what you think. Am I a partner?"

"Sure, Baron."

"Don't I make us the money?"

"Yes, Baron, you do. But we . . ."

"But—hell. I don't want to talk about it. Cancel our insurance with them. Do I bloody well have to do your half of this Deal, too? You handle all the business, right?"

"Right," I said, trying to keep the lid on this one. "But, Baron, they *want* to cancel our insurance."

He looked angry. "Well, frig 'em. Cancel out . . . we'll get another broker."

"Can't be done, Baron. This is the last one. Even Lloyds of London don't want us."

"Well, they can bloody well fug-off too," he sneered. "What's the matter —can't you handle it? Is it too big for you to handle, Jarn?"

344

THE DEAL

"No," I said quietly. "I can handle it, Baron, but you know it would mean that from now on we'd have to carry our own insurance." He thought that one over. A smile broke out on his face. He lit up at this simple solution. "Wonderful, kid, wonderful," he breathed, "I knew we'd figure it out together. The old partners . . . clicking again . . . huh?" The smile changed into the charming grin. I was now being conned. I was now being hypnotized. The Baron was pleased, so he felt he'd give me the greatest gift of all—his charm, his happy grin—I was again in the inner circle of his life and friendship. As he said, we were like brothers—better even.

The charm faded out and his facial expression went back up to the business level. He mused thoughtfully, then said, half to himself, "What did that premium cost a year, kid?"

"Oh," I answered, looking past his right shoulder at the rest of the people scattered about up forward on the deck, knowing what was coming. "I guess about seventy-five thousand, give or take a little."

"Well," said the Baron, still being the businessman, "it would seem to me, old boy—since I've saved us all this dough, I think I ought to have a little bonus." He looked sadly but contentedly out to sea. "I've been working pretty hard lately and I dropped a little money at Monte . . . 'relaxing' the other night."

I looked at him—my partner, who called me his best friend. I'd heard about the "little" he'd dropped at Monte in baccarat the last few nights—well over a hundred thousand. In an abstract way, if it hadn't been so repetitious, his continued *chantage* was brilliant. If it hadn't affected our picture, I could almost have admired his conniving, scheming capacity for extracting money from everyone—and always *sous la table*. It usually took a less direct form than this, but now he felt secure. He knew we had money in the bank, our new film was about on schedule. Yeah, the Baron felt pretty good.

But I knew we still had ten more weeks to go on this one, and one more film to do. One next year; and possibly one after. And then, with enough money, please God, I was going to get out of this asylum and make some good pictures.

He was still gazing out over the harbor, the absolute monarch of all he surveyed. If he had been insured and the films done and a lot of things different, I would have happily, correctly, and absolutely shot him right between the eyes. I'd put the bullet right where the eyebrows came together . . . I could see the little hole, blue around the edges where the bullet went in. Well placed, dignified, it wouldn't hurt him at all. He'd never even feel the fresh air that would finally enter his head. But I gave him my "boyish" smile—you see, we could both do it—I grinned. "I guess we can work something out."

"Grand," he beamed, "simply grand. You're my boy. I know I can always count on you."

"Absolutely," I said, "absolutely."

The Baron turned and started to walk back toward his guests and his "crew"; smiling, laughing, kissing his way to the Italian star. She smiled. He smiled. They went into their act . . .

"You're simply wonderful!"

"Oh, no, *you're* wonderful!"

The verbal strokes and caresses continued. With my boyish smile still hanging to my face by an eyelash, I walked over to the rail and looked out to sea. The smile dropped off and into the sea as if it had never been there. I stood by the rail until I felt someone come up and stand beside me. A husky-sexy voice said, "Did you tell him?"

I turned around to look at this girl—this girl that I'd loved, this girl who had literally changed my life. She was beautiful beyond description. The body of a goddess, the face—yes, the face—well, the face . . . However, she now looked as inviting to me as a bad agent. I said as she stood there looking at me, "You'll get the part, don't worry."

"I'm not worrying," she said. "But did you tell him?"

"No," I answered. "I didn't. It wasn't the time."

"*Ecoute*—listen, *mon ange*, now is the time—the time is now. I *must* know that I have the part. It's more important than the world to me," she finished.

I looked at her. "Yeah, I know. How's the kid?"

"What?"

"How's the boy?" I said grimly. "You remember—my son—our son, if you want to be technical."

"Oh, that again."

"Yeah, that again, and again. Listen, *mon enfant*," I said quietly, "why do you think I see you? Why do you think I'm giving you this part? Because maybe I want to sleep with you? Now, I asked you how's the boy, and how's the boy is what I meant."

She gave me a girlish laugh. "You still get angry with charm," she breathed softly. "You've spoiled me for other men, Jarn."

"Balls," I said.

"See . . . see what I mean?" she purred.

"Save it," I said, "save it for the picture. You know, that was your trou-

346

ble—you've always acted far better off the screen than on. If you can call it acting . . ."

"*Cochon* . . . pig . . ." she spat, with a smile you could have used to slice bread.

"Well, that's better. Now that you've used up some of your girlish charm, let's get back to my question—about my son, not about sleeping with you—that can be done any time."

She looked at me coldly for a minute and then, here came the switch. Her lovely violet eyes started to melt, started to get the little electric glow. Tears were starting to form in her eyes—a trick I had come to know and, in spite of myself, was still strangely moved by this. But there was a long history of too many things badly done, of too many days and nights, warmed over in my mind's eye.

I looked away from her around the yacht, seeing people start to gather on the afterdeck for the prelunch cocktail hour, where they would drink their fill from a common trough and all *oink* off to various nooks and crannies in the boat and "couple"—if they still call it that.

I turned back to the piquant little face looking up, the lips trembling slightly. She glanced furtively around for a moment; seeing nobody close by, she said softly, "Once you wanted very much to sleep with me— once you ——"

"Uh-huh," I said. "But that was then, and this is now." I looked down at her. "It bothers you, doesn't it? You can't quite believe that that body, that beautiful case, that lovely and exciting package you carry your dingus around in, is no longer desirable." I figured that her insides—that wonderful place between her thighs—must be made out of leather or elephant hide (although it never felt that way). It was tough and had been used literally hundreds of times—and I mean used hard in every sense of the word. But this beautiful body, this beautiful case, which she kept in perfect shape by continued exercise and constant massage, was really something.

She was an all-right product that did well what you could read on the label. Satisfaction was, and had been for me, absolutely guaranteed. I understood that for others the guarantee was equally satisfactory.

She took a step toward me. With a lovely little smile, she put her arms around my neck, pressing close against me. I could feel the two still pert and firmly-in-place little breasts pressing against my chest. An immediate and sudden warmth was between us where our bodies touched—thighs, belly. I looked down at her. Her head was tilted back. I could see the beautiful line of her throat, the long lashes, the violet eyes half closed, that sensual veil starting to slide warmly across them. It was amazing how she could turn it on. You felt that it was done by remote control, by a will so powerful than at any moment she wanted, the whole ambiance could be turned on.

"Listen, angel," I said huskily, "it's too early in the day for this sort of thing—and it's much too late in life for us."

She pushed me back quickly and slapped my face—not hard, but with a sting that hurt, as she meant it to hurt. She turned quickly, saw that a few people were watching, laughed gaily, and said, "Oh, Jarn, you shouldn't propose things like that before lunch. You're naughty, simply naughty."

The lovely body-case, carefully holding what it held, moved off, her slender figure moving lightly, sensuously. She leaped prettily over the low rail to the lower half deck, was gallantly caught by the Italian actor with the muscles. He held her high, much longer than was necessary, then slid her down gently, their bodies touching everywhere possible. She went along with the act. He gently let her to the ground, and arm in arm they joined the rest of the *cochons* at the trough. It looked like it was going to be an interesting trip.

The gong rang for luncheon and the twelve sought-after and highly respected guests, the "inner inner crew" who were to eat in the luxurious splendor of the Baron's dining room, walked in with dignity. The rest would be served under a lovely flowered canopy on the afterdeck. They were the insecure ones—they were the royalty "without papers," they were the starlets without contracts. I watched as the select few started to enter the large dining room amidship, a look of disdain, of a secure knowledge of their exalted position, on their faces. The caste system prevailed on the Baron's yacht, and I—along with the rest of the hypocrites—entered the dining room where sat the Baron, already enthroned, indicating to each with a grandiose gesture, his place at the Baron's table, at his groaning board. We all sat down.

The Jamaican cabin boys immediately started bringing in the drinks. The calypso band started somewhere off in the prow of the boat. I could feel the engines starting to turn, and the beautiful yacht, with its more beautiful people, moved royally and with dignity out of the harbor of Monaco.

The Jamaican cabin boys now came in, removed the empty glasses, carried in the different bottles of wine, set them correctly on the table. Then, with a flourish you wouldn't see at the Tour d'Argent or at Monseigneur, or at the finest restaurant in the world, in came two tall Jamaicans. They wore white jackets and white gloves and were carrying between them a large and highly ornate silver tureen of soup. Just beyond, came the

THE DEAL

French-Chinese chef, his white cap standing two feet tall. He was carrying, with the proper reverence, a smaller silver tureen, and with a great flourish, and many little graceful gestures, served the Baron himself. This was the Baron's "specially" prepared soup.

As the chef served the Baron, little comments flitted around the table regarding the Baron's exalted status, his living like a king. I watched the Baron, fascinated. I knew what was coming. He took a spoon and, with delight on his face—anticipating what was to come—tasted the hot soup. Steaming, it touched his lips. He tasted it, thought about it, decided he liked it, then swallowed. Finally, nodding to the chef with a benevolent wave of dismissal, said, *"Très bon, très bon."*

The Chinese chef nodded, smiled; his eyes met mine for a minute. He glanced shyly the other way, then his glance dropped to the floor. He made a polite little bow, turned, and gracefully made his way from the dining room. I turned around and looked at the Baron. I don't think the distaste showed on my face. I hoped not. You see, I knew how everything was. Everyone fell to the soup. I couldn't eat mine. I sat there watching the Baron, who was eating and talking happily. I remembered the first time I had seen the Chinese serve the Baron from that personal tureen. This bag of nails stuck like this . . .

We had just finished a picture. The Baron hadn't done too badly and, all in all, I thought maybe we had a winner. The Baron wanted to go on a cruise and, happily, he sounded very rational, so we planned a trip—just a bunch of guys—we were going to take the boat out and do some deep sea fishing, a bit of sailing, some underwater scuba diving—you know, clear the air—a lot of poker and a little normal drinking to be done. But, running true to form, after three or four days the Baron started to bully the crew, finally gave orders to the Captain that we should sail for port.

The Captain told the Baron, yes, we could go back to port. It would take us probably sixteen hours to get there.

The Baron said, "Those are your orders. I *command* you to return this vessel to port."

The Captain looked at the Baron a little strangely, but said, "Aye, aye, sir." The Baron then retired to his own luxurious stateroom, where I knew what was going to happen.

Later that afternoon—after the Baron's attorney (the American one) and a couple of the other hangers-on had drifted off to retire to whatever they retired to; and Saul Baum, who'd been awfully quiet on this trip and hadn't made too much of a nuisance of himself, disappeared; and the

Hollywood public relations man had faded away—I was finally beginning to like the trip. It was the first time that things seemed to be going normally. It seemed too good to last—and it didn't.

It was about four-thirty in the afternoon. It was perfectly beautiful; the sun was slowly fading just before starting its descent; the water was becoming a pale blue-green. Far off in the distance you could see the clouds starting to settle. It was lovely and it was quiet . . .

Then I thought I'd better go down and see what was happening with the Baron, so reluctantly I left the rail, walked back up the deck, through the doorway, and started down to the Baron's stateroom. I knocked on the door. No answer. I knocked again. No answer. I opened the door and stuck my head in.

"For Christ's sake, can't a man have any privacy?" the Baron snarled and whirled around—the needle still stuck in his arm.

I never said a word. I walked over and sat down in the big chair and looked at him quietly. He was plainly surprised that I didn't say anything.

"Well, Jarn boy," he sneered. "What's the matter—cat got your tongue?" I still didn't say anything. By now he'd turned away from me, walked back into the bathroom, where I could see him putting a little alcohol on his arm. Then a little cologne. Then, very carefully, he rolled down his sleeve, turned around and came back out, walked over and sat down in the other big chair.

"You're quite a little enterer, aren't you? You're quite a little fellow to come in when you're not invited, aren't you?" I still hadn't said a word. As I watched him, I could see the thing start to hit him. It was funny to see— "funny," but not at all humorous.

It was a strange thing; I could almost see him take on a glow. First his face became a little damp and the moisture started to form on his upper lip and just at the bridge of his nose. At this time, at the place on the top of his nose where you might have said he'd just removed his glasses, two spots appeared as though he had pinched himself on the bridge of his nose, very hard. The ends of his ears were turning a sort of pale white, even though he had a tan. Then I saw everything had hit bottom; I knew the thing was really "main-lined" for him. His nose got that waxy look I didn't like, then the machine rang "tilt" and he was ready.

"What are you looking at, Jarn boy?" he said, in full control, the heavy-menace stare hard at work.

"Not a thing," I answered. "I'm not looking at a thing. A nothing. You get the picture?"

He leaned back slowly. This was a scene he enjoyed. We'd played it several times. Thank God, this time we were playing it on the boat and not on the sound stage, not when there was something important to do. At least, I knew the worst that could happen was the son-of-a-bitch would fall overboard—and even that I wasn't able to insure him against, because sometimes I felt an urge to help him on the way. This was not one of those times. He truly hadn't done anything yet. It was his own life; although unfortunately, mine was mixed up with his. I didn't feel betrayed—I'd been over the jumps before, finding out too much about my fellow men too fast— much too fast. I learned that the good moments, the "truth" moments, are hard to come by. And they fade away quickly. Almost anyone can show you how rotten life is. The Baron was showing me with a flowery example.

The Baron sat there, looking coldly, thoughtfully at me; then he started that grin . . . "Well, aren't you going to say something, Jarn boy? Don't play the Iceman, we're here alone. The boat's sailed, kid. Give me the lecture. What I'm doing to you," he finished grimly.

"Not a thing, Baron, not a thing. It's what you're doing to yourself. Oh, you're going to louse me up; you have in many ways already." There were some lines that would fit here. The Baron didn't know them, probably. I sat there watching him glow with "horse." I thought, he proffered all his goods to save and thrill his body, destined to that living grave. Boy, that was the horse—that was the mare—the female the Baron was always trying to ride. The reason he did it and the reason he kept it up was—he knew he could conquer when he was on it—"horse." He could shoe any mare, anywhere. That was another of the Baron's unfortunate faults.

There was a knock at the door.

"Come in," the Baron snarled, with his usual grace—when he was about twenty minutes down the line, the main line. The door opened and in walked the French-Chinese cook. These two hated each other with exquisite delight—the Baron, because he knew that the French-Chinese chef was possibly more intelligent than he was; also that he always seemed under perfect control. The Baron truly had never been able to make him angry, although more than once he'd gone about it with the definite idea of making this poor fellow jump overboard or commit suicide. He went to the ultimate length in this by seducing the chef's beautiful little Chinese girl friend. This, of course, stuck out a yard when one day, in a burst of charming enthusiasm —loving all and wanting to be loved by all—(I remembered that was Jason's theme song: Loved by all, loved by all—a song in a dirty bathtub) . . .

It was when the Baron had given this party for the "crew." He'd let everyone invite his girl friend, mistress, or wife on board. I must say he gave a grand party. A lot of wonderful food. The liquor flowed like liquor, especially around the Baron, and this was a pretty big flow. The chef had brought on board a lovely, doll-like Chinese girl.

Well, as I said, it was a cinch what would happen. The Baron, his nostrils flaring, moved in for a "limp kill." He escorted her all over the boat, showing her this, pointing out that, and was charm itself. When it got to the point of showing her his stateroom, I knew what was going to happen.

The chef (his name was William Ching) was watching impassively. His face had a look of shy disappointment. Then Ching looked up and saw that I was watching him. He made a little bow of acknowledgment. When his eyes met mine, I could see the hurt in them, even though French-Chinese fellows are supposed to be able to disguise their emotions. (In my view, this is entirely false. When a man's hurt, he's hurt. Some show it more, some less, but if it's a deep-down-in-your-belly hurt, you show it, Hector, you show it.)

I turned and started briskly for the door that led down into the Baron's stateroom. Just as I reached the door and would have pulled it open, William Ching was at my side. "No, Monsieur Jarn," he said quietly, "no. It was my error to have brought her along. I should have known, but I was lulled into a false sense—" (Here, he started speaking French)—"I had lulled myself *en sécurité.* I didn't believe that she would be this taken with him. She has mentioned the Baron many times, but . . . I just didn't think this out well."

"Well, Christ, Bill, "you're a man, you're a *formidable* fellow. Now, let's look in on some pretense or other. I'll go with you. First of all—"

He stopped me, saying quietly, "No, Monsieur Jarn, this would be inadvisable . . . you know *Monsieur le Baron's faiblesse,* you know his many weaknesses. I had warned and advised Sing Woo, my fiancée, not to go, not to be separated from me. Obviously, this is her decision."

"Well, listen, I'll go in and—"

"No, Monsieur Jarn."

He turned and started walking back up the deck. I called after him, "Bill, *attend* . . . just a moment." He stopped. We walked over to the rail together and stood there, looking out to sea. "You know this isn't right," I continued.

"As I have said," he answered calmly, now completely under control, "this was my error. This, in a way perhaps, was my testing. I have proven myself wrong. I did the unfortunate thing of showing the Baron a picture of her. Since then he has asked me many times to bring my fiancée aboard. Until today, and until the friendly spirit that seemed to pervade the boat, where I felt *en sécurité*, I had, by devious means, avoided this that has occurred today."

"Well, Christ, Bill, if it was my girl, I'd be in there . . ."

Here he shot me a look of . . . almost hatred. "Would you, Monsieur Jarn? *You* would."

I couldn't meet his eyes, because I remembered a couple of times when . . . well, there it was. There wasn't anything else to say. He looked at me steadily for a moment, then he turned, and silently walked toward the galley.

Now, that's what had happened between the Baron and William Ching. So when the Baron, now on his "horse," riding bumpily over the humps—but the humps were being smoothed out considerably by the charge he had just taken—started browbeating Ching, it was the wrong thing to do. He cursed him, and then worse—he got up, walked over, grabbed hold of this elegant, intelligent, and thoroughly nice fellow and literally threw him out the door —saying many things that never should have been said.

That night at dinner I was late. The Baron was already in the huge dining room, seated in the baronial chair. I could see through the slanting blinds and the jalousies over the window—everything was in full progress; Saul Baum singing away; everyone with the silver tankards; the American attorney doing very well. Just as I walked through the small entryway that led immediately into the serving area for the state dining room, I almost bumped into William Ching, who was leaning there, quietly in the shadow. I couldn't see exactly what he was doing, but he was in a crouched position. He stood up hastily, and at that moment one of the ship's lights tiltcd. I could see the Baron's favorite silver soup tureen resting on the small stool that was used as a serving tray. And I saw more—William Ching had been delicately and daintily peeing into the Baron's soup.

I had started to shout something. He looked at me, carefully arranged himself, put the lid on the tureen, and said, "It's symbolic, Monsieur Jarn. It's symbolic. This is how I despise and hate this man." And then, as he would have turned and left for the kitchen, the Baron chose that moment to come bursting out the door, saying, "Everyone else is eating. Where in hell's my soup? Oh, Jarn boy . . ." He reared back, surprised. "Where have you been? You know I ordered dinner for seven o'clock." I couldn't say anything. I looked at Bill Ching. Bill Ching looked at me and the Baron said, "Get in here, you yellow son-of-a-bitch! I told you that I wanted my soup hot and immediate." Bill Ching's eyes met mine.

Then Ching shyly looked down and murmured, "As you say, *Monsieur le Baron, je suis à vos ordres*. I am at your orders, sir." He walked into the dining room and set the tureen of soup in front of the Baron's place.

The Baron sat down, waved me to a chair, took the silver lid off the tureen, served himself a generous portion of the soup and commenced eating. William Ching, who had backed up three or four steps and stood just out of the light, watched the Baron eat.

Bill Ching looked at me, I looked at him. He nodded slightly, turned, and with dignity left the room.

Several days later, I was getting ready to have lunch. There had been many arguments on the boat and I always, of course, remembered the episode of *la bonne soupe*. On this particular day, the yacht was moored in the harbor in Villefranche. The Baron and I were having, for once, a sober luncheon, discussing calmly what work had to be done that afternoon and the following morning. In came William Ching—bearing a tureen of soup . . .

I started. His eyes turned to me, and just the whisper of a smile touched his face and disappeared. He put the tureen of soup in front of the Baron, turned, and said to me, "Monsieur Jarnigan, your soup is coming. You see, sir, Monsieur le Baron likes his *épices*—that is to say, very hot—spiced more than you would like it."

I looked at him in fright. He must have seen it, and again the whisper of a smile touched his face. He bowed and left the room, and immediately returned. He placed a small tureen before me. I looked at him. He looked at me. It was at this happy moment that the Captain came in and said, "Monsieur le Baron, I would like to speak with you. It is a matter of urgency with respect to the mooring of the yacht. Since a United States battleship will be in late this afternoon, we must change our position."

The Baron immediately got up, left the table, and walked out on deck with the Captain. So there I was with William Ching. He almost grinned. I said quietly, "Listen, Bill, you and I are friends and we've had no trouble. But, since I'm the Baron's partner, how do I know you don't pee in mine?"

"Oh," he gave that faint smile again. "We all like you, Monsieur Jarn. Guaranteed, as you say, no pee—no peepee guaranteed." He smiled, bowed, and left the room. I must say I was afraid not to eat the soup after that, or the next time I might get it.

THE DEAL

The Baron came back in. We both started eating the soup. I had to take Bill Ching's word that mine was all right, but as I sat there, not too hungry, it was awful to watch the Baron eating his soup with gusto—what was worse, he liked it.

I excused myself, and went out on deck. I heard laughing voices and people started coming out of the dining salon. I watched the couples breaking up and going to the staterooms for the night. I knew the party was over. I knew it would not be long before the babies were locked and bolted in their sleep, in twos and threes. The yachting trip would be over in the morning.

So, "horsed" or not, the Baron and I were on our last few reels. Something had to crack. We were on a knife-blade. What to do . . .

There was nothing left but prayer. And I don't do much of that anymore . . . because I don't do it well enough . . .

"Well, you can try," *Someone* said.

"Good Christ," I said aloud, startled.

"That's a fair start, Jarnigan," *Someone* said. "And you are correct— Christ *is* good. Now continue, please, Jarnigan. If you get stuck, I'll help. Remember, I'll always help."

I looked around, then said quietly, "Good. Christ . . . I need help . . ."

39

The Baron had bet a lot of company dough—our company's dough in France—that he would walk on the water one night across the Seine from the *péniche* that is moored near the Pont de St.-Cloud. I knew that the Baron had been working with Sasha Kisorska, who was our underwater cameraman expert. But I hadn't figured on this kind of a trick.

The Baron had twenty of the crew at work blowing up small floats and attaching them to a raft. He also had a half-sunk raft lead-painted, and some Ping-pong balls, which he wasn't sure he was going to use, because they wouldn't stay far enough below the surface.

I was at the studio when I got the call—from a guy I'd always called Dry Nose. He had a nose spread all over his face—looked about the size of a turnip and was about as useful.

To furnish a little more background on this, it had all started because there was this Basque fellow—a guitar player who was kind of doubling as the maître d'hôtel–headwaiter on this *péniche,* where they serve wonderful paella. Now the Basque, who was called Alfred Jesus, was in truth a walker on the water—or slightly below. He had a unique trick which had its taste of originality. At the end of one of his concerts, if there was a goodly crowd, he had his large guitar filled with blown-up condoms. I knew that this was what had given the Baron the idea.

At one time I said, "Listen, Alfred, I heard this rumor that the Baron is going to try to walk on the water. Don't let him Christ-it too far, and above all—if he gets to it, don't let him drown." Then added, "At least until after this picture is over." I looked hard at Alfred, who was hastily arranging himself into a position of dignity. Now this was hard to do, because he had been practicing with the guitar. "Alfred," I said sternly, looking him in his slightly crossed eyes, which he wore courageously, "now if this trick has to be done, I'm relying on you for the Baron's safety." I took a step forward.

The little *péniche* moved and swayed gently because a big, or *grande, péniche* from Esso was going by. Alfred, without losing his balance, never batting an eye, took a step forward and said with dignity, *"Monsieur Jarn, je suis toujours à vous ordres*—always at your orders. But Monsieur

THE DEAL

Baron offered so much money and a part for me in this film you are doing; he said that if I would help him do this I would receive many days work and many francs."

"When is this caper figured for?" I asked conversationally.

"Oh, it seems to be tonight. It is the Baron's *idée fixe* once he obtained from me my secret, which is the blowing up of *les capotes anglaises*—the condoms, as you call them. Since he found this, he has been enchanted with the idea."

I looked at Alfred, trying not to laugh. I looked out across the Seine. I said, "The Baron's pretty enchanted all the time. However, enchanted or not, how does he figure to do this, or am I to assume that this was your idea?"

Alfred Jesus hastily denied any participation at the outset of the Baron's *grande idée fixe*. Alfred trying to look firm only looked more helpless. He turned to Dry Nose for support. Dry Nose deftly took the ball.

"I'm telling you," said Dry Nose, "the Baron is down on the *grande péniche;* he is going to try and walk on the water. Now, I figure that he ain't that pure, being like he is and all, but I figured I had better give you the word." He continued quietly: "You see, Monsieur Jarnigan, sir, he made some kind of a bet and he swears he'll not float—he'll really *walk*. He says he'll walk across the Seine."

"Yeah"—I looked at Dry Nose "how's he going to do it?" The way I asked made Dry Nose uneasy.

"*Merde,*" he sang, using up most of his French vocabulary, "It wasn't *my* idea."

"Listen, Dry Nose," I said quietly, "I can get you warm for two, chilled for three. Don't French me. I want it all . . . and I want it now . . . Now is the time, right now."

Dry Nose swallowed. "I'm just giving you the word." He stiff-voiced on, "You see, he made some kind of a bet with that Freddie McHenry group, and it's big money." He fell silent.

I walked back over to the edge of the boat and looked out over the water. There, with all of the residue that is in the Seine, was a guitar. Yeah, a guitar. You see, Alfred Jesus, who shilled for the boat "walked on the water" nightly; did it for the tourists, who then got carried away. Alfred practiced a lot. So, after being blessed and crossing his circumcision and himself with hundred-franc notes, he, Alfred, would step bravely and gaily off the boat. He did well enough, because he had had this ingenious idea to fill his pockets and his pant legs and his guitar with blown-up condoms. He was a great user of the condom, except for the real *capote anglaise*. He had

THE DEAL

purchased plenty of these condoms at the Petite Pharmacie de St.-Cloud, which I remember well.

So I now understood where the Baron had gotten his idea. He figured if Alfred could half walk on the water with his pants, his pockets, and his guitar filled full of condoms, the Baron, being a star, a money man, and a genius besides, would figure out a better way. He would improvise, refine, improve on Alfred's plan. The Baron assured himself he would be able to walk across the Seine. Now, he knew that he couldn't literally walk on his feet, but, as I learned later, the bet was, he must cross the Seine *holding himself out of the water*. Further, to make sure that he didn't use his hands, he was to carry in each a crisp loaf of French bread, which must not under any circumstances become damp.

Dry Nose was running out of gas, so Alfred grabbed the ball. "Again, Monsieur Jarn," he said, looking injured, "Monsieur le Baron offered so much money because I figured a way that he can stay definitely above the water without moving his hands."

"How's that, Alfred?" I asked. He watched me slyly. Again a case of the cunning dog who knows that he has successfully tricked the master. He walked carefully over to the deck double door, leaned down and picked up one of the heavy hold doors. As he raised it, he motioned to me.

I walked over and looked down, then stared in amazement. Looking down into the hold was really a sight to see. It looked like a galley of midget slaves having a New Year's Eve party. There were at least fifteen children of ages six to twelve blowing up condoms. They were working at full speed, as if the Russians were at the gates of the city.

The condoms lay in the hold like fluffy cotton. The work tables were long planks, each lying across two barrels. On top of each plank, at the far end, was a basketful of cellophane-covered candy suckers for the little blowers. These suckers were balanced carefully on the end of each row. The deal was five blown-up condoms tied well and not leaking air or any-thing—one sucker. The assembly line continued.

I stared at them aghast. "When does it stop?" I said to Alfred.

Alfred almost snapped to attention; then, in an organlike tone, "When *Monsieur le Baron* walks on the water." He said this reverently, almost crossing himself.

"Listen, Alfred," I snarled, "I don't mind *you* walking on the water. You got your guitar full of these rubbers and maybe *you* can do it, but you better see to it that nothing happens to the Baron if I can't break up this thing. You walk on the water tonight, and you walk on the water without the guitar."

359

"But my guitar, it's part of my act. It keeps me afloat," he wailed. "You know in truth, Monsieur Jarn, I am not the most formidable of swimmers."

"That is regrettable, Alfred. We should hate to lose you. But this must be done."

Alfred took a step back and said with dignity, "It shall be arranged and taken into account as you have indicated."

"Listen, Alfred," I continued, "I don't want the Baron walking on the water tonight. We've got to have more time to frame this dingus. Another thing, Alfred, I'm a little surprised about. Aren't you a Catholic?"

"Yes," Alfred said proudly.

"Well, then, man, it's easy." I leaned over closely. "Now, you and I don't want to do anything sacrilegious, right?"

"Right," he echoed.

"Well," I continued, as convincingly as I could, "any walking on the water around here, especially since you're a good Catholic, is only in connection with, and in the performance of, your work—*votre travail*, right?"

"Right," he sang again. Actually, he said *"Dac."*

Because we were speaking French, I continued in the vernacular. "Well, you know that all the Disciples and the Apostles were in favor of this sort of thing, but this is an entirely different matter and we don't want to do anything sacrilegious, do we?" I said, shaking my head from side to side. I waited and gave him a fix, looking him right square in his crossed eyes as he said, "No, Monsieur Jarn. Maybe you will think of something. Perhaps you have the possibility to arrange that Monsieur Baron does *not* walk on the water?"

"I shall try, Alfred," I said solemnly, "I shall try. We shall see. But you are to do nothing until you have word that I have arranged something. Understood? Agreed?"

"Understood and agreed. I permit myself to remind you, Monsieur Jarn," he said, almost popping to attention again, "I am at your orders—at your orders, sir, in their entirety."

I left.

●　●　●

I got the word from Saul Baum that the Baron would try the walking on the water the next night. Saul didn't want the Baron to drown either. His job, his total security, were tied up in the Baron.

After I found out that the Baron had finally prepared for his "walk on the water," I had gone down to the *péniche* next to the Pont de St.-Cloud to

THE DEAL

find that the Baron was there before me. He was already in his outfit. Everyone had been properly bribed. The Baron looked like Oliver Hardy's father. The flight-suit he had on was blown out; condoms were sticking out of every possible square inch—all of them sprayed a dark gray.

He was hidden in the hold, where he could step out easily and then, showing that he could hold his hands in the air, make it across the Seine. As he turned around to look at me, his face and head looked about the size of a pea sticking out of his fantastic suit. His pants, made of olive nylon Army cloth, were so inflated that when he walked I had to laugh.

"Jarn," he said with dignity, or as much dignity as anyone could have standing in a flight-suit full of blown-up condoms. "Jarn," he repeated sternly, "I fail to see any humor in the situation."

"You're right, Baron," I gasped, "you're absolutely right. Any guy who would laugh at a reasonable man who is, number one, in dark makeup; who is, number two, in a commando outfit; who has, number three, blown-up condoms practically sticking out of his ears, between his legs, and crammed into every nook possible in that suit—less what have popped, if that is the noise I keep hearing; who, number four, has these things tied around each foot—and who wants to speak of dignity and of seriousness, of walking on the water—well, I agree a guy shouldn't laugh." Here the Baron looked at me in amazement.

The Baron said, "You do understand, Jarn. You really do," he finished with a gasp.

I looked at him affectionately. "I leave you without a word," I said, offering him my cigar cutter with the long needle on. "You put this to good use and nothing will be said about anything. I'll do the needful upstairs."

"Would you, Jarn—will you really help me?" he said, getting up bloatingly, balloonly, condomly, definitely, and unsteadily.

"I will," I said firmly. "And here, Baron," I said, "you may have what in my view is the finest condom pricker in Paris." I handed him the cigar knife. I started away. The Baron stood up. I knew this from the squeaks of the ballooned condoms.

"Jarn," his voice rang out in the best John Barrymore–Jared Throne tradition, "Jarn, you are a prince, an icy prince of darkness, but a prince nonetheless." The Baron kept on talking.

I kept on walking. I went up on deck where I saw the Basque, the Alfred Jesus, the true walker-on-the-water, with his guitar already full of condoms. I approached him without making the sign. "Listen, you Basque bastard, I'm repeating this"—kicking around two of the condoms that would never leave the boat—"don't let him Christ-it too far and, above all, *don't*

let him drown"—then, quietly—"at least not until the picture's over."
Alfred again arranged himself into a position of stern readiness. Ready to
do his duty. A brave proud look on his face. (This is hard to do with condoms already blown up with air, coming out from under your arms and
between your legs) I said, "Alfred, I'm sure you realize the seriousness of
this occasion."

"It is realized, Monsieur Jarn, all is realized. But as I said the other
night, I am at your orders. Nothing will happen to the Baron, and with this
dark night—who knows?—he may have a chance to do it."

"Alfred," I said quietly, "on a dark night or a light night, or on any
night, the Baron is the one fellow in the world who has *no* chance to do it."

The bet had been made. The Baron had to go completely across the
Seine holding a *baguette* in each hand and holding them both above his
head as he crossed—thus "walking on the water" and without resorting to
any manner of swimming. The bets were ready. The fellows from Fred
McHenry's racing stable were all at the far end. Albert had showed rare
judgment in shining the searchlights in such a delicate way that they shone
directly into the faces of the people betting against the Baron.

Alfred said, worriedly, "Monsieur Jarnigan, I fear that all is in readiness
and we must proceed." The lights were turned on, the orchestra, limited
without the addition, the handsome addition, of Albert on the guitar, struck
up a tune. It certainly sounded nothing in the world like a hymn, but it
made the noise. It was time for the Baron to go. I leaned over to my
side of the deck, far away from the bettors. I could see clearly, since the
lights were shining from above and beyond me. I saw the Baron come out
on a plank teetering forth from the lower deck.

He turned, and I could tell that it was with regret that there was no audience. He made me a gesture, a brave sign holding the long *baguettes* in
both hands, the bread that would soon be over and above the water—
not cast on it. Now the Baron was preparing himself to walk to glory. He
looked at me, gave a dignified bow, stepped off—and promptly sank like a
stone. The Baron disappeared completely from view, of course taking the
bread under with him.

And then a strange thing happened. From here and there and from more
places than it was possible to imagine, blown-up condoms began popping to
the surface. The only way I could figure it was that the Baron's suit had
broken and released all of the children's blown-up balloons payable one
sucker for five blow-ups.

I hollered for Alfred, I wasn't going to jump into that dirty water; but it

THE DEAL

began to look a little serious, since the Baron hadn't come up. Now I didn't know if this was from a delicate sense of shame on his part, but I knew it behooved me to get hold of Alfred.

"Alfred," I yelled, "get the hell down here—the Baron's still under."

I hadn't waited more than a few seconds, when I heard the splasn. Without the guitar, Alfred had entered the water where the Baron had gone under. It was an interesting sight to watch what happened. Alfred came up first, then the Baron, looking absolutely thin in comparison to the way he'd looked a short while before. The old flight-suit, which had obviously been purchased from an Army supply post, had split every which way. The Baron, looking like some monster who'd lost weight and was ready to shed its skin, laboriously clambered over to the lower part of the boat.

The whoops and the hollers going on from the other side, where the winners were under the lights, was a delight to see. Now someone with a burst of enthusiasm had paid the men who had worked the lights to put them on the water. Happily, his friends did not see the Baron, who by now had ducked out of sight, but on the Seine there has never been such a picture. Somehow, in Alfred's scrambling in letting the lower gangplank down, our bountiful supply of blown-up condoms which had been in the hold now wafted out on the river. Now we had gray, green, and the classic white. Balloons such as had not been seen since the Americans landed in Normandie and the celebration in Paris when Ernest Hemingway arrived, were in such abundance that it is difficult to describe the scene. . . . "Rubbers on the River of the Seine Blues."

I went down to the lower-deck. I got Alfred. Told him to get the Baron out of the boat. To take him across the other gangplank—the car would be waiting—and to take him over to the studio and get him cleaned up. In the meantime, I'd go upstairs and see what I could do to settle my partner's debts. He hadn't walked on the water, but then he hadn't drowned either. So it looked like the Deal could continue tomorrow.

• • •

The Editor never thought big enough to steal all of the Baron's cash, his bonds, and the film negatives. Without question, in this respect the Baron really had him completely hypnotized. He was so overwhelmed and subject to the Baron's every wish that, although he could have literally ruined the Baron, his thoughts against the Baron were petty and of no consequence—piddling things. If he talked back or cursed the Baron, out of earshot of everyone, he considered it a victory. He then smirked and

363

thought well of himself. I don't think that for the period of thirteen or fourteen years he had worked for the Baron he had ever made a move, taken a decision, or had a thought that he hadn't first cleared in his own subconscious how that thought, move, or decision would affect the Baron . . .

The Baron kept the Editor's wife on salary as a secretary. This cute, kittenlike little blonde was good to have around. Since her recent marriage to the Editor, the Baron had used her from time to time, for many things, with the bridegroom's complete and contented sanction. The Editor was a born loser. When his bride would complain that the Baron was using her "harshly," the Editor would snap, "Open your mouth on this and I'll pop a tooth out of it." He was firm and manly with her.

Sometimes the Baron would fire the Editor because he—the Baron—looked "lousy" in a close-up. This, of course, was not the Editor's fault, but because the night before the Baron had been either drunk, "horsed," or intertwined with something or other.

On one occasion, when we were shooting the picture in Paris, and the Editor had again been "fired," he came up to me in the studio commissary at Billancourt in the Bois de Boulogne. Without being invited, he came over to my table and sat down. Happily, there were very few people in the large dining room.

He had been drinking and looked terrible. He poured out his troubles to me. And then, following the normal channels that these conversations always took, he requested money. After I refused, he moaned, "What am I to do?" Finally, after looking round the dining room, he furtively took a small pistol out of his pocket, put his hands under the table, and, pointing the gun in the vicinity of my stomach . . .

"You see this?" he whispered softly, with menace, in the best gangster tradition.

"Yeah," I said, "what do you want to do—sell it?"

He moaned again. This time in anger. He looked dangerous.

"Listen, kid," I said. "If you use your bean I'll try and help you again, but if you start cutting up in here, well . . ." I let this drift away, seeing he was getting nervous. I continued, "If you want to stick around you're going to be polite and not yell and not threaten and not pull guns on people and little things like that. It can make you unpopular . . ." I was talking loose and big, but didn't feel it. This silly bastard was rickety-brained enough to shoot me.

The Editor sighed. He looked down at the gun, then put it back in his pocket. He looked back up at me. He had the silly, sappy grin of a weak man trying to be strong. He said, "I'm going to get the Baron." The strained smile on his face looked as empty as a new-dug grave.

It peeled off when I said, "The grin don't fit you, Hector." He laughed the laugh of a pessimist who has contentedly found that things have turned out badly. I figured I'd try to laugh him out of it, since I sure didn't want him to interrupt the Baron on the sound stage. I made my laugh friendly, but it never reached my eyes. I was watching him.

He said, "You act like this is funny, but me—I don't laugh."

"Listen," I said, "the world is filled with people who don't laugh. Maybe you're one more, but it doesn't count. This Deal is not like you think it is, and you're not going to do anything."

His face started to crack up. He looked like he was going to cry. To continue to blast him at his expense wasn't funny anymore, because he was the born loser who had endured much—especially with that wife—with the valor of mediocrity. Had he been a nicer fellow he should have been spared the mockery and the "wearing of the horns." He had a lot more than film to cut.

And that's the way it was, one afternoon—with me trying to complete the picture.

After the Editor left the commissary, I got to brooding about what the son-of-a-bitch had done while we were in the middle of the previous picture, the second one of our Deal.

He had stolen the negative of our first picture and hidden it in one of the Baron's vaults, and I hadn't been able to do anything about it at the time, or even wanted to confront the Baron with the knowledge of it.

This was a touchy business because only the man who checked the negative into the vault (presumably the Editor) could get it out, no matter what.

I needed it now. I'd been counting on the income from distribution rights to it, whether from Wormser, who had first refusal, or someone else. That was another thing. If Wormser wanted to hurt me, he'd exercise his first rights, but withhold distribution. Of course, he'd then be withholding money from the Baron (and himself), as well as from me, and I couldn't guess if Wormser would go that far.

But I sure as hell needed money as we went ahead with the third movie. In the end, I decided to try to raise money another way—from my legal-financial friend, Jules Molotov. I met him later that day in the lobby of his hotel, and he side-stepped the hint beautifully, so I had to come right out with my need.

"Hell, Julie, you can give me the seventy-five G's. That will give me seven more days shooting."

"Can't, son. I can't, Jarn."

"Well, why the hell not?"

"Well, son, she spends money faster than the Baron. She's a rough diamond. You ought to see her spend dough." He leaned over closely toward me. "You ought to see her, period." Here, he leaned back, looked thoughtfully past my right ear and sighed, "Jarn, when I'm with her . . . I just . . ." Here, he breathed heavily and lapsed into silence. Then he gave me another thoughtful look and confided, "Jarn, you wouldn't believe how lovely she is," he said.

"Nope," I said, too harshly, "I don't. And, I don't need to."

"Listen, Jarn, you ought to get yourself a woman like Miriam."

"No, thanks . . ." I cut in.

He went on as though I hadn't interrupted him, "Then you wouldn't be so hard and mean and cold. Christ, you don't trust your own mother."

"Well, maybe not," I said. "Then, I'm not in business with her . . ." Julie didn't know everything. . . .

I had been down—not out, but sure down. Maybe that's where I belonged, but I didn't figure that way yet. I just needed to keep going, to keep the "under the line" going. That called for ten thousand dollars a day . . .

That's not a lot by normal picture standards. But when your star is the Baron, who has a history of nonperformance, and your picture is way over budget, you have to have a lot of money. I called the lab, the banker, the Suisse Syndicate man, who was selling off part of the picture. But the *bruit*—the noise—was all over Paris and Hollywood, and that meant everywhere. I called Darryl—couldn't reach him; Jason Wormser was warming himself by the fire that was burning me—getting gleeful reports, blow-by-blow disaster reports from some fink on the picture. (Think pink, think fink. He was; and he did. A pinko-finko. But he got the reports through.) So, no place to turn. I had one last card; but I didn't want to play it. I needed about seventeen days work and I could finish the picture.

I had called my mother. "Mom," I'd said, "I'm in trouble."

"Well, son, you all right? Not sick or anything?"

"Nope, but I need a lot of money."

"Yes, son . . ."

"Mom, you don't understand . . . I need about two hundred thousand dollars or I'm dead. The picture's costing me about ten thousand dollars a day. There's nothing left for me but prayer and I'm prayed out. Anyway, I don't do it very well anymore."

"I don't like to hear things like that, son."

"Mom, do you have any ideas?"

"Yes." A long silence. "Is it *that* picture again?"

"Yeah."

"Don't say 'yeah'—I've told you, Jarn."

"Yeah, I know. Listen, Mom, forget it. Mom, I don't know what's the matter with me—I don't mean to worry you. I'm glad you're O.K. . . . . I'll call you next week. Forget what I said. 'Bye."

I hung up.

I had received a bank draft the following Friday in my favor for one hundred sixty-five thousand dollars. The letter with it said only, "Here is sixteen and a half days, son—all I could manage. Love, Mother."

Mother was not only Mother . . . she was a gentleman!

But now I stood there looking coldly at Julie. I figured I'd lie to him a little—there was no sense in him knowing that in my pocket I was holding that sixteen-and-a-half-days check my mother had forwarded.

While I was thinking this, Jules Molotov was looking at me closely. ". . . . Well, *my* mother is worse. Wouldn't help me a bit. She even sides with Miriam against me. Can you figure it? I guess all mothers are bitches," he said to me. "You know how the Baron feels—bitches!" he said, nodding complacently and looking at me for agreement.

The Baron had said, "I get mad, I get mean—angry-mean—when people mock my dignity." He hiccuped. "Like my mother. She's a bitch . . . she ruined my father, who was a coward, and that's a ruin. So what does that make *me*, Jarn boy?" he burbled on, "if a five-letter woman marries a six-letter man? How many letters in 'ole son-of-a-bitch'?—Because that's what she was, and that's what *I* am, Jarn boy."

I looked at Jules; I again touched the wallet in my pocket that held my mother's check. I said, "Well, maybe you're right, but this isn't helping me with what I asked you, Julie. What about the seventy-five G's? You can get it back in about thirty days. What say?"

"I don't see how I can, Jarn," he said; "you know this Miriam's got me so boxed up I don't know how to fence with her. Why she even got me to put the lease on the new building in her name."

I thought this over, remembering that the only thing Miriam could possibly know about a lease, especially a million-dollar lease, was that lease is

367

a word that rhymes with grease. And grease was the "sexygel" she put in her diaphragm. So when her husband talked about a lease, through her mind's eye ran a montage of actors, of lawyers, of rented suites and having all of the locks and bolts oiled with sexygel-grease. So, the lease was in her name and Jules Molotov was again being led around by his dong. I looked at him. He was still awestruck by what he'd been thinking. "She's wonderful—simply wonderful," he moaned.

"So you can't help me out, huh, Julie?" I plowed on. "Me that put you in a pretty good position. In fact, if we're going to lay it on the line, you wouldn't even be talking about Miriam if I hadn't switched the Deal so you handled all of the Baron's and my business, instead of just working for me. You noticed, Julie, I said *for* not *with*, because that's the way it was. Now you're not giving me real service—except the kind of service they used to talk about on the ranch, some time ago."

His eyes bugged out. He took an attitude. He said a few legal things— in-respect-tos, and in-connection-withs, and whereases—some lawyers' gobbledygook which amounted to nothing. He now looked and barked and acted like a spaded dog who has seen everything, expects nothing, and gets it.

I turned around and walked away from him, through the door of anger, and found only disappointment. I knew now unless something unforeseen came up, I wouldn't finish the picture anyway. I glanced back at Julie. The revolving doors went around, but the expression on the little lawyer's face had slammed shut. I thought he smiled. It looked like a cracked butterfly's smile. His bleak eyes were set like stones. Yet hope was boiling in his veins, which would go unrewarded. Jules Molotov, tired unto death, weary now with fear, exhausted by his apprehension of Miriam leaving him, heard the rush of blood, and the bump-bumping of his heart. He walked awkwardly to the chair by the desk . . . Minutes passed. At last, Jules rose slowly.

I saw him turn and start back across the lobby, knew that he was going back to the suite and Miriam. Knew that he must have felt as though he'd betrayed me—and he had. He carried his guilt and his heavy thoughts like an ungraceful, ponderous ass. He was carrying more than his share of the load. But upstairs he'd have his swim in the velvet pot; and then, when the sex effort had riddled him down and was over, he'd start to feel hungry.

I left. I walked on down the street, thinking about the tribe. I wouldn't mind being a member of the tribe. I didn't want to be a "maven." Everybody's a maven. I'd just like to be a member, except I was rejected once. So I'd just better go ahead and roll my own hoop, I thought, stick in with my own bag of nails. That was the way I'd have to play it. Of course, there was another way . . .

Later, after Miriam's and my intimacy became more intimate, Miriam told me about Jules—and when I say she told me—man, she told me. She slipped the dagger of intimate knowledge into my sleeve to use in conversational deadliness against her lawyer-husband. Miriam had, strangely enough, a sort of dignity betraying Jules her husband. Which nonetheless did not change the effect that it would have. Jules didn't need that. Who does? Only Christ had to be kissed and taken . . .

40

I was sitting in my office when the door opened and a guy walked in, unannounced—something that I never did like.

At first glance he looked like an actor dressed especially for a gangster picture. He was a thin bird, but not memorable in any special way, except for some store teeth which didn't fit.

"Are you Jarnigan?" he asked.

"Yeah, who are you?"

"That ain't important. I just want to make sure who I'm talking to before I say what I'm supposed to say."

"Look, I don't know what you're supposed to say or why, or who you are, or who sent you. But I like my visitors to check in with the secretary—and I'd suggest you do that." Then I added quietly, "I'd do that right away."

"I heard you was kind of tough, I heard you was pretty sandy," the thin bird said, clicking his store teeth like he had plenty more to say. I waited. He surprised me by just standing there and looking at me quietly. He clicked them a couple of times more—*click, click.* He said, conversationally, "I wasn't told to *do* anything to anybody this time. I was just told to look you up and give you the word. We will need the negative of the picture or all the money. You get the idea, Jack?"

I watched him for a minute. His hands were down at his sides. He only ran about five foot ten. Very thin. Couldn't have too much muscle. I got up. I acted as though I were looking out the window and looking the other way. Instinctively he followed my glance, and I jumped him. I hit him on the jaw the way you hit anything you don't like. It was like swatting a fly. He went over like a bale of straw. He was as light as a feather. When he lit, his overcoat broke open and a forty-five bounced out of a holster. A wrist about as thin as a pool cue snaked out for it. I stepped down hard, ground my foot; he let out a moan, then clamped the store teeth on his lip, turned and looked up at me. "You didn't need to get tough, Jack," he said, "I wasn't going to do nothing. I wasn't told to do nothing. I was just told to give you the word."

I looked down at him. I pressed a little harder with my foot. He grimaced again. I reached down and picked up the forty-five; stepped back,

371

taking my foot off his wrist. He sat up. I walked over to my desk and sat down. He sat there on the floor looking at me and then he got up. I said to him quietly. "I don't know if you were supposed to come here and talk, and I don't know if you were supposed to come here and do anything. And then again, maybe I hadn't thought about it one way or the other, but I'll tell you something, Hector; to me, you're a fellow I can do without in my office. I'm going to keep the gun, you can get some more iron. Now you take off. I don't know which one of three groups is sending you, but I'd like to. Would you care to let out a little information on that?"

He said a dirty word.

I stood up behind the desk. "Maybe I'm playing this wrong with you, Hector. Let's you and I have a talk."

I opened the drawer, put his gun in, closed the drawer, snapped the lock, walked around the desk, went over toward him, and said, "Okay, wise guy, I was going to let you down light—now, you tell me or you get hurt."

He took two steps back. This put him right up against the mantel—he couldn't go any farther. "Geez, Jack, I didn't know we were going to get into this hassle, I was only supposed to give you——"

I cut in on him. "It ain't a question, Hector, of what you were to give me. I want to know one thing, and I'm only going to ask once. Who sent you?"

He looked at me for a moment, licked his lips, shot a glance at the door, and knew he'd never make it. "Well, I, well . . ."

I balanced on the balls of my feet, opened up my shirt collar, turned slightly so that I was half away from him; my right shoulder dropped a little. I said, "You want it hard, Hector? You're going to get it hard." I reached over with my left hand and grabbed him around the neck, around the shirt, with the tie and the collar all in one fist. He still hadn't said anything and as I started to hit him, he grinned. "You can't make me talk, I won't talk. You know why?"

"No, why?" I sneered.

"Because I don't know anything. They gave me five *mille* to come over here and say what I said. I said it. I don't know nothing. And nothing you can do can make me change that story."

I released his collar, stepped back a couple of paces, and studied him. "Well," I said quietly, "let's see about that."

I believed him when he said he didn't know—but I was still puzzled why the Syndicate, or the French co-producer, or the *avocat* would send a red-hot, with all the B-picture mannerisms, to tell me what he'd told me.

THE DEAL

"Take off, Hector, and don't come back," I said.

He looked at me sadly. "This is just another job to me, Jack. I done what I was told. Next time I may come to see you on my own." He looked at me calmly.

"You do that, Hector. I'm trying not to let that bother me."

He gave me another thoughtful look and strolled to the door, saying, "I like that iron, Jack. If you ain't afraid, you could leave it at the concierge."

"For whom?"

"Just say Matty. I'll have it picked up. You see, with me, Jack, it's nothing personal—just another job." He looked bored.

"Hold it, Matty," I said. I walked back to my desk, unlocked the drawer, took his gun out, unloaded it, put the clip back in and tossed it over to him. He caught it neatly. It disappeared. I grinned at him coldly, "That will save you a trip. Next time, if you pull it on me, you better use it. Now, dangle."

He smiled back at me, just the faintest trace of a dry smile. "Maybe some day I can return the favor, Jarnigan. 'Bye."

He walked out. He was a strange, cool number. He sure wasn't afraid. Now, who sent him—the Suisse Syndicate men, the French co-producer, the *avocat*, Jason Wormser—the Baron? Christ, what a mess! I turned out the lights. I went back to the studio.

41

That afternoon I'd almost had a fight with Saul Baum, who was plenty sure of himself and, more important, sure of his contract and long-term association with the Baron, knocking heads, frightening people—more of a bodyguard and bully than a stunt man. A big man, well over six-four— would weigh in about two hundred pounds.

In the deserted studio and on the sound stage with no one present—me trying to block out what could be shot tomorrow without the Baron's presence—Saul came onto the quiet sound stage and walked sure-footedly toward me. He passed through the empty "tavern" set, walking carefully between the empty tables toward me where I was sitting under the camera. He had a nasty look in his eyes, as if he wanted to fight with somebody and thought I'd do . . .

He came across the rest of the space between us—softly, like a cat walking on a wet floor. He spoke quietly, his voice purring with menace—the careful, unhurried, underplayed voice of the gangster-picture tough guy— movies have made them all like that: "The Baron can't come. I'm here in his place. You got a message for him, you give it to me." He smirked. "Well?"

I looked up at him. I had known this guy for many years. He'd been a stunt man at the studio for some time before the Baron had latched onto him, and I knew he'd do anything at the Baron's bidding. I didn't know how far he'd go. He was watching me carefully. "Now listen, Saul," I said, "I've got nothing to say to you. I know you're doing what you were told. Now I am telling you, go on back to the Baron and tell him I expect to see him within the next hour. We have to take a decision on this picture. Hell, man, you ought to know that."

He gave a little half-smile, still in control. "You ain't said nothing that's said anything yet," he said quietly.

"Look," I answered, not wanting to have an explosion right then, "I want to see the Baron. I want to see him now. I sent for the Baron. I didn't send for Saul. You don't look like the Baron."

He smiled. "Well, you might say that up to a point I *am* the Baron."

"Well, Saul, I'm beyond any point you're at. Now shove off—and tell the Baron I'll meet him here at eight o'clock. We've got some night shooting to do. And get him here sober."

THE DEAL

"Listen, Mr. Producer," he hissed, "I take orders from the Baron, I don't take orders from you."

"Well . . ." I said, "maybe we'd better do something about that."

He took a smooth step backward, balancing lightly on the balls of his feet. "You want to try now, Mr. Producer?"

I shook my head at him sadly, "Always the brawn . . . always the muscle. . . no brains . . . no class . . . no anything . . . just muscle. Now get out of here, Saul, and I mean *now*! You get that message to the Baron we'll forget all about your tough-guy act now."

"Listen, Mr. Producer," he said again, as though I hadn't spoken, "I don't like you. I never have liked you. You give too many orders. You think you're always in control. I've got news for you . . . the Baron don't like you either."

"That isn't news," I said. He kept on talking. I tuned out. I was thinking, as his words kept purring on: Was the Baron far enough gone to send this clown to try and do something? Was the lad that far off? Had I been that wrong?

I started to stand up. He slid forward quickly and stiff-armed me back onto the camera chair. I sat there. He said, "Don't get up, Mr. Producer, or I'll chill you." I looked around. He had me by two inches and twenty pounds. He was in great shape. I looked around farther and saw a spanner on the camera dolly. I looked at it. He looked at it. Just as I started to get up, he tensed, and a voice said, "*Well—are you two men rehearsing?*"

Saul spun around as if someone had touched him with a hot poker. I got up quickly—backed two steps to the left so I'd be in a better position . . .

My brother walked in closer to the light. He didn't look at me. He had a nice grin on his face. He said, "What's the matter, Saul boy? I only tuned in on the last. What's your beef with my little brother?"

Saul said, "Listen . . ."

My brother said quietly, "No, Saul, you listen." He carefully removed the raincoat he was wearing, dropped it gently on the floor. "Let's back it up twenty feet and replay this scene. I came in where you said something about 'Mr. Producer.' Now, Saul, that wasn't nice. That sounds sarcastic. You know my brother's name. It's Mr. Jarnigan to *you*, bum. Let me hear you say it . . . *Mr. . . . Jarnigan.*"

Saul flicked a quick glance at me—looked quickly back at my brother. Saul said, "I got no beef with you, Mo."

My brother said quietly, "That's where you're wrong, Saul boy. You got a whole lot of beef with me. I heard enough. Now, my brother said to deliver a message to the Baron. I didn't hear you say Yes, sir, Mr. Jarnigan—so I'd like to hear it now," he continued conversationally.

Saul looked back at me, took a half-step back, close to the camera dolly. "I ain't going to fight two of you."

My brother shook his head sorrowfully, "Saul, Saul, why persecuteth thou you?—you're not going to fight two of us—you're not even going to fight one of us."

Quick as a flash, Saul's hand reached out, grabbed the spanner—he started to raise his arm for a blow. My brother took a half-step forward, set himself, and threw his left. It was a perfect punch—knees slightly bent, shoulder bent, straight arm, wrist stiff. I don't think that blow traveled over ten inches. It sounded like you had slapped water with a flat board.

Saul, who hadn't quite straightened up, went down. My brother danced forward and stamped his foot carefully in the middle of Saul's wrist. He turned to me. "Come on, kid, let's get him out of here." He turned and picked up his coat, threw it over Saul, who was now shaking his head. My brother whispered to him, "Saul, you and me and my little brother have words to make. We know the negative is gone. It worries my little brother. I don't like to have him worried. We're going up in the hills and talk it over." He turned and for the first time grinned at me. "Kid, get the car and pull it over to the stage door. Best if we don't make this too noisy."

Without a word I turned, crossed the empty sound stage, out the door, got the car. Came back and opened the door just in time to see my brother with the spanner in his hand backing Saul gently toward the exit. He shoved old Saul into the car with a remarkable lack of restraint . . .

We started driving through the studio gate. I waved to the old French guard, who waved back. Then we started up the mountains, away from the shore, headed for the Grande Corniche. When I hit the turn that leads to St. Paul de Vence, I swung the big car to the left and up into the hills. It was just starting to get dark . . .

We crossed over a country road. I turned in and pulled the car to a stop. Saul was now making protesting sounds, talking to my brother. I got out of the car. My brother pulled Saul out from the other side. I was amazed how quiet he was. Far below, I could see the lights of the cars going from the studio toward Nice. It was completely quiet. The moon had started to come up and I thought to myself, What a Deal . . .

Saul backed up. It was a good name for him. He must have looked very much like his biblical counterpart. He was a bigger man than my brother, who said quietly, "Okay, boy, back up a little more." My brother's hands and arms were hanging loosely at his sides . . .

377

THE DEAL

Saul backed up, feeling better now, full of beans and plenty of gas. The smirk started to climb back on his battered face. He said, "Do you guys think you can get away——"

My brother took a quiet step forward and kicked Saul correctly and deftly in the groin—just like that. There had been no pause, no uncertainty. Saul's eyes popped out of his head half an inch. He gasped, spat out, and was trying to hold himself together. His sense of pain was dropping him down. He looked as though he were trying to scream but couldn't make it. This struggle within himself went on for a second—then he fell . . .

My brother grunted, looked at me, then commented evenly, "He's soft."

"No," I said, "he's not soft. He's hurt. Any man can be hurt there."

My brother said, "Are you complaining, kid?"

"No. I just——"

"Hold it," my brother said sharply. "Nothing's going to happen to him, nothing *too* bad. He's tough. He's a stunt man. He's a man who points out to me that I'm my brother's stooge. He's the man who does the dangerous tricks for the Baron. So far, all I've seen him do is hit drunks, slap two girls around, and carry the Baron home to bed. But he's tough—he'll tell you so."

Saul, by this time, had pulled himself up to his knees. He was taking deep breaths. "Now, tough guy," my brother said, "we're up in the hills. We're in beautiful France. It's a beautiful night. Sing me a night song. Where is the negative of my brother's picture?"

Saul just looked at my brother—still on his knees, his mouth half open, breathing heavily. My brother walked carefully over to the car and switched on the spotlight. He aimed it directly below Saul. It made a big circle of light almost as though it were a prize-fight ring. He walked back toward Saul and the light, and after a long silence—disturbed only by the heavy breathing of Saul—my brother dropped the heavy spanner, a two-foot iron rod, directly in front of Saul. He said casually, as if nothing had ever happened. "There you are, tough guy, make your move."

The side of Saul's face where he had scraped the gravel was a mass of blood. I couldn't see it too well, but looking at it in the light I knew it was there. His hands were working now. What that kick in the groin had done to him seemed to be subsiding. He looked away from the light—then suddenly, with a rush like a football guard, dove for the spanner, and got it . . .

My brother kicked him squarely in the face. Saul flipped over on his side, clawing at the dirt, shaking his head back and forth, a groaning sound coming from between his lips. He still had the spanner in one hand . . .

THE DEAL

My brother kicked him on the elbow. Saul howled—the spanner dropped down on the ground in front of him. He twisted around and came up on his knees; his face was white in the glare of the spotlight. He shook his head. Very carefully he started to stand up. He swayed a little, then spread his feet, hunched his shoulders, and attempted to get in position.

My brother taunted, "Come on, stand up, tough guy. Like you say, you're the Baron. I'd like to do this to that baby, except my brother needs him for the picture. You're a tough guy. You've got the Baron behind you. You've got your 'crew.' Come on, let's rehearse a scene. I'll stand in for my little brother. You don't mind doing it with me. It would be the stooge and the stand-in. I'll make you look good, boy—let's take a whirl at it . . ."

Saul lunged out in a tremendous movement toward the spanner. His hand barely touched it when my brother hit him a horrible blow on the back of the neck. As he fell, my brother jumped on the middle of his back. Saul yelled. My brother said, "Saul, that don't bother you?"

I said, "For Christ's sake, Mo, don't kill him!"

"Who's going to kill him?" my brother answered. "I don't want to kill him. I want him to talk. He don't want to talk. He's against talking to a stooge who's only working for his little brother. He's a tough guy."

"Well, just don't kill him," I said.

"Nix, not me—nix, kid, I wouldn't do anything bad like that. This is an honest fight. The stunt man against a stooge. He outweighs me by plenty pounds and he's tough."

Saul said groggily, "I ain't fighting the two of you."

My brother spoke up. "You ain't fighting anybody yet. I'm waiting—and I won't let my brother hurt his hands on you. Come on, tough guy, let's go. You've got a lot of power left, you're full of beans . . ."

Saul got up slowly, like a man trying to climb up out of a well. He shook his head and tried to pull a handkerchief out of his pocket; failed that and wiped off his face with his sleeve. He was wobbling back and forth, then suddenly he made a kick at my brother's stomach. For a second it looked like it was good . . .

My brother stepped back gracefully, grabbed the leg, pulled and twisted. Saul started to scream and my brother said grimly, "Not bad. I let you go that far when you had the spanner. You didn't figure on just kicking me without that iron in your hand . . . Let me show you what a mistake that was . . ." With a sudden turn, Saul's body seemed to arch into the air and tangle sideways. First, the left side of his head and shoulder struck the ground—the rest of him seemed to melt. My brother grabbed hold of the other foot and turned it as though he were closing a big valve on a boat.

THE DEAL

Saul began to flop around on the ground like a marlin on a gaff. Even when his face was covered in the dirt, the screams went on. It sounded as though tires were screeching to a halt on cement. My brother put more weight on the turn; he spread Saul's legs. Saul tried to gasp, finally gave another scream—the sound came out as though a saw were tearing through wood . . .

My brother looked at me through the dust and said, "Kid, this is some workout. Maybe I ought to be a stunt man—more dough than being a stooge, huh?"

Saul moaned, "I quit. I'll talk. I'll tell."

My brother did something else and twisted the leg in the opposite direction. Suddenly, Saul went as limp as a wet towel. It was like seeing an old horse floundering on a hot day. Saul fainted . . .

This bothered my brother. He released the foot, stepped back two paces, breathing heavily. He glanced casually at Saul, who was out for good, turned back to me and said, "Kid, loan me your handkerchief." I handed it to him dumbly, then reached into the car, got my scarf, and threw him that too. Blood was all over his hands. He looked down at the unmoving stunt man. "Tough guy," he said under his breath. "Too much wine, too much Baron—no guts."

"Listen," I said, "why don't we let him talk?"

"Maybe," my brother agreed, "maybe he's ready now." He bent down, looked carefully in Saul's face. By now Saul's eyes were open and he was blinking. My brother said, "Can you hear me, boy? Can you hear me, stunt man?"

He stepped back and kicked Saul in the ribs—not hard, but with a certain flair. After the third kick, Saul's eyes came back into focus. "Come on, stunt man, pull yourself together. I'm not going to pop you no more." Saul, fearfully and slowly—the one cut eye half closed, the other completely filled with dirt—carefully started to pull himself to his feet. Suddenly he was old. It seemed to take him several minutes to get up. He grabbed the air reaching for something to hold on to.

"I was telling my brother that you ain't tough no more," my brother said conversationally to Saul. "He says you won't talk. I say you will."

"I'll talk, I'll talk!"

"Don't shout," my brother said. "Nobody asked you to shout, nobody even asked you to talk—not really—my brother just wanted a little information from the Baron. But if you insist—yeah, in fact you *can* tell us . . . I'd do it now if I was you. Start out with 'Mr. Jarnigan, *sir* . . . I apologize for my miserable conduct toward you this afternoon.' Can you say that?"

380

THE DEAL

Saul looked as though he were confused. My brother took a step toward him. Saul lurched back, almost fell over. "I'll . . . I'll talk . . . Mr. Jarnigan, I'm—"

My brother stopped him. " 'Mr. Jarnigan, *sir*.' "

Saul choked.

"Christ, Mo," I said, "let him talk."

"No—he's got to be polite."

For the first time I saw how pale my brother's face was. I saw the hate that for a moment turned from the stunt man and looked directly into my eyes; then, almost embarrassed, my brother turned away as though he were ashamed I had seen such a look on his face. He looked back at Saul and said gently, "Now you can try again . . ."

"Mr. Jarnigan, *sir*, I——"

"O.K.," my brother said, "cut the babble. Where's the negative?"

"It's . . . it's . . ."

"Go ahead," my brother said.

"It's on the yacht. It's . . ."

My brother said, "You were thinking, Saul. I can see it." His fist lashed out; he hit Saul square in the mouth—a tooth popped out and went flying over into the bushes. Saul went straight back and fell heavily, like a tree. He never moved . . .

My brother walked back toward the car. He leaned against the fender. He walked back over, picked up the spanner, and laid it carefully on the ground beside Saul. "When he wakes up in a minute and sees that, he'll say anything we want him to."

"But I only want to know where the negative is."

"Well, that's for you . . . and I'll bet he wants to tell us. Guys are nice like that. I don't believe in forcing a guy to talk if he don't want to. You got to ask him nice. You got a cigar?"

I fumbled in my coat, couldn't find any, walked over to the car, opened the glove compartment, took out a couple of cigars, handed him one, lit mine—found my hands were shaking. He very casually bit the end off his cigar, spit the end out. I lit my lighter, held it to the end of his cigar. He saw my hand was shaking . . .

He thoughtfully watched the end of his cigar catching fire; then his eyes glanced up, as if we'd been talking of the weather. He smiled. "Well, it's cold up here, kid. Get your coat."

He drew heavily on his cigar. I reached over and flicked off the spotlight. My brother looked out over the hills and down toward the lights in the harbor. "You know," he said softly, "it's pretty up here in the hills at night. When I get old I want to buy me a little house up here—and do nothing but smoke cigars, drink red wine, and watch those lights."

I looked at him. "You know, big brother, I could use a drink."

My brother looked at me keenly for a moment; his face had started to take on a little color. He grinned the grin I had known all my life, and said, "Yeah, I'd like a drink too"—as though he'd never had one in his life—"but I got to remember to stay in shape. This picture isn't finished yet, you know."

"I know," I said quietly, "I know . . ."

Saul moved a little. My brother looked down at him indifferently, then he looked back up at me. "Kid," he said, "let's ask old Saul to tell us where your negative is." He added pensively, "We better take him with us, just to keep him softened up until we get it. Then—I think I'll let you buy me that drink."

He grinned at me then. He walked over to where Saul was by now sitting up and looking around, carefully avoiding touching the spanner. "Come on, Saul boy . . . rise and shine. We're going to pick up my little brother's film." He continued, quietly, "It would be nice if you'd give us the address." He reached down and jerked Saul half up. Saul was now in a kneeling position in front of my brother. "Saul boy . . ."—there was menace in the quiet way he said this; he was looking down at the upturned, bruised, and bloody face . . .

"Saul," he continued, "you are on the air."

Saul went on the air . . .

He milked himself dry. He told us that the Editor had taken the film negative and put it in a private laboratory under his name alone. The Editor alone could get the negative, and so had control of our picture.

We scraped Saul up, poured him into the back of the car, and with him still telling us things—many things—we drove back to the town, with me listening to everything carefully; making mental notes of Saul's soliloquy. The facts continued, then the replay turned to babble. I tuned him out as we entered the studio gates.

Later at the studio, I got a call. A voice that "clicked" when it talked (named Matty) told me where I might find somebody who might know something about my property . . .

Sam Neely, my brother, and I got to the two men that the Editor had hired to hide away the work negative for good. One guy got away; we got the other one. But now I had to make him talk. I couldn't waste too much time, since the Baron was still among the missing. Everything I had was riding on recovering this negative. I asked the tough guy for the last time where the laboratory was, so I could get to the Baron and let him know I had recovered the work negative and he couldn't leave France. Then he would have to complete the picture.

We strapped this guy in a chair, still plenty tough. He kept yelling, "You can't make me . . . you can't make me tell . . ."

I had to take a decision. I knew that it would take too long to let my brother or Sam work him over. Something had to be done, and fast. The guy said, in a tough, resigned manner, "Nothing you can do can make me talk, Jarnigan—and the Baron's gone."

"He's not gone," I said. An enormous weight was on me . . . the months, the heartache, the emotion, and such a big part of me that had gone into this picture, this Deal—and this clown was preventing me from recovering what was mine. A cold light was burning in my head. "Listen, you poor prick," I snarled, "I'll make you talk so fast you'll sing any song I want. For the last time, are you telling me where that laboratory is? Yes or no?"

"No!" he yelled.

"O.K., Sam. Hold him and unzip his fly. You know, tough guy," I told him, "you've seen too many motion pictures, too many shows. I'll show you how it's *really* done. You'll talk. You'll talk fast." I reached in my pocket, pulled out my lighter, and said, "Grab him, Sam, pull him out and hold him." I flicked on the lighter flame.

A look of terror came over the guy's face. His mouth opened . . .

"You're too late, Jack," I said, and I ran the lighter all over him.

He talked. He talked and would have sung, except finally he was out— out cold. I didn't want to burn him completely off with the lighter, but I sure wasn't going to lose that negative. Sam and my brother were both looking at me with the first real fear I had ever seen in them. They were now afraid of how far I'd gone, and they didn't know how much further I'd go. Now, as the rage started going away, it was hard to believe I'd done what I'd done. It had been a terrible thing to do. I knew it had given my brother a shock.

Driving back to Paris, I was tired. I started to doze after all the excitement. I half slept. I remembered some advice my brother gave me years ago, about my own dong . . . That had been a bad thing. Nobody should do that—should be so uncontrolled as to turn into an animal. Man, I I wished it was over—it seemed so endless. I slept . . .

• • •

THE DEAL

. . . and how you swam in the Walnut River, below where the sewer came in—though you didn't think about things like that then; you didn't even know about them—and the dead dogs, the bottles, and the condoms later, floating down lightly, with a lot of "lost" in them. But again, unknowingly, you dared and were dared. You fitted the used condoms on your little dinker, made love to a shiny black African princess fashioned out of the soft dark mud that made up the riverbanks—better than clay, and warm from the sun. And if an occasional root or stone got in the way and you felt a little pain from the thighs of the mud princess, that was— well, life, that was—and you tried to think . . .

And then, oh hell, let's go screw Darwin's sister; she's got pimples— she isn't black and shiny and princess-muddy, and she won't let you use the used condoms on her—you wondered why. She said, "It's the feel, Jarny, don't you see? . . . it's the feel." I held on and tried to agree with her. She was three years older than I, and I was sure she was plenty smart about that.

"I love you," I said.

"Don't tell me now," she breathed, "don't tell me now."

"When?" I said, "I'm trying to do like you ask."

"You don't come until I tell you," she answered . . .

"All right," I lied. I already had, and was looking down at her with interest . . . She was long and ugly, and she sweated something awful. She smelled like a can of silver polish. She started to moan, and grabbed me closer. "Now, Jarn, now . . ."

"Oh, sure—sure, Lois," I said . . . I'd gone long before, but when her eyes rolled up in her head and she kind of shook, I figured it was the time, so I pinched her buttocks hard with my hands, and said "Oh, oh!"— and tried not to laugh . . .

"Did you feel it, Jarn? Did you feel it, my sweet Jarny?"

"Yeah," I said, "I did, I sure did." I tried to pull away . . . she held me, her eyes became more alert . . . "And it's our secret, Jarn—our secret, yours and mine." She breathed out heavily and tried to pull my head down to kiss me.

I pulled out, half fell over, making more of it than it was. I said, "Sure, Lois, between you and me." But I thought—between you and me and Red, and Gene, and Augie, and Paul Graham, and all of us condom hunters. I said, "Sure, I won't tell—I know what you mean." I got up and walked past the bed, over to the screen porch, and peed out through the screen. It sprayed around . . . I remembered my older brother saying, "Just hold the

384

end, pee hard against it and then let it go; it's a sure way to avoid the clap." I had studiously followed my brother's advice; so I held and sprayed and held and sprayed, and what came from the first-story porch was in Morse code . . .

However, my brother was wrong; that wasn't the solution . . . I got the clap anyway—but of course I didn't know it then . . . I gave Lois a lingering, promising good night . . . After all, a fellow has to be debonair when he's thirteen years old . . .

* * *

I was awakened by Sam Neely, "Jarn . . . Jarn, you're home." I got out. I stood looking down at my brother and Sam, who were watching me carefully. "Good night, kid," Sam said quietly. "I'll see you Monday."

I had forgotten it was Saturday. I looked at my brother, nodded—I didn't say anything. I turned around and walked toward my apartment entrance. My brother and Sam both called out "Good night, Jarn" and "Take it easy, boy." I didn't turn around or stop walking. I just threw up my arm in a wave of dismissal. I went inside. I heard the car drive off. I went upstairs. I went into my apartment. I sat down in my chair. I was ashamed. I was going mad . . .

42

It was a cold and damp Monday morning after we burned the Editor's thief. There was a mist blowing in off the Seine, crossing the road and hanging like a fog. I drove through the studio gate. I let the boy park my car and walked over through the double doors and onto the sound stage. It was dark inside, difficult for me to see. I walked over to where there were some lights, where they were setting up for the first shot of the day. Out of the shadows stepped my brother. I took a look at him. He didn't look normal. His eyes were glassy. He said, "Kid, I don't feel so good. I'd like to talk to you."

There were many times when my brother hadn't felt good. Usually it was because he'd had too much juice of the grape or had had a bad night.

"I'm busy now. I can't do it now. I'll see you in the office later." I said coldly, still ashamed of burning that guy Saturday night.

"But, kid," he continued chokingly, "this is important. I've got some things I'd like to tell you about the other night and all . . ."

I spun around. "You didn't hear what I said, I told you I'm busy. Now go on over to the office and get Madame Henriette to fix you some coffee —I'll talk to you after a while." I looked him straight in the eye. He started to say something, shook his head slowly, then he turned away from me.

I walked on back to the lights and started to give instructions about what I wanted to be sure and finish, and about where the first two or three setups were to be. After twenty minutes of discussions, when I knew that the first three shots were lined up (we'd marked where the camera should be) I talked briefly to the head cameraman, Marc. We talked over the business of the next two days' work. Then pretty soon one of the three assistant directors came up quietly, a French boy we'd used chiefly to run errands and get coffee—a nice kid trying to learn the picture business. He respectfully nodded. "Monsieur Jarnigan," he said, "your brother is on the phone."

I frowned, "Listen, tell him that I'm busy and I'll talk to him later." I turned back to Grignon and the boy walked off. About five minutes later he came back and said, "I excuse myself to disturb you again, Monsieur Jarnigan, but it's your brother and he insists that you talk with him."

"You tell him·that I'll be up to the office in a half hour. To take some coffee. Tell him I said just that—to drink some coffee." The boy walked off, shaking his head. Marc looked at me for a minute.

"You know, Jarn, your brother didn't look too good this morning."

"Have you ever seen him look "too good" when he's hung over?"

"I don't mean that," Marc said. "I mean, he just sat in the chair quiet. I said hello and usually he talks and we kid around a little. He didn't say much—he acted like there was something on his mind. He didn't look like he was hung over to me."

"Well," I said, more annoyed, "Marc, let's just finish blocking these things out and I'll go on up." To myself I thought, If it's a hang-over—or if he's drunk, or been drunk, I'll punish him a little, I'll let him sweat. I'll let him know that I'm certainly more than just brotherly annoyed at him; because it's been too many times—too much of this. So I'll just—I'll just pop it to him a little, let him sweat it out . . . Yeah, let him sweat it out. I was still ashamed of the way I'd become. I blamed everybody for the way I was now. And my brother was the closest and best target. He couldn't, and wouldn't, fight back. You see, he was still my big brother and he truly loved me.

Another thirty or forty minutes had gone by when I heard a flurry at the stage door. I looked up, the door burst open and the production manager came running down. He said, "Monsieur Jarnigan, Monsieur Jarnigan, you're wanted right away up in the big building, your office—something's happened to your brother. I think they said he had a heart attack."

I dropped the script book. Dropped my coat, which I'd had over my arm, and cut out at a dead run for my office.

As I got to the office, Mme. Henriette was standing there, pale as a ghost. "Monsieur Jarnigan—*hurry!*," she said. "In the conference room."

I ran to the conference room . . . threw open the door . . . got into the reception room. And there was Jules Molotov, the assistant director, Jack Clement, and another fellow I didn't know. They all started babbling at once. They all looked frightened and pale. They kind of stepped back, away from me. Even Jules Molotov at first . . . then he came up to me—slowly . . . his eyes looked sick. He was saying something I couldn't understand. "Jarn . . . Jarn."

I looked down at him.

He said brokenly, "He's gone, Jarn."

I looked at Jules for a moment—didn't answer him. Then I pushed on by and went into the library. My brother was lying there on the big leather couch. He looked like he was either asleep or passed out. I thought the

THE DEAL

room was very stuffy. The assistant director, Jack Clement, was just standing there now. He looked at me, he had a strange look on his face. He started to say something and I said, "Well, what's the matter, Jack, and who the hell is *this* guy?" I said that looking at a strange guy I'd never seen before. "Look, Jack, will you get the hell out of here. I know how to take care of this. I've seen him through a lot of these things. He's just had another attack."

They both looked at me warily, then sidled out the door very quietly. I heard the door close. The room wasn't too well lit, there were a lot of scripts and books all around the room, heavy furniture, a thick rug, and the sort of musty, closed smell of a room that is full of well-meant intentions, but has been used too much.

I unconsciously took this in as I stood there looking across the room at and past my brother. I didn't want to get too close. I took a step away from him and then saw a chair that was in an oblique position away from the couch where he was lying.

I took the few steps there, sat down so that I was about twenty feet away from my brother. I sat there and just looked at him for a little while and then I said, "Hey, boy . . . hey, boy . . . you out or you just faking again . . . that's it . . . Listen, kid, now I'm not going to get sore, so you can cut out the act. Everybody's out of the room so let's lay it on the line . . . tell me what happened. I'm not going to get sore."

There was no answer from my brother. He didn't move. I got up quickly from the chair and walked over to the cupboard, where I knew there was some brandy and glasses.

"All right," I said, talking a little too loud and a little too fast. "All right, I'm going to have one with you. This has been a son-of-a-bitch of a weekend for me too. Now you just take it easy there, Mo. I'm going to get us a drink." Saying this, I took the bottle and two glasses and walked over to the table that was at the other end of the room and carefully set the glasses down and the bottle. I poured out two drinks. I picked up one of the glasses and carried it over toward him. Then quietly, without looking directly at my brother, I set his drink on the table next to the leather couch. Still without looking at him, I turned around, walked back across the room, picked up my drink, and sat down in a chair. I emptied the glass of brandy at a gulp, got up, went back over to the table, got the bottle, came back over and sat with the bottle of brandy in one hand, and the empty glass in the other. I looked over at my brother's figure lying on the couch.

"Oh, come on, kid. I told you, they're all out of the room now. Come

389

THE DEAL

on . . . down the hatch. Come on, you old son-of-a-bitch, you never turned down a drink in your life. Listen, Mo . . . listen, that's good brandy . . . that's good brandy." I choked, I was having a hard time talking.

"Listen, kid," I went on, "I told you and I'll tell you once more—I'm not mad, I'm not mad at all. I just want us to have this drink and talk everything over like you want to, because you know I'm kind of alone here on this thing and I've got some stuff I need to talk over with you. Now come on, take your drink with me and let's go ahead and talk this problem over. Now come on, please . . ."

I looked away from my brother. I walked over to the window and looked out. I wasn't seeing anything. I turned around, came back, poured myself another big drink of brandy, drank it. I set the bottle and glass down quickly and said gruffly to my brother, "All right, listen, boy, I haven't got all day to waste here. I've still got a picture to make. You called me, now here I am, so come on . . . come on there. Get up and have your drink and let's talk and then go on back to the stage."

There was no sound from the couch. I took six quick steps across the room. I grabbed the glass of brandy that was on the table next to the davenport. I leaned down and raised my brother's head. His eyes were open. He wasn't looking at me. His head was very limp, I was surprised how heavy it was. I lifted his head and put the glass of brandy to his lips and I poured it. He didn't open his mouth.

I whispered to him, "Now listen, kid. Take a drink of this and you'll feel better. I told you this is good stuff here and you're wasting it. Come on, kid, I'm not going to fuss at you. I won't bitch anymore. I won't bitch anymore, I promise you I won't. I won't bitch anymore, I promise, I promise, I won't."

I was kneeling now beside the leather couch, my arm was under his head, I was holding it up, I was talking to him without looking at his face. Then, I heard the door open behind me. I heard Jules Molotov say, "Jarn, Jarn, what the . . . what the . . . what are you doing?"

I turned around and snarled, "Get out of here, you son-of-a-bitch. Get out of here."

"Jarn, listen," Molotov said. "Jarn, don't."

I turned my head quickly and threw the glass of brandy at him. He never moved. I took a better look at him. I could see now he was crying. "Get out of here, you son-of-a-bitch. Get out of here, you Jew bastard. My brother and me are talking and we don't need any interference. We don't need any legal advice, so get out of here and let us alone."

THE DEAL

Jules took the three steps over and tried to put his hand on my shoulder and he said, crying, "Jarn kid, Jarn boy. Your brother's dead. Don't do this, don't take it like this."

I stood up quickly and I shoved him. I snarled, "Don't say that to me, you bastard. My brother isn't dead. I guess I ought to know him better than you. I know when the big son-of-a-bitch is faking, he's faking, that's all. He's scared I'm going to ball him out, and I will. You just get out now."

I gave Jules another shove, started him toward the door, and hollered again, "Now you get out and stay out." I pushed him through the door and slammed it. I turned around and stood in front of the door with my back to the door looking over across the room at my brother. I couldn't see him clearly. I stood there for what seemed to me to be a long time. Then I walked over so I could sit in the chair and not be too close to my brother, but where he could *hear* me. I sat there for a minute, then copped a plea.

"Listen, kid. He's gone—he won't bother us anymore. Now you listen to me. I'm in awful trouble, so you've got to snap out of this and come on . . . come on . . . come on out of this where you can help me now. Hell . . . hell, you're the oldest. Hell, you should be taking care of me instead of me always . . . having all the time to take care of you. Well, I'm just not going to do it anymore. I'm warning you," I said loudly. "Now, by damnit, you're older than I am and you're going to stand on your own two feet, I'm not going to help you anymore. You're going to help me. I've looked up to you . . . I've looked up to you all my life, ever since you were a lousy football hero. You were always bigger than me, you were always a better fighter, but you son-of-a-bitch you never changed—ever. You've been a lousy football hero all this time, through every one of these deals. All you've been doing is riding around on my back and I'm sick of it. So I'm giving you notice right now" (this said more calmly), "unless you snap out of it and you lay off the flit, and you lay off all of this no-help that you've been giving me . . . because you got to start taking care of some of these problems . . . because man, I'm alone. I'm so lonesome today, I could die. I don't have anybody to really talk to, so you see every time you get drunk and pass out like this, then I just got nobody."

I got up and paced the room carefully avoiding the leather couch. (Then, apologetically) "Now you see, kid—there I got mad again. I was blowing off, but now enough's enough, so come on, boy, just say something and let's have that drink, and we'll talk it all over. Then we'll go on back to the studio and get back to work."

391

THE DEAL

My brother hadn't moved. I got out of my chair and I walked two or three steps over toward the leather couch and then, I don't know why, I just couldn't walk very good any more.

The next I remember I was . . . I was down on my knees beside the couch and I had my brother's head in my arms. I was talking to him. He didn't react at all. I was trying to talk back to him. I said, "Now listen to me, I want to tell you for the last time, I'm sorry and I won't be mad at you about this, but listen, don't do anything—don't do anything bad to me. You just can't leave. You just can't leave because . . . I can't be alone here. I need you and you just can't go out away from me now. I'll tell you" (I said confidentially) "I'm going to change your deal with me and my deal with you. I'm going to cut you in on all of my part of it. I won't even cut you in on the trouble part. I'll cut you in on the top part."

I was patting his cheek now and rocking him gently back and forth. I wasn't looking at him. I continued quietly, "We just won't have any more trouble anymore, you and me, but please, boy . . . please. You always said to me there weren't no two or three guys good enough to take us in a deal, or in a fight or anything. Well, man, that's why, you see, that's why that you can't leave me, because you can't go back on your promise . . . you can't leave me, because I'm in a fight now, see, and it's a bad fight. You never walked out on me before, and if I promise you that I'm not going to holler at you anymore and bitch at you for getting drunk—hell, you can get . . . you can even get drunk, a little . . . you know, kind of take it easy. Listen, I won't even argue if you *get* drunk if we're going to talk business, but just let's talk it over now . . . please . . . come on. Come on, kid."

I put him slowly down on the couch, his face turned toward the wall. I half straightened up. "All right, listen. Now you're not going to walk out on me on this Deal. I won't let you do that. I'm telling you, right now. You stay like this . . . you keep this up and I'm going to get Jules. I'm going to tell him all the stuff you've done."

I turned around from where I was beside the couch and hollered at the top of my voice, "Jules! Jules, get in here, come on in here—I want to tell you something."

I must have been screaming, from the way that door broke open, and in came Jules Molotov, the assistant director, and that fellow that I didn't know. They came running into the room and Julie came over to where I was still half kneeling and I guess crying. I looked up into Jules' face, I said, "Julie, this bastard brother of mine, I've been telling him that I'll let go all of the bad stuff but he's got to straighten out and I'll make a new

THE DEAL

deal with him. Now I'm giving him one more chance. I'm going to leave now. I'm going to walk out of here."

Now I stood up. "You get him out of this library and take him over to his place and sober him up, because I can't do it, I just can't fight this here . . . and Julie . . . Julie, just get him on out of here and get him home. Now can I rely on you for that?"

Jules looked at me in terror. I continued, "Now don't answer me. *Don't tell me anything* and don't *ask* me anything. Just get him out of here and sober him up; I'll take care of him in the morning, and you tell him so. Now I'm going home and I don't want anybody to bother me. Just sober him up. Will you do that, Julie, will you do that for me?"

Jules looked up at me. The tears were streaming down his face. I was surprised to see him crying like that. I never thought he felt much deeper than a lawyer's brief. But he was crying while I kept trying to say something to him.

Finally I said firmly, "All right, that's it. This is Jarnigan telling you. Get him out of here, get him sobered up. He's to be at the studio tomorrow morning. I don't want to hear another thing now, not another thing." And with that, I turned around, walked out of the room, slammed the door, out down the hall and through the street exit, not into the studio.

I had left my coat and hat on the stage. I walked off down the street, I didn't wait for the car. Sam Neely yelled at me, I waved him away. I kept walking down the street in the direction of the Place de Neuilly where there was a *bistro*. I walked across the street, a lot of cars were honking, I guess I hadn't crossed where I should have, but I just kept going till I got to the bar. I walked in. The bartender was a short, squat pig of a man with a blind eye. He came over, made one or two inffectual swipes with his towel, and said, *"Monsieur?"* I said, "Give me a bottle of brandy and a large glass."

"Monsieur?" he questioned.

"You heard me. A bottle of brandy and a large glass."

I don't know how long I was in that bar. I carried the bottle of brandy from the zinc bar over into the corner, took one of the tables and sat there drinking, and from time to time looking around. I was aware that some of the other customers were looking at me but no one dared to come over to the table.

After what must have been an hour, since more than half of the brandy in the bottle was gone, I heard a commotion at the entrance to the bar. To my great surprise, in walked Jules Molotov, the assistant director, and—I never could have been more surprised—in walked the Baron.

393

THE DEAL

Behind them vaguely I could see some other people from the picture, a couple of members of the crew, but I wasn't too clear as to who was there. All I knew was that Jules Molotov and the Baron were coming over. The next thing I knew, Jules said, "Jarn, Jarn, we've been looking all over for you. Listen, you have to get home. Come on."

"Hi, Julie," I said, in a half-a-bottle-of-brandy voice. The Baron went over to the bar and asked for a bottle of something—I don't remember what it was. He came over and sat down, took the bottle that he had, took the glasses, poured a shot for Jules Molotov and a big one for himself; then looking at me steadily drank down half a water glass of something.

"Jarn, I'm sorry. I'm certainly sorry," the Baron said. He acted like he didn't know how to talk. He acted like he was talking to a stranger. "Jarn, I'm certainly sorry," he continued saying, "I . . . I don't know what to say at a time when there's so much trouble."

I cut in on him with, "Why, Baron, what have you done now? What trouble are you handing me now?"

"No, kid," the Baron said, "now take it easy."

I mumbled, "I'm taking it easy. I'm taking it easy. What's the trouble you've done . . . you're sorry about trouble . . . what other trouble can you give me that we haven't already done; I mean had . . ."

I poured myself another glass of brandy, drank half of it off and looked at him. He looked fuzzy. The Baron glanced quickly over at Jules Molotov, who by now had picked up a chair and was seated with us. There seemed to be less noise in the room. I looked around, a lot of people were standing some distance away, but all of them were staring at us. There was mumbling going on. I looked back. It was the Baron still talking.

He continued, "Jarn, now if there's anything I can do . . ."

"Hell, yes," I said. "Hell, yes, there's plenty you can do. Just be on time in the morning and everything will go all right. Just come to the studio and be on time and everything will go all right, you know. Everything's all right."

"Well, Jarn," the Baron continued. He reached over and he put his hand on my shoulder, a friendly gesture for the first time in a long time.

I looked up. I saw a strange look in his eyes. It was kind of like the look way back in that hotel where he'd gotten a glimpse of religion and it scared him and maybe he was going to try and change something—but it never worked out, nothing ever did for him. He just kept patting my shoulder.

The Baron said again, quietly, "Listen, kid. Listen, Jarn. Anything I can do. Anything I can do to help, I'll sure help. I'll be on time in the morning."

"O. K. Big deal," I answered. "You're going to be on time. What's all the trouble about?" The words were slurring now and what came out was, Wassall-thuh-troublabout.

"Jarn," the Baron said, very solemnly, "What I'm trying to say is, I'm very sorry about your brother. I liked him and I'm sorry."

"Well, you loused him around some but just take it easy with him, he's all right, he takes a drink too much once in a while, he's all right, so just you take it easy with him now and he'll be all right. I know that. So you be on time, and be there early on time in the morning and that'd be fine. I'd appreciate it, and my brother appreciates it."

I could see the Baron look at Jules Molotov and Jules look back at him. I could see both of them shaking their heads and Jules reached over and said, "Jarn, come on, son, let's go on home, let me take you home and—"

I cut him off with, "What the hell's all the overly careful things that are being said here? The Deal's O.K., Mo's O.K. . . ." I couldn't continue.

"Jarn," the Baron said, "I think Jules is right. Come on, I'll go with you and Jules. I'll drive you home. We'll take you home right now."

I looked at him and then I looked at Jules and back to the Baron. "I don't want to go home right now. I want to finish my drink and then I want to go back to the studio and check on what has to be done tomorrow, then I want to go home . . . Then I guess I should go home."

The Baron looked at me, turned around, and motioned for the rest of the people to get outside, then he looked back at me. He said, "Jarn, I'm sorry your brother's dead. I'm truly sorry. I wish I could do something . . . I can't, but I'm sorry."

"Wha . . . what'd you say?"

He looked back at me quietly and he said, "I'm sorry, Jarn. I'm sorry your brother's dead."

"Well . . ." I said, still not going along with anything, ". . . this Deal's killing us all . . . if that's right, it will kill you, it will kill Julie. This Deal kills us all."

With that, Jules got up; he motioned to Jack Clement, the assistant director, who had been standing in the back. He came over. So with Jack Clement on one side and Jules on the other, the Baron parting the way, they led me from the bar and we walked out into the street.

We were standing there together, just getting ready to get in the car. Sam Neely opened the door, looking scared. I was standing there just about to get in, the Baron on one side, Molotov on the other. Then the Baron said to me, "You want me to take care of the arrangements? Jules and I can do it. Do you want us to take care of your brother?"

THE DEAL

I looked the Baron over carefully, drunkenly, in the eye. The Baron said again, "Shall I take care of the details?"

I got into the car, then tried to close the door. The Baron said again, quietly, "Do you want me to take care of your brother . . ."

I looked at the Baron thoughtfully. "Fuck him," I said. And fell over on the seat. That's when the lights went out.

•   •   •

I was drunk. I was as lonely as the man who rolls up the false green lawn after the burial, after the brother's burial. The casket descends slowly on the sling and then you swing down onto the bar and resip your loneliness. Drop a nickel in the grave. A bad burial, a bad bourbon, although you regret them both no matter when they come. You can prepare for a disaster all your life, but when it happens you're not ready. So I talk and talk and try to wash and dry my conscience. I try to carry what's left of my soul in my hand, like a thin oily-sacked lunch.

The whole world would jolt; murmur sleepily, sigh gently, and ignore the leave-taking. Death, the overworked word we all fear, yet it is pounded into each pore of us from the first ass-slapped breathy cry to the undertaker's dry powdered work and drier powdered smile. ("The shoulders are too wide, the coffin will cost more, Monsieur Jarnigan.") He would like to say "each," he would like to bury twins, he would like to bury the world on the time-payment plan.

(Here the eyes heavenward. "He must rest comfortably, for eternity. You don't want him to 'sleep' [and how] on his side.")

"Oh, now, he wouldn't like . . ."

"I know . . . I know," the undertaker undertook to say . . .

I sat there thinking sad thoughts, I remembered some of the pictures that had been made and I thought of the friend of my brother who was a foreign producer who made several pictures. His pictures were always gloomy and gray. The screenplays he wrote all seemed to end up in Old Russia. And the plot was, a farmer goes out at night and is eaten by wolves and his wife and son and daughter walk through the next nine reels in the cow cakes and the horse apples of the barnyard, calling, "Father Nik, Father Nik, come home to us now, the clock in the barn is wrong."

The end of the story and the end of the movie usually was much more sad than that. The mother dies, is left out to be eaten by the wolves to save money on the funeral. Using that money, Ivan the son and Ivanska the

THE DEAL

daughter start a Pinsk branch of the 4-H Club with the money they saved from the nonburial of the mother and then the sunset rides off, and the theater lights will go up, *olé, olé!* I guess the brandy and the burial and the Deal are getting to me.

I turned and looked down at the bottle in my hand. It was empty. I was empty. So the brother's gone and things are like they are, and the Deal will continue. So I cry against the fate and pound my puny fists against what I knew could happen and what has happened. Love ye then the stranger, or should you send them away . . . I wish someone could send me away, far away. *So long, boy.*

There is now absolutely and truly no question, that I would be a better father, brother, or husband. I'm not too late for the first and the third. The brother part is gone now. And all I have left is the puny, feeble phrase "All men are brothers." All untrue, very untrue.

Even if I knew how many men have been through this "every-day, every-night hell," this "death by installments," it wouldn't cheer me any. Because it is me these things are happening to, it is me who is passing through these times, these days and these hours. I am not impressed with what has happened to these men in similar circumstances. There could be no similar circumstances. But even if there were, that helps me no more than the sorrow or the death of some other person would be helped by the knowledge of the death of the brother of the producer on the next sound stage. That brother had been a good man. We are all good men in a lousy word. So, you take it and you try to accept it. But nothing makes you accept it gracefully.

I remember my brother and me, when we were much younger—alone, on our own—were forced to get something to eat from the Salvation Army. We were hungry. We went into their building and were told to sit down and wait. Meanwhile an Old Man and an evil-smelling Old Woman came out and prayed over us. We were asked to read a passage from the Salvation Army–prepared Bible, and the Old Woman who smelled came over and breathed in our faces a copper-smelling breathy plea to join her in singing a hymn. Finally, they gave us some meat and bread. My brother ate and tried not to choke from crying softly and eating at the same time. I drank some of the sickly sweet coffee because it was hot and I was cold, but I wouldn't touch their damn food. My brother pushed some of the meat and bread into the pocket of my coat and then we left, wafted on by the copper breath of the Old Woman.

We walked out of the building and down the alley, past the cross that

THE DEAL

was neon-lighted to show the way to prayer, peace, and those sons-of-bitches in the Salvation Army building. Walking slowly, when my brother wasn't looking, I took the meat and the bread out of my pocket and threw it in the gutter. I hated those praying sons-of-bitches who tried to break us, and make me pray and sing and say things I didn't mean. I watched the bread float slowly away. By Christ, that's one supper I wouldn't owe to Jesus. I had cast the bread away, but not on the water.

43

There had been a delay and a holdup, or holdout, on the money to continue the picture. I had called a meeting in my office. All the vultures were there, but I was trying to delay things until my attorney and hopefully the Baron would get there to back me up in my demands.

I had to keep them in the office. I had to hold them until the Baron and Jules Molotov got here. I had to make them angry. Not angry enough to blow up everything. But angry enough to stay and hear me out. I was on a knife-blade. I took the plunge.

"I'm going to tell you babies the facts of life. I'm going to open up and tell you what you don't know about this Deal that you claim you've got a lot of money in."

At this, they shot glances at each other. I had their interest now. I needed to stall for time.

"So here's the way she goes, *mes amis*, here's the deadly *faiblesse*," I said, now speaking French. "You are rare and windy fellows. Your breath leaves much to be desired. Your letter writing, your contracts, and your speech are like a halitosis whirlwind. This is the nearest I propose to get to it. However, under the majestic image of this purple wind marching in a movement wholly *circulaire,* I see in a vision something of your mind. But the grand isolation of your thoughts leads you to express them in such words that may be gratifying to yourselves but have an inconspicuous and even unfortunate effect upon other people. In view of the enormous difficulty, the tremendous task of rebutting with people whose facts are in complete disregard of the truth—whose facts are based on emotionalism, exaggeration, and downright instability—this is a mountain to climb. However, since you have chosen to deal with me as a *gangster américain, alors, mes vieux,* my old ones, this is the problem that I shall attempt to resolve.

"In no attempt at brevity, although this is a word you do not understand, I have here very little to say that is not covered by a general adjuration to you to observe certain elementary rules. They are, roughly speaking, as follows: First, would you just stick to one lie at a time, just one excuse. It's easier for all of us to sort everything out if you do this. So, if a producer such as myself—with whom you are in difficulty, with whom your social relations are slight and timorous—if I should chance to find you playing with the money and the coins in my safe, don't try to explain that you are interested in rare and old coins, hoping if you give me the soft sell I might believe you. Worse, don't tell me afterward that you pitied me for being overloaded with these coins or contracts and were in the act of replacing them, that these priceless coins are all false and of no value, that you were only in my safe and in the contract files trying to conceal these things to save me from worry, and police prosecution. This might tend to make me feel that you are not completely reliable. Then it might be me who would turn on you and ask for police protection—or police prosecution.

"Now, this is not in any way an exaggeration of the way in which you have knocked the bottom out of any case you may ever conceivably have had in such matters as the Baron's contract, my contract, that had to go through the Centre du Cinéma and the various and sundry deals which have gone through this *con* here, from the Swiss syndicate."

Nobody moved—not a creature was stirring, as the fellow said. M. Gilot's eyes were an inch out of his head. He breathed with his mouth open. I plowed on.

"So, don't you see, men, that the very richness and variety of your inventive genius with respect to these contracts and all that you were going to do for me, as against all that you have done to me—'the finger' in every sense of the word—these varieties of excuses, apologies, and now demands upon me, throw a doubt on each and every proposition and explanation you make and, when considered in itself, *stinks*. However, since you persist in telling such lies as seen necessary to keep yourselves in good standing—not with me, but with the whole affair—there is an old axiom that you should follow: Don't tell lies to people who know the truth.

"When we are through with the question of your honesty or dishonesty, or my honesty or dishonesty, I think it's time that we had an understanding with respect to the downbeat and downgrading way in which you discuss me as the American and you as Europeans. Don't perpetually boast that you are cultured, in a language which proves that you are not. You claim and loudly announce to everyone who will listen, to everyone who walks the earth, that you are full of wit and that you have wisdom enough for the whole world. But I have found that people who have enough wit and wisdom for the whole world have wit enough for a whole contract or a whole written letter of commitment. You can't get through a contract, a letter, or even a paragraph without being monotonous, irrelevant, or unintelligible. In my view, you are self-contradictory and broken-minded, generally.

THE DEAL

"You also have that lovable quality of bringing out the worst in everyone with whom you contract. I never believed what you said about your superior motion-picture-making ability, about your culture, or even about the way you speak English or French, because of the way you say it. If a supposedly great writer says, "I don't make no mistakes in English, not me," well, I can understand his remark, but I couldn't endorse it. When I hear you Continental people speak, you Swiss-syndicate men, you middle-Europeans full of culture, you middle-European financiers *fauché* who don't know the truth, who are so crooked that when you die you will have to be screwed into the ground. I hear you say *'Je parlais le French language.'* Now to me, that might be comprehensible, but it is certainly not convincing.

"You speak of culture. You speak of culture when you are in a corner and can't explain away in several languages your dishonesty, but culture does, presumably, include the power to think. For less laborious intellects than your own, it is generally sufficient to think once. But if you will think twice or twenty times, it cannot but dawn on you that there is something wrong in the reasoning by which negatives and contracts are placed in a *safe* available to anyone who is smart enough to break into the safe; any friendly thief or co-producer can dip his fingers in the till when no one else is looking, because he can get in. My suggestion is: In your lying, make it more brief, cut it down to footage, cut the fat off it. If you limit your words, you might have more chance to be believed. If you confined yourself to single words, uttered at intervals of about one a month—that's twelve words a year—no one could possibly raise any rational objection or subject your words to any rational criticism. In time, you might come to use whole sentences without revealing the real state of things—without revealing how you have lied—how you have cheated.

"My heart is in my throat to dare to suggest anything to people with your great abilities and your undeniable dishonesty. However, when you mouth it up too much, you not only have talked it all away, but it's like that old expression in the Bible: You built yourself a trap of words and fell into it—what you didn't realize was, at the bottom there is a lot of stuff of which you are made. *Merde.* Pure shit, *en toute simplicité.*"

Just as they started to yell at me and jump to their feet, right on cue for once, in walked the Baron and Jules Molotov. The Baron never looked better—handsome, elegant, a superstar, and dead sober. He came into the room with elegant elegance. The Baron was a guy who owned and ruled any place he happened to be (except the bedroom).

"Messieurs." Baron bowed a little mocking bow. "My partner, Monsieur

401

THE DEAL

Jarnigan, says you are giving him a problem."* He frowned regally and stared them all down. *"Alors?"* he grinned.

The French co-producer said with a sick grin, "We've been having a friendly talk while awaiting you. Delightful. *Quel plaisir.*"

"How fortunate," the Baron remarked casually, "that you and my partner, Monsieur Jarnigan, are *sympathiques.*" His accent, like his bow, was faultless. He had conceivably been practicing both in some local bedroom an hour before.

"Did you ever hear the anecdote," he continued, with a friendly yet conspiratorial air, "about Monsieur Jason Wormser and your great André Gide? You see, Monsieur Wormser invited Monsieur Gide to Hollywood and offered him a fortune to write a little screenplay. But Monsieur Gide declined in this way: 'I regret that we cannot do business since you, Monsieur Wormser, are an artist, whereas I am really a businessman.'

"Well," concluded the Baron, with truly surprising deftness, "it is of course you estimable gentlemen who are so concerned about our work of art, whereas I—I confess it—will be satisfied with nothing less than a film that makes *money.*"

The neat twist was certainly not lost on M. Gilot. He was flattered and delighted, and the conference, which had begun in such a cold and ugly atmosphere, now began to warm up a little, although it was still no prairie fire. I could probably have gotten M. Gilot and his colleagues, at that point, to reduce their interest rates and invest it in the revolving fund for our picture.

And I thought the Baron had been most diplomatic, telling a story that linked the great French author with a philistine like Jason Wormser . . . especially since the actual interchange had taken place between Bernard Shaw and Samuel Goldwyn!

But whatever mixture of luck and wit had guided the Baron, he really deserved the credit for saving a delay on the Deal that time. When he was on the upswing and off the flit, you just couldn't ask for a nicer fellow.

Well, the bankers and the syndicate came up with the money. Good fellowship, goodwill, love, affection, and horse shit were again in full bloom. I started the wrap-up in Paris and gave instructions to the production manager, the assistant director, the cast, and crew for what should now be done.

After a final meeting in the studio, we left Paris to go to the south of France to complete the motion picture. The Princess had remained in Paris, but would fly down later. "15" came along; she held the floor—or the bed—and was the Baron's favorite now.

402

44

On arrival in Villefranche, the lovely old coast town in the south of France where the rest of the cast went to the luxurious hotel, the crew and technicians went to Les Maisons de Pension. I was staying in the villa of the Aly Khan, who had lent me his luxurious home overlooking the sea for the duration of the picture. The Baron had gone to his yacht where he had it moored in the yacht basin in Monaco. This being a Friday night, we planned to meet on Sunday afternoon to prepare for the resumption of the picture and to reschedule the shooting of the various sequences on location for Monday.

A few things bothered me, but that was par for the course. I was worried about the Editor, because after the scene that this guy had put over with me in the commissary at the studio in Paris, I knew that he was beyond the breaking point. I had told the Baron and the Baron's American attorney that this clown was desperate enough to really pull the chain on the whole operation with respect to the under-the-table money that had been given me for the Baron's and my account. Also, since the pulling of the gun episode in Paris, the Baron had become a little more thoughtful so far as the Editor went, didn't openly cut him down on the sound stage every time there was a blowup on the scene. The Baron had completely laid off the Editor's fluffy little wife and I imagine, between the Baron and the Editor, she could use the rest—the lay-off, I mean.

We had taken a trip in a privately rented limousine to the various banks and safe deposit vaults. We had rented a limousine, not wanting to use the cars assigned to the picture, since the four of us—the Baron, the Editor, the Baron's American attorney, and I—were trying to be as discreet as possible. We had picked up a lot of money.

There had been a terrible scene at my place between the Baron and the Editor—the Baron reacting to things the Editor said, the way a master reacts when a not-too-well-loved dog turns on his master and bites. The Baron had completely dominated the Editor for so many years that any show of rebellion on the Editor's part was not only astounding—the Baron considered it a direct affront to his charm, his ability to completely mesmerize whoever he wanted. So after these many years to have the Editor turn on him was a blow, difficult for the Baron to endure.

THE DEAL

But endure it the Baron did, since he knew that the Editor held various keys and signatures, powers which the Baron had given him, never for once doubting the Baron's own complete control over the Editor. Had it ever occurred to the Editor to be a thief on a grand scale he would never have had to threaten me with a gun, submit to the indignities which were his daily lot, or to turn over, with the grin the operating room sees, his wife to await the Baron's pleasure. The Editor could have gone alone, emptied the vaults, checked out the negatives, and absconded with a considerable portion of the Baron's wealth.

The Baron, always the foxy, tricky, untrusting son-of-a-bitch that he was, never let his right hand know what his left was doing. Or, the right "other" never knowing what the left "other" never did in any event. By reason of the Baron's three ex-wives, the various mistresses, "15," and the law suits that were continually floating around him—his lawyers met in the Coliseum every Wednesday—he had to have a pawn whom he controlled absolutely, and yet would not have his money, his bonds, or his "protection film negatives" in his own name. He never trusted his lawyer. He trusted no one but himself and his self-doubt was developed to such a point that he was in despair many times, which was another reason for the Baron's disturbed, overemotional, and completely unpredictable behavior on many occasions.

I, of course, knew where the money was. I didn't have the Baron's keys, but the golden hoop that kept rolling into the coffers of our film company in Europe during the last couple of years assured money to such an extent that it was unbelievable. Some was put in private accounts, some was buried in private banks, and some was just hidden.

We all made the trip in the hired limousine, covered thousands of kilometers, and returned to the south of France with two suitcases completely filled with French francs, Swiss francs, and Italian lire. We also had in excess of eleven hundred pounds of gold bullion. Another nine hundred pounds was hidden carefully in the Baron's yacht, in the third hold below the bilge line, covered over with tar. This, as the Baron used to say, was our "pirate gold," our "get-away" money. The only people who knew about the money hidden in the bottom of the yacht were the Baron and I and two Jamaican crew members. And the Baron had informed me that unfortunately those two had had accidents, had disappeared, in the course of the Baron's sailing around the Mediterranean ports and back and forth to the islands on trips he had taken alone . . .

On this particular Sunday afternoon, the Editor, in an absolute depar-

THE DEAL

ture from his usual quiet self, disrupted the meeting and was making statements dangerously close to what we, of course, did not want made public. I canceled the meeting and after a talk with the Baron decided I'd better handle this because we were balancing on a knife-blade. I calmed the Editor down, assured him we could work things out, and the Baron, the Baron's attorney, the Editor, and I left the hotel in Monaco to go aboard the yacht. We decided to take the thirty-mile run to the island of Marguerite and return late that night. That way we could have a long quiet talk.

From the beautiful yacht we could see the lovely hills of the coast fading into the distance. The sea was calm and I was sorry that things were like they were. It would have been a nice outing.

As it got along toward twilight, when the sky turned the unbelievably beautiful color that can only be found near the south coast of France or off the shores of Orracabassa on the island of Jamaica, we all sat, the four of us, on the afterdeck—the Baron and the Editor drinking straight Jamaican rum, the lawyer and I nursing our Scotch carefully . . . wondering what the hell was going to happen.

The Baron started to use his persuasive charm on the Editor. It seemed to be working. Basking in the warm and friendly glow of the camaraderie, feeling a sudden burst of warmth and affection for the Baron, the Editor's rebellion seemed destined to go down weakly without a struggle. Their fourteen years together served for something. I must say I admired and watched with interest, and a touch of amusement, the careful way that the Baron played the Editor. It couldn't have been more beautifully done—the way you play a marlin on the end of a line that you know is strong enough to pull him in. So you enjoy yourself and let the game go on as long as it is pleasurable to you. That's the way it was with the Baron and the Editor.

As the night drew closer, far forward, near the prow of the boat, we could hear the Jamaican crew singing, laughing, talking. For them, as always, everything easy, everything happy. Eat good, sleep good, love good, walk good. The Baron sat with a friendly, charming smile on his face, reminiscing, talking about past projects and how the Editor had always been his "little brother," and in his warm sudsy conversation of past glories accomplished by the Editor (completely untrue, of course) and of future motion pictures to be made, trips to be taken, the world to be seen, the women to be laid, the Baron continued with, "Why, hell, boy, you and I have just started. You were right to bring me up short, I deserved it, you should have done this a long time ago. I respect you for it and as for Joanie, I apologize. I apologize to you and I'll apologize to her."

THE DEAL

The Editor was overwhelmed, large tears filled his little red-rimmed eyes; in a voice unmistakably filled with love, affection, forgiveness, and remorse, he said chokingly, "No, Baron, no. You're my best and only friend. You've treated me like a fa—" He had started to say "father" and quickly changed it to "You have treated me like your younger brother and I appreciate it . . ." (Here the drunken, hiccuped sob.) "Old Editor appreciates it and Joanie too. You damn well have been white to both of us."

So with the Baron's lawyer looking on and me watching this scene full of emotionalism, absolute lies, an undercurrent of sickly sweet honey, a mixture of talky contempt, full of tears and flapdoodle, I switched my gaze from the teary-eyed sucker-mouthed Editor and looked straight at the Baron. This was a revelation. He had been drinking straight rum more than glass for glass with the Editor. I would imagine he had drunk at least a quart and a half of Jamaican rum.

He had given sloppy talk for sloppy talk, babble for babble, and now—he didn't know anyone was looking at him—he was staring at the Editor with a gaze of fixed hatred and contempt. His eyes were as bright and alert as if he had never taken a drink in his life, an amused smirk that he couldn't help was continually lifting the left corner of his mouth. This stiletto-point stare nailed the Editor in his deck chair. As I watched, once in a while the Baron said other friendly, caressive things, slowly assembling the beads and threading them, colorful baubles to rope around the neck of the Editor and drown him in a sea of false friendship, false affection, and two quarts of straight rum. It was a lovely sight.

It was getting dark now and time for us to try and get the scrambled brains together and go into the main dining room and have dinner. The lawyer went to his cabin. I talked briefly with the Baron and the Editor, making certain that the lid was on the conversation, that everything would be calm for a while. I went into my stateroom, thought I'd rest fifteen minutes before dinner. I must have dozed off, since I was awakened by a knock at the door and the steward told me that the other three men were already at the table and I should immediately come in for dinner. I went into the bathroom, washed my face in cold water. Shortly, I went into the dining room, where sat the Baron in the baronial chair at the long oaken dining-room table, the dining room being paneled, hung with fine oil paintings, where the rum or the wine or "tiger's breath" was drunk from huge silver tankards. The Baron had a silver tankard copied after Sir Henry Morgan the pirate's at Port Royal, Jamaica. It had a sterling silver whistle welded in the handle so that the Baron, who was more of a pirate than Old Henry,

THE DEAL

just blew the whistle and the cabin steward knew that he was immediately to fill the tankard of the Baron. The Editor was putting his tankard to good use. The lawyer was "playing cute" with his. Mine was sitting at my place on the table empty. I intended to keep it that way until I could take the temperature of this dinner conversation.

The food was served and was grand. The Baron had never been more charming. Even the lawyer loosened up. The Editor, flustered to be the center of attention, glowed like a neon sign. So, seeing that things looked under control I had my tankard filled and it looked as though it would be a nice comfortable party. Maybe everything would blow over. The Baron told stories and little anecdotes; the Editor swallowed everything. The attorney, who was eating everything in sight, was now drinking more than I had ever seen him drink, and the dinner went through to its logical conclusion.

When coffee and brandy were served, cigars were passed and the Baron got down to business. "Old boy," he said, looking at the Editor, "we have to make a deal. Under the circumstances you shouldn't be just the film editor on my pictures, you should become more of an assistant to the producer." Then, turning the charm on, and looking at me, the Baron said, "What do you say, Jarn?"

I grinned at him, "No comment. I want to hear the rest of this."

Anger peeped out for a moment from behind the Baron's eyes but was gone in a flash. He moaned and he said, "Old Jarnigan—always careful, always the Iceman when it comes to business." I grinned at him. I kept it a friendly grin. I waited. The Baron continued, glancing affectionately at the Editor, "Yes, boy, you should be an assistant producer. You know the business. You certainly know more than I do about pictures."

Here the Editor raised a protesting hand, nevertheless giving his head a little bow accepting the "goodish mead" of the Baron's gracious assessment of his meager talents. I looked at the lawyer, who was looking at me, a little concerned but still with a friendly glow on his face.

I knew something was coming. I didn't know what it was but I knew the Baron better than he knew himself and from the moment I had seen the look on his face when we were having drinks before dinner—the way he put that "look" on the Editor—I knew something was coming and was hoping I could handle it and keep the lid on whatever trouble there was. I watched both of them carefully.

Later, when we were far out at sea, the congenial, happy dinner conversation of the night began to take on overtones of menace with an undercurrent of hatred bouncing around the table. There was a continuation of talks between the Baron and the Editor. At one point, when the discussion came to a payoff and the cancellation of the contract the Editor had with our company, the Baron, his "charm" by now slipping badly, said to me, "I'll pay the little s.o.b. off. I'll cancel the editor's contract, but I want to keep the editor's wife under contract."

This, of course, pegged the rest of the conversation at the hatred level. During the argument, the Baron shouted, "All right, I'll make the payoff and I'll pay off in cash." He roared out of the room and returned with the two suitcases which he had locked in his stateroom. He hit both sides of the door coming back into the dining room. He opened one of the suitcases bulging with cash.

The lawyer knew an explosion was coming, and hastily withdrew. He left the dining room quietly and went down to lock himself in his stateroom. He would have nothing to do with this settlement, thank you.

Then, in the magnificent dining room of the yacht, the Baron, the Editor, and I started to talk over the settlement. We moved from the dining room to the main lounge and back to the dining room. All this time the money was on the table. Finally the Baron said to me, "Hand me the other case."

I lifted the case up and set it on the table, not knowing what the Baron wanted.

He emptied the two cases on the huge table and there, piled in front of the three of us, was a stack of money almost a foot high and a yard in circumference. The Baron sneered to the Editor, "Go ahead, take some—take what you think you're worth. This is the kiss-off."

The Editor's eyes were doing frantic things trying to keep from looking at all that money.

The Baron kept needling with, "Go ahead, go ahead, take some, take it all, take what you're worth. Do you know what *I* think you're worth?" Here he separated one bill from the pile and threw it on the table in front of the Editor.

I stopped the Baron. I told him that this was no way to arrive at anything, that we'd have to straighten this out. The Editor's contract had five years to go; his contract should be settled, and he and his wife Joanie should be allowed to leave the south of France and return to America.

The Baron during the previous conversation had threatened that the Editor would never work again. Finally, after much conversation, I was able to calm the Baron down. (The Editor was too frightened to do anything.) We agreed to settle the Editor's contract for one hundred thousand dollars.

The Baron kept adding, "That's for you *and* your wife in settlement."

THE DEAL

The Baron dictated a release that he wanted the Editor to sign. It wasn't a bad idea. I didn't know what this Editor, this crazy bastard, might do, especially since the gun-pulling incident. The Editor, badly shaken, signed the receipt, gave the release to me. The Baron grabbed both papers, looked at them, handed them to me. I looked them over, figured it would hold up. I placed the papers under a large candlestick and watched the payoff.

The Baron, carefully for as drunk as he was, separated one hundred thousand dollars worth of Swiss francs. He pushed them over on the table in front of the Editor with a broad gesture. The Baron looked at me piling the remaining money in one huge pile. In a grandiose gesture he brought his arm down in the middle of the pile of money, moved half to my side of the table, pulled the other half to his side of the table, saying, "You're my partner, Jarn. We split everything fifty-fifty and you're my best friend. Remember. Everything together."

I didn't see anything in that for me, so I let it drift with the tide. All smiles now, the Baron proposed we have a drink—as if this were something new. He went to the liquor cupboard, pulled out two bottles of brandy, poured a big blast in the Editor's tankard, sloshed some in mine, and practically filled his to the brim. He raised his tankard and said, "To the kiss-off, to the payoff."

I looked at the Editor's face and saw that this was not the thing to have said. I tried to smooth it over with, "Baron, that's not the way. The Editor's been a man, he's faced up to the Deal; he's being square with us. This isn't a kiss-off, a payoff, it's strictly a business arrangement we've made, a settlement we've made, a deal."

The Baron said, grandly, "I'll drink to that." Everybody raised their tankards. We drank. The Baron then started talking quietly to the Editor. Then he said, "It's too hot here in the dining room. Let's go out and talk."

The three of us left the dining room and went out on deck. The Baron seemed to be sobering up. He started talking nicely now with the Editor. We went over and sat on the deck in the stern of the boat. The Baron now talked about plans for the Editor's leaving and who would replace him. I heard the tears and flapdoodle stuff start to go on the air again.

I had a bellyful of this conversation so I walked down the length of the yacht and stood in the prow, letting the cool breeze hit my face. I could hear the Baron and the Editor talking, but muted, the sound of the yacht moving through the water muffling all sounds.

A few minutes later, I heard loud talking, then a scream. I turned and ran back to where the Baron and the Editor were now standing. As I ran up to them I saw that the Baron had an iron spike in his hand and was making thrusting and waving motions at the Editor, who was half his size. I shoved the Baron roughly away and pushed the Editor back into his chair. I said, "What's the matter with you two crazy bastards? Can't I leave you quiet for two minutes? Now knock it off or I'll wind you both up for good. I've had a bellyful. Get me?"

The Baron was angry and turned away; he went over to the rail.

The Editor just sat there.

I told the Editor that he should go to bed. I told the Baron to take the night off and go to bed. I just wanted to keep the lid on this thing so we could turn around and go back to port.

Suddenly, as though you'd pulled an electrical switch, the Baron walked over the Editor, stuck out his hand, and said "I'm terribly sorry. I don't know what made me say what I've said. I've never asked you before—please forgive me. I apologize."

The Editor's mouth dropped open; his surprise was complete. This was like the king begging pardon—asking to have himself excused by the lowest jester in the court. The little Editor stood up, stuck out his little paw and they shook hands slimily, like monkeys. An empty, futile gesture, although it meant something to the Editor.

I knew by the look on the Baron's face that he was moving another pawn in his never-ending game of "Baron chess." I turned and walked back over to the railing and stood with my back to the two of them, looking out over the ocean. I heard the Baron purring little quiet sympathetic words, little condolences, little regrets. I heard emotionally choked responses from the Editor, forgiving, blubbering—no character, a real zero. The gentle murmuring went on, and then there came that scream. I didn't jump more than ten feet. It was a terrifying wail.

I looked. The Editor was down on his hands, half his face was covered with blood, his left ear hanging from his head. The Baron had that spike in his hand and made another pass which by some miracle the Editor avoided. I ran to the Baron, caught him with a good left in the stomach. I couldn't strike the face—I needed the face in my picture.

The Baron sat down on the deck with a little *oof*.

I turned around. The Editor was crawling toward me, upright on his knees, in a moving praying position. "Don't let him kill me. Oh, Christ, don't let him kill me. I'll leave. He can keep the money. I'll leave. I won't say anything. Christ, don't let him kill me." He crept up, still on his knees, and held my hands, not trying to get up, only holding me in place as though to pin me down with his plea for help.

I felt a movement in back, turned in time to see the Baron sit down in

410

his own chair, and, by Christ, he was laughing. "Look at him," he laughed. "Down on his knees where he belongs, on his knees to the whole world, and to think this bug, this filth, this gum-clipped piss-ant would dare to threaten *me*."

I snarled, "Lay off, Baron, you've half killed him anyway, now for Christ's sake lay off. I don't know how we're going to square this one."

"What's the matter, joy boy?" he sneered. "You're the fixer, you're the business brain, you're the guy who arranges everything. A little thing like this half-killed nothing is no problem for a great man like you."

While this tirade was going on, the Editor had never stopped moaning, pleading, still from his kneeling position, "Mother of God, don't let him kill me—get him away from me—I'm afraid!"—and with that he fell over sideways.

The Baron jumped up.

I leaned down and turned the Editor over. There was a lot of blood but he didn't seem to be hurt too bad. His eyes were open and he was still saying, "Help me."

Again, in one of those blinding flashes, the Baron was cold sober. He leaned down quietly. "Terrible," he said, "terrible." He put his arm under the Editor's head and lifted him up. Together we set him up on the edge of the low rail to get a better look at the cut on the side of his head. I said to the Baron, "Man, you really clobbered him. Are you all right, Baron? Are you sober enough to hold him?"

The Baron said tersely, "Jarn, we have to square this."

"Square, hell," I said, "you've damn-near killed him. Hold him steady. I'm going to get the medicine kit."

The Baron looked me straight in the eye. "Hurry, Jarn, hurry. I've got him, everything will be all right."

I turned and ran about ten steps. I had just gotten to the stateroom door when I heard a loud moan, a muffled scream, a cry that raised the hair on the back of my neck. I turned and saw the Baron leaning out over the rail, holding the Editor's head down, two-thirds dangling over the water. Holding the Editor by his belt, he reached down, grabbed the spike and with a quick slashing movement of his arm—the way you'd kill a cat—he struck the Editor on the back of the head . . . the body plummeted straight down, like a stone, into the sea.

The Baron never moved. I stood there horrified and saw that the Baron had turned and was looking down at his wrist. The Editor, in the last movement he was ever to make in his life, as he tore out of the Baron's grasp, had clawed onto the Baron's wrist watch, torn it off, and carried it with him into the sea. I felt I stood there for several minutes. Actually, it could only have been a few seconds. . . .

I raced back to the Baron . . . cried out, "Good Christ, what have you done?"

He turned to look at me; his face looked numb. His lips scarcely moved as he said, "He took my watch."

• • •

I stared in horror at the Baron. I said to him, "Christ, we've got to stop this boat. We have to find him. Maybe he isn't dead."

The Baron, still acting funny: "Good, right; I'll give the order," and surprisingly after all that had happened, he ran beautifully, lithely, like a cat, across the deck, up to the second deck, and went through into the fo'c'sle. I kept looking back over the rail, cursing because I couldn't see. All of a sudden, I heard a roar from the engines, they sounded as though they were trying to tear themselves out of their moorings, and I felt the big craft shoot forward. I knew we were moving farther and farther away from where the Editor had gone under. Then, just as suddenly, I knew that no matter if we ever got this yacht slowed down, turned around, we could never find him.

The Baron came leaping back easily. He grinned, as if nothing at all had happened. "I guess old Cap got my orders wrong." His smile grew more serious and he said, quite normally, "You know, he does that sometimes. He gets my orders confused." Then musingly, as though to himself, "I'll have to speak to him about that some time."

I couldn't believe it. This couldn't truly be happening. I just wouldn't believe it.

The Baron calmly, underplaying everything, was talking with the surface numbness a man gets after being involved in an auto crash or surviving a plane wreck. He talked almost as though this were happening to someone else, not to us. He said conversationally, "So that's that."

I yelled, "Baron, that's not that. For Christ's sake, don't you realize you've killed a man?"

He turned to look at me as though I were a freak, as though I had said something completely out of context with our prior conversation. "What did you say, kid?" he said, looking at me as though he thought I were a little off.

"I said you killed the Editor. We've got to try and find him. Try to do something. I don't know how I'm going to square *this* for you."

He looked at me. "Square what?" He turned and walked over to where the bottles were sitting in their containers in the liquor table. He picked up a bottle of brandy, took a huge jolt directly from the bottle. He turned back toward me, leaning against one of the uprights of the boat, and said, quietly, "Kid, you should have seen him. When I was holding him there on the rail he forgave me . . . the silly bastard forgave me . . he thought I was crying real tears. Me, I was laughing. I never saw a happier look on a guy's face as when I hit him with the spike. He's probably the only film editor who's worked on my pictures who died happy."

I looked at him in horror. I hissed and snarled at him, "Oh, you bastard," I said, "you raper, you liar, you blackmailer, you bloody mucking murderer, you mother-fucker . . ."

After I had hissed and spat and snarled all of this in his face, standing about three feet from him, he slowly raised his hands and patted me on the shoulder. "Jarn," he said, with a boyish grin, "You're right about the rape, and the liar, and a blackmailer and maybe a murderer—I guess so; but a mother-fucker—no, definitely not. I have thought about it seriously, but do you know why I didn't . . . my mother never appealed to me." And with another boyish grin he turned away, took another drink of brandy and looked out at the sea. I could only stare at him in absolute terror. He was insane.

Suddenly he turned around. "Jarn . . . Jarn." He had a scared look on his face. "Jarn . . . I have to . . . help . . ." Then, without a sound he stiffened, his head erect, he fell over backward, stiffly, the way a tree falls. Nothing ever sounded harder than the way his body hit the deck. I rushed over to him. I pulled open his collar. I tore my handkerchief out of my pocket, wadded it into a ball, then, using a spoon which had fallen from the table, I pried open his mouth and stuck the handkerchief ball between his teeth. I looked to see that he hadn't swallowed his tongue. Oh Lord, oh Christ, oh merciful Lord, what could happen now?

I knew the Editor was dead. I ran back and leaned over the side to look back. It was impossible to see anything in the black water. And anyway, now it was something that I wanted nobody to see. I had to think. I wasn't bothered by *Someone*. The Baron moaned.

•   •   •

I sat there looking down at him. Once in a while he'd twitch or jerk a little and moan, then he was quiet for a while. I was looking out toward the night, toward nothing, when I heard a cough. I spun around.

The Baron was sitting up. He had taken the handkerchief out of his

413

mouth. He threw it over the side. He looked at me steadily. "Jarn . . . I'd like a drink."

I returned the look, then quietly I went over to the table, got the first bottle my hand touched, walked back over and handed it down to him.

After a few minutes he got up slowly and walked carefully over to a deck chair. He sat there drinking and looking at me quietly. "Jarn, sit down over here. We have to talk."

I went over and sat down in a chair opposite him. I watched him thoughtfully.

The Baron finally said to me, "Well, kid . . ."

I sat there looking at him. "I don't know, Baron. I don't know what I'm going to do, but this is one thing, this murder, this is one I can't square for you."

He looked me directly in the eye and said softly, "Square for *me*? Why kid, we're partners. *We* did this. You were there. *You* held him over the rail." He rose, drink in hand, walked past me, paused near an upright. "You must remember *that*," he said.

I snarled, "You lousy bastard, you'll take this fall alone. This is one time you're going to have to take it by yourself." . . . I stood up quickly.

He laughed. "Did you see him on his knees almost praying to you to save him? Do you remember when I was on *my* knees asking you to kneel and pray with me? My prayer never got me anything—his prayer didn't get him anything either."

Remembering all that had taken place during the religious episode at the Hampshire House—without thinking, remembering how he'd duped me, remembering that I had knelt and truly prayed for this lousy son-of-a-bitch —before I knew what I was doing I reached down, picked up the bloody spike, and aimed one at his head.

He leaned back carefully against the upright and with a coolness that was almost admirable he said, "What are you going to do with that, Jarn?"

I raised my hand higher, ready to bring it down not only on his head, but on the filth, on the death, on the contracts, on the Deal, on everything that he represented. I was ready to kill him. He grinned at me and said quietly, "You better do it . . . if you don't, your evidence is shot to hell. Your prints are on the spike too, his blood is on your hands, and the payoff was one we made for *our* company, *our* Deal, not just me. And Jarn"—this said quietly—"who do you think my lawyer is going to side with if this thing goes further?"

I looked at him with horror. It sank in. It was true what he said. He took

414

THE DEAL

two steps toward me, looked me in the eye, and said, "What about it, kid? Do you want to take a cut at it?"

I didn't move. Very slowly, as though touching a stick of dynamite with the fuse already burning, he gently, quietly, took the bloody iron spike from my hand, walked over to the side of the boat, leaned out and holding it carefully in his hand he opened his fingers slowly . . . gracefully . . . and the iron spike disappeared into the well of the sea. He walked back to the table, took a pitcher of water, pulled out his handkerchief, very carefully poured water on his hands, walked over to me, pulled my hands over to him, poured water over both very carefully, dried his hands, gave me two big napkins, and I, unconsciously, as if in slow motion, unthinkingly dried mine. He wrapped the napkins and handkerchief around a metal ashtray and dropped it over the side, then turned back to me.

He said, "Let's go inside." We walked, the Baron holding my elbow, into the cabin. There on the dining table were the two large piles of money and the one pitiful small pile. Under the candlestick lay the release and the Editor's receipt for himself and his wife, bought and paid for. Gently, like a brother, the Baron carefully pulled out a chair and sat me down, walked around the table and leaned over across the money; the light from the overhanging ship's lantern glinted on his face and hair. He very studiously divided the money that had been in front of the Editor's plate, fifty thousand dollars worth of francs in the direction of his pile of money, fifty thousand in the direction of my pile of money. With unbelieving eyes I saw him pick up the receipt and release from under the candlestick and, carefully holding them in the flame of the candle, watch them burn, his eyes gleaming. I sat unmoving. It was more than a nightmare, this most unbelievable thing that was happening.

He walked around the table, opened the huge silver humidor, took out two cigars, came back around, laid one in front of my plate next to my huge pile of money. He whispered in my ear, "They're the right kind, Jarn—panatellas." He walked back around the table, sat down in his chair behind his huge pile of money, He bit off the end of his cigar, leaned over, took a light from the candle, inhaled the smoke superbly, took a sip of his brandy, then leaning back in my direction, a friendly affectionate grin on his face, said, "Now, Jarn . . . let's talk about your script, *partner.*"

Be no mocker, for mockery follows them that mock, as Cyrus in Xenophon. In Plato, Socrates is described then to sink down with them of whom Elihu hath said, *"Momento moriuntur."* ("In a moment shall they die."

415

THE DEAL

Job 34:20") Yesterday I saw a fragile thing broken. Today I have seen a mortal thing die. Anger is not always a defect. Be angry, and sin not. This is the difficulty. In the case of the Deal, anger had its place, good and evil. The cooling-off period will let me finally know. Faults are either notorious or private. The Baron's faults gained common fame. But the executioner is not without charity as he takes away the life of the condemned. It is his duty, not pleasurable. The male ego is an agile, fragile thing. It's as thin as the fibrous membrane of a frog's brain.

We sat there smoking in the flickering candlelight. The Baron was talking . . . quietly. I sat there. I listened . . . quietly.

After we had arrived back in the port of Villefranche, the Baron was a little less brave than when he had whiffed the Editor. After the "tragedy" I rehearsed the Baron with what he should say to the Captain. I didn't worry about the lawyer. First, he hadn't seen a thing; and second, he'd do what the Baron wanted anyway. I sent the messboy away. He was childlike and could speak no French—could barely speak English. He was a Jamaican from the farm country.

After a while the Baron joined me on deck. He looked pretty wobbly. For the first time in a long while, I looked at him and did what I'd vowed I'd never do again.

"Baron, let's have a drink," I said, opening the last act—an act from which there would be no return. He looked at me in surprise. He sat down in a deck chair and looked up at me quietly.

"Yes, I think I could use a drink." He managed to say this as though it were an unusual occurrence. I sent the boy for the portable bar table with all the bottles firmly in their places, so the thirsty fingers could get at them. A little later we were sitting with drinks in hand watching the big yacht glide into her berth in the yacht harbor.

"Baron, we'll have to go to the Préfet and explain the disappearance and probable death of the Editor." He nodded his head, still looking at me, saying nothing. "I've talked to the Captain; the logbook reads exactly as it happened." For a moment he gave a start and sat up straight in the deck chair . . . his mouth opened, no words came out. I plowed on, "I told the Captain exactly what to write; I had your lawyer check it. He says it's all right and anyway, he didn't see or hear anything, only remembers the Editor was terribly drunk and not truly himself. He will swear to that." I added grimly, "If that's okay with you . . . I'm not boring you, am I, Baron? You know this bag of nails is really yours, not mine."

416

THE DEAL

For the first time the eyes became crafty, the look less relaxed, more alert. He said, *"Our* bag of nails, Jarn . . ." Then, more softly, "Our bag of nails." I watched him closely.

We talked over again what was to be said. It was clear to me that I was so tied up in this thing now that even if I wanted out, I couldn't get out without springing the trap on myself. An hour later we were in the Hotel de Ville and in the Chef du Préfet's bureau. We had told our story two or three times; the Baron, the Captain, the attorney, and I. Now we were to go up to the court and swear out the statements before a court reporter. A brief question-and-answer period, and then apparently it would be over.

We walked up into the old courtroom. There was a musty smell of lusts gone wrong, and paid for by misspent lies, greed, bitterness, and hate—all judiciously bottled up in the closed-in room. A court reporter was there; he must have had a cold. He blew his nose first, then wiped his eyes on one of the dirtiest handkerchiefs I'd ever seen in my life.

After a while the president of the tribunal came in. He was in a flowing black robe, much in need of cleaning. He mounted his bench, the other clerks of the court sat down, and we were ready to go. By politeness and protocol, the Baron got to tell his lie first. He sat there and lied beautifully, his voice low, with the proper solemn note of tragedy in it. He explained to the court that the Editor had been drunk and violent; that he, the Baron, had tried to reason with him, had tried to get him to go to bed. He glossed over the fact that the Editor had threatened me with a gun in Paris, and had threatened the Baron, who was his best friend and benefactor. He left out the part that the Editor became violent only after the Baron had literally chopped the guy's ear off with a marlin spike. The threats and screams from the Editor were not explained fully. For example, it was true the Editor had screamed; but only because part of his brains were being beaten out of his head. And the bed the Baron had wanted to put the Editor in was plenty wide, deep, and wet . . . and where the Editor was now, he wasn't cramping anybody. The Baron had seen to that. But the Baron droned on, and soon the Editor began to sound like Jack the Ripper.

The Baron finished sadly, "If I had only known . . . if I had only known he was that unbalanced."

The Editor was plenty unbalanced, when the Baron had him hanging over the rail with one ear hanging by a thread on his shoulder. But you couldn't have asked for a straighter drop; man, he disappeared without a splash . . . no lack of balance there.

417

THE DEAL

The Baron got out from behind the witness "horseshoe" and came back over to where we were; he sat down slowly, mournfully. Christ, Barrymore couldn't have done as well. "Man, you were great," I said, looking at him grimly, "just great . . ." He nodded his head.

"It's a sad thing, Jarn, and no mistake." The Baron had sold himself; he believed everything he had said.

Well, it rolled along like that. No bumps. The Captain sang his song. "Yes, the Editor was drunk and unruly. Not in a fit condition to be at sea." The Baron's attorney told practically the same story as the Baron's, although he hadn't seen a thing. But, working for the Baron, he lied just to keep in practice.

I stepped up and told my big lie like a little gentleman. "Yeah, the Editor was drunk, unruly, unbalanced. A finished man." (And how.) So with the lies folded neatly into the court records, and all of us getting ready to leave, I shot a look at the judge . . . *Monsieur le Président* . . . He sat there looking at us dryly. A smile hung lazily at the corners of his lips like cobwebs that hang loosely in the corners of an old ceiling. It was a musty-fusty smile, like his courtroom. There wasn't anything in it; he didn't even know it was there. It really didn't matter now, anyway. The case was closed: "Death by misadventure."

So the Baron lied and signed his statement, the Captain lied and signed his statement, because that's what the Baron told him to do; the attorney lied and signed for the Baron, to keep his client from stepping off for good; I lied and signed to keep my picture, save my contract . . . and deal my way further into hell.

45

It's Paris. It's night and I am alone, as usual. I am trying to work on script number three. I am desolate, and for the first time afraid of failure. I have swum the ocean and am drowning in three feet of water. The clock on the Ile St.-Louis church just in front of my window has struck three. The fire is burning slowly, giving off a yellow and fluffy glow; the expiring flames rise and fall, leap, then sink, puffing softly, back into the ashes. The watchman, forgetting the hour, is sleeping beneath the church. The laborious and the happy are at rest, locked and bolted in their sleep. Nothing awake but meditation, guilty thoughts, and despair. These ride tightly behind me, listening for sad revelry. The drunkard once more fills the destroying bowl . . . the cup that disarms and robs more than the thief, who's walking his midnight rounds. The suicide lifts his guilty arm and points the gun against his own sacred head. He will not fire. He hasn't even the nerve for that. It does take nerve . . . I know . . .

I won't waste more time, more of this night, but will continue my solitary walk; where vanity, ever-changing, but a few hours past walked arrogantly before me; where vanity in my own ego has kept me going like a parade that leads nowhere. The trumpets beat, the flags are damp, we go down an alley. But I march alone. The floor is creaking. The gloom hangs in every corner. There is a damp, musty-fusty smell blowing in from the Seine. The dying firelight feebly admits a blinker's gleam. No sound is heard but the solemn chiming of the clock on the church and, once in a while, a distant watchdog . . . a lonely mélange of sound truly not frightening anyone. All the bustle of human pride is forgotten. Certainly mine.

There must be some way to sort this out . . . You feel to mingle your tears with others' tears, you need someone to cry with. You know you're alone. You wanted it that way, and it's that way . . . Two or three times I've picked up a girl from the studio, brought her here. We sat in front of the fire. Gratefully; hoping that it would be different. It wasn't. We talk; we murmur; we hold hands with whiskey-tangled fingers—all very uninteresting. "Tell me it's great! Oh, it is . . . it is." (Here, the false and breathy sigh) Screwing anymore was rickety-lousy. You were like self-winding toys: You wound up the spring with Scotch and love talk, and unwound finally, bumping-thumping against each other; the orgasm a spitting disgust, hawked from a sore throat, bleah.

The murmurings are like a thin cutting of. lost love, spread on a slice of thin stale bread. There is a used nastiness in it, like second-timers with that friendly girl you knew. It doesn't help. Jarn—Jarn the Iceman.

It's later now. I've just finished taking a walk. I walked down Rue St.-Louis-en-l'Ile to the Pont. I watched the boats for a while. It was sad. I wandered back along the other side of the Ile, looking at the Seine, trying to figure what should be done tomorrow. I watched the cobblestoned streets becoming more damp as the mist fell. Seeing the noiseless people go through the streets, all nonexistent—the people and the streets. How few appear now. A little while ago these streets were crowded. But, those who appear now no longer wear the daily mask or attempt to hide their lewdness or their misery or their cunning; their craftiness, their building the trap of words and lies that lead nowhere. And those who make the street their couch find a short repose from wretchedness. These are strangers, wanderers, and poor producers like me whose circumstances are a disaster. The wretchedness of this night seems beyond enduring.

I am like the beggars I see in uncertain sleep, wondering which pharisee to ask for alms in the morning. I will beg and suck for money for one, two, or five more days' shooting. I'll beg . . . yes, I will. I have a disease of the mind—the picture business, the trying to finish at any cost. I see *les putains* walking back and forth; their gait is stiff and awkward. It is too late now for anything good tonight—or in their lives—and they know that. They are given up to nakedness and hunger. These poor, shivering girls, these females, who have perhaps seen happier days, may have been flattered and paid for their beauty. They must have been beautiful once. The great whore of the picture business was beautiful once. I love her still—this diseased beauty whose overripe body and Technicolor sores are surely killing me. I regret that I see *les putains* suffering wretchedness. For I can't help them or me, we are soulless, homeless creatures. But me? I won't give up. I'll go back to the bed and lick the wounds and pray a canted prayer, lap, lap, Lord. I wonder what to do tomorrow?

Do I now have to write in script number three? How can I become a successful producer? There are some. They have had some perfumed troubles. The slightest misfortune, the most imaginary uneasiness of these great men is aggravated with all the power of eloquence and held up to engage attention and sympathetic sorrow. Jason Wormser has a velvet wailing wall, a push-button wall. It is velvet (or flesh) you push into, or slide against. You bump up the sound track to help in your bereavement. You hump and thump yourself into sleep. Next day. You're still a king and not even ashamed . . . swell, huh? The poor weep unheeded; a poor man such as I weep but for myself . . . I feel persecuted by every subordinate species of actor or actress, of French co-producers, of false Suisse Syndicate men with no Swiss francs, no security—all are my enemies.

But the clock chimes again. Another night is past, another of those little limited portions of time which are allotted me and are numbering out my life. I want to stop awhile. I want to rest but there is nowhere to go. I'd like to think; and then think more deeply how I have employed this past week, this past year—this past time. The lies I've told, the subterfuges I have resorted to, to try and keep this film going; how I have advanced or deviated from the path. My time has certainly been lost, or worse than lost —misspent. This week I have neither been kind and helpful, truthful nor sincere. I have neither been friendly nor discreet. I have not taken to thiefdom with good grace. I have been ungracefully dishonest; and certainly not disinterested with the way I am literally "stealing" through this portion of my life. I have sunk my own ship. I have destroyed my own vessel by overloading it. And though it is filled with

> False silver and gold and precious stones
> and shooting scripts and actors' bones . . .

it will give a poor account of the voyage that I have charted.

I think I shall return to my apartment, light up the fire, and have another brandy or two or five.

"You've been getting profound again, Jarn," *Someone* said.

"That's right, I am. I know you're here and I'm not angry with you tonight. Please stick around. I've got a lot of things to tell you, and at least you listen: *How can I hide a murder?*"

•   •   •

I sat down at my desk. I looked at good old script number one and tossed it in the drawer. I looked at less good old script number two and tossed it in the drawer. I took out old script number three and looked at it with hatred and despair. I wondered if I ever could be allowed to work on a good one . . . or any kind of one again.

Think of the power of a writer. A million copies of a book read; one million pairs of eyes in front of, and slightly below, one million brains. The thoughts between two ears, encased in a bowl of bone, the two million eyes, the one million brains, and the ten million thoughts—if you wrote truly and well—were on your words. So it behooves you to look to your pen and not point your brainy, self-satisfied thoughts on the soft anvil of hypocrisy . . .

The next few days went on more smoothly. The Baron wasn't kicking up too much dust. I had geared everything down tight. So long as the Baron was working well, I wanted to finish as much footage as I could with him. Marc Grignon, my friend, said, "Jarn, we're doing pretty good. How're you getting along outside the picture—everything under control?"

"Yeah, Marc, things are 'copacetic.' The Baron's still 'flitting it' a little too much, but he hasn't sicked-up on the rugs lately." ·

"Fine, *cher ami, très bien.* If it's good for you, it goes well for us." Marc grinned and walked away.

As we pressed to get more film in the can, I knew I'd pay a price for every foot. Still, I didn't mind "paying off" the Baron with a little party for a few good days of work—if I could keep my eye on him while he tanked up and passed out, it wasn't a bad arrangement. Sam was still an expert at getting the Baron to bed. I had to really keep things quiet now.

When the Baron was on ice, I had only myself to take care of and . . . I was the Iceman.

On the other hand, ice can melt if exposed to too much heat. As I had discovered that night in the Baron's apartment when I first called the Princess by her real name, and she had tried to find out if I really was "an ice man."

So here came a replay, with the Baron passing out again at the party, and leaving the Princess very much on my hands . . .

I had Sam help me. We gathered him up and with Saul's help, we carried him upstairs. I left them there to tuck him in bed and see if they could clean him up a little. I walked back downstairs and the Princess was standing there—looking at me. I looked at her; it seemed that's the way it always was. She stood right where I'd left her when we'd taken the Baron upstairs; she was motionless now—in some sort of a fur coat that was held up close around her neck. She had gloves on her beautiful hands, she didn't have a hat. Her hair was falling gently on the side, and was part of the darkness of the night. Her eyes were like that, too.

"Well, that was pretty good work, Jarn. Looks like you're stuck with me. You'll have to drive me home." Her voice had a harsh note that it didn't usually have. I smiled at her.

THE DEAL

"Well, it looks like *you're* stuck with *me*. Do you have a car?"

"No. You have a car, haven't you?" she asked, starting to return the grin.

"I came with a man. What are you doing here?"

I answered, still grinning, "Well, I thought the Baron wanted to see me. But the way he was tonight, he couldn't see anybody," I finished.

"I didn't know he'd called you, Jarn."

"Well, I don't mind telling you, he didn't call. Sam Neely called and said he thought the Baron was in bad shape. He figured I'd better get out here if I wanted him on the set tomorrow."

"Did he say I was here?" she asked.

"Nope."

"Did you ask him if I was here?"

"Same answer."

"Well, are you going to drive me home?"

"Looks like I have to," I smiled. "You ready?"

We walked down the steps, out of the beautiful buildings that had been converted into this estate. We walked around the corner; there was some light up ahead, so we continued down a long corridor and came out in back of what used to be a stable. The cobblestones were gleaming faintly wet in what little light we could see.

"You know, Nic, I'm sorry about the Baron."

"You mean you're sorry he won't be able to work tomorrow?"

"Yeah."

"You're not sorry about anything else, are you, Jarn?"

"Maybe."

"Why don't you tell me you're glad to take me home, Jarn? Say something nice to me. Say something like 'Nicole, I'm so pleased to take you home'—somebody should be glad to take me home."

"Yeah," I said. "You know, you could avoid stuff like tonight."

She turned her head and looked at me. "How do you mean?" she said.

"Well, you know you don't have to drink with him, you don't have to go every place he wants to go, especially if you know he's going to get clocked."

"Jarn, you know him as well as I do. Where is there a place that he's not going to get clocked, as you say?"

"Yeah," I agreed.

"You know, I've even thought of marrying him," she went on in kind of a semi-serious voice. I think the unpleasantness of the Baron passing out on her was just beginning to get to her; which surprised me, because it had certainly happened before. Maybe there was something else. She cut in on

423

me. "You know, Jarn," she said, "I've truly considered marrying him. I've thought a lot about it. He's asked me many times," she went on, in this different kind of tense voice. Now, I knew that the Baron's passing out like that had gotten to her, but I didn't see what made this time any different. She stopped. I bumped into her.

"Sorry," I said.

"You know," she continued, "at odd times when nothing particularly agreeable would come into my mind—we all have those spells; but with the Baron, it would be a lot of money; you know, his yacht and the place in Jamaica, the place in the south of France, the little place in Rome that you know about—we stayed there, you remember, when we did the Anzio picture—there are places . . ." Here she stopped. I could see she was fighting something down so I decided not to interrupt her; better let her work it out of herself, if she could. "There are places," she continued, as though she hadn't paused at all, "places dotted all over the world—they're just one shot of brandy or one shot of something else apart . . ."

"Yeah."

"Can't you say anything else but 'yeah,' Jarn? It's not very articulate, you know." She looked at me with those beautiful eyes, glanced down, then looked up at me again.

"Nic, you sure have beautiful eyes." (Silence) I continued softly, "Have you ever thought to cut out on the Baron?"

She looked at me pointedly: "The Baron tells me you're like his younger brother."

I remembered words in the Bible: "And Judah said unto Onan, Go in unto thy brother's wife, and marry her, and raise up seed to thy brother." What a jumble of words that is. What a thing, that Bible. It is one of the books that I never get tired of reading. The Old Testament, men and women, their relationships, fields, sheep, famine, wars, years of plenty, Saul, David, Abraham, Samson—the strong men, honey, mead, barns. The thrashing of the lovers on the floors—come lie with me. And he turned unto her by the way and said, Go to, I pray thee . . .

The Princess cut into my thoughts. "What's your real name, Jarn?"

"That's it."

"No, I mean your real name. What did your parents call you?"

"Logan."

"Logan," she repeated.

"Yeah, Logan—but most everybody calls me Jarn. Why?"

"I just wondered."

"Sometimes I feel like a loogan."

THE DEAL

She laughed, "What's a loogan?"

"It's a guy who carries a gun for some guy who's graduated to the point where he doesn't have to carry one anymore."

"Are you a loogan?"

"I guess so. Yeah, I guess so. I'm a lot of things since I've been in this Deal, but, strictly speaking, a loogan is a guy who packs a rod for a guy who can afford not to pack one, but he's got to have someone walking behind him who can pick up the pieces if anything's dropped."

By this time we'd walked down the rest of the path that led to where I'd parked my car along with the rest of the cars. I opened her door. She got in without a look or a word. I closed the door and walked around to my side, got in, and started the car; backed up and tooled it out onto the road. She said, "Jarn, why don't we take a drive? You know, let's drive toward the Bois or down the river—anywhere." I nodded. I had taken a look at her in the light of the dash. Whatever it was, whatever you needed, she had it. She leaned back comfortably in the seat. "Do you have a cigarette, Jarn?"

"Uh-huh."

"Could I have one?"

"Sure." I reached into my side picket, took out a case, handed her a cigarette. She lit it herself from the lighter in the dash. We drove on quietly. She was smoking. Neither one of us was saying anything. I turned the car down a lane, down a slope with a high group of trees on one side; we passed over some of the cobblestone intersections and then, very far off, we could see the glitter of lights that looked down onto the Seine; the fog was almost gone, the cobbled lane here joined another intersection that went off to the right. I took the left, the small lane. It still was cobblestoned, but the car took the rough spots nicely. Once in a while we saw a *camion* parked, but it was closed up, with the tarpaulin thrown over the back end of the truck. For the night. They were waiting, of course, to go into the Halles in the morning. We passed the lights of a small nightclub, a *boîte*—there were a few people coming out, one of the pedestrians walked pretty close to the car. I gave him a blast, braked the car, blinked the headlights at him, heard a shout—"*Salaud!*"—but we continued on. I took a look at her. She hadn't paid any attention to this. I drove on for another five minutes without a sound from her. Finally, without saying anything, where the little lane took a turn close in by the river, I tooled the car over to the right, pulled up and stopped. She never said a word.

"Nic?"

"Yes?"

"Nic." Without another word, I moved out from under the wheel and

THE DEAL

into the middle of the seat. She turned her body a little away from me as if she were going to look out the other side of the car; and then directly and limply fell toward me without a sound. Her head was very close to mine. The eyes were closed, the face was dim; then I could see that she had opened her eyes, because I saw them shine. Then she lay back. The shine in her eyes was clearly visible in the darkness.

"Jarn . . ."

I put my arms around her. I could feel her hair against my face. I held her face in my hand and then gently pulled her toward me. The eyelashes were flickering now and then. I kissed her, hard, long. It was a hungry kiss. She opened her mouth, she began to tremble, her tongue was a darting snake between my lips. She kept on kissing me and I, kissing her. After a long time, when I couldn't get my breath, she put her hands up behind my head . . .

We stayed there a long time. We bumped knees, elbows, heads—and things. We touched all over everywhere—in and out of each other. The car was a safe place—it became larger—we became smaller. Finally, we were so locked up, so close together, we had all the room in the world, and for that too brief a while—we had that, too. I had wanted her for a long time, and she had been truly worth the wait.

Finally, in the gray and lovely damp, terribly cold, and awfully beautiful morning, I took her home. Paris and many things looked different . . . I started driving back to my apartment.

It would be difficult to completely explain about this girl. I thought I loved her so much it made my stomach hurt. I thought I loved her so much that salt had no taste—I wouldn't work, eat, or sleep—the life would be flat unless we were together.

I had told her this was dangerous. She had said, "Do you mean I'm never going to kiss you anymore?"

I had felt her lower lip, it was like warm velvet. I covered her. Then the smooth, silky jolt of a kiss.

She had said, *"Dupeletz . . . te pup."*

I loved her with all my heart, and my poor old soul, looking like a football that had been kicked around and scuffed, poured out silently—truth, trying to crack out.

Someone said, "Would you die for this girl, this lovely that you love so?"

"Christ, can't you ever let me alone?"

"I'll be around, Jarn, if you don't shove too hard . . . Don't file the evil down to such a fine point. Like you say when you are angry—a trait that

426

THE DEAL

must be overcome—if you are going to stick around, you are going to be polite."

"I'll be polite," I said quietly.

Well . . . the Princess—yes, the Princess; women make swell friends; you have to be in love with one to have the basis for friendship, and the Princess was, and had been, my friend. She'd shown it in many ways, many ways. But *l'addition*, the bill, always came. It was one of the absolute things you could count on. It was a simple exchange of values. You got something; you gave up something. For any good thing you ever got, you paid—*and how*. Your payment was sometimes you, or the learning of a thing; you paid for the experience, the "ifs," the gambles; the never-ending payments never ended. You enjoyed it, or you didn't, but that didn't make it any less true. The world is a good place to lie in, to buy in, to die in.

"Boy, you're a thinker today," *Someone* said out loud. "A real thinker, another profundity."

"Knock it off."

"Okay, it's knocked off."

I should never have started the conversation with *Someone* in the first place. Usually it's pretty good company.

"Until you get profound," *Someone* said. "Then you stink."

"Okay, I stink. You got any more things to tell me?"

"Nope, no more things—but we know, don't we, boy?"

"Yes, we do."

"We know what it's all about," *Someone* said, then finished quietly: "Settling-up time is coming, Jarn; I'm the fellow you'd better start trying to make a *Deal* with. Don't wait until the office is closed, boy."

● ● ●

It was a cold, gray, and damp evening in Paris. We were only thirteen shooting days from the completion of the picture. In these last months, the majority of the things that happened on this picture and with this Deal had been unbelievable. I had lost touch with everyone—I had lost touch with reality. I didn't know for sure what would happen with respect to the additional money I would need to complete the picture. The Baron was on the downswing. We were barely speaking. In fact, there were times even on the set when the Baron would be standing ten feet from me, and he would say to a changed Saul Baum, who was ever at his side, "Tell Jarn boy this . . ." or "Tell old Jarn the Iceman that . . ."

It was just one more point, one more thorn in the flesh; but if I could

427

hold out for these next two or three weeks, I'd finally be through with it, I thought, looking out of my apartment window, watching the *péniche* go by on the Seine, seeing the lighted windows of the cabins, steamed up to where you couldn't see in—and they wouldn't want to see out. It was going on toward seven o'clock. I decided to call the Princess for dinner—which was something I knew would be the *coup de grâce* with the Baron if he ever found out about it. Yet, since that evening with the Princess in the car, and since the Baron had been indifferent to the Princess for a while, I was trying to rationalize these phone calls. The Princess and I were no longer strangers—but something else, always, seemed to be cluttering up everything. I knew what it was—I didn't like it, but could no more control it than I could the sea.

I had spoken to her earlier in the day and told her that I would call around five o'clock. Since it was after seven, I figured we might have an early dinner and talk about anything—except this picture, or the Baron, or the Deal . . .

I went over to the bar. I mixed myself a light brandy-and-soda; I got a cigar going, I was grateful I still had a few of the panatellas from Jamaica. How stupid, vain, and insensitive you can become at the wrap-up of one of these pictures. Everybody's wrong—all wrong—and you are right, always right. And you derive such satisfaction from simple things like having a quiet drink by yourself and smoking a cigar in front of your own fireplace. I went over and sat down in the big leather chair, picked up the phone and dialed Nicole. It rang for a minute and then someone said, *"Allo?"* I said I'd like to speak to the Princess Nicole. The heavily accented voice said, "And who is speaking?" "Monsieur Jarnigan," I said.

I waited what seemed to me to be a long time, and finally, in a voice that sounded a long way off, "Hello, Jarn . . ."

"Hi, Nic. Everything all right?"

"Yes."

"I'll be by and pick you up in about an hour and we'll drive over to the Club Elysée and have dinner—or if you prefer, let's go to the Dinarzade and have some shish kebab and hear that beautiful Russian singer."

"Why didn't you call me at five o'clock?"

"What?"

"Why didn't you call me at five o'clock?" she repeated.

"Well, I didn't call at five because things went wrong at the studio and I didn't finish till a little while ago. Why? What's the problem?" There was another pause.

"Well, the problem, Jarn, is that I've made another date."

THE DEAL

This time it was my turn for the long pause. "Oh . . ." I said. "Well, all right, I'll give you a call some other time. *Bonsoir.*"

"Wait, Jarn . . . wait!"

"For what?"

"Well," she answered, "when you didn't call I thought maybe it was another one of those 'working all night' deals—you know, I've been waiting around for you every other night for the past couple of months; and half the time you either don't come or you don't call . . so you shouldn't be . . ."

"I'm not anything, Nicole."

"There," she said. "I know when you call me Nicole you are angry."

"I'm not angry," I said. "I'm just tired. I don't care if school keeps or not. I don't care how the picture goes, I'm tired. And I'll call you in a day or so. *Bonsoir . . .*" As I put the phone down I could still hear her saying, "Jarn, hello, Jarn . . ."

I hung up. I walked back over and got the bottle of brandy, fixed myself another drink, went back and resumed my place in front of the fire. Well, there it was. When you get to the point that you don't care if you see a beautiful woman like the Princess, you're ready for the high drop . . . As I was thinking this, the phone rang. I didn't answer. It kept ringing every five minutes for the next half hour. I let it ring. After the third brandy, knowing that I had to go out and eat somewhere—the cook was off—I remembered a restaurant called Chez l'Ami Jean. It was in Neuilly; I remembered it was not far from the apartment of Danielle Dumont.

She had taken this small apartment against the advice of her mother and myself, but one of the minor French actresses was sharing it with her. Her mother tried to keep a line on her. The French actress, who played supporting roles and who was only an adequate actress was, nonetheless, a nice girl. I'd given her a part in the last couple of pictures and had made arrangements through producer friends of mine to use her often, only because of her watching out for Danielle. Since the famous night that I had spent with Danielle and got my first "down" on the Baron, I had wanted to be sure that Danielle was all right without directly being responsible for her. Mme. Dumont had been satisfied with the deal I had made her, in paying off her property. Mme. Dumont's French attorney-lover was satisfied; I had let him draw the contracts for a couple of films and overpaid him. A dollar would have overpaid him. But all in all, I had kept the lid on that, and kept my lever, which I had used judiciously only the one time with the Baron.

429

THE DEAL

I decided I didn't want to eat alone, so I called Danielle. On the third ring, she answered the phone. "Oh, Jarn, Jarn," she said happily, "how *formidable* it is to hear from you! I have missed you . . . oh, I have missed you!"

"Fine, little one, me too. Are you busy for dinner?"

"Why? . . . are you asking me to go to dinner?"

"Yes."

"Then I'm not busy and I'll go," she said promptly.

"Good. I'll be by and pick you up in a little while."

"Just *klaxonnez* and I shall descend to avoid you having to climb the stairs."

"You are a thoughtful child," I answered. I hung up.

I had another brandy. During the next forty-five minutes the phone rang a couple of times more. I didn't know if it was the Princess or someone from the studio, but that evening I had had a bellyful of everything and didn't want to talk to anyone about business. I finished the brandy, turned out the lights and went downstairs, got in my car and started to drive out toward Neuilly to pick up Danielle.

I honked the horn—*dum dee dum dum, dum dum*—I klaxoned as she had requested a couple of times. When she didn't come down I didn't know whether she had heard me, so I got out of the car, slammed the door, and started the first flight up to "fourth heaven." I could never have made "seventh heaven" and as it was, the four flights of those straight-up stairs made me feel like an old man, and going downhill fast. When I got to the top of the stairs and went to her apartment, before knocking at the door I waited for my heart to get down in the low hundreds and the air to be a little less rarified. Not only was everything lousy—I was in lousy shape. I was full of tears and flapdoodle . . . or flapdoodle and tears; either way I felt like Mahatma Ghandi's father.

"You're drunk," *Someone* said.

"Well, if I am, I'm entitled to be."

Someone cackled, "Old Jarn the Iceman, old Jarn the raper, old Jarn the wino."

My breath had slowed down now. I was wonderful . . . I was fine. I "tightly" but more happily knocked on the door; I would be pleased to see this beautiful little girl.

After a few moments, the door swung open and there she was. "Jarn," she cried happily. "But you are here already! I was so excited when you called and I wanted to look nice for you. I washed my hair and it's taken

430

longer than I thought," she pouted prettily. She was dressed only in a little *en tissus robe éponge*. It was fastened at the waist rather carelessly. She wasn't dressed at all. I stood there in the hallway and said, "Is your friend home?"

"Oh," she said, *"non.* Simone is working tonight at Boulogne. They're *tourning* a *film de gangster* and they must *tourne* at night. She won't be home until daylight or later."

"Well," I said, "I assume it's all right if I come in, or do you want me to stand here in the hall?"

"Oh, je suis stupide. Quelle imbécile . . . entrez. Enter, Jarn. You must excuse my impolite behavior."

She took three steps backward into the room. I stepped in and shut the door. She pirouetted happily. The robe, in my view, swirled unnecessarily high, revealing everything that it . . . revealed. She was without coquetry; she was without shame; she was a beautiful child-woman who loved me— she had told me so repeatedly—who demanded nothing but only that we see each other from time to time . . . We had.

She sat down on the couch, motioned me to sit beside her. I removed my coat and threw it on the couch and took a chair. I sat down, took out a cigar and said, *"Permettez moi?"*

"Mais certainement, Jarn, of course smoke. *Tu es chez toi.* But you know that." Then she arranged herself carefully on the couch, making a lot of unnecessary little movements, but all very cute, and when she finally curled up and settled herself, she looked like a beautiful little white cat who is drying its fur. She was rubbing her beautiful long blonde hair briskly with a towel. I looked away and lit my cigar. If I hadn't done that we would not have gone out to dinner. I knew again I must be getting old because, there everything was. You couldn't find better, or as good any- where in the world, and here I was thinking about going to dinner and going home and rewriting the frigging scenes for tomorrow . . .

This brought to mind an interesting thought. All through this mother-of- a-picture I had to write the scenes three ways. You know, that's a son-of-a- bitch. I'd write the scene the correct way: everything normal, everything fine; then I'd write the scene with the Baron only half drunk—same scene but less dialogue for the Baron; making arrangements to let the other actors carry the ball—with the Baron only reacting or doing nothing except sitting or standing—if he was good enough to stand. Now the third and last way— which unfortunately I had to resort to so many times—that was my "leprosy" script on this picture deal. It was three times as large as the other

431

two. Each night before, I rewrote and adapted eight to ten pages of dialogue in each script, so that I was prepared for normalcy, half normalcy, or complete insanity. Thus we continued the picture.

". . . look so tired, Jarn." I realized that Danielle had been speaking to me, for how long I didn't know.

"No, *ma petite chatte,* not tired. Just thinking." I got up, threw my cigar in the fireplace, which was not burning—it having been replaced with one of those little gas stove affairs which burn you up if you stand close to it but don't give off any heat more than three feet away. I walked over and sat down on the couch next to Danielle. The drying of the hair business had almost finished and I said, "I invited you to dinner, remember? Don't you think you should get ready and let's go?"

Without a word she raised her little face to mine and kissed me on the mouth. She smelled soapy and clean, young and nice, lovely and desirable. I pulled back and said quietly, "You had better get dressed." She leaned back on her side of the couch, she sighed gently, fluttered her eyes and pushed back her lovely tawny hair. The mane of it fell back down over her eyes. She tilted her head and gave me a thoughtful up-from-under look. When she saw this hadn't hit me hard enough to grab her, she lowered her eyes shyly and said, "I like you, Jarn . . . you're not like the other producers I know."

"What other producers do you know, child?" I smiled.

"Well, Simone introduced me to some and I know . . ." Here, she thought prettily, then turned back around, kissed me quickly again and laughed. "You're the only producer I know. You are the only producer I want to know. You are the only everything I want to know." Then she laughed and I laughed with her. She kissed me quickly again, jumped up and ran like a child from the room, calling back as she left, *"Je suis prête dans cinq minutes."*

I called after her, "Well, if you're *not* out in five minutes, I'm coming in after you."

She stuck her pretty little head out the door, made a face at me, and said, "Then I shan't be ready in five minutes. I'll wait in here." She pulled her head back in the door.

"Well, then, you're going to be pretty hungry, because I'm waiting for five minutes and then I'm going to Chez l'Ami Jean and have a wonderful dinner and a bottle of wine that I'd hoped to share with you."

"I'm coming . . . I'm coming," she laughed. I knew there was a reply in that for me, but I grinned and let it drift with the tide.

Danielle did pretty well. She was dressed and out in ten minutes flat. She looked adorable in a short-skirted dress with a little cape effect, no hat. She pirouetted like a model, showing more of her lovely slender legs; tilted her head downward and said demurely, "Do I please you? Do I please you? I think I am very beautiful tonight. I want to be very beautiful tonight."

"*Petite toi,* I can safely inform you, without any fear of contradiction, in the whole of Paris—no, in the whole of France—no, *dans le monde entier,* you are the loveliest girl that it's possible to be with."

Immediately, she was not the child-sophisticate-mannequin; she was again eight years old and very thrilled; she impulsively came over and kissed me on both cheeks, saying, "*Oh, toi* . . . *toi* . . . you . . . you . . . you make me feel so wonderful, and I'd do anything for you." She then repeated, humbly—looking into my eyes, "Anything, Jarn." She reached up and kissed me. "Well, then." I smiled down at her and said over-quietly, "You'll let me go get something to eat and take you with me."

She stamped her little foot, "Oh, you are a monster . . . I hate you." And she turned and flounced to the door, opened it and—down the four flights, much ahead of me. When I got to the street I was there just in time to see her rush over to the car, open her side, get in and slam the door.

I walked slowly around the car, got in, started the motor and turned to look at her. She was staring straight ahead, her dear little face very serious.

"Are you all set?" I said.

"I," she replied with dignity, "am not speaking to you."

"Well, this won't make for a very good dinner conversation," I answered.

"Well—" Looking straight ahead she continued, "Oh, I intend to have a good dinner. I shall order everything. I shall order champagne"—with menace in her little voice.

"You do that, darling. You are entitled to it. The prettiest girl in Paris, in France, or in the world, is certainly entitled to champagne."

She turned and faced me, laughed gaily, and said, "You are terrible." Then slid over in the seat and sat as close to me as was possible. Looking up quickly, she said, "But I am still very angry."

"All right," I said, "we can talk about it at dinner."

"Good," she purred—and we drove off.

We arrived at Chez l'Ami Jean. I parked the car and we went in. Jean was an old and very good friend of mine that I'd known many years. He was from Arles and he loved the bullfights. Every year he went to Spain and followed this or that *torero* who was his star of the moment. I had made a documentary film with Luis Miguel Dominguin and his brother,

Pepe, and his future brother-in-law, Ordonez. The film was called *Les Toros*. I had lived for three months in Spain, working every day on this film, following these men closely and with admiration. They were the greatest stars in their own right. It was one of the most agreeable pictures that I had ever done. It had been pleasant all through. Everyone was normal. We were all happy making it because we loved the story and we loved the action of the bull ring. I suppose, to use the overworked phrase, we were *aficionados*. I had met Jean, who was in Spain at the time on his yearly vacation to follow the bullfights. We had become good friends, and while living in Paris I went to Chez l'Ami Jean often. There was never a bullfighter, good or bad, who needed to go hungry in Paris so long as Chez l'Ami Jean was open. I think during the off-season he truly had bad financial months with the *torero* heroes—who, unfortunately, were not always so heroic, but were certainly always hungry. It was all done with style and with much overenthusiasm, and unnecessarily rude commentary.

However, tonight Jean escorted Danielle and me to the far corner of the restaurant that he knew I liked. I didn't order dinner because Jean knew what I wanted. He made two or three polite suggestions to Danielle, who said, "I'll take whatever Monsieur Jarnigan takes."

Jean nodded, "You will do beautifully then, mademoiselle." She smiled up at Jean. I was amused to see that Jean took it very big. She turned around and was looking at the other people in the restaurant. He looked at me, saying quietly, "*Elle est magnifique, la petite.*"

"Yes," I said, "I am in accord with you, old friend. But she is the daughter of a friend of mine . . ."

"That I should have such friends," he said sadly, walking away. "That my friends should have such a daughter." He walked in the direction of the kitchen, looking heavenward, prayerfully.

Dinner was fun. Danielle looked lovely, made silly, amusing conversation. She was delightful and the two hours passed and for the first time in weeks I realized I hadn't been brooding over the picture.

We finished dinner and Danielle wanted me to take her to a discothèque on the Left Bank and when I refused, she was childishly angry with me again. "Listen, *ma petite gosse*, I have the work to do tomorrow. You have the sleeping to do. I'm taking you home, but one other night I would love to take you to your discothèque or whatever it is."

"Oh, really, Jarn, would you take me? I'd be so proud to have my friends see me with you."

"You have my *parole*, my word on it." She kissed me on the cheek.

I drove Danielle home, got out of the car, walked around, opened her

THE DEAL

door for her, and we started for her apartment door. When we got to the entrance, the concierge's light was out. It was usually just a dim glow in the cavern, which all concierges seem to use for light. Most of the concierges that I know live in constant twilight. Danielle had me firmly by the arm and started in and up the stairs. I stopped. "Don't make me walk the four flights, my little angel. I'm tired, I'm full of good food, I've had lovely company, and now I'll bid you *bonsoir* and return home."

She pouted. She said quietly, a little note of disappointment in her voice, "But, Jarn, I thought . . . that is . . . I wanted . . . Well," she continued, "I hoped you would come up and . . . and . . . have a good night-hat, as you say."

"We don't say 'night-hat'; it's 'nightcap'!"

"Well," she said annoyed, " 'hat-cap,' it's the same thing. Please come up."

"No; but I will come discothèquing with you next Saturday night." She looked at me steadily. Then demanding, childishly serious.

"Would you promise? Would you hold out your hand and spit on the devil and promise?" I performed the ritual. "Well," she said, firmly convinced, "now I know you'll take me to the discothèque Saturday night. I then permit you to take leave of me on the bottom step."

She held my arm and I walked over with her to the stairway. She walked up two steps, turned back, and we were standing face to face. She leaned over, she put her little arms around my neck, she whispered, "Jarn," and we kissed. It was a wonderful kiss . . . It almost made me carry her up the four flights—I know it could have carried me up—but gently I moved my head back. I kissed her softly on the nose, *"Bonsoir, petite ange. Bonsoir, petite toi, à moi. Et merci."*

"It's me should thank you," she whispered softly, "it's me who had the wonderful evening, although I am sad you must return to work, but now I will go upstairs and think about Saturday night, I will wear a new dress for you. I will look very lovely for you." She turned quickly and made two or three steps up the dimly lit stair. She turned back and whispered, "I only want to look lovely for you . . . just you."

"Danielle, I'll wait until you are up, then you will whistle and signal me you are inside."

"Mais, Jarn, je ne suis pas un enfant."

I laughed and said firmly, "Up you go; even if you are not a child, I will await until you are safely in your door—then whistle. We tell each other good-night, and then I know we are both safe."

"Tiens, me not safe!" Then, with a little lilt in her low voice, she said,

435

THE DEAL

"I'm only not safe with you, *tiens!*" And with that, she shot off up the stairs. I walked over to the other side of the entrance and pushed the *minuterie* which would allow two minutes of light before turning it off. I heard her say, *"Deuxième étage*—blouses, skirts, handkerchiefs, many lovely things."* All in the exact intonation of the lady elevator operator in La Belle Jardinière department store.

In a few moments I heard, *"Troisième étage,"* all on the same note; "film producers, men who must keep their promises, who must buy records they sell in a discotheque."

In another few moments, very faintly, I heard a little voice, *"Quatrième étage*—*chez moi."* Still on the same one note, "I am arrived. I am in *sécurité*. I am safe from everyone except Jarnigan. I open my door, monsieur," she sang as though it were a Catholic nun's chant, "I have the key in the lock, monsieur." The light went out. "Help, help, *au secours!*" she called. I punched the button again; the light went on, the little voice floated down, "My savior, my producer-savior!"

"Listen," I called up the four flights through the stairwell, "You'll wake everyone in the apartment."

"Très bien, very well. It would serve you right if I did."

"It isn't how it would serve me," I yelled back. "You'll be very unpopular!"

She called down in her dear little voice, "Just for saying I am unpopular, I'll tell you now, good night." She laughed gaily. *"Bonsoir,* Jarn," and I heard the door slam. I took two or three steps and that damn light went out. I have lived in Paris for many years and have never been able to time those bloody lights.

I burned my finger with my cigarette lighter finding the button release which would let me out the apartment entrance. I went out. I got into my car. I drove home.

46

I parked my car, got out, closed the door. I didn't lock the car; it was better if you didn't because if you did lock your car the kids on the Rue St.-Louis might just cut open the top of the convertible . . . not because they were mean kids, but because they just were great kids to nose around. I'd been living there a long time. I knew most of them and happily they liked me and didn't bother my car. The leader of the neighborhood gang on the street was a good friend of mine; he was called *un jambe Jeaneu*, which means "one-legged Johnny." He was a boy who, when an infant, had his right leg blown off at the thigh in a bombing raid. He'd had an artificial post fastened to the end of his leg and with that and a crutch, a very thin one, he was able to move around as fast as the other kids, and, because he had used these things since he was two or three years old, he could lick most of the kids. He used his crutch with dexterity. Most of the youngsters around that part of the neighborhood looked up to him because he was a "war veteran" and certainly knew all of the ins and outs of Ile St.-Louis.

He was an accomplished pickpocket and when there were weddings or funerals going on and the people going into the Church of the Ile St.-Louis, either properly sober because of the funeral or properly gay because of the wedding, Johnny moved quietly through the crowd, picking a pocket here, lifting a purse there. He did it very well. Later on, he'd come to me and say, "Monsieur Jarn, if I confessed to the church janitor—would it—be the same?"

"What do you mean, Jeaneau, what are you conning me for?"

"Well, I can't say this to Father LaRue because he would only be angry with me, but I figured since the janitor worked in the church, if I confessed to him it would be about the same—him working for the church and all." He laughed mischievously and went on. "I grease him every once in a while, I kind of split with him, especially when it's a sad funeral and if it's a rich *commerçant* they're putting away."

So little one-legged Jeaneau and I had our deal. He kept the kids away from the car and I tried to help him when I could. I was his *père américain*.

I went into my apartment and went upstairs. It was now a little after ten-thirty. I took off my coat and went into the library and started to lay out my three scripts, my three glories, for the following day. The Baron had promised to meet me later that evening; later for him meant twelve or one o'clock, but at least I wanted to go over a couple of things with him for the shooting, and since he didn't have to go to work till one-thirty the next afternoon, I figured I could impress upon him to learn the scene that was an important story point in the picture.

It took place in a courtroom on the big sound stage. He had some rather long speeches to make, a lot of lines to remember, and even with the help of the blackboards and other devices that I used to keep the dialogue in front of him, it always helped, if he was sober, to go over the things with him the night before.

When it was after midnight and still no Baron, the telephone rang. I got up from the desk and went over to answer it.

"Jarn?" It was Sam Neely.

"Yeah, Sam."

"Jarn, the Baron didn't meet me like he said. He had asked me to meet him in front of La Môme Michele's apartment and I've been waiting here since a little after eleven. He told me to meet him at eleven-thirty, it's now almost twelve-thirty. What should I do?"

I thought for a minute. "Well, Sam, stay there till one-thirty and if you don't hear anything, give me another call. Where are you now?"

"Oh, I'm in a little bar just down the street where I can see the entrance to La Môme's apartment, but he's not around any of these places either."

"Well, stick around, Sam. If he doesn't show up by one-thirty, give me another call. Then we'll have to go and find him, or rather, you'll have to go and find him because, boy, I got a lot of work to do. I can tell tomorrow we're going to use script number three." The telephone crackled.

"What's that, Jarn?" he said.

"Never mind, Sam. Stick there and call me if he doesn't show by one-thirty."

"Right, Jarn. Just what you say." He hung up.

I went back and sat down at my desk. I looked at script no. 1, which I liked. It had, in my view, good dialogue; I thought the scenes played fairly well and I would certainly have loved to shoot script no. 1 all the way through. I picked up script no. 2, which I used when the Baron was only half crocked. This of course cut down his dialogue and I played the scene on the villain or over the shoulder of the Baron, favoring the leading lady. Everything to keep the Baron in the scene and yet not have him say too much, not come in too close on him. With regret I tossed even no. 2 script back in the drawer and took out old no. 3. Old no. 3, so far as I was concerned, was filled with pages for the devil. This script was made with prac-

THE DEAL

tically no dialogue for the Baron, an awful lot of "seated" pantomime and was truly written for a star you knew would be incapable of performing, yet you had to have him in the scene. I loathed this script. It was about the size of the New York or Los Angeles telephone directory. I had tried to anticipate *l'imprévu,* as the French say, which means the unforeseen, the unexpected. I tried in this script to anticipate anything this bastard would do. I had this script written so if the son-of-a-bitch could even lie flat on the floor, I could still go ahead and shoot the picture. He could lie there and be a corpse. Some way I'd get old Marc the cameraman to lower the camera and shoot over past him so that one way or the other we were able to get footage. This, of course, lent a very "artsy-craftsy" look to parts of the picture.

In some of the rushes, I must say, I was congratulated for the unique and unusual angles that I had "directed" the cameraman to take. I took this, of course, with thanks, acted as though I had planned it that way. However, the cockeyed angles and the shooting up from under camera effects we were getting were because in the majority of cases the Baron himself would be at a canted angle, and, in order to make him look like what he wasn't, we would shoot a very unusual shot, hoping in this way to partially disguise the Baron's true condition.

So having put a good script no. 1 in the drawer, the so-so and half-way-good script no. 2 in the drawer, there I sat with old script no. 3, the leprosy book, the syphilis book, the book that to me was not inventive or ingenious, just sheer desperation.

The telephone rang again. I took a look at my watch. I was surprised to see it was already one-thirty. I knew that it'd be good old Sam, bless his heart. He was always on the button, especially with respect to the things he did for me. I could rely on him. At least there was that. I went over to the telephone and said, "Yeah, Sam . . ."

"Hey, how'd you know it was me calling, Jarn?"

I laughed. I didn't feel like laughing, but I laughed. "Oh, I just took a chance, Sam. What's the good word?"

"Well, that's just it, Jarn, I can't give you any good word tonight. The Baron isn't here and I kept an eye on the front of La Môme's apartment, even tried a couple of bars up and down the street. He just isn't around. What'll I do?"

"Well," I said, "forget about staying there in front of La Môme Michele's. Let's start to do the rounds—you know, go over to Jimmy's, go to Eléphant Blanc. I would look out in Neuilly, there's the Nain Bleu restaurant, and let's see—I know, why don't you go by the studio and look in the lodge, you know, the dressing room, talk to the cop at the gate; maybe he came in and is sleeping it off there. I guess that's about all. Let me know, Sam, let me know what happens."

"O.K., Jarn, just as you say . . . you know me, I play it like you want it. Right?"

"Right . . . Sam, I know, boy," I said tiredly.

"Hey, Jarn . . . you all right? . . ."

"Yeah, I'm all right."

"You sound like there's something wrong."

"Nope, everything's all right, just a little tired. I've been working on that . . ."

"Don't tell me. You're writing in that frigging telephone book you keep talking about."

"You pegged it, Sam, that's what I'm doing. Listen, boy, you try and find him. Go in those bars and look around and when you get him tell him I got to talk to him. Snake him out of whatever bar it is, even if you have to kind of nudge him along a little . . . he likes you."

"Right, Jarn, I'm on my way." The telephone clicked. Sam had gone on the mission that he'd been on many times before. I stood there looking down at the telephone in my hand. I placed it back on the receiver, walked over into the corner where I had the bar, poured myself a brandy, then went over to the mantel, got a cigar, stirred up the fire a little, and stood there. I lit my cigar. I waited.

I must have been seated in front of the fire for about twenty minutes, smoking and thinking about the work the next day, when all of a sudden the apartment door was shoved on. Then, a hurried knock. I got up and went over to the door, I opened it. In came the Baron fast like he was being chased. He was something to see. His hair was mussed, his eyes were as glassy as two marbles, he had no coat, he was covered with blood, on his shirt and all over his pants. He was spattered; he looked like he'd been sticking a pig. He went immediately over to the bar where he saw the bottles of brandy, poured himself a big charge and downed it and stood there holding the bottle. I looked at him for a moment and then went over and closed the door.

"Lock that, will you," he said in a voice that was certainly scared and didn't sound much like the Baron's casual and suave approach.

I locked the door and walked back to the middle of the room. I said quietly, "Baron, what the hell's happened? What have you been in, a fight?"

THE DEAL

He started to answer, then shook his head, turned around and went back over to the bar; he poured himself another big drink; he started to take the brandy bottle with him and realized that he had that kit that contained the false dong in his hand; there was a lot of blood on that too. He gulped down the glass of brandy and ran from the room and headed down toward the bathroom.

I knew there wasn't anything to do but try and find out what had happened. I didn't understand him when he'd babbled something about "I didn't do it, I didn't do it." It was hard to connect up anything that he said. I couldn't tell whether he was saying "I didn't do it" or "I didn't mean it," but either way, I knew that "we" were in some kind of trouble. I could hear a lot of noise and water-splashing in the bath. I walked on down the hall and went in the bathroom, left the door open and stood there watching him. He had thrown that case on the linen chest—tore off his shirt and undershirt, threw them on the floor, pulled off his pants, shorts, and shoes, undressed completely. He dove for the shower—but without the agility that he would normally have had. As he dove, his shoulder hit one side, his other shoulder hit the other side of the shower door and in he went. I was afraid he'd hurt himself, so I ran over to him, but he'd already turned the water on. He stood under the water, shaking his head, I don't think he knew whether it was hot or cold. In point of fact, it was cold.

I reached into the shower and adjusted the handle so that the water would be just warm. I walked over to where he'd thrown his clothes, I put all of the bloody things together. I knew instinctively we'd have to hide them. I went back down the hall and walked into the library, I poured another brandy—I needed it—and stood there wondering what kind of hell we were in, and how I was going to be able to straighten this out. I knew we had a lot of work to do in the afternoon, but I figured I'd better go back down and see what he was doing, I didn't want him to fall asleep in the shower even if he couldn't drown himself.

I went back down the hall into the bath. By now he was out of the shower, and strangely enough the Baron looked half sober. He turned to me when I came in and said, "Oh, hi, Jarn. Hi, boy." He shook his head. "I really don't feel very well." I thought this was the understatement of the year. I stood there watching him. He went over to the door. There on a hook were a couple of large toweling bathrobes. He said, "Can I, old boy?"

And I said, "Sure, Baron, go ahead."

He was still acting half like a sleepwalker but at least I was glad he was more calm. By now he'd put on the toweling robe; he wrapped it around him, took a deep breath, looked at the brandy glass in my hand, tried to grin the boyish, charming grin, but it didn't come off. It looked more like a grimace. He said, looking at my brandy, "I'd like one of those."

"All right," I said. "Put on those slippers, I'm going back to the library. Come on down and let's see if we can sort this one out." Without another word I turned and went out of the bath, back down the hall, and into the library. I got my cigar. I lit it. I poked at the fire a little bit, stirred it up. I threw on a couple of logs, walked over to the bar, poured him a shot of brandy, a small one, and stood waiting for him.

Pretty soon the Baron came walking into the library. He looked more calm now, he'd combed his hair, he had another towel in his hand, the robe was wrapped around him, he was shivering although it was not cold in the room. He walked over and stood in front of the fire a minute. I handed him his glass. He took it without drinking, turned around and looked into the fire, his back to me.

I said, "Baron, anytime you're ready." He never moved. He gave no indication that he'd heard me. I said, "Baron, I know you've had some trouble tonight. I also know the more time you give me to try and sort out the beads and string them for you, the better off we're going to be so . . . better let me know what it is right now."

He tossed off his drink. Then walking over to where the bottle of brandy stood on the sideboard, he poured himself a big one. He drank part of it and stood looking at me thoughtfully over the glass. "Well," he leered—I could see the second or third glass had got to him now because he had the "leeries." He put on half the heavy-menace stare along with the leer that now didn't slide off as it had done a couple of other times. I knew the Baron was set to tell me his version of the story and as usual I'd have to sort it out and see how much of it was truth and how much of it he was inventing. He didn't say anything for a while.

I looked at him and said conversationally, "Well . . ."

"Well . . . I . . . er . . . I . . .er . . ." he faltered.

"Go ahead, Baron, let's have it; whatever it is, the sooner I know about it, the better I can handle it."

"Well, you can't handle this one," he said.

"Well, Baron, you roll it out here in front of me and let's see if I can handle it."

"I . . . er . . . I've been out with Danielle." He looked at me, testing to see how I was taking this.

"Oh," I said. "'You'd better hold that one a minute, Baron. What's that got to do with the problem at hand? Your telling me you've been out with

442

THE DEAL

Danielle don't help us much. Try again." As I stood there looking at the Baron, I literally saw him turn green. I knew that he was going to be sick. I just pointed toward the bathroom. "Go ahead, Baron, you can make it. You'll feel better." Without a word he turned and rushed out the door.

I followed him slowly—he was down the hall and into the bathroom. Pretty soon I heard the sound of his being sick. I stepped inside, he was down on his hands and knees vomiting into the shower. I couldn't step around him because he was half stretched on the floor, I saw the needle and the bottle there but I couldn't reach over to get them. I did think I could hide everything else that was in the kit. I picked it up, I turned around, walked briskly down the hall, thinking to put the case in behind the books in the hall closet.

For a moment I stood there. Then I opened the case. I looked inside distastefully at the Baron's false dong. The famous false dinker. It was all bloody. It looked like he had gutted a horse with it. It was covered with blood. Even the straps, the harness, were covered with blood. I knew now without question what had happened. While the Baron was still vomiting—I could still hear him in the shower—I grabbed the case, wrapped it in towels. The case was about the size of a small typewriter. For no reason in particular, except I wanted this thing out of here, I went out the living room door, down the stairs fast; I unlocked the trunk of my car. In the turtle-back of the car I had two big metal cans that I used to carry two-thousand-foot reels of work print film. One of the cans was empty. I unlocked it, I put the case in, double-locked the steel case and then double-locked the back of the car. I turned around and raced back up the stairs and into the apartment. When I got inside there was no sign of the Baron. I went down to the bath. The door was closed and I heard the shower running; I thought, man, what a mess. And it wouldn't do any good to go inside. I went back down the hall to the library and stood there waiting, wondering what in the hell to do.

After about fifteen minutes, here came the Baron; but now he had on my other toweling robe, a dark blue one. He walked over to me and stood in front of me smiling. He had a white towel around his neck, again his hair was properly combed; it was in casual but not unstudied waves, so I knew that the Baron, at least in part, was back to "the norm" for him.

"Jarn, boy," he chirped, "aren't you going to offer your old partner a blast . . . a drink . . . the juice of the grape . . .?" The Baron said: "Jarn the Iceman, huh?—smart guy, huh?"

"Not unless I have to be," I said, "and don't fall asleep from that last shot in the arm, don't go 'main-liner dopey' on me."

THE DEAL

"Wha . . . wha . . ." he uttered.

"Don't try to be smart and clever now, Baron. Now is not the time to cutie-boots it. You're not the same fellow I left fifteen minutes ago."

"What?" A look of puzzlement came on his face. "What do you mean, Jarn boy?"

"Nothing, Baron. Fix your drink and then sit down. You and I have to talk." We were standing there just looking at each other. I said to the Baron, "You'd better sit down, boy, and tell me what's happened now." He went over and sat in the big chair that was the closest to the fireplace. He was shivering a little. I walked over to the closet, I got out a big robe, took it over and threw it on him. "Here—now suppose you start at the beginning."

He looked at me for a moment and he said, "Jarn . . ."

"Yeah."

"How long have you been home?"

"Well, I don't know, a little after ten-thirty, I guess. Why?"

"Well . . ." He looked back into the fire and sat without moving, without saying anything. The minutes seemed to go by. Heavily, I stood there waiting, wondering when he was going to tell me; but worse, wondering *what* he was going to tell me.

After a moment I said, "Well, now'd be a good time to start, Baron, it's getting late." I suggested more casually, "I'll see if I can help you."

"Huh?" He looked at me quickly. Then he said, "Could I . . . could I have another drink . . ."

"Do you think you need one, Baron?"

"Well, maybe you're right, Jarn." He looked back into the fire, then glanced sideways at me and said, "Jarn, we are in trouble." When I didn't say anything, he turned to me and looked surprised.

"Go ahead, Baron."

"No, Jarn, we are in trouble."

"You already said that. What kind of trouble?"

He leaned back in the chair, "Jarn, I pooned Danielle tonight." He said this quickly. He looked at me with almost hatred in his eyes.

"You what? Now come on, Baron, give it to me straight."

"I pooned Danielle, the little bitch. She's been after me so long, teasing me and all—well, I pooned her for fair."

"Yeah?" I said questioningly. "When did you do all this?"

Here he got that look on his face again, the half-sneer was back, the little smile that made the matrons shed their false teeth came over his face.

444

THE DEAL

"You thought you had that little woolly all locked up, didn't you, Jarn boy?"

"Now hold it, Baron," I said, a little frightened now, hoping it wasn't as bad as I thought. "Now, what'd you do? Let's really hear who you been with, Baron, because the time is going by. Now don't lie to me. I know you weren't with Danielle, because *I* was with her." He looked back into the fire. "Baron, how bad are you blipped? You didn't take more than your usual 'poke' when you were in the bathroom, did you?"

He turned around, a look of absolute dislike on his face. He said quietly, "You got it wrong tonight, Iceman, I'm not blipped, I'm sex-tired and confused."

I leaned over toward him. "Listen, Baron, now you listen to me. Who did you boff tonight with that plastic bat? You know when you came in your clothes were bloody like you'd won the pig-sticking contest."

He looked at me for a second and got quickly to his feet. The blanket fell on the floor. He walked over to the bar and poured himself a large glass of brandy. He said to me over his shoulder, without turning around, "You want one?"

"No, one of us has to stay sober, and right now you should lay off that flit. Now damn it, who did you rip up with your thing?"

He said quietly, still without looking at me, "I told you—Danielle, the little slut."

I got to my feet and said coldly, "You're a liar, Baron. You weren't with Danielle tonight. I told you *I* was with her."

"I know," he said quietly.

I didn't jump more than a foot. "You what?"

He paused, turned around. The look on my face made him change his mind. I could read it on the blipped, empty mask he wore as a face. He was brain-gnawing on something. He looked at me thoughtfully, almost soberly. "I said," he repeated quietly, "I know."

We looked at each other coldly for a minute. He looked like he was trying to sort something out, figuring what to say. Then he gave me a cold smile and said, "Oh, Jarn, I'm ribbing you. I know you want to know who I was with; well, don't be scared, it wasn't Danielle and it wasn't La Môme, although it should have been La Môme. I'll get that little piece too—for real. No—it was a little *putain* that I got in Neuilly on the way home from the studio." He poured himself another drink, got half of it down, shuddering, turned and started walking back toward me with his half-filled glass. He raised it up and said like a poet: "I pooned her in the park . . . I boffed her in the *bois* . . . I'm a poet, huh, Jarn?"

THE DEAL

"You're a prick," I snarled. I walked over and stood in front of him. Looked him straight in the eye, continuing harshly, "Now you listen, Baron, you'd better level with me. Who were you with, and how bad is it? You know we can't keep a lid on everything if you're really in bad trouble. Now, did you really just boff a little whore?" He nodded. "Well, did she call the cops, did she kick up a commotion?" He shook his head. "Are you shaking your head Yes or No? You can talk. You were sounding off grand a while ago, now don't go silent on me. Now is not the time to try and cutie-boots it."

I stood there looking at him for a minute, then repeated myself: "Listen, Baron, how bad is it? I'm asking you, did she call the cops, did she mention the police, did you pay her off?"

He sat down quickly.

"Who," he asked, "said anything about police? . . . said anything about cops?"

"Me," I said. "I said cops and cops again. And you damn well better tell me the truth, so we can get your story ready."

He turned and looked at me steadily. "Our story ready, Jarn boy. *Our* story. Remember, we are partners, we share everything. The money, the pictures, the dames, the boffs—"

I cut in on him, "Listen, Baron, you snap out of it, I want the truth and you might as well roll it out now." I added quietly, "I won't ask you again."

"Well, Jarn"—he walked over toward me unsteadily—"I pooned this girl, see . . . I pooned her in the woods, and I left her lying there. I put some money in her purse. Now, Jarn, don't look at me like that; because she was just a little whore; we made a deal and, like you say, I was regular with her. I left her some money in her purse."

"You told me that," I said.

He added quickly, "No one will know. No one will know"—here he hiccuped. Then said quietly, a trace of conspiracy in his voice—checking, taking a reading to see how all of this was going over with me, "Jarn, they can't trace me, so you can stop worrying."

I snarled, "I won't stop worrying until you get your story straight. Then I can get *my* story straight."

"She's as straight as she'll ever be now, Jarn boy," he said, much too calmly now for my taste.

"Well, Baron, then you're not concerned."

"Me . . ." he answered, "no, I've been right here with you all evening. I've been right here"—he looked carefully at me and said quietly, "I've been

446

here discussing my picture with you, oh . . ."—he grinned—"I've been here discussing *our* picture since about ten-thirty." He took a deep breath, he looked around a minute, he was getting pale from talking too much. He walked over and sat down in the chair. I followed him over and leaned down, "Baron, you'd better level with me. What was all that talk that you had pooned Danielle?"

"Just talk, Jarn boy, just talk. I wanted to fry you. I know you've got a thing for this little girl. No, nothing to it, except I'm tired and I want to sleep." Then he looked at me carefully and said, "But just in case, Jarn boy, you know . . . to avoid any trouble for your partner"—here he looked at me steadily and very formally—"I have been with you all evening."

Well, there it was again, I tried to sort it out, I thought over everything he'd told me. If he was lying, which I figured he was, one way or the other, I'd have to help him. I was in too deep now to even think of pulling out. If he went, I'd sure as hell go right with him, so I'd have to ride this one all the way. I looked down at him and said (locking and bolting myself firmly into hell): "All right, Baron, you've been here and we've been talking about the script since about ten-thirty. After I left Danielle I came here and you were here. Now listen, I'm going to take those bloody clothes and get rid of them. Did you really hurt that girl bad? There's enough blood; it looks like you might have cut her head off."

He leaned back in the chair and leered at me, "I pooned her, Jarn, I pooned her," he sang.

I shot him down with, "I told you, now is not the time to cutie-boots it, Baron. I'm going to get rid of those clothes. Where, I don't know—I'll get rid of them somewhere."

He looked at me and smiled, "It's awfully good of you, Jarn boy." Then he glanced around suddenly as though he didn't quite know what was going on. He got up, shaking his head, and walked down the hall toward the bath. I followed him. I handed him a laundry bag. I told him, "Now here's a couple of towels, wipe everything off, then throw the towels in the bag."

He walked over and sat down on the edge of the bathtub and put his head in his hands. I looked at him for a moment, then went over; I picked up the bloody clothes; there was a light silk shirt, some raw-silk slacks, an undershirt, shoes, socks, everything. The Baron stood up and was wiping everything off with the towels. It seemed to me there was an indecent amount of blood. I didn't see how there could be that much and not something serious happen to that girl. He didn't mention the false dinker, neither did I.

THE DEAL

"Baron," I said to him, "you really don't think this girl will kick up an explosion?"

He raised his head and looked at me steadily for a long moment. "No, Jarn," he said seriously, "I'm sure she won't."

I picked up the bag with the towels and the bloody clothes in it and walked over to the door. He stood up and walked over toward me. "Partner, be careful. I'm going to borrow some clothes, then I'm going right home. If there's any problem, call me. I'll do anything I can to help," he finished sincerely.

I looked at him coldly. "That will be swell," I said. I left.

I went down the stairs and out of the apartment. I had the laundry bag with the bloody clothes. I went down the street to my car and unlocked the back of the car and put them in. I locked the trunk of the car, got in and drove out along the Seine, clear beyond the Pont de St.-Cloud. I parked the car, well out of the way. I looked carefully around. I could smell the damp mist coming off the river. I opened the trunk of the car, I took out the clothes—I had removed the labels. Then I placed them in the other film can after carefully removing the two reels of work print that were in there and wrapping them in a blanket. I shoved all the bloody clothes into the heavy large metal case. I put in two snow chains I used when skiing at l'Alpe d'Huez, that I'd kept in the back of the car. Then, late as it was, looking carefully up and down the bridge to see that there was no one near, I walked to where I knew the Seine was over eighty feet deep, where the *péniches* pass. I carefully dropped the can over the side of the span. For such a heavy case, I was surprised that it made so little sound as it went into the water. No one would ever locate that . . .

I knew that in the other metal case, carefully locked in the back of the car, was the false dinker of the Baron. I drove back home. It was around 3:30 a.m. when I got upstairs. The apartment was empty. I undressed and went to bed.

• • •

A bell was tolling. A shaft of sunlight tickled my eyelids. I opened my eyes and saw through the window the sun shining brightly on the Church of l'Ile St.-Louis. Gentle clouds were touching other clouds of different colors, moving slowly across the hazy blue sky. I felt the rough blanket against my face. I started to get up, but, after all that had happened and trying to pound myself to sleep with brandy, I couldn't do it. So, I compromised. I rolled out of bed and half sat up. I leaned over quickly because my head

448

started off in left field. I had no more hoops to roll—I finally made it up on my feet. An achievement. I walked the crooked mile across the living room. I felt like a sick dog. I stopped in front of the big mirror over the bureau. I looked like a sick dog who can't eat his dinner, sniffs, but can't walk away from it even though it disgusts him. "You're a beaut this morning, Jarn boy," I said to myself.

"Yes, and how about you last night?" *Someone* asked.

"Oh, Christ, not this morning. I'm in trouble, so not any of that this morning."

"Yes, Jarn—Christ this morning and every morning. You're in trouble, Jarn; I want to be able to help you," *Someone* said firmly. "You'd better answer the door."

With that, I came to. The doorbell was buzzing. The clock said it was just after seven. The buzzing of the doorbell continued . . .

I finally went to the door, opened it, and there stood two policemen. The one in uniform was obvious. The other had that square, cold-block look; ready to be as tough or as nasty as the situation called for. This seemed to call for the neutral stage, because the French detective said politely, "Monsieur Jarnigan?"

"Yes, *oui*. What is it?"

"Monsieur Jarnigan, may we come in?"

"Well, I'd like to know what it's about. But, yes, you can come in if it's important."

"Monsieur Jarnigan, *croyez-moi*, believe me, it is important."

I stepped back, opening the door wide, and in walked the two policemen. I closed the door and ushered them into the library, motioned them to chairs, walked over and sat down at my desk and said, "Well, what's the problem?"

The detective spoke again. He seemed less at ease here in the library; which was very luxurious, than when he had been standing in the hall. He glanced around, noticing some of the paintings, noticing the furnishings. Then, in a more polite way, he said, "Monsieur Jarnigan, do you have in your employ a Monsieur Sam Neely?"

"I do," I said. "He's not only in my employ, he's also a very close friend. Is there something wrong? Has something happened to him?"

"In a manner of speaking, Monsieur Jarnigan. When did you see Monsieur Neely last?"

"Well now, just a minute. May I see your credentials and your card?" At this, he flushed, reached in his pocket, pulled out a leather case, and showed me his identification.

449

THE DEAL

"Your card says you're Inspector Pierre Fougerol. Jean-Pierre Fougerol. So, Inspector Fougerol, before I answer any more questions; I request you to tell me exactly the nature of your visit. Now—has Sam Neely been involved in an accident?"

"More than an accident, Monsieur Jarnigan."

I got up from my chair, walked around the desk, across the room over to the mantel. I selected cigars, offered them to Inspector Fougerol who was even more impressed with the quality of the cigars. Hesitantly, he took one. The other policeman in uniform took one and held it in his hand all through the rest of the conversation. After Inspector Fougerol was properly lit up—I was standing in front of the fireplace, smoking—I said, "I'd like to hear exactly what the problem is, Inspector Fougerol."

"It's very grave, Monsieur Jarnigan." Nodding his head seriously, "Monsieur Neely is under arrest for the rape and murder of a girl whom you also know. You see, we are well advised." Here, he gave himself a little nod of appreciation, thinking of the thoroughness of their police force. "We know many things. This girl—"

"What girl?" I said sharply.

"Mademoiselle Danielle Dumont."

I clenched my hand so tightly I broke my cigar. I turned and threw it in the fireplace. I thought to myself, So the Baron *had* done what he'd said first; he had pooned and pronged little Danielle to death. Oh, that bastard! I couldn't talk for a minute. Inspector Fougerol was very alert, saw that I was more than disturbed.

"Monsieur Jarnigan?"

"Yes, Inspector?"

"May we have a statement from you as regards this situation?"

"You may," I said. "First of all, I am shocked and grieved at this misfortune. This girl, this child, was a close friend of mine. But one thing I am absolutely sure of, and will stake my reputation and my money on, is the fact that Sam Neely had nothing to do with this tragedy."

Inspector Fougerol looked at me coolly.

"Do you have some other ideas?" he said quietly.

I shot him a quick glance and saw the sly and calculating look in his eyes.

"No ideas, Inspector, no ideas at all. Now, I'm going to call my attorney, Maître Gautrat; and then I will accompany you back to the precinct because I must talk to Sam Neely."

"This is precisely why we took the liberty to disturb you at this early hour."

I walked back over behind my desk and dialed Maître Gautrat. I motioned Inspector Fougerol to a chair. He nodded graciously and sat down.

In spite of the early hour, Gautrat's secretary answered the phone, and after a few minutes of good mornings, I finally got through to the great man.

"Maître," I said "we have a very serious problem here. I want you to meet me at the—" here I turned back to Inspector Fougerol. "What precinct?"

"Precinct of the Seine, Quai des Orfèvres."

"I want you to meet me at Quai des Orfèvres precinct. Sam Neely has been detained and apparently arrested for an assault, rape, and possibly a charge of murder. Yes, that's right."

Then Gautrat started asking me many questions. "Maître, I'm leaving as soon as I'm dressed. Will you meet me there?"

Maître Gautrat said he would meet me immediately. I hung up, turned back to Inspector Fougerol. "If you will permit me, I will get dressed and will be ready to leave shortly."

"We permit you. I pray that you will forgive this intrusion." Here he relaxed a little bit, "and may I say, Monsieur Jarnigan, you have my sympathy for this unfortunate affair which involves two friends of yours."

I started to thank him; but again I saw this sly, appraising look in his eyes. Inspector Fougerol had something on his mind. He didn't want to let it out into the light yet; he had something going, but he wasn't ready to spring it on me right away. I didn't know what it was. I didn't know if he knew of any connection between the Baron and Danielle as yet. I didn't know how much he knew. I turned abruptly, saying, "You'll excuse me," and walked out of the room.

Twenty minutes later I was shaved, dressed, and back with Inspector Fougerol and the uniformed officer. We left the apartment. I decided to take my own car and told them I'd meet them at the precinct. Inspector Fougerol was very agreeable and drove off ahead of me. At least I was relieved in the sense that apparently they hadn't connected me and the Baron at all ... or I didn't think they would have been as free in allowing me to get in my car and follow them to the station.

On arrival I was introduced to the deputy chief of detectives. The men were all sitting around in an open room. Some were drinking coffee. All were smoking Gauloises Bleues or another French-brand cigarette, awfully strong. After a little while I was ushered into the office of the chief of detectives. He didn't bother to get up when we were introduced. He sat there at his desk. He was a fat man. He had a loose-lipped smile, and a sappy expression on his face. His nose was long and fat and had hung over a lot of quick ones in its time. He had large, square yellow teeth, like a horse, but they hadn't grown in his mouth—it seemed I was always meeting the store-teeth boys.

He grunted "Bonjour, monsieur," motioned me to a chair. He knew my name, he'd had it all explained to him. But he asked me several questions with respect to the last time I'd talked to Sam Neely. He said he wanted to know all this before he could allow me to see Sam Neely. I told him my story once—and he listened. Then I told it again, for him to see if I had it down too pat—then I had to tell it to him again, to see if I'd changed anything from the first time . . .

After awhile, he got up heavily and walked out of the room, leaving the door open. I looked out the large door and then turned and looked out of the window, which was open. It was the false spring in Paris—the chestnut trees were trying to bloom. People walking on the Boulevard and on the quays next to the river. The Sphinx and the Belle Aurore—the two finest whorehouses in Paris, which were called Clubs with dignity—were doing a land-office business in fifteen-year-old virgins of every nationality. An "absolute" virgin—they'd even give you an Oklahoma guarantee it was so.

But I wasn't thinking of spring, chestnut trees, or walks on the Boule-vard. I was thinking of fifteen-year-old virgins like little Danielle. Christ, what a terrible thing—that poor, dear child! Good Christ, I wondered how this one was going to work out. I didn't know how to sort the beads out and string them this time . . .

I knew that the Baron had killed that little girl and somehow or other Sam had got mixed up in it. Now I understood why he hadn't called me. I sat down for a while. The minutes went by. Time didn't seem to be too important to these people. I had wanted to see Sam, but apparently there were some complications that they had to clear up before they were going to allow me to see him. I was still waiting for Gautrat to arrive.

About this time, the far door opened, and through the side entrance in came Inspector Fougerol, bringing with him another man whose appear-ance was really something to see. He was worth a second look. Inspector Fougerol came over and said to me, "Monsieur Jarnigan, may I present Monsieur Louis Merdeo. Monsieur Merdeo is a confidential and private investigator, who has been on a . . ." And here, he cleared his throat. He permitted himself a wry smile and said, ". . . has been on a confidential mission."

I didn't see anything in that for me so I let it drift with the smoke. I watched them both.

Inspector Fougerol continued, "It seems that Monsieur Merdeo had been assigned to survey the activities of Monsieur le Baron, who is, as I know, the star of your picture—widely acclaimed. Yes, indeed," he said to himself again, nodding sagely, "yes, widely acclaimed." Here he passed the buck to M. Merdeo. (He looked like his name.)

M. Merdeo stood there uncomfortably for a while. I just looked at him and waited to see what he was going to do. M. Merdeo started to go on the air. "Monsieur Jarnigan, it is a great pleasure to have finally made your acquaintance. I have observed you from afar—in my line of duty, you might say. Ha, ha, ha." Here he allowed himself a little laugh. Everybody seemed to be allowing themselves certain things. I sat back and waited. I knew something was coming. He continued, "I was in the small *bistro* in Neuilly when Monsieur Sam Neely was taken by the police. I had been trying to observe Monsieur le Baron, but unfortunately I had lost him. But I was in on the ultimate capture and arrest," he said proudly, "of Monsieur Sam Neely."

He turned around and looked at Inspector Fougerol as though he expected some sort of applause. None forthcoming, he looked back at me. "I may say, however, Monsieur Jarnigan, that I have observed you and have had a close association from a distance with Monsieur le Baron. I have been *suiv . . .*" Here he started to lapse into French and went back to his bad English, "I have been following him for the last few days."

Inspector Fougerol interrupted M. Merdeo. Again I thought, his name suited him perfectly. "Monsieur Jarnigan, it is now time that I pose a direct question toward you. I can see that apparently it is not you who had engaged Monsieur Merdeo to do his surveillance of Monsieur le Baron. Correct?"

I didn't say anything, but I nodded.

He continued, "Then I may asume that is correct?" I nodded again. He continued: "Of course, as yet I am unable to force Monsieur Merdeo to tell me who has engaged him to do the surveillance on Monsieur le Baron, but it would be helpful if you could shed any light on this little problem."

I looked at both these men. First, at the inspector; and back at M. Merdeo. I turned to the Inspector and said, "I wish I could, but I am unable to throw any light as to who has engaged this gentleman to survey the Baron's activities." But to myself I thought of three people: It could be the Suisse Syndicate boys. It could be the American attorney; just protecting his investment and client. Or, it could be my French co-producer.

Keeping this to myself, I looked back up at M. Merdeo and said, "*Alors,* well—what have you to say?"

"As you may know," he smiled with a self-satisfied smirk, "I cannot divulge my client's identity; however, as I have aforestated, I have been in close contact with the Baron . . ."

"Until tonight," I interrupted.

His face fell. "You have it correct, Monsieur Jarnigan—until tonight. I must confess Monsieur le Baron gave me the slip as neatly as has ever been done to me in my thirty-two years of experience as possibly the finest confidential detective in Paris." Again he looked around for some comment on this self-accolade; again none was forthcoming.

I said, "Your connection with the Baron may be incidental, accidental, or coincidental. Or, it may be a figment of your imagination. However, I must take it into consideration."

I said this to him quietly, then just sat there and observed him. He shifted uncomfortably under the scrutiny. He could not withstand the bead of careful concentration and observation that I laid on him. He looked like a whore's dog. His eyes were puffed out of his head. His beard was fluffy and white; it looked powdered; like unclean cotton candy. He was fat, flat; a blob. He looked like he had been spaded. He shifted again and looked at the floor.

I turned back to Inspector Fougerol. "Inspector, it is now time for me to see Monsieur Neely. I have been here almost two hours. I now insist to see Monsieur Neely—the reason for which you brought me here."

Happily, at this moment Maître Gautrat walked through the door. He snapped his fingers at the guard and said to me quietly, *"Suivez-moi,* Monsieur Jarnigan, *suivez-moi.* Follow me."

I did just that.

47

I was walking down the corridor, following the guard and Gautrat, on the way to see Sam Neely. I was trying to think of everything and nothing. Little Danielle was dead. The police knew by now that I had been with her that evening. They also knew that Sam Neely worked for me.

That lovely girl—not even a girl, a child. So the Baron did get her. So the Baron had pooned to death little Danielle with that plastic bat. He had been telling me the truth that first time—I hadn't believed him. Then he'd started lying. It would be hard now to make him remember what had happened.

Gautrat and I were taken into the cell-block where the dangerous convicts were kept. There were six cells, four of them were empty. The guard led us down to the far cell on the right side, and there, in the cell, looking forlorn and absolutely dazed, was Sam Neely.

The guard unlocked the huge iron gate—the bars two inches thick. Gautrat and I walked into the cell. Sam looked at me as though he didn't recognize me for a minute, and then jumped up. The guard clanged the door shut, and Gautrat waited, pointedly, until the guard had walked away. Then he said, "I'm Maître Gautrat. Monsieur Jarnigan has—"

Here I interrupted. "Sam, this is my lawyer. He's going to ask you some questions and you must tell him exactly what happened."

Sam looked at me. There was fear in his eyes. Then he said, "Jarn, I don't need to tell any lawyer anything. I want to tell you. I did just like you told me. I went to all the places you told me. And then, just on an afterthought, when I couldn't find him in any of the restaurants and the bars, I went by the studio. The guard told me I might try up at that little girl's apartment. I went up there. I climbed them stairs . . . and when I walked in, it was a terrible sight."

Sam continued slowly. Gautrat started to say something but I made a gesture for him to keep quiet. "Go ahead, Sam," I said quietly. I walked over and I put my arm around his shoulders, hit him roughly on the shoulder to let him know I was with him, and said, "Sam, you have to tell us exactly what happened then."

"Well, Jarn, I went in that room—the door was open—and there was that little girl, lying on the floor. Jarn, there was blood all over. I never saw so much blood! I ran over to her because she was shaking her head from side to side. I picked her up—I wanted to put her on the davenport—but she kept whispering, "No, Baron, no! No, Baron!" Well, I don't know what happened then except I was afraid. I knew I should get her a doctor and call somebody, so I just laid her down there on the davenport, and ran out the door, down the stairs to that little bar you know we've been in. The one not too far from the studio. I tried to use the telephone—it was busy. While I was waiting, I had a couple of brandies. Then, the next thing I know, here come the police and they just carried me right on down here!"

Now, for the first time, the lawyer Gautrat interrupted, speaking in his slow and not too good English. "Monsieur Neely, did you see anyone else near or around the apartment of this young lady?"

Sam looked at me, as though for advice. I just nodded my head Yes— answer everything.

Sam said, "I didn't see anyone. Everything happened so quick and I was frightened; I didn't see anyone." He turned and walked over to a bunk and sat down.

Gautrat said, "I'd best go see the lawyers who will do the interrogation. I also would like to know who has been assigned to the case. There's nothing more we can do here."

I said, "Sam, I'll be back. We have to see what has to be done to get you out of this."

I don't know if I looked guilty or not—I felt guilty. Sam didn't get up. He shot me a look—intense, pleading. "Jarn," he said quietly, "you don't think I had anything to do with that? You don't think I'd hurt that little girl, do you?"

I looked at him. "No, I don't, Sam. I *don't* think so. I *know* you didn't do anything." For just a second, a brief smile, a look of relief, came over Sam's face. Then the pained look came back. Sam just shook his head from side to side, then put his head in his hands. I said, "I'll be back to see you, boy." Sam nodded, Gautrat banged on the bars for the guard to come and unlock the cell-block door.

When Gautrat and I came back down the corridor out into the offices, no one could have been more surprised. In walked an apparition. As dapper as could be, looking every inch the movie star, in walked the Baron.

He said Hello grandly to everyone, nodded to Gautrat, although he didn't know him well, walked over and said, "Jarn, I heard about this. I got the news from the studio. What a terrible thing. I know you couldn't be involved—I came right down, partner," he added smiling courageously.

In the background, Inspector Fougerol, M. Merdeo, and a couple of other inspectors—I assumed the other man was a lawyer—were all coming back into the room. They heard the Baron as he said, "Jarn, we have to get this straightened out. I hear they've arrested Sam Neely."

I looked at the Baron. Quietly, "That's right, Baron, they have."

THE DEAL

"Well, kid," the Baron said, "I'm awfully glad you're not in any problem. I explained to the inspector here, while you were in talking with Neely, I was in your apartment until late last night. We were talking about the script—so I knew you couldn't be mixed up in anything. However, this is such a terrible tragedy—just terrible," he finished solemnly, looking around the room for sympathy.

He got what he wanted.

The police inspectors were very impressed that a star of the Baron's magnitude was in their precinct—was there in the station office, talking to them. They explained more about the crime than was necessary. The Baron, who continued acting horrified—was the perfect superstar portraying tragedy, grief—was also at the same time giving the absolute impression he was ready to do anything—anything—to help his friend Jarnigan, and Jarnigan's friend, Sam Neely.

I listened to him saying some of these things. I stared at him in amazement. He turned his head and caught my look. He returned the look—straight in the eye—very pale, very strained. He knew that I knew what he had done.

So there it was. The police, the inspectors, and even the lawyers, were overly polite. Maître Gautrat had now told me he was going to talk to the judge, the president of the tribunal, also the chef du préfet. The Baron and I were planning to leave. We'd all meet later in the day and consolidate our plans to see what could be done to save Sam Neely.

It was at this point that Inspector Fougerol came over and finally shot the bolt I knew he'd been saving. I had no idea that it was what it was. Very quietly he said, respectfully, "Monsieur le Baron, I wonder if I might speak with you privately for a moment?"

The Baron looked at me, looked down at Inspector Fougerol; for a moment, fear was in his eyes; he hid it successfully from everyone except me. "Why, of course, Inspector. What may I do for you?"

Inspector Fougerol answered, "It is an affair of delicacy . . . if we may speak in private."

The Baron reared back, "I have no conversations in private in which my partner, my friend Jarnigan, cannot assist." Saying that, he walked in the direction of the door that Inspector Fougerol had indicated, taking me firmly by the arm. We walked into the private office where I had been when I came early that morning.

Inspector Fougerol closed the door and walked over to his desk.

The Baron stood there, looking very elegant, very calm, very secure. I watched. I knew something was going to happen.

THE DEAL

Inspector Fougerol said, "Monsieur le Baron, will you be seated?"

"Non, merci," said the Baron, now coldly polite and watching everything; trying to look at me and at Inspector Fougerol at the same time. He said, "Inspector, what is this 'affair of delicacy'?"

Inspector Fougerol, the mask of politeness now dropping from his face, said, "Monsieur le Baron, Monsieur Sam Neely had made an interesting statement to us, one, perhaps—" here, a little politeness came back into his voice—"perhaps that you might clarify."

The Baron said nothing, just kept looking at the inspector.

"Well," the inspector continued, "Monsieur Sam Neely said, when he picked up the Danielle Dumont girl to place her on a sort of divan or couch —he swears that at this time the girl was alive, and that she was saying, 'No, no, Baron, no!' "

The Baron went about three shades paler. He looked at me. I gave him back the look. I didn't say anything. I only shook my head No. The Baron turned back to Inspector Fougerol . . . "I am surprised at this statement. I am also surprised that you make this insinuation."

Inspector Fougerol leaned back in his chair and said, much too calmly for my liking, *"Cher monsieur,* we are on a matter of extreme importance—a matter which involves the death of a girl, a matter which must be solved. Every word, every possible situation that could throw light on this terrible thing must be looked into." He gave a minute smile. "I'm sure you understand, Monsieur le Baron."

The Baron looked at him. Then a slow smile started on his face. He said, "You're right, you're absolutely right, Inspector. You must forgive me. This is the first time I have ever been involved in something of this nature." He glanced at me quickly, then back to the inspector. "I had heard, of course, that this girl had been violated, raped; and that this was the cause of her death." Here he looked at me almost in triumph. He continued, "I had heard rumors that Sam Neely, who in truth is not a friend of mine, had made this statement, had said that this girl had mentioned my name. It is for this reason I asked my attorney to come here— unfortunately, he has been detained outside the city. But we will ask for—and I demand now—to be examined by your police physician, your police doctor; this can easily prove beyond a doubt my innocence in this terrible, terrible thing."

I looked at the Baron. Here he was again, the superstar. It was plain what was going to happen. Inspector Fougerol was taken aback. The Baron firmly insisted. I went over and dropped down into a chair. I heard the two of them talking; pretty soon the inspector took the Baron out of the room at the Baron's insistence. The idea was that they were going into the medical examiner's office. I sat there. What would happen now, a moron could have guessed.

After about twenty-five minutes back came Inspector Fougerol with the Baron. The grin, the smirk, the arrogant look firmly in place. Inspector Fougerol was all apology, all delicacy, completely awed by the Baron's absolute friendship. Impressed by the grand way in which the Baron had suggested that he be physically examined. He was not angry; in fact, seemed grateful to prove that he had absolutely nothing to do with the death of Danielle Dumont. And prove it he had indeed. Inspector Fougerol found out, and wrote into his report, "It would have been an impossibility for Monsieur le Baron to have been the cause of the death of the Danielle Dumont girl. Monsieur le Baron is physically inadequate to have caused any such wound or wounds . . . our examination, thus far, indicates he is not involved."

What he did not write, and what I saw later, when Gautrat gave it to me to read, was the vindication of the Baron, based on his physical examination. This left more than a suggestion of guilt on the part of Sam Neely, based on *his* physical examination . . .

After we left the police precinct, with me planning to meet Gautrat that afternoon to help Sam Neely, I was driving, with the Baron sitting quietly beside me looking straight ahead—not saying a word. When we were almost to my house, I said, "Baron, I've got you cold. I know you killed Danielle; maybe you didn't mean to, but she's dead just the same. And hidden in a safety deposit box with one key I've got your false dong with her blood all over it, where you stuck it into her, you rotten lousy bastard." I was shouting now. He never even turned to look at me. "Well, you're for the high jump now. I am going . . . "

"Jarn," he cut in quietly, "I've got an idea—a way out for both of us."

"Christ," I snarled at him, "you think I'll cover this for you? Do you think I'm going to let Sam—"

"No, Jarn," he cut in quietly again. "I think you'll listen. I think we've both got too much to lose. I think you will hear me out."

I shot a quick look at him as I drove up in front of my apartment. I stopped the car and shut off the motor. "Not this time, Baron. Not this time."

He looked at me with a leaden stare and said, "So you are going to break it off in me, huh?"

I looked back at him with whatever kind of a stare I had at the time, "Christ . . . you broke it off in yourself. You've asked for this for so long I don't wonder you are finally surprised to have to pay off."

THE DEAL

He sat there looking at me vaguely, uncomprehendingly. I stared at him, not knowing how this disaster would fall on me now. I remembered back, a thousand years ago, seeing him at Jason Wormser's big studio in Hollywood. The superstar, the "slick star savior" for my many picture plans. He had been grand, gloomy, sullen, arrogant. He had sat upon his throne, a short-sceptered king; a knight wrapped in the unhappy solitude of his own peculiar problem. He had ruled the studio then. At his touch executives crumbled. Stunt men reigned. Suckling actors played the clown to his caprices, his wildest thoughts; his colored and bent whims changed reason to absurdity. He reigned supreme, ready to forsake the friend, deny the favor. The Pharisee's arrogant prayer, "I thank thee, God, that I am not as other men"—and he really wasn't.

So watching him now, sitting there beside me with that calm crazy look in his eyes, waiting for me to guide him, to tell him what to do, to cover up everything again, to put the velvet lid on the trouble that was coming. I looked at him coldly. I had a final horrible idea. Maybe there was a way out of this velvet hell. I said to him, "Baron . . . let's go upstairs and talk."

Slowly the fear started to go out of his face. "Anything you say, Jarn boy."

* * *

We were sitting now in my apartment, looking at each other, the Baron was making me a counterproposition, trying with the charm and the soft sell to convince me of what maybe I wanted to be convinced of, because I wanted to save the Deal. Hell, we had already covered up one murder. Even *Someone* wouldn't put his nose in this one—no, I was screwing myself tightly into hell alone. I knew for certain now that the Baron had pronged little Danielle to death. I also knew that Sam wouldn't have. We sat there just looking at each other.

The Baron opened the act . . . Satan the persuader: "Listen, Jarn, you think I'm just a moron, with no dong and no brains. Well, boy; you're wrong on both points. You're wrong on both counts." He shot me a quick look, to see how I was taking this. I just sat there watching him. He stopped and lit a cigarette, waved the smoke away; then continued conversationally, as if we were talking about the script of the picture. "Listen, Jarn, let's see how bright you are. Now here's the deal. I know you like those. First, I'm not so sure Sam didn't prong her too. But you . . . you always want to think the worst of me. Me, your partner, who's made you money and—"

THE DEAL

"When?" I snarled.

The Baron went calmly on like he hadn't heard me interrupt him. He continued, "Me, who took you out of the artsy-craftsy producer class and made you what you are."

"Yeah," I said. "When did you do all this for me? And even if you did, Baron, you can't cover *this* up. Now I'll—"

"Right, Jarn boy," he cut in, "and right again, I can't shake the whole thing out, then sweep it right under a French rug." He moved his chair a little closer toward me, and continued smoothly, "You remember, Jarn boy, we smoothed that one over on the Riviera, you remember that, don't you —the Editor? So, Jarn, if I go, you go. But Christ," he said excitedly, "now I remember, old chap—I remember, dear boy." A look of cunning came over his face, exaggerated cunning, letting me see him get the thought, *I saw you hit the Editor with a spike.*

The Baron then described the murder of the Editor, exactly as it happened, only he put me in his place, so that in the telling, I, Jarnigan, killed the Editor. The Baron continued, "Sure . . . that's it, I was drunk, I was "horsed." All I remember," he went on vaguely, now full of his act and going on with the scene, "all I seem to dimly recall is you hitting the Editor on the head with the spike—then dropping him overboard, and I . . . the Baron"—here he struck a pose. It was better than any scene he'd ever played in any picture he'd been in. Holding the pose he continued calmly and majestically, "Unhappily . . . I've been in your power ever since. That's why I'm going to pieces, Jarn boy. That's why I'm getting worse and worse. I worry, I hate to cover up a murder. I hate to know that the Editor lies"—here he struck another pose—"in a watery grave, with his head caved in, and your wrist watch in his hand." Then, throwing back his head like John Barrymore he said, "But I stick t'me friends."

I watched this dirty son-of-a-bitch playing out a scene and believing it more and more each time that he continued, getting a little filth idea here, a little more insane and dangerous idea there. Then a look of amazement must have come over my face. I could literally feel my face pale and tighten. A nerve was twanging away in my cheek like a guitar string. The son-of-a-bitch's eyes started becoming glassy. He talked, he talked, he was selling himself. He was conning himself into it. In five minutes, he'd be rockbound convinced that I was the killer. He'd be certain and would swear in any court, that I was the killer of the Editor. This rickety-brained bastard, my partner, was already wild enough to tell it that way. He knew it . . . and I knew it . . . Dear Christ, was this going to be another part of the Deal?

We were seated in my trophy room off the study. On the walls there were mounted heads, some guns, some knives. Specifically, some knives from Guadalcanal that had been hung on the wall with the dates of the capture of certain islands. The knives were made from Japanese bayonets and were razor-sharp. I was sitting there watching him; the Baron got up, walked over to a big chair—a high-backed chair from Spain, made out of a heavy wood, muchly carved. He sat down. Leaned back, half closed his eyes, a contented little smile on his face. He watched me. I must admit he had played a hell of a scene and certainly had convinced himself that so far as he was concerned, I not only was in this thing with him, but a little more conversation with himself, as he'd just had, and he'd be protecting *me,* he'd be hiding and covering up for me. For the moment, the question of the death of Danielle Dumont and of Sam Neely being arrested for the murder of this little girl, didn't bother the Baron at all. He was so full of the fact that, in his own mind, he was certain it was old Jarnigan the Iceman, old Jarn the raper, who had killed the Editor. And here we were, the Baron and Jarnigan, in the middle of a rape, and another death. With the Baron again as innocent as a lamb. He was a big star, set upon by a producer who had him in his power.

As I watched him sitting there, I got up and walked away; started looking around the room as though I had never seen it, trying to figure out what to do. The way I was feeling then, I'd just as soon blow the whistle on the whole Deal. I didn't know how much more of it I could take. I knew this son-of-a-bitch would say anything to stay out of trouble. Just then he quietly said to me, looking every inch the star, "Jarn boy, what are you so upset about? You know that I'll protect you. You know I'm your best friend, as I've told you many times." And here he said, with a self-righteousness that was terrifying, "I know you're my best friend. You're the best friend I have in the world. I trust you, Jarn, I trust you. That certainly shows why I'm ready to do anything for *us* . . . partner. Now I know maybe you're a little mixed up, Jarn," he continued, as though talking absolutely to himself, "I know you've been under a terrible strain, so from now on I'm really going to be a partner. I know that I've made some unreasonable demands, but I thought, as always, you'd be able to handle it. Hell, you're Jarn the Iceman, you're old Jarn the fixer. I didn't think there was anything that could bother you. But now that you've got this problem . . ."

Here I gave him a quick look of hatred. All of a sudden it wasn't even the Baron's problem anymore! He had just said, *But now that you've got this problem.* To me, Jarnigan. I looked at the Baron. He saw the hatred in my eyes, and he recoiled.

THE DEAL

It brought him back to some semblance of sanity, because he said, "Jarn, we have to cover this up. We have to work on it so that Sam Neely—" Here he got another idea. The Baron was full of ideas, but nothing could alter the fact that he had killed that child with his plastic bat, and now was trying to get me to frame my best friend who had now been arrested for the murder. This was now "the Deal" that the Baron wanted to continue with. Wanted me to sort out and arrange for him. When I didn't react fast enough, he said, "Y'know, Jarn, I'm scared. I'm afraid I'd better go to confession." Here he laughed. "Or maybe," he continued, "go to the préfet of police, because I don't know if I'm doing the right thing. Perhaps I shouldn't continue to hide my partner's guilt, because then I share that guilt equally." Here he sighed heavily, "It is a burden, dear boy. Yes, perhaps that's what I should do. Though it would grieve me. It would make me very sad. But perhaps it's my duty." Here he put a look of stern diligence on his face and said, "Yes, I should do it."

He started to rise from his chair, smiling to himself, and that broke it. That tore it. Way back in the far-off corridors of my mind, something snapped. I shoved him back in the chair. I literally sprang over to the wall and tore off one of the razor-sharp knives. *By Christ, I'll kill him, I'll kill him now* screamed through my mind. Then it will be all over. The clank-clanking of my brain, boiling like steam over a vat, like pulling a cat through a sewer pipe and strangling him. I was back very quick. I put the knife against his throat. I pressed the knife against him. I had him by the throat. Snarling, hissing at him, I said, "Oh, you filth. Oh, you motherfucker. Oh, you impotent whore. I've had it. Now you've got it." I pressed the knife more firmly. An ounce of pressure more, a hair's pressure more, and that would do it.

"Jarn, Jarn," he said quietly, and that brought me back to reason. If the Baron had yelled or cursed, if he'd pleaded, I'd have slit his throat like you cut a melon, and he knew it. And what was worse, I knew it. "Jarn," he continued quietly, "there's a way out of all of this. First, we are partners and then, you're my best friend. I can never forget that." Then continuing still more quietly, "Or let you forget that." Here he touched the knife. "If you want to pull that knife across, this is what you must do." And very gently, he reached up his hand, placed it firmly around my wrist, and said . . . repeating himself, "If you want to pull the knife across, pull it across like this." Suddenly he yanked my arm, and if I hadn't jerked the knife away, he'd have made me cut his throat from ear to ear.

He laughed out loud in pleasure. "Jarn boy." And then went off in another spasm of laughter. Strange laughter. "Dear old Jarn," he said.

463

Then more quietly to himself. "The waste, what a waste. You know," he said quietly, looking up at me thoughtfully, "if you'd really do it, you'd be doing me a favor." Then, almost sadly, "You won't do it though. You won't do it, Jarn." He sighed again. "So, instead, would you fix us a drink?' He grinned suddenly and laughed. "And let's 'partner' our way out of this . . . partner." He laughed boyishly. "You know, Jarn," he whispered, "we *can* do it." Then daintily, with one finger, he pushed delicately at the blade, gently moving it away from his throat.

I held it firm at first, but a little away from him, then I dropped my arm and walked over to the table and laid it carefully down next to a book.

He looked at me with a grin. Then, in his friendly "voice to charm the dead," he said, "Jarn, here's the way out for you first; and then me second." Then he had another thought, and added, "And here is a way out for old Sam.

"Now, here's what we do. First, my suggestion is, I'll sign you a letter of confession, or," he continued more firmly, "or we go together. Now, I *want* to sign this letter. It gives me a kick. You know, it's kind of like 'coming.' Now, second, we go get your money—your bloody money, that you would go, and are going, to hell for as fast as you can." He continued casually: "In a lot of ways, Jarn boy, I truly think you're worse than I am. Nonetheless—since you know that word," he added—"thirdly, I'll get Sam the best criminal lawyer. I'll pay the lawyer's fee and we can get him off. I'll pay, Jarn. It's that or—" Here he got up, he walked quietly over to the table, he picked up the knife, he turned around and came back over and sat down in the chair.

Very slowly, he reached down, he picked up my arm, then reached for my hand, he pulled it over and put the knife in my hand, closing the fingers around it tightly; then, with the other hand he raised my hand with the knife firmly in place and pressed it gently against his throat. Then, turning his head so he could see me, smiled at me and said quietly, "Now you pull that—and that's one way—or we pull together and we all get off. And that's the other way." He continued pleasantly, "The last way, you're free and you're a rich man." He smiled to himself. "A rich man. A little more tarnished, but nonetheless, rich."

He turned and looked me full in the face. "Now, Iceman, it's up to you. Let's see who's got the guts. Let's see who's the real faker, who's the real man." He looked around the room for a moment, strangely. A little disturbed, a little annoyed. Perhaps like he wasn't quite sure what he was doing there. Then he shook his head, opened his eyes very wide for a second, looked up at me again and said nicely, "Y'see, Jarn"—here he gave me the sincere smile, the honest look that he got when I knew for sure he was leveling. He continued quietly, "Y'see, Jarn, I truly don't care, one way or the other." And he didn't.

After awhile I walked back over to the table, and again put down the knife. I opened a drawer and got out some paper and a pen and said quietly, "All right, Baron, here. Now you write this." He grinned at me. "Don't be dictatorial, Jarn boy. I know exactly what to write. Then, if you wish, you may edit, rewrite, as you always do, and I'll sign it. Done?" Here our eyes met for a long moment. My eyes dropped first and I said, looking at the floor, "Yeah, yeah, Baron, I'm done. Go ahead and write."

He turned in the chair, put the paper on a table, adjusted the pen, said quietly, "Anything you say, Jarn boy." Here he grinned again and, whistling gently under his breath, began writing—slowly, correctly—and the pact was made. We were both doomed.

I walked over to the liquor cabinet, got out a glass of brandy, poured myself one, poured him a big one, took it over to him. He never touched it. I walked back over in front of the fireplace, I reached up on the mantel, got myself a cigar. I bit the end off, lit it. Stood there, quietly looking at the Baron, watching him and thinking. He was writing easily, as unconcerned as though he were writing a letter to a girl friend. I thought, Why shoot him down.

You see; I didn't want to tell the Baron *I didn't kill him just because I didn't know how to clean it up afterward.* The evil thoughts breathed—the words burned: Go ahead . . . do it . . . what have you got to lose? (Only my life.) Only that? Well, then . . . you're giving up nothing . . . so why not proceed?

But if I could have sorted out the beads and strung them—well . . . But a good producer can't kill his star. He can't do anything like that. He always needs the second sooner, the inch farther, the contract signed—and ours was.

The Baron kept on writing. I kept on watching him, wondering how long it would take me to go the rest of the way into hell . . . I found out shortly.

• • •

The next day I went back to see Sam Neely. By now, he was in "murderers' row," the block of condemned cells; but he wasn't in the "sick cells" that they keep for the ones who are to be executed. He wasn't there yet.

Sam didn't seem as glad to see me as I thought he would be; perhaps he suspected what I knew, which would be reason enough.

I said, "Hi, boy." He looked at me grayly. I continued, "I've hired you the best lawyer that there is in Paris. I got you Maître Gautrat. You know he's the best. He's got a fifty-grand fee, just as a retainer. I don't know what the rest will cost."

Sam looked at me for a minute like he wasn't too sure what I had said. He looked away as though he were embarrassed. Then he talked away toward the window, which was so high up you couldn't see out. The bars were placed close together. It was only to let the air in. Like a wound.

Sam said: "The Baron was here. He paid me a visit. He told me that *he* gave Maître Gautrat fifty grand as a retainer for me. He told me he wanted to see me out of this. I thanked him. I didn't tell him what I am telling you." Here Sam turned and looked me straight in the eye. "We both know the Baron, Jarn. I want to know why all of a sudden this son-of-a-bitch put up fifty grand for me. He wouldn't give me the right time when we were working on the picture." His voice lowered. "Why, Jarn, why? You got the answer? Why is the Baron so big-hearted? He don't lay out for anybody."

I looked at Sam and then I looked around the cell. It was built for four convicts, and there was only Sam in this one. I walked over and sat down on one of the bunks. I looked at Sam quietly for a minute. I saw he was perspiring, yet the cell was almost cold. "Well, Sam, I'm trying to help you. Baron keeps telling me a thing that kind of bothers——"

Sam had been looking at me hard. Now he cut in: "Jarn, you're not the Iceman now. You're talking funny. Why? It's not like you to talk funny."

I looked at him coolly. "Well, I'll tell you what's not like *you*," I said. "It's not like you to tell me how I am." I walked across the cell, turned back, and said quickly. "Sam, you got the best lawyer in Paris, and I'm going to see that everything is all right. Will you just take it easy?"

Sam looked at me for a minute as though he didn't know me. He turned and walked over to the other tier of two bunks. He sat down and started to put his head in his hands, thought better of it, and calmly looked up at me. "I don't know what you're doing, Jarn," he said quietly. "You know I'm with you like I'm *always* with you. Nobody loves you better than me, except old Mo—and he's gone. But you gotta let me in on the inside. I gotta know why I'm here and why you're keeping me here. There's something going on. That slick son-of-a-bitch Baron would of never come down here, talking big, unless there was something." Here he stopped. He started to get up and then glanced at me for a moment, put his head down in his hands and said quietly, "Jarn, you're not table-topping, boy. You're not leveling with me. I don't mind staying here. I don't mind doing anything for you that's needful to be done—but I gotta know *why*, Jarn."

THE DEAL

Here he looked up at me, and for the first time I saw tears in Sam Neely's eyes. I'd known him all my life and I'd never seen him like this. It was a plea. It was a crying-out from inside for me not to shatter what he thought of me. "Jarn, listen," Sam said, trying to keep his voice level, "What's the problem, Jarn boy? You and me can talk it out. Nobody here but you and me. You know what we always said. There's just us . . . now that old Mo's gone."

Sam kept on talking quietly about my brother, who I knew was gone for good. The thing I was doing to Sam was dragging on me, down deep where it hurt, like I was hurting my brother again. I resorted to the thing that a guy resorts to when he knows he's doing something flat-out wrong. I said, with a calmness I didn't feel, "Listen, Sam, you got to stay here for a while. I'm trying to square everything so's to get you out for good. There are some people who think you're not too clean in this."

He started as if he'd been whipped. "Who . . . people . . . what people?"

"What do you care, as long as I ain't one of them," I snapped at him. "Now, it's going to take some dough and some time. If the Baron saw fit to tell you that he cracked for the fifty, that's all right by me. You know we got to do a lot of things to keep this guy in line. I just didn't figure on so much tro—"

He cut in on me. "I know, Jarn, I know. But just let me in on what we have to do. I don't like sittin' in here. I been in jail for little stuff—you know, knockin' some guy on the keist. But nothin' like this. I don't mind being in jail for fluff stuff—fights and all—maybe sticking a guy a little if he gets to cuttin' up on you. But this thing I don't like. I don't like it one little bit. I wouldn't have hurt that little girl for nothing. I liked her."

I looked at him closely, "That's what the Baron said." I waited a moment, then continued, "Sam, listen. You got to do what Gautrat tells you. I'm talking to him every day. You're going to be sprung, and for good. Now, you take it easy. I've got to leave and I won't be back for four or five days—I've got to take a little trip—but I'll take care of everything like always."

Here Sam looked at me as though he knew what was going on. I couldn't say much more to him because I was angry—with myself; and with him, for being so close to the truth. In fact, not close . . . right on the button. Old Sam knew me and I knew him. I hated what I had to do. I said, "Sam, I'll be talking to you in a couple or three days."

He tried to grin and couldn't. He said quietly, "Jarn, I'll be here, boy. I'll be here." He turned around and walked into the corner of the cell; he never said another word.

467

THE DEAL

I called to the guard, rapped on the bars and said, *"Venez, je suis prêt, ouvrez la porte."* The guard came over, and he opened the door. I said, "Sam, I'll see you very soon." He just waved his hand. He never turned around, never said a word. I left.

Sam stayed in "murderers' row" at the Prison de Santé, Rue Jean Dolent, awaiting my return. He was bewildered, frightened. He knew, and I knew, he was innocent; only he didn't know that I knew. He just figured I hadn't been trying to help him as much as he thought I would. Man . . . he didn't know. And I didn't know what was happening while I was flying to Switzerland. Fate took it here. Fate played it badly.

• • •

It was in the prison of the Santé and the guards were going down the corridor, walking toward that group of "sick cells" in which are kept only the men who are going to die . . . who have been condemned to be guillotined. It was six o'clock in the morning. The guards looked sleepy and didn't like their work. When they were thirty yards from the small door that leads into the group of three cells holding the three men who waited, or who slept, or who dreamed, the guards quietly removed their shoes and laid them in a pile in the hall, then tiptoed softly toward the small door where the guard who was in the lead—and who had a stomach-ache every time he was in the lead to open this door—quietly put the key in the lock, turned it, and with a rush the three guards entered the cell.

The three men who were waiting were on their beds. One was sitting up and acted as though he could not see, the second was moaning in his sleep, and the other was quiet. This was Sam Neely. They took the first man, the one sitting up. He began to protest—he screamed. The man who was sleeping turned over and sat up. There were two guards on each side of the man who was to leave the cell. He knew what had to happen. He started to moan—his knees sagged and he lost control of his sphincter muscles and the guards let him drop. They were disgusted, and the guard who had been sick to his stomach turned—walked out into the corridor and said, "Bring him along . . ."

Sam Neely wasn't going to be executed—yet. But in order to get a confession, he had been put in with the condemned men who were actually awaiting death. Sam was only waiting to be *tried* for murder . . . either life imprisonment or death. He didn't understand, he didn't care either way. Jarn had dropped him. Jarn wasn't sure of Sam, or he'd have done more

468

and wouldn't have let Sam stay there without some word . . . some vote of confidence.

An hour from the door-opening for the condemned convict, it was all over. It isn't too important now to explain what happened. But then, moving down the corridor, his heels ringing briskly as he walked, came the priest. He was admitted to the small cell wherein sat the two men, Sam and the Moaner—the other having left, never to return. After a word with the man who was still moaning, but a more contented moan, as if he had delayed something for a while—like when you feel like vomiting you are able to delay it and have a less bad time, which makes you feel easier—the priest walked over to Sam, who had been quiet, and said to him, "You know the . . . the time is short, relieve your soul and confess. Although I am not allowed to insist, I urge you very strongly . . . relieve your soul."

Under the light from the top of the cell, perspiration stood out among the few remaining hairs on top of the priest's head. Sam looked at him and found that if he squinted his eyes a little, the head looked gray. The father continued, "Don't go to God with this on your soul . . . it's never too late." He waited for an answer but nothing came, and he said, "Don't meet God in this fashion. You must approach God slowly and reverently with clean hands and a pure heart."

Sam's lips moved. He opened his mouth, started to speak . . . but no sound came.

The father leaned toward him and said, "Yes, Sam . . . tell me!"

The faintest trace of a smile started to change Sam's mouth. It was a good strong mouth, and as the smile slowly started, the muscles which had been so tense began to relax and he said, "If I have to step off, I will know for sure, what really you're not sure of, because if what you say is true, I will see God. But I don't think I will see Him because if there is a God, this wouldn't happen to me. I am innocent. I didn't kill that girl, and if the God that you pray to—who you aren't sure of, and who I could meet before you do—is really there, He knows it. So He can't be much of a God if He is there and if He lets me take it."

The priest leaned back . . . a shocked look was on his face, but his voice was calm. He said, "I understand your feelings, but you will be forgiven. Even at this moment I am sure you are forgiven." Sam said tiredly, "Man, you still keep it up. I wish I could just let you know after it's all over, to see your face and to tell you what a mistake you and God made." Sam turned his face to the wall, saying, "If you want to help me, get Jarnigan to come down here." The father tried to talk again, decided not to, and walked out.

THE DEAL

Later that afternoon, other feet came down the hall. They stopped outside the door—the guard was motioning to the woman who was Sam's mistress. She had tried, but she couldn't convince the priest. She said very little. She had waited for Sam and resented all this. She was a devout and overprayerful Catholic in her silence. Soon a guard came and led Sam through the maze of bars and corridors and there they were, face to face, old Sam and his mistress—they looked good and friendly together. They looked like they belonged together, and the woman spoke to Sam as if she were a young girl.

"Darling, I talked to the father . . . now I believe you, I believe you, but you can tell me anything. I love you, but this makes me hurt in my stomach—not hurt in my heart, because my heart doesn't feel anything—it's dying and will be dead if they finally do this to you. But please tell me. I'll help you, and what helps you will help me. The father said it will be a mortal sin if you don't tell, because if you do, then you will be saved and we'll be together again."

Sam looked at the woman. His eyes studied every feature of the face. The nose that was a little too large, the eyes lovely but maybe a little too close together, the lips with just a trace of lipstick which didn't follow the line. He remembered she always tried to make her mouth look a little bigger. In spite of himself, he tried to act like everything was okay, kid her out of it, but nothing worked. None of the senses worked. It was as if he were enveloped in smoke which had deadened everything. Smoke without a smell, without a taste, that dulled his brain; so he just listened to her talk. He looked at her and said gruffly, "Do you think I killed her?"

She answered grimly, "I hope not, but if you did you must tell."

He said, "I tell you I didn't. Look in my eyes and tell me—do you think I killed her?"

She looked in his eyes. The look held. The minutes tiptoed by. There wasn't a sound. Then she said, "The father said I must make you tell."

Sam looked at her. His big old head started moving slowly from side to side in a negative reply. He turned and without a word left the screen which was in front of the bars, which were in front of other bars, and walked back to the guard. He stood there quietly, like an animal who is waiting to be led to the left or to the right, or to be told to wait. The guard led Sam off. The woman held on to the bars, watching him go. It was quiet in the cell-block.

48

This was what was happening while the Baron, his attorney, "15," and I were on our way to Switzerland. The Baron and I were making a simple exchange of values. His life, against finishing the picture and giving me all the money owed . . . In exchange, I'd give him his "confession" letter, plus the key and a signed safety deposit signature card so he could get his false dong from the Chase Bank in Paris.

When the plane got over Geneva, the fog was thick. We were unable to land on time. We circled around and thought we might have to go clear to Montreux; but the fog started to clear; finally we were able to land at the airport in Geneva. Of course, we were too late to get to the bank. A limousine met us at the airport, so the Baron and I (with the Baron's entourage), Mlle. Quinze ("15"), and the Baron's American attorney, all went to the Palace Hotel in Geneva. We checked in. The Baron and his entourage took a large suite. I took another one, farther down the hall. We were to meet the following morning to go to the bank.

The Baron wanted to "talk it over some more"—he still would have liked for us to continue as partners. He still insisted soberly that I was the best friend he ever had. Again I thought, if I had been his best friend—God help him. The Baron's lawyer said a few things and anger began to work its way into the conversation. I didn't want the excitement that seemed to be brewing cause this settlement to be talked to death, so that a disaster could happen. Anger hung in the great hall like smoke. Again a layer of steam on a boiling vat. I tried to speak quietly, although now I didn't have to; yet I wanted to keep the lid on this discussion. Suddenly, the Baron straightened up, looked me straight in the eye. "All right, Jarn," he said, his face very pale. "All right, nine in the morning."

As we separated in the big corridor, the Baron called back, "Well, Jarn. We just missed it. You're not nervous, are you, boy?" he grinned.

"No, Baron, I'm not nervous. Just a little tired," I said, looking at him calmly.

"I'm tired too," he said. And in fact he looked it. His nose was like a barometer so far as I was concerned, and anytime it got that waxy look, I knew he was either in for a bad one, or had already started one.

He waved airily and said, "Be pure, Jarn," and walked down the huge

471

THE DEAL

corridor with his arm around "15," toward the entrance of their suite. His attorney followed at a respectful distance.

I went down to my suite. The boy already had brought up the bags. I rang for the valet and asked that a fire be built in the fireplace. Pretty soon, with the fire going, and after a brandy, I was standing in front of the fireplace smoking a cigar. I decided I'd better call Paris. I put in the call, and after about a twenty-minute wait, I got hold of Maître Gautrat.

He came on with the operator: "Hello . . . yes, the connection is quite clear . . . I would be grateful, operator"—Gautrat's voice came over the wire, very faint. We started talking. He sounded like he was in Willcox, Arizona.

Finally, he said, *"Oui, Jarnigan, ton ami, ça va. Tout va bien."*

"You mean, Sam's all right, then?"

"Didn't I just say so?" Gautrat complained. "You speak French."

"I know, *maître.* I know, but I'm tired." We talked for a while, then hung up.

After knowing that everything was as under control as it could be in Paris, I walked over and sat down in the chair in front of the fire and started to make plans for the bank the next morning. I knew that the Baron and I should be there early so we could finish our business. Then I wanted to take the plane immediately back to Paris.

Sitting in front of the fire, smoking a cigar, I wanted something to read. I looked for a Bible. There wasn't one. It's the only great book you can return to weeks or months or years later in your life and in all your life not be sadly disappointed, even if you yourself have changed. You are not the same—boy, young man, or man—at the moment of truth, of course; in that book the truth is there, always . . . in other books, seldom—in fact, rarely.

In other books, the wonderful parts you remember are remembered because you rewrote them to suit your age, your time, yourself. Later, you bemoaned their loss in the book you thought you'd read.

But I found a book—it was *The Letters of André Gide*—some were interesting, some were full of the brilliance that Gide once had, some were downright dull and bitter and sounded like an old woman complaining because she is out of it forever—all dried up, the juices gone, waiting, but still a clanking wind, thinking, reliving things emptily, alone . . .

It must have been around one a.m. when suddenly there was a loud pounding at the door. I went over and opened it. It was "15." She was crying and crazy with fear.

472

THE DEAL

"Jarn, Jarn," she wailed. She had nothing on but a thin little robe. She was barefoot.

"What's the matter?"

"Oh, Jarn, come quickly! Come! Something's happened!"

She turned and ran back down the hall in the direction of the Baron's suite. I followed.

When we walked into the suite, the Baron's American attorney was there, his usual poise badly shaken. He was hysterical, trying to remain calm. I looked over and was shocked to see the Baron half lying, half sitting on the floor. He was leaning against the divan. There was a perplexed look on his face, which was waxy white, and shiny from perspiration. He didn't look up as I entered—he seemed to be trying to work out a problem, and not doing too well at it.

I walked over quickly and knelt down by him. He didn't recognize me. He didn't say anything. It looked to me like he was in a state of shock.

I spun around and said to the attorney, "Have you called the house doctor?"

The lawyer and "15" both started babbling at once. "15" came toward me and was pulling at my shoulder; completely ignoring the fact that her robe was wide open. She was as naked as September Morn, but not a bit coy. She was scared, and with good reason. I said, "Well—did you for Christ's sake call the doctor?"

"Oh, no, Jarn, no," she wailed. "You see . . . I mean, what will I do? He's never even . . . oh, Jarn . . . help me, help me!"

I whirled around and slapped her sharply to bring her out of it. "Now you sit down and shut up," I snarled. "Or go over and wiggle your ass in front of his face like you've always done; if he ain't dead, he should perk up. Or what's left of him should perk up."

"Oh, Jarn," she wailed, and fell into a chair.

The attorney sat on the other side of the room, crouched down in his chair. He looked like he was going to jump.

"Now listen, you legal prick," I snapped. "You get a doctor *now*! And I *mean* now! Out! Go get one! The concierge will help; but you take the car to the Geneva Hospital and bring the doctor back. I'm going to call emergency by phone. Now get going!" He looked at me fearfully. I took a step toward him—he fled for the door.

I crossed over to the phone and got the operator. *"Ecoute,* operator, there is an emergency here. A heart attack. Call the Geneva Hospital at once and get the best physician or doctor. It's the Baron."

I waited and heard a cackling over the phone as she passed this on.

473

"... *Oui, madame.* Baron. *La Vedette.* Big Star. He's had an attack. He may be dying. This is an emergency call ..."

With that call, and with the attorney gone for help, it was all I could do. I went over to the Baron, who hadn't moved. I leaned down to him.

"Baron," I said.

He blinked his eyes.

"Baron! Can you hear me?"

He never moved.

"Oh," wailed "15," "oh, Jarn! Is he ...?"

I shot a look at her. She shut up, as though a hand had been clapped over her mouth.

I went around the Baron. Pulled over a low chair. Sat down close to him and tried to prop him up. He leaned back and for the first time he seemed to focus a little better.

"Baron, can you hear me?"

He took a gasp-breath; then hoarsely said, "Yougoterall ... all goterall ... I am ... and you bastar ... don't, can't ..."

"Baron, listen!" I said.

He started to turn his head slowly from side to side. Right—left—twitch. Right—left—twitch. Still trying to say "Go to hell."

I was breathing hard. The back of my neck was wet. I had already sweated through my shirt even though the room was cold. *I couldn't let this man die!* I had to keep talking to him. I started to speak to him quietly—anything to keep him alert. I had to keep a contact with him. I had to keep him interested. Christ, I had to keep him *alive! I had to!*

"Listen, Baron ... Baron, can you hear me?"

He kept up the turning of the head and the twitch movement. But it didn't seem to me that it was quite so bad now. I jumped up, ran across the room, grabbed an opened bottle of brandy, came back, and put the bottle up to his mouth. He never moved. He never knew that I had a bottle of brandy close to his lips. You see, the Baron had never achieved the stern task of living. And perhaps now he never would. He had been over and under the ropes; winning most of the time; sliding through life on a greased chute; the poor brandy-bruised face a ruin; the eyes peering unseeingly out at the world through the oyster-phlegm haze of his life. But perhaps now, as his soul coughed away the phlegm and the haze, he was seeing more clearly than he ever would again. He coughed ... harshly ...

"That you, Jarn?"—this quietly, hoarsely. He shook his head slowly, I put the bottle down. I looked closely at him. His eyes were now like the eyes of a sleepy cat, a dry mind thinking things out drily. Then his eyes seemed to start to glaze a little—go out of focus—I had to keep him alert. So I picked up the bottle and pushed it firmly against his lips, and poured. And, by reflex, he opened his mouth and I got a good charge of the brandy down him. He gagged and said again, "Goterell." And, then swallowed. But after a few minutes—me watching him closely—his head started to slow down, it almost stopped the turning and the twitching. A little color came back into his face. I turned my head and said, "Listen, kid. Listen, Quinze . . . Get that operator and tell her to call again, to get that doctor over here right away!"

"Oh, Jarn," she sobbed, "is he going to die?"

"Not if I can hold on to him, he ain't. Now dammit, call that operator for the doctor!"

She came over and stood looking down with a scared little face at the Baron. The little tearstained face. The robe completely open. The little fifteen-year-old breasts pert and beautiful. The little belly—flat. And the other—there, all there. No health cure, but the Baron didn't notice. He had been in, and around, and seen every part of her. Maybe the Baron had even loved her in his way. She had lasted longer than most. But now he looked at everything—at nothing.

"Listen, Quinze," I said. "Call that doctor, then get some clothes on. I'm not going to tell you again."

I started to get up. She stumbled backward and ran from the room. And soon I heard her babbling into the phone. I looked back from the doorway through which Quinze's voice echoed; glanced down at the Baron. I was shocked to see that he was looking directly at me . . . a strange look. Intent. Calculating. Deadly. His color was almost normal. He winked at me.

"Jarn," he said quietly.

"Yeah?"

"Sit down, Jarn." This softly, for the Baron. But at least he was coherent.

I pulled a stool over next to him and sat down. Just as he drew himself together and started to speak, there was a rapid knocking at the door. I jumped up and went over to the door, where I let in the attorney, a doctor, and a male nurse carrying a lot of equipment. The doctor, full of importance, walked slowly over and stood looking down at the Baron. "Doctor," I said, "will you please examine him at once." The doctor, fully aware of the dignity of his profession, gave me the proper stern, reproving glance, cleared his throat and went into slow-motion action.

After a brief examination, the doctor said to me, quietly—with his stethoscope still in one ear—"Any slight exertion will kill him as though he'd been shot—he can't be moved."

Then he stepped to the phone to get the ambulance crew, oxygen tent, stretcher; prepared a syringe of adrenaline still talking on the phone. The male nurse hurried out.

I went back. The Baron was still half lying, half sitting quietly on the floor. He had answered questions Yes or No by nodding; and he had understood what the doctor said. Any movement, any excitement, could send him over . . .

Quinze, the doctor, and the attorney were now in the other room with the door closed (for quiet for the Baron). The Baron and I were alone; I had stayed with him. He gave a feeble smile. "That's right, kid. That's right, Jarn boy. Stay with me . . ."

Then the Baron started to talk, slowly, quietly, about everything—about the Deal. About the murder of the Editor; the death of my brother; the rape-murder of Danielle; Sam Neely in the death house. The Baron finished, saying, "All this. All this, Jarn, and you still want the Deal. You still want the dollars in that bank. Then you'd be all set, and we're all square. Is that right, Jarn? Then you'd go your way, Jarn boy—and I'd go mine?" Then, more quietly, "Well, you know, partner—" Then he gasped, "Get . . . me . . . some . . . brandy!"

Brandy! I got up, quickly went to the sideboard, got another bottle—and had trouble with the cork. I heard—sensed—a movement behind me. I spun around. There was the Baron, standing there shakily, both arms outstretched as though he was reaching out to choke me. He stared at me for a moment. I dropped the bottle in surprise. He looked down at the bottle and back up at me, shook his head slowly, and said "Hell." Then fell forward.

I caught him. He laughed softly, "No money, Jarn. No bank. No Deal. Now, Jarn, what I want . . . what I want . . . I want, you son-of-a—" He waved his arms like a windmill, his body twisted to the side as though caught in a wave of big surf. It took him a week to fall . . . with me steadying him . . . with me pleading and yelling for the doctor . . . saying to the Baron, "You can't die! You can't die, you bastard! You got up—you did that on purpose! Oh, you mother—" I was half insane.

He grinned and said, whispering hoarsely, "Lousy picture . . . Lousy partner. Lousy Deal. Whole world lousy. Damn lou . . . I . . . I . . ."

I didn't care, I couldn't see too well; I didn't know if I was crying. I knew the son-of-a-bitch was dying, was going out. His eyes, not completely alert, were staring at me fixedly. I truly don't think he cared . . . I think this was the way he had wanted to play it.

The Baron was speaking, quietly: "Jarn, I didn't mean to hurt that little girl. Christ knows I didn't mean to kill her . . ."

THE DEAL

I was kneeling beside him . . . "Oh, you bastard," I said, still crying. "Don't think you're cleaning everything up because you're maybe going out: *Sorry* don't cut it! *I didn't mean to* don't cut it . . . You bastard, you've fucked up all our lives—and your dying now only fucks it up more! Hold your strength, save your lousy heart—Christ knows what a son-of-a-bitch you are!"

"*Stop* that!" *Someone* thundered. "Jarn, you knock it off. I mean right now," *Someone* said, dangerously quiet now. "This man is dying. And you're right—Christ knows him. He knows you—and you're alike. The only difference is, you haven't *literally* killed anyone yet. Now you help him!"

"Help him!" I cried.

"*Help* him!" *Someone* commanded firmly, "and help him now!"

I looked at the Baron's face closely through the mist of the anger tears.

He felt my look; he tried to speak. All that came out was, "Jarn . . Jarn boy. Now what I'd like . . ." *And out he went* . . .

But I was talking to him, "Listen, kid—listen, Baron. I got the word—I was part wrong. Listen, Baron. Listen, you son-of-a-bitch . . ." (I can cuss him—he ain't here) . . . the hell he isn't . . .

"Baron, man, just suck in your belly and take a breath." (Here, getting up on my knees.) "All right, man, I'll do you a new Deal. Just stop fucking the dog. Stick around—at least, wait and hear me out . . . I'll go back with you and we'll try and square it. Hell, man, you're sick . . . (and how) . . . maybe Gautrat can get you . . . get us off . . ."

Death was a hair's breadth behind his eyes. It peeked out slyly, warily, as if looking for, or sizing up, the rest of us.

I wiped my eyes and looked at him. The now-dead eyes . . . half open . . . stared incuriously at everything . . . at nothing. The way he lay there, he was so flat you expected blood to start leaking out from under him. He couldn't just lie there like that and be dead. Too much had happened. He had caused too much trouble. Like I said, "You can't leave yet . . . it's not finished."

"It's not finished . . . oh, you lousy bastard . . . at least, let me keep fighting you to finish this Deal . . . if you are dead and finished, it's done. *Oh, you bastard* . . ."

I was the only fighter left in the ring. I was locked in the empty office of the world all night. Now I'll call and call for help, and no help will come. No evil friend to open the lock; no golden key to call upon, so I rang the bell at the doorstep of the world. There was no one home. The earth had died from a lack of warmth . . . The Baron was dead.

477

THE DEAL

It was true . . . he was really dead. That made the Editor, my brother, little Danielle, and now the Baron . . .

You try and hear a breath—to soak up the last traces of a man's life with a sponge. I sat down on the floor next to the Baron.

"Well, you did it," I said, talking to the dead face that was getting deader by the minute. "You really fucked the dog for good with this trick. I knew you were a foxy bastard, could think up more ways to not finish this picture—but now you've really frigged it up for good."

The mask of death was beginning to set his face into hard, sunken ridges. He looked older, shrunken, and somehow smaller. Yet his face had a dignity it had never had in life. I sat there, studying him. Well, I'd get Sam off. All easy now—old Sam was safe.

I got up slowly and walked over to the other door. I opened it and called the doctor and the attorney. I said, "He's all yours. Hang it on the wrench." I walked out, and down the hall to my rooms.

49

How much loyalty can a dead man use? Did I owe him anything? Yeah. There was one thing. I'd have to think about it. After I'd used it to get Sam Neely off, maybe I'd just put the false dong in the Baron's coffin. There would be a lot he could use it on, where he was going.

I had called the airport; the plane would be ready on an hour's notice. I was numb, I couldn't quite grasp it yet. The rubber bell was tolling—no gong. No noise. Everything unreal. I went over and looked out the window.

There was the lovely view of the mountain overlooking the water. The lake of Geneva was quiet—as motionless as a sleeping cat.

I thought of the Princess and I thought of Danielle. I thought of the times that I could have been a better man. I could've said, "And let you cry—quiet and lonely—no sighs, no remembrances of things past." There is nothing to come; in every sense of the word. There is always a way to blunt the needle if you like blunt things, and blunt rhymes with the Other—and you certainly like those. You know plenty. There are more in your head— an abundance, an overwhelming amount of *"les cons."*

Someone said, "One of these days, Jarn . . . but you're sure a problem, son." I heard a sigh. I'd left the window opened. I looked out. It was cold. Far below, on the mountain road, the little cars shivered by, their headlights pushing each other across the face of night. The world sneezed. God bless you.

Now that he was dead, I thought back on the Deal. Of the times I had looked at the Baron as though he were a pitiful thing, a trapped fly with one wing under a glass cover. In the neat and nasty way he had sometimes slipped through his life, he had had the faculty of disturbing you, of making you embarrassed, uneasy—like a retarded child or a malformed and wounded dog. A man who was mad with the rabies of sex; with a misguided ambition, chasing after himself, searching for his dong, and frothing at the mouth. Man the animal, his tail cut off, all donged-up and no place to go. (Well, he has a place to go now.) So the Baron, with his false dinker, screwed himself tightly and directly into hell.

And the Deal ended up a clamor of eunuchs and ghouls of fagolas and fools; all were fruity bats, hovering over horse apples. And I was the worst of all. Maybe that was why I was standing there crying . . . quietly . . . no sound—no anything.

● ● ●

I was finished now with everyone, and everything . . . except strongbox 10976. Man, how I hated to give up that.

I sat in a little Geneva park waiting until nine a.m. and wondering if the trust company would possibly break, suspend, or at least bend their rules. But I knew they wouldn't.

When I finally walked into the manager's office, I had the impression that the little guy knew my story, and had heard it too many times before. The sanctity of his eventual turndown gave me a religious chill, as if I had been excommunicated.

"I guess this is fitting," I told him. "I guess this is the way it has to be . . . We should maybe take communion—partake of the eucharistic body of the strongbox. Of box 10976, which can't be entered into."

Here the little manager blushed back and forth and said, "But Monsieur Jarnigan, I implore you, I pray you, do not cause a disturbance. You seem to be distraught."

"Well, hell, having over eight hundred thousand dollars in that box, knowing that it's yours and not being able to get in there and get it, has a tendency to make a fellow a little nervous—you know how it is." I said this, of course, in English, and his English wasn't perfect. He got the gist of it, however, and continued in French:

"But all was explained carefully when the arrangement was made. Only with both keys can we get in the box. No waivers, verbal orders—only you and Monsieur le Baron together can get in the box." (Well, there it was.) "When can Monsieur le Baron meet you here for the opening?" the little manager asked.

I looked at him quietly for a moment. "The Baron will be late—very late. Oh, we'll meet again. We are both screwing in the same direction."

"You mean going," interrupted the little Swiss banker.

"Yes, you are right. I mean, we are *going* in the same direction." I left the vault. Then, walking out of the offices of the safety-deposit section of the bank—"I hope to see you and Monsieur le Baron together soon; we await your orders," the little banker called after me. I nodded and waved good-bye. I went outside, got in the hired car and returned to hotel.

After leaving the bank and returning to the hotel, I put in a call to Gau-

480

THE DEAL

trat in Paris. I told him not to talk, just listen, and put the secretary on the extension to take notes. I told him the Baron was dead, I couldn't get the money from the box. But now, most important, I had a letter signed by the Baron, that the Baron had killed Danielle Dumont; also I would deliver to Gautrat the plastic dong of the Baron as conclusive evidence, positive proof of Sam's innocence. Gautrat was calm, quiet . . . said practically nothing to me. I told him I was leaving for Paris at once.

Now I just needed to pack my bags. I had left the Baron's attorney and "15" at the Palace Hotel in Geneva. Now, on my return from the bank, the attorney was full of confidence. His way was now clear. He would handle the arrangements for the Baron. He would also handle "15" (and how). When I went to the Baron's suite to get some papers and tell him what arrangements to make, they both came out of the bedroom, disheveled and out of breath. They did not look sad.

"I'll see you in Paris, Jarnigan," the American attorney said—full of gas, legal as hell. His fly completely open.

"Only by appointment, man, only by appointment," I said, looking at him coldly.

"Listen, Jarn," he said judicially, "we have a lot to discuss, a lot to talk over between us, you know . . ." He finished with a leer, standing there full of himself, but trying to put down the elation of now being in control, of being number one (and he was). Now he held some power over the Baron's remaining assets. And to top it off (in every sense of the word) he was winning the Baron's "15"-year-old-assed asset. (She had been won in advance.) He was already so bloody conceited as to be unbearable. Now as he spoke he was sure of himself, all the facts were straight, he was debonair, he was perfect; until I said, "By the way, counselor, your fly is open—if you care." His hands moved frantically to repair that problem. "15" moaned, "Oh, Jarn." I said quietly, "You deserve each other." I left . . . quietly. I went downstairs, paid my bill, tipped everyone too much. All were lined up with friendly condolences.

The driver in the hired car said nothing as he drove me to the airport. He told me good-bye as I tipped him (also too much). He thanked me breathily. He had been eating garlic. I had been drinking brandy—heavily. Good-bye driver . . . good-bye Switzerland . . . good-bye Baron . . . good-bye money . . . *so long Jarnigan.*

I got on the plane quietly, if unsteadily. It is hard to convey the dejection accompanying the discovery, when you see yourself as you are. It is life

481

at the low-water mark with the mud flats plain for everyone to see. You see dull, stark mud—matter everywhere. You are increasingly conscious of what it means to be an animate producer in an unmalleable world. You are lonely, you are certainly lost. The self-pity leaves you a possible avenue of escape. Men can hope for more, producers can afford that illusion of interpenetration, comprehensiveness of being, which alone gives meaning to existence if you are in the picture business. When you have once identified yourself with that, you are lost. It is difficult to gain new assurance on the ultimate question—Hector, can you still make a good picture? Can you make a good picture without a star, without the Baron? Well, you have to face up to it, you have to see.

I searched for some way to define what I felt . . . I was like a fellow who gathered raindrops and tried to make an ocean. Or to dream of sleep . . . to try and capture sleep. I began to think after I talked with *Someone,* there's nothing to fear. There are no underworlds or overworlds, there's only *the* world. I hoped I could handle it better. I'd take the evidence back to Paris and I'd get old Sam out. Then we'd see what would happen, but I'd sure do anything to get Sam out. I'd straighten everything out in Paris. I'd get Gautrat and we would go to the police . . . I could then make . . . another Deal.

50

But this is what was happening in Paris in the Prison de Santé while I was flying from Geneva.

It was night . . . again three guards were going down the corridor. Once again, they removed their shoes and advanced in stocking feet toward the small door. The guard in the lead inserted his key, and threw open the door. The other guards rushed in.

Although the guards had not come for Sam on this occasion, he was ready. He stood up deliberately and held out his arms, and, had not a word been spoken, would undoubtedly have left the cell, walked down the corridor. But the guard with the queasy stomach, now thoroughly confused, looked at another guard. "Are you sure it's him? I hope he doesn't do like the last one . . ."

Then Sam yelled . . . it was loud . . . it was a horrible scream. It broke loose all the quiet that had existed in Sam until now. He grabbed the guard on the left, put his hands around his throat, and held on. The guard who had been sick to his stomach grabbed Sam by the hair and one ear. The other guard started beating Sam over the head. The guard with the delicate stomach pulled the hair and pulled the ear and tried to stick his fingers into Sam's eye.

In the corner, the other convict, whom the guards should have taken, bundled himself up into a little ball on his bed. He put the end of the blanket in his mouth and began chewing on it. The sick-stomach guard pulled and pulled. The other guard beat and beat. Sam's hands moved tighter . . . closer . . . tighter . . . finally the body of the guard whose throat had been crushed in Sam Neely's hands fell to the floor.

Feet were running down the corridor, heavy feet. Guards rushed into the cell. They held Sam. The sick-stomach guard called for the doctor. The doctor came, followed by the priest, and after one look said, "He's dead!" The room was quiet. The breathing was heavy. For almost a minute no one said anything. Looks darted from the body of the guard on the floor back to Sam . . . but Sam was quiet again.

Suddenly, other feet came down the corridor to the cell . . . feet that were in a hurry, that tapped out authority with each step. It was the assistant warden. "What has happened?"

The doctor said, "Sam Neely just killed the guard."

483

THE DEAL

The warden looked at the body of the guard, then up to the face of Sam. He said, "Dear God, I started running because of the excitement. I was coming here to give you the word. We have conclusive proof that Sam Neely is not a murderer . . . my coming here was to end his being kept in death row. He was to be released." He thought he had said he had come to give the news of Sam's innocence twice, and yet his brain was trying to accept what had happened. His mouth kept forming the words, "I was coming here to arrange his removal from this cell-block." Two other guards came in.

They all looked at one another. Sam looked at no one. The priest turned his face to the wall and said, "Mother of God." The guard with the sick stomach was sick again. The guard who had been beating Sam on the head, sat down quickly on the nearest bunk. The other guards who were in the room shifted their feet. Sam just stood there . . . quiet . . . no emotion.

The warden said, "Carry the body out . . . I must call the préfet's office." They all filed out, leaving Sam, who had still not moved. The convict in the corner still had the blanket in his mouth. The door of the cell slammed shut, and because of the door being shut, the cell was almost completely dark . . . there was no sound. Sam Neely stood there and waited. He wondered if Jarnigan would now come to get him.

More feet came down the hall . . . well-shod feet . . . sure of themselves. They walked to the door of the cell-block. The guard came . . . nodded respectfully . . . Maître Gautrat walked in. He went over to Sam and said, "I didn't believe you; I'm terribly sorry—I regret I didn't believe you." Sam didn't say anything. The lawyer said, "I'm having you moved to another part of the prison; after that we must talk."

Then Sam looked at him and said, "I don't want to talk. I want to see Jarnigan."

The lawyer said, "I understand, but this is one thing you must leave to me."

Sam said quietly "I left it to you once. I told the truth . . . I said what you wanted me to say."

The lawyer started for the door—turned back and said to Sam, "You will be moved this afternoon, then we must talk."

Sam didn't answer. Maître Gautrat left the cell.

It was quiet in the courtroom. It was a very unusual hearing. The evidence had been given. The guard who had beaten Sam on the head had talked. The guard who was sick to his stomach had talked. The widow of

484

THE DEAL

the dead guard had said what a fine man he had been . . . how devoted to his work—and it was true, he *had* been a fine man and he was dead in the performance of his duty. All through the talking, the president of the tribunal had listened, had been quiet, not wanting to, nor really being able to, start to think of a decision. Sam sat behind the table, looking at neither the guards nor the people who listened. He was looking for Jarnigan. Gautrat stood up. He looked over the people in the court. He walked forward slowly and stood in front of the president of the tribunal. Now came the summing up. Maître Gautrat said: "This man is not guilty of murder . . . wrongfully he was waiting to be killed . . . this man who was being held in murderers' row for a murder which he didn't commit. This man—who at eleven-thirty on the night of the eleventh, strangled to death the guard Hervé Maulé, who we admit was doing his duty—this man was innocent. He alone knew he was innocent, so those guards who came to take him—where he didn't know—for something he hadn't done, in his eyes were his enemies. He was being held and tormented unjustly, wrongfully. Whether by a man or by a government, the deed and the result for him is the same.

"I say to you, when a man knows that he may be killed, and is fighting for his life with no weight of guilt on his mind or on his soul, he is rightly defending his life, and I turn in a plea for my client of 'Not guilty by reason of temporary insanity.' It is clear that what he did was to protect his own life, which up to eleven-thirty on the night of the eleventh was completely free of any crime whatsoever. Temporary insanity, the right of self-preservation, was his right. He *was* not a criminal. He *is* not a criminal. I demand that the court return a verdict of 'Not guilty.'"

The lawyer turned and walked back to Sam, standing directly over him with one hand on his shoulder . . . he looked full into the face of the judge and said, "The defense rests."

Sam looked at the judge. The judge looked at Sam. Their eyes locked and the minutes murmured by with their fingers to their lips . . .

This was what was happening as I sat there and watched from the back of the tribunal. I'd been in the courtroom the whole time, but I'd been unable to go and talk to Sam. I had told Gautrat everything. I was sure he'd get Sam off. And he did. The verdict was "Not guilty by reason of temporary insanity." Privately, the judge and the prosecuting attorneys had been shown the Baron's letter of confession and the "evidence." They were horrified, and were understandably sorry for Sam Neely.

There was no way, unless there was a stunt man, to finish the picture. I

485

knew that this was the last act of the drama of the complete dissolution of the Baron-Jarnigan Motion Picture Productions Limited. All of the stupidity, the loose and tiny morals of the Baron, all of the savagery and the badly thought-out maneuvers of Jarnigan had combined and had wound up into "nothingness."

In the picture business, as in everything, mercilessness and muddleheadiness are met together. Unrighteousness and unreasonableness cannot kiss each other. The tempter and the tempted, even though they agree, only end up a blank. A hundred and eighty feet of film that can't be backed up. A blank. A nothing. A disaster.

I talked to the distributors and tried to get them to go along with me; even though the Baron was dead, I figured I could finish with the double. Their distributor inequities had deprived them of any dignity, of any compassion. But finally, with the Baron's death and the Deal broken, it seemed to be something that had happened thousands of years ago. It seemed to speak in parables. There was the hammering of spears and the smell of bad, musty, crusty makeup—all the juices dried, everything gone.

When I had first made the Deal I didn't want the Baron's life, nor did I want him to have mine. The girls he brought, that came to and fro, talking of Michelangelo, were all angels—but angels with their wings clipped, angels naked and open to our view. The Baron's trumpet blared loud and clear in conversation. It was only later that I found there was no real trumpet, no mute, no song. So the dissatisfied and unsatisfied angels flew off, sadly but with dignity. And, being heavily paid, said nothing. They wouldn't explain of their unsuccessful attempts to play the Baron's trumpet. So, with money between the feathers of their wings, and nothing between the feathers of their thighs, their flights took them to other nests. I completed their poem:

> Their flight took them to other nests.
>   All took these angels to their breasts
> And now their nests were lined with gold
>   They had no fear of growing old.
> You couldn't call them whore or strumpet,
>   For who could blow the Baron's trumpet?
> Completely happy with their loot,
>   Their deal . . . to play the Baron's flute.
> My deal was grand, no doubt, no maybe.
>   Oh, fool! Your dirge was "Melancholy Baby."

51

The rich stingy man or a miser can't use his hands to reach for money to give.

I tried to borrow . . . I tried to sell out . . . I tried to *hypothéquer,* I tried to make any financial deal I could on the picture to give me eleven more days. But my bankers, my rich attorney, my wealthy "friends" . . . immediately had nothing. On the occasion of my desperate request, my plea for help, their riches made themselves wings—as Solomon put it—and flew away." But these false friends . . . these pharisees . . . gave freely to me windy and insignificant charity. They lent me advice. This was without value.

I spoke to them . . . rather, I pleaded with them. The talk of friendship should not be broken when money . . . or lack of it, enters the scene. I said, I have to have this to survive, without it I am done, finished, ruined. You are my friends, give me some help. Good Christ . . . don't give me more advice. I was told from every side, "Impossible at this time," "Impossible period," "Take your licking, profit by your mistakes." "What doth it profit a man?" Well, I could damn well tell them what it would profit me. I didn't need quotes or advice—that wouldn't get me one, two, or five days more shooting, that wouldn't get my film done. A well-phrased and sympathetic turndown would not pay the laboratory costs. Good advice and counsel couldn't pay the actors or pay for the costumes.

● ● ●

Let's talk about my rich and good old friend Clinton King. Clinton King, a pretender to godliness, a seeker of the word and the throne, judged my pitiful story as I rolled it out before him. I was precise, coherent, rhetorical. My pitch relied on securely based facts—and his friendship. He, as my trusted benefactor, could hold title to everything, have liens, notes, immediate ownership, full control of monies lent, only he would sign checks.

"Young Jarnigan, my dear young friend," he tolled, "it's a pity you find yourself in this predicament, that you should be in such desperate straits."

"Yes, sir," I sucked, "yes, sir, and I'm ashamed to request this amount this fast. But you see, sir . . ."

THE DEAL

"Son," the old voice quavered, "you couldn't have come at a worst time. Money is very scarce," he admonished. "These taxes, these damnable, unforeseen taxes . . ." His kind old voice scalpeled. He sat there watching me bleed-out in front of him, my words lying uselessly on the floor, beggar-shabby. My old friend, this man-of-mouth financier, this mouther of charities, could advance me no loans, but would pray with—and for—me.

"The prayers of a righteous man availeth much," he intoned. He mouthed many sayings, he talked a lot. Did he think he could help me with that? . . . Did he think his tongue could lick me up and out of trouble? . . . then carry me to the bank? The old formal hocus-pocus—don't give the beggar a quarter . . . rather, help him out with your prayerful blessing, sing him a sixpence psalm.

"Listen, Clint, what will your prayer and your advice sell for? What will it buy? How many feet of film can I get for your pick-nose prayer?"

I left him and went to the home of a wealthy banker—who had known the Baron well, who liked both of us. I said to the Baron's financier friend, "You know, *cher ami,* true friendship must undergo and withstand the shocks of adversity, so don't stay sore because the first picture doesn't bring you money. Let your friendship turn to affection. Let your banker's hand give with largesse, even though the calloused foreskin of your heart says Caution."

I was pretty loaded, but either he came in with the dough or he didn't. I should have been more careful, but my time was running out and the golden hoops had broken. I grinned at him, "Well . . ."

"I just don't know at this time, Jarn . . ." Then, changing the subject, "My, that was certainly sad about the Baron. You must miss him terribly."

"Terribly," I said. And walked out.

I was dead . . . my prayers for help hadn't entered his ear, and if they did . . . the one ear was readier to let them out than the other to take them in. He had a closed, gnarled bronze fist, but he had a closer, harder heart.

From such turndowns . . . my friends' denials, while protesting undying loyalty . . . the song "That Old Gang of Mine" became for me "That Old Gangrene of Mine."

I had one last chance.

• • •

I went to Barclay's Restaurant near the Rond-Point to meet Luconovitch to try and borrow some money on the picture, to continue the picture. I walked into this elegant restaurant—a trough wherein fed the neither pure nor impure. As I entered the private salon—the dining room for "business meetings" and more clandestine deals—I saw Paul Raymond, the private banker, the financier. He was noted firstly for his immense fortune, secondly for the immense interest he charged, and thirdly for his immense peculiarities. Four years ago, I had made a lot of money for Paul Raymond, at usurer's rates, on my first picture. He was a fat, effeminate, soft fellow, always smelling heavily of perfume. He had a large moon-shaped face; black, velvety cowlike eyes; black and wiry curly hair, like a Negro's; and —he looked like what he was. Yet, though he was all of these things, he was clever and shrewd; could cheerfully cut your heart out while thinking of other pleasure.

Paul Raymond was seated alone in a corner of the dining room—his upholstered sometimes-office in this velvety rendezvous for lovers. Paul looked up and saw me walking in his general direction. He hastily reached into his upper coat pocket and, from behind his lace handkerchief, took out his dark glasses, put them on, and looked the other way—out the window. With his dark glasses on, this of course made him invisible. I grinned and walked up to his table. I stood there, looking down at him. He fidgeted and turned around quickly in mock surprise. "Oh, Jarn," he said quickly, a look of phony gladness, of counterfeit surprise, on his face, "I didn't see you."

"How could you? You've got dark glasses on and were looking the other way." I grinned. He made the first move.

"In point of fact, I'm pleased to see you," he said primly, managing to look pleased. "I've got a big deal coming off in about three months"—this said pointedly—"and then I'd like to make another picture with you." Here, he removed the dark glasses, folded them neatly and placed them carefully back in his pocket, behind the lace handkerchief. He looked up into my eyes sincerely.

"Well," I said, "I'd like to talk to you about something else—about the Deal I've got *now* . . . You see . . ."

"*Oui*, I have heard about your troubles, Jarn," he simpered. "Who hasn't?—you being Jarnigan and all." He saw I wasn't buying the flattery and hurried on with, "If I hadn't been in this other *affaire* where all my money is blocked for the next three or four months," he mentioned this again firmly—then, more sadly, "I'd have come to see you, Jarn . . ." Then the voice became lower, "You know I've always liked you . . . really fond of you . . ."—his voice trailed off—". . . and because we are friends . . . but unhappily, I'm now too . . ."

"You've made your point, Raymond."

"*Oui*, yes, it's terrible," nodding his fat head sadly, but now being safely over the hump of a possible approach for borrowing his money, he beamed. "Jarn, do have lunch with me," he said girlishly, over-enthusiastically.

"No, I'm lunching with Luconovitch."

"Oh," he gasped, "that crook. What are you doing with *him?*"

I sat down. I gave Paul a steady, thoughtful look. "I am trying to get him to advance me some money on my film."

Paul leaned forward and lisped like a bitchy fat woman, "Jarn, he's a crook."

"You already said that."

"Oh, but he is . . . he *is!*" If he had been standing he would have stamped his foot. "He's uncouth . . . he's vulgar—and he'll surely cheat you, Jarn . . ."

"Yeah, but his money ain't blocked."

"Jarn . . ." Here he looked down; then impulsively reached out his fat-woman's hand, with two rings on the wrong fingers; he stretched out his arm and, in a furtive gesture, put his hand on mine. He gave me a quick, searching look, his wide, soft cow-eyes flashing. I took my hand out from under his and gave him another thoughtful look. I grinned at him.

"Don't play with my emotions, Paul," I said, sarcastically. "I'm only an innocent lad."

"How much money do you need, Jarn?"

"I thought your money was all tied up." I said.

"Oh, it is, it is . . . it's tied up like I told you . . . but . . ."

"Well, if your money's tied up, what difference does it make how much money I need? What are you doing—shopping?"

"Oh, don't be like that," he said girlishly. "I'm asking because . . ." Here he looked away—then he gave me a look, his eyes flashing. "Perhaps there is a way I can help."

"Listen, Paul, the only thing that can help me is money. Now what did you have in mind?"

"Well," he said softly, primly, "it's just that I don't want to see you get involved with a horrible man like Luconovitch."

"I'm not going to get 'involved' with him," I said, "I just want to make the least kind of cutthroat deal I can make to get an advance on my percentage of the picture."

I looked around the restaurant. People were coming in now. Luconovitch was already late. I figured he'd show if only to have lunch, since he knew

THE DEAL

I was picking up the tab. Even with me giving up all of my percentage—since news of the Baron's death and gossip about the stopping of the film and the many difficulties I was having with the Baron's picture were, as they say in French, *dans toutes les rues de Paris*—I wasn't overly optimistic, but I was desperate enough to try anything. I *had* to have that money.

The waiter came up, and Paul Raymond said, "Have a drink, Jarn; let's have a glass together."

I turned to the waiter, "Bring me a brandy-and-soda, will you—and a cigar."

"I," said Paul the ped, flashing a look around the room, "will have champagne. *Garçon*, a bottle of Dom Perignon." The waiter walked away. I sat there, looking around the room, wondering what the hell I was going to do if Luconovitch didn't show up; he was about my last hope. The waiter came back with my brandy and cigar and was doing a lot of unnecessary fussing with Paul's bottle of champagne . . . getting it properly iced. They were talking back and forth; I lit my cigar and sat looking around the room.

"You know, Jarn," Paul said, becoming a little more daring, "I've always had a sympathy for you. I've always . . . well, I've always had . . ." Here he looked heavenward and said girlishly, "I guess I've always had a sort of *thing* for you." I didn't say anything, I just kept watching him. "Jarn," he said impulsively, with all your problems and all, do you know what you should do . . . do you know what *we* should do?" he said.

"Keep talking, Paul."

He ducked his head in two or three little nods and then went on, more excitedly. "You're having many problems; I can see you're worried. I hate to see you worried, Jarn. And I'd truly like to help." He said this very fast. "Now, what I think would be good for . . . both of us . . . you remember my villa that is in Cannes? Well . . ." When I didn't say anything and just kept looking at him, he paused for a moment, then went on softly. "I think we should go there; and there we can work out a solution to all of your problems. I'm sure that I could arrange some money and who knows . . . perhaps I could even arrange to finance another picture for you."

When I still didn't say anything, he became a little self-conscious; he leaned back in his chair, looked at me for a moment, drank his whole glass of champagne at a gulp, then leaned over to me and said, passionately, "Jarn, I have a confession to make." I nodded. "I don't have my money blocked. I only said that when you came in and started talking with me, but then—you know my affection for you, of course—it's now getting the best

491

of me and I'll confide in you the truth. My money isn't blocked. I have it all, and I will help you if you'll go with me—or rather . . ."

Here he watched me carefully, thinking perhaps he'd gone too far with his proposition. He leaned back and said more quietly, "What I mean to say, Jarn, is this: I think that to correctly resolve your problems—and knowing how important the completion of this terribly expensive film is—it would be wisdom for us to go to the coast together; we could stay at Cannes for a week and resolve all the difficulties. In the meanwhile," he said, dealing out his last card expertly, "I can take care of the expenses and we can say you are starting the picture next Monday morning. With this announcement, all of your distributors—and you know, I know who they are," he said in a conspiratorial voice—"all of your distributors will call me and I will say, Yes, my company is definitely taking over the financing of your picture . . ."

When I still didn't say anything, he didn't know whether to be more nervous or more sure of himself. He was balanced on a knife-blade. The waiter started to come up and refill his glass; he motioned the man away in an irritated manner and then quickly poured himself another glass of champagne. He drank half of it, and leaned back in his chair, twirling the half-empty glass in his fingers and looking at me appraisingly, half concerned and yet half expectant. He waited. I finished my brandy, motioned to the waiter with the glass; he scuttled off. I turned back and put a fix on Paul. I was looking at him steadily when the waiter came back. He filled my glass and backed up, saying, "Would monsieur like to order?" I turned to him and said, "Not now, but you may bring me a bottle of brandy immediately." The waiter rushed off. Paul looked at me.

"You see, Jarn," he said sadly, "look at you, my dear friend. It grieves me, it makes me sad to see you so depressed and drinking your problems away . . . or rather, trying to," he continued. "This is what I want to avoid, this is why I truly want to help you," he said, and he swallowed. His fat throat shook; he had a dewlap under his chin and it vibrated with sincerity and emotionalism. I finished my glass of brandy still looking at him, and the waiter came up, set the bottle on the table. I motioned him away. When he was out of earshot, I poured myself another glass of brandy, but I let it sit there in front of me. I looked at Paul thoughtfully and said, "Paul, let me get this straight. You're proposing that we go down to your villa on the Riviera—that we stay in Cannes for the week and then you help me resolve my problems."

"Oh, that's correct, Jarn!" He gushed, "That's absolutely correct. We can discuss all our business affairs, we can discuss . . ." Here the words came tumbling out of his mouth, bumping into each other, leaping over each other as he was making his pitch. He burbled on, I let him go. The velvety silken filth poured out of his lips as he became more and more confident—more brave. There he sat, the predatory female—or worse—what he was.

"Paul, I want to tell you something."

He leaned over the table closely. "Yes, Jarn . . . yes."

"If you'd have made me a direct proposition—if you'd have said to me, Listen, Jarn, I want you to go down to the Riviera with me, I want you to go over the jumps with me. . . I like you; you're a man of the world—let's get together. Try me . . . try me . . . try it . . .' If you'd have said, 'Jarn, I know you're disappointed in life, I know your finances are at their lowest ebb—in fact, they're nonexistent—I know and have heard rumors that you and the Princess have finished'— Oh, don't say anything. I know, because you hear everything. Yeah, all of you hear everything. If I wasn't sure you had heard, I wouldn't have taken it the way I'm taking it."

"Why, Jarn," he said quickly, "what do you mean?"

"Now just be quiet, Paul," I said, "I haven't finished . . . If you had made me an out-and-out proposition, saying, 'You need two hundred fifty thousand dollars to finish your picture—this is what I want to do—come with me to the Riviera—let's talk over your proposition—' . . . but the way you did it, you propositioned me like a whore. And worse—you waited until I was down; you waited until you thought I was absolutely at an end, where I was ground into the dirt—you thought that I'd accept anything! Even filth like you! Let me tell you something, Paul*lette*, there's only one place I'd go with you—I'd like to go hunting with you!"

He drew back, "Jarn, I don't know what you mean. I don't know what you're saying."

"You know what I'm saying, and you know what I mean. I said, and I say again: Boy, would I like to take you hunting! Make you have one of those hunting accidents you read about every weekend during the season. You know anything about hunting, Paulette?"

"Well, Jarn," he said, trying to draw himself together, becoming a little afraid, "Jarn, I . . ."

I looked at him coldly. "Now you be quiet, I haven't finished. I want to explain to you how I see this hunting trip of yours and mine . . ."

After this exchange I turned back and looked carefully at Paul the ped's face. I said, conversationally—calmly. "Paul?" He didn't answer. "Paul, I'm speaking to you."

"What is it, Jarn?"

"Did you ever do any hunting?"

"No."

"Well, did you ever *see* any hunting?"

"What do you mean?"

He drew back, looking at me fearfully.

"Well, I mean, did you ever see any hunting?"

"No—no, I haven't," he pouted.

"Well, Paul, I'm going to tell you how it is. You see, there's a hunt that goes on in Fontainebleau, or past the forest of Rambouillet. It's a boar hunt—a pig hunt. You start early in the morning and the beaters go through the forest. You're on a point where you can see a pretty good distance both ways. Then, after a while, with luck, a boar will go by—a large pig going very fast, and later there'll be the sows. Now usually, in the middle of those sows, and slightly in back of the run, there'll be a mother sow; she may run to one thousand pounds in weight. Well, I set my sights on this big sow's belly and I gut-shoot it—because this doesn't spoil the meat but it knocks the sow off its feet. It's stunned, and you're able to walk over and carefully shoot it in the head before the kidneys and the gall get mixed in with the blood and spoil the meat."

Paul turned away, his face pale, a sick look on it.

"Well, what I'm getting at is this, Paul. This gut-shot sow, this pig, is the way you're going to be if you ever speak to me again. If you see me on the street, run away! If I come into a bar or into a restaurant where you are, you'd better leave! If you see me in a restaurant or bar, don't come in."

After all that brandy, my face was numb. I leaned over, looked him in the eye, and said, "Paul, if I ever see you this close again—if I'm ever within arm's length of you—as sure as God made little apples, I'm going to rip your guts apart! You'll be like that gut-shot sow, and I'll be there to shoot you in the head."

Paul dropped his napkin, he upset his glass—the waiter came over. I shooed him away. Paul leaned his bulk back in the chair and stared at me, his face pale and sweaty; his eyes had a sick look. I picked up my cigar, relit it; blew the smoke in his direction, and said, "Paul, do you remember what I told you about being in the same restaurant with me?" He didn't answer. His eyes grew more fearful. "Well," I said, "I'm going to smoke my cigar, turn around and look out the window and feel sad. Then I'm going to turn back around in about a minute. If you're still here, you're going to get what I promised you."

With that I turned around. I heard fumbling, scratching movements behind; I heard the chair fall over and I turned back around in time to see

THE DEAL

Paul moving hurriedly, hastily, bumping into people on his way out the door. The waiter came up hurriedly. "Something wrong, monsieur? Something wrong?"

"Yeah. All wrong. All very wrong," I said. "Bring me another bottle of brandy and clear that away; take that champagne back."

The waiter looked around and then said, *"Monsieur Raymond . . .* he is coming back, *non?"*

"Mr. Raymond," I said quietly, "is not coming back, no. Get the brandy."

I sat there drinking brandy, drinking coffee—drinking brandy. Was this all there was?—did it all stop here? There seemed to be truly nothing left.

Even *Someone* had apparently walked in the other direction . . .

And after death, hell could be riding down in a lonely wicker-basket elevator; a rosy overhead light you couldn't read by; a sense of wrong-doing and of down-going, because, after you reach the forty-five number, you end up in a restaurant—a fixed grin, polite idiocy, and hatred for yourself and your life—because, after all, you made it yourself . . . dyed . . . glasses supposed to make you look studious, but which only make you as open and defenseless as an oyster or a clam. (Drop the net, the lemon, or the Tabasco—I'll squirm.)

The waiter came over—now a grinning corpse who fitted his coat to his body like a coffin. He smiled. "Is monsieur ready to order?"

I was. I did.

52

It was weeks later. Sam was out. I finally went to see him at the apartment where he was living with his mistress. I walked up the three flights, knocked on the door. The door was opened by the mistress, who eyed me with a little suspicion, which was understandable. I walked in. There was Sam in his old gray sweater. He had on his boxing shoes and looked in good shape. A little quiet. All he did was nod and say, "Hi, Mr. Jarnigan" —not sarcastic, just leaving everything open for me to answer.

I walked over to him. "Sam," I said, "here's the way she goes. You know what the score is. The Baron's gone. I guess everything's gone. " I said these words without self-pity, just stating fact. I took out the keys to my car, which I knew Sam loved. I took out the papers that I had signed that morning with the *notaire*.

"Sam, here are the keys, and here are the ownership papers for the Rolls. Here's another little package." I handed him a brown manila envelope that was wrapped and properly sealed. He looked at it for a minute. He didn't touch it. He didn't take the keys either, or the paper. I continued, "Sam, you got that Rolls. You got twenty-five thousand dollars in this envelope. It's in cash. I took it out of the Chase. You know how we used to do that."

He started to grin and then he stopped. I plowed on. "Now, the way I figure it is this. You've been telling me all the time since you came to Paris that you wanted that limousine car and chauffeur's operation here in Paris, if you had the Rolls and three Cadillacs. That would give you four sets of wheels, make you plenty of money, so it looks like you're set, boy."

Sam still hadn't touched the keys or the car papers, and he wouldn't touch the money or even look at it. "I'm taking off, Sam. I'll . . . I'll be back over soon. I'll be talking to you. I'm sorry you had that lousy ride. It couldn't have been much fun." I turned away. I couldn't say any more. Sam just sat there looking at me quietly. He didn't say anything. As I left I said, "Sam, you take it easy, boy."

I started out and I heard, "You take it easy too, Jarn." I closed the door quietly.

I went back home . . . I didn't feel like anything. All I wanted to do was curl up and hide somewhere and go to sleep. When I'm ready to die—and we all have to—I won't like it, but I'm ready if it'll help and if it's the thing that has to be done. Old Jarnigan's father never raised a boy who would be afraid—and yet that's a lie, because I *am* afraid. But banking on *Someone* . . . I'll fling my arms out and above like swinging across a pool and jump into the nothingness of whatever it is. I know I'll be caught, weighed, shook out, and then, hopefully, be able to explain or talk away my badly used life—the three talents wasted. But since He knows everything, I can save Him that. I'll just say and know He'll either shake me out and wring out the water or ignore me as evil. I don't think He'll do that. I truly don't think He'll do that. But in all fairness, He sure should shake me plenty.

Man, looking back without being dead—yet wondering if I have the courage to do it—because it does take that—I'd sure like to heal up and change around a couple of things I have left undone. There's always something to finish. An argument unsettled. A girl unkissed. And if you think of your life for a minute, while you can still breathe and feel and love, then you should approach God reverently, not violently, as I'm planning.

• • •

It seems to me, in retrospect, that my youth has thundered by in silence, as unnoticed as a parade down the wrong street with muted trumpets and unskinned drums. I sail on the ship of silent sadness only, because what I have talked and thought about is, or was, unworthy of sound. I have been vain, arrogant, thoughtless, proud, empty. Cymbals sounding with cotton swabs. A clay "flub" . . . a flub is a bivalve of missed opportunity. I have spit a pinky dentist-shot into the gums of eternity. How can you do that? So you roll your rubber-tired hoop and I'll roll mine and we can bounce down to the rubber-tired hell together. All filmed in Technicolor.

However, I am grateful for all that *Someone* has let me see, to know that so much is waste, is a "spit" for "come," and a "nun" for some.

Someone said, "Jarn boy, sometimes you get pretty close, I know that; that's why I'm here—because you're thinking like you are.

"Hell," I said.

"Sh . . . sh," *Someone* said, "I don't want you mad or saying that word. Incidentally, hot shot, I'm saving you from that. I only wanted to say to you that, at least for today, you have done fairly well and I'm glad you're trying."

"Well then just, for Christ's sake, knock it off."

"All right . . . all right." And then *Someone* laughed.

THE DEAL

"Stay with it, Jarn boy, I'm with you, good and bad. And though you've vexed me many times it *ain't*, as you so incorrectly put it, that you roll your hoop and I'll roll mine. Jarn, you keep on rolling your hoop and I'll try and see that it stays straight."

"Oh . . . oh . . ."

"Don't say it," *Someone* said. "Listen, if you want to do a little cussing tonight and you don't take the name of the Lord in vain . . . well, Jarn . . ." and here I heard a deep sigh. The breath of a feathered wing.

Someone continued: "If you want to swear a little tonight, I won't listen. I've become very close to you, Jarn. In point of fact, I'm with you now; I was, and have been with you all your life, and when you finish here, I'll be around to 'give the word for you.' "

"Christ, man," I said, "I don't want any favors. The favors were all gone out of me a long time ago. You can't even find soul in the dictionary—in the definition part."

"Don't worry, Jarn boy, I'm here; *and I'm there*, when you need me; but now you need rest. You sleep, because I'll watch and all will be well."

I listened for a minute—then, "Okay, okay, that's good. Thank you."

"You're welcome, Jarn," *Someone* said.

I slept. I dreamt . . .

Jason Wormser came to see me. First, to gloat. Second, to try and buy up everything for nothing. He chanted with glee. "You do everything wrong, get everyone's balls in an uproar—then you need old Jason to save your bacon, to save you smart-assed young pups."

Good Christ, I said to myself, do I finally have to sell everything to this pharisee, this gloating old man whom I want to dislike—perhaps more so because, maybe, he's been right?" Good Christ, whom I feel sometimes to summon, is not to be disturbed by this infamous prayer . . . I'll say "Judas priest" . . . Judas—the great *farceur* . . . "the kisser," "the hung one from a tree" . . . but not in any other sense . . .

Actually, Judas was a fagola who didn't make out any way. He was a suppressed one. He needed help but . . . none was forthcoming. Judas' brother had gone to Jason Wormser's forebear and asked for some bread. He was refused. So Judas' brother said, "Listen, Jacques"—he used the French, even though they weren't around then. He said, "How do you figure this guy?" And Pontius Pilate Wormser said, "Well, what has he done before . . . I mean," he said judiciously, "what are his credits?"

"You mean for kissing?"

"Christ, no."

499

"You can't say 'Christ, no.' He, or it, hasn't been invented yet."

"Well . . . Judas priest."

"That's better."

"At least we are dealing with someone we can touch . . . if you want to."

"Are you going out to watch it?"

"Yeah."

"Me too; let's walk up to that hill together."

"Listen . . . hell, if they stick him with that pointed stick and put those nails in him . . ." Here Milord the Fairy said, "Now you hold on, right there," the girlish voice continued, like Peter the Fool . . . "the nails were wood spikes. I definitely gave orders for wood spikes," he added delicately, like an actor disdaining the discussion of a sandy play . . . "It won't hurt much," he added, sadly.

"Listen, you know what?"

"No—what?"

"I see . . ." the other said, casting a quick glance up to the Cross, then back to his friend, "this is a bad 'deal'—it won't take. This guy they're sticking had them going."

"Horse shit, if he was going to have done something about it, he would have done it already." The friend looked at him. He continued haughtily, "If you don't believe me, ask Ernest Hossenfeffer. He was always in on those things before anyone else except J.C. . . ."

"Who's that? . . . What Justice of the Crease can say anything?"

"How can you get a 'Justice of the Crease' out of 'J.C.?' That means Justice of the Cunt—go ahead, laugh—don't you get it?"

"I get it. I get it. But why the hell should we ask him?"

"Yeah, he's up there, man. Ernie Hossenfeffer has a lopsided visa in and out. Old Ernie has fooled them all with colored baubles, but not as much as he's fooled himself."

"How's his face?"

"Fuck his face."

"He would have," the other said calmly, "but he couldn't reach it. Let's have a drink."

"Okay," I said dreamily, "but some day I've got to lay off that brandy and finish that picture. I can do it. I just need to get a double—hell, I'll bull it through some way. What's your best offer, Jason? You Pilate you . . ."

53

When I awoke the next morning, I knew I wanted to try to complete the picture, using the double of the Baron. The French double made many unreasonable requests—which I granted, since he looked enough like the Baron to be his brother.

So, we were shooting the burning ship, the burning docks, and the dangerous stunt of the Baron swinging on a rope from the top of the mast out over the water and jumping onto the dock.

After much preparation, with five cameras shooting the crowd scene, fires burning, smoke and wind machines going, I gave the signal to the Baron's double. He swung from on the top, from the high mast, out over the water, dropped on the docks, and—absolute disaster again!—he broke his leg.

I didn't know what other misfortune could fall on this poor picture. We rushed the double to the hospital, then I called all the actors and extras who played the parts of the seamen. There were about thirty-five men dressed in character. I lined them up. I chose the one who was the tallest and in rough physical outline matched the Baron. I paid off the second double, and on the following night rehearsed the shot; set the thing up again—cameras turning, fires burning, wind and smoke machines going, the second double swung out over the water, made the drop awkwardly but finally was able to do it—under the cover of smoke, fire, and the action of the extras. I finished the scene.

I now needed dialogue from the Baron, who, being six feet under, couldn't talk clearly. Unfortunately, the last scene was a love sequence where the two lovers, the Baron and the leading lady, were reunited; and in the scene, the Baron must say, "But darling, you should never have doubted my love for you. You know I love you and I always will . . ." Then the fade-out and the end of the picture . . .

I told my film editor and sound man to print up every foot of dialogue sound track I had; then, from nine different voice tracks, I made up the Baron's love scene. I took some words with the Baron calling to the men on the boat; I took some words out of the courtroom trial; I took some words where the Baron talked with his friends; I reprinted some dialogue track in different love scenes. From all this, I got the phrases correctly made up so the Baron said, "But darling, you should never have doubted my love for you. You know I love you and I always will."

However, the Baron had spoken each word in a higher or lower voice; the courtroom voice brisk, the friend's voice persuasive, and the love-scene voice very low and seductive. So, although the right words were said, what came out was a voice speaking in several different registers and several different moods. I had a Movieola broken down and reassembled with a foot accelerator so I could run the film faster or slower; running the voice track through the Movieola—some places faster, some places slower—to at least get an even register. This still was not satisfactory.

I then sent a camera crew to the south of France, knowing that the two ships, one of which I had purchased, were still in port. I had the camera crew photograph the ships on a stormy and windy day—later on, putting in flashes of lightning and thunder sound effects.

Finally, when the picture was finished, the Baron—who had never played this love scene, who was buried in Hollywood, California, at the time— played it beautifully, even though the storm practically drowned out the dialogue. It was in this way that I completed the last scene of the picture. In retrospect, I thought how fine it would have been if I could have re-cut and re-shot some of the dialogue in real life for the Baron. It might have made his life easier; but then, to keep from getting too profound, I remembered I should re-do a lot of my own dialogue tracks, and words should be put in my mouth that I have never said—which some day, if I live long enough and become a better man—I still might be able to say. It would never make you happy. Maybe there was no happiness in it either.

Now, with the picture completed, even though it was finished with a double, I had to attend a meeting with the bankers, French co-producer, Suisse Syndicate men, and the various attorneys. The distributors were also backing out of their contracts, claiming the picture was incomplete. Everyone wanted all the money back.

They wanted the picture. They wanted money—all I had—also for me to sign notes and my life away for the rest. And they wanted releases.

This was what was happening in the office. . . .

Old Jarnigan, the victim, was now in the Syndicate man's office. All was ready for the signing of the releases. All the original documents were in front of me. I sat there looking at the faces watching me. The Baron was dead, the picture was in doubt, the jackals were there on the other side of the desk looking at me carefully. They knew they were killing me. They knew that they were tearing the flesh off my bones, then scattering the bones apart. They were taking back all the money and the unfinished picture. They were dealing out justice to the "American gangster" producer. They were making me an example. Dealing out my death sentence with the stern and arduous impartiality of men who are in no danger themselves.

I looked at Gautrat; he was pale but calm. He gazed at the documents as though he had never seen them before. As the papers were placed in front of me, carefully, almost stealthily, I looked down at them, knowing that when I put my signature on them I'd be completely ruined. Not for the Deal—but forever.

Gautrat was watching me carefully. You see, he knew me well, for a long time and through many crises, but never one like this. Where before, some way, by some magic—not by God's, or my God (whom I turned away from, who nonetheless had allowed me to slide through)—where *Someone* had talked and I had babbled back (a wordy-windy nothing, a puny payoff prayer), yet I slid through, as before. But now was now. Not even a pooped-off prayer could come to help me now.

I looked up, and was dumbfounded to see, or *sense*, my brother standing in the corner. He looked in good shape, somehow younger and slimmer. I couldn't make him out too clearly, because of my anger. He watched me a moment, then he grinned, nodded his head, and gave me the go-ahead sign, with his fist clenched. I remembered what he'd said, "Nobody can beat the two of us, kid." I looked hard at him—Christ, my eyes were going bad —I could almost see two of him. He nodded again, turned around, and fixed an icy stare of dislike on the men threatening me, the jackals waiting to finish me off for good . . . or for evil.

I looked at the set of men opposite me. I looked at Gautrat. I stood up. I carefully picked up the releases and looked at them. Then, without a word, I reached over the big desk, I picked up the neat stack of contracts and papers, tore each of them in halves and quarters. As the shouts of the startled, shocked, and angry men grew louder I walked quickly around the desk to the fireplace and threw the papers into the fire. I spun around after seeing them burning. Three of the men were on their feet now, one running toward the fireplace, then dropping onto his knees, reaching toward the flames—moaning and hissing directly at me. I shoved him away roughly; he fell over on his side, still moaning.

But now my brother came over and stood by me. We were ready. Gautrat never moved. I spun around and faced the men. "Tell me I can't get away with it," I snarled. "Tell me what trouble I'll have. Tell me about lawsuits and jail, and fines and jail. Listen, those papers are gone—to hell with any copies, they are unsigned, and you babies aren't so clean either. That was hot dough, that was tax dough. So we are all going to take the bath together. Not old Jarn alone any more. Not old Jarn taking the fall solo. We all have a piece of an unfinished picture; and I've got a dead partner."

I took two steps toward them, still snarling. "Tell me about troubles . . . tell me . . . I have had mine; you've got yours now. You've got yours and mine and I have just exchanged my old ones for new ones." I looked at them. The shock was wearing off now. Surprise and shock were changing to cold and studied hatred. Now was the dangerous time. Now would come the death threats—or worse. I waited.

The Suisse Syndicate man asked quietly, "Did you ever kill a man, Monsieur Jarnigan?"

"Yeah."

"How did it feel?"

I didn't say anything.

"Some men like it."

I didn't say anything again.

"Nasty feeling, isn't it?"

I looked at him. I didn't smile, I didn't frown. I didn't do anything except to think, Would the Editor *float up*?

"I'd lay off that one, if I were you. But since I'm not you, I'm telling you, I'd drop that one."

He looked away, then back at me.

Then he said with icy politeness and his undertaker's smile, "Monsieur Jarnigan . . . Monsieur Jarnigan . . ."

I waited.

He looked at me steadily and continued, "Do you know why we haven't had this little meeting before? Do you know why we've waited this long after your associate's unfortunate demise?"

"Yeah," I said, "you couldn't find me." I watched them—all of them. Then I started to talk. I went ahead and showed how I had them completely and absolutely screwed. Now they'd *have* to listen to the Deal the way I wanted to make it. They'd have to come over to my way of thinking and give me the support that I needed to swing the Deal legally.

It all seemed easier now that the Baron was dead. I was the surviving partner. Maybe that's it. Maybe that's the ticket. Let them die off. It shouldn't take too much more time or be too much more hell. Maybe I could, in some modest way, help them along. This damned Deal, this mother-of-a-Deal, it was killing me as sure as day. I looked around the room. I had them cold and they knew it! I had the sole signature. I could play them the way you can kill a nonflying pigeon as it walks out of the trap.

I looked at the French co-producer and knew he didn't have a prayer of staying out of jail now. I had my own papers, I could send him there. He looked at me with a sickly smile. He looked at me and heard the door clang shut. I had him—I had them all, and by Christ I was going to *finish* them.

I laughed out loud. I felt good inside. I had a hard skin over what was left of my soul—a callus where the heart had rubbed it. That's what had happened to me since going on with this Deal. I could look at any sort of crime—rape, blackmail, extortion, and even murder—without seeing anything in it except my name on eighteen feet of film as a producer—any crime covered up for a main title. For what you see on the screen actually for five seconds would last in your head for years. But me getting a charge, getting a glow out of this filth, this mockery of everything decent— that's what the Deal had done to me. After being brought face to face with all of these things, the unreal realities, the incentives, are blown away like mist in a wind. The correctness in life is gone, and gone again. That, perhaps, is the most punishing blow of all. What remains just disappears. Not like a brass band, not like the babble of the five-highball voices, it disappears softly, a faraway, unimportant sound, like distant footfalls on dead leaves.

As it says in the Bible (Deut. 10:16), "Circumcise therefore the foreskin of your heart, and be no more stiff-necked." In the Deal, it hadn't been a stiff neck I'd had to worry about.

I looked at all of them again. I walked toward the door. I said—to the open door, not to the men in the room: *"Messieurs, l'Affaire est finie . . .* the Deal is finished."

I left.

Strangely enough, I slept well, was up early and getting ready to leave. Gautrat's office was making all arrangements about my apartment. While I was packing, I came across my three scripts—Numbers 1 and 2 and the old leprosy script. How faraway and yet how friendly they seemed now. They had tried to help. Like the fellow says, "A motion picture is like a love affair. Almost any fool can start one, but to end one beautifully requires considerable genius." Of course, if your star dies in the middle of your picture, with no insurance and other details—this can have its annoying side effects.

For the last few weeks I had been in contact with a good friend of mine. He was the son of the vice-president of Haiti—one day, hopefully, its president. I had two stories, good scripts that could be made on the island, because they showed the country and the government in a good light. The government officials up to the President liked the scripts, wanted to cooperate—I could use the army, the boats, the people—even the Tontons Macoute. My friend Joseph Bulla had sent me letters and papers, all very official-looking. I'd had Gautrat check with the embassy and consulate in Paris. It all seemed to check out.

I was going by car down to Marseilles, to stay at the Hotel De Noailles, a lovely old hotel on the Old Port, and wait for the ship that would take me to Haiti. It was due to sail in four days . . .

I had called the Princess. She had left for Rome—she didn't call to tell me good-bye. I was offered a social picture to do in France, but now I didn't have the money, the script, the inclination, or the manners. No, I'd just leave for Marseilles.

The Baron's attorney called me at the office. He and "15" were going to New York. I felt like warning that grand city. I saw Saul Baum at Fouquet's—his hair dyed blond. He looked fierce and fawning, over a girl of sixty covered with rocks and warts. (He wouldn't notice the warts. The rocks shone beautifully.)

So, that afternoon the car I'd hired started the drive from Paris to Marseilles. "I love Paris every moment . . ." I still do. But I didn't mind leaving her.

54

When I got to Marseilles, I was glad to see my two friends, the brothers who own the hotel. We had a drink; my bags were sent up to the suite. I planned to do nothing until the boat sailed. That's hard to do.

The next afternoon I was sitting in my living room in the hotel. There was a knock on the door and in walked Sam Neely, followed by a porter and another guy. Sam said to the porter, "Put the bags in the corner." The porter did that; Sam tipped him and after he had gone, said to the other guy, "Okay, Herb, drive her back gentle. Mr. Jarnigan don't like anybody to drive her but me. Watch the oil pressure, and when you get to Paris, take it to the Rolls garage and leave the extra keys and papers at Maître Gautrat's—you know, where we was yesterday. Got it?"

The guy nodded. "Got it, Sam, what else?"

"Nothing, man, here's your dough and thanks for the aid. It's cheerful to have a man you can depend on." Here Sam grinned, handed the guy some notes, the keys, and some papers. "Bye, Herb—be seein' you."

"Hold onto the left one, Sam. Give us a buzz when you're back," Herb said, "I'm always around." With that, the little guy touched his cap to me, hit Sam on the arm hard, and left the room without looking back.

During all this time, I hadn't said a word. Sam went over to the low table in front of the fireplace. There he dropped the large envelope, which I knew held the money I'd left him. He dropped some letters down on the money package, and said casually, "I stopped by your place and got the mail." He sat down, looked at me. "Where we going, boy?"

For the first time since he'd come in I spoke. "I don't know where *you're* going, but I'm going to Haiti."

He looked at me steadily. "Great. What's it like?"

I just looked at him. He turned, looking away from me and into the fire that was almost out in the fireplace. "Well," he said quietly, not looking at me, "I worked her over pretty good, all ways. Then I figured I'd better get on down here. Gautrat told me the boat don't go till Saturday. He also dropped the name of the hotel. But, hell, I could of found that . . ." Sam talked on. I watched him . . . he just wanted to know where, and for how long—just polite talk.

I told him why I was going to Haiti; how my friend the vice-president's

507

son, had offered me a deal for a motion picture and possibly a television business there; and that the government would give me an official contract for the exculsive motion picture rights for the whole country. It sounded like a great deal, I told him, and I wanted to do it.

Sam walked over, opened a grip and pulled out a bottle of brandy, went over to the table and got a couple of glasses, poured us both a drink, and went back over to the fireplace. He tossed off his drink and stood looking into the dying fire. When he turned around, his face was drawn and he looked kind of out of breath. As he walked over toward me I noticed his shoes were untied. He said quietly, "Jarn." From the way he said it I got up. I stood there looking at him, knowing what was coming. "Yeah?" He looked down, then back up quickly.

"Jarn, I've got to know." He looked me straight in the eye. "If the Baron hadn't taken the big one, would you have let me take the fall?" He swallowed.

I stood looking at him. He swallowed again, this time hard; but kept looking at me. Nothing was as quiet as that room. Time murmured and whispered by. I walked over to him; I stood there, looking in his face. The muscles in his jaw were moving.

Finally I said quietly, "I . . . don't . . . know." Sam swallowed again. His lips looked dry and cracked, and we stood there staring at each other.

After a minute, Sam turned away. He went over and stood looking quietly out the window at the boats in the old harbor. Pretty soon, he turned around and came walking back. He stood there looking at me thoughtfully. Slowly, he stuck out his hand. Then that dry, cynical grin that I had known all my life started over his face. His eyes were moist with brother-affection.

"You're table-topping now, Jarn." He grabbed my hand. "Listen, Jarn, I've got to tell you. Son, I know you, and I know this mother-of-a-Deal like you do; so if it's any comfort—and I figure you could use some—if I had been in your shoes and in your place, I don't know but what I'd have done just like you did." He added quietly, giving me a long, steady look, "I'm leveling, Jarn. You understand? It's done. Gone. Forgotten." He started shaking my hand. "*All gone*, little brother."

As we shook hands, I was the first to turn away . . . because I couldn't talk. I couldn't see too well. Damned eyes going weak on me again. I said gruffly, "Sam, your damned shoes are untied."

He turned around and walked over to a table, came back in a minute with two of my favorite cigars. He stuck one in my mouth. He flicked his lighter and as the flame burned, I only watched the end of the cigar as I puffed, slowly starting it to burn correctly. I couldn't look up. Sam lit his cigar.

Then, finally, I felt his hand on my shoulder. I looked up into his eyes. He started to smile and the smile changed to his wonderful, friendly grin. The brother-grin. He said quietly, "Well, when are we going, Jarn boy? What's the deal?"

I tried to return the grin . . . I couldn't. But I loved him as my brother. He'd taught me more in the last few minutes than I'd learned all my life.

I remembered when I was a boy, Aunt Jessie taught me this poem:

> When a man ain't got a friend
> And he's feeling kind of blue
> And the clouds hang dark and heavy
> And won't let the sun shine through,
> It's a great thing, oh my brethren,
> For a fellow just to lay
> His hand upon your shoulder
> In a friendly sort of way.
>
> Makes a man feel curious
> Makes the teardrops start,
> And you feel a sort of flutter
> In the region of your heart.
> You can't look up and meet his eyes
> You don't know what to say
> When a hand rests on your shoulder
> In a friendly sort of way.

I turned away, walked over and looked blindly through the window. I thought I'd have to tell *Someone* about this. Maybe then he could explain to me the workings of this kind of a Deal . . .

I turned back to Sam. The grin was still there. It looked even better and this time I could grin. I stuck out my hand. We shook hands again. Hard. I said to him, "Sam, let me fill you in on this. This time we've got it made, son. This time nobody can beat us . . . after we get there. Now, you have to do just what I tell you."

"Jarn, I always do like you say, and that's the way she is."

I grinned at him. "I got an idea. Here's how she goes."

Sam grinned and settled down to listen.

"Now listen good, Sam. Here's the deal."

55

Sam and I got to Haiti . . . we liked it. The Haitians are something to see. I like them. They are something to look at and think about. The dark ones slowly turning copper, then *café au lait*, then light velvety brown. Dark, tanned, small-nosed features, the Haitian women, beautifully, warmly, wetly, if not lovingly, getting the race lighter and lighter. "Out of. many, one people."

This slender girl was overly pretty to look at. She had a dance in her body. I said to myself, "what do you pay to be a good man? What does it cost to be a good man, a just man, a poon man . . . two dollars? Go to sweet velvet hell on Saturday night, get good old God on Sunday morning, then . . . sing with remorse "The Old Rugged Cross," the poontanged hymn to be sung next Saturday night—"Poon, poon, beautiful poon."

I walked out of the bar and saw a brown and golden girl cat lurking in the shadows. Come out pussy . . . come out young lovely thing. Good cats walk good. White hot nights . . . sweet mama mangoes . . . de life, mon . . . de life. . . . What a Deal.